Born in Orkney in 1887, Edwin Muir is best known as a poet. When he was fourteen his family moved to Glasgow, and *Poor Tom* reflects something of the trauma of that experience.

J. F. Hendry was born in Glasgow in 1912. He was an influential poet and editor of the New Apocalypse movement in the 1940s, along with G. S. Fraser and the young Norman MacCaig.

Gordon M. Williams was born in Paisley in 1934. After he left school he became a reporter and settled in London. His other books include *Walk Don't Walk* and *The Siege of Trencher's Farm*, filmed by Sam Peckinpah as *Straw Dogs*.

Tom Gallacher was born in Dunbartonshire in 1934. One of the most successful Scottish dramatists of the 1970s, his plays include *Mr Joyce is Leaving Paris* (1970) and *Revival!* (1972). *Apprentice* is the first in a series of three books following the career of the same character.

Dr Liam McIlvanney is a Lecturer in English at the University of Aberdeen. He has published on modern Scottish writing and is the author of *Burns the Radical: Poetry and Politics in Late Eighteenth-Century Scotland* (2002). He is General Editor of the Association for Scottish Literary Studies and a reviewer for the *Times Literary Supplement*.

Growing Up in the West

POOR TOM
Edwin Muir

FERNIE BRAE: A SCOTTISH CHILDHOOD
J. F. Hendry

FROM SCENES LIKE THESE
Gordon M. Williams

APPRENTICE
Tom Gallacher

★

With an Introduction by
Liam McIlvanney

★

CANONGATE
CLASSICS
110

Don't Read.

S.o. else has already "done" this one.

Poor Tom first published in Great Britain in 1932 by J. M. Dent & Sons Ltd, London. Copyright © Gavin Muir 1982. *Fernie Brae: A Scottish Childhood* first published in Great Britain in 1947 by William McLellan & Co., Glasgow. Copyright © J. F. Hendry 1947. *From Scenes Like These* first published in Great Britain in 1968 by Secker & Warburg, London. Copyright © Gordon Williams 1968. *Apprentice* first published in Great Britain in 1983 by Hamish Hamilton Ltd, London. Copyright © The Estate of Tom Gallacher 1983.

This edition first published as a Canongate Classic in 2003 by Canongate Books Ltd, 14 High Street, Edinburgh EH1 1TE. Introduction copyright © Liam McIlvanney 2003. All rights reserved.

The publishers gratefully acknowledge general subsidy from the Scottish Arts Council towards the Canongate Classics series and a specific grant towards the publication of this volume.

Set in 10 point Plantin by Hewer Text Ltd, Edinburgh. Printed and bound by Nørhaven Paperback A/S

CANONGATE CLASSICS
Series Editor: Roderick Watson
Editorial Board: J. B. Pick, Cairns Craig, Dorothy McMillan

British Library Cataloguing-in-Publication Data
A catalogue record for this book is available
on request from the British Library

ISBN 1 84195 262 1

www.canongate.net

Contents

Introduction

In Alasdair Gray's *Lanark* (1981) there is a now infamous scene in which a young man explains to his friend that the inhabitants of Glasgow do not live there imaginatively, since their city – having produced nothing more than 'a music-hall song and a few bad novels' – hasn't been used by artists.[1] There are two things that need saying about Duncan Thaw's thesis. First, it is needlessly pessimistic about the imaginative capacity of ordinary Glaswegians. And, second, it isn't true. Glasgow *had* been used by significant artists – from Catherine Carswell and George Blake through to Edward Gaitens and George Friel.[2] One aim of the present volume is to press the claims of the neglected tradition that Thaw – and by extension Gray – chooses to belittle. It does so by bringing together four powerful West of Scotland fictions, written for the most part before the appearance of *Lanark*, and, in one instance at least, written in a style that palpably influenced Gray's great novel. We will understand Glasgow fiction – indeed, we will understand modern Scottish fiction – better if we stop viewing *Lanark* solely as a watershed and restore that book to its rightful place in a longer tradition of Scottish urban writing.

The major successes of this tradition – its moments of insight and power – have tended to fall in the perhaps predictable territory of the *Bildungsroman*. The story of a sensitive youth negotiating the path to maturity in a brutal and intractable environment is a venerable staple of urban fiction, and Glasgow writers have used it widely. Still, a genre is what you make of it, and a number of Glasgow writers have made very significant things indeed from this familiar scenario. We think of Edward Gaitens's chronicles of a Glasgow-Irish upbringing in *Growing Up* (1942) and *Dance of the Apprentices* (1948); of Alan Spence's vivid limning of a child's-eye Govan in *Its Colours They are Fine* (1977) and *Stone Garden* (1995); and of James Kelman's masterful studies of boyhood in stories like 'Fifty Pence', 'The wee boy that got killed' and 'Joe laughed'. The works collected here form part of this tradition, and together they offer some insight into the business of growing up in the West of Scotland over the first five or six decades of the twentieth century.

Poor Tom (1932) is one of the foundational texts of Scottish urban writing. It inaugurates that vigorous wave of 1930s Glasgow fiction whose highlights include Dot Allan's *Hunger March* (1934), George Blake's *The Shipbuilders* (1935), James Barke's *Major Operation* (1936), the short stories of George Friel and – not least – McArthur and Kingsley Long's notorious *No Mean City* (1935). As it is the earliest, so *Poor Tom* is the best of these books, remarkable both for its psychological acuity and for its pioneering treatment of slum life and socialist politics in the years before World War I. For all that, its initial reception was hardly ecstatic – the first edition may have sold as few as eighty copies[3] – and it remains less well known than it ought to be. Perhaps, like Muir's other novels, it still lies in the shadow of his celebrity as a poet. When a great poet writes a novel we almost desire to see him fail. Success in this second arena seems somehow to diminish his lustre in the first: he can't have been such a great poet if he is also a competent novelist. In Muir's case, the position is further complicated by his high standing as a critic, so that we often approach his work with a hankering for hierarchy and with the kind of priorities indicated in the title of Margery McCulloch's 1993 study; *Edwin Muir: Poet, Critic and Novelist*. Indeed, Muir the novelist has often to cede the floor not merely to Muir the poet and critic, but to Muir the autobiographer, and there is no doubt that Muir's novels have suffered from being habitually judged alongside the autobiographical writings, as if the principal merit of his fiction lies in the light it throws on his life.[4]

All this is to suggest that Muir's novels haven't always been approached on their own terms and in their own right. And yet such an approach must be made, for Muir's fiction is a far from negligible aspect of his achievement as a writer. For a few years on either side of 1930, Muir worked primarily as a novelist, producing three works of fiction in the space of half a decade: *The Marionette* (1927), the 'symbolical tragedy' of a mentally impaired Austrian boy and his grief-stricken father; *The Three Brothers* (1931), a historical novel of the Scottish Reformation; and *Poor Tom* (1932).

Poor Tom charts the tensions between two Orkney brothers – Tom and Mansie Manson – who have moved to Glasgow with their mother and cousin following the death of their father. As the novel opens, Tom catches sight of an ex-girlfriend, Helen, arm-in-arm with Mansie, and the brothers' long estrangement begins. The brothers' quarrel may have its roots in a deeper antagonism – Tom is a maudlin, splenetic drunk and Mansie a rather priggish convert to socialism; Tom is the family black sheep and Mansie a model of sobriety – but the catalyst is Helen. When Tom, in a stupor of drunken self-pity, stumbles from a tram and injures his brain, Mansie blames himself. Tom's subsequent illness – he contracts a brain-tumour after his fall – prompts Mansie to scrutinise not just his relationship with Helen (which had been motivated less by affection than by its intoxicating air of transgression) but his own rather under-examined conscience.

It is here – in Mansie's self-analysis, his halting inventory of his spiritual estate – that the novel finds its true focus. Though not much of a thinker – in some ways, indeed, a fairly shallow character – Mansie has been jolted into pensiveness. Above all, he comes to question his political creed, the rather nebulous and sentimental socialism which has taken the place of his Baptist faith. For Mansie, socialism is a method of 'diffusing' his benevolence so as to avoid having to expend it on any particular individual. He combines a generalised sympathy towards the 'bottom dog' with a shudder of revulsion at the actual people who 'sat about collar-less and in their shirt-sleeves, and washed themselves down to the waist at the kitchen sink'. Tom's illness confronts Mansie with a concrete instance of suffering, a stubbornly unsympathetic victim who – like the noseless beggar sometimes seen around the city – inspires in Mansie a physical dread. In due course, what Mansie comes to realise is that his vaporised, indiscriminate benevolence actually hinders him from giving due attention to his dying brother, and that the socialist heaven on earth – unlike the conventional Christian salvation – has nothing to offer the man who, like Tom, will perish before its inception.

Given its preoccupation with such themes, it is tempting to describe *Poor Tom* as a novel of ideas, but this would be misleading. Certainly, as Margery McCulloch argues, it is an 'overtly philosophical' book,[5] but its philosophy concerns emotions and half-formulated perceptions as much as coherent ideas. Muir's great achievement in the novel is to find a series of compellingly vivid images to convey the often wordless visions of his characters. One can say of *Poor Tom* what Muir himself says of Kafka's *The Castle:* 'everything happens on a mysterious spiritual plane which was obviously the supreme reality to the author; and yet in a curious way everything is given solidly and concretely'.[6]

Be that as it may, Muir's method in *Poor Tom* has its pitfalls.
The fact that, for most of the novel, the two principal characters
are not on speaking terms rather limits the opportunity for
meaningful dialogue. Partly as a result of this, the novel suffers
from a condescendingly intrusive narrator. Critics have complained that Muir is too eager to articulate *for* Mansie and Tom,
that there is too much telling and not enough showing in the
novel. This is true, but one could equally argue that the forensic,
third-person approach pays significant dividends here; for one
thing, it conveys something of the detached, impersonal state of
these characters, their curious alienation from their own emotions
and actions. The distanced, third-person narrative – viewing the
characters from the outside, treating them as laboratory speci-
mens – is not just legitimate but apposite, for this is how the
brothers view themselves.

If Tom and Mansie are the protagonists of the novel, the most
rounded minor character is the city itself. There is an amplitude, a
generosity in Muir's depiction of Glasgow that distinguishes *Poor
Tom* from the more one-sided and pejorative treatments of the
city in *Scottish Journey* (1935) and *An Autobiography* (1954). The
Mansons may seek to blame their troubles on 'the corrupting
influence of Glasgow', but it is clear that Tom was a restless
drunk and Mansie a shallow prig long before the removal from
Orkney. Glasgow's slum districts – the loathsome Eglinton Street
in particular – inspire some classic Muir invective, but even here
Muir largely avoids the kind of hysterical rhetoric that marks
similar passages in the *Autobiography* ('the damned kicking a
football in a tenth-rate hell'). He also responds with real enthusiasm to the bustle and vitality of the city, its whist drives and
Socialist dances, the fervid debates over Nietzsche and Shaw.
Douglas Gifford sees Muir's treatment of the city as deeply
ambivalent, arguing that, in *Poor Tom*, 'Glasgow is simulta-
neously positive and negative'.[7] This is true, though it is not
clear why Gifford should regard such ambivalence as a 'weakness'
when, on the contrary, it represents a properly complex and fluid
response to a many-sided city. A more damaging inconsistency,
perhaps, lies in the characterisation of Mansie who, as P. H.
Butter observes, spends much of the book as an amiable dullard,
only to rise at sudden junctures into vertiginous flights of philosophical speculation.[8]

Despite such glitches, however, *Poor Tom* remains a forceful,
cunning book. Perhaps, in addition to its philosophical intensity
and its lively treatment of place, what impresses most about the

novel is its careful craftsmanship, its meticulous construction. I'm thinking, for instance, of how religious imagery is threaded so subtly through its pages; of how its key incidents are so deftly foreshadowed (when Mansie describes Tom as 'always stumbling against things that hurt him' he innocently anticipates the accident with the tram); of how Muir sets up an intricate series of parallels – between, for instance, Mansie's 'defenceless clothes' during a liaison in the woods, and Tom's 'crumpled blue trousers' as the doctor conducts an examination. There is, on top of this, an often brilliant use of symbol: the 'naked' iron bedstead that reproaches Mansie when Tom has abandoned their shared bedroom, or the pristine bowler hat that speaks of Mansie's fastidiousness. This is a novel of poetic reach and intensity, a novel that repays multiple readings and that reinforces our sense of Muir as one of the century's truly significant Scottish writers.

Fernie Brae: A Scottish Childhood (1947) is the only published novel by James Findlay Hendry, a writer who, partly due to his lengthy residence abroad, is culpably little known in his native land. Born in Glasgow in 1912, and raised mainly in Springburn, Hendry studied modern languages at Glasgow University in the thirties, though he left without taking a degree. After the war, during which he served in the Intelligence Corps, Hendry left Scotland (like the hero of *Fernie Brae*) and travelled widely in Europe, Africa and North America, working as a professional translator and interpreter, before becoming Professor of Modern Languages at Laurentian University in Ontario. He died in 1986, on the verge of returning to Glasgow for good.[9]

An eclectic writer, Hendry's output includes a volume of stories, a biography of Rilke, a handbook for translators and (as editor) *The Penguin Book of Scottish Short Stories* (1969). Like Muir, however, he was principally a poet. He was the key figure in the wartime New Apocalypse movement, which countered the political poetry of the Auden school with a verse of extravagant and often mystical opacity. A number of Scottish poets – Norman MacCaig, G. S. Fraser and W. S. Graham – also participated, but Hendry was the prime mover, composing the New Apocalypse manifesto and co-editing the movement's three anthologies: *The New Apocalypse* (1939); *The White Horseman* (1940); and *The Crown and the Sickle* (1943).

While the New Apocalypse was a short-lived affair, some of its ideas and practices – a delight in the visual and the visionary, a preference for the image over the concept, a belief in the regen-

erative potential of myth, and a deep distrust of the machine age –
continued to inform Hendry's work and are powerfully apparent
in *Fernie Brae*.[10] Towards the start of the novel, there is an episode
in which the young protagonist gently places a number of caterpillars into the drawer of his mother's sewing-machine, only to
discover the 'stench of green death' on the following morning. As
well as being a plausible naturalistic incident, this is a classic New
Apocalypse symbol: organic potential destroyed by the machine.

In *Fernie Brae*, Glasgow itself is a machine, a sordid contraption
of iron and stone, crushing the life of its trammelled inhabitants.
The city is a parody of nature; its chimneys wag like 'wasted
grain', its trains cross the landscape 'like black slugs'. The hero,
David Macrae, inhabits a tenement district penned in by a
cemetery, a grassless park and two vast locomotive works. The
irony here – that the locomotive workers rot in their places while
the engines they fashion circle the globe – is dryly drawn: 'Engines
from [the Cowlairs works] went to India, China and South
America. The majority of the men who built them did not even
go down town.' The city is a penitentiary, its spiked iron railings
the symbol of its purpose. From the schoolroom, with its clan-
gorous bell, to the factory, with its pitiless siren, the city is an
instrument of subjection, a device for enforcing obedience to 'the
mechanical cackle called civilisation'.

Like Edwin Muir, Hendry views the Industrial Revolution and
its concomitant urbanisation as a massive cultural trauma, a
catastrophe that menaces Scotland's very survival as a nation.
At the novel's outset we learn of the process by which 'the Scots,
in the gathering wheels of industry, lost historical vision and
perspective'. Cairns Craig is wrong, I think, to perceive in this a
Scotland cut off from the process of history.[11] Rather, what
Hendry depicts is a Scotland dangerously ignorant of the baleful
history whose patterns and antagonisms it mechanically repeats.
David's 'feeling for historical faces' (he has an aunt who looks like
James VI) is repeatedly borne out in a novel whose pages resound
with the din of dead battles. The Glasgow district of Battlefield
takes its name from the defeat of Mary Queen of Scots by the
forces of John Knox. For David Macrae, nearly four hundred
years later, the district is 'still a battlefield', still governed by a
punitive ethic of iron discipline and masculine aggression. The
embers of Clan warfare and the spark of Covenanting zealotry still
cast an angry glow on a Scotland riven by factional hate. As surely
as Stephen Dedalus, David Macrae is struggling to wake from the
nightmare of history.

And yet, all is not bitter in *Fernie Brae*. There is a good deal of humour, as well as vivid and tender vignettes of childhood: street games and old rhymes, fishing trips with a joking uncle. There is an alertness to the city's unlooked-for beauty – to 'the liquidity and lability of everything' after a shower of rain, or the glorious liveries of the brightly coloured trams. What is most impressive here is how Hendry avoids relaxing his vision into a nostalgic soft-focus. Incidents that another writer might have exploited as cheery set-pieces of tender reminiscence – penny soirées in the church hall, visits to the cinema for the children's matinée – are always refracted through David's own distinctive consciousness and so retain an edge of strangeness. Crucially, too, Hendry's fragmented and elliptical style reproduces the often mystified perspective of childhood. Events occur with no apparent cause. The motivation – and even the identity – of certain characters is frequently obscure. In this way, Hendry avoids triteness and sentimentality to fashion a fresh and often disturbing work of fiction.

Fernie Brae is a considerable artistic achievement in its own right, but it is also of interest – as I intimated earlier – for its influence on the greatest of all Glasgow novels, Alasdair Gray's *Lanark*. While there is no mention of *Fernie Brae* in *Lanark*'s 'Index of Plagiarisms', the two novels do have a great deal in common. The topography of *Fernie Brae* – the northside tenements, the cemeteries, the Infirmary, the locomotive works – is substantially that of *Lanark*. The secondary school which features strongly in both novels is the same one: Whitehill in Dennistoun, though Hendry, in a satirical twist somehow suggestive of Gray, has changed 'White*hill*' to 'White*hall*'! The character of David Macrae – unsporty, awkward with girls and possessed of an innocently subversive honesty (he scandalises a teacher with his assumption 'that soldiers won medals for killing Germans') – is almost a prototype of Duncan Thaw. Macrae's experience at Glasgow University, alienated by a bored staff and a tired curriculum, anticipates Thaw's frustration at Glasgow School of Art. (Both characters leave without taking their degrees.) On a wider level, the novels share a political outlook. Hendry's vision of technological civilisation as a monstrous Leviathan squeezing the globe in its bloated tentacles has clear affinities with the satire in Books 3 and 4 of *Lanark*. Indeed, the young Macrae's perception of the Bank and the Church as the 'same institution' may well anticipate the sinister 'Institute' that dominates life in Unthank. Even Thaw's impromptu seminar on the economic basis of the

Italian Renaissance is articulated first by David Macrae. Clearly, the connections between *Fernie Brae* and *Lanark* deserve a fuller discussion than I have space for here, but even this cursory treatment does, I hope, reinforce the significance of *Fernie Brae* and underline its status as 'one of the few great Scottish novels of the 1940s'.[12]

Perhaps the bleakest of the four books collected here is Gordon Williams's cold-eyed *Bildungsroman, From Scenes Like These* (1968), which was runner-up for the Booker Prize in 1968. A darkness that is more than merely physical is apparent from the opening words:

> It was still dark, that Monday in January, when the boy, Dunky Logan, and the man, Blackie McCann, came to feed and water the horses, quarter after seven on a cold Monday morning in January, damn near as chill as an Englishman's heart, said McCann, stamping his hobnail boots on the stable cobbles.

There is a lot going on in this opening paragraph. First, we encounter two characters who are defined above all by their level of maturity. Dunky Logan is 'the boy', and the novel will follow his progress towards what passes for manhood in his society. Among his models here is Blackie McCann, whose nickname reinforces the darkness motif and whose sonorous boots carry a promise of violence. Hard physical labour will be important in this novel, and so too will the atmosphere of casual bigotry, though the bigotry – in a rather deft irony – rebounds onto its perpetrators: there are plenty of chilly hearts in this novel, but none of them belongs to an Englishman.

The novel charts a year in Dunky's life. Fifteen and fresh from school, he has newly started work at Craig's farm. As one might expect, given the title's sardonic nod to Robert Burns, this is no bucolic idyll. Hemmed in by a factory and a lawless council estate, the farm is a 'sharny old relic hanging on against the creep of the town'. The green Ayrshire of 'The Cotter's Saturday Night' seems a world away. There is no rural piety here, and no reverence for nature. There is no organic relationship between man and animal. When old Charlie, the Craigs' faithful carthorse, has worn himself to the bone after eleven years in harness, he is not put out to pasture; instead – like Boxer in *Animal Farm* – he is despatched to the knacker's. The flensing of Charlie – recalling similar passages in Archie Hind's *The Dear Green Place* and Edwin

Muir's *Autobiography* – is one of the most harrowing episodes in the novel.

Not that the human workers are treated with much more charity than Charlie. When Daftie Coll proves surplus to requirements he is paid off with a scant week's notice – and this after eight years' service to the Craigs. 'Farmers can't afford all this sentimental blether' is Dunky's verdict, and neither, it seems, can anyone else. There is a brutal, Hobbesian tenor to life in Dunky's Kilcaddie. Bickering, back-biting, mutually jealous, the labourers on the farm are like ferrets in a sack. Family life is a bitter joke ('Family! Don't make me laugh' says Dunky's father), but no one is smiling at the round of flyting and fighting and even incest rendered here. Not even in sex do these characters find communion – the act is either an animal function or a weapon in the class war. Only once – in the maudlin crush of boozers in the bar on Hogmanay – does anything like a community emerge, and even here violence is never more than a jogged elbow away. This is a moral landscape almost devoid of natural human sympathy, and it's small wonder that the casually ubiquitous rhetoric of damnation ('MCCANN DAMN YE!', 'hellish keen', 'Damn and hell, it's cold') gradually acquires a more sinister resonance.

According to Isobel Murray and Bob Tait, Dunky Logan is 'doomed to a dead end', but the matter may not be as cut and dried as this.[13] For much of the novel, Dunky is a borderline character, divided not just between country and town ('he wasn't one or the other'), but between the 'self-mutilating ethic'[14] of Kilcaddie and a wider horizon of learning and opportunity. His old teacher's opinion of Dunky – 'always the realist' – is actually wide of the mark, for Dunky is not merely a devourer of adventure stories (he alludes to Stevenson on more than one occasion), but an A-grade dreamer, a kind of Ayrshire Billy Liar. The problem is that, like everyone else in Kilcaddie, he fears and distrusts his own creativity, his dreams and 'daft notions', his 'silly-boy imaginings'.

What Dunky needs – and what Kilcaddie fails to give him – is a socially respectable outlet for his abilities. School is no help here. Nicol, the well-meaning dominie who wants to make Dunky his protégé, is a non-starter as a rôle-model. Desiccated, nit-picking, effete, he merely confirms Dunky's perception that 'Education was something you went in for if you weren't good at anything else'. Moreover, for all his Nationalist radicalism, Nicol remains – like the teachers in Hendry, Kelman and Gray – an instrument of the state, 'stage one in the disciplinary process'. Nicol aside, there

is no-one in Kilcaddie who might foster Dunky's ambitions.
From his friends and relatives he meets nothing but levelling
scepticism and brutal derision. A key incident comes when his
uncle Charlie discovers Dunky's secret diary – 'the chronicle of
the life of Duncan Aitchison Logan, plus some information
appertaining to his interests' – and proceeds to read aloud from
its ingénu pages. The torment of this incident leads Dunky to a
spiteful, self-abnegating pledge: 'They *wanted* you to be as thick
and dim as they were, so he'd show them he could win the
Scottish Cup for ignorance. He'd grow up into a real moronic
working-man and balls to them.'

Dunky is true to his word. In the troubling final chapter he
turns himself into a caricature, a lumbering parody of lumpen
masculinity. The mordant irony here is that, having spent the
novel striving to become a 'real' man, Dunky winds up as a
simulacrum. 'Like' is the final chapter's pivotal word: 'It was like
a man to have mates like them'; 'It was like a man to stand at the
bar'; 'It was like a man, to have a good laugh about other people's
hard luck'. For all his earnest pondering of the subject, Dunky
still doesn't know what manhood is. He is left with a rôle, a dog-
eared script, a 'collection of poses'. He is still adrift in the novel's
final scene, stood with his drunken mates at an Old Firm match,
venting borrowed rage in a long barbaric yawp: 'He held his
hands high above his head and roared and roared until his throat
was sore.' This final image is a grim one, and it makes us question
what Dunky has learned in the twelve months covered by the
novel. In some respects, the swaggering thug on the slopes of
Ibrox is a long way from the nervous boy of the previous year,
feeding the horses in the winter dark. From another perspective,
however, very little has changed; Dunky is as far as ever from a
proper conception of manhood. And one thing is certain: it's still
dark.

In an oeuvre that solicits the epithet 'uneven' – it ranges from
'serious' literary fiction to detective novels and 'avowed potboil-
ers'[15] – *From Scenes Like These* stands out as Williams's triumph.
This is Williams at the top of his game. The prose is disciplined,
sharp and pungent, and has none of the sub-Joycean flourishes –
the frantic punning, the sequinned word-play – that vitiate *Walk
Don't Walk* (1972) and *Big Morning Blues* (1974). It's also a truly
courageous novel, one that coldly interrogates the kind of Caledonian machismo in which Williams was often culpably willing to
indulge; his interviews are full of windy hard-man rhetoric, and in
one he commends his forthcoming football novel – *They Used to*

Play on Grass (1971), co-written with Terry Venables – for showing that 'not all novelists are faggots living in Hampstead'.[16] The best answer to this kind of posturing is the penetrating intelligence of *From Scenes Like These*, in which the true cost of such witless bigotry is relentlessly and movingly anatomised.

With Tom Gallacher's *Apprentice* (1983), we move north from Ayrshire to the 'precipitous streets of Greenock in the 1950s'. *Apprentice* is Gallacher's first work of prose fiction and the opening instalment of the Bill Thompson trilogy, which continues with *Journeyman* (1984) and *Survivor* (1985). When his sequence of Clydeside stories made its appearance, Gallacher was already in mid-career as a playwright, his prolific output throughout the seventies and early eighties including radio plays, adaptations of Ibsen and Strindberg and original stage plays like *Revival!* and *Mr Joyce is Leaving Paris*. This theatrical 'apprenticeship' leaves its mark on Gallacher's fiction. His faults as well as his virtues are those of a dramatist: his mise-en-scène is effective, his dialogue has polish and point, but his characters can sometimes seem overblown and 'stagey', and they are rather too ready to state their case in loudly impressive soliloquies.

The form adopted by Gallacher in *Apprentice* – the short-story sequence – is one with a distinguished pedigree in Glasgow fiction, having been used with some élan by writers like Gaitens, Friel and Spence. Gallacher's sequence is tightly constructed: there are five stories, one for each year of the narrator's apprenticeship, and each centres on a different character, one of the 'spirited, funny, maddening people' whom Bill encounters as he serves out his time. We are thus confronted with the paradox that, while *Apprentice* is the only text in the present volume to feature a first-person narrator, its narrative focus is the most diffuse and decentred of all. Bill Thompson is less concerned with his own ideas and fancies than with observing – and where possible learning from – those around him. He is not simply an apprentice engineer but an 'apprentice human being'. He is also being inducted into an unfamiliar culture, undergoing an 'initiation – into adoptive Scottishness'.

For Bill is an outsider, a young Englishman from a moneyed background, the well-spoken product of a minor public school. His father, a consultant engineer, worked his way up from Clyde yards and wants Bill to benefit from a Clydeside apprenticeship before he joins the family firm. Bill is thus, as one of the locals points out, 'More of a *visitor* than a real apprentice', and this

external perspective is crucial to the functioning of *Apprentice*.
Neither credulously sympathetic nor antagonistic to the lives he
chronicles, Bill maintains a perspective that is not so much
objective as disinterested. Through Bill, Gallacher also avoids
the danger of narrative condescension. When an anthropological
note creeps in – as when Bill describes the habitat and manners of
the natives, their standards of hygiene and their courtship rituals,
or muses on the 'foreign language of industrial Scotland' – this is
tempered by Bill's awareness that his own accent and manners
seem equally outlandish to the inhabitants of Greenock.

Bill's status as a temporary resident, a 'fanciful outsider who
just happened to be passing through', throws into relief the
predicament of the locals, for whom the prospect of escape seems
impossibly remote. This note of pessimism is worth stressing,
since it is easy to miss amid the bantering exuberance of Gallacher's Greenockians. Though its touch is light and its tone often
quietly celebratory, there is a good deal of darkness in *Apprentice*.
Its concern with what James Kelman calls 'everyday routine
horrors' – losing a child to the dampness of the slums, lacking
the cash to put food on the table – is marked. There are also some
disturbing episodes which verge on the histrionic – the matricide
of Delia Liddle, for instance, or the madness of Isa Mulvenny,
who winds up as a kind of Greenock Miss Havisham, a tenement
Mrs Rochester, pining for the husband and the son who have
forsaken her. What keeps these scenes on the near side of
melodrama is the contrast between the extravagance of the action
and the precise, unflustered prose in which it is rendered.
Throughout the stories, indeed, we encounter a prose whose
almost archaic formality ('She again essayed the disdainful tossing of her head') registers Bill's distance both from the demotic
language of those around him and from the raging disorder of
their lives.

As befits a fiction centred on a shipyard, the actual processes of
labour have their place in *Apprentice* – as they do throughout
Growing Up in the West – but here the focus is resolutely small-
scale and intimate: the turning of a valve, the cleaning of an oily
sump, the drilling of a brass plate. There are no grandiose
panoramas in *Apprentice*. Gallacher knows that the human frame
is not ennobled but diminished when viewed against a backdrop
of gargantuan machinery, that the great cranes of the yard render
the workers 'insignificant and identical'. Accordingly, there is no
naïve 'Clydesidism' here, no earnest hymning of the riveter's
glory, no paeans to the epic stature of the welder. The swelling

chords which overwhelm a novel like George Blake's *The Ship-builders* are thankfully absent here. Even where the characters do rise to feats of heroism – as when Andrew Mulvenny risks his life to close down an unmanned rolling mill – we never mistake them for paragons. An unmannerly braggart and a domestic bully, Mulvenny remains incorrigibly human.

While it would be unfair to describe Bill Thompson as a misanthrope, he isn't quite bursting with affection for humanity at large. He is one of those who are 'not charmed by their fellow men in the mass, in the crush, or in the queue'. This preference for the discrete individual may help to explain the striking fact that – alone among the books featured here – *Apprentice* contains no reference to socialist politics, to Clydeside's culture of labour activism. *Apprentice* is political in depicting a world of brutalising poverty and exploitation. But the world it depicts is not itself political. There are no firebrands in its yards, there is little sense of class solidarity, and there is almost nothing in the way of political consciousness. We hear some truculent and knee-jerk resentment of Bill as a 'stuck-up' Englishman, a born member of the boss class; but no one in these stories believes conditions might be improved except on a personal level, through petty crime, emigration or a 'college education'.

Thrown back on their own resources, Gallacher's characters must improvise responses to the chaos in which they move. One might say of these characters, not that they are emptily theatrical, but that they are – for the most part quite knowingly – *actors*. They hold themselves together in a collapsing world by maintaining a certain persona. From the aristocratic labourer Lord Sweatrag ('He was acting. He was certainly acting, but with what *style*') to the impossibly brash Delia Liddle (whom we first encounter in a theatre), these characters are playing out a rôle. It is a mark of Gallacher's tact as an artist that he refrains from dictating where such rôles begin and end. Despite its surface crudeness, then, there is decorum in Gallacher's characterisation, a refusal to claim any definitive knowledge of the person behind the persona. Bill Thompson sets this tone in his rueful preface, when he acknowledges his limits as a narrator, pointing out that his perspective on the people he sketches is partial and contingent, that 'what was true of them outside my personal intervention and knowledge is missing'. And this, it may be, is the cardinal lesson of the book: that in the business of understanding other people one can never be an adept or an expert, but only and always an apprentice.

*

The great triumphs of Glasgow fiction in the 1980s and beyond – the successes of Kelman and Gray, and the subsequent achievements of Janice Galloway, Jeff Torrington, A. L. Kennedy and Andrew O' Hagan – have encouraged a drift towards cultural amnesia. While the glories of the now engross both readers and critics, a whole tradition of antecedents and exemplars is slipping out of view. And where earlier urban fiction *has* received critical notice, it has sometimes been glibly disparaged as gloomy and unadventurous, a drearily homogenous 'Glasgow school of crisis'.[17] It is to be hoped that *Growing Up in the West* will complicate this picture, testifying as it does to the verve, variety and ingenuity of West of Scotland fiction in the decades prior to the 'Glasgow Renaissance'. And this – the high literary quality of the works collected here – is the central point to emphasise. If these books have a claim on our attention, if they deserve to be rediscovered and re-read, it is firstly because of their literary merit. They are four finely realised works of fiction. Beyond that, however, they can do us the service of correcting our foreshortened perspective on the literary past, reminding us of a time when the Scottish urban novel itself was growing up in the West.

NOTES

1 Alasdair Gray, *Lanark: A Life in 4 Books* (London: Picador, 1994), p. 243.
2 On Glasgow fiction generally, see Moira Burgess, *Imagine a City: Glasgow in Fiction* (Glendaruel: Argyll, 1998), and the same writer's *The Glasgow Novel: A Complete Guide*, 3rd edn (Hamilton: The Scottish Library Association, 1999).
3 Margery McCulloch, *Edwin Muir: Poet, Critic and Novelist* (Edinburgh: Edinburgh University Press, 1993), p. 28.
4 Critical studies which treat Muir's fiction and autobiography together include: P. H. Butter, *Edwin Muir* (Edinburgh: Oliver and Boyd, 1962); Elgin W. Mellown, *Edwin Muir* (Boston: Twayne, 1979); and Margery McCulloch, *Edwin Muir: Poet, Critic and Novelist*.
5 McCulloch, p. 29.
6 *Selected Letters of Edwin Muir*, ed. by P. H. Butter (London: Hogarth Press, 1974), p. 67.
7 Douglas Gifford, *The Dear Green Place? The Novel in the West of Scotland* (Glasgow: Third Eye Centre, 1985), p. 7.
8 See Professor Butter's introduction to the 1982 Paul Harris edition of *Poor Tom*.
9 *Chapman*, 52 (Spring 1988), a special Hendry number, contains much useful information on the writer's life and work. See also the biographical note to J. F. Hendry, *Marimarusa* (Thurso: Caithness Books, 1978).

10 On the New Apocalypse, see J. F. Hendry, 'Apocalypse Now: The Image and the Myth', *Chapman*, 31 (Winter 1981/ 82), 45–54.

11 Cairns Craig, *The Modern Scottish Novel: Narrative and the National Imagination* (Edinburgh: Edinburgh University Press, 1999), pp. 124–5.

12 Douglas Gifford, 'A New Diversity', *Books in Scotland*, 26 (Winter 1987), 6–14 (p. 14).

13 Isobel Murray and Bob Tait, *Ten Modern Scottish Novels* (Aberdeen: Aberdeen University Press, 1984), p. 123.

14 Craig, p. 54.

15 Murray and Tait, p. 143.

16 John Lloyd, 'A Novelist in the Mirror: An Interview with Gordon M. Williams', *Scottish International* (August 1971), 22–8 (p. 28).

17 This term was coined by Beat Witschi in his *Glasgow Urban Writing and Postmodernism: A Study of Alasdair Gray's Fiction* (Frankfurt am Main: Peter Lang, 1991).

Liam McIlvanney

POOR TOM
Edwin Muir

PART ONE

PART ONE

WHEN ONE EVENING in the early autumn of 1911 Tom Manson saw his brother Mansie coming out with Helen Williamson through the gate of the Queen's Park in Glasgow, he stopped as if he had been given a blow on the chest. He told himself that he must be mistaken; but, no, there was no doubt about it; Mansie and Helen were walking along there like old friends. They had not noticed him, but with their faces turned towards each other went off along the park railings towards Pollokshaws Road. Behind his incredulous rage Tom felt honestly alarmed for them; they were so completely unconscious of their danger; they had no idea that they had been seen! But then, as by the single turn of a screw, his fury completely flooded him, sweeping out everything else. He turned and walked down Victoria Road. 'By God, I'll get even with him!' he thought, but no expedient came to his mind, and his anger took another leap upwards.

He pushed open the swing-door of a pub and went up to the counter. The barmaid smiled at him; he could see that all right; but at the same time it was only a distant glassy re-arrangement of her features, so he paid no attention to it but ordered a double Scotch, and when that was swallowed, a second one which he drank more slowly. His anger now quite filled him, yet when he turned into Garvin Street and neared his home it took another leap upwards, lifted him up with it, so that he seemed to be walking partly on the air. Slamming the house door behind him he made at once for the room where he and Mansie slept and began to haul his clothes and belongings to the parlour. The sound of furniture banging brought his mother from the kitchen.

'What are you doing, Tom?' she cried. 'You'll break the bit sticks o' furniture if you're no' careful.'

'Leave me alone!'

'But, lamb, what's the matter?'

'If you think I'm going to sleep another night in the same room as that—' He had to stop, for only one word would come to his tongue, and he could not speak it out before his mother. So in revenge he said: 'I'm leaving tomorrow. I'm going to ship on the first liner I find.'

'But what's wrong, Tom? Tell me what's wrong?'

'Leave me alone!' he shouted. 'Can't you leave me alone!'

His mother turned, and her bowed back as she left the room filled him with despair. No, he would never be able to leave this hole! He was chained here. He went through to the bedroom again and carried his bedclothes to the parlour, threw them on the horsehair sofa, and stood staring at them. A key turned in the outside door, and someone stepped into the lobby. He stood rigidly listening. There were voices in the kitchen and then steps in the lobby; but it was his cousin Jean who entered.

'What idiocy have you been up to now?' she asked. 'Do you know that your mother's crying in the kitchen?'

'Leave me alone,' said Tom. But now he spoke in a merely sulky voice.

Jean looked at the bedclothes piled on the sofa: 'A fine mess you've made. Are you going to sleep here?' Then she turned to him, her voice changing, and asked: 'Tom, what has happened?'

'Oh, it's no business of yours.' He went across to the window, and looking out said: 'Well, if you want to know, Mansie's walking out a lady that used to be a great visitor here at one time. I caught them coming out of the Queen's Park.'

'What? Not Helen Williamson?'

'Yes, Helen Williamson.'

'But it's absurd! It's impossible!'

'Well, I saw them. Haven't I told you?'

Jean was silent for a moment, then she asked: 'Did they see you?'

'They were too much occupied with each other.'

She stood looking at him: 'But what's to be done now?'

'That's not my affair. I'm going to ship on a liner tomorrow.'

'Don't talk nonsense. You know you've got to consider your mother. But I never thought Mansie was such a terrible fool as that!'

'Well, do you expect me to live here after this?'

Jean stood thinking. Presently she said: 'Go for a walk. And I'll make your bed and put this room in some order.'

She began at once, turning her back on him. At the door he said: 'At any rate, it wasn't my fault this time.'

'Who says it was your fault?' Then she burst out: 'That woman will be a curse to the both of you! I never liked her.'

'It's his fault, not hers.'

'Do you stick up for her still? But I don't deny that it's Mansie's fault. I'll have to tell your mother, I suppose.'

Tom walked rapidly up Victoria Road. But when he came to the park gates again his rage met him like a wave and turned him automatically in the opposite direction from the one that Mansie and Helen had taken. With his mother and Jean there he would never be able to get back at that creeper. Velvet-heeled creeper! Scented velvet-heeled creeper! Rows of black, spiked railings spun past him, and he struck at them with his stick. Like a prison, these neat streets and numbered houses and genteel railings. Why had his father hauled him back that time when he had tried to run off to sea? He had actually got to Blackness, was on the boat, tucked away all safe in the forecastle; and then his father came, the very skin at the root of his nose white with anger; and he had got out of the ship again and into the cart, and his father had driven him home to the farm, five hopeless miles. He had been sixteen then – a fellow was far too much at the mercy of everybody at sixteen! – and then his father had had his first heart attack, and that had put a stop to all hope of running away to sea. And when his father died there was his mother to look after, for Mansie had done a bunk to Glasgow long before that: the creeper always knew how to sneak out of things. No wonder he had taken to drink when they had gone to Blackness after his father's death; he knew every stone in the streets and hated every one of them; but when you got drunk your nose wasn't brought up against them at every turn; it seemed to give you some hope. Oh, why hadn't they let him go to sea? They hadn't known what they were doing.

He was walking now through a wide park dotted with groups of young men in shirt-sleeves playing football. And as if in response to his release from the constriction of the rows of railed houses, he saw himself again, as he had often seen himself, standing at the prow of an ocean-going ship in the solitary morning watch, standing bare-footed and with uncovered head in the wide flapping trousers and blue jersey of a sailor, a cigarette between his lips, a foreign look, the look of one who has seen many lands, on his face. The circle of the sea horizon rose and sank with a slow turning motion like a great coin lazily spinning, and within that ring of danger he was secure, for danger itself was a shield, turning aside all that was equivocal and treacherous and creeping. Yes, that was the life for him; but his father had not known and his mother would never know what a thirst a fellow could have for the sea, so that he seemed to choke on dry land, choke as if a dry clod were rammed down his throat. The sea, or the Wild West with a revolver at your side, some place where you knew your friends and your enemies, knew where you stood.

But suddenly, while he was still in mid-ocean, the turn of Helen's neck as she looked up at Mansie rose before him. Damn and blast her! It was as if she had given him a blow between the eyes, and he, lying on his back in the gutter, were asking her in pure astonishment why she had done that. And he would have given up everything for her. How good he had felt at that party, the first evening they had met! But he mustn't think of that. Still, when she wouldn't tell him her address, by God she had been perfectly right! Better for him if he had never found it out. A damned fool, too, to have wandered round Langside every evening that week in the frost and cold, among all these new streets, great blocks of redstone they were, with genteel railed gardens in front. Of course he hadn't met her there. But on the Sunday he had got up good and early and gone to the church she attended. Well, he had asked for his medicine pretty thoroughly, right enough. He had looked all round the church, but couldn't find her. He might have given it up as a bad job then; but no, he had to wait on the pavement when the service was over, and after a while out she came. He had hardly dared to step up to her, the soft fool; he didn't know at that time that she was the sort that would kiss and canoodle with anybody. But it was all easier than he had expected, far too damned smooth and easy altogether, and she agreed to go for a walk in the park with him without winking an eyelash. Might as well have given him her address at the first go off; but that was like her. And then it was a long time before he plucked up his courage and got it out – a nice sunny day it was, after the frost – but out it came at last: 'I love you.' And his voice had trembled: was there ever such a fool? It had made her catch her breath all the same; but then she had replied in that superior way of hers: 'How can you tell that? You don't know me.' But he thought he knew her better than anybody had ever known a girl, and that began it. Yet even then he hadn't dared to touch her, or to kiss her, for weeks and weeks. Still, that had been the happiest time he had had with her. Better if the thing had always stayed at that stage. For her kisses drove a fellow frantic, and she didn't seem to know it. Flung herself at you and thought she could go on doing that till the cows came home; kissing and nothing more. Thus far and no farther. And after it was over she would just pat her hat to rights again, looking as superior and genteel as ever, and that was that. How could he have stood it? No wonder he got violent that night in Maxwell Park; he was beyond himself, he couldn't help it. But then he had crept and crawled before her, licked her boots, told her he was a waster, and promised never to offend again. And after all it wasn't any use, for she kept as stiff as a poker, never gave him another chance, took no pity on a fellow. And now she was kissing and canoodling with that creeper. By God, if he had guessed that would ever happen he would have known what to do; he would have paid no attention to her objections; that was how to treat tarts of her kind. A proper soft mark he had been.

Now he was among streets again. His anger, which had winged his feet, now fell like the sudden ceasing of a wind. He felt tired; a drink would do him good. He pushed open the swing-door of a pub. As he sat drinking, and the comforting equivocality of alcohol spread through his mind, he gave himself over more and more completely to the thought that he was a waster, as though it were a consoling thought. It didn't matter what happened to a poor devil like him; let them kiss and canoodle. But then – for even a waster must take some measures of defence against his enemies – he suddenly saw that he must get back before Mansie; it was a point of honour, a point of honour that a creeper mightn't understand; but it would be indecent if he wasn't home before Mansie, if he wasn't sitting at home and waiting for him. So Tom got unsteadily to his feet.

But as he approached Garvin Street a long forgotten memory of his childhood came back to him. A big lout, the son of a neighbouring farmer, had lain in wait for Mansie one evening. Mansie had stood with a terrified look on his face, refusing to fight; but Tom, although he was only a little boy at the time, had flown at Mansie's tormentor screaming: 'You're no' to hurt Mansie! You're no' to hurt Mansie!' And everybody had laughed, and there had been no fight. And now Mansie had given him a stab in the back. Without provocation. His elder brother that he had always looked up to, that he would have done anything for. 'By God, I'll get even with him!' he said as he went up the stairs, but it was only the repetition of an empty phrase. And when he opened the door he felt so tired that he walked straight through to the parlour – driven out of his very room, by God! – and forlornly went to bed.

After a long and inconclusive debate with his mother in the kitchen, Mansie wearily betook himself to his room. He had denied that there was anything between himself and Helen, denied it as indignantly as if he were speaking the truth; and indeed what he had told her was partly true at least, entirely true in fact if you only counted the time up to the moment when, yielding to a silly impulse – it had become far too much of a habit with him, dash it! – he had stooped down and kissed Helen on the mouth. He knew it was a mistake the minute it was done, knew it as soon as he found her in his arms, knew it while her lips were still clinging to his: a silly goat to have got himself into such a fix for the sake of a moment's pleasure. But then, whether it was the total abandon with which Helen fell into his arms, as if she had been fatefully poised in a perilous equilibrium that only one touch was needed to destroy, or whether it was the slightly terrifying thought that this was Tom's girl, whom it would be wicked to trifle with, almost blasphemous to embrace unless one were driven by an irresistible passion that excused everything: all at once they had both become serious, they had looked at each other like con-spirators suddenly bound together by a fatal act that they had not foreseen a moment before, revealing them to each other in a flash, so that it would have been useless, even perverse, to pretend any longer. This wasn't like his other affairs with girls at all! The frightening thought had shot through Mansie's mind while He-len's lips were still pressed to his. There was no turning back now. A serious business!

And now, as he lit the gas-jet in his room, he thought again, listening involuntarily for any sound from the parlour where Tom was lying: A serious business! But all the same what he had told his mother was true. Helen had only come to him for help and advice. And besides, it was a dashed shame of Tom to have lain in wait for her, stopping her and speaking to her like that: the poor girl was frightened out of her wits and didn't know where to turn. Tom should have taken his dismissal like a man. Why, it was two months now since she had told him that it was all over between them! And yet the fellow still went on persecuting her, even stopping her in the street: that was carrying things a bit too far. Still it was dashed unfortunate that Tom had seen them that evening. It was like him, all the same; always stumbling against things that hurt him, always getting himself and other people into trouble. Well, he had only himself to blame; Helen would never have had him back whatever happened.

Mansie glanced round the bedroom. It had a strange naked look. Made a fellow feel quite queer, that empty iron bedstead; something ugly and threatening about it. Things would be dashed uncomfortable in the house now, with Tom in that state of mind. Mansie slowly took off his clothes. Unpleasant going to bed with that thing standing there by the wall as if it were watching you. Wish Bob Ryrie were here to keep a fellow company. Bob would be able to advise one too. He turned his back on the bedstead. A serious business! And he was to see Helen on Saturday afternoon. He almost wished now that he had not fixed up that appointment with her; but there was no drawing back; the damage was done; Tom had seen them, and there would be no use in trying to convince him that—

Putting out the gas, Mansie slipped into bed, carefully avoiding the iron bedstead still reproachfully and threatingly exposing its shameful nakedness to him in the light of the street lamp outside. For a long time he lay awake thinking of Helen and Tom and wishing that Bob Ryrie were there with him. He felt forsaken and unjustly treated, like a child locked as a punishment in an empty room where damaged and disused pieces of furniture are kept. But at last he fell asleep.

TWO

Since there's no hope, come let us kiss . . .
DRAYTON

IF TOM MANSON had had the ability to crystallise his vague feelings of betrayal connected with Glasgow he might have said that he was betrayed by a kiss. For it was a kiss, or rather a special kind of kiss, known perhaps only in Puritan countries which have been thoroughly industrialised without being civilised to the point requisite for an industrialised population, that was one of the chief causes of his later misfortunes.

Like all born lovers of freedom Tom had always been irked by a countless number of things which tamer natures adapt themselves to without inconvenience. His father's farm had irked him because it was stationary, because the seasons followed one another, because the soil had to be ploughed and the harvest reaped; and the little town of Blackness had begun to irk him as soon as he felt that he knew every stone in it. For on the farm he had at least felt the horizon round him wherever he went; but here his sight was bounded by arbitrary walls, and if he got drunk oftener than he should it was partly because then the houses lost their stability, rocked lightly like ships at anchor, and seemed on the point of floating away; and this fluctuating barrier was far more endurable than the rigid walls that sobriety raised about him. Sometimes as he walked home at night after a spree he would kick a particularly massive stone in the wall, at first to convince himself that it was as solid as it looked, and finally in anger at its unresponsiveness. Next day his imprisonment was always harder to bear.

When at last his apprenticeship in the engineering shop was over and he could go to Glasgow, the hugeness of that city became an image of inexhaustible freedom. For a year he was enchanted by the variety and strangeness of Glasgow. Even the unfamiliar conventions pleased him, and he set himself eagerly to acquire them. And although he came from a northern island where people's speech had still a ballad frankness and young men still climbed in through their sweethearts' windows at night, he soon learned what words might and might not be addressed to a respectable young Glasgow typist. Like almost everybody, indeed, who, coming from a relatively primitive state of society, seeks to adapt himself to one that is more complex, he made the error of taking the new conventions at their face value and fell from his natural frankness into a fantastic propriety. One thing in particular helped to make his attitude to women excessively correct. A man who has been accustomed to steal to his sweetheart under cover of night insensibly comes to associate love with loosened hair on pillows and matches clandestinely struck, and the sight of a young lady, correctly dressed, walking towards him through the crowd, which he has been watching for the last ten minutes, awakens in him quite a different train of thoughts and conducts him into a world from which there is no bridge to the world of love as he has known it. And that bridge being unthinkable, he comes in time to conceive of the transition to the physical rites of love as a perfectly arbitrary step not provided for by the convention, a blind leap out of one world into another, a violent settlement of a question for which there is no legitimate solution. Tom, in other words, simply could not imagine himself lying in bed with the stylishly dressed girls whom he walked out – at least while he was walking them out; or rather he could not imagine the process which would lead to that consummation: day and night attire having for him almost the force of two absolute conditions – the present in which he was embedded, and the past from which he had been roused for ever. And even when he fell in love with Helen his feelings still remained in this suspended state, and it was only when she granted him a little more than he had reckoned upon that Glasgow and its conventions began to irk him: the small draught of freedom represented by a special kind of kiss was enough to make him feel his bonds.

They must have kissed sooner or later; but while in the world which Tom had known an ardent kiss was only the prelude to a more intimate caress, to Helen it seemed to be the end. And the passion with which she flung herself upon it had something of despair and renunciation. It was as though in a fury of make-believe she hoped to transform it without anyone's knowledge, even her own, into that ultimate surrender which she allowed to enter her imagination only as a legendary happening. To Tom this final and sterile kiss, rehearsed so often, gave a momentary appeasement, an appeasement which was half torture, however, for it seemed to have so little meaning; it was followed by a feeling

of apprehension which he could not shake off. It was as though he
had gone with Helen into the house of love, thinking at first: This
is only the ante-room, but presently discovering that it was the
only chamber in the house. For though there is another door in
the inner wall of this room so much frequented by young couples
in the larger towns of Scotland, a door leading presumably to
other chambers, when one examines it one finds that it is only
painted, very realistically, on the wall. There is even, it may be, a
handle affixed to this door, but if there is, the handle is false too, it
turns round and round accommodatingly as long as one chooses
to turn it, but nothing happens: it is wooden, the ante-room is
wooden, the whole house is wooden, a long narrow wooden shell
with a splendid façade. Behind this façade, in such a long and
shallow room, Tom and Helen performed their passionate and
sterile rites.

Yet at certain moments, when two lovers strain against the
painted door, there must come, no matter how convincingly their
conscience assures them of the contrary, the urgent knowledge
that the door is real after all, that other rooms lie beyond it, and
that if they could awaken they might find themselves, with fear
and trembling, but with definite relief, ensconced there. And
while to all appearances they are quite happy in the bright room,
and feel privileged to be there, in secret they are thinking of those
other chambers whose existence they never admit to each other,
and which have become a subterranean domain through which
their thoughts can licentiously roam while they stand so chastely
clasped. In time their embraces become merely a device to gain
them admittance to that place, where they can wander in solitary
thought, and where, if they ever met, they could not greet each
other. So as they stand pressed so closely they are as far apart as
secret drinkers indulging their craving in shameful privacy. Once,
it is true, when desire first threw them together, they gave
themselves when they kissed, but now, while still pretending to
give, they are merely filching from each other something they are
ashamed of and wish to hide. So when she casts herself into his
arms with the splendid gesture of one who surrenders everything,
offering her breasts to him as though each were a precious gift
which he must accept with homage, she is merely making a breach
in her own body through which that secret world may break in
and become a private garden where she can wander at her
pleasure, but where she had no further need of him, where indeed
he would be a burdensome intruder, now that he has been the
means through which she has found her way into it. And when she

kisses him she closes her eyes as though to hide something, and if she could she would conceal her face as well, for she cannot keep the waves of passion from flowing over it, from rippling under that smooth mask like the muscles under the hide of some lovely animal.

Such secret pleasures are exciting, but they leave a sense of guilt towards the object that was employed to produce them. Tom was filled with shame that such thoughts should come into his mind when he was with Helen, and told himself that he was a waster. He felt that he had desecrated their love, and the fact that she did not know it made his treachery only the worse. Yet sometimes, almost drowned by his self-reproaches, a feeling that he had been betrayed would rise in him; and then the country girls that he had lain with, frank whether in conferring or refusing their favours, would seem to him innocent compared with this Glasgow girl, superior as she was to them, and unassailable as was her virtue. And if they had been within reach he would have gone to them to be cured.

But, although he observed them, the conventions of the city were still strange to him, and so he accepted this as one of them. Certainly it seemed a queer arrangement that young fellows courting should go about for years with their senses aroused under their clothes and pay no more attention to it than to a slight physical inconvenience, a corn or an attack of indigestion. But no doubt they got used to it; perhaps it was a normal drawback of love that had to be accepted with the rest; still it was queer to think of so many of them, dressed in their best, bow ties neatly in place, every button fastened, trousers creased, and all the time— The Rabelaisian picture, comic and yet sordid, imprinted a sheepish grin on his mouth whenever he realised that he was one of that ignominious army. It was a quite definite sense of solidarity, and although it humiliated him it gave him a satisfaction as of revenge, though on what or whom he could not have said. It was unpleasant to remember Helen at those times.

But to Helen those limitations of love were far less irksome. As she climbed the stairs, turned the key in the door of her lodgings, lit the gas in her room and absently looked round her, she still breathed that richer atmosphere which the touch of Tom's lips and arms had distilled, an atmosphere that she inhaled effortlessly through every pore of her body, giving her a dreamful sense of lightness. It was only when she was undressing, still in a dream, that the weight of her body began to return; and the undoing of her corsets, and all the trifling acts of liberation which had to be accomplished before she could lie outstretched in bed, were like a series of infinitely complicated petty problems that she could never hope to solve. When at last she lay between the smooth sheets, every inch of her body seemed weighed down by a separate burden, lay there dead and impenetrable, a foreign load attached to her, a trunk which was of no further use, for it had been ethereally decapitated; and her lips, on which the savour of Tom's kisses was slowly fading, seemed alone to harbour any life, seemed alone dedicated to love, a solitary beacon in the darkness. When she turned on her other side for relief it seemed an ignominious thing that she had to turn all her body; it was a conscious and deliberate act that was shameful and also in some way perilous. And she plunged into sleep like a stone falling into an abyss.

Sensual images came to her very seldom, but when they did they were brutally vivid. She saw Tom before her stripped naked, his head cropped like a boxer's, his flesh leaden. But worst of all were the times when his nakedness was persistently obstructed by some trifle, a collar fastened by a stud round his neck, or a sock on one foot; for that was like a dismemberment, as though the collar severed his head from his shoulders and the sock darkly conjured his foot away. These startling materialisations terrified her at the rare moments when she remembered them, and it seemed impossible that she should have seen or imagined them – she, the girl who stood in the ante-chamber of love.

It is in the hand that the human will is most unequivocally incarnated, so unequivocally, indeed, that we are often held responsible even for its involuntary motions. So when Tom raised his hand and almost imperceptibly touched Helen's breast, that breast which so often had been flung at him by the blind engine of her body, crushed against his so firmly and long that he could hear the beating of her heart; when he raised his hand to those softly outlined spheres, the act had all the appearance of deliberate violation, of Luciferian blasphemy. She was so outraged and incredulous that he at once stammered an apology. Finally she forgave him, but that was the beginning of their rupture. For when she had crushed her breasts against him it had been in involuntary obedience to the compulsion that threw their bodies – no, perhaps not even their bodies – that threw their souls together. And although she was perfectly conscious of the thrill of the impact, and indeed enjoyed it secretly and deliberately, yet no action takes on the indelible stamp of responsibility until it is acknowledged by some other human being; indeed until then one cannot even be sure that it ever happened; and Tom gave no sign, perhaps he had not noticed. Helen was too absorbed in her inner sensations, however, for such questions to present themselves to her except in the vaguest terms. But when Tom raised his hand against her breast as though against herself the cloud was torn asunder; she felt naked, and she could not fling herself into his arms again in such complete obliviousness of what she was doing. It was after this that she began to dream of Tom without his clothes.

THREE

WHILE TOM DREAMT of adventures, Mansie's reveries were filled with hosts of friends, and his most comforting thought was that with the years their numbers would increase. Yet he never took the first step; he merely held himself expectantly open, and this of itself was enough to tell anyone who met him that here was a real friendly fellow, and to put the more sensitive into a position in which an advance into intimacy was unavoidable. But nobody except undesirable people ever wanted to escape the tacit invitation. Mansie was like one of those actresses to whom bouquets seem to fly of their own accord, and to him each new friendship was indeed a sort of bouquet which he accepted without affectation, privately conscious that he deserved it, but far too decent a fellow to let the slightest sign of this appear. His life was passed among his friends as in a garden exhaling an almost sensible fragrance and warmth; and it filled him with pleasure to know that no corner was uncultivated, and to look forward for a whole week, aware that every evening he would be in some sheltered arbour of this pleasance which expanded in an ever wider concentric ring as the years went on and yet remained intimate, resembling a private estate.

The thing that puzzled him most was how he had got on so well in life, how he had come to be promoted over the heads of men older and more pushing than himself, and he was occasionally troubled by the thought: could he be a sly fellow after all, sly perhaps without knowing it? But these thoughts came to him only in moods of dejection: they were really too absurd. Next morning he would contemplate his business career half in wonder and half in gratitude, and acknowledge frankly how lucky he had been, for his popularity with his employers and with the customers was pure luck! And fortune itself seemed then the paragon of decent fellows, and he cherished for it, though invisible, exactly the feelings one decent fellow cherishes for another who has done him a good turn.

It was somewhat the same feeling that had led to his conversion and his membership of the Baptist Chapel. This had happened a little after he came to Glasgow. There had been a great revival, several men in the warehouse had been accepted by Christ, and Mansie, already so popular with decent fellows, felt assured that he could not be turned away. Perhaps too he was afraid that he might be missing an opportunity of bettering himself, and this was a point on which his conscience was really strict; for bettering himself was associated in his mind with disagreeable effort, with such things as asking the manager for an increase of salary, and to evade such difficulties made him almost fear that he might be a man of weak character. So he went to the revival meeting and was quietly saved. Afterwards he was very glad he had done so, for the uprush of ecstatic feeling that followed had taken him quite by surprise, and again he felt that gratitude, this time tinged with a degree of awe, which one decent fellow feels for another who has done him a good turn.

He read very little, contenting himself with the *Glasgow Herald* and the *British Weekly*, and did not regard himself as a 'literary fellow'; yet he would have been distressed to be found wanting in reverence for things which were deserving of it, and when the Reverend John McKail in his sermon one Sunday quoted, as though in independent confirmation of his own views, 'God's in His Heaven, All's right with the world,' Mansie felt that there must be something in this fellow Browning and in poetry too, although from all he had heard it was a rather profane business; and picking up *Great Thoughts* one day from the desk of one of the clerks in the office, and finding in it extracts in verse from great names, such as Tennyson, Browning, Coventry Patmore and Dante, extracts in which encouraging counsels were expressed in perfectly understandable words, he nodded his head in appreciation of those great men who could descend for a little while from their 'poetry', and say something to help a simple fellow like himself. That was true Christianity. Over one of the sentences, not in verse, he actually chuckled: 'Hitch your wagon to a star.' What things those great writers thought of! He would have to tell Bob Ryrie that one.

He was as nice in his habits as in his taste for literature. A spot of dirt on his sleeve was enough to make him unhappy, and when occasionally he went out for a country walk for the sake of his health, he always came back, no matter how muddy the roads were, with his black shoes speckless. Clumsiness in others annoyed him; so that whenever Tom returned at night with another wound, the sight of the bloody bandage smeared with oil and grit angered him and sent a thin rush of blood, as though in resentful

answer, to his own cheeks; and somewhere in his mind the words
took shape: 'Great clumsy brute!' For it was all so unnecessary!
To live and dress quietly was simple enough, one would have
thought, and it wasn't as if he approved of display, or put a rose in
his buttonhole except when he was going to meet a girl. He liked
his suits to be of a soft shade of fawn, his neckties to be quiet; and
if his circular stiff collar was smooth as glass and white as snow,
and his circular bowler hat had the burnished sparkle of good
coal, and his shoes were impeccable, he felt he need fear nobody.
Yet he disapproved of the travellers who put on a la-di-da
Kelvinside accent; that was going too far altogether; and although
he tried to speak correctly, in what he took to be English, he kept
something plain and unassuming in the intonation: for it would
have seemed to him offensive presumption to pretend to be
anything but an ordinary fellow like anybody else. And besides
it was only decent to the English language to pronounce it as it
was spelt.

A young man, good-looking and neatly dressed, who sets out
conspicuously to be decent to everybody, will be greeted with
decency on every side; the world surrounding him will obediently
turn into the world of his imagination, and in that world, if his
own decency and his faith in the decency of others are sufficiently
strong or blind, he may live secluded as in a soft prenatal reverie
for a long time, and if he is fortunate for all his life. Mansie lived in
such a world, and except for an occasional harsh echo from the
tremendous world outside he was happy in it. Tom was the most
constant jarring presence, but being constant, allowance could be
made for him, and the disturbance, if not avoided, yet foreseen.
The only serious threat to Mansie's happiness came from those
moments, and they were infrequent, when he found himself
morally in the wrong. That this should happen seemed to him
not only undeserved, but even unnatural, and then he could be
very harsh on whatever acquaintance might happen to threaten
the inviolate image of his decency. He had, however, a happy
capacity for forgetting things; he could forget Tom while he was
actually talking to him; and he forgot those other disagreeable
moments so completely that, searching his mind, it would have
been difficult for him to remember that anybody had ever accused
him of an action even slightly incorrect.

And how quietly and yet intensely happy was his life! When,
returning in the evening in the tramcar from the semi-exile of the
day, he saw his friends like a glorified host awaiting him, friends to
whom for the calm rest of the evening he could devote himself,

sometimes it seemed too much, and a lump would rise in his throat. But recollection gave him a joy almost as intense; for instance when he remembered the moments that big Bob Ryrie laid his scrubbed and scented hand on his sleeve, and, his face as near as a girl's, put him up to some business tip; then the memory of the urgent affection in Bob's voice and eyes would fill him with embarrassment, and he would feel almost as though he had listened to a love declaration. Often, thinking of the way in which Bob inclined his head as they walked slowly side by side, in Mansie's mind a very early and apparently inconsequent memory would rise, the memory of a picture of the disciples in a child's Life of Jesus which his mother had read to him; and there one of the disciples was shown with his head lying on another's breast. Somewhere in Mansie's mind was the definite knowledge that the other figure was Jesus Himself, yet as Bob was confused with this recollection the idea that it should have been Jesus was in some way blasphemous; and it seemed to him a more reverent thought that the second man had been merely a disciple. And while he was dreamily absorbed in this thought, his business round would suddenly appear a sort of pilgrimage, and he himself a humble disciple doing good to people. A real nice fellow, Bob, anyway.

Yet although Bob was so good a friend, something in Mansie shrank from according him more than the privilege of one friend among many; for he had a profound need to diffuse painlessly in an ever wider concentric circle every impulse within him that was urgent or painful, to vaporise himself hygienically without leaving any muddy residue; and to do this he needed many friends. There is one impulse, however, that is so palpably localised in the body that all the arts of the vaporiser must fail; and like most single young men living in a Puritan country, Mansie was sometimes hard beset by sex. He tried to fight it, he vaporised heroically; nevertheless there were hours in which, most incomprehensibly and undeservedly, his mind was besieged by lascivious images, and it was during one of those periods that he went, at Bob Ryrie's suggestion, to an address for men only at the Southern PSA. He never went back again, and for some time there was a slight coldness between Bob and him. The Wesleyan parson had talked so much about 'control' that Mansie had not known where to look; then the word 'sex' had rolled roundly and often through the church, followed by the Biblical term 'seed' – and that was really going a bit too far; it had almost turned his stomach. And in the back seat of the gallery a crowd of young boys – hooligans they must have been – had sniggered so much that at last the preacher, getting quite red about the gills – Mansie could not understand how that vulgar expression had leapt so nimbly to his tongue – had had to rebuke them for their 'filthy minds'. These Glasgow people were really a funny lot.

But soon after this, before the impression left by the PSA had faded, unexpected relief arrived. At the YMCA Sunday afternoon meeting he had admired a girl secretly for a long time, glancing across at her where she sat among the other girls under the long row of windows at the opposite side of the hall. Yet he had never dared to speak to her, for obviously she was a superior girl, perhaps even a school-teacher. She was tall and dark, and her clothes had a ruthless perfection of cut; and individually all those things daunted him. Then one day he caught sight of her approaching on the pavement, and when half-defensively and half-hopefully he put up his hand to his hat she smiled and stopped. And in a few moments he found that they had arranged to go for a walk that evening.

It was the last Saturday of the Glasgow Fair. The city had that spacious look which is given to great masses of stone when the cares within them are suspended; the very houses seemed to be breathing a more rarefied atmosphere (perhaps it was merely that no smoke was ascending from the chimneys), the children's shouts rose with unusual clearness, and even the regular boozers who on this vacant Saturday night got drunk because after all it was a Saturday night, seemed forlorn and ineffectual figures wandering about in a mere dream of intoxication which they were striving to make real: in vain, for the sober crowds whose presence alone can prove beyond doubt to a man that he is drunk had inexplicably melted away. On this one Saturday night in the year a drunken man wandering through the solitary streets, where the summer evening still lingers, may carry on for a long time a peaceful metaphysical debate with himself and at the end of it not know whether he is drunk or sober; and finally he will go to bed more in perplexity than anger, yet with the indefinable feeling that the world has changed.

Mansie and Isa took the tram to Maxwell Park, from which they intended to walk to the Pollok Estate. On the top of the tram, which was almost empty, Mansie felt, as he always did when he was committed for the evening to a single companion, a doubly vivid consciousness of all the friends whom he had left behind and whose company he was in a sense sacrificing, and a trace of bitterness came over him at this girl for being the cause of such a separation, a trace so faint, however, that presently it passed into the resolve to get all the enjoyment he could out of the evening. The paths and woods of the Pollok Estate were deserted, and the sense that he was walking here almost alone with this girl intensified the pleasurable feeling which Mansie received from nature, a feeling compounded of a vague melancholy and a solid conviction of religious comfort. After he had carefully spread out the light raincoat that he always carried with him in provenance, they sat down on the grass behind a line of bushes which screened them from the road. Mansie generally kissed, at some suitable moment, the girls he took for a walk. The moment came, he kissed Isa, and then the dreadful thing happened. What was this woman after? Was this a way for human beings to behave? As if fleeing from violation the trees and bushes around him that had stood tranced as if in anticipation of the coming Sabbath receded to a remote distance, leaving him to his fate . . . yet the worst moment of all came when, turning away awkwardly on his side, he had to readjust his clothes, while behind him he heard a surreptitious rustling. Yes, she could be as discreet now as she liked, he might pretend that he was only brushing the dust from his coat: nothing could hide the vulgarity of this final end; and he felt as though he had been transported among the working classes, who sat about collarless and in their shirt-sleeves, and washed themselves down to the waist at the kitchen sink while the rest of the family sat at the table eating, and the word 'proletariat', which Brand was so fond of using, came into his mind, an ugly and yet meaningless-sounding word. A rush of unavailing pity for his defenceless clothes, which had been so rudely violated, almost blasphemed against, came over him; and he was sorry for hers too. To treat a beautiful summer frock like that showed an insensitive, almost a brutal nature. What need had she for pretty clothes, if this was all she wanted? Any shawlie in the streets was better dressed for it.

Isa had got to her feet and said curtly: 'Well, are you coming?' The light seemed to have faded very quickly: how long had they been lying there? They walked side by side and in silence between the vague trees. Now and then he flicked an invisible speck of dust from his coat sleeve. Suddenly the terrible fear fell upon him that his bowler hat might have lost its polish, might even have been dinted; and he took it from his head and anxiously ran his palm round it. His clothes seemed to sit less well on him; he put his hand up to his necktie and was surprised to find it in place; but his shoes, he knew it for a certainty, must be covered with dust, and a feeling of despair came over him, and he said under his breath: 'Well, they'll just have to wait till I get home.'

The security of home for a moment floated before him, but the sinking at his heart had already forewarned him before the dreadful question leapt to his mind: How could he face his mother now? He saw himself stealing into the house, having walked about until he knew she would be in bed; and he would have to forgo her welcoming smile tonight when he was so much in need of it. Even the cleansing of his shoes from this dust, the witness of his delinquency, would no longer be a symbolical act, emblem of his nicety and the purity of his house, but a sordid utilitarian stratagem to conceal his transgression from his mother, and from Tom too, for Tom would exult in his fall. Suddenly the thought 'Tom has done this' shot through his mind, and an indeterminate and yet vehement gust of anger rose into his throat – anger which demanded a direction and clamoured to be fed, and which he deliberately fed now with the thought (though he knew it to be false) that Tom had tricked him into this, that Tom had in some way by his evil communications caused him to do this. Tom probably liked it; with his low passions he would. And the feeling that Tom had done what he himself had just done was a greater affliction, and gave him a deeper sense of degradation, than the impure act itself; and suddenly he remembered, as something which he had no longer any right to remember, his mother laying her hand on his head, after her Sunday reading from the child's Life of Christ, and saying: 'That's my good boy.'

And how was he to face all the fellows and girls he knew? They were walking now along the railings of Maxwell Park, and he was glad that night had fallen, for his appearance seemed to have shrunk, had grown tarnished and mean, and every time his knees bent there was something abject in the jack-knife-like action of the joints. If Bob Ryrie were only here with him instead of this girl! The picture of the disciple laying his head on the other's breast floated up as from a drowning sea of shapes trying to smother it and sank again, leaving Mansie's head slightly inclined, as though in desperation he were resting it on the soft evening air. And assemblies of young men in clean raiment and with brushed hair, at YMCAs and Bible Classes and Christian Endeavour meetings, appeared in his mind row upon row: there in those decent ranks he would be secure, there he would be clean.

By now they had come within reach of the lighted tramcar at the terminus, and as Mansie stepped into the diffused glassy radiance from the windows he shrank for a moment as if stung.

Isa climbed the stairs without turning to look at him, yet she was careful that her long skirts should not float out behind and disclose any glimpse of her ankles. Well, he had seen a lot more than her ankles, he thought, shocked at his own sudden cynicism. Yet, sitting now in the lighted tram, she looked so proud and unapproachable that what had happened that evening seemed a blasphemous impossibility, and when, seeing the conductor approaching, she said coldly, 'I get off at Strathbungo,' it sounded like a reproof of his disrespectful thoughts, and he felt like a servant receiving an order, and hastily thrust his hand into his pocket for the coppers. Nothing he could do now, not even the simplest action, that did not seem vulgar! She was like those nurses, he thought. And he remembered the hospital where his friend had lain, and where the nurses had had just that same insolent and distant look. Yet his friend had told him that they were ready for anything, and knew all about a chap, and quite callously exploited their knowledge, and had as little respect for the decency of the human body as an engineer had for the works of a machine. And they smoked too. Did she smoke? he was wondering, when her voice startled him: 'Have you lost your tongue, Mr Manson?' The impudence! He could not keep the blood from flushing his face, although he knew she was looking at him. 'That's my business!' he rapped out, but she merely turned away her head with insulting slowness and looked out through the window. Just like a nurse. When the Strathbungo stop came in sight he got up silently to let her out, and silently made to follow her, but when she reached the top of the stairs – they were alone in the tramcar, and only the conductor could hear – she turned and said: 'I don't need your company any further, thanks. Good night.' And she disappeared.

'All right, then! All right!' Mansie exclaimed to the vacant lighted seats in front of him. And after a while, when the tram was already slowing down for the next stop: 'Good riddance!'

Yet after all he did not feel any discomfort when he met his mother that night, nor indeed when he saw Bob Ryrie and his other friends next day. For one moment when he was left alone in the tramcar, the thought – which seemed to have deliberately bided its time until that woman had gone – the appalling thought, How could he, a professing Christian and a Sunday-school teacher, face his God after this? had risen up before him and seemed to fill the lighted top of the tram, which for a moment had a glassier look than ever. Yet the fact that God already knew comforted him in some way and made his offence seem more ordinary. And an ardent plea for forgiveness that night freed him with extraordinary ease from his distress. And when he met Bob Ryrie next evening he was surprised to discover within himself, instead of shame and embarrassment, a secret sense of condescension. He even mentioned casually the name of Isa Smith. What sort of a girl was she?

Bob leant towards him and said earnestly: 'Don't you have anything to do with her, Mansie; I know about her. She'll go the full length with any fellow, and when it's over that's the last he'll see of her. Queer! Gets them to the point, and then looks clean through them the next time she meets them in the street!'

Mansie met her a few weeks later, and she did in fact look through him. 'Just as if she'd scored off me!' he fumed. 'The other way about, I think, my dear girl!'

Yet it was Isa who had scored, for Mansie had fallen, and she had only fallen again. The celerity too with which he had got rid of his remorse, while it eased his mind, disquieted him at the same time. What sort of a fellow could he be not to feel up or down after committing a sin like that? And sometimes to reassure himself he would again ask God's pardon, though he could never feel sure that this might not be an act of presumption against God, an indirect reflection on God for having forgiven him so quickly, and for so completely having removed any trace of remorse. Almost like over-complaisance, almost like collusion! The very thought, the very thought of such a thought, was blasphemous, and now Mansie really did not know for what he should pray to God, nor in what terms his prayer could be couched. Yet his soul seemed to be begging him for something that he could not give it.

The other effect of his offence was more practically difficult to deal with. For he knew now that he could get relief – and with alarming ease – from the stress of desire, and so he was no longer safely enclosed within his own confusion and torment of mind: the door of temptation stood wide open. Girls, even the most faultlessly dressed, even the most unapproachable and nurse-like, were accessible. During the next few years, in spite of an unwearied fight, Mansie fell more than once and less involuntarily than the first time. And curiously enough he too, like Isa, could never afterwards bear the sight of his partners in guilt. To have continued such connections would have seemed to him indecent. How a fellow could deliberately, with his eyes open, go on associating with a girl after it had happened once – planning out their indulgence, perhaps even unblushingly talking it over together! – he simply could not understand such a thing. But if it were always with a different girl it might be called unpremeditated at least, in fact almost a surprise; and if one fell always with a different girl, it was in a way a first fall every time. And the ease with which one obtained forgiveness was almost uncanny.

Yet now and then Mansie still felt the lack of the remorse that would not come. It was as though there was a vacuum within his soul, and at its centre, completely insulated and quite beyond reach, a tiny point of pain.

As he lay thinking of the past evening and involuntarily glancing every now and then at the iron skeleton of the forsaken bed, the memory of that first hour of guilt haunted him, and it was as though something far within his mind, so far within that he could not reach it or stop what it was doing, was trying to weave some connection between Isa and Helen. He had the feeling, at any rate, that something was being woven, something implicating him and yet beyond his control, and the words shot through his mind, 'I'm in for it!' as he thought of Saturday, when he was to meet Helen. And he knew that he would go to the appointed meeting-place in spite of everything, of the scandal, of Tom, of his mother and Jean, and of the opinion of all good fellows.

FOUR

But ye loveres, that bathen in gladnesse,
If any drope of pitee in yow be,
Remembreth yow on passed hevinesse
That ye han felt, and on the adversitee
Of othere folk.

CHAUCER

THEY CAUGHT SIGHT of each other at the same instant; twenty yards of the Central Station separated them. People hurrying to their trains, message-boys, porters, crossed the line stretched between his eyes and hers, but it did not waver, and as he walked straight towards her he seemed to be following a beautiful and exact course which cut through the aimless crowd as through smoke and only reached its end when it joined his hand and hers. At first, when they were too far off to read each other's faces, their eyes had been filled with doubt and questioning; but now love had risen round them and enclosed them like a wall, and within that perfect security they could once more look questioningly at each other, no longer with dread, as a few moments before, but with delight at the thought of the strangeness which it was their reciprocal right to explore. And so keen was their desire to do so that the suddenly arisen citadel of love within which they now stood became an objective fact whose consideration they could calmly postpone.

But the joy of discovery had also to be postponed when presently they found themselves in a crowded third-class compartment of the Gourock train. Helen sat in the corner, Mansie sat beside her; they were silent and gazed out through the window, scarcely seeing the things that fleeted past their eyes: the backs of sooty tenement buildings with washing clouts hanging out to dry from kitchen windows, the neat red-gravelled suburban stations sweeping smoothly past as if on runners, sharp bridges, coal trucks, a red factory wall. But when, after Paisley, the train ran through the flat farm-country, and they saw the yellow cornfields half-reaped, and the red and yellow woods, they felt that it was for them that nature had transformed itself in this strange and brilliant way, for the last time they had seen the country it had been an ordinary green. Now everything was dry and bright; the stubble fields glistened, the ancient castle of Dumbarton on its rock across the river seemed to give out an infinitesimal sparkle as of impalpable dust, the jewelled leaves rested on nothing more solid than the air, were held in it as in a translucent crystal, and the trunks and branches of dried wood rose unencumbered, as if they no longer felt the weight of their shining burden. Yet this aridity was not that of barrenness; the dust on the roads beside the railway lines seemed as rich as seed, and the coloured leaves fell ceaselessly as though they wanted to bury the earth. At Langbank gardens rows of deep and bright yellow flowers flashed by, then the inky tenements of Port Glasgow passed, almost unseen, before their eyes, and Greenock rotting patiently between the beautiful hills and the majestic firth. Nevertheless when they emerged from the stifling tunnel, and for a moment the estuary of the Clyde flashed upon them like a turning mirror before the train ran into Gourock station, they felt as though an oppression had been lifted.

Yet now that they walked along it, they scarcely saw the estuary outstretched like a great blue stone, nor the near houses, nor the dark hills on the opposite shore; for the desire to know and make known had again taken possession of them, and they reached the end of the long and empty promenade as though it had melted into air before them, so open were their minds to each other, and so vivid were the images that they contemplated there. They felt that they must know everything, but still more strongly that they must tell everything; for in the suspended calm which preludes desire, a calm in which passion is so subtly diffused that it is bodiless, they had been so transmuted that they were conscious of nothing within them that needed to be hidden; and at the moment there was indeed nothing. After they had walked on in this way for a while they stopped of one accord and looked round them. They found themselves on the shore road gazing across at Dunoon and Innellan, and they watched for a little a paddle-steamer passing down the estuary towards Rothesay.

'Isn't it lovely?' said Mansie, as though drawing her attention to a sight that had appeared just at that moment; then, 'Will we have a rest?'

She did not reply, but left the road and clambered down the sloping banks of the cliff until she reached a shelf of dry turf. Beneath them the sea's surface ran smooth and unbroken to the

opposite shore several miles away. And lying there they were
frozen to the same immobility as the sea; it was not a frame of
flesh and blood but a transubstantiated body that he clasped; for
though they lay for a long time like this they felt no lessening of
their trance-like ease, nor did his arms grow tired, so perfect was
the equilibrium that reciprocally upbore them, an equilibrium as
of a double trunk growing out of the ground where they lay. When
at last they sat up, it was as by a single impulse coming from
without, as though a voice had called to them both at the same
moment; yet even then they could not break the spell binding
them, and they remained silently leaning against each other while
their eyes gazed out across the firth. Sometimes their faces turned
of one accord and they kissed; the trance deepened and when they
awoke it had kept that deeper darkness, and now it was a little
more difficult for them to move their limbs. Only once did the
spell threaten to break, letting in the menacing world. Mansie had
been playing with a locket hanging at her neck; he opened it idly
and saw inside a twisted strand of black hair. Something far
within his mind said: 'That is Tom's hair.' Helen sat up and
snatched it from him. 'I don't want it! I don't want it!' she cried,
as if in answer to an accusation he had not made, and she tore the
locket from the chain and flung it into the sea. He looked at her,
hardly aware yet of what she had done, but she said: 'I won't have
you made unhappy,' and again leant towards him, closing her
eyes. And while he was still wondering that she should carry about
Tom's hair clasped in a locket, and still thinking of Tom's hair
drowned in the sea – that gave one an uncanny feeling, as if part of
Tom had been drowned without his knowing it – the spell stole
over him again, the trance held them suspended, and when at last
they rose and walked back the flashing arc made by the locket as it
fell into the sea had been lost in the web of their dream, woven
into it like the curves cut by the seagulls in their flight and the
constant lines of the Highland hills opposite.

They had tea in a little tea-room on the sea front. They did not
speak much; fragmentary pictures of seaweed and rocks flowed
through Mansie's mind, he felt the salt scent of the sea air, and
still remembered with surprise and delight Helen in her smart
clothes sitting on that piece of common turf among the rough
rocks and taking up a few ordinary pebbles in her hand as though
it were the most natural thing in the world; and although with her
fine clothes she belonged to a quite different world, calling up a
vision of lace-covered sofas and curtained rooms, she had fitted
perfectly into the picture and had gone splendidly with the sky

and the sea and even the gritty little pebbles. Nor did the grease-spotted tablecloth in the dingy tea-room destroy the unshakable harmony between her and her surroundings; yet when they were out in the street again they did not take the road they had taken that afternoon, but turned their backs upon it and climbed a steep lane leading to the hill behind the town. And now as though with the closing in of the day something else which they did not know were closing in upon them, their trance became blinder, and when, reaching the top of a winding path, they saw a rowan-tree with its red berries burning in the last rays of the sun, and beyond it a field of corn transfigured in the same radiance, they looked at that strange scene as from a dark and shuttered room, and it seemed a momentary vision that must immediately vanish again. The sky darkened over them as they lay in the heather, and now they clung together until all their limbs ached. At last she rose abruptly, and as they descended the hill once more all the heaviness that had so strangely left her body during the day returned, slackening her limbs, and she leant all her weight upon his arm as though to break it.

The train was crowded, and the country lay in darkness. The other people in the carriage were weary and silent. Now and then a smile flitted across Helen's face, and her gloved hand sought his. When they walked out of the Central Station in Glasgow, the lights, after the clarity of the spaces they had left, seemed to float in a fume of dust and noise; and that acrid infusion now entered into their trance, troubling and thickening it, so that when they reached the end of the close where she lived they stood for a long time in a blind embrace which was neither happy nor sad, yet from which it seemed unendurable that they should ever be torn.

It was only when he was nearing his home that any external thought broke into Mansie's reverie. The memory of the locket falling into the sea returned very distinctly, and with it a rush of urgent anxiety for Tom. He remembered his own humiliation that evening after Isa Smith left him in the lighted tramcar. Tom must feel like that too, only far worse. It was terrible to cast off a fellow like that, terrible to cast a fellow's hair into the sea; women were hard, and he could not help blaming Helen and even feeling a little afraid of her. Yet that day had wiped off for good his humiliation with Isa Smith; it had washed everything clean again; 'a clean page', the words came into his mind. But then he saw that division and atonement, wrong and right, were mingled in the love that bound Helen and him together, and this made the bond still stronger; it could never be broken. He stole softly into the house, as softly as one might steal into a place where a victim is still secretly bleeding; he hoped that Tom had not heard him, for it was very late.

FIVE

BRAND AND RYRIE had dropped in for the evening. They sat in the kitchen talking to Mansie and Jean. The table had been cleared and pushed against the wall. Brand was holding forth as usual.

'And I tell you you can't be a Christian without being a Socialist,' he said, looking across at Mansie with his cold blue eyes. They were so cold that they seemed made of glass.

Mansie looked doubtful. 'I don't see that,' he said.

'Don't see that either,' said Bob Ryrie.

'That's because you've never thought about it,' Brand went on. 'What did Christ say?'

Mrs Manson, sitting in the armchair by the fire, looked up. The tone in which Brand mentioned Christ disquieted her; he brought out the name as he might have brought out 'Smith' or 'Mackay'.

'What did Christ say? That you're to love your neighbour as yourself. Is it loving your neighbour to pay him starvation wages, as lots of your churchgoing capitalists do? As I've told you before, it's the churches that have got to be converted first.'

'Yes, to Socialism,' said Bob Ryrie, giving Mansie a wink.

'And why not?' Jean retorted. She did not even glance at Bob Ryrie, but kept her eyes fixed on Brand.

'I thought myself that the churches were out for Christianity,' said Bob, still to Mansie. 'I may be mistaken, of course.'

Jean shrugged her shoulders.

'And so they should be,' Brand seized the lead again. 'That's just our quarrel with them. What have they done all these hundreds of years they've been in existence? Have they helped the weak? Have they abolished poverty? Look at the slums of Glasgow. You've never faced the problem yet. What did Christ say—'

'In 1872,' said Tom sarcastically, entering in his stocking soles and going to the fireplace to get his shoes.

'Tom, Tom, my lamb, you mustna' say things like that,' said Mrs Manson, bending down to get his shoes for him or to hide her face.

Brand looked at Tom with blank uncomprehending eyes. 'What did Christ say?' he repeated. 'That we're all members of one another. That's what any Socialist will tell you. That's what we have been preaching for the last twenty years. And they won't see it. And the Christians are the worst of the lot.'

'Fine Christians you Socialists are!' said Tom, pulling on his shoes. 'I suppose you consider Ben Tillett a Christian?'

'If he helps the weak he's a Christian.'

' "Oh God, strike Lord Devonport dead"!' Tom intoned, jeeringly. 'There's Christianity for you. And he gets a crowd of ignorant navvies to repeat it after him in public.'

Bob Ryrie shook his head at Brand: 'No, that wasn't right, you know. A fellow can go a bit too far.'

Brand glanced at Jean; then he turned to Tom: 'I'd like to ask you a question. Are you on Lord Devonport's side or on Ben Tillett's?'

'I'm on the side of the poor devils that are starving on account of Devonport's and Tillett's damn foolishness.'

'That's all very well; but who's fighting for better pay for them, and who's fighting against it?'

'I'm for better pay all the time, but—'

'Wait a minute. What did Ben Tillett mean when he prayed to God to strike Devonport dead? Did he have any ill-will against Devonport? Not at all. He wanted to stop all these men and their families from starving. There's thousands of women and children starving because of Lord Devonport. You never think of them; you only think of him.'

'Oh, you can twist anything round,' said Tom, bending his red face over the shoes. 'When a Socialist does a damned measly action it's bound to be right!'

'I think it was a silly thing to do,' said Jean. 'Besides, if you think it was right, God evidently didn't, for He didn't answer their prayer.'

Tom laughed. 'That's logic for you, Brand,' he said. 'See if you can find an answer to that.' He got up and walked out, and presently the front door slammed.

Brand seemed taken aback. Then he looked across at Mansie again: 'Well, as I was saying—'

THOUGH JEAN WAS four years his junior, Mansie had a great respect for her opinion and felt singled out when it supported his; and so her dislike for Bob Ryrie, a dislike which nothing, it seemed, could alter, deeply disappointed him and even shook a little his own regard for his friend, although he would not admit it. After Bob's first visit to the house – it was a few weeks before Helen broke with Tom – he asked Jean a little uncertainly what she thought of Ryrie. She put her nose in the air and said: 'You feel he's offering you a coupon.' The blood rushed to Mansie's cheeks; it was as though he himself had been attacked, and he replied: 'Bob's a gentleman! And he's the kindest-hearted fellow you'll meet.'

'Well, he can keep his kindness to himself,' said Jean, and it was clear that she did not consider Bob in the first class.

This was a very small class, but to her a definite one, and indeed the only one she was able to tolerate. She could not have told what qualities people had to possess to belong to it; yet she thought in classes, and so the very first thing that she might be expected to say when asked such a question as Mansie's was, 'He's a pure third-rater,' or 'He's tenth rate.' But Bob was Mansie's best friend, and so the exasperated figure of speech escaped her, and she felt irritated at Mansie for forcing her to speak 'in conundrums'.

Oh, no doubt this Ryrie man was kind-hearted; he let you see that only too clearly; he let you see it in the way he shook hands, in his anxious hopes that you might like Glasgow – as if Glasgow belonged to him! – in his gentlemanly attentiveness, which made you feel that with his eyes he was supporting you in the mere act of living, helpfully assisting you to breathe and endure the immense strain of sitting upright in your chair. And Jean had sat up straighter, had braced her shoulders to hold off this smothering load of solicitude which was about to crush her. No, she could not stand the man, she could not stand his brown eyes with their protective glance, nor his brown moustache waxed at the points, which also seemed in some way an earnest of masculine protection, but became slightly limp, in spite of its waxy rigidity, when the protection was blankly ignored. She could not stand his brown tweed suit, which recapitulated again the note of enveloping protectiveness and gave out the delicatest aroma of tobacco and peat, a faint, pleasant and yet oppressive emanation of somnolence. She wanted to yawn, felt that she would like to go straight to sleep, and her voice when she replied to his polite enquiries sounded remote to her, like a monologue heard when one is half awake. And neither could she stand his neatly shaven face to which the bay rum still clung like a transparent film, making his cheeks look as though they had been iced; nor his scrubbed and manicured hands, nor his pipe for which he apologised, nor the way he inclined his head, like a servant awaiting orders. A fatuous ass, a pure tenth-rater, she told herself, and she was angry with Mansie for having such an acquaintance, and angry too that she could not say so more unequivocally.

But she was quite unequivocal enough for Mansie, and he felt both insulted in his taste and hurt on Bob's account. For a fellow who made people feel that he was offering them coupons could hardly be considered first rate, and it was a galling reflection that his best friend was not first rate. Of course it was all a misunderstanding of Jean's, all due to Bob's kindness of heart; and besides she hadn't seen him at his best; no, it was a pity, but Bob hadn't been at his best. All the same the coupon stuck, and now Mansie could not help remembering that when he met Bob first he too had been a trifle nonplussed, maybe a little put off even. They had met at the Baptist Chapel a little after Mansie's conversion. Bob had begun to pour out information on him right off in the helpful voice of someone directing you to a strange address, saying, 'You should go there,' or 'You should join them, a nice set of fellows.' Mansie had felt quite rushed. Yes, it seemed impossible for Bob to say anything at all without making you think that he was lending you a helping hand; even when he told a funny story he seemed to be making you a present of it, so that you might win social credit for yourself by telling it to someone else; well, perhaps a fellow who was so genuinely anxious to help as Bob got into the habit of talking in that way and just couldn't help it. But later Mansie had stopped thinking about it, and especially after Bob had taken him to that church soirée where all those Boy Scouts were. For they were exactly the same, all eager to help; he couldn't make them out at first, thought they were dashed forward; but then he saw it was all quite genuine: when you lived in a big place like Glasgow you had to be on the look-out for opportunities to help people, that is if you had any decency in you at all; you might need a helping hand some time yourself. Jean didn't realise that yet; she was new to Glasgow and didn't know how hard life might be for a girl there, not to speak of temptations. He didn't care whether Bob was first rate according to her silly notions or not. She could dash well think what she liked

But in the ensuing months Jean showed no sign of getting over her aversion; it became more frank, and so it was no wonder if Bob didn't do himself justice; he hadn't a dog's chance. All the same he was a dashed sight too anxious. After all, had he any need to go to such pains to please Jean? He actually seemed to be quite put out because Jean didn't take to him, and he couldn't help trying again, getting more and more red in the face every time; no, he didn't show to advantage then.

Nevertheless when one evening after Bob had left Jean turned to Mansie and said: 'I object to people making eyes at me because I'm your cousin,' Mansie flared up and shouted, 'He's too dashed good for you!' He had had no intention of saying such a thing; it just jumped out, and for a moment he felt quite taken aback.

'Well, you'd better tell him so,' replied Jean. 'He bores me stiff.'

'Everybody else in the house gets on with Bob. Why shouldn't you?'

'He doesn't make eyes at them.'

'You flatter yourself if you fancy he's making eyes at you!' Mansie became angry again. 'He's only trying to be humanly decent.'

'I prefer people to keep their distance.'

There was no use talking to her, that was clear, and when a few evenings later Bob said with a slight catch in his voice, 'Mansie, I'm afraid I'm making no headway with your cousin; I've done my best to be nice to her, but it's no use,' Mansie replied, 'Don't you bother, Bob. You've been too dashed considerate to her. Yes, by gum!' But then he suddenly felt embarrassed; they walked on without looking at each other; and when Bob broke the silence it was to speak of something quite different.

After this Bob was careful to treat Jean with distant politeness, and the change in fact seemed to take her somewhat aback. Mansie decided that Bob had got the better of the exchanges after all; but that was nothing to be surprised at, for Bob could be quite the man of the world when he chose to take the trouble. And Bob's superiority remained unchallenged until David Brand appeared. By bad luck Bob happened to drop in that evening after Brand had been holding forth for more than an hour, and the sight of Jean sitting listening with her eyes on Brand's face seemed to knock him flat. He began to talk to her in his old confidential tone; she stared at him in surprise for a moment and then snubbed him; but he was completely rattled and couldn't stop until he had been snubbed three or four times. Then he got into an argument with Brand about Socialism; but Brand just played with him, giving Jean a look every now and then; and at last Bob simply turned tail and had to console himself with a long and helpful talk with Mansie in the lobby. Mansie had never seen Bob at such a disadvantage, and was sorry he had ever invited Brand to the house.

He couldn't understand what Jean saw in Brand anyway. A striking-looking fellow, no doubt about it, with his Roman nose and his yellow hair; but there was something queer and cold about him; you could never think of him as a friend. Mansie had met him first at a YMCA dance. It was in the men's cloakroom, Mansie was standing before the looking-glass putting the finishing touches to his necktie, and some fellows were discussing the Insurance Act. 'What do you say to that, Brand?' someone had asked. Mansie turned round at that moment, and he saw a tall, lanky young man raising his head, which had been bowed over a dancing-pump that he was pulling on. 'I think it's claptrap,' came the reply in a falsetto voice, but Mansie was so astonished by the beauty of the briefly upturned face, which was now bent over the other pump, that he continued to stare in a trance at the smooth flaxen hair presented objectively to him, its fairness and the even masses in which it lay reminding him somehow of butter. Afterwards he saw Brand dancing; he was a very bad dancer and seemed to talk to his partners all the time. It was not until near the end of the dance that Brand strolled up, stood beside him, and made some remark about the heat. 'Lots of nice girls here,' Mansie said, not knowing what else to say; but Brand replied, 'I'm not interested in females, I'm here to make converts.' Females! thought Mansie, so it must have been Socialism that he was spouting to them! and as a new dance was just beginning he rushed away.

But next Sunday afternoon at the YMCA Brand fastened on to him, seemed in fact to have taken quite a fancy to him, and although Mansie didn't really care much for the fellow, no doubt about it he was a dashed handsome figure to be seen with. But though Brand was a brilliant success in the Church Literary Society, he didn't make a really deep impression on Mansie until that evening in late spring when they went to see *Arms and the Man*. And it wasn't because Brand laughed at all the right places, looking round him contemptuously, that Mansie was impressed; what struck him was a sentence that Brand dropped carelessly as they were walking to the tramcar; he said, 'I think I'll have to write a play too.' Then Mansie realised all at once that Brand lived in a completely different world from him. For to Mansie the writing of a book or play, even one he could understand, was a mysterious act, he simply didn't understand how it was done; and yet here was a fellow who after being at a play one could make neither head nor tail of simply said: 'I'll have to write a play too!' Mansie felt excited, yet was resolved not to show it, but to reply in the same tone. 'You should, Brand,' he said. 'I think you really should.'

Brand was in fact very handsome, and that was probably enough to give Jean an immediate respect for him; but what won her final approval was the fact that he carried his handsome looks almost scornfully, as though he ignored them; for that seemed to her the perfection of good taste. And so it might have been had he merely ignored them, magnanimously declining to employ them to his advantage; but it would be nearer the truth to say that he was completely oblivious of them, and that they were thrown away on him and so bereft of all meaning. They were like a thankless gift that he was always trying to forget, that he even did his best to deface; for he had so little respect for his exquisite features that he was continually knitting his brow like a schoolboy and twisting his mouth into peevish lines that deserved to look mean, and would have done so in any face less perfectly formed. When he did this, such treatment of a rare physical miracle gave one a sense of ingratitude, even of desecration; nevertheless it was ineffectual, for no matter how he scowled, the lines instead of disfiguring his face merely fell effortlessly into new patterns of symmetry, one more interesting than the other. No, he could not escape from the beauty that had been so unwelcomely thrust upon him.

But though he could not rid himself of it he could refuse to impregnate it with life. So his face was like the photographed faces of actors which seem to be mutely begging for a rôle to bring them to life and add expression and character, no matter of what tinge, to those unemployed features with their tell-tale vacancy. And Brand's face sometimes struck one as that of a man waiting for his rôle, a rôle that should have been his life, a rôle that he would never find. His talk, too, was as trite as that of actors or popular preachers who after declaiming as though in another world, 'I am dying, Egypt, dying,' or 'Ho! every one that thirsteth, come ye to the waters' have nothing left to utter in private but the stale clichés of political and social snobbery. It shocks one that they should do so with such flat conviction. But what shocks one still more is the recognition that after all they are merely acting another part, an innate and compulsory part which has no connection whatever with Antony or Hamlet or Othello, with Christ or Paul. The conversation of Brand seemed to belong to a part such as this, a part which did not suit him, which was false and even badly played, and yet had been imposed upon him so imperatively that he would have to act it all his life. But his words had also the sonorous emptiness that is so often found in the conversation of men who spend their lives advertising commodities which they have not made and will never use, but who nevertheless become mechanically rapturous upon the virtues of those commodities whenever a prospective buyer comes in sight. It had that false and portentously edifying conviction; but also, somewhat incongruously, a touch of the flat assurance of a school-teacher imparting to his class information that means hardly anything to him; securely supported in a sense of right when he asserts that Milton is the greatest English poet after Shakespeare (although Milton bores him), or that man's chief end is to glorify God (although he has never in his life felt the slightest impulse to glorify God). And Brand was a school-teacher.

So it was only in their form that Brand's opinions differed from those of a gentlemanly actor or an unctuous business man. He had been brought up in a Socialist family; his father was an atheistic Marxian; and only when he was twenty-five did David discover Christianity. The discovery was so novel that the ideas he encountered seemed novel too, not unlike those of Ibsen and Shaw, and in his mind Christ was enthroned between those two contemporary idols as a great advanced thinker; a position which, Brand was really convinced in his heart, conferred fresh glory on the New Comer, though he was fond of saying – to impress people with his brilliance – that Jesus was the most advanced and revolutionary of them all. Yet he felt that he had done Jesus a favour in promoting Him to such company, and so he spoke of Him with involuntary condescension; but then he spoke of everything with involuntary condescension – it may have been because he spent so much of his time in teaching. And besides, the people he had to teach now were Christians, and they simply did not know the rudiments of their own subject! So he had to make the matter as simple as possible.

Yet it may be that he could not help making it simple; for a man who has to simplify knowledge for several hours a day to suit minds of twelve or thirteen often ends by simplifying everything; he may acquire such a love for simplification that only simplified ideas give him pleasure. And in fact the more elementary a truth was the more pleasure Brand found in uttering it; and if he could impart to it a sort of flashing triteness he himself was dazzled, as though he had achieved an epigram. So when he came across the axiom, 'God is love,' it was not the statement itself that thrilled him, but the tellingly terse form in which it was couched; and he did not see anything blasphemous in this treatment of a saying which all the wisdom of the world is insufficient to comprehend. For a school-teacher of the conventional kind may not only admire simplified statements; he is capable of falling in love with them simply as statements. He falls in love with them as the commercial traveller falls in love with gypsum, clinkers, or asbestos jointing; for though he can make no more personal use of them than the commercial traveller of those wares, yet they are the things that give meaning to his deliberate and rational activity as a human being. But his love is less humble and passionate than the love of a commercial traveller for asbestos jointing; for he has a monopoly of his goods and the commercial traveller has not, and he can pass them on to the recipient without being obliged to exercise the arts of persuasion, whereas his commercial brother has to summon all his eloquence, has to plead, to propitiate, to dazzle. So when Brand made any simple assertion which his interlocutor refused to accept on the spot, he had a habit of saying: 'I'm telling you.' After asserting that Jesus was a Socialist or that the Kingdom of Heaven was within you – if you voted intelligently – he would add, 'I'm telling you,' and it may be that, yielding to habit, he once or twice capped even the sublime axiom, 'God is love,' with this unseemly addition. For he could not utter even that saying without seeming to clinch something, without appearing to be making a point.

All this, however, is only the outside of Brand, and what lay behind it would be hard to say. It is questionable indeed, whether anything lay behind, for the thing one was most vividly aware of was a want. And in that want there must of necessity have been some deficiency of sex. Nothing else could have made him such a glittering and vacant fool; for even a hardened libertine, if his attention were seriously drawn to the sentence, 'God is love,' would see at least that it was a very extraordinary statement, even if he did not understand it. But to Brand it was not in any way extraordinary; it was an obvious truth contained in a simple sentence of three words. So his lanky body with its unselfconscious and yet ungainly movements was that of one unaware of life; his bones beneath the clothes of a tall man were the shameless, raw bones of a boy of twelve or thirteen. He had also the shy affectionateness of a boy; but he had no charity, for charity is an adult virtue. And catching sight of his inarticulate limbs stretched out like a cry for help as he half lay in a chair, one saw all at once that his words were not after all those of an actor or a teacher, but those of a bright boy of twelve, and one forgave him and felt sorry for him, no matter how intolerable his arrogance may have been a moment before.

It was probably his sexlessness that attracted Jean. Had she known it was sexlessness, it is true, she would have been repelled. But being herself passionate and yet self-repressed, she saw in Brand's demeanour only a scornful superiority to the fatuity of desire. She hated sentiment, she hated the disorder and disingenuousness of love, she hated, above all, women who got left with illegitimate children; she hated them with the naïve hatred of one who passionately disliked ambiguity. So Brand's logical advocacy of women's suffrage and common-sense exposition of religion appealed equally to her; they seemed to exclude all sentimentality. She began to go to women's suffrage meetings with Brand, then to plays, then to Socialist demonstrations. He never touched her or treated her like a woman, and she felt that she had come at last to know a rational being. Nobody else in the house liked Brand, and perhaps that made her go about more constantly with him than she would otherwise have done. It also made her oblivious of the strange state Tom was in.

SEVEN

A MAN WHO has desperately fought for the possession of an unattainable object finds himself in a very strange position when he realises that it is worthless and that his desire for it has suddenly vanished. Then it may appear to him that he should be perfectly happy again; for the cause of his suffering is removed, and the things that once gave him pleasure are still to be had; he has only to stretch out his hand for them. The sun still shines; friends, music-halls, saw-dusted pubs, the lights and crowds of the city, the excitements of football and wrestling – all these exist unaffected by the experience he has passed through. Everything seems to be as it was before; yet something has changed: a hole has yawned in his world, and through it all the warmth that used to be in things has drained away, leaving them cold and empty. He feels the heat of the sun on his face and the backs of his hands, but it is stopped there as by an icy casing; it does not warm his limbs. He breathes the sharp autumnal air, but it is thin and bodiless, an invisible empty something that he draws into his lungs; and although there is no danger of its failing him and he inhales it automatically, yet he finds that breathing requires a slight effort, an effort that tires him, for it is meaningless. His friends too have become curiously external and objective, have receded into a different dimension like figures in a painting, and for the first time he notices lines in their faces that he had never noticed before, lines which, if he were not outside the picture himself, might make him dislike those people. Nor do the jokes of music-hall comedians give him pleasure, for all that he can see in them is a mechanism for producing the automatic spasm of laughter; he sees this clearly, although he is far less capable of analysing his impressions than many of the people who laugh. Sometimes in the midst of wrestling he suddenly surrenders to his opponent's grip where he could have jerked himself free; for the knowledge that the stronger must inevitably overcome the weaker makes all resistance meaningless, and his mind refuses to strike out the sudden inspiration that would extricate him, for that too seems irrelevant. And the feeling that nothing is involved but two fixed units of animal energy, incarnated ludicrously in two sweating bodies, disgusts him, and he stops going to the club.

Seeing that so many things are empty, although still perplexingly palpable to his eyes and mind, he falls back on the most simple and gross and therefore dependable realities in his life: on necessity and deliberate pleasure. He rises every morning to go to work, because he must; and he drinks, because drink, if taken in sufficient quantities, can be relied upon to produce an effect as independent of the unstable human will as a natural law. So he clings to drink as the one solid thing in a world that has become insubstantial. Yet he does not drink to forget, but simply to comfort himself: to fill the vacuum within him with a warm and friendly presence, with something that will lie down and coil itself snugly inside him like an affectionate, sleek, soft animal, say a little black puppy. He feels then so intimately united with a cordial and caressing presence that he prefers to sit alone over his beer or his whisky, so that nothing so incalculable as human society may interfere with his pleasure.

But the fact that he has become a solitary drinker shows that other things besides the things he sees and hears have gone empty and blind: his ideas, his very actions. His actions have lost their content, have become neutral, so that now he does without scruple things of which once he would have been ashamed even to think. So when one evening Tom Manson, while sitting before the fire in the empty kitchen, caught sight of his mother's purse on the mantelpiece and got up and looked inside it, he did so casually and absently, as one turns over an illustrated paper in a doctor's waiting-room. And when, seeing a number of coins inside, he took one out and put it in his pocket, it was a self-evident and yet unimportant action, the mere shifting of an object from one place to another. He felt neither guilty nor elated, he hardly felt interested, and the fact that presently he put on his shoes and went out to the pub at the corner of the street was only an accidental effect of his original action – if it could be called an action – and not the proof of any design. When he had drunk the half-crown he felt warmed and comforted, but that was all; the coin was gone, and it had such an indirect relation to the glow he felt within him that it might never have existed at all, far less have been stolen by him two hours before; he scarcely gave the matter a thought. Had he kept the half-crown, or had he spent only part of it, no doubt his conscience would have smitten him every time he heard the jingle in his pockets; but the half-crown was gone, and by next evening the effect was gone too. Yet when next evening his mother complained that she must have lost a two-shilling piece he said to her: 'You should be more careful with your money; you leave it lying about too much'; and he meant what he said. And on Saturday he gave her an extra five shillings for his weekly board: 'Got a bonus this week,' he said.

But Mrs Manson continued to leave her purse lying about, until one day she discovered that a pound note was missing. That was a serious matter; she could not get over it, and her lamentations drove Tom into a fury. 'It serves you right!' he shouted. 'Can't you look after your money?' And on Saturday he did not give her anything extra; it was her own fault, and he needed all his money for himself. After that the purse was not left lying about.

Yet the thought that Tom might have stolen the money never entered Mrs Manson's head; she could not imagine anyone she knew doing such a thing; and when she read in the newspapers of thefts what she saw was the stylised image of a thief, a being so different from the people she knew that had she interrogated her imagination she would probably have found him furnished with a distinctive cut of clothes, a subtle and inconspicuous livery. So she never suspected Tom, although Mansie was continually complaining of his thefts. Now it would be Mansie's ivory-headed stick that was missing, now one of his ties; he would find it next morning crumpled up and flung on the floor of Tom's room. The fellow might at least take care of one's things, if he insisted on pinching them! Mansie suffered in silence for a while, and when at last he complained to Jean and Mrs Manson, Jean remained silent and Mrs Manson said quite unexpectedly: 'I never thought you twa boys wad be enemies.' That silenced Mansie, and he could not complain to Tom either, for they were not on speaking terms; and besides, in the midst of his anger sometimes he felt strangely touched by those naïve thefts; they were so childish, they were what a little boy might do to an elder brother who did not love him. Occasionally he was actually alarmed at Tom's familiar use of his things; it touched one so intimately, it was like a threat, and it was unnatural too, quite unlike Tom; and the thought would come into his mind: Tom must be very unhappy. But then his exasperation, tinged with a little dread, would return again, and seeing that his mother and Jean refused to do anything he spoke bitterly of his wrongs to Helen.

Tom's own feelings when he took Mansie's ties and vests might have been expressed in the words: 'Why should he have everything?' and although he was not consciously aware of Helen as an item in that everything, no doubt it was she, and she alone, that was at the back of his mind. So his open use of his brother's belongings was not merely a silent announcement that Mansie was outside the pale now, with no right to protest, whatever was done to him; it was also the symbolical declaration of a claim to have unconditionally all that Mansie had, and Mansie had been wise in seeing a threat in it. A very indeterminate and quite powerless threat, however, almost a fictitious one, for the Helen that Tom wanted was not the Helen who had passed into Mansie's possession, but an illusion, once cherished and now dead, which his brother was powerless to restore to him. He did not know what he wanted from Mansie, and so he took whatever he could get.

EIGHT

ONE EVENING MANSIE decided to walk home instead of taking the tramcar as usual. He had been in the office all day giving an account of his last quarter's work and going over the possibilities of opening up new custom during the coming weeks; the manager had been very pleased with his report, but Mansie felt cramped and a little stifled after sitting all day in the poky office – the manager had actually insisted on sending out for dinner – and now he wanted to stretch his legs. And besides he was curious to find out how Eglinton Street would strike him now after such a long time, for passing through it in the tramcar every evening was quite a different thing from walking from end to end of it on foot. Months and months it must have been since he had done that; not more than once or twice since he had been taken from the office and put on the road. What could have possessed him to walk home through that street every evening during those first months in Glasgow? Of course, it was Bob Ryrie; Bob had told him that he must take exercise for the sake of his health. All the same Eglinton Street was a queer place to take exercise in; not much health to be picked up in Eglinton Street. It had made him feel quite low-spirited at times, especially when he was tired. Well, he got enough movement now as it was without having to walk through Eglinton Street.

He crossed the Jamaica Bridge. Dusk was falling and the lamps were being lit; they ran in two straight rows up the slightly rising street, and those in the distance hung in a soft moony haze that was almost fairy-like. The pavement was damp and sticky, though there had been no rain, and now it seemed to him that it had always been like that. After passing through on the tramcar, too, one felt uncomfortably near the ground down here, as though walking along the bottom of a gully which was always slightly damp, while a little above the level of one's head ran a smooth and clean high road. When a tramcar sailed by with all its lights on he felt tempted to run after it.

Astonishing the number of dirty squalling children that were down here, down here the whole time by all appearances, for you never saw them anywhere else, perhaps they never got up at all, poor little beggars. And the way they yelled and screamed was enough to scare you; wasn't like a human sound at all. Yet you never heard them when you were passing on the tramcar. And into Mansie's mind came a phrase that the Reverend John had been fond of using, a phrase from the Bible: 'Crying to the heavens.' Perhaps that was what the poor little beggars were trying to do, their voices sounded so desperate; but their cries remained down here, all the same, seemed in a way to belong to this level, perhaps never got as far even as the house roofs, seeing that you never heard them in the tramcar. A terrible life for those youngsters. And the girls in shawls; walked straight at you, made you step out of their way pretty quick, and even then brushed against you intentionally as if to say: If you walk here you've got to take the consequences. And you never saw them speaking to these poor little kids, not even speaking to them. Wouldn't like Helen to have to walk through this street, by gum! A difference between this and that shore road outside Gourock.

Maybe it would be best to take the tramcar at the next stop after all. He hesitated, but to stand down here frightened one; walking was bad enough, but standing was far worse; and so before he had time to weigh the matter he abruptly went on again, and as he did so he felt angry. A fine kind of street to be in a Christian town! Blatchford was quite right, by gum; streets like this had no right to exist, people could say what they liked. A warm cloud of stench floated into his face, he hurried past a fish-and-chip shop, and in a flash Eglinton Street rose before him from end to end as something complete, solid and everlasting; it had been there all the time, he realised, and it would always be there, something you had to walk round every morning and evening, that forced you to go out of your way until at last you got used to your new road and it seemed the natural one. As he passed the shop, whose crumbling door-posts seemed rotted and oozing with rancid grease, something made him glance up. Yes, there in the next close mouth she was standing, the great fat red-haired woman with her arms clasped about her overflowing breasts as if to keep them from escaping. Queer, he had clean forgotten her. But there she was, and it seemed to him that she too had been there all the time, standing at the end of the close and keeping them from escaping; and she too was something that one had to walk round, a fixed obstacle that could never be removed. He hurried on. Terrible to have to live down here; but the street was mounting, the houses were thinning, the crowds were thinning too, only a few had managed to struggle up here where he was; and they were better dressed, they were like himself, they lived in the suburbs. And his confidence began to return, and with it pity for those poor beggars who were shaken together down there to the bottom of the street like rubbish at the bottom of a sack. A church. Queer to see a church here. A group of young men, clean-shaven and with mufflers round their necks, stood bristling on the pavement and stared at him without moving aside. He stepped into the street – still muddier, still nearer the ground down here – and made to walk round them; but then he changed his mind – these fellows had to be taught a lesson! – and so he strode straight across to the tramcar halt at the other side of the street and stopped there as though waiting. He wouldn't give them the satisfaction of think-ing he had stepped off the pavement for them!

But he had to wait a long time, for all the tramcars were full. Now and then he glanced across at the bristling group on the other pavement; it was almost dark now, but they were standing under a lamp-post and he could see them quite clearly. The stream of home-going pedestrians flowed more thickly now along the pavement, but where the group was stationed it made a bend, wavered, turned aside, and then flowed on again. Mansie's anger mounted and mounted. A set of hooligans! And the sight of that long, living, helpless animal stretching away under the rows of lamps until it was lost in a dirty haze, stretching so far that it seemed tired and weighed down by its own dragging length, but yet flowed laboriously round this small hard obstacle when it came to it, made him far angrier than his own discomfiture had done. Tom wouldn't let himself be shouldered aside like that, by gum he wouldn't! He would teach those young hooligans a lesson; he would send them flying! And Mansie longed for Tom to appear, and when at last he got on to a tram in which there was only standing room he blamed the roughs for that too, and his anger flamed up again. *They* flourished in the slums, those hooligans, it suited them down to the ground, they were in clover. It was time to put an end to these plague spots; for that was what they were, just plague spots. But those other poor beggars at the bottom of the street, it was no joke for them; a fellow couldn't close his eyes to the fact; they were a problem. Blatchford might be an atheist, but he was quite right there, people could say what they liked. The words of Gibson in the office came into his mind: 'And what about the poor bloody little children?' but he did not smile this time; Gibson was a bit of a card, and an extremist too, but by gum he was right. It was enough to make a fellow join the Clarion Scouts. And as he got off the tramcar at the corner of his street he half wished that it was Brand he had to meet that evening, instead of Bob Ryrie.

NINE

IN A HOUSEHOLD consisting of four people a state of armed silence between two of them is like the opening of a hole in the middle of the floor. They have all moved about at their ease, they have sat where they liked; but now their chairs are pushed back against the wall and when they speak to each other it is across a gulf. Arithmetically the silence between Tom and Mansie should have affected only themselves, and the possibilities of intercourse that remained were obviously considerable. Mrs Manson and Jean could still speak to everyone in the house, and Tom and Mansie could each speak to Mrs Manson and Jean. But though it was on this strictly arithmetical foundation that the new domestic arrangements were based, for there was nothing else to base them on, the subtler effects of the silence were inescapable. One of these was irremediably to reduce the size of the family. When both Tom and Mansie were in no one could talk naturally, and so they were always wishing one of their number away. For then the family was reborn again; a family, it was true, that had been lopped, and suffered from an unuttered bereavement; yet nothing unites a household more selfishly and tenderly than the absence of one of its members. And if Mansie and Tom, the inconstant links in that constant chain – by turns the bereaved and the absent – felt their position an equivocal one, that only made them identify themselves more eagerly with the family while the chance was given them. They did so as if under the approaching shadow of extinction, as if they were taking a last chance.

Or at least it was so at the beginning, before the new state of things had hardened and been accepted with the selfishness of habit. Then Tom, already careless of himself, very soon became careless too of what his mother and Jean thought of him, and began to use the house as a mere convenience. It was Mrs Manson who suffered most, for Jean and Mansie were very often out during the evenings. But even when Jean was in talk was as constrained now in Tom's presence as it had once been when both he and Mansie were there. For by some mysterious leger-demain Tom seemed to evoke by himself, as he sat morosely over the fire, that gulf in the middle of the floor which they both wanted to forget.

And Tom was in the house a great deal. His weekly routine had become so mechanical that it could be calculated beforehand. By Tuesday night he had drunk all his wages, except for the few shillings to take him to and from his work, and from Tuesday to Friday he sat over the fire every evening, staring into the coals and doing nothing, yet bitterly annoyed if he was interrupted in that empty occupation. He seemed to find a peculiar satisfaction in the warmth and silence, a satisfaction without pleasure, however; indeed a strictly impersonal satisfaction. For it was not himself that he warmed there, but his grudge against Mansie and Helen, and as this was a private duty rather than a pleasure it was only natural that his expression should be austere and jealously guarded. Sometimes, partly out of old habit, partly out of joyless self-indulgence, he took out his long cherished dreams of a free life in the colonies and warmed them there too. But by now they had become as cold and empty as everything else; they were like pictures hung up on the wall and shuttered in with glass; and even when he thought of ships, often all that would come into his mind was the neat little model of a liner high and dry in its glass case in the window of a shipping agency in Renfield Street. All this was no longer a possibility in his mind, hardly even a dream, simply a picture; yet he took pleasure in contemplating that picture with his mother sitting so near him quite unaware of what he was doing; it was a malicious, almost a revengeful pleasure.

The family had to make a show of unity when anyone came in, but that was quite easy, and the insincerity it involved was actually enjoyable; for when one after another the whole family had spoken or replied to the visitor, the invisible gulf seemed to close; it became a merely private abyss that existed only while no spectator was there to see it. They all felt this particularly when Bob Ryrie called; but Brand, being absorbed in himself, left them in their isolation; and besides Tom was always quarrelling with him. It was partly Brand himself that he disliked, partly Brand's ideas; and when Brand brought out as a last appeal, 'You must give the bottom dog a chance,' Tom would retort, 'You can say what you like, but there'll always be wasters, and why should decent chaps have to pay for their damn foolishness? They've too damn much done for them as it is.' And the fact that Mansie was coming more and more to agree that the bottom dog must be given a chance winged Tom's anger; such sentiments in Mansie seemed the most open and shameless hypocrisy.

Jean, to Brand's surprise, always took Tom's side in those arguments. It was partly an indirect demonstration that she considered Tom ill-used, partly an act of loyalty to the family. And when she joined the ILP she told Brand that Tom must not know about it. But such things cannot be hid; Tom soon came to know, and, although he did not reproach her, he felt that she had betrayed him, and he no longer argued with Brand, but simply ignored him. Mrs Manson too was hurt by Jean's action, and it was only when Mansie as well as Brand assured her that Socialism was Christianity in practice, and that the Reverend John himself was coming more and more round to it, that she was content to be uneasily reassured.

Nevertheless Jean's action was to her only another proof of the corrupting influence of Glasgow. In her heart she blamed Glasgow for all the misfortunes that had happened since they had come south, though she did not say this for fear of being laughed at. Yet it was inconceivable to her that had they all stayed in the surroundings she knew and trusted, Mansie should have taken Tom's girl. It was simply the portion of the corruption of Glasgow allotted to them, their private share of the corruption that was visible in the troubled, dirty atmosphere, the filth and confusion of the streets, the cynical frankness, hitherto unknown to her, with which people here talked of their privatest affairs, their fathers and mothers, sisters and brothers. She could not understand them or their ways, and she grew shy of talking about Tom and Mansie even to Jean, and especially after Jean joined the ILP. For with that Jean had identified herself with Glasgow; she had become by deliberate choice a Glasgow girl, and – who could tell? – perhaps she would no longer even understand. And when one evening Mrs Manson found Robert Blatchford's *Britain for the British* in a drawer in Mansie's bedroom, it seemed to her that she no longer understood her family and that Glasgow had taken them and made them almost as strange as itself.

But worse was her fear of all the machinery, machinery she did not understand, and with which Tom was so unavoidably associated. Indeed Tom had now more accidents than ever; his hands were perpetually in bandages. He had always been reckless; he was now indifferent as well; but what exposed him most of all to accidents was the fact that, feeling shut out from everything, he felt shut out too from the very work he was doing every day, and so never penetrated within it to that security which work itself seems to give. He never reached that almost trance-like abstraction which we envy in the workman bowed over his bench, enclosed in his task as in a private Eden where time no longer exists, so remote and calm that even a child will become quiet and hesitate to speak to him. Tom remained outside, and this made him irritated with his tools, and in his irritation he began to treat them disrespectfully, began indeed to acquire an impatient scorn for machinery wherever he encountered it. Nothing, however, punishes disrespect more promptly and ruthlessly than machinery, and when Tom was brought home late one Saturday night with his head bandaged and his blue serge suit covered with mud, it was because he had treated a tramcar with insufficient deference. He had been drinking; yet while descending the stairs to get off he had provocatively kept one hand in his trouser pocket, using only the other as a support. When, after what seemed to him a long time, he found himself lying in dirt and water in the street with a crowd of strange people round him, he naturally enough felt cold and miserable, for it was the middle of November; but he also felt a little frightened. These people standing round meant well, he could see that; yet he was helplessly exposed to them like an exhibit, and the overpowering stream of kindness that they poured down on him was like a threat and filled him with sudden panic; he felt as though he had been lynched in some strange way, lovingly and tenderly lynched by the assembled YMCA. So that he was glad when a young man raised him up, asked his address and led him home. Someone had bound up his head, which felt stiff, tight and wooden, and it was with surprise that he felt under the bandage a quite soft, pulsing trickle.

Next day was Sunday. Sunday morning was always a bad time for him, and he lay in bed gloomily listening to the church bells jangling; there were loud pompous peals with blank intervals which filled him with apprehension, and busy fretful nagging little bells that went on and on; it was like a tin factory gone mad. His head throbbed, and when he rose to draw up the blinds he felt so queer that he walked over to the mirror instead. Christ! he was looking bad with that bandage on his head and the black rings round his eyes; he looked a real waster. And he went back to bed again without troubling even to pull up the blinds: a real waster, and he would never be anything else.

He refused to see a doctor, although for several days his head hummed and rang, and at the back, where the wound was, there clung a lump of pain; it felt like a clod of hardened mud that would not be dislodged. At last the pain went away and his scalp healed. And in spite of his indifference, his relief was so great that he resolved to pull himself together and go straight.

When Mansie first heard of Tom's accident he was very angry. A fine way to behave, the fool would break his neck some time yet! But when Tom began to go straight, keeping decent company, dressing neatly and taking a drink only now and then, Mansie became ashamed of his annoyance. He expected every day that Tom would suddenly turn to him and say something, for the fellow was completely changed, he had quite a different look about him; and when Tom gave no sign of speaking Mansie felt a little hurt. But on one account he was sincerely relieved by Tom's reformation; for now he felt there was nothing to prevent his joining the Clarion Scouts. With a brother who was a waster he would never have been quite sure; it might have looked a bit fishy, for lots of people looked upon Socialism as fishy. Pure prejudice, of course; the crowds he had met at Socialist demonstrations were a very decent lot; welcomed you too, no side about them, a friendly set of fellows. So Mansie decided to take the plunge; with Bob joining at the same time one felt better about it. And once his application form was filled in and sent off a surprise awaited him; it was as though the Masonic circle of decent fellows had widened infinitely all at once, and he felt as a visionary democrat feels when he sees everywhere hosts of free and intelligent electors spring up at some great extension of the franchise, hosts of free and intelligent electors where before there had been a dull and slavish mass. The very distinguishing marks of decent fellows were radically altered, the old marks seemed inessential and ridiculous, and it was almost by a whole world of decent fellows that Mansie now delightedly saw himself surrounded. You had only to look below the surface, and even those hooligans in Eglinton Street might turn out to be much better than they seemed.

PART TWO

TEN

THE PROCESSION WAS gathering in George Square. It was a
warm still May morning; a few white clouds floated far up in the sky.
As Mansie turned the corner of St Vincent Street he saw, far away,
the banners languidly waving in the square, waving in silence, for
no sound came from those parti-coloured rectangular blocks of
human beings, which from here looked as peaceful and dumb as the
rectangular buildings frowning above them. Mansie's footsteps
rang sharply in the deserted street. It was the first Sunday in May.

As he drew nearer, and on the motionless rectangles isolated
points of movement started out and spread into an imperceptible
ripple running along the whole line, he wished that Bob Ryrie had
not had to call off at the last moment; but a fellow could not take
risks with a bad cold. At last he reached the procession and
paused on the pavement, feeling very exposed while he looked
around him distractedly for some face he knew. A voice quite near
at hand shouted his name; it was like a lifeline thrown out to him
where he was standing on the pavement. Why, there were the
Clarion Scouts almost under his nose, and he hadn't seen them!
He smiled back and hastily fell in at the rear beside a white-faced
pot-bellied man whom he did not know.

And immediately he was enclosed in peace. It was as though he
had stepped out of a confused and distracted zone into calm and
safety, as though the procession had protectively enfolded him,
lifted him up and set him down again on the farther bank of a
tranquil river among this multitude who like him had reached the
favoured land; and the people who passed on the pavement with
averted or hostile or curious eyes, on their way to church or
merely out for a walk, had no longer any power over him; for they
were still wandering out there in exile, out there on the pavement,
and he was safe, at home and free. Yet one thing still troubled
him: that he was in the last line of the procession, so that the
threatening world yawned at his very heels; but when a new
contingent from the Kingston ILP marched up and stationed
itself behind him his security became perfect; he was embedded in
fold after fold of security.

So that now he had leisure to look round. A little in front of him a bareheaded man in a brown velvet jacket and knickerbockers was carrying a child on his shoulder. It was a little girl, and when she turned her head to look down on all those strange faces her yellow hair glinted in the sun. Mansie could not take his eyes from her, and when the procession began to move, when, in a long line like the powerful and easy rise and fall of a quiet surge, the ranked shoulders in front of him swung up and down, bearing forward on their surface that gay and fragile little bark, unexpected tears rose into Mansie's throat. But when presently from the front of the procession the strains of the 'Marseillaise' rolled back towards him over the surface of that quietly rising and falling sea, gathering force as it came until at last it broke round him in a stationary storm of sound in which his own voice was released, he no longer felt that the little girl riding on the shoulder of the surge was more beautiful than anything else, for everything was transfigured: the statues in George Square standing in the sky and fraternally watching them, the vacant buildings, the empty warehouses which they passed when presently they turned into Glassford Street, the rising and falling shoulders, even the pot-bellied, middle-aged man by his side; for all distinction had been lost, all substance transmuted in this transmutation of everything into rhythmical motion and sound. He was not now an isolated human being walking with other isolated human beings from a definite place to a definite place, but part of a perfect rhythm which had arisen, he did not know how; and as that rhythm deepened, so that all sense of effort vanished in it, he no longer seemed even to be propelled by his own will but rather to be floating, and with him all those people in front and behind: the whole procession seemed to be calmly floating down a sunny river flanked with rocky cliffs on either side, floating like a long wooded island where the trees stand in orderly ranks and breathe out fragrance and coolness to either shore. His arms and shoulders sprouted like a tree, scents of spring filled his nostrils, and when, still gazing in a trance at the bareheaded man with the little girl on his shoulder, he also took off his hat, his brows branched and blossomed, and he could not help remembering that statue of Moses he had seen in a shop window with the little horns rising from its forehead; they were barren, shrivelled to dry bone, they would never know anything like this. And as he looked round him, seeing and yet unseeing, it was transubstantiated bodies that he beheld everywhere; and it did not matter that on many of those faces were the marks once traced in some other world by greed and humiliating servitude and resentment and degradation, that many of the women's bodies were shapeless, as though they had been broken into several pieces and clumsily put together again: it did not matter, for all outward semblance was inessential, all distinction had fallen away like a heavy burden borne in some other place; all substance had been transmuted. And although the pot-bellied man by his side spoke to him now and then, and he replied, he could not have told what was said; for words too had lost all distinction and become transparent in this state where speech and silence had equal meaning.

They passed the crumbling houses of the Saltmarket, where women in shawls and men in mufflers stood at the close mouths and stared at them, and it seemed to Mansie that they too were changed, in spite of their jeering laughter, and that only one little thing was needed, a thing as easy as the lifting of a finger, for all those men and women to join the procession, to step on to the floating island and be in bliss; and he thought of the hooligans in Eglinton Street: he would have liked them to be here too; there was room for all. Even when the procession reached the Glasgow Green and that great harmonious being voluntarily broke its body as for some unknown sacrament, crumbled for some mysterious and beneficent purpose into isolated souls again – even then the spell did not lose its power, and Mansie wandered from platform to platform, where Socialist orators, still transfigured so that he scarcely recognised them, spoke of the consummated joys of the future society where all people would live together in love and joy.

It was only in the evening, when everything was over and he was walking home, that he began to wonder whether he had talked a great deal of nonsense during the day; but even that fear did not trouble him, for everything was allowed. He was almost glad that Bob had not been able to come, and that he had plunged into this business by himself. As he walked up Eglinton Street he thought: Nothing can be the same again. And passing the great red-haired woman standing at the end of her close, he did not make his usual detour, skirting the edge of the pavement, but kept straight on, almost brushing her with his shoulder. Nor did the young hooligans bristling on the pavement have any power to harm him now; yet as he wanted to please even them he stepped eagerly and with a smile into the street when he came to them, and though one of them asked truculently: 'What the hell are you girning at?' all Mansie could do was to go on smiling, until another of the youths interposed: 'Let the young fella alane. He hasna' hurt you, has he?'

But when Mansie opened the kitchen door and saw Tom sitting by the fire in gloomy and rock-like apathy, it was as though he had run his head against a wall; he paused irresolutely at the door and then went through to the parlour and stood looking out at the people passing. As he watched them his blissful security slowly came back. He stood like this for a long time.

ELEVEN

Und dass mein eignes Ich, durch nichts gehemmt,
Herüberglitt aus einem kleinen Kind,
Mir wie ein Hund unheimlich stumm und fremd
HUGO VON HOFMANNSTHAL

AT FIRST IT seemed to Mansie that the revelation vouchsafed
him on May Day must last for ever. As it happened the first blow
to it came in a few days and from those who had shared it with
him. On Wednesday evening he eagerly set out for the Clarion
Scout rooms. But when he ran up the stairs and burst into the
rooms the atmosphere of enveloping acceptance was not there to
meet him; nobody paid any attention to him; in the twinkling of
an eye they had all dwindled to their former size again; they had
all fallen back; and Sunday and all that had happened in it might
never have been! He wandered dejectedly from group to group.
They were discussing the procession: apparently it had been a
disappointment. Mansie listened, at first with bewilderment, then
with interest, then to his surprise with pleasure, for as his
exaltation of the last few days gradually oozed out of him and
he returned to a more comfortable size it was actually a relief – he
couldn't but admit it to himself, it was an undeniable relief,
though it left a sort of empty feeling somewhere. His feet were on
the earth again. Strange how easily you slipped back into your old
feelings! And when a man turned round to him and asked how he
had liked his first procession, he said carelessly: 'Oh, it was quite
all right in its way.'

Yet when he left the Clarion Scout rooms he felt cheated and at
a loss. The best part of the evening still lay before him, and all at
once it seemed quite blank – he had nothing to occupy himself
with; an evening wasted! So he resolved to walk home. But
coming to Eglinton Street and seeing all those people fallen back
again, all those dirty children still crying to the heavens – they
would cry for a jolly long time before they got any answer, poor
little beggars! – it was more than he could bear; and at the strident
voice of an open air evangelist at the first street corner he abruptly

crossed to the other side and waited for a tramcar to take him home. As he sat on the top of the tram he reviewed again his feelings on May Day, and now they filled him with alarm. Something far wrong with the whole business; something soft and sticky, almost indecent! The disciple laying his head on the other's breast rose into his mind; he had been jolly near doing that himself, by gum! Almost made a complete ass of himself. What would the people he knew have said if they had seen him? And a still earlier memory stirred insinuatingly in the grounds of his mind. But he pitilessly repressed it: an unhealthy-minded, unnatural young beggar he must have been then! Had to take care. Dangerous to let yourself go like that. That fat man he had walked beside in the procession, couldn't even remember now what he had said to him, might have said anything, given himself away hopelessly. The disturbing memory stirred again, rose a little, vague and sickly, and seemed to float down his mind like the procession floating down Glassford Street, becoming involved with the rising and falling shoulders, which now gave him a sensation almost of sea-sickness. He would take dashed good care that he didn't go to another May Day! But all the time he was on the tramcar he could not get that early memory out of his mind.

It was a quite vague memory, and concerned an affair that he had had, and should not have had, with a little girl from a neighbouring farm when he was six. He had had no consciousness of guilt, or only a sense of it as purely fanciful as the comedy he was playing; and indeed, seeing that sex was still unawakened in him, and he was only acting, he was probably as innocent of any actual or even possible offence as a character playing an enigmatic part in a story. Yet he had felt environed by guilt, and this had made him carry out his games in secrecy. At certain stages children seem to live in two separate worlds, both of which are real. In one world, the world which included his parents and all other grown people and himself, a place perfectly familiar to them but full of perplexities for him, Mansie knew that what he did was, in spite of its simplicity, a sin of awful dimensions; but in the other country where he lived with his playmate there was no evil, or a purely fictitious evil which he could summon before his mind only by make-believe. So accompanying the clear knowledge that he was disobeying his father and mother, was the feeling that he was committing a fabulous sin, a sin which was not a sin to him, but to some shadowy figure – it might be God – in a world only visible to his elders.

In his memory, and more especially during the years of adolescence, this episode seemed to him, grotesquely enough, the most shameful in all his life. He could no longer remember the feelings that had accompanied his acts, and he seemed to himself simply to have been a very nasty and unnatural little boy. Unnatural, for now he could only see those games, played in a world where the powers of sex were still unawakened and so nonexistent, through the eyes of a youth whose thoughts were penetrated with sex and his awareness of it, and in this distorting medium his childish play acquired not only a shadow of perversity, but even something of the disgrace of impotence; and when, after joining the Clarion Scouts, someone told of the agapemones of the early Christians, those promiscuous love-feasts in which lust seemed so strangely mingled with piety, innocence with vice, universal love with sexual perversity, that period of his childhood wavered up before him again. The forms taken by his games, however, were by then almost completely effaced from his mind, and all that remained was a thickly-woven cloud, corporeally oppressive, and both bright and dense, like a golden nightmare weighing on his mind. Yet at the same time he felt that this cloud lay deeper in childhood than any other memory he could summon, lay there, ring-shaped, in an almost terrifyingly secure and still zone, at that very heart of childhood into which it is perilous even for children to venture too far. Its radiance was richer than the light on the little green hill behind the house where he had lain so often and watched the ships passing over the sound in the shadow of the black islands – passing so slowly that he could discern no motion in them, and yet saw, with a feeling of wonder, that they had moved. The towering hills changing from black to dark blue of the neighbouring isle, the little red coat with the yellow buttons – a red and yellow so absolute that they seemed to exist not as mere qualities but as living things, quivering like flames and glowing like flowers: these he remembered vividly; yet they faded almost to the hue of an ordinary memory if the thought came to him of that rich and bright cloud in which, as in a trance, some part of him for ever beyond his reach still lay imprisoned; so that the memory awoke in him a vague need to struggle and free himself from something or other, he did not know what.

He and his playmate had already turned to other games when his father took a farm on the mainland. And then, without warning, the guilt, which had been hanging, a small and distant cloud in the sky, and should with the discontinuance of the offence have dissolved and vanished, fell upon him in a clap.

It was after the time of the sheep-dipping. His father had warned them all against touching the sack in which the sheep-dip was kept. The sack was laid out in a field at some distance from the house; the sheep were dipped, and the empty sack was burned; but for a long time afterwards Mansie could not rid himself of the obsession that the poison had got on to his hands. He washed them in terror many times a day until they had a wasted and transparent look. At first it was the poison that he tried to cleanse from them; but as time went on he washed them in a panic, as though he were purifying them of something that he had long since forgotten, some mysterious stain which could be erased only for a moment and immediately returned again; like the *Book of Black Arts* which you could drown in the sea or burn in the fire, but would always be found lying in its place in your trunk if you had once been so unfortunate as to possess it. Every day was filled with alarms and trepidations which invisibly lay in ambush and did not leave him even when he slipped suddenly round a corner to avoid them, or locked himself in the dark cupboard where he hoped they could not enter. He did not know from what source they came or what brought them on him; for by now he had completely forgotten the little girl, and when he thought of that time a comforting blank, which yet disturbed him as if it concealed some treachery, was all that his memory gave back. He could not tell his father and mother of his fears, and so they enclosed him in a silent world whose invisible terrors he had to face by himself. The knowledge that there were things in which his parents' help, no matter how anxious, could be of no use to him, bewildered him most of all; the feeling that he lived in a blind place was perpetually with him; yet this blind place was only a thin film surrounding him, from which if he ran very fast and very far he might be able to escape; and his cousin playing a few feet away in the sun, and his mother taking his own head on her shoulder in the firelight, were in that secure world, and yet he was outside. The only way he could think of escaping his terrors was by running very fast until he could run no farther; and when he fell and bruised himself he felt that the blood trickling down must, as by an expiatory rite, bring him back to the ordinary world where other children too bruised their knees and bled. But these accidents staved off his invisible alarms only for a little, and deceived him.

This period in his life was one of real and urgent terror. How long it lasted he could not tell now, but it must have been towards the end, when his fears were thinning, and twisted gleams of the real world appeared again as through running glass, that his mother had taken him out to the back of the house to see the lamb. He had been ill, of what he could not remember, and this was his first day out. As between two folds of cloud he could still see the black lamb beside its mother against the spring sky. The lamb was weak and tottered as it ran; the soft black wool covering its gawky body, the lacquered little cloven hoofs, the soft eyes, which still had a bruised look, appeared to have been just made; and the lamb seemed both surprised and glad to be on the earth. And suddenly, as though it had come for this, a black lamb cast up without warning on the green sward, it charmed him out of his nightmare, and he saw the young sky and the great world out-spread. The lamb paid no attention to him and yet seemed aware of him; it played like a child who feels its mother's eyes upon it and in its inward dream is telling her something which it wants her to know. The dark cloud returned again, but soon after this it must have vanished.

So Mansie sat on the top of the tramcar smoking a cigarette; and the ship passed and did not pass, the little red coat glowed and glittered, the two hands cleansed each other and yet were not cleansed. And over all hung the ring of golden cloud with two long lost figures, himself and the little girl, hidden at its heart, hidden there and past all help. He shrugged his shoulders as if shaking himself free of something, he did not know what. But even while he did so he felt his helplessness. Somewhere beyond his control the ring-shaped cloud of childhood touched the ring that had encircled him as he floated in bliss on his island down the stony defiles of the streets of Glasgow, touched it and melted into it; and now he could scarcely tell what filled him with such apprehension, the apprehension evoked by things born irrevoc-ably before their time, or made of too soft and perishable sub-stance. He resolved again, definitely, never to go to another May Day.

DURING THE WINTER Mansie and Helen had been assidu-
ously attending Socialist dances and whist drives. Helen had
hesitated at first, but when she was at last persuaded to go to one
of the monthly dances given by the Clarion Scouts, the number of
well-dressed people, the liberal sprinkling of evening suits and
smart low-necked ball dresses, reassured, impressed, even a little
awed her; and besides during the evening Mansie introduced her
to several school-teachers of both sexes. She was agreeably
surprised; it was clear that a girl who respected herself could
come here without fearing that she might regret it; indeed she felt
that she had risen several steps in the social scale, and so – for that
is invariably the corollary of such a feeling – was delighted to have
at last found her true level. If doubts recurred during the evening,
when she came in contact, during a set of quadrilles or lancers,
with the more proletarian elements, she was immediately reassured, say, by some white-haired old lady, obviously of superior
station, who sat regarding with good-humoured amusement the
rude but well-meant antics of the more obvious working class;
and these rough men and stern-looking women, of whom she
would have been slightly afraid otherwise, became harmlessly
transformed into a chorus of comic yokels in a play; there was no
real harm in them, they were doing their best, and before the
evening ended she too was smiling experimentally at them,
conscious that that was the right thing to do in this more elegant
and emancipated society into which she had stepped.

It was a revelation; and there was nothing now to prevent
Mansie and Helen from flinging themselves into a whirl of dances
and whist drives that lasted the whole winter. And as though that
exhilarating rush of movement were a revolving fan winnowing
the chaff from the grain, its last revolution cast them strangely
clean and light into the lap of an early spring. It may have been
merely the discovery that things which they had hitherto regarded
as wicked were not only permitted, not only harmless, but good
for one; in any case the whole atmosphere of their thoughts and
feelings cleared, the brooding twilight which had meant happi-

ness to them at one time rolled back, some life process reversed its course, and they found themselves in calm and luminous light, the light of a sunny Saturday afternoon. They were happy without misgiving; that was all. The faint shadow of apprehension that had darkened all their pleasures, that had made even dancing an enjoyment to be indulged sparingly if one were not to tempt providence, had been danced clean away. They had danced themselves into a new world.

But though it was dancing that most radically transformed their ideas, some credit must also be given to Socialist thought. Yet even that they seemed to absorb more through their bodies than their minds; and while they whirled on the smooth floors of a consecutive flight of brilliantly-lit ballrooms, from the throng of other couples revolving round them were flung out radiating intellectual sparks which softly pelted them and in course of time adhered; so that without knowing how it had come about they presently found themselves convinced that the world belonged to mankind, and that in collaboration with mankind they might seek and confidently expect to find happiness there. They seemed to possess far more things than they had ever done before, but they were quite unable to distinguish between those that were actual and those that were merely potential; for if anything the latter were the more real to them, and gave them a pleasure quite as solid as corporeal substances could have done. For suddenly all the suffering in the world, all the evils which they had once accepted as ordained, were revealed as remediable – things that could be 'abolished'; and for their liberated minds, still a little dizzy at the new prospect, the step from the possibility of a remedy to the accomplished cure was a short and dreamlike one, and they might be easily forgiven for taking it. With half their minds, the half that was freed when their day's work was done, they lived in the future as some people, especially in youth, live in poetry or in music; and so, breathing in anticipation the more spacious air of the coming Socialist state, they had no need to con books on economics, thick volumes which in any case the consummation of Socialism itself would providentially abolish; no more need than they had to open the works of Nietzsche and Shaw to acquaint themselves with the attributes of the Superman, seeing that they already felt far closer affinities with him, as merely another inhabitant of the future, a sort of neighbour, than with the previsionary phenomenon of mankind. And if it had not been that all young Socialists of his time without exception read Edward Carpenter's *Love's Coming of Age*, Mansie would not have read that either; for any limitation of his floating ideas, even on free love, was an interruption of his undifferentiated delight, a violation, a disfigurement. And in fact Mansie was shocked by the book, and did not hand it to Helen after all when he was finished with it. He was still more shocked than he had been one evening when a clever young fellow in the Clarion Scouts told him that, according to Nietzsche, the Superman would be as different from man as man was from the monkeys. The idea displeased Mansie; that wasn't how he saw it in his own mind at all. He felt he disagreed with Nietzsche.

Yet all this dwelling in the future did not lessen Mansie's benevolent friendship for mankind, or for the trifling part of it that he met; and if the future revealed a world in which humanity, every evil abolished, was at last free and glorified, it was in unjust social conditions that the decency of decent fellows shone most eminently, and he still felt that he was surrounded by a great host of decent fellows. Indeed now they seemed more decent than ever, for his vision of a transfigured humanity cast a reflected radiance back upon their faces, and sometimes he could see in a flash how gloriously they would shine out if poverty and adversity and dulling toil and servitude were lifted from them. It was like a pain at his heart. Why should such things be? Why should injustice and hate and suffering and strife continue? Why should not Socialism come now, in the twinkling of an eye, and put the world's sorrows to rest?

In the spring they went for rambles into the country, sometimes with the Clarion Scouts, sometimes with a more select party made up for the occasion. Bob Ryrie often went with them, and Helen was charmed by his gentlemanly attentiveness, which made her feel that with his eyes he was supporting her in the mere act of walking, helpfully assisting her to climb over any stile, it did not matter how low, anxiously hoping that she would enjoy her ramble – as if he were responsible for it, the absurd fellow! His brown eyes with their protective glance enveloped her warmly, and even his brown tweeds, which gave out the delicatest aroma of tobacco and peat, were like a soft buffer against every shock, and she felt secure and irresponsible behind them. To Mansie Bob was enthusiastic about her. 'A superior girl!' he said, and it was at his suggestion that Mansie ceased to take her to the Clarion Scout rambles. 'A bit rough and tumble,' Bob said. 'Playing football in a field's all right for you and me, even if it's on a Sunday. But for a refined girl like Helen—' So they made up a small party every Sunday and went out to Strathblane or the Mearns. They were very happy.

Yet though such a revolutionary change had taken place within Mansie and Helen, anyone perusing their actions would not have found any sign of it, for conduct too lay for them in the future. So although they devoutly believed in free love it never entered their minds to put it into practice; and had Mansie attempted any of the liberties with Helen which had caused Tom's downfall, she would have been just as indignant again, in spite of her emancipated ideas; still more indignant, indeed, for she had fled to Mansie as a refuge from those very perils. But she had no need to fear Mansie. For in this atmosphere disinfected by the future, an atmosphere generated by Ibsen, Shaw, Nietzsche, Carpenter and Wells, but whose fantastic possibility was unbounded even by that fact, for Mansie had not even read those writers, it became quite easy to dissipate in an ever wider concentric circle every impulse that was urgent or painful, to vaporise oneself until one was conscious of no residue. Never before had Mansie felt so free.

When a disturbing fact, a case of objective suffering, an illness, say, in the family, impinges on the consciousness of anyone in Mansie's state, at first it is a distant and muffled sound heard by the physical ear while the mind is securely asleep, and for a while the mind tries to weave it into its dream. Until the moment comes when the phantom shadow becomes so gigantic and affrighting, so far more oppressive than the objective fact itself, that with a start the sleeper awakes.

THIRTEEN

ONE EVENING A few weeks after the May Day procession Mansie was sitting at the kitchen window reading the evening paper until it should be time to go out. Tom was crouching over the fire with his elbows on his knees and his head in his hands. His presence did not disturb Mansie, for though they still did not speak to each other all the tension had gone out of their silence; and even when, as sometimes happened, they brushed shoulders as they passed each other in the lobby, that was a mere chance which could not be avoided in a small flat.

Tom gave a muffled groan now and then, but even that did not disturb Mansie very greatly; it must be one of Tom's headaches, for Tom had been having a great many headaches lately. But when Tom began to rock his head from side to side, still holding it tightly clenched in his hands, and emitting a long quivering sigh that ended in a loud groan, Mansie became alarmed; he laid down the paper on the table and half raised himself from his chair. Should he speak to the fellow? This looked serious! Why had his mother and Jean gone out this evening of all evenings? Perhaps he should really speak to him? For Tom's rocking had grown faster now, it went on and on as if he couldn't stop, as if he actually didn't know what he was doing. And Mansie was on the very point of opening his mouth – this couldn't go on! – when Tom turned an unrecognisable face to him, a bloodshot face over which some dreadful change had come, so that it looked like somebody else's, and gasped: 'Get a doctor, for God's sake!'

'I'll get one at once!' Mansie burst out, almost taking the words out of Tom's mouth. He should have spoken before! 'I'll get one at once . . . What's the matter? . . . Wouldn't you feel better lying down?'

'No, no!' groaned Tom, and as if speech had released something he beat his head against the wall and burst out: 'I don't know what it can be! I don't know what it can be!' He turned a blind face to Mansie, and Mansie saw with terror that in his wide open eyes the eyeballs were rolling round and round like wheels that had flown off their axles.

'Don't do that, Tom!' he cried. Good God, what could it be? 'Let me help you across to the bed.' He put his arms under Tom's armpits, pulled him up, stumbled with him over to the bed and carefully lowered him, laying his head on the pillow. He looked back before he rushed out; Tom was lying still.

At the second attempt he found a young doctor who was willing to accompany him. When they entered the kitchen Mrs Manson and Jean were standing by the bed still wearing their hats and coats.

'What has happened, Mansie?' said Mrs Manson. Her face was white and she looked at him reproachfully. The doctor went forward to the bed. Mansie told what had happened, and involuntarily added: 'I don't know what it can be.' It sounded almost like an exculpation, but for what?

While she was listening Mrs Manson kept her eyes fixed on the doctor. The doctor was bent over Tom as if engaged on some secret and sinister task, bent so low that they could not see what he was doing, could see nothing but Tom's crumpled blue trousers and grey stockinged feet.

At last the doctor straightened himself and turned round.

'I think I can give him a powder that will ease the pain,' he said, and he turned to Mansie: 'You'd better come back with me for it.'

'What is it, doctor?' asked Mrs Manson.

'To be honest, Mrs Manson, I can't say yet. I'll have to give him a second examination tomorrow. No need for worry meantime. The powder will put him to sleep.' And the doctor made resolutely for the door.

Outside he turned to Mansie. 'I'll tell you what I would like,' he began in quite a different tone. 'I would like your brother to go into the Western Infirmary for observation for a week or two.'

Mansie's heart sank. The infirmary! Could it be as bad as that?

'Will you try to persuade your mother that it's the best thing to do? He'll be well looked after and quite comfortable.'

Mansie promised with a sinking heart. After a pause the doctor asked: 'What sort of life has your brother led?'

A queer question to ask a fellow! Mansie replied: 'He's an engineer by trade.'

'That wasn't what I meant. I've a definite reason for asking, and you can help me by being perfectly frank. Did he go about with women a lot?'

Mansie's face grew red. He looked at the people passing as though he were afraid they had heard.

'No. He had a girl once, but they haven't been keeping

company for some time now.' Why had he said that? A stupid
thing to say!

But the doctor still persisted. What *was* he getting at? 'Can you
tell me whether he ever went with – er – loose women?' then as if
taking a plunge, 'with prostitutes?'

'My brother would never do such a thing!' Mansie burst out.
These doctors! Bad as the nurses, the way they spoke about
things. But he felt relieved; if the doctor connected Tom's
headache with that he was quite off the track.

There was silence again, and then the doctor asked, as if
casually; 'I noticed a slight scar on his head. How was that
caused?'

As if it had been waiting for this question Mansie's heart
stopped. If it should turn out to be that fall from the tramcar
this might be serious, by gum! He told the doctor what had
happened. But the doctor merely said: 'Well, all that I can do at
present is to give him a powder. But make it clear to your mother
that he should go into hospital for observation.'

When Mansie returned Tom was already feeling a little better;
he took the powder obediently and was soon asleep. Standing by
the bedside Mrs Manson turned to Mansie and said gravely: 'I'm
afraid this is a serious matter, Mansie.' Why did she look at him
like that again? What had he done? Still it was good, in a way, that
she should take it seriously; it would make the doctor's suggestion
less of a shock. And after standing out for a time she agreed at last
to Tom's going into the Western Infirmary.

A week later Tom was taken there, and a suspended calm, the
calm that follows an inconclusive crisis, descended on the house.
Tom was in good and secure hands, Mansie reflected; that was
one comfort at any rate. But when one evening, while they were
alone in the kitchen, Jean turned to him and said: 'Mansie, what if
it's a tumour on the brain?' he burst out angrily, 'Don't talk such
nonsense!' It was indecent to say such things. He got up abruptly,
stuck on his hat, and left the house.

FOURTEEN

AFTER LEAVING THE office Mansie parted from Gibson, saying: 'I'm going along to the Reformers' Bookstall.' He would put off the journey for a little while at least. But instead of making for the bookstall he wandered down Hope Street. It was deserted, for all the law offices were already closed. A belated message-boy, a sheaf of blue envelopes in one hand, hurried past him with the anxious look of one who has fallen so far behind in a race that he has lost all his companions. Mansie's own anxiety stirred somewhere, threatened to awaken, then sank again.

He walked on in the chasm of shadow between the tall buildings; but when he came to the corner of West George Street he stepped into a level drive of light; the roofs and smokeless chimney-pots glittered, and looking down the hill he saw a yellow tramcar floating past amid a hurrying crowd of men and girls in bright dresses. And anxiety came over him again. He would have to take that tramcar some time; he couldn't put it off indefinitely! Nevertheless he continued on his way, went into the Central Station and stood at the bookstall, his head half-turned to look at the crowds hurrying to their separate platforms. They seemed all to be flying to one point, like filings drawn by an enormous magnet. After the morning dispersion which had scattered them to their distant outposts, evening was gathering them together again, and on the faces that passed him there was a look: 'We are coming.' Yes, it was all very well for them. He thought of Tom and stood staring at a book on the stall which he had noticed there months before, and its persistent futile presence filled him with discouragement. 'You and me,' it seemed to be saying.

He bought an evening paper and walked out through the side entrance, crossed Union Street, climbed on to the open top of a yellow tramcar, and sat down in the back seat. Now that he felt himself being irrevocably borne home, he tried to banish from his mind what he would find there; for the twenty minutes that were still left seemed an invisible suit of mail which, if he refrained altogether from thinking, might soundlessly close round him, encasing him for the encounter. But it was of no use, for already he saw himself standing unprepared on the stair-head with the latch-key in his hand, and the same feeling that he would have then swept over him, a sensation of simultaneous collapse, as if everything within him were loosened and falling, and he himself were being precipitated through the solid stone landing where he stood. He was awakened by a sudden brilliance; the passengers looked like a glorified company dizzily charging through seas of light: the tramcar was crossing the Jamaica Bridge and the rays of the westering sun showered over it. He looked at the Clyde winding eastwards in radiance, and saw down in the river a fantastically elongated shadow car with a cargo of spectral and aqueous passengers. Beyond the moving shadow ran the little suspension bridge where the noseless beggar had stood. 'Eaten away,' the words came into Mansie's head. For the wide gaping nose cavity had actually looked as if it were being devoured by incredibly tiny indefatigable armies, and it was against them that the look in the man's face was protesting, and not against the people, all of them with complete faces of every variety of shape, who passed him daily. And his voice! A subterranean snuffle rising to a soft hoot as of swirling wind in a chimney; but never any intelligible sound. The poor beggar had stood there in hard frost too. Mansie had always given him a few coppers, though he had had to overcome a physical repulsion first; and now sitting on the tramcar he remembered that he had been offended at the man for not seeming to be aware of it. Well, a man who had lost his nose couldn't always remember to behave like a man who had lost his nose. Maybe put up his hands sometimes to scratch it, and it wasn't there! A dashed unpleasant shock. But he had looked in a funny accusing way at you sometimes; made you feel uncomfortable. Then he had gone and never appeared again. What could have become of him?

Mansie twisted his shoulders to shake off such disagreeable thoughts. He would fix his mind on something more cheerful; but instead it flew forward to Tom waiting at home, as though the beggar had been cunningly leading him there. Well, there was no good in burking the fact; Tom was out of the hospital now and waiting for him. These fellows sitting here on the top of the tramcar weren't returning to a brother with a tumour on his brain! Idiotic the way Jean's silly words kept running in one's head. He felt all at once violently exasperated with Tom. What need had the silly fool to go and get a tumour on the brain? That was where he landed himself with his dashed recklessness. The tramcar was rolling up through Eglinton Street, and Mansie's eyes fell on the fish-and-chip shop with its door-posts rotten and oozing with rancid grease. He looked to see if the great red-haired woman was standing in the next close as usual, with her arms wrapped round her over-flowing breasts. Yes, she was there, talking to a laughing ring of young girls in shawls, still holding them in; but they would escape some day, and then there would be a fine flop! Nice thoughts to have when your brother was. But all the same she would always be there, nothing could shift her, just like something you had to walk round every morning and evening, forced you out of your way, until at last you got used to your new road and it seemed the natural one. He remembered Gibson's words again: 'And what about the poor bloody little children?' A blackened steel railway-bridge rushed smoothly towards him and passed over his head. The tramcar stopped at Eglinton Toll and turned up Victoria Road. Suddenly like a gaseous fluid dread pumped itself into him, filling him up so tightly that there seemed no room left for the air he tried to draw into his lungs. Four stops, and he would have to get off.

He descended and walked very slowly up Garvin Street. Dashed nonsense! Tom was getting better. At the close mouth he stopped again. Half of him was still out in the street, and to draw it back to him from its freedom, which he shared as a poor man, standing at the lodge gates, shares a fine estate, – to force this half of him to coalesce with the other which was about to walk resolutely into the close and up the stairs, was a task for which he had to summon all his strength as for the pulling in of a heavy weight. With a jerk he turned and climbed the stairs to the first floor. There he was, standing with the key in his hand; but the sensation of sinking through the floor did not come; he had paid that debt in the tramcar; and now his mind was strangely clear, so that when he inserted the key in the lock and turned it his act seemed a purely intellectual one, faintly suggesting the shining revolutions of the stars. As he hung up his hat in the lobby he felt quite indifferent to his brother. 'What must be, must,' he thought, and walked into the kitchen: 'Well, Tom? Feeling better?'

Tom was sitting at the table eating ham and eggs and drinking tea, and at that prosaic sight Mansie's mind fell through octave after octave until it rested on something like reassurance.

'Yes, I think I am,' Tom answered with his mouth full.

Mansie took his place at the other side of the table and glanced at his brother. He was astonished. He had expected some change, but this was a clean knock-out. Tom had grown fat. His thin face with the daring line of the cheek-bone and jaw was round and soft now, and the skin seemed darker and coarser, as if there were an admixture of infinitesimal specks of mud in the grain.

Mrs Manson set a cup of tea and a plate of ham and eggs before Mansie.

'Isna' he changed, Mansie?' she asked. 'Isna' he looking weel?'

Tom made a movement with his hand as if he were warding off something.

'But you are looking better, Tom.'

'Well, don't make such a song about it, mother,' said Tom as if ashamed. 'You might talk about something else.'

'But I'm that blithe about it!'

Mansie unobtrusively studied his brother. Something queer about the fellow's face; yes, must be the eyes. Tom's eyes had an intent, almost pleased look, as if he were listening to something inside him: something ticking – Mansie could not keep the thought out of his head – ticking and ticking. Suddenly on this face that he was studying a very quick spasm ran from eye to chin. But it did not seem real somehow; and indeed it was not caused by real pain, but perhaps by a faintly vibrating memory, even a dream of pain. Yet Mansie felt profoundly cast down all at once; it had looked almost like a threat. Then the expression of intent and pleased watching returned again. So might a condemned man sitting in chains listen to the rain beating on the window of his cell, and tell himself that so long as he listened to that regular drumming no harm could come to him, for when it was raining – raining as it might rain on any day – how could anything happen, how could the blow fall? And he did not know why, Mansie felt disquieted by that pleased expression on Tom's face.

The evening light was streaming in through the window on to the table. Mansie shifted nervously every now and then to get out of it, and its warmth on the backs of his hands was like a spidery film that he longed to tear away. His mother sat in her chair by the empty range looking into Tom's face. Mansie felt apprehensive, almost scared, at the expression in her eyes, for although of course Tom would get better it was almost asking for trouble to be as confident as that. His heart sank at the thought that the pain might return after all, and pushing back his chair he walked to the window. There, looking out into the backyard as if that put a barrier between him and his brother, he said: 'So the pain's quite gone now?'

His mother threw him a warning look, but Tom replied quite coolly: 'Yes, I haven't had any for more than a fortnight now.'

Mansie asked him how he had liked the nurses; a queer lot, from all accounts.

'Oh, they're all right,' said Tom indifferently.

'Well, you'll just let your mother look after you now, my lamb,' said Mrs Manson. 'We'll have the whole hoose to oursel's. You'll get up when you like, and we'll live like grand folk.'

'All right, mother,' said Tom impatiently. Then as if he had something really important to discuss he turned to Mansie: 'They told me I was to go for walks. Have you anything on this evening?'

'No, nothing. I'll take you— I'll go for a stroll with you if you like.'

In the lobby Tom turned to Mansie with a pleased look: 'I've been putting on weight. Twelve pounds!'

As they were walking along Garvin Street Mansie thought he noticed something queer about Tom's walk, but told himself that he must be mistaken. At the corner of Victoria Road Tom stopped and carefully surveyed the street before crossing. They wandered slowly in the direction of the Queen's Park recreation grounds. And now Mansie saw – and his heart almost stopped – that Tom was really walking very strangely. His feet, flung out with the old impetuousness, seemed to hang in the air for the fraction of a second before they returned, a little uncertainly, to the ground. It was as though the additional weight of his body had made him a little top-heavy. He walked very carefully with his eyes fixed on the pavement a few steps in front of him, as if there, no nearer and no farther, lay the danger that he must circumvent, a danger that continuously advanced with him as he went on.

From the gate the recreation park stretched before them, in the distance rising to a grassy sunlit hill, behind which rose the irregular ridged roofs and chimneys of Mount Florida. In the eastern sky beyond floated a few pink fleece-like clouds, deepening at their centres to hectic rose. Shouts came towards them on the still air, mingled with the thud of footballs and the sharp click of bats. They walked over to a seat where they could watch a game of cricket. And soon the vigilant inward look had quite faded from Tom's face; for now he followed almost with anxiety the ball as it flew from the bats of the players, followed it with tortured hope as if in its flight it might carry him into another world, a world where everybody's head was as sound as a nut. This could take him out of himself, Mansie was thinking, and his mother couldn't! 'Tits, man. Hit it! Hit it!' Tom kept muttering impatiently. A band of schoolboys were running about, and sometimes in swerving they almost knocked against the seat. For long intervals they would play at the other side of the field; then for a little they would circle round the seat as persistently as a swarm of bees. At last Tom muttered in a tearful voice: 'Go away, damn you! Go away!' The boys were back again. Suddenly, just in front of Mansie, one of them tottered and fell and Mansie saw a cricket ball bounding away at a tangent. The boys stood round, quite silent all at once, the batsman came running across. Tom got hastily to his feet and said: 'Come away! It isn't safe here.' Mansie rose and followed him.

'Fine rotters you are!' the batsman panted, bending over the boy. 'Walking away when you see someone hurt!'

'My brother's ill,' said Mansie.

'Oh! Sorry!'

Mansie turned back to see if he could help. The boy was lying on the grass, his face transparent, his breath quick and soft as if he were inhaling an infinitely subtle atmosphere. He looked like someone to whom something fortunate but very strange had happened.

The batsman raised his head: 'Run to the pump for some water! Here's my cap. Hurry!'

One of the boys flew away.

'It hit him here,' said another, pointing to his collar-bone.

The batsman felt the neck of the unconscious boy with his fingers. 'No bones broken. It must have been the shock.' And as though those words were a magical formula, his voice was quite confident now. He wiped the sweat from his face. The boy opened his eyes, which had a bruised and wandering look.

'All right again?' asked the batsman in a matter-of-fact voice.

'I suppose I can go now,' said Mansie. Without waiting for an answer he walked across to Tom.

'Where did it hit him?'

'On the collar-bone. He'll be all right in a little. He fainted.'

'It's lucky for him it didn't catch him on the head! Serve him right. These damned kids shouldn't be out playing so late as this, anyway.'

Tom walked on. The accident was merely an accident, and soon the boy would be walking about again, none the worse. At the thought he felt the disease within his head like a grub clinging to him. He would never be able to shake it off, and yet he did not know what it was or where it was; he put up his hand to the back of his skull, which was hard and blank, like a wall. 'And it might have hit me on the head!' He did not notice that he had spoken the words aloud until Mansie gave him a warning glance. He walked on faster, his left leg swinging out jerkily. All at once his head seemed terribly vulnerable; a slate might fall on it from a house-roof, a chance stone flung by a boy might hit it. Or he might stumble and fall and ruin everything now that he was getting better. The sweat broke out on him. I've got to be very careful, he thought, at this stage. He jerked Mansie back by the sleeve. 'Can't you wait a bit! Don't you see there's a car coming?' They were at the corner of Victoria Road. A tramcar was slowly approaching from the direction of the park gates; it was still a good distance away. Presently it ground past them, continuously pulverising some invisible and piteous object which hovered just above the dust in front of it, and Tom felt the pavement thrilling with a menace that had been and was over. They crossed the empty street.

'You've got to be careful when you've just come out of hospital,' Tom said half-apologetically. 'A pretty poor game, wasn't it?' But immediately his thoughts closed him in again, and Mansie's reply was cast back as from a wall.

'Come in and sit down!' Mrs Manson cried as soon as they entered the kitchen.

'I'm going to bed, mother,' said Tom coldly. 'The doctor told me to get as much sleep as possible.'

'Ay, just do that, lamb.'

Mansie went through to the parlour and stood looking out of the window. He breathed quickly as though he had been running, and an intense longing drew him to everything his eyes fell on: an old man walking peacefully along the pavement, the windows opposite with their dingy lace curtains, the impalpable white sky. He felt hollow and cold, as if all the warmth in his body were being drained out through the glass panes into the street below him, and was wandering homelessly there like a lost dog eager to attach itself to any master. Eglinton Street. The pavement was coated with a thick layer of liquid mud, into which one's feet sank with a humiliating feeling of discomfort and shame. A frightening place, Glasgow! Every winter his father's farm had been like a thin raft riding on nothing but clay and mud. Terrible clinging mud; but he had escaped, he had found a firm foothold on the dry clean streets of Blackness. If he were only back there again! He felt tired out as though he had been walking and walking to get to the end of Eglinton Street, to get past all those houses, all those people who kept looking at you.

He began to walk up and down the room. Must get out of this! His mother came in.

'He's going to bed,' she whispered. 'Did he say anything to you?'

'No. He didn't say much.'

'Isna' he looking better?'

'Yes. Mother, I think I'll go out for a turn.'

'Why? Have you an engagement? Come in quietly, then, and be sure not to waken him.'

She was offended. He turned to the window: the light was running away from him as through a sand-glass. His mother's soft footsteps receded. He stole into the lobby and softly closed the outside door behind him.

He hastened up Victoria Road. The park was still open: thank God, the park was still open! For a moment he had half thought of going to the Clarion Scout rooms, for he wanted to lose himself among people and wash away the remoteness with which Tom had touched him. But the park with its trees, its flowers and its crowds, all sending out the same glow, drew him unresistingly. Inside the gate he was caught by the crowd coming away from the band enclosure; he let himself be carried along by the weight of the massed bodies round him, his limbs became slack as under a stream of warmth, and life ran back into his veins. He went up the main avenue and turned along the terraced gardens, from which the scents were pouring in a steady stream, perfuming all the air, perfuming his very breath. Once more his arms and head seemed to break into blossom, and it was as though he were floating, an anonymous shape, in the half-darkness. From the blacker shadows came low voices and now and then a laugh which seemed startled at its own sound; and a warmth radiated out to him from the populated darkness, and he was glad that he could wander here alone, without Helen. And again the warmth of his body flowed out, but freely and blissfully now, filling the twilight, stretching from horizon to horizon, a web as perfect and delicate as the tissue of a moth's wing, except for one point, a point no bigger than a burn made by a red-hot needle, a blackened point of which as he walked on he was scarcely aware, so distant and so tiny did it seem. But when he emerged from the tree-shaded gardens to barer ground and saw the street lamps far away in Pollokshaws Road, that distant harsh burning leapt so viciously at him that he turned round hastily into the scented darkness again. But now the park-keepers' whistles blew; a rustling came from the trees; voices that a moment before had sounded sweet or care free all at once became matter-of-fact, and the laughter had a note of embarrassment. It was over. They were going home, just going home, after all. Surely the park-keepers might have waited for a little longer? Mansie mingled with the crowd moving towards the gate. It seemed to be carrying him irresistibly on a wave from which there was no escape, and which must inevitably wash him up on that stair-head, where he could do nothing – nothing at all – but take the key out of his pocket and turn it in the lock. A fine life for a fellow! How long was this to last?

FIFTEEN

TO BE SEEN out walking in the company of a man with a physical infirmity makes one self-conscious, it may be even a little ashamed, as one is ashamed of an acquaintance who is shabbily dressed. But if the man should be your brother the matter touches you far more nearly, and you may actually have the feeling that there is something wrong with your own clothes. You take off your bowler hat with a puzzled and absent air and run your palm round it to make sure that the polish has not been tarnished; your stiff collar feels uncomfortable; and when anyone passes you stare carelessly ahead as if nothing were the matter and perhaps throw a casual remark to your companion, signifying by your unconcern that nothing is really the matter with him either, whatever appearances may say.

If your companion's infirmity is one that makes it obviously unsafe for him to be out alone, your self-consciousness may become acute. You fancy that people are staring suspiciously at you. 'Something wrong here,' their eyes seem to be saying; 'that poor fellow should be at home or in hospital.' And when they see what pains he is taking to walk smartly, as though nothing were the matter, planting his heels on the ground with jerky regularity, and reminding one of nothing so much as a sergeant-major blind to the world dazedly upholding the dignity of the British Army, they look reproachfully at you as though you were wantonly making a public exhibition of this friend of yours, whoever he is.

But this is only at the beginning of your apprenticeship, and soon you discover that there are other people who glance at you with interest and sympathy, first at your companion and then at you, clearly thinking: 'A good, kind-hearted young fellow, that.' They are mostly men whose hair is turning grey; but women of all ages also notice you, and the eyes of the younger ones seem to be saying: 'What a pity that that poor young fellow's life should be wasted in looking after a helpless invalid!' And if the girl is pretty, sometimes you sadly return her look, return it without the slightest danger that she will think you are trying to pick her up; for the society you are keeping now makes you immune, puts you indeed in what might almost be called a privileged position. So you can woo as many pretty eyes as you like without any risk of encountering either disdain or, what would be almost shocking, coy encouragement. Still, being a decent fellow, you sometimes feel a little ashamed of being the sole target of this battery of sweet glances, and would like to deflect some of them to your companion, who needs them far more than you do. Then you cannot help half turning towards him, feel tempted indeed to raise your hand and wave it in his direction, like a performer in the theatre wafting half the applause to his assistant, without whom he could do nothing. But your assistant never receives a single glance. Women are really a queer lot!

Yet this, you know all the time, is only on the surface; all this is unreal: the running fire of sweet glances no less than your rôle to which they are merely the response; the reproving stares of respectable citizens no less than the hang-dog air with which they immediately saddle you; for all the time it is your brother Tom who is spasmodically strutting there by your side, and all the time you are Mansie Manson. None of those people know that, none of them can ever know what that means; for it is a truth so simple and irreducible that if you were to try to explain it you could only repeat your original words again; a secret so securely sealed that even if you gathered all the people in the Queen's Park together and proclaimed it publicly to them, they would be no wiser.

And so as Mansie Manson walked by his brother's side in the warm summer evenings through the Queen's Park or the recreation grounds, he could freely think of whatever came into his mind, respond to glances, put on an interesting or an unconcerned air; for that was all secondary and idle, so deeply was he aware the whole time that this was his brother Tom and that he himself was Mansie Manson. Even his shame at feeling ashamed of walking here in public with his brother was idle; it was a detached and objective response which did not really touch him; he felt it almost by an act of choice; and it seemed to him that if he cared to make a different choice he would not feel it at all. And the fact that he could quite calmly think of Helen too, and plan where he would take her next evening, was equally idle, seeing that in any case he had to occupy his mind with something. For Tom left him completely to himself, left him far more alone than he would have been unaccompanied; by his absorption in himself Tom seemed to be silently imploring him for heaven's sake to discover something of his own to think about, it did not matter what. For all that Tom wanted was to escape notice, to ignore and be ignored, so that in peace he might listen to that internal ticking which reassured him so profoundly, and keep his eyes steadily fixed on the path a few steps in front of him, where lay, no nearer and no farther, the risk that he must avoid.

Yet there were bounds to this suspended freedom in which Mansie walked beside his brother, and they were reached when in musing over Helen he remembered with quickened pulses the savour of her kisses and the contact of her body. It was as though a peril had sprung up at his side, and he would glance quickly at Tom, terrified for a moment lest Tom had guessed his thoughts. And, his eyes still hypnotically fixed on Tom, on the left leg jerking out, hanging in the air for the fraction of a second and returning a little uncertainly to the ground, he would think, 'There's no turning back after this. We must get married when Tom is well again.' It seemed in a sense their duty to Tom, an acknowledgment of the greatness of his misfortune. Yes, if they were to treat this business idly it would be a wanton insult to Tom. They were bound together now, and as soon as Tom was well again they would announce their engagement and get married. Of course while Tom was ill they could not even announce their engagement: Helen agreed with him there. But what if Tom were never to get quite well? What if his leg were to jerk like this for the rest of his life, or even for the next five years? They couldn't postpone their marriage for ever! After all, it wasn't as if Tom's illness was their fault. The position was unfortunate, certainly; it was a problem. Well, there was no use in worrying about it at the moment. Tom would be all right again, no doubt, in a few months. Ridiculous notions that came into one's head!

Yet the idea of marriage disturbed Mansie, and particularly since he had begun to suspect that Jean and Brand were thinking of it too. For being married to Jean would be no joke; she would take it in deadly earnest and she would make Brand take it in deadly earnest too; she would stick to him through thick and thin; 'till death do us part'; it absolutely scared you. No, when you thought of Jean marrying, you saw that marriage wasn't a bed of roses by any means; it was a very serious business, almost terrifying, like joining the army. And yet it attracted you in a queer way too: burning your boats. Well, if Helen and he did that, surely that would wipe off everything. Tom could have nothing to complain of, surely, after that.

Mansie had only one really uncomfortable moment during those promenades. As they were walking through the recreation park one evening, whom should they meet but Helen. When she saw them she started visibly and seemed to be looking round her for something to hide behind, and in her confusion she actually remained standing where she was. Mansie stopped too, equally at a loss, and mechanically raised his hat. A fine figure he cut, standing there with his hat in his hand! Yet what could a fellow do in the circumstances, but simply lift his hat? Then Helen abruptly walked on, and putting his hat back on his head again Mansie followed Tom, whose left leg he saw jerking busily in front of him. Mansie fell in by his side without speaking: an unfortunate business. Tom's face was red, and all at once he exclaimed furiously as though nobody else were there: 'The common bitch!' And he brought down the point of his stick with a grinding crunch on the gravel of the path. The blood rose quite slowly into Mansie's cheeks; he felt as he had done at school when he was reprimanded before the class, felt like a schoolboy who must patiently let his face grow redder and redder and look more and more foolish without being able to answer a single word. Yet he did not resent what Tom had said; on the contrary he felt on Tom's side; there was a secret between them now from which Helen was shut out and with which she had no concern; and in any case what right had she to fling a fellow's hair into the sea like that! He would never be able to tell her how Tom felt, of course. Would have to put her off with some story or other.

Tom made no further comment on the incident, and their evening walks continued undisturbed. Bob Ryrie sometimes joined them, and then Mansie walked along with a still greater feeling of detachment; it was as though Tom were completely taken off his hands, and anyone passing might have thought that Bob was the solicitous brother and Mansie merely a friend good-naturedly keeping him company. Of course Brand never volunteered his society; to bother about illness was beneath him, didn't come within his scheme of things, hadn't anything to do with Socialism; yes, to him Tom was just a chap that would never be of any use for the movement. Bob was far more of a Socialist at heart, though he couldn't argue your head off like Brand. A queer fish to think of getting married to. It would be a dashed funny marriage. But if Bob couldn't spout all sorts of theories, he could make Tom talk, and that took some doing. Tom liked his company, cheered up like anything when Bob appeared. Jean, of course, pretended not to notice, never even thanked the fellow;

but Bob was never given the credit that he deserved. And walking along Mansie listened to Bob drawing Tom out, telling funny stories, or discussing last season's football form; and for a little they were all happy.

SIXTEEN

THE FIRST FEW weeks after Tom's return from hospital passed in a Sabbath calm. All the life in the house seemed to slow down with the slowing down of Tom's bodily movements, bringing a compulsory relaxation in which even anxiety for the future was lulled to sleep, a sleep which had to be watched over with bated breath, as one watches through the protracted crisis of an illness. It was a tension which consisted in a deliberate avoidance and postponement of tension, and it demanded somewhat the same effort that is prescribed in exercises for completely relaxing the muscles of the body.

Yet although in this Sabbath-like daily communion with her son, serene as the dawn of a new dispensation, Mrs Manson drank comfort as from a fount that had been sealed for many years, and although the thought that he might never get better did not enter her mind, often she gazed at him with sudden alarm. True, Tom's slowness had something restful, something deliberate and leisurely, as though he were quietly reflecting on what he should do next – as he had been doing, for instance, before he got up a minute ago from his chair and walked over to the window to look down into the backyard and up at the sky, where the white June clouds were floating. And it was pleasant to see with what contentment he enjoyed his ease in bed every morning, like a good boy who has been told that he must lie still; and when he got up the leisurely care with which he put on his clothes was pleasant too, he so obviously enjoyed it. It gave one quite a sense of ease and order to see him spending such a long time on everything; on shaving, for instance, and knotting his tie, and brushing his hair. Yet even when that was done, and he had put on his waistcoat and jacket, even then he was not finished. For then he would sit down to a new occupation he had found, one that he kept to the last and seemed to enjoy most of all. Seated erect in his chair by the fireside he would take a little file from his waistcoat pocket and carefully file and polish the nails of his hands, which, after their long idleness, were nearly as white and smooth as Mansie's. And it was when he was busied in occupations as harmless and reassuring as this that Mrs Manson would gaze across at him in sudden alarm.

The days of a sick man who is able to walk about, dress carefully and attend to his appearance, have something of an aristocratic seclusion and spaciousness. His infirmity may confine him to a pair of small rooms, but for the spatial freedom that he is denied, Time, Time in which he can do nothing at all if he chooses, richly recompenses him, translating itself into a new and more satisfying, because more amenable, dimension of space. And so when, instead of madly rushing through the far-stretching temporal vista represented by a day – in a fury to reach the end of it, as most people seem to be – one travels at one's leisure and by easy stages, it is a form of luxury, a privilege that one cherishes, an aristocratic privilege. For when there is abundant time for everything, it becomes a matter involving one's personal dignity that everything should be done without haste and planned in due sequence. And although at bottom all Tom's watchful delibera-tion, which kept him from ever making a sudden movement, was caused simply by the necessity never to lose a beat of that internal ticking to which he was listening all the time, and which was merely the non-arrival of the pain that he dreaded and hoped would never return, the deliberation of his movements gave him genuine pleasure, the pleasure of being master both of them and of such an abundance of time. And besides, in moving with this controlled slowness one cancels, one makes merely accidental, the fact that one could not move more quickly, no matter how hard one tried. It may have been this that Mrs Manson divined when she glanced at him with that look of alarm.

In the afternoon, if it was fine, they went out for a short walk. Like everything else that Tom planned, the hour for setting out was carefully chosen; it was the dead time between the dinner rush and the dismissal of the schools, when very few people were about. Keeping to the quiet side-streets they would walk slowly along, conscientiously enjoying their constitutional, meeting little but an occasional nursemaid push a perambulator. At one time Tom could not have helped casting an appraising glance at these girls, but now he never even lifted his eyes from the point on the pavement where the danger lay; indeed it seemed beneath his dignity. Still, there were certain afternoons, afternoons on which he was more silent than usual, when he did actually lift his eyes for no more than an instant to shoot a rancorous glance at the plump healthy faces of those girls; and as though his resentment had been automatically communicated to her too, his mother would

make some indignant and meaningless remark about those brazen Glasgow hussies. And they would both walk on sheathed in
rancour, a rancour that was disgust for all that was young and
healthy. On those days they would turn back sooner than usual, as
though they had found an immense bank of discouragement lying
across their path.

Almost every afternoon their road led them past a school and,
looking at the empty concrete playground, automatically there
rose in Tom's mind, afternoon after afternoon, a memory of a
Sunday walk with his mother long ago which had taken them past
the little country school that he attended. The playground was of
turf and not of concrete, and in the clear afternoon light he had
peeped in through the gate at the warm, ragged grass, worn bare
in patches and no longer pounded by the feet of his schoolmates,
but lying lost and vacant; and he seemed to be looking at something forbidden. He had glanced up fearfully at the classroom
windows, and his head felt hot and tight again, as if stuffed with
warm wool; the feeling one would have if one were shut in a
clothes-cupboard. And he had run after his mother very fast and
taken her hand. Sometimes he wondered now whether she
remembered that walk, but there was nothing in it for her to
remember; it was like scores of other walks to her. And at the
thought an intense feeling of regret would rise in him; it was as
though he had lost something which could never be found again.

For no apparent reason this memory sometimes evoked another, the memory of a young man, the son of a neighbouring
farmer, who had come home from Edinburgh to die. Tom had
been a mere boy at the time, he could not have been more than
nine, and it had seemed very strange to him that this young man
should have come home 'to die'; it was as though he had chosen
not only the place and the time, but death itself, and had returned
deliberately to accomplish that sad and strange duty. By chance
Tom and his father had met the cart which was bringing the dying
man from Blackness to his home; he was sitting on a bag stuffed
with straw, and his large, lustrous and very sad eyes were not
looking at the fields and houses he had not seen for so many years;
he had not looked even at Tom, although Tom was standing in
front of him on the road, a strange boy that he had never seen
before. And in a few weeks the young man had died; and playing
in front of the house Tom had watched the funeral procession
winding along the distant road to the churchyard; but the sight
had not seemed sad, but only very remote and strange, like the
things that happened in the old ballads his mother sang.

Remembering all this now, a blind hunger for the home he had
left swept over him. O God, would he ever see it again? Why had
he let himself be trapped here among these miles and miles of
houses? And he could hardly walk! He could never escape by his
own strength; he could never run away to sea now, even if his
mother were to give him full liberty and bid him go with her
blessing. Why had his father hauled him back that time? Why had
his mother set her face against his going? They had not known
what they were doing. And while this wave of despair engulfed
him he went on planting his feet carefully on the pavement, kept
his eyes fixed on the point a few steps in front of him, and listened
without losing a beat to the inaudible ticking on which everything
depended. But in a few minutes he felt very tired, stopped, said
'I'm tired,' turned round, and made for home, anxiously followed
by his mother.

This relatively serene interlude lasted almost for a month.
Then, without warning, Tom had another attack. Coming so
unexpectedly and after such an interval, it threw him into confusion, his powers were strangely scattered, and it took him
several days to assemble them again. Mrs Manson had to implore
him to leave his bed, where he seemed to be hiding. When at last
he reluctantly obeyed, he fell into a deeper pit of despair, for now
he felt palpable difficulty in controlling his limbs, he could no
longer conceal it from himself. What could it mean? What on
earth could it mean? He did not bother even to shave or put on a
collar, but sat by the fire and only at long intervals lurched to the
window to gaze up at the sky, or to the front room to watch the
people passing in the street. Yet as the days went by and there was
no sign of another attack, he plucked up courage again, shaved
and dressed himself carefully as before, though a little more
slowly, and even went out now and then in the afternoon with
his mother.

But another attack came, once more unexpectedly, and after
that another; the circle seemed to be narrowing and narrowing,
until, except for his outings with Mansie in the evenings, its
circumference was the house. For he no longer felt that it was safe
to go out with his mother; she could not help him if anything
happened; she was not strong enough. And anything might easily
happen. For his slowness would no longer obediently translate
itself into a pleasant leisurely deliberation; it was a palpable defect
that he had to struggle hard to overcome, without being able to
judge, even then, in what measure he had succeeded. For his
sense of time had curiously changed; it was indeed as though he

had two measures of time now. Everything he did seemed a little too late. For instance if he stretched out his hand for the newspaper lying on the table he was often surprised that his fingers should not reach it until a quite definite interval had first elapsed; it was almost as though he had miscalculated the distance. And even when he opened his mouth to say something, the words seemed already said before he heard, as in a dream, his tongue laboriously and quite unnecessarily repeating them. Everything he did seemed to be an unnecessary repetition, retarding him, obstinately delaying his thoughts before they could move on to something else; or rather everything seemed already done, and all that was left for him was to watch this repetition, this malicious aping of each one of his actions after it had already taken place. And this really frightened him. Suppose when he was out with his mother a boy should run into him! He would be lying on his back before the hand he tried to raise in defence left his side; and he saw himself lying in the street with his hand – too late! – raised against nothing, raised against the sky. A terrible state to be in!

This hiatus in his movements was quite perceptible to anyone who watched him, and if Mansie and Mrs Manson had not grown accustomed to it very gradually, from its first beginnings, they might have been far more anxious than they were. Jean was the only one who saw clearly the hopelessness of Tom's state, and as the summer wore on she kept more and more to the house in the evenings, seeing Brand only once a week. It was as though she foresaw the end and was silently preparing for it. She said nothing to the others, however; for if they too were to become convinced that Tom would never recover, the house would be unendurable. Yet she was bitterly disappointed by Brand's indifference to Tom's state. They had talked about it one evening, and Brand had pointed out that Tom had always run his head into things, and that it was asking for trouble to get off a tramcar in motion when one was drunk. He had actually used the word 'drunk', and without the least notion that he had been insulting; on the contrary he had looked to her for approval, with his triumphant debating air. It had almost made her sick, and she had flung at him: 'Oh, you're a fool!' And that had really penetrated his hide. He had fallen into an offended silence, and they had parted with few words.

Yet she had been unfair in reading into Brand's words a particular indifference to Tom, for he was indifferent to everything 'personal', and scarcely found any interest even in himself except for the fact that he was an advocate of Socialism, a fact of which for some reason he was inordinately vain. And she had been unfair too in feeling insulted by the short and pungent word with which he had designated Tom's state; for he had been thinking in all innocence of nothing but the most telling way of stating his views, and the word 'drunk' had in the context an artistic and logical appositeness which, even if he had divined Jean's susceptibilities, he would have found it hard to forgo; it would have been like a violation of his aesthetic sense of fitness. But so intent was he on the general question that he had never thought of her feelings at all. Besides, she had deliberately introduced a personal matter, had wantonly embarked on the kind of talk that he called gossip, and that it was gossip about dying made it only the more inexcusable. For death was one of those questions which did not interest him even in their general aspect, seeing that it could never be solved and so to think of it at all was a wasteful expense of time. 'I'm only concerned with evils that can be remedied,' he was fond of saying whenever any of those metaphysical problems which trouble even the most ignorant of mankind were brought up. And he would glance round him with a look of conscious rightness, asking for approval like a bright child repeating an incontestable maxim.

None the less, Mansie's coldness and Jean's outburst of contemptuous anger shook him. He felt at a loss in this atmosphere where the personal had unaccountably grown to such dimensions, overshadowing and bleaching all colour out of the general, and making even the most clinching argument hollow and unreal. Jean listened to him still, but as she listened he could feel his authenticity oozing out of him, could feel himself, a militant Socialist, fading to an almost transparent insignificance, so that when he sat in the kitchen with Mrs Manson and Jean and Mansie and Tom, sometimes he could hardly convince himself that he was there, no matter how hard he talked. Nor indeed was he actually there to them except as a troubling succession of words, a sequence of syllables in an imperfectly known foreign tongue which one followed with difficulty, or was content – for it did not really matter – not to follow at all. So it was no wonder that in pained perplexity Brand should at last cease to visit the house, and fall back on his weekly meeting with Jean. And no sooner was he gone than he was forgotten; and if once in a few weeks someone said with a surprised air, 'David Brand hasn't been in for a long time,' the words were as empty either of relief or regret as a newspaper paragraph containing a piece of unimportant news from a distant country. It was as though he had faded to such complete nonentity before the reality which preoccupied the household that the removal of his visible presence made no difference, created no void. And indeed in his last visits he had become – an unprecedented experience for him – almost silent as well as null.

SEVENTEEN

THEY WALKED ALONG the still canal. The sun had set long since, but the light was still ebbing. As it faded it became more and more transparent, so that what was left was not darkness, the darkness that the eyes expected and almost longed for, but an unearthly stationary clarity into which every object rose distinctly but blindly, as though already coiled in sleep within itself and turned away from all that was round it. The water in the canal shone like polished steel; it shone blankly, as though nothing but itself were there. In front, quite far away, another pair of lovers were walking with their arms round each other. Nobody else was in sight. It was midsummer.

'He's been queer since the last attack,' said Mansie. It was always at this hour, when the light was fading and their faces were turned towards Glasgow again, that they talked about Tom. They never mentioned him by name.

Mansie had taken his arm from Helen's waist when he began to speak about his brother. The pair away in front were still walking with their arms round each other.

Helen looked at him but made no reply. Mansie walked on for a little, then he said: 'He seems to be thinking of something all the time. I've done my best to rouse his interest, but it's no use.'

'Maybe he'll come round by himself,' said Helen. 'He was always moody.'

Mansie was silent again. Then he said: 'Yes, he may come round by himself. I wish I understood him. But he never tells me anything. He goes his own road, as he's always done. I've never known all my life what he would be up to next. He was always reckless.'

'Yes, he was terribly reckless. Sometimes I've almost been afraid of him, Mansie.'

Mansie frowned as though the words displeased him and said: 'He's never hurt anybody but himself.' Then after a pause: 'It was hard lines that this should come just when the fellow had turned over a new leaf.' And after another pause: 'He's greatly changed.'

Helen made no reply. The darkness was now falling at last; one could no longer see whether the two in front had their arms round each other.

As if encouraged by the darkness, Mansie said presently, speaking into it as one speaks into an unlighted room knowing that someone else is there: 'Well, there's this comfort: when he recovers he'll be a different fellow.'

And Helen's voice answered cheerfully at his side: 'Yes, and then everything will be for the best after all.'

The confidence in her voice made him uneasy for some reason, but there was nothing more to be said. And when they had gone on for a little farther in silence he put his arm round Helen's waist again. It was a reassurance.

EIGHTEEN

Und die findigen Tiere merken es schon dass wir nicht sehr
verlässlich zu Haus sind in der gedeuteten Welt.

RAINER MARIA RILKE

WHEN HE WAS twelve Mansie had had a curious experience. It
took up only a few minutes, but afterwards it seemed to have filled
the whole of that summer afternoon, and to have coloured not
only the hours which followed, but the preceding hour as well,
which became a mysterious time of preparation whose warnings
he had not heeded.

'That strange afternoon' was how he thought of it, and the
strangeness had begun with the class being dismissed after the
dinner hour. Some state event had just been published, an
important event, for it had to do with the royal family, yet human
and touching, for it might have happened in any ordinary household; and this perhaps was what had made the teacher's voice, for
all its reverence, sound almost confidential when he asked the
class to give three cheers. Yet there had been something unreal in
the teacher's elation, and although the class were glad to get such
an unlooked-for holiday, and felt grateful to the royal family, the
three cheers had a hypocritical ring. Afterwards Mansie's companions had decided to spend the afternoon in town, and he had
taken the road alone. In the bright afternoon sun the road looked
unusually deserted; on the fields the men and women seemed
more active than usual, as though they had just begun the day's
work, a day in which time had been displaced in some curious
way, making everything both too early and too late. So even the
wild flowers along the roadside were unfamiliar, as though they
had sprung up that moment, supplanting the ones that should
have been there. Still, this was the road he had always taken, and
so he went on.

It was in the little sunken field sloping down to the burn that it
happened. There were generally several horses in this field, and
he had always passed them without thinking. This day, however –
it may have been because of the displacement of everything, for

the shifting of time had subtly redistributed the objects scattered over space as well – there was only one horse, a young dark chestnut with a white star on its brow. Mansie had almost reached the footbridge over the burn before he saw it, for it was standing half-hidden in a clump of bushes. They caught sight of each other at the same moment, and Mansie stopped as though a hand had been laid on his forehead: into his mind came instantaneously, as a final statement of something, the words: 'A boy and a horse.' For out of the bushes the horse looked at him with a scrutiny so devouring and yet remote that it seemed to isolate him, to enclose him completely in the moment and in himself, making him a boy without a name standing in a field; yet this instantaneous act of recognition came from a creature so strange to him that he felt some unimaginable disaster must break in if he did not tear his eyes away. This feeling was so strong that his body seemed to grow hollow. Then slowly the stone dyke by which he had stopped grew up, wavered, and steadied itself; he put out his hand to it, the stones were rough and warm, and this gave him courage to stand his ground a little longer. But now as he gazed on at the horse, which still stared steadily and fiercely at him, he seemed on the point of falling into another abyss, not of terror this time, but of pure strangeness. For unimaginable things radiated from the horse's eyes; it seemed to be looking at him from another world which lay like a hidden kingdom round it, and in that world it might be anything; and a phrase from a school book, 'the kingly judge,' came into his mind. And how could be tell what it might do to him? It might trample him to death or lift him up by its teeth and bear him away to that other world. He took to his heels and did not feel safe until he was at the other side of the footbridge, with the burn behind him.

At the time Mansie was not of course aware of all those feelings; he was merely filled with terror of something very strange, and felt – though this perhaps was a deliberate fancy – that if he had waited a moment longer the horse might have carried out its sentence on him. But when, several months later, he happened to look at a portrait of John Knox in *The Scots Worthies*, the long face, still more elongated by the wiry, animal-looking beard, transported him to that field again, and he felt afraid of the eyes gazing out at him from the flat smooth page. And one day in Glasgow many years later he caught sight of a plaster statue in a shop window and suddenly felt dizzy, standing on the hot pavement; and although a tramcar clanked past, throwing sharp beams from its windows into the dark window of the shop, he again felt transported to that distant hot still field, and the sound made by a message-boy running past echoed in his ears like the sound of his own feet on the little footbridge. Strange! he had clean forgotten that afternoon. In a little he saw that there were two names outlined in rough relief at the foot of the plaster cast: 'Moses' and in smaller letters 'Michelangelo'. Michelangelo was a great man; the Reverend John often mentioned him in his sermons. Queer how solid the beard looked, just as solid as the head, all of a piece like the head of some strange animal, and the two funny little horns on the forehead were like blunt pricked ears. Uncanny, the thoughts that must have been in the mind of the fellow who made that thing. And yet the Reverend John thought a lot of him, so he must have been a Christian; all the same one simply couldn't think of a Christian bringing out a thing like that. Almost frightening! And later, when he picked up *Gulliver's Travels* one evening in Brand's lodgings, the book fell open at a very queer picture, 'The King of the Hou—' something or other, it was called, and it showed a horse sitting on a throne with a crowd of naked shivering people before it. Mansie could not take his eyes off it. The horse's front hoofs drooped clumsily and helplessly from the legs outstretched like iron bars; but the massive haunches, too heavy for the frail throne on which they rested, were powerful and majestic in spite of the curly and somewhat mean legs in which they ended. A queer picture; if he hadn't been ashamed of exposing his ignorance he would have asked Brand about it. And later still, when the Reverend John gave a sermon on the Pharaohs, there rose in Mansie's mind, a little obscenely, a picture of those powerful wrinkled haunches and that long, austere and somewhat stupid skull, so hard that it seemed to be made of granite rather than bone. If *that* were set on a throne of justice, by gum you would have to sit up! Not much friendliness about justice of that kind. Made a fellow shiver when he thought of it. Seemed to take all the stuffing out of a fellow.

The autumn holiday had come; Tom did not yet show the hoped-for improvement; so there was no possibility of Mansie's getting away for the week-end. But on Sunday, as Tom said that he intended to remain in the house, Mansie resolved to take a walk in the country. As he shaved he went over in his mind all his acquaintances; every single one of them away, he decided bitterly; of course one could hardly expect them to stay in Glasgow simply because— But still it rather let a fellow down. In morose resignation he took the tramcar to Killermont, pleased that there should be hardly anyone in it but himself; yes, they were all away

at Rothesay or Dunoon or Helensburgh, and it was right that the
other passengers in the tramcar should look ashamed and furtive;
all except the conductor, of course, who had a right to be there.
Still, the fellow showed his contempt for them a little too plainly
when he shouted jokes from one end of the almost empty tramcar
to the other, as if only he and the driver were there. Like these
Glasgow keelies.

But when, having walked through Bearsden, Mansie turned
into the footpath over the gentle hilly grasslands leading to
Strathblane, his spirits began to rise; perhaps after all he would
meet some solitary rambler from the Clarion Scouts; somebody
would be sure to be on the road. He would have a rest when he
came to Craigallion. But when he approached the gate leading
into the field where the pretty little sylvan loch lay among its half-
ring of trees, he stopped short, for a young horse was standing
behind the gate watching him. Everything grew still and bright,
the long grasses by the roadside became quite motionless, and the
wooden bars of the gate looked all at once so solid that no effort
could ever prevail against them; they ran smoothly from side to
side of the gate like a goal which one might touch, but never pass.
No, he could never go through that gate. And suddenly, staring at
the chestnut horse standing behind it Mansie thought, and it was
as though an oracle or a Pharaoh had spoken: 'Tom will die.' The
shock of the thought made him feel a little dizzy; he looked across
at the bald crown of Dumgoyne: it was very bare, he had never
realised before that it was so bare. So far away too, and this gate
and this horse were so near. Why was one thing in one place and
another in another? A complete riddle, the way things were
scattered about on the face of the earth, hills and houses and
rocks and gates and horses. Why shouldn't the hill be here and the
gate and the horse somewhere else, in some peaceful distant
place? And what was a hill anyway? A clumsy big thing without
conceivable use to anybody. Yes, it was ridiculous that a horse
should be standing beside a gate. Things were just dumped down
anywhere and anyhow; you had literally to pick your way among
them, to walk round them and be very careful even then, for you
couldn't even be sure that they would stay in the same place; lots
of them moved, and some of them rushed about at a great speed,
tramcars and things like that, and at times, in spite of all the space
in the world, they banged straight into one another. If a horse like
that were to let fly at you with its hind hoofs you would just curl
up.

With a rush of relief he realised that he need not go through that field, need not pass through that gate, for the road he was standing on would take him by a roundabout way to Strathblane: you could get to places after all if you made up your mind! And as he walked on, not once turning his head to look back at the horse, he felt as though he had circumvented Fate and perhaps done Tom a good turn he would never know of. But presently the refrain returned again: 'Tom will die. Tom will die.' It was outrageous to be pursued by such thoughts; besides they didn't seem to be his at all, they didn't seem real. They were like something you read about; why, maybe this was what people meant by poetry? And once more he felt relieved, for poetry wasn't real life; it was imagination. Yet it was strange this had never happened to him before, there was something dashed funny about it, and he tentatively tried the words over again; they didn't commit him to anything. 'Tom will die. Tom will die': the refrain beat on, filling his ears as he walked on slowly amid the brightness and silence. Then quite unexpectedly the hills trembled and dissolved; tears were running down his cheeks. Yes, he knew it now! Tom would die! And he gave himself over to his grief, seized upon it as though it were a precious draught he had long been waiting for and must drink to the end lest it might never return again; and he let the tears flow and when they showed signs of stopping started them afresh with the hypnotic beat of the refrain: 'Tom will die. Tom will die.' What was he doing? It was almost like an act of treachery to his brother! Yet his tears were not real tears, they didn't count, they didn't mean that Tom would really die. What on earth could they mean?

The fit passed. He washed his face in a little wayside stream, washed it shamelessly and matter-of-factly as one might wash one's hands after a dirty but necessary job. Yet when he thought of Tom now everything seemed more hopeful. He felt better, and he was convinced that Tom was better too, that Tom had at last improved, perhaps since that morning.

Turning the corner he came upon a pale milky-faced little man in rusty blue serge, who was bending over some weeds by the wayside. It was Geordie Henderson, and when he looked up and nodded Mansie was almost sorry for once to meet someone he knew. A nice fellow Geordie, of course, a kind soul in spite of the way he liked to talk about frogs and the survival of the fittest and the freezing-out of the whole human race in a few million years. Still Mansie's heart sank when he saw the soft pale milky face, a face so pervasively milky that even the blue of the eyes had the opaqueness of soap-suds. And pitilessly ignoring Geordie's wel-

coming look he walked on with a curt 'Nice day.' Everything
seemed to be scattered in confusion again like boulders on a vast
plain. That dashed horse! And Henderson with his invertebrates
and his amoebas and his protoplasm! What use were such words
to a fellow? And Geordie's milkiness seemed to shrivel into small
dry grains, like the new kind of milk that was sold in tins: dried
milk, they called it. That was all Henderson was, just dried milk.

And Mansie remembered a Sunday ramble with Geordie. In
the middle of a field where cows were grazing they had come
upon a huge rock six feet high. The rock looked funny enough
there in all conscience, but when Geordie began to talk learnedly
of how it could have got there, that was surely making too great a
song about it. The rock had been carried there, Geordie decided,
by an ice block that slid across Europe at the end of a glacial
period. That was science, of course, and Mansie had listened
respectfully, but at the same time he couldn't help thinking: All
very well to blether about this rock, but, when it comes to the
point, how did anything get where it is? And on the top of this
recollection he remembered the feelings he had had when his
father removed from the farm in the island to the one near
Blackness. Yes, he had felt just the same then looking at the
new countryside – though he had clean forgotten about it: that
everything was a little out of position, that things needn't have
been as they were at all. The sea needn't have swept in just there,
the hills needn't have been just that shape; and the same with the
farmhouses: they were set down just anywhere, and one of them
was planted in a position that it made you uncomfortable even to
look at: it was about two-thirds up the side of a hill, when of
course it should have been either at the top or the bottom. But
then he had got accustomed to all those things, and in time it
seemed quite natural that they should be as they were and where
they were. They seemed at last even to have a sort of plan; yet if he
were to go back now and look at them again he would find that
that was pure fancy. Still it was a dashed uncomfortable thought.
Made a fellow wonder where he was.

Terrible to think too of those millions of years stretching in
front, for what with things moving about as they did and even
taking different shapes (according to Geordie), how on earth
could a fellow know where he was? Even those historical Johnnies
that they taught you about at school, Cromwell and Henry the
Eighth and Napoleon and so on, would never be able to stick to
their places for good; they would all have to shift, no matter how
hard they fought against it. In a million years they might be

anywhere, out of history altogether maybe, for how could the schools go on teaching history as far back as that? Everything on the earth now would be forgotten, things changed so fast. Maybe even Christianity would be forgotten, perhaps even Christ Himself, or at least He might become one of those nature myths Geordie was always blethering about. Even that was possible. And then there were earthquakes to be taken into account; always something else when you thought you had provided for everything. Suppose Palestine were to subside and be covered by the sea? That was quite possible. And he saw on the sunken reef of Calvary a luminous Cross covered with jewelled sea creatures and glimmering phosphorescently in dark blue waters. A phrase he had heard somewhere, 'sea gods', came into his mind. Would Christ become a sea god then instead of a nature myth? And he saw fleets of submarines circling round the silver-dripping Cross, fleets filled with strange-faced pilgrims from a distant age: worshippers of the amphibious god. Queer thoughts that came into a fellow's head. Well, he wouldn't like to be the last Johnny left to be frozen out. At the thought he almost felt inclined to turn back and seek Geordie's company.

When he reached the tea-room in Strathblane he was glad to find the tables crowded, glad that he had to sit down at a table where two young men were eating. And when he ventured a 'Lovely day' he was grateful that the two young men said something friendly in return, for he had a sense of having come back from such a vast and watery distance that the very look on his face, the very air he carried with him, might well scare any decent fellow. He basked in the friendly over-crowded atmosphere of the tea-room, drank in like an immaterial refreshment the jokes flying about, almost reverently masticated the thick floury buttered scones, as though they were friendly and helpful substances humbly offering themselves to him, voluntarily sacrificing themselves to prove that the earth was a great and kindly living thing and not a plain of boulders and rocks.

Comforted, he went out into the garden, sat down in a deckchair, and lit a cigarette. For a long time he lay in a dense cloud of animal comfort, his mind blank. The crystalline evening light fell in a calm and frozen cataract on the little garden, the thick rhododendron leaves rose into it rigid and shining, the roses gleamed lustrously as though wet with spray. Steadily the slanting cataract fell, but on the uplands to the east, on the high level fields, its fall quickened to a race of light, a wind of pale fire flying over the sward, which it turned golden as it ran onwards to the

invisible walls and roofs of Glasgow. There too it would bring
radiance and peace, and even if there were some house of sickness
or pain there, it too would be drowned in that serenity; the little
stubborn point of pain must dissolve in shame amid such peace. It
was like paradise. All this talk about natural selection and protoplasm didn't seem very real now. Dried milk. He got up, said
good night to the waitress, and set out.

He climbed the slope to the gate of the field in which lay the
little loch. He looked up; he could scarcely believe his eyes: that
dashed horse was at *this* gate now! Could he never get away from
it? He walked straight up to the gate; he looked for a moment deep
into the white star in the middle of the horse's brow; it was remote
and pure as a planet in the sky, and it gave him a queasy feeling at
the pit of his stomach. Then he lifted his walking-stick and said in
a quivering voice: 'Get out, damn you! Get out of this!' He swung
his stick, the horse tossed its head, shied, turned round, and,
flinging up its hind hoofs, slowly trotted away. Mansie climbed
over the gate with his legs trembling. The horse was not far
enough away yet for his taste, so he picked up a stone and walked
towards it. 'Get out!' he shouted again, making to fling the stone,
but now the horse finally cantered away quite casually without
looking at him. Mansie felt very tired; yet he walked on rapidly
without looking to right or left, took his way mechanically through
gates and down lanes and round corners, until he found himself
at Killermont, where a lighted tramcar was waiting. This business
of Tom's might turn out to be serious, he kept thinking. Have to
see whether anything can be done. Maybe a specialist should be
called in. He longed for Wednesday, so that he might talk with
Helen about it, for he saw in a flash that she alone could help him.
He hurried home almost in a panic. But Tom was neither better
nor worse. He had had a quiet day.

NINETEEN

Warum? Wofür? Wodurch? Wohin? Wo? Wie?

NIETZSCHE

A MAN OF our time who is converted from a Christian creed to one of the modern faiths takes without knowing it several centuries at one leap. He launches himself out of a world in which the church bells are still ringing, reminding him of the brevity of his life and the need for salvation, and in the twinkling of an eye he is standing in a landscape from which thousand-year-old lights and shadows have been wiped clean away, a shadowless landscape where every object is new, bright, pure and naked; and while he is contemplating it the medieval bells, still ringing, die away to a thin, antiquarian jangle in his ears. The astonishing thing is that he should be able to execute this feat without becoming dizzy. Yet often it is accomplished with trance-like ease, as though he were flying; and that is because during the brief time he is in the air he has been metamorphosed with chemical rapidity and thoroughness, and so it is a new man, perfectly adapted to his new surroundings, who lands at his mark. He has experienced a change of heart. And although between the creed, say, of a Baptist, the most narrowly indivi-dualistic of all creeds, and that of a Socialist, which is commu-nistic through and through, there lies the gulf between the religious and the secular, as well as several centuries of human thought, the convert behaves in the most natural manner as though he were merely stepping out of one room into another furnished more to his taste.

The difference between the world he has left and the one he enters now is perhaps simply the difference between Why and How. And perhaps he has had no choice. For if a man lives in a large modern city where existence is insecure, and change is rapid, and further change imperative; where chaos is a standing threat, and yet in the refluent ballet of becoming every optimistic idea seems on tip-toe to be realised; where at the very lowest one must put one's best foot forward to keep up with the march of invention and innovation: the How challenges at every turn and one is irresistibly driven into its arms. Once there, however, one finds that the Why has become an importunate and niggardly claim, holding one back; and so without scruple, indeed with a sense of following the deepest dictates of conscience, one casts it off, and with it apparently all concern for the brevity of one's life, the immortality of one's soul, salvation, and God. Strange how easily all this can be done!

To fulfil itself the Why must conduct us to the definite end of its seeking; but the How leads on and on through the endless mutations of endless appearance, as if it were set upon circum-navigating a world into which one dimension too many has entered, so that it can never completely describe its circle. Nevertheless the How goes on striving towards horizon after horizon, each of which, like a door, merely throws open another circular chamber, and after that another, and after that another; it casts horizon after horizon behind it like great spent coins, interesting now only to the antiquarian. At first the convert finds nothing but delight in the potentialities of this new world where he can lose himself a thousand times and always find himself again; but as time goes on infinity itself, which seemed the most imponderable of things, begins to weigh upon him like a massive vault, walling and roofing him in; and though it surrounds him at an unimaginable distance, sometimes it seems uncomfortably immediate, for after all there is nothing very substantial between it and him, and so he may run slap into it one day at the corner of a street, although it appeared to be millions and millions of miles away.

To run slap into infinity is a momentarily annihilating experi-ence; a man who chances to do it no longer knows where he is and cannot account even for the simplest objects round him. Quite irrational questions spring up: 'How am I here? Why is this thing in this place and that thing in that? Why does one moment come before or after another? Am I really here? Am I at all?' And he hastens to put something between him and an infinity that is annulling him, something so vast that it will fill all space and time and leave no gap anywhere for that dreadful hiatus, that mad blank like the abyss between two breaths one of which may never be drawn – that hole into which he and all things may fall and never be found again. He seeks a How that will fill the cosmos, a How so great that it almost seems a Why: he embraces the universal process itself, although, accepting the jargon of his age, he may merely call it evolution.

People of traditional religious feeling are mystified and repelled by such terms as the religion of humanity, the religion of science, the religion of evolution. They cannot understand how anyone can put personal faith in the universe, call upon it for personal aid, and look towards it for personal salvation; and to do so seems to them not only blasphemous, but also simple-minded. Yet such a thing is easy to comprehend, and that simply because once man has fashioned a How of cosmic proportions it reinstates in his mind the problems, the very terms, of religion. He broods once more over immortality, though it may be merely the provisional immortality of humanity's linked generations; and he recognises the need for salvation, even if by that he means nothing more than the secular consummation of human hopes. Heaven itself, removed from eternity, which has become void, indeed nonexistent, appears again as an infinitely distant dream of the earth's future, a dream so deep that the shadows of sin and death have almost vanished into it, have been almost, but not quite, dreamt away. Nor is the dogma of grace definitely abolished; for the almost providential appearance of the saving How rescues the believer, if not from damnation, at least from imminent absorption by a blank cosmos, and he reposes in the universal process as the Christian reposes in God.

So it is quite understandable that the emotions with which he contemplates this How should be religious emotions, or at least should run so exactly parallel to their counterparts that a fallible human being may easily confound them, or even hold that *this* is the true and *that* the false. And this is what generally happens at the beginning, until the hour of doubt, which every genuine faith has to surmount, somewhat blankly strikes. Then there may fall on the believer a fear which the How, in spite of all its majestic inclusiveness, is impotent to relieve. And it is not merely the fear that can be caused by the recognition that this How, this pseudo-Why, is itself in process of changing, so that one has none but shifting ground beneath one's feet – for one can get accustomed to that sensation and even acquire a liking for it which may last for the years of a man's life: no, it is a far deeper and yet vacant fear, the fear that if one were to comprehend the How from beginning to end, seeing every point in the universal future as luminously as the momentary and local point at which one stands, and seeing oneself with the same clarity as part of that whole, the universe might turn out to be merely a gigantic crystalline machine before which one must stand in blank contemplation, incapable any longer even of looking for a Why in it, so finally, though inexplicably, would that one thing be excluded by the consummated How. A man who has realised this fear, yet who longs for a faith that shall transfigure life, will be betrayed into a final mad affirmation, and in the vision of the Eternal Recurrence will summon from the void a blind and halt eternity to provide a little cheer and society for blind and halt time, and so alleviate its intolerable pathos.

It is a fear such as this that sometimes hovers round Socialistic dreams of the future. Like the visions of the saints, the Socialist vision is one of purification, and arises from man's need to rid himself of his uncleanness, the effluvia of his body and the dark thoughts of his mind. Yet the Socialist does not get rid of them in the fires of death, from which the soul issues cleansed and transfigured, but rather by a painless vaporisation of all that is urgent and painful in a future which is just as earthly as the present. The purity of the figures in his vision is accordingly the purity of the elements, of the sea and the winds, of air and fire, perhaps in rare moments of a scented flowering tree; it is a chemical or bio-chemical purity, not a spiritual. It is what is left when man eliminates from himself all that is displeasing, unclean and painful; and that residue is finally the mere human semblance, deprived of all attributes save two, shape and colour: a beautiful pallid abstract of the human form. Yet it might still be a negative vision of perfection if it were not for one thing, that the dreamer is unable to think away from all those multitudes of lovely beings death and dissolution; and as mortality never seems more dreadful than when it is beauty that it consumes, the more radiant the vision of a transfigured humanity becomes, the more deeply it is tinged with fear. Until something, perhaps the dread of death for one he knows, opens the dreamer's eyes, and he sees that all those future generations of whom he has thought are only ordinary human beings without entrails. And with that his vision of the very earth upon which they walk is disastrously and yet beautifully changed; it is a world of glittering rocks and flowers, of towering pinnacled rocks and waving hills of empty blossoms: a barren world, for without the digestive tract and the excretary canal how could there be flourishing orchards and fields yellow with corn?

Yet this dream teases him persistently, for it need change only once more, he thinks, and it might after all become the beatific vision. But when it does change something very different is left him – an empty world, the symbol and precursor of that which will come when all life has been frozen from it. And it seems to him that his vision has been made of the wrong substance, and he begins to divine why over it the shadows of fear and mortality should fall so heavily, far more heavily than in the indeterminate light of his own days.

TWENTY

Qu'as-tu fait, O toi que voilà
Pleurant sans cesse,
Dis, qu'as-tu fait, toi que voilà
De ta jeunesse?

VERLAINE

AFTER ALL MANSIE did not speak to Helen about Tom's state when he met her next Wednesday evening, and several weeks passed without anything happening. Then one night Tom had a very severe stroke. When he awoke late next morning the pain was gone, but for a while he did not seem to know where he was. He stayed in bed all day, ate the food his mother gave him, but when she asked whether he felt better only stared gloomily at her without replying.

His gloom still lasted in the evening when Mansie returned. Mansie sat down at the table to his kippers and tea. A fellow had to eat whatever happened. After he had finished he went over to the bed: 'Come, Tom, buck up . . . Would you like to see the doctor?'

Tom replied: 'I won't see any doctor. It's all up. I'm done for.'

Mansie glanced in alarm behind him. Thank God, his mother wasn't in the room. Well, this settled it; a specialist would have to be called in now. He had been quite right that evening after all, walking back from Strathblane. He said, but his words sounded empty, like words cheerfully spoken when everything is over: 'I tell you what, Tom, we'll go along and see a specialist. It's my opinion that this doctor fellow doesn't know what he's talking about. There's a professor in the Western Infirmary, Bob says, that knows more about a fellow's head than anybody else in the United Kingdom.'

'All right, fix an appointment with your specialist if you like,' said Tom glumly. But in a few minutes he became more cheerful, and when Mansie returned next evening he was clothed and sitting expectantly by the fire.

'I've fixed it up,' said Mansie, 'Friday afternoon at three.'

A flush overspread Tom's face and quite slowly faded again, leaving him very pale.

'Nothing to get anxious about,' said Mansie. 'Just like a visit to an ordinary doctor. Only that this fellow knows what he's talking about.'

Presently Mrs Manson came in and was told the news, and at her exclamations of delight they all became gay and even Tom forgot his watchful gravity. But when in a little while he got to his feet to walk out of the room, all his gloom fell back upon him again. For he was feeling damned unsteady on his pins today, far worse than he could remember ever having felt before; no use trying to hide the fact. Mansie was sitting beside the window. Whatever was Tom up to? Why was he doing that with his legs? Pretending to be drunk, or what? And a purely automatic smile appeared on Mansie's face; it was so dashed funny, the way Tom made one leg waggle while the other was quite steady! Mansie came to himself: Why, the fellow was far worse than yesterday! And he was about to get to his feet when suddenly Tom turned to Mrs Manson and said: 'He's sitting there laughing at me! And I can hardly walk!' Mansie started from his chair as though it were a place of shame:

'No, no, Tom, I wasn't laughing! I swear to God I wasn't.'

'You were. I saw you,' said Tom sternly. Then, as if that question were settled, he went on: 'Lend a hand here. I need to go to the water-closet.'

Mansie put his hand under Tom's left elbow and helped him across the lobby. Tom's body felt curiously soft and jointless. They pushed their way clumsily through the narrow door of the water-closet, their feet making a loud scuffling noise on the linoleum. Mansie turned to go. 'Stop here,' said Tom, like a master speaking to a servant. Mansie stood leaning against the wall of the narrow little room with his eyes on the floor.

But when Tom turned round presently Mansie was surprised to see his face all blubbered with tears.

'I've wasted my whole life, Mansie,' he said, and it was as if he had decoyed Mansie here by a childish stratagem for this confession. 'I've made a complete mess of it. And now I'm done for.' His red unshaven chin quivered like an old woman's, and with trembling hands he tried to fasten the buttons on the front of his trousers, but then let his arms fall helplessly by his side. Mansie looked over his shoulder at the backs of the houses opposite. He kept his eyes fixed out there, so that some part of him at least might be out of this cell where he was standing with his brother.

He answered in a deliberately careless voice: 'No, no, Tom, that's all nonsense.'

But Tom went on steadily as though he were preparing for a long and serious talk, during which even the buttoning of his trousers could wait; though that omission evidently troubled him, for his hands kept wandering to his buttons, but without closing with them. Perhaps what had started him was simply a confused sense that this room was the one in the house best suited for heart to heart masculine confession, for talking freely without any risk of being interrupted by the women; perhaps a vague memory of maudlin confidences to tipsy friends in the privacy of public-house urinals had risen without his knowledge to his mind. At any rate he went on: 'It's the God's truth, Mansie. I know what I'm talking about. I might have gone to the Colonies and made good long ago. Might have had a wife and kids by this time. A home of my own. God, what a mess I've made of my life. And now—' But there, when he seemed to be well set, he broke off with a sob and tried again to fasten the buttons of his trousers, but once more helplessly let his arms fall.

Unendurable pity rose up in Mansie. 'Here, Tom,' he said, and he bent down hastily and fastened the buttons. Then he put his arm under Tom's; 'And don't say you're done for! Remember we're going to the specialist on Friday. Dash it, it isn't your fault that you're ill! You'll be all right again soon.'

Tom dried his tears, and they returned to the kitchen.

But now Mansie had to hurry away to keep his appointment with Helen. And such a mechanical thing is habit that he did so almost as though he were going to an ordinary assignation. But as he sat in the tramcar, suddenly he felt that something extraordinary must happen. As if that confession in the water-closet, that prison confession, had united him to Tom as they had never been united before, he felt in his own body that Tom was dying, felt death in his own flesh, and it was almost with a dying man's eyes that he saw Helen now. What did she matter? Tom was a complete wreck; helpless as a child. His younger brother. And she had flung his hair into the sea, and he, Mansie Manson, had looked on and said nothing. What could have come over him? What could have made him do a thing like that? Worse even than smiling at Tom's helplessness. How could he have done that either? He hadn't meant to, but how could even his face have smiled? Couldn't trust even yourself, it seemed. A terrible position for a fellow to have got into between that girl and his brother. Oh well, everything was smashed up now. Tom was dying, and if he died he would be between them all the rest of their lives. Mansie's heart contracted and seemed to grow very small. They would have to give each other up, never see each other again. It seemed a fortuitous thought, and it was with astonishment that he suddenly saw: that was really how things stood! Oh, why was Tom dying on them like this? But the cry seemed to be dead before it rose; it was a purely hypothetical cry, enveloped in layer after layer of impotence like the struggles of a patient under an anaesthetic. He felt wooden and stupid. What was the use of feeling when everything was smashed to pieces?

Helen was waiting for him at Eglinton Toll. At the sight of his pale face she hurried forward anxiously and asked: 'What's wrong, Mansie? Are you ill?' He saw the mouth and eyes he had kissed so often and they seemed so natural, so intimate, so inevitable, like a permanent part of his world, that his limbs lost their woodenness, he became again the Mansie who had stepped on to this pavement so often before and looked at that mouth and those eyes, and there seemed no reason why he and Helen should not have their walk as if this were any other evening, no reason why they should not simply go on having their walks indefinitely. But then she asked in the expressionless tone into which she fell whenever she spoke of Tom: 'Has he had another attack?' And Mansie's limbs became wooden again, and he said woodenly: 'Yes.' Then he added: 'I must go back to him at once.' He had not intended to say this, and he was a little scared at his own words; but suddenly it was all unbearable: the tram ride to Maxwell Park, and the weary walk with Helen through the dark or lamp-lit roads. No, he couldn't talk about Tom to her if she was to speak in that terrible voice. He would write.

'If he's ill,' said Helen, still in the same voice, looking away, 'of course you must go back to him.'

Oh, why couldn't she call him Tom for once! He was his brother, after all!

'I'll write,' he said. Then he was silent again. There seemed nothing to say. But then, as if he were remembering a piece of news that he had overlooked, he went on: 'He's to see a specialist on Friday.' Now there was nothing at all left to say, so he said: 'I think he's dying.'

'No, no, Mansie, you can't mean that!' she cried as though he had tried to wound her.

'I'm almost certain of it,' he said stubbornly. Was it his fault if Tom was dying?

'But I never thought – I never thought—' her words died, she looked at him as if for help, and then glanced away.

People and cars were passing. What was the use of standing here? And to put an end to the unbearable silence he said: 'I don't know what's going to happen after this. I'll write,' and without his being able to help it there was a threat now in the words. His heart, as he stood there, seemed to be hardening by a perfectly arbitrary process over which he had no control; he could do nothing but stand and let it grow harder and harder. It seemed a pity for her, certainly; he felt sorry for her, but he could find nothing to say. No use.

'Good night,' he said. He took her hand, which was cold and nerveless, and let it fall again. It seemed a wanton act of cruelty – his hand was so hard, and hers so soft and defenceless. Well, he hadn't meant to hurt her. He said again: 'I'll write,' raised his hat and turned away and left her standing at the corner.

That was over. He felt very tired. He might as well go home.

TWENTY-ONE

THEY DESCENDED THE steps before the hospital and walked along the red gravel path towards the cab that was waiting for them. Presently Tom asked without lifting his eyes: 'What did he say?'

The specialist's words were running in Mansie's head: 'I can do nothing. It may be a matter of months, possibly of weeks.' Mansie cleared his throat: 'He says you're just to go on . . . just go on quietly,' then he took the plunge, 'and it will get better in time.'

Tom listened with his head to one side as if weighing Mansie's words, but he did not look up, and even when they were sitting in the cab they still avoided looking at each other.

'Go on quietly!' Tom said at last to the floor of the cab. 'Is that all he said? It's easy for him to talk!'

Mansie gazed out through the window at the sooty front-garden railings spinning past. It was a dull November afternoon. Why had he said that about going on quietly? A child could see through it, and he was astonished and a little shocked that Tom hadn't. But Tom was really as helpless as a child, couldn't even fasten his buttons. He replied with an effort: 'Oh, he said you weren't to worry. That's the only thing that might do harm.'

It was as though he were talking to an object that had Tom's shape and was able to reply in Tom's voice, but that was all: an object that you carted about in a cab and had to deliver like a package at its destination. It didn't matter what one said now, and yet it was hard work to say anything at all. Tom asked:

'Did he say how long it would take?'

And mechanically Mansie responded: 'He said it might be a matter of months, but possibly of weeks.'

The specialist's very words! He had given the whole bally show away! But Tom seemed actually reassured by his answer.

After a pause Tom said: 'Do you know what he asked me? Asked me if I had gone with loose women!' Mansie glanced at him in alarm. 'Fancy asking a fellow a thing like that!' Tom went on. 'A funny set, these doctors, I must say!'

'He had no right to ask you that!' exclaimed Mansie. It was going a bit too far, and the fellow dying! 'It was a dashed insult!'

But he was thinking: That was the first thing that Doctor Black had asked too.

Tom looked out through the window: 'Oh, I told him off all right. Still, it was a damned cool thing to ask a chap.' The cab was rolling along Sauchiehall Street. 'I see they've opened a new cinema there.'

'Yes, cinemas going up all over the show now,' said Mansie. 'Money in them too. Pay as much as 40 per cent, some of them.'

But Tom seemed to be profoundly dejected all at once. Hadn't been in a cinema for a long time, poor chap. Would never see the inside of one again. The thought brought the presence of death very near. Mansie glanced at his brother and hastily turned away his eyes again. What could one talk to him about? A matter of months, perhaps of weeks. This cab was taking a terribly long time. Only Union Street still. If you could only get out and walk: do something!

The dull afternoon brightened; they were crossing the Jamaica Bridge now. Tom put his head out through the window and sniffed as if he felt the sea air. The rusty funnels of a tramp steamer showed over the low parapet of the bridge. Tom sat with his head just inside the window; he seemed turned to stone. Then he lay back in his corner with a thud. Thinking of the sea, no doubt, poor beggar. Eglinton Street. These squalling children. You could hear them here all right; seemed to be right down among them. Orange-peel on the pavement. The red-haired woman. As usual. Everything unchanged. Would this cab never get there?

At last the cab stopped. There was the close, right enough. And Mansie eagerly pushed Tom up the stairs as if he still feared that he would never get him delivered. Mrs Manson was waiting in the doorway.

'It's all right, mother,' said Mansie. 'The specialist expects he'll be better in a matter of weeks, but it may be months.'

It came quite easy now. Queer how easy a fellow got used to it. Tears started to Mrs Manson's eyes, and she silently took Tom by the hand. They went in. Delivered safely.

When Tom was settled in his chair by the kitchen fire Jean made a sign to Mansie and left the room. He found her standing by the window in the parlour. 'No hope,' he said, and he repeated the specialist's words.

'Your mother mustn't be told,' was all that Jean said. Then she went back to the kitchen.

Mansie walked through to his room and lay down on the bed.
Took it out of a fellow. Wouldn't like to go through that again.
Helen. Have to write to her. But he lay where he was without
moving. Too dashed tired. He awoke with a start. Why, he must
have fallen asleep; it was quite dark. He got up and lit the gas.
Have to write that letter. The thought exasperated him. Well,
better get it over. But there was no letter-paper in his room. Dash
it, what if there was none in the house! That would be the bally
limit. At last he found a writing-block in the kitchen, and ignoring
his mother's advice that he should write in comfort at the kitchen
table, bore it back to his room, sat down on the bed and with a
resolute air took out his fountain pen. But the sight of the letter-
block reminded him of all the letters he had written to Helen,
letters beginning with terms of endearment that he could never
use again, and the strength went out of his fingers. It couldn't be
true that he would never see her again! That couldn't be the
meaning of this letter that he was going to write to her! It couldn't
be! Tom couldn't be dying on them like this! Dash it all, were they
doing any harm to anybody? It seemed hard lines that they had to
give each other up because Tom got a clout on the head falling off
a tramcar. But as though this were merely a rhetorical protest by a
spectator watching an impersonal process accomplishing itself,
his fingers gripped the pen and wrote the words, 'Dear Helen'.
Fatal words; for at the sight of them his heart hardened and he
went on setting down one short sentence after another, as though
he were doling out in minute doses some strange and dreadful
substance – for it did not seem to come out of him at all: 'Tom has
seen the specialist today. The specialist says there is no hope.
Tom may live for a few months, or it may be only weeks. In these
circumstances I feel we cannot go on. It would be better not to see
each other again. I hope you will forgive me and see that this is not
my fault. I think you will agree that we cannot go on. I trust you
will be happy in the future.' He stopped and gazed at the written
page. He felt very tired. Should he add anything more? What
more could he say? He pondered for a moment and then signed
his name. A queer end to that day on the cliffs outside Gourock!
Oh, dash it, dash it! Must stick to the house and Tom now.
Enough to keep any fellow occupied.

He put on his hat, went out to the corner, and dropped the
letter in the post-box. All the tramcars were packed with people
returning from their work.

PART THREE

IN THE NATIONAL Gallery in London there is a picture of Christ in the Garden of Gethsemane by Giovanni Bellini. The dawn is wakening and on the high hill to the north the walls of Jerusalem are rosy against a night sky sullenly dissolving away. The garden, a coign of clean and carven rock, a little wave-like shell of stone, lies in a hollow where the shadow is like clear water. In the cup of this shell recline the three disciples in a slumber that looks more like a trance, so rigid are their postures, so blind and rebellious their faces. To the right the basin swells up to a thick frill of rock, where, overlooking the ultimate curved crest of the wave in whose trough the sleepers lie, Christ kneels with arms upraised towards the dark mountains, His face turned away from His followers. He is a powerful, deep-chested man with reddish-fair hair and beard, and one can see that the bars of the cross will take a long time to break Him. In the middle ground, between Jerusalem's hill and Gethsemane, a handful of soldiers are straggling along a country road. The road does not lead towards Gethsemane but runs at right angles to it, and one might imagine at first that the soldiers are making for some other destination, until one sees that the road presently bends round. Christ's eyes are lifted to the mountains. Has He seen the soldiers? It is impossible to tell; but if He should turn His head, it will not be the familiar fields and roads that He will see, but a stage on which He can watch, as if it were somebody else's, the unfolding of His personal fate. And where the road bends towards Him the soldiers will become taller and He will see that their eyes are fixed on Him.

Somewhat like this is the apparently fortuitous and yet deliberate approach of a disease which intends to remain for a long time with its object, and can afford at leisure to fulfil its purposes. All that the watcher may discern at first is a tiny moving shape at the head of some remote mountain path. He watches it with an uneasiness that he cannot explain, for the road forks many times before it passes his house, and there are many populated valleys among the mountains to which it may be going. Presently the

path is hidden behind one of the peaks of that country, a
mountain so high and broad that it blots the very memory of
the traveller from his mind. But several days later he again
remembers and looks up towards the mountains. Nothing is
moving, the road is bare, and he is about to turn back and walk
into his house, when, far nearer than he had thought of looking,
he sees the traveller still steadily walking on. His heart contracts;
for although still a long distance away, the traveller is now in his
valley. When, still at the same deliberate pace, the moving figure
turns up the path that leads to the watcher's door, the watcher
retreats a little within the threshold as though to hide himself, and
peering out still hopes: Not for me! For my mother, my wife, my
child! But not a word is spoken when at last the visitor's shadow
falls across the threshold stone; the householder's body stiffens
for a moment, but then he sits down on a chair and stares at the
clear swathe of light falling uninterruptedly now across the doorway.

Afterwards he has no need to strain his eyes looking for his
visitor, for they are never separated. Yet he still keeps an anxious
watch, but now it is on his wife and mother and child, for though
he still lives in his own house, and has indeed inscrutably become
a prisoner there, everything has become strangely remote, for his
new companion now bears him away on a spectral journey in
which all that was once familiar to him recedes to a fabulous
distance; and when his wife Helen or his mother speaks to him,
often he does not answer, for they are so far away that even if he
were to shout his voice would never reach them; and besides his
visitor's silence so encompasses him that he has grown into it.

At the beginning he manages occasionally to shake off his
companion's voiceless converse for a few hours; but the return
to it is dreadful. But most dreadful of all is that when he takes off
his clothes at night and stretches himself on his bed – from which
his wife has been banished, for he has entered on his celibacy – his
companion lies down quietly beside him and takes him in his
arms. Every morning automatically proffers an instant's hope;
awakening he lies looking at the floor, on which a little strip of
light is already stretched, and, his mind vacantly clinging to it, he
wonders why the hour should be so late and he still in bed; then he
remembers, and the hope stealthily emerges: he cautiously puts
out his hand and feels the arm around him. He lies for a little
staring into the face beside him on the pillow, and then as though
in defiance he feels his arms and the arch of his chest, which are
still powerful in spite of all that his enemy has done. He savours

his defiance for a little; it is a luxury that he has learned he may safely indulge, for such things as these do not move his companion to retaliation; he may even curse, if the inclination takes him, more, he may insultingly ignore his companion altogether. But all this liberty freely allotted him is only a cheat; suddenly he gazes in front of him as though he had remembered something unpleasant, gets up, and puts on his clothes. As he does so he cannot help once more prodding with the tips of his fingers his arms and legs, which still look round and strong; yet now he is not so sure; he has grown fatter; it is as though he had assumed a new casing of fat as a protection against his enemy, had retreated behind a quivering wall of fat; but it is unavailing, a stupid ruse of the dumb body, and he has ceased to believe in the efficacy of the tissue that so warmly laps him round.

When he sits down to breakfast under the anxious eyes of his mother, once more it is an act of defiance to his visitor. He eats greedily, yet it is an unnatural act, for it is only his body that is eating, and he is aware of the chewed balls of food being driven by a deliberately perverse act of the will down into his stomach, there to enrich his blood and secrete fat to plump his skin. For what? And he feels for a moment that he has been treacherously feeding his enemy. His palate is flat and wooden, and he rises from the table with a hollow nausea, as though he had been participating in an unclean rite. Going outside he walks up and down before the house, slowly, for his left leg jerks forward and swings back again in a strange way, drawn by some external force he has never hitherto been very clearly aware of; it is the force of gravity. He looks at the trees and the stony mountains; once they were a source from which he could draw an infinite supply of health; the cool breath of the leafage refreshed him, the hot breath of the burnt rock lulled his senses; but now everything is hard and sterile; the trees are dead wood and even the leaves are sharp; when autumn comes they will be sharp as blades. His eyes seek the pool lying in shadow in the hollow below the house; he would like to sink far down in it, for then he might get relief; yet he can scarcely tell now whether in that thought of relief the thought of death may not have quietly concealed itself. Nevertheless he feels assuaged, looking at the pool; but then his eyes stray again to the unfriendly trees and hills, and he turns and sees his wife and his mother standing at the door. They too are unfriendly now, for they cannot help him; nothing can help him, neither the cool morning, nor the embalmed evening air. He goes in, the women making way for him, and sits down on the hard chair beside the

fireless hearth; for the dead wooden arms of the chair on which his
hands rest are no more dead than all those trees standing in their
thousands with drooping leaves in the heat; they are nothing but
wood, nothing but wood to the core.

So his stationary journey conducts him to more and more arid
and waterless regions; but in his dreams his progress is sometimes reversed, and the presence he has been so long accustomed
to once more advances upon him as though for the first time. But
now it advances with rushing speed. He is in a vast city and he is
safe for the moment, for he is lying in a small room at the end of a
high-walled street so narrow that it scarcely gives room for a man
to pass. His sleep is alarmed by a distant sound, the ghostly
brazen clank of some vehicle rushing through the streets. It
seems to be miles and miles away, in some distant suburb.
Where can it be going? What strange load can it be carrying?
He hears it boring its labyrinthine way through stony gullies lit by
electric moons like clocks all pointing to the same blank hour; he
tries to waken himself, for what if it should be coming to him?
But he cannot tear his eyelids open, although the dinning now
clashes round him like the waves of a brazen sea, sinking and
swelling as the house blocks muffle it and set it free again. Then
with a glare of lights the tramcar flashes down on him and hits
him full on the head; he puts up his hand and screams. At last he
opens his eyes; people are standing round his bed; yes, there they
all are, his mother and the rest of them. He looks round;
everything in the room is where it had been before; everything
is quiet; but his companion has laid his hand, gently, on his head:
the laying on of hands. And now, while his mother busies herself
with wet cloths, he knows that he must set himself to endure a
long ordeal. The pressure is gentle still, but gradually it in-
creases; he sets his teeth, the pain softly bores in and in, he breaks
out into words at which his mother turns her face away; but it is
of no use, and like a child being whipped he sobs, begging for
relief for this one time: the pressure tightens. And to a shadow
standing in the dim gaslight he cries: 'Shoot me, Mansie, shoot
me!' But then as though his companion were only after all
tickling him in a particularly ingenious way, his limbs begin to
jerk, his face grows red with humiliation and agony, the cry 'Oh
Christ!' bursts from him, and his arms stretch out like rods, his
fingers clench the edge of the bed, the pupils of his open eyes roll
round and round like planets whirled out of their orbits, and a
long and trembling sigh is expelled through his nostrils, which
quiver like those of a snarling dog; it is as though in that long sigh

he were trying to breathe out the hard ball of pain. In a little his leaden stupor passes again into sleep.

He awakens next morning shaken and relieved, for having broken him the pain has left its habitation. He lies on in comfortable vacancy, lies longer than usual, and in a half-doze almost forgets his companion. Towards midday he rises and still half in a dream walks up and down before the house. Behind the walls of his dream the trees and hills have receded, and he realises that with a leap last night has borne him on for another great stretch of his invisible journey. And although his senses are still drugged, and he refuses to emerge from the lulling stupor in which he walks, he cannot keep his heart from turning over; yet that spasm is ineffectual and irrelevant, like the straining of a body under an anaesthetic. When he tries to think now of what he would like most in the world, he discovers that his desires cannot reach back beyond the time of his captivity; if he could but be as he was yesterday he would be happy, and the days when he fearfully scanned the mountain path seem an impossible dream.

At last he reaches a stage in his changing progress where he can tell no longer in which world he is moving, that of humanity clothed in the same vesture as his own, or that of his unearthly companion. When neighbours come to the house he looks at their sunburnt faces with distant eyes and cannot quite conceal his aversion; his glance appraisingly runs over their shoulders, arms and legs, as it might over a horse which he would not buy at any price, knowing that it cannot be depended on. Nor do his eyes change whether it is male or female that is reflected in them; he may stare a little longer than is seemly at the outward spout of the women's breasts, but a sick man has privileges, and although those spheres may bring to his mind, now arid as dried bone, the thought of gushing fountains, their existence seems as mechanical as that of a spring bubbling up and maintaining incessantly its glassy bell-like shape by a perpetual feat of illusion; and besides he has no longer any desire, parched though he is, to drink of those waters. For now he lives in a world of impersonal forces, a world where anything less than infallibility is insufficient and almost shameful, and where there are only straight lines. He has grown so far beyond the normal human stature which men call maturity, that even those who pride themselves on having put away childish things seem to him children or at best clumsy adolescents. For much as they may talk of necessity not one of them understands the word 'must'; and although they admit perhaps that there is no appeal against and no reprieve from the powers that rule their fates, they are incapable of believing it, for they still hope to escape. And when his mother, perhaps out of over-anxiety, fails to understand some casual sign, he gives her a deadly look; but it is not lack of love or solicitude that he hates her for; it is lack of infallibility, for infallibility is the only thing that can save a man beset by infallible forces.

When he sees this, it is the beginning of despair. Yet sometimes he thinks that if he were a clever man he would be content to give all his mind to the foiling of his enemy, content to pass the rest of his life up to old age in that impersonal and stationary combat; and if in the midst of the fight he should be snatched away by some irrelevant accident, a vulgar epidemic or mere old age, he reflects that he would go willingly, for that too would be a triumph over his enemy. For it is no longer death that he is fighting, but the infallible consummation of an objective process.

So he has to think impersonally and infallibly, and not like ordinary people ruled by such blind motions as love and fear and pity. Yet sometimes it seems to him that this very impersonality which he opposes to his enemy is merely the last capitulation, the habituation to the inevitable. Then in terror he seeks an escape, he flies back to fallible human contacts, and with lowered eyes, ashamed and threatening, dreams of admission to his wife's bed. But it is a sad and unnatural physiological experiment, a trivial post-mortem ecstasy in an automatic hell where only the flesh still lives. Afterwards he may lie by his wife's side while the tears flow down his cheeks, but then with averted face he finds himself in his own bed, where he remains in a despair so profound that he does not even notice his companion lying beside him.

In this final redoubt of despair, beleaguered by forces which are neither cruel nor benevolent, but merely pitiless, at the very last moment he appeals to a power beyond them, a power as infinitely loving as they are infinitely without love. And although hitherto he has clearly recognised his sufferings as a dispensation from God, now he appeals to God from them and sees no contradiction in his appeal. Yet – for he has learnt cunning – he does it stealthily, so stealthily that, in spite of his wild desire that God should hear and answer him, he leaves a last hope: the hope that God may not have heard. For if God were to hear and yet not answer, his faith might perish, and dying he might despair even of death. At last, when no answer comes, the hour of resignation breaks in gently and brutally, destroying everything but itself; and he is resigned to all, to God, to his persecution, to his agony, to the fabulous waterless regions through which he is now more and more dizzily whirled, and to the thought of the death of his body.

This last stage is so hateful to human eyes that even the involuntary object of the metamorphosis can hardly be contemplated without a faint but deep feeling of aversion. Those who are nearest him have now perpetually the look that can be seen in the eyes of people returning to their house after saying good-bye to a son or a brother who has set out on a journey from which it is unlikely that he will ever return; it is a look in which despair, resignation and a trace of relief are mingled. And although he has not actually gone away, but still lies there in the bed, they take no pains to conceal this look; they gaze upon him, tenderly but with a little aversion, as on something whose presence is inexplicably troubling, with those eyes that have already said farewell. This aversion lasts until the final moment of metamorphosis. But then hatred both of death and his victim falls away, and in astonishment the living see that something stranger than they could ever have imagined has been accomplished. And looking at the face, so remote now that even the white sheet that touches it seems to have far more of the pathetic associations of mortality, they are wafted on to a shore so strange that they can find no name for it; they stand on the very edge of Time, they stand there as in a sleep, and dread lest they might awaken and Time be no longer there with them.

TWENTY-THREE

IN A HOUSE of sickness, as in any house, the ordinary routine of the day must be observed. The breadwinner must get up in the morning and go to work; the meals must be on the table at the appointed hours; fires have to be kindled, floors swept, beds made, brass scoured, dishes washed and dried. Yet all those daily offices whose very monotony once gave a sense of comfort, as though they were a perpetually renewed covenant securing the day's peace and order, become meaningless once the covenant has been repudiated by the other invisible party to it, and is left in one's hands, a useless piece of paper whose terms nevertheless bind one, strangely enough, as absolutely as before. So even the simplest household tasks which Mrs Manson had performed with automatic ease for many decades would on some days rise up before her as alarming problems that she needed all her skill to solve, and she would look round the kitchen as if everything in it – the range, the brass taps, the pots and pans – had grown strange and hostile; and it was a mathematical labour to move the table from the wall to the middle of the floor, and to remember the number of dishes, of knives and forks and spoons, she had to lay out on it. Even when, shortly after Tom's visit to the specialist, Jean threw up her job and took over most of the housework, Mrs Manson was still dazed by the little that remained for her; the routine of the house had become a piece of recalcitrant machinery whose workings she had painfully to foresee and provide against, and it inspired her with something of the dread that she felt for all machinery: for the tramcars rushing about the streets, for the cash tickets neatly shot out like little sneering tongues by the automatic cash registers in the shops, for the dreadful maze of machinery through which, since he came to Glasgow, Tom had walked for a time miraculously unscathed, until at last it struck him down. Often she would stop in the middle of the morning's work and say: 'Oh, why did we ever come here, Jeannie?' But she had asked the question so often that she never waited for a reply, but simply resumed her work again.

Tom became more and more incapable of controlling his

limbs, and a few weeks after his visit to the specialist he had a
severe stroke and next day collapsed on the floor when he was
getting out of bed. As they lifted him up he said something, but
his speech was indistinct – it was as though his tongue were
swollen   and Jean and Mrs Manson could not make out his
mumbled words. This made him very angry, he gave them a
furious look and refused to repeat what he had said. For some
time he lay in silence. At last he said, very slowly and deliberately:
'Give – me – a – drink – of – water,' as though he were repeating a
difficult exercise, and when Jean hastily ran and filled a glass at
the tap he looked at her reproachfully, for her quickness was a
wanton exposure of his new infirmity. So now he must lie in bed
and have everything done for him.

After this even Mansie gave up hope. Yet a few days later he
wanted to call in another specialist, and his mother and Jean had
to plead with him for a long time before he gave up the idea.
Surely there was something that could be done! It was terrible to
sit there with idle hands and resign yourself to the whole business
like his mother and Jean. But it may have been that he simply
needed to spend to the last penny the money that still lay in the
bank for his marriage with Helen. And possibly the very fact that
the sacrifice was quite useless, that he took no risk whatever in
throwing away all his money on Tom, made him all the more
eager to do it: it was a sacrifice without even an object to qualify it,
an absolute act uncontaminated by consequences. In any case he
was fantastically generous during those last few weeks, supported
the whole household uncomplainingly on his shoulders, gave his
mother every Saturday a far larger allowance than she needed or
could use, and was offended when she chid him for his extravagance. It was dashed hard lines for a fellow to be taken to task
for trying to do his best for his brother! But it was for another
sacrifice that his mother and Jean felt most genuinely grateful.
Mansie did what he had never done before; he stayed in the house
evening after evening. He had grown thin, and his mother sometimes actually pushed him out through the door and made him go
for a walk.

At the beginning of an illness, when the presence of the sick
man in the house is merely a disagreeable fact, one flies for relief
to society which offers the most complete distraction, to people
who do not even know that one's brother is ill; and one is grateful
that such society should exist and that one has so many and such
diverse friends. But when the illness takes the last turn and enters
the short dark high lane that narrows steadily to the final point, to

nothing at all, the household of the dying are gradually stripped to the skin, to the bone, are stripped of feeling after feeling, of friend after friend, until nothing and nobody is left except the thoughts and the friends that still come to bear them company, that consent to sit here with them in this oppressive prison half-light between the narrowing walls, and voluntarily cut themselves off from life. And any friend who makes that sacrifice is a visitor from a higher sphere, for a household of the dying are like a band of outlaws. Society has turned away from them in its irresistible onward course, and if one has put one's faith in society and dreamt of its end when all men will be happy and beautiful and without pain, one feels cast off by the universal process itself, a stone unworthy of the builder of the world, a pariah like the noseless beggar selling matches on the bridge. And when your friend talks of the world outside, he seems to be telling you of things which no longer concern you, of a country you have left where great things are being done in which you can have no part. And in your home-sickness for it there is the bitterness of the rejected.

It was now that Bob Ryrie showed his true mettle. Every evening he dropped in, if only for a few minutes, to sit and talk by Tom's bed. He faithfully reported the football match on Saturday, and every evening had some new funny story to tell. And he seemed to know exactly what to say to Mrs Manson as well. Even Jean's manner changed towards him, and one evening when Mansie was putting on his hat in the lobby he heard her saying in the kitchen, in reply to Mrs Manson's customary eulogy of their visitor: 'Bob? Yes, he's a trump.' That was high praise for Jean, and next evening Mansie told Bob about it. But although Bob was obviously pleased, he remained quite cool, accepted the compliment, one might almost say, as his due. Well, Jean hadn't treated the fellow very well, but all the same he might have shown more appreciation.

Still, Mansie was very proud of Bob. But it wasn't so easy to explain why Brand should have begun to come about the house again. Nobody wanted him in any case; even Jean didn't seem particularly pleased to see him. After staying away all the summer when Tom was able to move about and talk like a human being, it was almost indecent of him to come to the house now when Tom was pinned to his bed and unable even to protest. And it wasn't as if he came to see Tom; didn't care a hang, seemingly, how the poor chap was. Besides one couldn't take him in to see Tom; Tom couldn't stand the fellow; and so one had to sit with him in

the parlour and talk about the ILP and Guild Socialism – his latest
fad, what would the weathercock take up next? Almost seemed as
if he wanted Tom out of the way before he came to the house
again. Still, he appeared to be put out about something or other;
always telling one to go for walks and look after one's health.
What was that that he had brought out the other evening? Some
quotation from Ruskin: that you should help those that could be
helped, not those that were past help. Him and his quotations.
Well, if Jean married the fellow she had less sense than he gave her
credit for.

But Brand still continued to visit the house and to ask with
anxious looks after Mansie's health.

TWENTY-FOUR

A YOUNG MAN whose heaven has recently altered its position, shooting down from the transcendental to the historical plane, is likely to be thrown into greater bewilderment even than other human beings by the fact of death. For until a year ago death and heaven have been so close to each other in his mind that only an unimaginable something, infinite yet infinitesimal, divided them; but now they are separated by an immovable expanse of quite ordinary time, by days, weeks and years just like other days, weeks and years, and there remains nothing to connect death which is here with heaven which is merely somewhere else. The secular transplantation of heaven, which should have brought it closer, has removed it to an inaccessible distance, so that not even man's last desperate resort, not even death, is of any avail. And as your mind, no matter how ignorantly, demands a meaning for everything, even for death, you may feel at times that your brother is doing something quite unnatural in dying now, and that, to have any meaning, the act should at least be postponed – say for a few hundred years: postponed until he has first known what life can be. It is as though he were dying in a provisional chaos where neither life nor death has yet completely evolved – scarcely even dying therefore, but simply falling into a bottomless hole that swallows everything and gives no sign. And if you suspect in your heart – even though it is palpably untrue – that you have robbed your brother of his girl, you may feel now that you have cheated him of his legitimate death as well, and substituted for it something small and commonplace without his knowing what has happened.

If Mansie Manson felt this, he was hardly aware of it, for his most articulate sensation was one of painful and embarrassed repugnance, a repugnance that muffled without softening the icy and majestic dread which heralds the approach of death. And that he should feel this embarrassed repugnance was inevitable, although he did not know it; for the new creed he had embraced was different from all the older faiths of mankind in one startling respect: that it did not take death into account at all, but left it as an arbitrary fact, a private concern of the dead. It took death so little into account that it could comfortably transform death into a mere moment in the progress of life towards its Utopian goal, a necessary and indeed progressive factor in human destiny; for how except through death could the ever-advancing armies of the generations relieve one another? It socialised death so radically as to forget altogether that it is human beings who die, and that all human beings must die. It transmuted death into another kind of life, so that, pitifully isolated in your ego and in time, you could still believe that you would live on in the lives, as pitifully isolated, of the legatees of your breath; or that, consigned to the earth, you would enjoy at least a sort of immortality in the fortuitous flowers that might spring from your dust, a chemical or biochemical immortality through which finally, it might be, you would enter in some appropriate incarnation into the chemical bliss of your far distant Utopia.

Not having any great intelligence or sincerity of mind Mansie Manson was quite incapable of perceiving this; as incapable as he was of seeing that, in spite of its extreme Utopianism, his faith contained as necessarily as the strictest Calvinism a dogma of reprobation. A dogma of reprobation far more sweeping, indeed, than Calvin's, for until the gates of the earthly heaven are opened all who die are automatically lost. Automatically, for it does not matter whether you have striven for that heaven or perversely turned your back upon it; in either case you are lost 'by a just and irreprehensible, but incomprehensible, judgment': Calvin's words used in another connection apply with just as overwhelming cogency to you.

All this Mansie might have discovered had he chosen, or been able, to understand the Marxian interpretation of history, which for all its harshness is the true theology of every Utopian religion. But he was quite incapable of understanding it, or of seeing that the penalty for certainty in any faith, heavenly or earthly, is some form of predestination, involving election and damnation. He accepted the inevitability of the heaven with which Marx's economic doctrine had presented him, but he disliked Marxians as heartily as a popular religious enthusiast dislikes theologians who insist on demonstrating the necessity of hell. They were a set of sordid-minded materialists who kept nice people out of the movement.

Yet now that Tom lay on his back unable to stir or to speak, passively submitting to the automatic process of death, Mansie, while still clinging to his far distant heaven, felt that Tom was

incomprehensibly and irretrievably lost, lost as one might be who
had died on a world frozen to rigidity long before this world came
into existence. Heaven still floated before him at just the same
point in the future; it had not changed its position by a hand's
breadth; but it was as though he realised for the first time exactly
how far away it was.

And then, in a clap, the feelings that he had had on the Sunday
when he walked to Strathblane, and many times in his childhood,
returned again. He felt as he had done when a boy, looking at the
farm planted precariously on the side of the hill, that the position
of his heaven was in some inexplicable way wrong, so deeply
wrong that it filled him with apprehension. He felt that it was not
where it should be; yet when he dreamt of another station for it he
became blind and could see nothing but a shining vacancy. It was
a vague sense of ill-ease that he felt, and it never hardened into a
definite thought. But had he been able to read his mind he would
have found, strangely enough, that what he longed for was not to
bring his dreamt-of heaven nearer, so near that he would be able
to see it outspread before him and cross its frontiers and be
received finally within it, stepping out of a dying world into one
new born, but rather to raise his heaven to some position high
above itself, to lever it upwards with his eyebeams to a height
where it would no longer be in Time; for so long as it was in Time,
Time would sunder him from it. And with his sense of separation
his old dread of chaos returned, for chaos is universal separation;
and at the uttermost end of the blind longing to lift his heaven
from the distant future place where it stood so implacably, there
must have been the hope that if it could be raised high enough,
uplifted to an inconceivable height, Time would once more
become whole and perfect, and a meaning be given not only
to present death, but to all the countless dead lying under their
green mounds, so that the living and the dead and the unborn
might no longer be separated by Time, but gathered together in
Time by an everlasting compact beyond Time. All that he felt was
an uneasy sense that even the perfect future state was not all that it
should be; but when, brooding on Tom's certain death, he said as
he often did now, 'Well, there's no use in expecting a miracle to
happen,' he was probably thinking, without knowing it, of a
greater miracle. But he had no hope that it would happen.

TWENTY-FIVE

BOB RYRIE HAD finished his account of the afternoon's football. He got up and said: 'Well, so long, Tom, see you again tomorrow.' In the lobby he turned to Mansie: 'Can I speak to you for a minute?' and he pushed open the parlour door. Mansie followed him and lit the gas. The venetian blinds were not down, and the blank window looked like a hole let into the room, leaving it perilously exposed.

Bob cleared his throat. But after all he did not speak for quite a while. At last he said: 'Helen's been to see me.' It was the first time that Helen's name had been mentioned between them since Mansie had announced the breaking of the engagement.

Mansie stared at the floor. He was standing beneath the chandelier and the light falling on his head again made him feel exposed. She's gone to him next, he thought. Hasn't wasted much time. She'll never be at a loss for anyone to take her part, by gum! 'Well?' he said.

'Mansie,' said Bob, 'is it all off between you?' He added hastily: 'Helen's been going through a pretty rotten time, you know.'

'It's all off,' said Mansie. 'And I can't discuss it.' The exposed window troubled him; Bob and he seemed to be standing there as on a stage. Almost like rivals.

'All right, Mansie, all right. I don't want to interfere. But I thought you would like to know— Well, we won't say any more about it.'

They stood in silence for a few moments; but the window still troubled Mansie, and as if confronting a danger, he walked over to it. There, looking out into the foggy darkness with his back to Bob, he said: 'Bob, do you think I'm to blame in this business?'

Bob cleared his throat again: 'This business? You mean Helen?'

'No,' Mansie jerked out, swinging his arm towards the kitchen, 'Tom.'

'Come, come, you're overwrought, Mansie. You're getting fancies into your head. I can say this, and I defy anybody to deny it: you've done everything a brother could have done for Tom.'

'Yes, yes, I know,' said Mansie, still looking out through the window. Then he burst out: 'If it hadn't been for my going with that girl this might never have happened! I wish to God I had never set eyes on her, Bob!'

Bob was silent again. At last he began in an embarrassed voice: 'I don't see—' Then, as if taking a plunge: 'She broke with Tom long before that, you know. She would never have gone back to him, whatever happened. And besides – I don't like to say it now – but it was Tom's own fault. She was actually afraid of him; she told me so herself. If Tom had any grudge against you, it was all pure imagination. And he knows it now. And besides Tom was always a little too fond of a glass; you know that as well as I do. He might have tumbled off a car on his head any time these last two years. It was sheer good luck he didn't do it before.'

Mansie listened vigilantly. Bob was certainly pretty cool about the business! He said: 'Well, it may be.' Then he burst out: 'But a fellow would like to be sure!'

'Mansie, you never did anything intentionally against Tom. Keep that fixed in your mind. It's only his intentional actions that any fellow can be held responsible for. You shouldn't stick to the house so much, you know. Makes you begin to fancy things. Well, I must be going.' Bob looked at his watch. 'I'm late. I'll have to hurry.'

Mansie escorted him to the door. Earlier in the evening he had had thoughts of taking a turn with Bob himself, but Bob was evidently in a great hurry to meet someone else. Who could it be? A girl? And suddenly Mansie knew: it was Helen. He glanced into Bob's face. 'Well, good luck, Bob,' he said, and he could not refrain from adding bitterly, 'I hope you have a pleasant evening.'

'Right!' said Bob hastily. 'Right! So long, Mansie.' And he turned and literally flew downstairs.

Mansie returned to the parlour. So Bob was off for a pleasant evening. Kissing and cuddling. First Tom, then me, then Bob. She should be satisfied now, by gum. Made you want to spit. But it was downright indecent to go straight off to Bob, to one's best friend. Was she to make trouble between all the fellows she could get her claws into? By gum, she wouldn't do it this time, she wouldn't make trouble between him and Bob; he would see to that. Though Bob might have shown a little more delicacy. It wasn't like him. But that woman had got round him, and she was equal to anything. Kissing and cuddling and Tom dying. And she

couldn't even have forgotten the feel of Tom's kisses yet! Well, he
was glad he had cleared out. Hard lines on Bob, in a way; almost
as if he had been let in for it; but he dashed well deserved all he
got, behaving like that!

Mansie went on walking to and fro between the window and
the door. The fog outside had grown thicker. He let down the
blinds. Kissing and cuddling. A fellow couldn't stay here evening
after evening! Must go out once in a while; Saturday night too; all
Glasgow out enjoying itself and him chained here. Might try a
music-hall, the Pavilion or the Alhambra, and be among people
and see and hear something cheerful for a change. Kissing and
cuddling. A fellow couldn't go on like this! A fine life! He went
through to the kitchen. His mother and Jean, sitting before the
fire, looked up; Tom seemed to be asleep.

'I think I'll go out for a little, mother,' he said, 'if you can spare
me.'

'Do that, my lamb, you need a change.'

But when he was sitting on the top of the crowded tramcar
suddenly he felt discouraged. All the seats would be booked up;
no hope of getting one at that hour; what was the use of trailing
from one music-hall to another? So he got off at Gordon Street
and wandered into the Central Station. But nobody was there; the
book- and tobacco-stalls were closed, and the electric lights hung
blankly high up in the fog under the roof; the place looked as if it
hadn't been used for years. He walked out into Union Street.
Although the station was deserted the pavement here was packed
from side to side with a moving mass of people, and looking down
from the steps he saw bowler hats and upturned faces on which
the electric lamps shed a fitful glare, coating cheek-bones and eye-
sockets as with a luminous and corrosive oil. The pavement,
though completely filled, gave passage-way for two sluggish
processions that moved in opposite directions, and from where
he stood these two processions seemed to be standing each on a
long raft that moved with them at a steady speed to some
destination that could not be imagined, bore them away without
paying any regard to their wishes; for some of them had the air of
unwilling captives, while others seemed impatient at the slowness
with which they were carried forward. Yet though their progress
was so inexorable, it left time for a group of young men here and
there to shout inviting or lewd words to the girls on the other raft
as it floated past, words that evoked stony stares or tittering or
raucous laughter. But at the same time these two rafts bearing all
that human freightage floated just a little above the mud, were

only a thin partition over a bottomless quagmire, and through the planks the mud oozed up and clung to the passengers' shoe-soles, though their heads were so high in the air. If the whole business were to collapse! Mansie pushed his way through the moving mass and stepped on to the roadway. Safer there, though it was damp and sticky, like Eglinton Street. There was no help for it; one had just to walk right round a crowd like that. Swaggering there under the electric lights and shouting filth at each other. And people dying!

He came to the corner of St Vincent Street. The street lay before him completely dark and silent, a blank wall of fog, and he plunged into it as though a thin paper wall hiding oblivion or nonentity. But the zone in which he found himself was not completely blank, as might have been thought; for as he walked on there went with him a small intimate circular area of clarity, a private area in which he was far more alone than he could ever have been in a room. And with a shiver of fear he knew that he could no longer escape, here in this perambulating privacy, from the thought that had been trying to catch him all evening. Was he to blame for Tom's death? Oh God, could he be to blame? He turned a corner as if to escape from the question. Where could he be now? Tram-lines. Must be West Nile Street. Hard if a fellow was to be held responsible for a thing he never intended! Never even in his thoughts! Was it his fault that Tom took a glass too much that night and stumbled as he got off the tramcar? What had he to do with that? How could he have helped it? (Dangerous things these cars; must be careful.) And was it just that Tom should have to die of a tumour on the brain simply because of that one clout on the head? Seemed a pretty heavy punishment for taking one glass too much. And maybe it wasn't Tom's fault at all! The car driver may have had too much drink himself and stopped the car with a jerk; that often happened. And was that Tom's fault? It was the car driver's, if it was anybody's. And Tom had to die for it after all these months with that pain in his head. And just after the fellow had turned over a new leaf too. Seemed dashed unjust.

Mansie turned another corner and passed a church. Its grimy walls had the look of many city churches; as though they had been defiled by innumerable passing dogs, or by a long succession of drunken men overcome by need and pathetically willing to find any wall a urinal. That church in Eglinton Street. Those hooligans were still standing there, no doubt. As cocky as ever. Nothing happened to *them*. *They* were allowed to do what they dashed well liked seemingly. By gum, they would know how to treat a tart like Helen, all the same. For that was what she was, in spite of her refined airs. Tom was quite right in calling her what he did that evening. And now she was walking with Bob. In the fog where nobody could see them. Safe and cosy. Took dashed good care that nothing ever happened to *her*. *She* never went through Eglinton Street. It was simple fellows like Tom that had to pay the penalty. The menacing thought came nearer. He quickened his pace. Women! They always knew how to go scot-free. No, he wasn't to blame! He was dashed if he was to blame.

He came to an open space. Tall shapes rose round him in the fog. George Square. High up, the electric lamps flung down cones of bluish light on the stony heads and shoulders of the smoke-grimed statues. It was dashed uncanny, all these figures standing there without moving. Standing there for ever so long, some of them for a hundred years maybe. Must seem a queer world to them if they were to waken up now, frighten them out of their wits, think they were in the next world. That tall one was Burns, couldn't even see his head. No electric light in his time, maybe no fog either. The banks o' Doon. I'll steal awa' to Nannie. And then this. The world was a terrible place, when you came to think of it. Burns had some dashed bad hours in his lifetime. All these women he got in the family way. But none so bad as he would have if he were to waken up here now. Like johnnies frozen stiff and cold; the last fellows left on the earth might look like this. Would the earth be covered with fog then? Scooting through space, dead, the whole dashed lot of them, frozen stiff in the fog. Nobody left to care a hang for the poor beggars.

An immense pity for all those figures staring into the fog, left stranded there in the fog, came over him, and he felt a longing to see human faces again, even if it were only those people parading Union Street.

But when he reached Union Street again and saw the two solid streams of human beings still mechanically flowing, apparently quite unchanged, although now different bowler hats, different cheek-bones and eye-sockets were borne on the dim surface under the misty electric lights, he took the first tramcar that came as though it were an ark riding an advancing deluge about to engulf him. And as he sat on the top of the lighted tramcar he felt somewhat as if he were in an ark, felt almost grateful to the other passengers for allowing him to join them, for picking him from the jaws of danger and taking him into this company of decent fellows. Yet he did not speak to the man sitting beside him, for all those up here in this lighted, enclosed, moving chamber were united by a strangely intimate consciousness of one another, and all at once the knowledge came to him: They have all gone through it. And he was filled with pity for them, a pity quite without patronage, for he himself was included objectively in it. Yes, they had all gone through it. A great weight rolled from his heart.

TWENTY-SIX

JEAN AND MRS Manson were changing Tom's bed and body linen.

'Oh, his poor, poor ribs! It breaks your heart to see them sticking out o' his skin like that, Jeannie.'

'Hush, mother, he feels no pain now.'

'Oh, why does he sigh like that? It's terrible to listen to him sighing and sighing as if something was broken inside him and he couldna' stop. His poor, poor legs. There's no' much flesh on him noo, Jeannie.'

'He's at rest now, mother. It's like a sleep.'

'How white his skin is. He had aye a fine white skin. Ever since he was a bairn.'

'You must think of us now, mother. You still have Mansie and me. Mansie has been a good brother.'

'He could lift me up wi' one arm once, and noo I can almost lift him mysel'. Do you mind yon evening when he lifted me up on his shoulder and wadna' let me doon again? I was frightened oot o' my wits yon night, Jeannie, I can tell you. He was aye so fu' o' fun. Oh, Tom, Tom!'

'There, it's finished, mother. He's comfortable now. Sit down by the fire and rest.'

DINNER WAS OVER. Jean was still softly busied with her house-work, which gradually, however, seemed to be coming to a stand-still, and then everything would be at rest; for after her long battle Mrs Manson was lying in her room almost as motionless as Tom outstretched to his full length in his coffin; they were both lying there with only a wall between them. Mansie sat by the kitchen fire; he felt relaxed and drowsy; everything was settled, all the funeral arrangements were made. And as the definitive accomplishment of any long and laborious task, even if it be a death, automatically produces a feeling of satisfaction, the satisfaction of something completed, Mansie could not keep a little content from mingling tormentingly with his other feelings. He found relief for it, he almost seemed to escape responsibility for it, in the thought: 'Well, Tom is better out of this.' But that was not exactly what he meant, nor did the reflection that his mother was relieved now from the long strain quite seem to absolve him; queer thoughts a fellow had, thoughts that didn't seem right when one's dead brother was lying in the house. And under his drowsy relaxation uneasiness began to stir. He glanced across at Jean. What was she thinking? Was she thinking the same thing? An overpowering longing seized him to look in Tom's face again, to reassure himself finally, to see once and for all, even if at what he saw a fear should start up that he would never forget all his life. And he furtively glanced at Jean, to see that she was still intent and busy, before he left the room.

At the parlour door he waited for a little, then softly turned the handle. The sharp scent of lilies met him, and darkness, for the venetian blinds were down. He stood in the doorway breathing in the scent of the lilies, in which the sharpness of death itself seemed concentrated, and it froze him, so that it was with icy fingers, fingers so numb that they did not feel like his own, that he mechanically closed the door and opened the slats of the venetian blinds, letting in the dull December light. He turned and walked back to the door again before he dared to lift his eyes to the place where the coffin stood; he must have a way of retreat behind him. Then, exerting all his strength, he lifted his eyes.

The light was dim, but Tom was there, almost within reach of his hand. He saw the face with startling vividness, more clearly, it seemed to him, than he had ever seen it before; and as if death had restored Tom to himself, tranquilly reinstating him anew in his body, which had been usurped those many months by a mad and suffering pretender, Mansie realised, as if for the first time, that this was his young brother. How handsome and fine-looking he was! How serious and distant and proud! So this was his brother. Mansie gazed at the face opened to him in death, and all the things that he had been unable or too dulled by custom to read in it while Tom wore it as one living identification mask among many others, a useful everyday mask announcing that here was a fellow called Tom Manson – all these qualities, now absolutely simplified in death, and in that process themselves become absolute and pure, were written clearly on his face, and Mansie saw that his brother had been strong and generous and brave. No, he had never known Tom, never known that he was like this though they had grown up together and lived in the same house. But indeed Tom looked changed, he looked younger, as though in putting off life he had put off at the same time all that had thwarted and defaced it, all that had clouded the lofty fate for which, his brow declared so clearly now, he had been born.

Mansie stood without moving, breathed in the scent of the lilies, and no longer felt any desire to go away; for though he knew that he was standing here in the parlour with his dead brother, something so strange had happened that it would have rooted him to a place where he desired far less to be: the walls had receded, the walls of the whole world had receded, and soundlessly a vast and perfect circle – not the provisional circle of life, which can never be fully described – had closed, and he stood within it. He did not know what it was that he divined and bowed down before: everlasting and perfect order, the eternal destiny of all men, the immortality of his own soul; he could not have given utterance to it, although it was so clear and certain; but he had a longing to fall on his knees. It was not death that he knelt before; he did not know indeed to what he was kneeling, or even whether he was kneeling; for his head might have been bowed by the weight of immortality, by the crushing thought of that eternal and perfect order in which he had a part. He did not go down on his knees; perhaps a sense of shame restrained him; he stood with his eyes fixed on Tom's face, though now he scarcely saw it, and everything seemed clear to him: he saw his long struggle to justify himself towards Tom as a perverse and obstinate and yet quite

simple error, inconceivable in front of this greatness; he understood why he had felt, after the May Day procession, that his
happiness had been made of the wrong substance; for nothing less
than death could erase all wrong and all memory of wrong,
leaving the soul free for perfect friendship: and, his heart pierced,
he knew that Tom could never have completely forgiven him but
for this, no, never but for this. Never while they both lived could
he and Tom have found that perfect friendship for which every
human being longed; for even if Tom had freely forgiven him,
memory, which only died with the body, would have remained
between them. No, never on earth could that dream be realised;
he saw this with perfect clearness; yet now he was no longer
ashamed of his feelings on May Day, though in the twinkling of an
eye they had become as pathetic as the make-believe of children
trying to penetrate, in all reverence, though quite aware of the
deception, into mysteries beyond their understanding. But this
was only a dim intuition which he was incapable of grasping, and
all that he felt was that he was glad he had been there with the
others.

Again the longing to kneel down came over him, imperiously
bowing his head, so that now he looked at the carpet, pensively
absorbed as one might be in the presence of an old friend whom
one can treat like oneself; and as if in the stillness of the house all
the walls had fallen, he saw Jean sitting in the kitchen by the fire,
and his mother lying in her room under the gaslight, and they all
seemed to be together in one place, he and Jean and his mother,
united in boundless gentleness and love, like a family in the Bible.
Bob should be there too, and Brand should come, and Helen
should come. And at the thought of all the people who should
gather to the house, as in the evening all the exiled workers are
gathered to their homes and to themselves, he felt embedded in
life, fold on fold; he longed to go at once and look at Jean, as if she
herself were life, sitting there by the fire; he wanted to experience
again, like someone learning a lesson, all that he had already
experienced; for it seemed a debt due by him to life from which he
had turned away, which he had walked round until his new road
seemed the natural one, although it had led him to places where
all life was frozen to rigidity, and the dead stood about in the mist
like the statues in George Square. He was in haste to begin, and
with a last glance at Tom's face, which he could only dimly
discern now, for darkness was falling, he left the room and closed
the door after him.

FERNIE BRAE: A SCOTTISH CHILDHOOD

J. F. Hendry

And see you not that bonny road
That winds about the fernie brae?
That is the road to fair Elfland
Where you and I this night maun gae.

'But Thomas, ye maun hold your tongue,
Whatever ye may hear or see,
For gin a word you should chance to speak
You will ne'er win back to your ain countrie.'

(Old Scottish Ballad:
Thomas the Rhymer)

FOR
MAMIE

I

HIGH CARTCRAIGS, BUILT in 1789 as a school for the children of planters and known therefore as 'The Black Boys' School,' stood out of the neighbouring village of Shaws, on an eminence going by the name of 'The Green Knowe.' As the River Cart ran near, it was given the name of High Cartcraigs by the villagers, before being left to its lonely resources.

The French Revolution came and went. In the long field opposite, the local guard drilled to resist the Napoleonic invasion and set their bonfires. No invasion came.

The village prospered, mainly from customs-dues and the traffic of carriages and coaches entering Glasgow from the South. 'The Rocket' held its trials, and a railway was built through the meadows which had hitherto been only a gigantic yellow mirror for the sun. As the Scots, in the gathering wheels of industry, lost historical vision and perspective, High Cartcraigs lay at last in a backwater, between tram lines and a railway bridge, above the old toll-house known as 'The Wee Roon Toll.'

It was silent now, though once it had been full of life. On the other side of the street, like merry bells, there still came the sound of 'The Smiddy.' Uphill lay the Green Knowe where generations of courting couples had strolled. On the ground floor lay the school proper, and on the first and second floors the dwelling of the dominie. In the mornings the class-rooms were filled with children's voices singing or at prayers, or else chanting lessons. During the interval they danced about the garden, climbing the apple trees and the rowans, and in the evenings, when they had all gone to bed, there could be heard the voice of the dominie himself, as he read aloud the Scriptures.

The district, authority has it, is famous all over the world as the haunt of 'The Queer Folk.' It is mentioned in Burns and in Kipling; doubtless occurs in Scott, and, according to the Parish of Eastwood, is known even to lonely Boer farmers on the veldt, and to pedlars in the markets of India, anywhere, in fact, where the queer folk have set foot.

It is Covenanting country. That is not uncommon. Maps of Scotland are dotted like pirate flags with the crossed swords indicating battlefields, and one district in Glasgow still rejoices in the name of Battlefield. Drumclog, too, is a sound and a sentiment that still means something in Scottish ears, and the harsh Covenanting strain that severed horsemen from their saddles with a claymore was still a presence in the Shaws. Across the fields lay the 'Beheading Stone.' In the Art Galleries, crowds stood before the bloody picture of the murder of John Brown of Priesthill; and, just as David still seemed to hear in his grandfather's tones, the voices of children in the school-room and the dominie's theological ramblings, so he felt himself sprung from these scenes of terror and carnage.

Upstairs, he read books bound in leather, like wallets or sporrans. *The Scots Worthies*, *Wilson's Tales of the Borders*, or *Rollo's Ancient History* impinged powerfully on his mind, like the heavy wings of some great, dark eagle in whose inscrutable eyes there lurked a drama unassuaged. He was glad to run away from such pictures as these books provided. Clan battles, golden eagles and illustrations to the Last Judgement were too full of ancient sin to inspire anything but terror in the boy, and when he had read too much, he ran into the sunlight of the garden.

There he walked up the path between the flowers, chrysanthemums, the colour of burnt sugar, and tea-roses. Strange they should be called tea-roses. Some of them were white and beginning to wither. The rot was spattered on their petals like flakes of rust, or dried tea-stains.

He set down his glass jar and waited for the butterflies. There were several cabbage-whites fluttering high in the air, little dancing parachutes, at the foot of the garden where no one ever went. Once he had gone, through trees with cobweb claws, to look over the wall, against his grandfather's orders – straight into a horse's face!

He would wait for them to come up.

Now he idled about the grass, kicking the tops off dandelions. Suddenly there was a spark of flame. For a moment he could not think; then, madly, he darted at it. A red admiral! A red admiral!

'Bobby! Bobby!' he shouted to his cousins in the house. Never had he seen one before. It was smaller than a white, with a web of black spots on the tip of each blood-red wing.

He careered after it, banging his net down on dandelions,

cabbages, sometimes even on a clucking hen; but the red admiral rose high over the bristling, mossy wall by the blackberry bush, in a ribbon of unfurling fire, and disappeared in a dance of sparks.

Angrily he threw the net down.

'It's twopence wasted!' said Bobby. 'I catch them with my hands.'

'You couldn't catch a red admiral with your hands! It's too quick!' David said.

'Yes, I could!'

'Oh no, you couldn't, Bobby!'

Sandy, the smaller, a little blonde with a face like the letter V, gave one of his Jack-in-the-Box giggles. He always sided with David, and that made Bobby fly into a tantrum, a veritable explosion of whimpering impotence. Coiling his lips in rage and snorting tears, he aimed a blow at Sandy.

'It's not a butterfly-net anyway! It's for catching baggie-minnows!' he screamed.

'This is a new kind,' shouted David, catching his arm. 'And if you touch Sandy, it'll be the last thing you'll ever do!'

Off stamped Bobby in a fury of mortification.

'He's going to cry to Bessie!' mocked Sandy merrily, a mischievous gnome.

Bessie was their foster-mother.

Together they built a tent of sacking round the rowan tree, which, though they did not know it, warded off devils from the house of turrets. That calmed David's nerves, upset by Bobby's outburst. The tent beat out the last heat of the sun and smelt of straw and earth.

Then they made a sortie to catch the butterflies snowing on the soft undulating soil among the potato blossom. When they had caught one, they returned to drink some soda from a halfpenny packet, through a tube of licorice.

'Shall we make some sugarolly water?' David asked.

'What's that?'

'You cut up the licorice and put it in a glass of water till it melts. It's great!'

'There's no time,' said Sandy. 'The sun will soon be down and the butterflies will go home.'

'Home where?'

'I don't know. Sometimes they sleep on the wall alongside the blackberry bushes.'

'They're moths!' exclaimed David. 'I've seen them. Big tiger-moths! Ugh, they look awful!'

'What's the difference?'

'What's the difference? A moth has a thick body and small wings. It's greedy, and ugly. A butterfly's wings are wide and transparent and beautiful. It has a thin waist and furry shoulders, and only wants to enjoy itself.'

Down they went again into the garden, but this time there was an interruption.

'Dauvit!' came a gruff voice. 'Come oot o' the totties! You tae, Sandy!'

It was their grandfather, revered figure in hat of tweed with moustache and beard that seemed of the same material, only not woven so well, strandy and straggling, with the same tobacco strands.

'If ye want to help,' he went on, 'get the caterpillars oot o' the cabbages. Or dig up the wireworms!'

'What are you going to do?' said David boldly.

'Burn this rubbish.'

Grandpa's grey eyes twinkled frost.

'Burn the rubbish!' they whooped. 'Can we help to gather it?'

'All right!'

The old man nodded, still standing, bowed, a scarecrow in the field of destiny.

As they stood watching the flames, he patted David on the head and said: 'Ye're a good lad, David.'

Soon the magic of the garden mingled in the scent of the smoke from weed and bracken. In its purplish coils, so thick he could almost feel them, the dreaming boy saw ripe-red rowan berries on a branch of fern. Sparks danced at their heart like red admirals and green sap burst from the rind of burning trees like the birth of apples.

He stood with Bobby and Sandy round the fire as it mounted, but they saw nothing of his vision, except the westward sun aslant on the red and purple flames that gradually dimmed its valour. His eyes streamed smarting tears of smoke in the lazing evening. He had some of that fire and some of that sun in his jar.

Looking down, he saw the butterfly stalk up the wall of glass, clinging on hair-fine limbs, like spores of thistledown. Its green eyes, dabbled with black, stared huge as two revolving eggs; and the coiled trunk in between them seemed a fairy circus-whip, through which it sucked a nectar from the flowers.

That was part of his fire and sun, a memory of his grandfather's library near the attic where he ate 'cheugh jeans' and

read *Tom Finch's Monkey* or *Nansen's Farthest North*. So high and
so quiet was it there that he travelled for hours in another
hemisphere. The books were large and dusty, bound like ledgers
and full of mysterious reckonings and figures dealing with the
world of space and time, but he could not always follow the
argument, sitting in the attic, near the sky, wiping the dust from
their bindings that somehow became the dust of stars to guide
him, as the heavy tomes loomed, purposeful as the prows of ships,
swinging into seas of silence and of wonder like those that once
met Nansen.

Continents and years unfolded like a map below.

Somehow the garden was one of those continents. His grandfather was Nansen in the Arctic, with frozen eyes and beard, the
years' hero. And he, David, was the fire and sun through the trees
in the orchard, the butterfly winging towards he knew not what.
Seas of silence? Chill ice-caps? He was unafraid, for Nansen had
gone there before him, and now his grandfather too was there.
What did it all mean?

His grandfather was smoking a clay pipe, full of thick black, and
he wore mittens. His gardening was done, and he stared medita-
tively at the forest of potatoes and at the little orchard where the
apples fell mysteriously on to the grass as if from a pendulum,
marking the passage of time.

'Stick in, son,' he said. 'Stick in.'

That meant 'Work.'

He turned and scraped his boots before going into the stone
corridor of the house. They were caked with crumbs of earth.

David followed him in.

'What did ye do wi' the wireworms today, grandpa?' he asked.

'I hackit them wi' my spade,' he said. 'They're deevils. Deevils!'

'Shush, will ye,' shouted his grandmother; 'I cunny hear a thing
oot o' this contraption!'

She was twiddling the cat's whisker on a crystal set, now and
then adjusting the Ericsson headphones.

'It's a blessing to her, Teenie,' said his grandfather to his
mother. 'She listens a' day. Ye maun thank Jock for buying it.
I hae nae time for sic-like new-fangled nonsense.'

They all sat down to tea.

Suddenly his grandmother slapped him across the face with a
crumpet and laughed out loud.

'My, bit ye're a glaikit bairn!' she cried. 'Cuddy-lugs!'

She was to him a prehistoric monster, sitting there mouthing
incomprehensible language.

'Here's a saxpence see. Noo awa' an' buy yersel' some cheugh-jeans!'

He went up to Gates', the sweet shop, and bought a soda-fountain, a penny 'negative' and some scented cachous. After-wards he played 'Colonel Bogey' on the gramophone, while his grandfather read the Bible.

The sneck of the door lifted and his uncle walked in.

'Evenin', fauther!'

The old man looked up, but did not answer. His mother began to weep in a corner to herself. David ran out.

At the back, in the wash-house, were books in large packages, tied with string, and reaching up to the ceiling. Mr Wood had bought them at the barrows.

Exploring the garden, he found the nest still there, but de-serted, on which he had once laid a stone when the eggs were in it. He was very young then, but the memory still haunted and tortured him. There were earwigs still in the washing-poles, spiders on the walls, and two ancient rusting bicycles – one of them a penny-farthing, the other a walking bicycle without pedals – still leaned against the tower, gradually falling to pieces. The sunflowers were his friends. They were hairy and strong and wore their petals like dog-collars.

He looked in at the window. His grandfather was still not speaking to his uncle. He was 'grumphing.' David conceived a dislike for his uncle. He lived in a modern house.

'Cartcraigs wasny good enough for him,' his grandfather said.

It did not seem to matter that they were both elders in the Kirk or that his mother cried. What could have happened?

'Auld fule,' he heard his grandmother say. 'Him and his buiks. Ony yin wad think *Scots Worthies* was aboot decent folk. Geordie Telfer o' Trongate, who wears a lum hat wantin' a croon! Or Tinker John, who sells umbrellas and fortunes, or even Blin' Harry. But whit are they? A pack o' auld prelates! Wishart an' ithers as ill-kent. Ye're nothing but a John Grumlie. Dae ye hear?'

That was a 'flytin'.' It was terrible to get a flytin'.

David walked alone among the cabbages, turning over the great ears of leaves to inspect the back, and picking fuzzy caterpillars from among the straggling veins. You had to look close, for they looked a part of the hand of cabbage, green and struggling in an agony of light, like children severed from the wrist of stalk. These, too, he dropped, numb and cringing little questions, into a jar as glassy as his eyes with wonder.

When it was quite dark, his mother appeared at the back door, thirty yards off.

'Come, David!' she called, vague as a bird in the wood. 'Time to go home!'

He placed the net over the jar and walked towards her, plucking the heads off flowers on the way and dropping them nonchalantly inside. Food for the butterfly in its transparent cell.

In the tram going home he knelt on the seat, looking out of the window. It wasn't sore, for his stockings were pulled over his knees. He wore his little glengarry. He should have had his rifle by his side, too – the one that fired a bullet of cork – plonk! – on a piece of string. Instead, he clutched the long cane with the net at one end, like a forlorn sceptre.

'Look!' he shouted suddenly. It sounded like 'Luke.' 'There's a student, mother!'

He had been watching for them. It was Charities' Day, when University students all dressed up collected for the hospitals, but to David a weird day, full of irrupting red admiral magic. He looked down again at the butterfly in his jar. It lay crouched on the bottom, antennae turning this way and that, as though listening for a possible way of escape from the mirage.

Outside, Red Indians were pushing policemen off point-duty. Negroes with upraised axes were chasing motor-cars. Their tram was filling with strange creatures he would have liked to capture and keep in his jar. They flashed colour in all directions, like deep-sea fish he had seen once in an aquarium.

It was like Daft Friday.

He held his breath. A huge man in a blue and yellow costume shook a tin before his mother, and he dropped a penny in the slot.

At the back where the conductor usually stood was a resplendent being in blue blazer and velvet-tasselled skull-cap. Irrupting magic. That was being young. These people could do as they liked, and lived a life of laughter and sun like any red admiral.

'What will you be when you grow up?' his mother whispered over his shoulder.

'A student,' he breathed, 'like that man over there, with the velvet tassel.'

The thought was so daring he could scarcely bring himself even to think of it.

'He got that for playing football,' his mother said.

Now the tram swung over the river, blue sparks shooting from the pole on the wire. This was the part of the journey he liked least, when the centre of the town was revealed, like the rotten core of an apple, as a mass of warehouses, factories, coal depots and chimneys, looking like the animals he found when he turned over a stone in his grandfather's garden.

Trams were called 'caurs.' There were blue cars and red cars, white cars and yellow cars and green cars, a whole hierarchy of cars in this medley of colour in the town. Red cars went to Pollokshaws and Thornliebank, so colour was the real guide, not the direction on the roller-tape in front. People were known to each other by the car they took, and between, for example, the blue car people and the red car people, a gulf was fixed wider even than that between the muffler and the white-collar workers, for red cars went through the city, but blue cars went through the Gorbals.

He savoured the names on them. BALORNOCK. That lay out of the city to the North. It was a vast area of new factories, new tenements and soft asphalt, yet with stretches of green grass along the canal. He repeated the name to himself softly. It was forlorn and beautiful, and had grief in it, and even death. It imprisoned a day in his life when he had seen a rock-pipit there. Balornock. And they went to the deep quarry where a boy was drowned, and wondered at the fatality that lay in the sheer silent water.

His head swam. He felt he was going to be sick.

When they arrived home at last, the students were gone.

'Do you remember being lost once?' his mother asked him. 'In the town?'

'No.'

'I went to the Police Station and phoned all the hospitals. When I came home you were waiting for me over there, on the stairs.'

'Was I?'

'A lady had asked you where you lived, and you said: "8 Avelato Teet, Pimbim." You couldn't say "Laverockhall Street, Springburn," so you said "Pimbim."'

In the chill lane of smoking tenements he covered the butterfly to keep it warm, but once in the small kitchen he took it out. It would be better here than in grandpa's garden, he thought.

'They live longer in houses, don't they, mother?'

'Yes,' she said, taking off her hat, to light the fire.

'I can feed it on flowers and sugar and milk. It'll soon be tame and live a long time.'

He took it up in his hand. The powder-grains spread on his thumb a metallic glitter, and the wings shone, glazed.

'Oh, look,' he cried. 'It can hardly fly! Have I hurt it?'

He stood the jar on the dresser and watched the butterfly agog on his thumb. 'It's beautiful,' he thought. Oh, he hoped it would live in the cold of the grimed tenements if he brought it flowers. The wind would not blow so hard. It was his youth. Every Saturday in the garden. Every butterfly he would pursue.

Gently, he turned to the contortions of the anguished caterpillars. From their blunt, blind heads, and from their diffident bodies, too, would one day stream that irrupting magic. They would all be married to the sun. Carefully he placed them in the long button-drawer of the sewing-machine and stuffed its compartments with leaves of fresh green lettuce. The butterfly itself he allowed to fly about the house. It was his friend, the magic he must tame and make his own, the good and true.

Darkness fell, and he closed the drawer and sealed the jar, piercing holes in the cardboard lid to let in air.

Next morning before breakfast he opened the drawer, and at once little beads of corruption assailed his nostrils and eyes. Drawer, lettuce and caterpillars were one stench of green death. Never would they know the freedom now he had meant to give them. He had made them prisoner only in order to see the actual irruption of the magic, and now the magic itself had flown away.

In the chill jar he saw the butterfly, his inspiration, lying too in death. Over its fallen brittle petal the boy wept.

II

Next day, a ghost out of the history book knocked at the door, carrying a box of rock. It had a face exactly like King James the Sixth of Scotland First of England, and sure enough it was his Aunt Bessie.

Entering, smirking, she gave him a red stalk and a white stalk, which he held up like candles till he puzzled her out. She was not Glasgow, they said. She was Edinburgh. She lived somewhere inside the Castle Rock. Some women, he noticed, had faces like scones, and tartan does not improve the complexion. He could not understand her native girn. Like his grandmother's language it was tribal and strange.

Afterwards, he was very proud to have for an aunt the only woman in Scotland to look like King James, except that she wore no ruffle and had not bothered to grow a moustache, which was pending, but now he felt so bored he made a tent below the bed, took his rifle, said he was Jack Logan and was going back to France. It was always awkward in France. There was not much room and you had to sit with your knees up to your chin. He decided to take a bit of leave, and crawled out from under the bed valance.

She was still there. She was Sandy's mother. She stood looking at him sideways, with amusement, as if he were a stuffed teddy-bear. When she spoke, the words dribbled from her thin mouth in a meaningless sing-song. At any moment he expected her to tumble over her wilkies like a clown.

'What do you think of Jenny Campbell?' she asked, folding her hands like Alessandra in *The Birth of Venus*. 'Going to New Zealand?'

'She's daft,' said his mother, succinctly.

'Her brother had a call, she says.'

Up and down went the voice in endless variations.

'Hm!' said his mother, with staring eyes, 'I ken the call he had.'

It was all slightly incomprehensible. It was like looking in the bird house at the Zoo. He knew Jenny Campbell. She had brought him a yellow chicken once, and a boat with real cotton-wool smoke coming out of the funnels. She was a Sunday-school mistress.

'Are you going to the saree tomorrow?' asked his aunt, with a simper. 'She'll be there.'

'Dae ye tell me that?' said his mother.

He was going. He had his ticket. It was blue, and in black capitals on it stood the inscription:

PENNY SOIREE
ST ROLLOX CHURCH
TEA CAKES CONCERT ADMIT BEARER ld.

'What's a saree?' he asked.

'It's a place where everybody does as he likes,' his aunt cried. 'A ceilidh, only better.'

For no apparent reason his mother began to recite:

> How wad ye like tae be me
> Going to a penny soiree;
> A lump of fat
> Stuck in my hat;
> How wad ye like tae be me?

It was like all the other exciting words he saw in the town when they passed through it on Saturdays coming from Pollokshaws. There was the BONANZA, where they secreted Santa Claus in a gigantic free shop full of lucky dips, and the COLOSSEUM, where people had to be urged to take something for nothing by means of huge posters, and streamers, and then, when they did so, were arrested.

These were the opposite of the Bank and the Church. His mother took him to the Bank on Saturdays and to Church on Sundays. They were next door to each other, and for a long time he thought them part of the same institution. They formed part of the same taboo. The furniture in the Bank was massive – like the furniture in the Church – oak and ebony. The doors, which David opened for his mother with both hands, were gigantic and swung open only very slowly. The men inside were clad in black, the lighting was subdued, and obviously operations of great significance were going on. The only difference was that no one sang out of the bank books as they did out of the hymn books, and none of the men in the bank delivered a sudden sermon from a ledger, although they looked as if they might at any moment.

On the counter stood a text: 'Take Care of the Pence and the Pounds will take Care of themselves.'

He disliked church himself. The first time he had gone, a figure had appeared in the pulpit and he had asked: 'What is the man doing in the wee box, mummy?'

'Sh!' she said, and stuffed into his open mouth a cough drop, which he at once took out and found to be the shape of the moon.

The Bank was far more interesting. It was full of strange contraptions. There was a little white wheel like a mill-wheel, upon which they wiped their fingers instead of licking them, when they had to count sheets of dirty paper. He would have liked one of those. It would have saved him licking his own fingers when he had to strip the paper from treacle toffee. He watched the wheel spin round and dip into the water below. There was also a sponge sitting in a tiny basin which they used for the same purpose. It was not so good, for sometimes it gave out a horrible shrill squeak. Still, it was all part of the ceremony and rites like the altars, and organs, and choirs, and shaded lights, and thick carpets, and palatial arches, and furs, and bated breath, and self-conscious coughing. He did not like it at all.

The ticket was glossy as a negative of Tom Mix.

'Be sure and come,' Jenny had said. Her hair was knotted and dry, but white too, like the cottonwool smoke.

The whole affair was full of contagious fever. Jackie Boyd was going. So were the Richardsons. Everyone took it for granted he was going too. He did not remember being asked, except by Jenny.

Darkness fell on an evening of frantic washing and donning of best clothes, and there followed the long trot along Auchentoshan Terrace in complete obscurity but for the dandelion lamp-posts, towards the gates of St Rollox Church, normally chained and padlocked like Barlinnie Prison, and thick with flakes of dust and dung. It never occurred to him that St. Rollox had been a saint. Who had ever heard of St Rollox the Good? Or even St Rollox the Bad? Across the road he saw the great engine-yards of St Rollox where his grandfather had worked for half a lifetime, one of a thousand blue-clad slaves who carried the lamp of Aladdin round the monstrous locomotives, oiling the various parts. His grandfather had had rheumatism in his finger-joints. No one oiled his various parts. He was no engine, though at times he was expected to be. He wasn't even the patron saint of the railway as the dim St Rollox might be at best. He was only a man, as David doubted St Rollox had ever been.

The gates were open. The huge pseudo-medieval doors were folded back and a golden light shone forth, as if from the depths of a cave. It was like a bazaar. Sometimes they had a bazaar in church, where everyone raffled and rifled and ruffled, but the minister was not a very good Ali Baba. At the entrance, like a drinking-trough, stood a stone bowl for the 'offerings.' He dropped his own coin in with a loud clink, and, holding his breath, passed through. For a moment he stood as if blinded by the glare of light and the wave of sound that hit him before he could gather himself together and look round.

The pews were packed with shouting, screaming, kicking, singing, gesticulating children of every shape and colour. At each end of the various benches sat a Monitor, acting as a kind of breakwater. The church was more crowded than it had ever been in its life. Of that he felt sure. Over the altar had been built a kind of stage, conveying the impression of a built-up fireplace. Ninety per cent of the howling mass of infancy went neither to church nor to Sunday-school, preferring to spend their time in stealing or breaking windows, but this was different. It was a soirée, a desecration, a demonstration they were accustomed to in the street and which they normally called 'a rammy.'

Suddenly he caught sight of Jenny. There was her brilliant smile, deriving from a profusion of teeth, and the dry wisps of her hair. He sat down in the tightly-packed pew next to her and a bespectacled girl with eyes like a fish. She gave him a paper bag. Some of the boys had already their noses in theirs, as if it really were a nose-bag. He opened it and saw that there were cakes inside. Carefully in that barrage he counted them. There was a rock-cake, two cookies, and a doughnut with the remnant of a blob of jam still sticking in it. No snowball. No meringue.

Silently he placed it on the ledge where the Bibles usually lay. There came then a tremendous roar that made him jump.

The tea had arrived.

Above the mad clamour he could hear the kicking of seats and a dull stamping on the floor, accompanied by a monotonous chant: 'WE WANT TEA! WE WANT TEA! WE WANT TEA!'

There were baskets of cups. There were jugs, pails, canisters, bowls, kettles of tea. When at last everyone seemed supplied and replenished and refurbished, the inevitable bun-fight began. Pieces of paper dipped in tea flew through the air in hard pellets. Thick as hail they fell. To escape, one had to bob down on one's seat. David was struck on the neck by a particularly unpleasant missile which flattened when it landed.

Looking round to find who had thrown it, he saw it was hopeless even to try. Boys were standing on the seats. Others were leaning over, or bobbing and weaving in mischievous delight. The girls either imitated them or screamed.

Turning round again to his cup, he was shocked to find that someone had placed a cake in it, and stuffed it well down with paper, dragged along the floor so as to be good and dirty. He gave up.

'This is the last time you will see me!' said Jenny Campbell, above the din. He could not hear. 'I'm off to New Zealand,' she shouted. He could only see the bun of her hair.

Cakes followed the pellets in an endless stream. The whole church was a menagerie in which the screaming never ceased for an instant.

DAVID! WILLIE! ELSIE! ARTHUR! COME OVER HERE! LOOK! OY! HEIGH! HEY! YOOHOO! AAALLEEEC!

She gave up trying to tell him and merely smiled at him.

It seemed senseless, but it was only a soirée. It must be a part of religion, like the St Rollox Works.

Now the organist began to play, and they pelted him too, as if a Bacchic or Dionysiac frenzy, or perhaps some ancient dance of warlocks had finally thrust through the years of miracle play. Not until the choir appeared did they run out of ammunition. They were tiring in any case, and these were their friends and relatives. They were, all together, the chorus, and the tragedy was about to begin, the family tragedy.

The choir sang a few hymns, and it was the turn of the concert proper. There were conjurers and singers and Highland dancers

wearing breastfuls of medals, funny stories and recitations by
blushing boys, and finally the choir again. It was a variety show,
except that there was no Punch-and-Judy.

'I shall not see you again after tonight,' said Jenny Campbell
huskily. Feeling under the seat, she produced a large box, which
she handed to him. When he looked at her to thank her, her eyes
were full of tears.

'I'm going to New Zealand with my brother. He is a preacher.'

He did not like to say 'I'm sorry,' as it did not sound right, so he
said 'Is New Zealand very far?'

'Very far. I may never come back, David. But I shall always
think about tonight.'

It seemed incongruous. A penny soirée and New Zealand,
where the butter came from, in the Maypole Dairy. He remembered seeing a cow from there in the window. Suddenly they all
stood up and sang 'God Save the King.' Most of the children were
too sleepy even to look at the orange they received at the door
before being ushered out into the cold night.

He hurried again past the cemetery of St Rollox, and past
Sighthill Cemetery, the orange lying in his hand like a harvest
moon, and felt the dead had risen and were hurrying after him.
They couldn't have. It had not been a resurrection, only a mirage.
He ran faster to keep up with the Richardsons. St Rollox would be
barred and shackled in dust and dung tomorrow and for ever as it
had always been.

Long ago, his father had told him, there was a soldier who
struck a boulder with a sword and transformed it into a warrior.
There were the lines:

> Dar thighedh sluagh Tom na h'iubhraich
> Co dh'eireadh air tus ach Tomas?
> (When the Hosts of Tomnahurich come
> Who'll rise first but Thomas?)

His father said that was Thomas the Rhymer. He had been
stolen away into a Far Countrie.

On he ran through the shrouds of mist and rain, back to the
gaslit sunshine of the house.

'Yesh,' his Aunt Bessie said, 'he used to live near me. I kent
him fine. He wrote the lines your mother told you:

> How wad ye like tae be me
> Going to a penny soirée,
> A lump of fat

Stuck in ma hat,
How wad ye like tae be me?

Thomas, he thought, must have disappeared through falling
under the seat at a soirée and never been missed when they locked
up the kirk.

III

Horror-agog and frog-eyed, Mrs Greig appeared at an open door
in the close, with upraised broom. David ran and ran. Out into
the street, where he fell and slashed his knee on the jagged flints.
His sister wept, thinking she had caused the fall; but it was Greig.
The very name was the bark of the china-dog on his mother's
mantelpiece, a soul-splitting crockery-cackle, a porcelain yelp –
Greig! – as though the toys he played with had all come rantingly
alive.

There they were, barking and shivering from the strands of her
tinselled grey hair, her lidless grey eyes and protuberance of teeth:
'Greig! Greig!'

At any moment she, or others as evil, might seize hold of him
and pinion him with sightless glance, and he would drown, die,
dissolve in the wave of terror emanating from the nothingness of
the fish-scale of those eyes. Always, coming downstairs after that,
he stepped on pins and needles past her door and watched with
awe the brass nameplate brazen on the varnished wood.

Only love overlaid these symbols of terrifying neutrality, so that
he began to forget them, although, when sitting in the swing at the
kitchen door, he could not enjoy the forward lurch into light for
fear of the backward swing into the darkness of the corridor. They
existed therefore as a background. They were the second plane to
his behaviour, the undercurrent, in mortal combat with the
friendly manifestations such as the aspidistra plant, which, every
Sunday morning, grew a bar of chocolate wrapped in silver paper.
Its leaves curled like dark green plumage out of the back of a black
stucco swan. That was a miracle if you like! So engrossed was he
with the shiny crinkling paper illuminating the depressing wet
plant that he left unexplored the gap between its being there and
not being there. To be sure he went into the room sometimes on
week-days, but only because he was hungry for chocolate. Never
for an instant did he doubt. As soon as he saw the dried tubers of
the plant quite bare, he withdrew again silently, chill as the earth-
mould round it.

It was probably owing to the aspidistra plant that he became aware of detail on the smallest possible scale. There were the contorted, pseudo-oriental designs on the chairs in the room. The material was green and the design in relief. He ran his fingers along the edges. In the interstices was no fur. It was horrible. Nor did the springs give. The arms, also fur-covered, had a carved wooden base. They were particularly horrible.

The fireplace contained brass shovels and brushes, all highly polished. The ebony clock on the mantelpiece was equally highly polished, and had a maddening re-echoing tick, as if the makers had wanted to prove that it was going. The floor was clothed in a thick black rug of sheepskin. Thus everything within the four walls was either bald and polished wood or covered in dense hair. The only available means of salvation in the whole jungle of fetish was a small organ, which, however, could in no time blow up a storm of incredible volubility, especially if you pulled out the stop marked – was it? – could it be? – BASSO VOCE? He liked pulling that. It had a smooth velvety touch and slid out, effortless as a feline claw.

At times the boy imagined that if he pedalled hard enough he would blow the whole room to fragments. Even 'Onward Christian Soldiers,' however, failed to do that. All that happened was that, given particularly loud pressure, clouds of dust flew out as if it had not been an organ but a vacuum-cleaner.

He was astonished. He climbed down from the music-stool to peep inside behind the pedal. Yet, though he held it down, he could see nothing. It was a cave. It might easily have been a home for mice. Bobby had said that haystacks were cows' houses. He began to hoard things in it, forbidden objects, pearl buttons, toy soldiers, naked bobbins of thread made into steam road-rollers. It was a hollow mountain wherein dwelt the enemies of this existence. Sometimes he took them out and the soldiers fought in the sheepskin jungles of Brazil, the steam-roller tore a path through the carpet, the pearl buttons opened up before his eyes a silver mine.

Normally, this was discouraged, and he was not supposed to go into the Room at all. There were sacred occasions, however, in the evening just before a party, or on an especially cold Sunday, when the fire was lit and he was allowed to perch on a square stool with a leather top, about three inches high. A 'party' was when your mother baked all afternoon, running here and there, ironing, wrestling, fighting down live dough, like a sculptor or a surgeon attending a childbirth, into the oddest shapes and consistencies.

He was amazed at the transformation in the scene, and at the Sisyphean labour of his mother over tiny biscuits and slabs of shortbread which afterwards she dabbed like Auld Nick himself, with a hot fork. 'If a thing's worth daein, it's worth daein weel,' she said. Their shapes intrigued him. Animal biscuits bore each the outline of an animal in white icing, on a brown background. Shortbread had to be beaten all over to reveal little wrinkles and eyes, whilst cakes were fashioning themselves into birds and baskets. Yet tempers were short. Metal moulds for cakes were short. And the oven was much too small for her ambition, where David stood stirring the porridge with the spurtle.

The 'party' itself was far less interesting than the tea. It consisted only in sitting around the fire playing whist, with cards advertising the CPR. On the backs of these were maple leaves and pine trees. On the face was a glazed real photograph of the scenic beauty to be found on the Canadian Pacific Railway. Dapper canoes throughout the pack sped over rockbound lakes, and weary travellers struggled up towering mountains. Sometimes in these scenes David sensed a brooding air of helplessness and emptiness which was distressing. Even the slopes of the Rockies repelled him, and not because of any threat of an avalanche from a crack in the card. They had merged with the shaggy empty room he lived in. He was certain that even from the train they would thrill him no more and no less than the sheepskin rug, and resolved to avoid Canada, if he could, in the future.

Easily the most mysterious person for miles around was 'The Gude Man.' Pale, delicate, bob-haired Peggy Robertson, the girl upstairs with eyes like a mole when she had died, had, his mother explained, 'gone to the Gude Man,' an apparently desirable end which nevertheless cost all concerned many tears.

Her mother was much more concretely terrible than the 'Gude Man,' who seemed an ineffectual sort of fellow at best. She had had a portion of her cheek-bone removed – presumably for reasons of tuberculosis – though this was never mentioned – with the result that she stared through his dreams like an accusing phantom, the immense hole in the centre of her cheek tightening the single jawbone into desperate resolution. She, too, was a symbol; she was Eros oppressed, a monster with no definite features except those imposed on her by the terrible disintegration of her suffering.

The 'Gude Man' seemed to be ignorant of all this. He was someone you had to be kind to, or perhaps for, whenever you happened to remember. Sometimes David thought he was MacLacherty, who came sailing down the street every Saturday on a pony and float with a bell, selling apples or coal-briquettes in the intervals of his song: 'Aippuls, Fine Ammerrican Aippuls!' – or 'Coal Brikets! Coal Brikets!' – according to whether he spun the sun or fine threads of mist and rain.

At still other times the 'Gude Man' was the back-court singer, that modern troubadour, 'Ye Banks and Braes,' who sang the song of the same name in a tattered army greatcoat. He was old, with a drooping moustache of the Ming Dynasty, and no hope in anything except perhaps a drink. He therefore sang with considerable feeling the old lines:

> Why do ye chant, ye little birds.
> And I sae weary, fu' o' care?

Counterpart of the 'Gude Man' was, of course, the 'Bad Fire.' This never meant much to David, because he could not see how a fire could be either bad or good. It was either a fire or it was not, and if it was a fire it was in a grate, and that was an end to it. So the threat 'You'll go to the Bad Fire' held no terrors for him, being a piece of futile adult whimsy if they did not believe it, and superstition if they did. He had nothing but contempt for those who stood in need of a mythical fire to buttress their sagging authority. His father didn't.

He did not know his father at all at first, except as a man of mysterious movements, who occasionally appeared in the Room when he was plucking the bar of chocolate; one who had to be served with sausages and mince as soon as he came in. A man of colossal appetite, with bulldog face, he ate in short rushing bites. His bushy eyebrows, drawn down in a frown of wire, and his jaw, thrust out as if harbouring fangs, made David rather afraid. Yet there proved to be surprising things about his father that gave him confidence and made him happy to sit in a chair on the landing awaiting his arrival, watching the lamp-lighter clatter up the stairs with his ladder and torch, which he placed, plump, on the gas-lamp to puff it – splutter – into an incandescent hiss of brightness.

One of these things was that his father rarely if ever struck him. His mother was not so sure in her behaviour. She was capable of anything when she shouted and shook her fist at him, as on the day when he had been playing football, in spite of her admonition: 'Don't kick your toes away again!'

Normally he played just the same, standing after the game at the corner of the street to let the wind blow the sweat off his face, and wiping his boots with a piece of paper. Once, however, he had forgotten to wipe off the mud, and like a fox she snapped: 'Wait till your father comes home! He'll give it to you! Just wait!'

'Can I have a piece on jam?' he asked.

'No, you can't. I've had enough o' this. I'm fair sick o't,' she girned. 'It wad gar ye greet.'

At that he knew she was serious. His mother never used the phrase 'sick o't' except with particular venom and emphasis that carried conviction. He slunk about the kitchen now with perturbed but fascinated glance, watching her black smoothed hair, like an Eskimo's, her sharp face, like a bird's when she turned in wonder and held her head on one side, screwing up her eyes in unspoken benevolent inquiry. Now there was no wonder visible, only, it seemed to him, boundless savagery. He began to sob, wandering round the house disconsolate and condemned, feeling his inner guilt and thinking of the coming thrashing – the unrestricted, unpredictable effects of it on all the love around him.

At nights he prayed to the Gude Man: 'Make me a good boy, for I am a bad boy.' His mother told him to do that. Perhaps it was really the Gude Man's fault that he was bad, but his was to be the punishment.

He heard his father's knock. 'Rat-tat-a-tat!' and the quick decided downtread of his boots in the lobby. The stocky figure with the dome-like head appeared and his father threw a cap on the bed in the wall, took off his jacket, revealing arms and bunched muscles like an elmbole, bare to the rolled sleeves, opened up his waistcoat and glanced round merrily.

'Weel, whit's new?' he asked as he sluiced the water over his head and neck at the sink, arms bent like a surgeon preparing for an operation.

'David's been a bad boy today. You'll hae to gi'e him a beating,' said his mother, equally active and laying knives and forks for the meal, hastily, almost timidly.

He stood white-faced, waiting.

'No,' his father panted, between gulps of air and great gasps as he rinsed eyes and neck with the towel, face red now as if he was throttling himself in that circular movement of rubbing. 'He's a good lad you know; if you say he's bad . . . there must be some mistake.'

'There's no mistake,' said his mother, looking at him with needle-eyes as she poured the tea and lifted the kettle from the hob. 'He's been the deevil. I mean it. I'm fair sick o't. Ye'll take him into the room!'

David held his breath. This was a threat. No one was taken into the Room except for a deliberate thrashing.

'No, no, there must be some mistake,' expostulated his father. 'We'll talk it over. He's a good lad really, you know,' until David could scarcely credit his ears. Surely his father must be either a fool, or – very, very wise? He began to walk around with his shoulders squarer now, feeling perhaps his father was right and he really was a good lad, and even if he wasn't he mustn't let his father down since he seemed convinced of it. Who knows what might happen if he found out his mistake? It might kill him. He might kill David.

His mother said he was 'spoiled.' He thought of a yellow cabbage leaf in the dustbin. That was 'spoiled.' His mother spoiled him. She picked his ears with hairpins until his father told her to take off her shoes and go in her stocking-feet. She combed his hair with a short bone-comb that was double-edged, and she cut his nails to the quick. She was to him the ogre out of Jack-the-Giant-Killer, who walked on stilts across the stage and laughed right into their box.

Everything settled again into place, the clear fire in the grate, the shining knobs of the oven handles, the hissing gas-mantle, the fender where he sat and read Sexton Blake and Dixon Hawke, hoping his father didn't see, because he said it was nonsense, although it belonged to this world of mysterious light and shade, of half-forces only dimly understood, of the balance and eternal war between 'good' and 'evil,' 'love' and 'fear,' his father's hands, his mother's kisses, both their voices; and the china dogs that never barked but looked as if they might; the horror of the dark; the rusting engine in the Low Park that cut your knee and hands if you slipped – between, in fact, the things that you knew and which knew you, and the things you could never know, the things that were rigid with mechanical, rebellious hate.

In the warm kitchen his confidence returned since his mother seemed to have forgotten the apparent ferocity of a moment ago.

'Can I have the tissue-paper from the bread, mother?' he asked.

Still resentful, she thrust it towards him and he pinned it by two pins to the table-legs at the end of the little wooden table. This was another piece of friendly magic. The tissue-paper round the bread was brown and transparent and crinkling. If you pinned it up to the end of the table and put a candle behind it, you had a cinema. You could show the shadowy silhouettes of 'scraps' and figures cut from papers.

Once right in the middle of the theatre his grandfather appeared. He could tell by the apparition of the long, phenomenal knees. To his delight, his grandfather sat down between the table and the bed and was the whole audience! His head was the gods; his knees were the Grand Circle, and his feet the Stalls.

The gods laughed when the marionettes moved in all their stilted gravity. Their actions did not matter. They could not do any harm. Set in the proper frame of the proscenium, they were insulated in space.

Their performance consisted chiefly in fighting and kissing. The figures bent over and embraced or jostled and pushed each other down. There was not much more they could do. The stage was rather small, and their reflexes therefore limited. Yet what they lacked in spontaneity and action they made up in character and exotic interest. There were coloured scraps borrowed from his sister, of Japanese ladies in nightgowns, combs and fans, winking penny-in-the-slot eyes, and pirates with their heads in turbans and a mouthful of fish-knives. There was a pale newsprint Charlie Chaplin, whose face was composed of spots, and a tomboy Pearl White in breeches. The trouble with the latter was that if you licked her too hard, you saw instead of Pearl, the printer's ink on the loss of the Titanic, which to David was as large and tragic as a broken mouse-trap.

Between the acts there were no divisions, as there was nowhere to go had there been an interval. The cardboard theatre, which had formerly housed a gigantic pair of shoes, was not made to run to a curtain, did not perhaps believe in too great a severance from the auditorium. It was all a pleasant muddle really, rather than a play, and it ended abruptly whenever dinner was ready. The characters could all be scrapped at once. Often they would be cremated. There would be plenty more tomorrow.

His grandfather said it was a fine show, and he should know. David looked up his steep sides, amazed to find an adult so receptive.

'Are ye comin' out to the Shaws on Saturday again?' his grandfather asked.

'Oh yes; we always come out on Saturdays.'

'Ye'll hae tae bring the theatre wi' ye!' the old man said, patting him on the head.

'He'll come,' said his mother, 'if he's no' on the training-ship by then.'

He knew the dread word. It was what his father said when he

took him into the Room. He knew where the training-ship was. It was at Helensburgh. It was full of boys who had no fathers or mothers, or were too wild, and it was covered with black-and-white squares like Nelson's *Victory*. His father knew the captain.

'He doesn't want to go to the training-ship. He told me,' his father said.

The prospect was terrifying.

Dissatisfied with the figures as they were now, because they would not stand up to their fate, David licked them and stuck them on the back of the screen until their faces and forms shone through like shades from beyond, dim ghosts struggling into life. To make the image clearer, he would bring the candle closer until, catching the paper-screen, it wrapped the whole faint theatre and marionettes of paper in a tongue of consuming flame, and David leapt back terrified, and his mother screamed.

The training-ship! Would it be the training-ship?

The china-dog barked.

Yes! Yes!

IV

When, after much daring, David discovered that he did not live in a palace-yard but in a small kitchen, which did not contain a theatre, a tent, an aeroplane and a racing car, but a table, a bed, a sewing-machine and a round-backed wooden chair, the realisation was something of a blow, and he tottered out to play in the streets.

The girls let him play with them at *hooses*. That was keeping house, but it was not much more fun than really being in the house. Boys played *bools*, with steelies, glessies, plunkers and jorries. They played *rubbish* and *tig* and *conkers*. *Tig* was It. *Conkers* were chestnuts. *Rubbish* was anything in your pocket, hairpins or halfpennies or buttons, thrown against the wall. If you were nearest, you threw up the rubbish in the air and if you caught it when it fell, you could stick to it. They had *peeries* they flogged, and coloured metal singing-tops if they were rich. They played *moshie*, a queer game of marbles involving three holes in the ground, spaced out evenly. Into each of them the marble had to be rolled, the opponents being, if possible, knocked away in the process. When one boy was going up to the top hole for the third time, this was called going up for *snooks*, and ended the game. David never found out what *snooks* were, but they seemed definitely worth going up for.

The girls were nicer at first. They had dolls, and you were a big

doll, and they played *peever*; or 'baw-beds,' which the English call
'Hop-Scotch,' imagining the Scots to be a hopping nation. They
wrote on the pavements in large letters of chalk *no more playing so
don't ask!* They played *bee-baw babbetty* and sang:

> Bee-baw babbetty,
> Babbetty, babbetty,
> Bee-baw babbetty,
> Babbetty babbetty bowster!

or:

> Ring a ring o' roses,
> A cup a cup o' shell,
> The dog's awa' tae Hamilton
> To buy a new bell.

or again:

> Is it hauf past ten
> An' is the morning dry?
> Hiv ye got a haddy
> Or onything tae fry?

They had their own songs and their own rhymes. When they
chose someone in *tig* to be *het*, they all stood against the wall and
were counted:

> 1, 2, Buckle my shoe.
> 3, 4, Shut the door.
> 5, 6, Pick up sticks.
> 7, 8, Lay them straight.
> 9, 10, A big, fat hen.

and the famous:

> Ickerty-pickerty
> Pies a-lickerty
> Pumpaleerie-jig.

These were magical incantations, recited with pride and fervour by the umpires, like Druids chanting a spell. Some were just
nonsense-rhymes:

> Dan, Dan, the funny wee man,
> Washed his face in the frying-pan,
> Combed his hair with the leg of the chair,
> Dan, Dan, the funny wee man.

There were hundreds of them. One of the girls from upstairs, Minnie Robertson, took David to school on his first day. The first day was all right, but afterwards began the real process of education, during which the boy was stripped, ragged, scruffed, strapped, caned, booted, upended, frog-marched and generally fired and tethered into a semblance of correct deportment as conceived by the Big Five (not the Yard), and the microscopically-graded Civil Service.

Not that there was a chance of the products of this school going into a bank, even to deposit coppers from a Home safe, or into the Civil Service, even as cross-eyed telegraph-boys. They were much more likely to go into Millar's the grocer's as roll-boys, and come out again with a leather-skull pad on their basketed heads and a floury face, like a Crab' Upcraft, or into a butcher's, to work up from slitting papers to a pig's throat, cheeks becoming bloodier with insolent health and dogs running cheerfully after them, even in quite a strange town, and in 'civvies.'

Unattractive as were the exits, however, they came to resemble Heaven to the boys, principally for four main reasons:

I They were outside the spiked iron railings ringing in the school. These grew in that particular shape in order to tempt the boys to climb over, so as they could tear their trousers and legs. They were iron plants that lived on boys.

II It was a different part to play in the drama of life, a part in which one's lines were to 'nip' fags, take a bird out, and be free-and-easy to swear, spit, puff, gurk, and generally act the tough man without any goddamned headmaster taking up the challenge to see if you meant it.

III It was a free country. You didn't *have* to do anything. Anyone could cheat, swindle, steal, graft, bully and blackmail his way to the top as long as he had the drop on the others and did not believe in a group.

IV Dammit, it meant for you you threw away your school-cap and the trousers that shaved your legs for longs and a workman's 'cady' and muffler. You had silver in your pocket to jingle – till you reached home anyway – and you brought in a 'wage,' like a loaf.

At schule they called him many names. He was 'Liar Liar Lickspit in ahint the caunlestick,' ninny-numbskull, soly-bungler. He was a rabble-dazzler, a tammy-tousler, a shitty breeks, a wee shauchly shaver, a dram doddle, and a scrim-shanking rapscallion skulldugger. They wrote that in their books.

Among these kittly kilties and busby-jumpers and chittering german gomerils, he was a laggardly stock jobbing sycophant, a doddering, backscratching, mealy-mouthed tub o' guts. That was what the English teacher said. He said an Aberdeen fish-wife had shouted it in his hearing. The boys thought up the answers, but they were only a set of tatterdemalion buncombe-gestators, hindlehoggish flibbertygibbets, toddlywinking corybants, snuff-snifters, privy pullulators.

Before boys were allowed to 'leave' school, they had by main force to pass an examination, not an examination related to anything in the scheme of things, just 'an examination.' The questions were not just questions either. They were Questions. They helped to create the whole complex of Questions in the world outside. They helped to make the whole Earth unhappy if it had not a Question to solve.

Boys left, their heads positively buzzing with Questions. They never remembered being given any list, however modest, of Answers.

Describe the cogitations of Harold before the Battle.

Construct a sentence to illustrate the use and significance of the word 'Fiddlesticks.'

Parse Harold in the above question.

'Do you know Wee Rosa?' the boys said. Wee Rosa who? Wee Rosa Hooses.

That was what the boys said, and why in this caste-foundry, 'education' to them meant less than half a toffee-ball.

The first thing to learn was The Bell.

When The Bell started ringing it was a warning that in five minutes you would be late and marked absent and need a line from your parents or why did you come. This taught you obedience. It meant that in after life, every time you heard a Bell, you would start running, whether it was a fire bell, a hand bell, a door bell, a telephone bell, a church bell, or, in the Alps, a cow bell. Primeval things, such as washing, having breakfast, or even putting on one's clothes, had to be dropped as soon as The Bell rang. This was the main reason why so many otherwise decent, well-behaved boys arrived at school snot-rotters, eating pieces, extracting soap from their dingy ears, or even tucking their shirts down the front of their trousers.

He always had to run to school. He was always running, at the beck-and-call of Mr Bumbletory, Francis Ponce, Jack Botabol, and old Joshua Midriff.

He rarely had time to dream or seek release from that iron obedience. He must 'get on,' they said, though they never told him where to go.

Yet it was in Petershill that he first learned to look at the city round him, and from Petershill that he began to explore the wastes of streets, stretching for miles away into the distance.

His own street, Laverockhall Street, he discovered, lying between Springburn and Provanmill, formed part of a pastel-desert in which blocks of tenements rose like the standing-stones of some primitive megalithic civilisation. Burns mentions the laverock often, but no laverock had been heard there for generations. Before the invasion of this stone cataract, the birds had retreated as once they withdrew from the ice. Few of the kirtled shawlies among the inhabitants even knew what a laverock was.

Towards the north spread Paddy's Park, a high waste of soil many acres in extent, on which few blades of grass ever grew. It was pitted with trenches dug by children, which invariably filled with rain-water and rarely drained. To the south there sprawled the Caledonian Railway Locomotive Works, known locally as 'The Cally,' with girders in place of poplars, and vast arenas of oil-drums. This, too, pinned down in idleness hundreds of ravaged acres.

Asphalt on the streets and pavements expanded like rubber into blobs of tar for boys to play with during the long afternoons when hooters and sirens were silent.

On the western side, Sighthill Cemetery hemmed in the living as well as the dead; whilst far to the east, the furnaces and chimneys of the famous Cowlairs Locomotive Works completed the design of a jagged human pen. Engines from there went to India, China and South America. The majority of the men who built them did not even go down town. Their tendency towards escape was termed 'romance' and had to be built into their craft, or dissolved in tears and blows on a Saturday night at the 'Kelpie Inn.'

It was a compact piece of territory, all the more so since every trace of spontaneous nature, including flower-pots on window-sills, had been blacked-out by smoke or erased by the knives and bibles of inhibited industry. Flowers in these former fields meant only arum-lilies under bridal-veils of glass in the cemetery. To the boy, therefore, something symbolic clung to the figure of the stone-mason at the corner, who broke up all forms of the stone that was paralysing and throttling the life of the city, and shaped it into Celtic crosses. He should, David felt, have been turned loose on these terrible streets and on these walls, chalked with scorpion-like inscriptions. He might have made of them something more than condemned cells.

Masses of men in blue dungarees, shambling daily out of the 'Cally,' blackened mess-tins in oily hands, darkened the streets with sullen purpose. Masses, shambling without direction, like cattle moving along a country lane, bestirred themselves in his dreams and tried to break free of the iron monster they served.

Only the wonderful Clydesdales, with cornflowers in their manes and tails docked, trampled urbanely about their patient business. Their shoes, rising to a rhythmic crescendo as they tackled the innumerable hills at a brave trot, provided a background of music to the discordant sounds of the city. They had manes like lions. They dominated in their very nobility those warrens of cobbles and those hills of rain; and in the summer, as if the winter of work had not been enough, they carried the children from neighbouring Sunday-schools into the country on an annual trip. Benches were placed back to back on the carts. The carts themselves were painted resplendently in red or blue or green, and the horses, apparelled as no circus-horse had ever been, wore great towering bridles hung with arches of flowers and bells, on a shining harness of leather and brass fit for palfreys, and their ears and manes were decked with blossom. These festivals had a pagan origin like much in the city, but to children and horses both they were unforgettable, and, though stigmatised by chimneys and the belching fires of Cowlairs as a dream, were more significant by far than the meaningless plodding existence led every day by horses and men alike.

His grandfather had worked in the 'Cally' until, amid fumes and clanging fires, consumption had painted his cheek like a clown's, and his hair shone like snow. The place now meant to the boy a concrete hell that beat through his heart like a dynamo. Even if he had to run away, he felt, he must not let himself be engulfed in this morass of mad injustice. He had been on one of the trips when a child, and never forgot it. Carters and their horses were knights without armour, wandering among canyons of furnaces and yards where thistles grew, towards their final encounter with the caged engines of disaster.

Laverockhall Street, however, was wiser than some of the other streets. The buildings in it were of red sandstone. That was warmer than the crumbling yellow stone, like caried teeth, of poorer Bedlay Street, which after four o'clock in the day became a veritable Bedlam of ragged, running urchins, intent on any and every form of reckless mischief.

Though he, too, had to run, and had no time to dream, it was in Petershill that he learned to look at the horses and the men, and unconsciously to listen to the fury and the meaning of their labour.

Through the long, frozen windows and the tall forests of railings, he gazed at them in his dreams, hearing the sound of hooves coming up the long white ribbon of cart-track from Garngad. 'Glasgow,' he said.

Glasgow or Glesca or Glesga or Glasga or Glasgie go the iron hooves on the cobbles coming out of St Rollox, for the horses in the streets outnumber the Lord Provost and are louder than the riveters of the Empire. The bird that never flew and the fish that never swam, the tree that never grew and the bell that never rang are all buried in this city of whistles and sirens once called 'Glaschu.'

If it were one of its own ships, he felt, or even only a stowaway, it might go somewhere, instead of pulling the imperial cart up Buchanan Street. As it was, the rains fell through the square, aslant like Zulu spears, and Queen Victoria sat in her shroud, an old shawlie in a drunken Band of Hope. The bailiffs had moved in. The carts were carrying off her furniture in crates. Her hens were locked in wooden cages. The corridors of her home were lanes in a vast Goods Station. The cock crew. Her palace was a pumpkin. She was old. So Glasgow or Glesca or Glesga or Glasga or Glasgie went the iron hooves of doom in her rooms, for carters in bell-bottomed trousers outbid bailies in brass, and spit on their hands as the rain spits in the Clyde.

TWO

I

AT SIMPSON'S, JUST before the Low Park, where a charging bull had put its foot through McAra's barrow, they sold sugarolly straps like Miss Miller's tawse. It was a sweet idea. Tawse you could eat! He remembered the legendary strap Miss Miller had, boiled and sprinkled with pepper, they said, every night. He did not believe that, though Miss Miller herself, with her silvery hair, her flowery complexion, baked face and billowy skirt, was definitely like a little edible figure, the verimost sweetie-wife. She was like the cousin of old Millar in the dairy, that lacteal Clemenceau.

Since the affair of his Aunt Bessie, David was always seeing relationships in faces where in fact no relationships existed. Sometimes at home in the evenings they played a game of cards called 'Happy Families,' and the faces in that horrified him. There was Master Potts, the painter's son, and a horrible spectre, Miss Potts. There was Mr Bunn, the baker, and the frightful Miss Bunn. Miss Miller, he thought, had probably looked like Miss Bunn when she was young, her hair all done up in a prim pagoda. Most frightening of all were the chimney-sweep and the butcher with his cleaver. They were linked in David's mind with the pictures of the prisoners in the Bastille which he had seen in a copy of *A Tale of Two Cities*, filthy, hungry spectres with rolling eyes, devils which were to him more real than the ineffectual oddities represented by the others. It was not pleasant to think that in the time of Dickens, when children like himself were being ordered to sweep chimneys, their terrified portraits were liable to be put on a card for the parlour amusement of those whose chimneys they kept clean, and who represented 'good taste.'

The cards had been badly produced, with the result that the lips were shapeless and slobbering, as if the people concerned must be constantly wiping off blood. They were the ones who, late at night at the corner of the street, called after him: 'Pussyfoot, Pussyfoot!' Mr Grant was one. He said that too.

With his penny on Saturday he bought a sheet of dabetties. He liked the name 'dabetties,' and rolled it on his tongue as he did the transfers themselves before sticking them on the back of his hand to glare at him, green and blue and yellow and red, in the garish colours of nightmare. They had odd faces too, but friendly ones. When you moved your skin they did funny dances.

There were other words he had once thought 'funny,' like 'dabetties,' in that improbable world where to be funny was not to be amusing but to be strange or even beautiful. There was, for example, 'glabber.' That was a noise made by striking mud with the flat of a spade, or with one's hand. It was the mud itself, the original perhaps of which the Scots 'glaur' was only the contraction. He had never heard it used except by other children.

Always there was a world struggling to break through, a world on the verge of the freedom it had once known, a world struggling to be born, of speech and action, of forgotten sights and sounds, the world of the horses and the carters, of the Cally workers when the siren blew, of Master Potts and the Happy Families, and the filthy spectres and Miss Miller, and his father, and grandfather, and his grandmother's language, and MacLacherty, and 'Ye Banks and Braes,' and all his children friends. Especially in words and action did he feel that imprisoned world, against which were set the school and Midriff and Ponce and Botabol, policemen and magistrates and draughtsmen who designed better engines than houses.

There was 'fankled.' His kite's tail was often 'fankled.' It was wound in such tightness of confusion that it was almost impossible to unravel and perhaps a knife would have to be used. That was 'fankled.' A lot of things in the world were 'fankled.' It was better not to think about it, his father told him.

'Let me tell you a baur,' he said. That it was. A baur, a story worth telling, sometimes amusing, always vital, and with point, true with a poetic truth.

There was Cording. He was 'fankled,' too. He lived at the top of the street and was top of the class, a bright boy with curling blond hair, who always sniffed and looked incredibly woebegone. His innocent eyes were inwardly puckered as though he could not bring himself to believe that the world was actually as it appeared.

'Ingins' had no such qualms. A small, wizened creature with a face like a crab-apple and a mouth as firm as a trap-door, he made his world as he wanted it. David fought a battle with him one day after school.

'You? I could beat you with one hand tied behind my back,' he said.

'Aw right,' said Ingins, in his precocious bass, 'I'll fight ye at four!'

The dread challenge was out. There was no shirking. A pack of screaming boys propelled him out of the stone building and down the steps into the stone quadrangle shouting: 'A fight! A fight!' He was scarcely aware of what was happening. It was out of his hands entirely. It was not his fight any more. It was a 'school' fight.

He shaped up. Ingins danced before him like a firefly and suddenly smote him on the nose. It had always been his weak spot. Now it began to bleed. At once a horde of boys parted them. 'Ye're beat!' they shouted at him. 'Na, ye're beat!' The first to draw blood, it seemed, won. He hadn't started. It was his own private fight, didn't they know? He was amazed.

Afterwards, Ingins was much nicer, and saw him home.

'Oh my! Will ye see to that boy?' his mother shouted, putting down the teapot when he arrived, nose bleeding still. 'Oh my! What I've to stand! Take him into the room I tell ye. He's been like that the haill day!'

'Whit's up wi' ye, wumman?' asked his father, glancing ferociously. 'I work the whole damned day and hauf the nicht and this is whit I get when I come hame! Gimme some peace! Haud yer tongue!'

'Now!'

His mother glared at his father, and David could see from the angle at which she held her head in admonition, and from her eyes, staring in a wild concern, that for some hidden reason it was all she could do to restrain her tears. She looked as though at any moment she might fly into fragments like the world. 'Don't address me like that in front o' the weans. I'll not stand it!'

Precision in speech was characteristic of her anger. David's bowels melted into water. He wanted to cry and hug her, let his father thrash him, anything to release his mother from that awful strain of temper and pathos. His father, however, only glanced up once, but penetratingly, eloquently, interrupting his eating and sucking of gravy, to say: 'Hiv some eighteenpence. Is the war gettin' intae ye?'

The ugly tone, and the slang, eighteenpence for sense, cut her like a whip. Her head sank as she turned aside in a paroxysm of sobbing, and a finger and thumb stabbed her eyes to stay the flow of tears and weakness.

'It's aye ma faut,' she sobbed. 'When you shoot oot yer neck of course it's different. Ye gave poor wee Meg a squint wi' yer roaring last week though!' This in an accusing crescendo.

These changes of front bewildered the child. He tried to follow, to see some sequence in the behaviour, to gain some insight into the causes – but they eluded him, as did the friendly and the enemy mysteries. It seemed as though his mother was now the china dog; as though everyone, even his father, lived on the verge of an inhuman madness, exuded from the whole incalculable world of iron, glass and crockery.

'Naebody tae think o' the puir wee lambs but me,' she muttered, with contorted face, and led him off to bed. What had happened? Outside he heard the moaning whistle of the long and crawling trains.

'If I don't dae a' thing myself, it's no' din at a'.'

Their mother loved both children and husband with more intensity, perhaps, than any of them suspected. Busy all day as she was, her heart was wrung with anguish for them. She was a proud woman. Her father, a man of education and real calibre, was not one who had learned how to count and how to spell merely in order to make more money; money he abhorred; but a Scotsman of the old school, loving education for its own sake, for the deepening knowledge and consciousness of reality it brought, and for the philosophy it gave him, wrung from religion.

She had seen him walk daily into work, seven miles, and seven miles back at night, for earnings that were meagre. She had noted his Spartan habits and his generosity to others in need, with its small, if existent, reward. Whilst idolising him for that, and because he was capable of real and lasting affection, she had resented the fact that often his children had had to suffer as well as he himself, because of that very uprightness, in a world that had no room for a scholar and a gentleman. His son, for example, had had a good education, although he had not gone to a university but into a bank. She had married, and been twitted by her sisters for marrying 'below her station,' the man being only an 'engineer' and coming from a line of 'engineers,' who were the opposite of scholars. Sometimes she thought it was true. Sometimes she thought she had missed the finer things in life by marrying as she had, that she had been forced to miss them because her father had not had the foresight or the financial ability to make possible a good match.

Yet she loved her husband, and still loved him. There was something impressive and appealing at the same time about his finely-chiselled lips and jaw, something direct, that would not be put off with evasion and pretence any more than her father could be put off by these, although he lacked perhaps her father's sensitiveness and culture, being more interested in engines and mechanical contrivances of every sort. It had impressed her when he disappeared for two years after overhearing her sister call him a good-for-nothing, and returned with nearly three hundred pounds in the bank. Not that money interested her, but one had to be careful, and she was so afraid now that the same would happen in her own family, money would go to those in need, to his parents, for example, and they themselves might be in want. That she could not stand. Love and pride forbade it. Not selfish pride, not pride of race, but the pride of her blood, individual self-denying pride typical of her stock.

When David was in bed she returned to the kitchen in silence. After the implied rebuke she was smarting and contemptuous. At moments like this she felt she could leave him without the slightest remorse.

On the grate she noticed some sparks of soot, and that gave her the opportunity for a fresh outburst.

'There'll be a blaw doon here the nicht!' she said snappishly, looking up the chimney and pulling the vent to and fro as she did so. 'It's a good job we're leaving. The chimney would have tae be swept.'

That, too, she hated. All the dirt of it.

'Mair expense.'

Her whole surroundings, in fact, were loathsome to her, the room and kitchen in the noisy tenement; the gossiping, occasionally drunken, neighours; the dirt; the work and worry . . .

She had to rise at six with her husband, because she did not like him to make his breakfast alone, being afraid that he would skimp himself and go out into the cold with nothing on his stomach. While he lit the fire she would fry some ham-and-eggs in the little yolk-encrusted pan and 'mask' the tea. They never had much time for conversation in these early hours, when the light, like consciousness first breaking on the world, filtered slowly through the little panes above the sink.

There was never much time for conversation even in the evenings.

'Funny thing happened the nicht,' her husband remarked. She waited intently, ready to pounce. 'A went to see that shop I've my eye on. Ye remember I telt ye I mentioned it tae Alec.'

Alec was his employer, a man who owned several machine-shops. She nodded impatiently, listening and watching his features.

'Well, he'll no' sell noo.'

So that was it.

'Hm. T-t-t-.' She nodded her head backwards and forwards several times as if, whilst expecting something of the kind, she could still scarcely credit it.

'He promised it tae you for £250 didn't he?'

'Aye. There's something funny aboot it. It's a nice shop. A good cycle and sidecar trade could have been built up in it, and maybe a garage one day; and there's plenty o' space.'

Now she walked about, poking the fire, turning down the gas, laying back the bedcover, all, in her agitation, little meaningless gestures.

'You're aye the mug!' she flashed out at last, though as yet she did not understand anything except that he had missed an opportunity.

It was all part of his stupid goodwill, she felt. He would never get on. 'The deil provides for his ain!'

There was her ancestor, who had been imprisoned as a Convenanter, after signing the Solemn League and Covenant in his blood in Greyfriars Churchyard. That was a pride of shame he had turned into victory. In the dungeon of Crookston Castle he had made a model in wood of his prison which was now in the possession of the laird. She, too, made a model of her prison. Thoughts like these were so much air to her husband. He in his mind was comfortably off working twelve, sometimes fourteen hours a day for six pounds a week, not seeing his children at all from Friday morning at six till Sunday morning. Nor was that all. Out of his small wage a pound went to his parents living at the coast, and though they needed it, his own father being an invalid, they were not as grateful as they might be, or even as thrifty. Her children and her family were the sufferers. He might at least think of his children!

'The man must have been tipped off by Alec!' he said suddenly, and the effect was like a rocket.

'T-t-t-t.' She was looking up now, eyes staring, as she said herself of others, out of her head 'like pot feet,' her hair thrown back in part challenge, part ecstasy.

'I tell ye. I tell ye,' she muttered in a contralto crescendo, though what she told was not clear. 'He's no' slow, is the Big Yin. He's no' slow. That's aye the wey o't. You're aye Johnnie A'thing!'

Little meaningless phrases accompanying meaningless gestures such as putting the boots on the 'spars' of the table and tucking in the tongues, snapping down the lid of the tea-caddy, wiping a piece of dust from below the threepenny bank, gestures devoid of any purpose save the expression of her excitement and indignation.

'You're too oaft, that's what's the matter wi' ye! Too saft!' she hissed, and again tut-tutted, her pale face and raven hair weaving a witch of her anger.

He knew what was coming and unloosed his collar, throwing it with the bow-tie atop the coal-bunker, habits and undress she hated. The whole house oppressed him now. He felt there was no room. He was being choked. His mouth set grimly. The coal-bunker behind, serving as a dresser, stuck out in the middle of the kitchen. The folding-bed was let down like a medieval bridge; the table was larger with the wings up, and the sink shut off the window.

There was hardly room to swing a cat in. And now his wife was nagging because he would not break with his boss, or because he wouldn't demean himself by asking for higher wages.

'I really don't know how I stand it! I really don't!' she wept, eyes like slits and her face twisted into the grimaces of a clown with tears and grief in place of grease-paint.

'Some day I'll just give wey a' thegither; I know I will!'

'Listen, Teenie!' He leapt up angrily now. 'You're too damned weel aff, and that's a fact. One o' they nichts I'll come hame drunk! – I'm no' Tom Foy!'

It was the direst threat possible to utter, but who Tom Foy was no one knew. He was a mythical figure, a fool, as Johnnie A'thing was a helpless creature at the service of others.

'Speak like that tae Alec, no tae me,' she whimpered, and still he failed to see her real desire and need, as indeed did she. Comfort to her meant little. Love meant everything.

'I'll dae that when it's time,' he said, his face a mass of thunder. 'No' afore. I ken I'm makin' him a fortune. £100 a week an' mair clear profit. I know he could never dae it himself, the big midden. Whit does he know about machinery? I ken he's cheated me oot o' startin' up for myself, gie'n the man a backhander and tell't him I'm no tae hiv the place. I ken he's a' you say he is, and that he needs me, but Teenie, we need him noo tae!'

It was a last appeal and she spurned it.

'I don't dae it for him! It's for the sake of the faimily and the auld man. I love them. I'm like one o' the brithers, Teenie, and the auld man's like a faither tae me. Alec's in charge noo, the only black sheep among the lot, but I canna leave the noo, jist because o' that, no' as long as the auld man's still alive!'

There were six brothers in the Falmouth family and Macrae had almost grown up with them. Mrs Falmouth had first taught him to save money in a bank.

'Dae ye think the auld man disnae ken his son is stealing the business aff him?'

'The Big Yin's gettin' the benefit though. Allow him!' said Mrs Macrae bitterly.

Alec Falmouth, her husband's immediate boss, was The Big One to all and sundry, often indeed Big Mick, meaning he had a high conceit of himself.

'Mother!' David called from the room. 'Mother!' terror flooding him like a sea there in the moonlit dark of the Room and the jungle of green doom.

'Shut yer gub!' shouted his father, roused by frustration. 'I'll gi'e ye a skelpit leatherin'!'

His wife seemed to crumple.

'Sh! The neeburs!' she hissed, but it was too late.

'Damn the neeburs,' he shouted again.

Meg, blonde and scared mite, looked up blinking in the gaslight through her sleep, from the bed in the wall, and began to cry almost before she was awake.

'Lie doon!' he bellowed at her, now thoroughly roused. Normally this terrified his wife into silence and a beggar's humility, but tonight, because of the child, she became suddenly passionate.

'Don't you raise your voice tae her. I forbid it. Don't address my children like that!'

'*Your* children?'

Macrae laughed with unaccustomed bitterness. He was rarely bitter, and when he was, it was painful to see how it hurt him, when you loved him, and with what dignity he bore it.

'Go to sleep,' he thundered again, though less loudly.

In a blind access of rage she slapped him across the face with the back of her hand, forgetting her heavy signet-ring, which left a weal on the skin.

He paled, staring at her for a moment. It looked as though he might strike her down with one of those hamlike fists, in a boxer's swing, and stretch her senseless; or as if she might snatch up a poker. Anything.

Instead, he quickly seized cap and jacket and stormed out, slamming the door behind him.

Again David shouted. 'Mother!'

What was happening? He glimpsed the shadow of assassins in

the corner, lurking strangulation; the walls, precipitous cliffs, made him giddy as he lay looking up at them. China-dogs and brass fire-set and black sheepskin rug all went dancing through their misery, evilly pitching and tossing inside his mind.

From the ebony eagle clock the hour was beaten out flat, eleven times.

'Mother!' he cried again, to save her – but she did not hear.

Her head was bowed as the sobs shook her.

II

The day's ritual began. In the morning the children had to be roused, David and Meg, David for school, Meg to crawl around on errands of mischief, opening the drawers of the sewing-machine, tearing in two David's collection of cigarette cards, whimpering, wetting.

She washed up. There was the scrubbing of pans, with nothing to relieve the prospect from the one window but wickedly spiked iron-railings below in the yard, caked with rust, smoke-blackened; and beyond, the rusting iron 'Billy' on the mud-flat they were pleased to call the Low Park. When she looked from the window on to this back-court, paved with tar and gravel-studded, hearing children shout 'Throw me down a piece on jam! Throw me down a drink! Throw me down my barrow!' she was always afraid of seeing someone impaled on the railings. There were five such 'courts,' all separated one from the other into little caged kingdoms by these spear-like stanchions, over which boys swarmed and which they tugged and kicked and pulled until they were wide enough to slip through. Once a boy in the next close had missed his footing as he was climbing and the rusted spearpoint, caked with soot, had sharply entered his groin. Fearful.

Nevertheless she washed and watched. At the head of the court they shared with twelve other families in the tenement stood a low brick wash-house with an iron boiler and two primitive tubs. There wives raced every day in brown shawls and fought like sparrows as to whose washday it was.

'You washed last Friday!' Mrs Robertson was screaming, pulling at her board.

'It was Thursday! It's ma turn noo!' retorted Mrs Boyd, a small woman whose red hair gathered in a bun, pale, freckled face and thin wormy lips impressed one with their wasting bitterness.

She never liked scenes. Rather than squabble meaninglessly out there, arousing hates and gossips capable of destroying her home, she would withdraw into her kitchen to wash as many clothes as possible in the sink, until her quick, unquestioning hands were split and cracked with hacks from long immersion in water, and the gathering forks between her eyes fought against the dim light. The wet clothes would hang to dry on the pulley as she opened the window to let the steam out of the narrow kitchen that was their living quarters. The white things could be done afterwards at night, in the wash-house, when nobody was likely to interfere.

On the wall hung a picture, *The Marriage of Cana*, which she disliked intensely. It was a reproduction of an engraving, containing a crowd of people in togas.

'Were you married at Cana?' David asked, seeing her look at it.

'No,' she said. 'That's in the Bible. Christ turned water into wine there.'

'Are you glad Dad and I came to live with you?' he asked again.

'Of course,' she said.

He was half-way through his porridge before he asked again: 'Cana is in Heaven, isn't it?'

'No,' she replied. 'Why?'

'Its full of pillars and people undressed and music.'

'There's *no* marriage in Heaven,' she answered gravely. 'Neither marriage nor giving in marriage.'

Did that mean his father and mother would not know each other there? Or if they did, that they would not care for each other? It was all very strange.

'Oh we'll all know each other and be together again,' his mother stammered impatiently when he kept on, 'but there's *no* marriage in Heaven!'

He was surprised at the vehemence of her.

Once David was packed off, the dusting began of the Room, where the best furniture was kept in almost holy adoration. It never occurred to Mrs Macrae that the injunction 'Worship no graven image' might apply as well to furniture as to statues, or that there was an affinity between the taboos and totems of Indians and the frantic collection by Europeans of objects they neither used nor intended to use, because they were too valuable or lent a sense of glory to their owners through the mere fact of possession. Nor did she realise that in both social systems, the ancient and the modern, the result was identical, deification of an object, and consequent slavery of the spirit, ultimately in the most complete and terrifying sense.

Never in her wildest dreams did she imagine that her son was obscurely terrified of just these things, nor would she have understood if she had. No one went there except for a formal reception or a formal thrashing. Dusting the organ, she remembered with fervour how David had once thrust out his lower lip and wept when she played 'Jesus Loves Me,' Sentiment, she thought, had mysteriously touched him, but it was the lugubrious dark-green of the room, underlined by the heavy Venetian blinds, the aspidistra and surrounding darkness which cramped, sickened and made the child afraid, much as the railings, the gossip and the quarrels did her.

After supper of an evening, when she really wanted nothing more than to sit down, or at least have the long delayed conversation with Macrae, the loving small-talk and the retailed gossip, she had to wait till he read his paper by the fire, or did his calculations and plans, illegible scribblings covering pages, up and down and sideways, without rhyme or apparent reason.

She despised him for their untidiness, while she hated him for not seeing how much she wanted to talk to him. She never had time for a paper. If he was in a good humour, which to do him justice was very often, she could perhaps take the nails out of his trousers and sew on buttons, or prevail on him to change his suit so she could wash it or have the shining patches of oil taken out.

It was up to him to speak now, she wouldn't, she decided.

The children knew there had been a quarrel. It had engulfed them willy-nilly, interrupting their sleep, making David doze at school till the teacher threw the chalk at him and asked if he delivered milk in the mornings or why was he so tired?

The outer world burgled him at school. Gone were the days when he could let his imagination run riot in hundred-part stories which he told to his friends grouped round the chimney on the roof of the wash-house in their back-court. To reach the class before the Bell stopped, he had to run across the street and up a narrow, crazy lane, uneven and full of puddles, between the backs of wash-houses the walls of which he had learned to 'dreep.' This had become a race twice a day against his own doom.

School itself was the greatest shock to pristine wholeness. This was being 'educated,' learning you were a hopeless fumbling fool at sewing patterns of strips and scraps of coloured paper, that you would never be anything else; that the scissors and glue and weaving and intricacy of thought and shape and loopholes in design were all forever beyond you, so no use trying. Confidence and wholeness were in the myths around you, in the family, even in the 'Gude Man,' myths not in the sense of untruths but in the sense of space, the standing back of all these things that there might be room to breathe, a wider environment necessary if life were to expand like a flower and not simply be crushed at the outset.

Now at school he had suddenly learned that he must not dream or feel or imagine anything, but think, fit into shape, make coloured patterns and cardboard models from rigid enervating lines. Sometimes there were ridiculous coloured beads to be strung along a thread. These forms of eyestrain always took place when the rain made everything dark outside, falling in a fine ceaseless sheet against the window-panes, and the naked gas mantles hissed through the tired classroom. On all these dreary days he would be kept behind, and the teacher would bicker at him, as though the only thing worth doing in the world was fashioning strips of coloured paper into a pattern.

Yet there were many things he liked. Today, for example, the essay Miss Miller gave them, the little, thin-lipped, marble-eyed woman in blue overalls who presented him every Friday with a penny for what he had written. Then there were the stories of Danish mythology, of Sigurd and Thor in Valhalla. He would have liked more of these. They came at half-past three, and the whole shaggy class sat silent and intent for half-an-hour. Gaels all of them, they had never heard of their own giant Cuchulain who waited down the river, and no one ever told them of Tir nan Og, the Land of the Young.

Occasionally, too, there was question time, for fifteen minutes, before four o'clock, when picked pupils competed against each other in asking and answering questions. David often won by asking questions culled from the columns of the *Children's Newspaper*. Then he would wander home pleased, forgetting the awful mistake he had made in saying that soldiers won medals for killing Germans.

Today on the way home, however, he dawdled, balancing matters up, the quarrel and the scraps and the essay. So young, he still saw no interval between things. Old train journeys to Fairlie were swallowed in tunnels of memory, and he saw only the winking Xmas tree Aunt Nan had stood in a bare, dark room, exciting and crackling as tangible stars, swimming in the smoke of his imagination. That was a symbol of sheer pungent beauty he could never forget. Why the quarrel, though?

On he walked, past Sneddon's hardware shop, smelling of varnish, brown paper and Mr Sneddon's moustache. Over there was Millar's dairy, where Millar himself lived in a large can, wearing a face of sour milk dried in scones and singing 'Soor dook! Soor dook!'

At the corner stood the grocer, a huge fat man, exactly the shape of one of his outsize sacks of flour which he shovelled into a poke. He was wearing a white apron, had a bald head, side hair, and drooping whiskers, like white meal.

David was afraid to go into his shop, even for animal biscuits. If he did, Storey was sure to say, with a walrus grin, from the depths of his tun-like stomach: 'Coo's lick!'

That, he learned, meant his, David's, hair. Black and watered, it curled in a tangled knot on the point of his forehead and could not be shed, giving him the appearance of a plump, if junior, Mephistopheles.

The more concrete the contours of the city, the more disturbing they always were. The scented imagery of the Fairlie Xmas tree became hard tinsel at the window of an orphanage on top of a hill in Glasgow. Twice a year his mother made him gather all his broken toys together, with others she said he didn't want, and they went in a tram to the orphanage. 'Always remember the poor little girls and boys,' she said to him, although they were by no means rich themselves. She need not have repeated it so often. He knew everything she would say. He knew what she would say to-day – about the dinner. He knew what it was for dinner.

Home now, down the lane, past the blackened ash-bins with their spluttering tongues of burnt paper like torn-out roots, he idled, unwilling and afraid to have his food. The 'sausages,' links they called them, would be cold, he knew, and floating in little bergs, narrow floes of grease. He would choke over them, almost vomit, as his stomach turned.

'What are you boking at?' his mother would yell. 'Eat it! It's good food and you should thank the Lord for giving your father strength to earn it.'

That was true. He had no idea what was wrong, and accepted the suggestion that he himself was. But his stomach would not hold it, he knew. He daren't be sick, and yet he daren't refuse. What could he do with the links? Put them in his pocket probably, as he had done before, to throw them down the lavatory later, where they looked at home anyway.

He pushed open the door and went in. His mother was kneeling on the floor with pail and cloth, washing the linoleum.

'Your dinner will be cold, but you'll eat it!' she remarked, pushing with her head towards the table. There it was at the end.

He had to stand now, while she slopped around his feet great blobs of water, up and down, as he stared at the grease. Cold fog drifted through the open window and he could smell the steam from the waxcloth. Only a miracle, he felt, could save them all from the coming explosion.

'Eat it!' She thrust her head up from between his legs, glaring at him so closely that he could see the prongs in her forehead.

'I can't! I'll be sick!' he whimpered. 'I'm not hungry!'

Then, thinking better of it, as he saw the table laden with potato-scones, treacle scones, muffins, tarts, pancakes, crumpets and morning rolls: 'I'm only hungry for the cheese-cake!'

'The cheese-cake is for your father. Take a soda-scone!'

They were the only ones he disliked, soda-scones, like Mr Millar who lived in a can.

'Was it dry when you came in?'

'Aye.'

He picked up a potato-scone. It was useless to argue.

They picked him last at football seven-a-sides, with a look of indifference or even disgust on their faces, during their 'slave market' selection of players. Even Johnnie Robertson, of the otter eyes and deer-like movements, who could punch you round his back and had a great respect for David's father because he had once been an amateur boxer, would only tolerate him, and sometimes left him out of cricket matches altogether. Then he would field desperately, at long-stop, hoping to attract attention by catching out a crack bat and be acclaimed by both sides.

'We're flittin' tonight,' said his mother, panting with her efforts at swabbing the floor. So that was it! He was struck dumb. It meant a new environment altogether, but he was too miserable to think of that. He would lose his friends, the lamplighter who came sweating upstairs with his ladder and a blue smock and funny peaked cap, like a porter's, to give him a 'shine' in the face with his lantern before climbing up to lay it on top of the close lamp so that 'pouf' the dark stairs leapt into spluttering brightness. He was 'Leerie-Leerie Light the Lamp.'

He would lose Charlie Paterson, a tall boy in a short black jersey and shorter trousers, who had unquenchable curls, ate 'saps,' and lived in an attic in curious intimacy with trains, which chugged on the mat and whistled along the line outside across the street. He would lose Jackie Boyd, with the red hair and freckles, whose face was like a 'ginger nut.' Above all, he would lose the little niche five feet high up on the corner of their block of

tenements, facing the sun, where the boys placed their penny
negatives to develop into the sun-burnt faces of film stars.

'Oh, leave it if ye cunny eat it!' said his mother with a girn. 'We
have to be ready at eight. The van's comin'. An' the kitchen's like
a dog's breakfast!'

'Can I go out and play now?' he asked. His last play, when all
the streets fell silent as condemned cells.

'Awa' ye go! Safe win' tae yer tail!' she said, and that was
gracious consent.

Out he ran, over the sobbing wooden doorstep and down the
pipe-clayed stairs of red. Santa Claus came flying with his
reindeer to the sound of the sewing-machine overhead, on his
way to Iceland. He was William Farnum 'Smashing Barriers,'
Eddie Polo leaping cataracts, Tom Mix galloping over the Low
Park slapping his own haunches till he fell on broken bottle-
glass that poisoned the torn palm of his hand to purple
gravelled skin.

He wept, wending his way home holding up his hand like a
rabbit, in the company of two sympathetic maidens.

'Oh my, I'll skivver the liver oot o' ye!' said his mother. 'Day
and daily I tell ye no' tae run across the street, day and daily!'

'Nip it, nip it!' his father said, and bandaged up his hand. 'He'll
have to bathe this in Condy's Fluid.'

He wept again, but afterwards he was a hero. Remembering he
would have to leave all this behind, he went to the lavatory to
think about it, resolved to take a last look round before going, so
that he might carry as much with him as possible.

The lavatory was dark. So was the corridor. He hated the
corridor. It was all draped with his father's coats, like so many
ghosts. He hated swinging back into it on the swing. Yet what he
hated more even than swinging back into the darkness or cutting
thin strips of coloured paper, or eating cold sausage, was being
washed in the sink in front of the window in the evenings when
the curtains were drawn back for all to see and the yellow
gaslight blared, revealing him to all his companions in a cold
shower, as they stood watching him one storey up, laughing at
him, shouting up at his nakedness: 'Ho-ho, wee Mac! Look at
wee Mac!'

That was the rack and that was tragedy in almost a dissolution
of personality. It was seven times worse than being in the stocks or
horse-whipped through the town, yet his mother seemed entirely
ignorant of it all – was she made of china? – and went on rubbing
and scrubbing, even to waving down at them, inflicting on him far

more than the tortures of the stinging soap that blinded his eyes with foam and tears.

'Scuddy!' she said, slapping him. 'You're scuddy!' Then he felt like:

> Wee Willie Winkie, running through the toun,
> Upstairs and downstairs in his nightgoun!

But there was no escape.

He went to bed, dreaming through the concretisation of shadows, of the Low Park over which they had played out their curious, grim wars; of the Wandered Building, a lone tenement standing on the other side of the Park, like one of the American flat-iron buildings built by engineers, not architects. These were all grim stages and grim monsters, that thrust up through the green grass of his dreams like pitiless barbed-wire battlefields. He would have no truck with them. Even if his father were an engineer and his great-grandfather had built the Forth Bridge and another cut the First Trans-Scotland Canal, he would have no truck with them.

He called out many times to his parents in the kitchen: 'Good-night!' to see what they would say. There was never an answer, though there might be a shout: 'Go to sleep!' And he drifted uneasily into a land where the 'Shows' came with their lights and music and games and caravans and lulled his fancy till his mind, almost broken up, like a dissecting-map by the hammer, through any quarrel, was like a pool into which a stone had been thrown. The ripples widened, exploding fantastically into ever expanding circles, seeking perhaps their own cause, only to launch themselves against some unyielding shore, as waves or dreams or reflections, like those in the green and red bottles in the chemists' windows, where, they said, babies swam before they were born.

III

It was not that he had been unhappy in Laverockhall Street. There was the constant serenity of Saturday morning to buoy him up, when the flint streets filled with the cries of flower and fruit vendors; of giants in leather jerkins carrying coal on backs of black-dust; or of carters with vegetables, and mysterious old women, who deposited miraculous baskets on the doorstep, full of china and pots and vases. They were called 'bowel-wives.' 'Bowl-ladies,' said his mother. They might have come from Spain or Africa, so ageless and so gipsy, so knowledge-laden and so redolent of energy were they. Sometimes his mother took a jug from them, and somehow a jacket of his father's would be missing next time he looked for it, since these incalculable Furies dealt in old clothes, like moths.

While his mother was washing up floor and sink, polishing taps to bright gold and battling against voluminous dust, he would be sent out then into the warm sunshine to the Co-op, against which his father harboured some inscrutable animosity, to buy a six-pennyworth of 'snowballs.' These were small cakes, with macaroon on the top and jam inside, which were indescribably sweet when hard. Eating them was like biting icing. Remembering, too, was biting icing, sweet and sometimes agonising, as the sugar sought out a hidden nerve.

And there were the Saturday afternoons when he still went to Pollokshaws with his mother, in trams full of the odour of chrysanthemums.

'One day we'll live there,' she said. It was the opposite of all Springburn stood for. It was old Scotland, a garden of gold bees and breasts of fruit, bright as a patch of sun in the drab life of these streets, and inspiration.

On the wall there hung a little picture in an ancient Celtic frame of a man wearing a tam o' shanter, sitting on top of a hill. Beside him lay a collie dog, and underneath was a poem he had written. The chorus was:

> Eirich agus Tiuginn O,
> Eirich agus Tiuginn O,
> Eirich agus Tiuginn O,
> Soraidh slan le Fhionnairaidh!

That was one of his ancestors. Now they had all to go. He knew now why the old man looked so sorry as he gazed at Fiunary.

He was sitting on a fernie brae like the Green Knowe.

His games, too, had been inspired by the solitude of his own imagination. Besides the theatre and the rudimentary cinema, the tents below the bed and the wars in the park, there were the weekly magazines he read increasingly, the *Union Jack* or the *Gem*. Sitting by the oven-door of the grate, so thrilled was he reading these that he would not have been surprised, turning over one of the pages, to find it suddenly soaked in blood. That was what his father called them – 'Bloods.' Dixon Hawkes or Sexton Blakes he threw angrily on the fire, but he would buy for David himself *Comic Cuts* or *Boys' Cinema*.

He had few toys, therefore, to take away, apart from some

soldiers with wooden legs, more often than not headless as well, so that he felt it was unjust if not indeed slightly ludicrous to expect them to fight well, or even to submit to conscription. He did not want a Meccano Set like Jackie Boyd next door. Unlike his father, he had no aptitude for such intricate, concrete mysteries. Their skeletal construction seemed to him the bones of nightmare. What he desired was the flesh and blood of dream.

It was the same with games outside. Always he fought to preserve something of his own world. He had sat for hours on the roof of one of the wash-houses, by the broken smoking chimney, grotesque as a boar's head, telling stories of fictitious heroes to his comrades, to Willie Hodgins, to George Milne, to Alec Patterson. If they showed any signs of impatience, he would lard it with more excitement. If they made to move away and 'dreep' the wall – which was hanging by the fingers full length and then dropping – he would call after them: 'It's a hundred-part story! You can come back tomorrow.'

He liked Hodgins. He was a small boy with a pale but plump face and serious brown eyes, exactly 364 days younger, so that for one day every year they were the same age.

The art of story-telling he had learned from Mr Johnson who lived up the next close, and filled the night with the hideous laughter of his Indian war cries and tales of Black-feet and Sioux.

'Sou-ix,' he would say in two syllables, 'Sou-ix,' gnashing his jaws and licking his lips till David could *see* the Indian in his face, conjuring up in the lanes of shadow black and blanketed assassins.

He was leaving Petershill and wee Ingins, 'Onions,' with the crab-apple face; the toffee-balls made by Tammy Anderson, a man in a cap and huge waistcoat surmounted by a watch and chain of gold or toffee. Tammy always coughed sharply. He had a very red face, and a black moustache. His eyes were brown as two of his own toffee-balls and as pointed.

'Cheugh-jeans,' said his father. And there was Bill, who had fallen through a plate-glass window from a dyke, and had his leg encased in plaster of Paris, the street hero.

'How would you like *your* leg in sticking plaster and stucco?' they shouted at him.

He was leaving them all, Bill and George and Alec, the red close and the smell of pipe-clay and the iron banisters, leaving the swarming street cries of a community where he had begun to feel at home, to go and live on Balgray Hill.

The air was better on Balgray Hill, his father said. For some reason, the people on Balgray Hill thought themselves better than other people. For one thing, they lived in houses that were larger and had gardens. They were 'semi-detached,' and they were near Springburn Park. It was almost like their own park, they were so near.

They could go every evening, instead of every week-end like other people. They 'commanded' a view of the city, as if it appeared only when they wanted to look. The wind was keener.

They lived in another world, his father said.

When they finally left Laverockhall Street it was certainly the beginning of the end of the world he had known. He was sitting in the back of a delivery van with knives and bolts and screw-drivers jangling in his ears and over his head, lying on his back, unable to sit upright, with the light coming in through chinks. The van was a clanging mass of metal travelling with the speed of light. He could think of nothing but the people and the places he was leaving forever, and how long was forever?

As soon as he stepped out of the van he felt friendlier to his sister. In the past he had ill-treated his sister.

'Beat it!' he had said. 'You can't play with us. You're not a boy. Boys don't play with girls. Go on, beat it!' And he kicked his toes away at football, his mother said. When he stood at the corner of the street to let the wind blow the sweat away before he went upstairs, his sister put out her tongue and shouted: 'I'm going to tell! I'm going to tell!' His sister was a 'clipe.'

Here she was his only link with anything. He took her hand and together they went into the little garden and sat among the gooseberry bushes. It was nicer than Laverockhall in a way. There was a lovely new private wash-house for his mother, his father said; green dreams in the grass, and from the garden next to them they could hear the cooing of doves.

It was summer, and they ate one or two hairy gooseberries, like strange and minute crustacea. If they peered through the bushes they could see a high house, from which came the sound of piano-playing. They were very high up. David felt very elevated. It was like Alec Patterson's, high and empty and somehow mournful in the waning light, as they looked down upon the plains of the city where the tall chimneys stood like trampled wasted grain and the whistling was the whistling not of birds, but of trains that slowly crawled along like black slugs.

They sat blinking in the light. Suddenly, they heard a voice: 'Would you like to see Ian's pigeons?'

Looking over, they saw a girl's face peering at them through the

bushes behind the white-cemented wash-house. She was like a
cannibal, unkempt, teeth large and protruding, and eyes bright
with glee as she stared at them, relishing the liberty or the new
sensation they brought.

'My name's Jessie,' she announced, and as she stepped out,
they saw she was short and plump, with yellow skin like an old
woman. She wore a tattered gym costume.

Behind her, appeared her brother.

'This is Ian,' she slavered.

'They're ma pigeons,' said the scarecrow behind her, edging
forward.

His nose was running. He wiped it frequently with the sleeve of
his jacket. The seven-league boots he wore pinned him to the
ground, which perhaps explained the mud on them. His blue and
white striped tie was hanging out of his waistcoat and his collar
was open at the neck. Watching the small, shrunken face, coppery
as a pear, and the hair curled under the skull-cap on the back of
his head, David conceived an intense dislike. It was as if he were
looking at a rabbit.

However, they obviously expected him to be friends. He was
made to feel he and his sister were adopted, so together they
stumped through the mud of the back garden, up four wooden
steps, to find themselves in a maze of boards and planks and hen-
coops and dovecots and toolsheds, with tumbledown whanging
fences leading to a wheezy gate which in its turn gave on to a
disused quarry.

All over the back of the quarry were similar ramshackle con-
structions, a nightmare of fictitious and largely fortuitous privacy,
where families scrabbled not for gold or oil, but for a stake in
stony soil, like soldiers under a barrage with entrenching tools.

For the moment David was too occupied to notice that they
had merely exchanged the barren Low Park for a disused quarry
as a playground.

He tried to tell Ian some stories, but found his tales engulfed in
the feathers and down and eggs and shit that seemed to be the sole
components of this new world.

During the long summer they played from early morning till late
at night, and the sun did not go down till midnight. It was the
Land of the Midnight Sun. They went up to Springburn Park and
fished for baggies with a butterfly-net. They picnicked on lemon-
ade and biscuits and hunted frogs among the yellow jungles of
broom beneath the bamboo flagpole. High above the smoking

city, like a pyre or an ancient sacrifice, higher than the highest chimneys and masts of the fiery forest, they swayed in the wind on the 'swings.'

They wandered through tall palaces of glass in the Botanic Garden with jam jars, canes, and flushed faces, alone with the aristocratic tropical plants of Africa; staring into fountains rusting with goldfish, walking along duck-boards like gangways, sitting under sweating palms, wondering at the change in the climate, and coming out of a dream and walking down wide avenues of trees and cushion-flowers in an almost empty wonderland larger than Pollokshaws, yet full of the same sweet geography.

He went on these excursions with his sister and the Seymour clan – of whom there were five. On other days he played on the lot with Adam Hamilton, a boy with porcelain features and a light blue jersey, who always seemed on the verge of tears. He had a brother called 'Hammy,' whose head swung like a pendulum in a tick, or tilted backwards like a globe, and whose eyes squinted though he always grinned. 'Hammy' was popular because he was supposed to have a wild temper, but Adam whimpered too much about the 'hammering' he would give you to mean it really.

David read the papers to find out about Music in the Parks. There was a small column about it. He never 'read' the papers. He did not know what they were about. He wasn't old enough to read them; but he read the column about Music in the Parks.

It said:

GLASGOW GREEN: Scottish SCWS Band.
KELVINGROVE PARK: Besses o' the Barn Band.
QUEEN'S PARK: Round the Clock Concert Party.
ALEXANDRA PARK: Scottish Light Orchestra.
SPRINGBURN PARK: Band of HM Scots Guards.

In Springburn Park they played under a bandstand like a Chinese pagoda. Along the road, however, lay school, waiting to put a stop to all this nonsense. It consisted of two stone buildings and a ramshackle structure of red corrugated iron nicknamed by the boys 'The Tin Building,' which was really called the Higher Grade Department, exactly as if it housed a lot of salmon.

During the first week there he met his friends and his enemies, Chick McDougall, the chick being ironical; Galt the bully, with a mouth like a bear. He was a beefy youth. The calves of his legs terrified his schoolfellows. Not that he was very much of a bully.

Scuffles with him never got beyond the stage of handing round pepper in the classroom instead of snuff, or of rolling up his handkerchief, tying it tight, cutting the end in strips, dipping it in vinegar and cracking it round your knees to make you jump. He was not as bad as some of the masters – Stalker, for instance.

The teachers, Mr Bumbletory, former laird of Burriecrassie; Francis Ponce, the Science Master, formerly full of indiscriminate if rambunctious female fructification, a believer, they said, in tart for tart's sake; Jack Botabol, the salmon-tanner and mind-reader in English history, bowed at the Head, old Joshua Midriff, descendant of a somewhat long line of baked-bone manufacturers, who rammed into the barbarous empire of children he had the dishonour to command every known law, so that they might know exactly what it was they were breaking besides adult adulterers' hearts.

It was a famous school, as David found out. In its time, which was mainly before now, it had produced galaxies of pan-handlers, corn-chandlers, and haberdashers; a man who made a living by getting out of a straitjacket of mail for a wager; a policeman who swallowed his whistle when wetting it; three honest clerks; 76 greengrocers; 3,594 fitters; three pumpkin-purveyors; one apothecary; six heretics; one professional and highly-qualified burglar; as well as 65 members of the leisurely dispossessed classes, 22 bookmakers' touts, three pimps and a beekeeper. There was really no end to what it might produce. Oh, and a plumber who became a minister to stop the evil leak.

These were but a few of the testators of ability, the inheritors of the cobbles that ran down the lane.

Once it was Cardboard and Stalker was walking up and down in front of the class. One of the boys had wet himself with excitement although it was only half-past three. Stalker had been in the war. He had a 'gommy' leg. His face was long and dry and vicious, like a clean-shaven wolf's. He would eat you up. Once he beat up Donald Levens.

On top of his desk lay a pile of models from last week. He picked up one. There was a breathless silence.

'I don't know what this is supposed to be,' he said. 'I asked for a tray. Look at the corners! Not even gummed up properly. Look at the outside! All finger marks. What the hell is it, Graham? What is it?'

He stalked up and down. He was six feet.

'Please, sir, a tray,' whimpered Graham, holding his stomach. There was a muffled series of snorts from the others.

'Out to the floor, boy,' roared Stalker.

At those terrible words the chaps looked at each other fearfully. A few wriggled uncomfortably in their chairs as if they had had it. David sat quite motionless, holding his breath, hoping he would not be noticed before four, when it would be too late. His model was a wreck. It was to him the continuation of the torture of the coloured paper and incomprehensible design of childhood. The measurements were beyond him. He lived in another dimension, outwith measurement. Paste stuck to his fingers like fish. He could not always borrow the scissors, and anyway, he had no idea what he was supposed to be making. Sheriff was cleverer. So was Geordie Low. They did it all. He had to wait until they had finished to see what it was, and then it was usually too late to put it together rapidly himself. Out curled the strap like a snake from Stalker's hip-pocket.

'Crossed hands, Graham!' Swoo-oosh! Smack! Smash! 'Back to your seat!'

Stalker smiled. It was a quarter to four.

'Here we have a beauty!' he said. 'It's fit for – hm, let me see—' He held it up. Then suddenly he let it drop, raised his gommy leg and stuck his foot through it. 'The wastepaper basket!' he screamed, in a horrible war-cry.

'Whitna lovely drop-kick,' whispered Easton.

'Easton, the floor. And you, Macrae. It's *your* model!'

He picked up the rest of them, trays, boxes and pin-holders, reading out the names of the owners like the lists of the condemned. 'Murray, Gregg, Carter, Frame, McDougall, Galt!'

They all trailed out to the floor, crowding to the rear so that his arm would be tired when their turn came. For ten minutes, only the sound of the strap like a steady waterfall could be heard in the tired classroom, and the weeping of a few boys not terrified into silence. Stalker knew it was close to four. He meant to have them all strapped by then. It was a game he played, cat and mouse.

When the gong sounded for the Relief of Mafeking, Stalker picked up his things and left, and the boys stampeded over desks, kicking models, throwing maps, yelling and fighting in the unutterable glee of tension released.

David ran home along Edgefauld Road and along the back into the kitchen. Jenny McArthur was in. She was consumptive and had large teeth. Everyone treated her with peculiar indulgence because she was going to die soon and they were not. But she did not die. She, too, went to New Zealand.

'Is ma tea ready, mother?'

'There it is, see, at the end of the table.'

He still ate standing up at the end of the table.

'Can I have a penny?'

'Whit for?'

'The Wellfield.'

He was quick. He wanted to be off. Jenny McArthur was looking at him with amusement, like his Aunt Bessie.

'I haven't a penny in my purse.'

'A halfpenny, then. A halfpenny and a jam jar'll do.'

'There's one in the scullery. – Don't scliff!'

The scullery had a bunker. On the top was the bread-bin. Jars were stacked there, jam still clinging to their washed sides like little pimples.

Outside he met Fagan trotting to the same destination. They arrived together at four-twenty. Inside the hall was a seething mass of boys, whistling, shouting, jostling, chewing, spitting, and fighting, and running up and down the narrow corridors like thunder in the clouds.

'I'll gi'e you a hammering!'

'Whit, you?'

'Aye, me.'

'Where's Mac?'

They sat at the back, drenched in cat-calls, sneers, and the winged threats of snakes and eagles.

It was best before it began, because then the hall you knew was full of a happy anticipation, and nothing could really go wrong.

No programmes were announced for matinées.

As soon as the lights were lowered a loud cheer went up, almost extinguishing the gas-jets, and they descended into a miraculous darkness. They saw Buck Jones stopping a runaway stage-coach, but at the most exciting moment of the chase the lights went on again and they gazed at each other like strangers, stupid in that sobriety. Shouts arose, like the shouts of awakened sleepers.

'Hoy, hoy! Lights! Whit's the big idea?'

The manager strode on to the stage wearing a bow-tie and the face of a snarling lynx. His bedraggled hair, but for its dryness, might have been a wig.

'Silence!' he bawled, 'or I'll clear the hall and give you all your money back! *And* your ruddy jam jars!'

That was an old threat of his. It stilled them at once.

'Is Willie Macfarlane here? His mother wants him at the door.'

'*Macfarlane! Come on, Macfarlane!*' they shouted '*Buzz off!*'

A small figure, bowed with grief, huddled out.

'He's tae mind the wean!' a voice cried out.

There were a few laughs at the sally, and then there spread again before their hungry eyes the panorama of a dream, as they rode through six sun-drenched reels.

When they came out, it was dark and raining. Drugged with wonder, they stood for a moment, but could think of nothing else to do. There were no 'Shows.' They had no money for a Tizer, and they did not know there was such a thing as a public library, so they launched out into the rain and the shock was just like being in the Baths. Round the back and up over the trenches and uneven ground to Hill Street they ran, all the way home, bracing themselves against the drenching and the chill in their shoulders and knees.

The lot was their usual playground, though not at night. It stood between the wings of tenements, where they chalked up wickets on one gable end. Sometimes they had to run if a slop came, and then it was easy to get through the bent paling into Hughes's close. They were safe there, Hughes said, because the slop couldn't get through the paling and he didn't dare come in the close. It was their close – Hughes's close – very pink and very private. You could only get in if you were with Willie.

If you had 2d, Mrs Denham was next door who made tablet. It was like a speak-easy. You only had to knock and ask. She hadn't a shop and you just had to know.

'Here's a googly!' shouted Hughes. He had long lanky legs and a very thin nose. He walked with a bounce, his legs were so long. He could swallow anything, like an ostrich, and his hair stood up on end like an ostrich's when he was annoyed.

He had buck teeth too, which snarled when he smiled. He was a fast bowler, but Adam Hamilton clouted it.

'Run! Catch it; oh, catch it! Oh, butterfingers!'

Bunny Fergus ran for it, his podgy little legs knocking against each other at the knees in their eagerness as he ran. He was short-sighted and fat. His peering through his glasses gave him a constant frightened look which his bulk should have dispelled. He pelted on, knees wavering ever more wildly until he stumbled and fell, hands outstretched in an attitude of prayer – to receive the manna of the ball.

It dropped past him like an egg.

'Yah, butterfingers!' shouted Hughes, his hair like a cockatoo's. 'Yah!'

Hoohoohoo, tittered Fagan behind his hands, the cunning eyes full of glee.

Bunny blushed.

It was Saturday afternoon. Somehow the atmosphere was totally different from that of Laverockhall Street. There was no flood of grimy men pouring out of the Cally or St Rollox, no hurrying of dense crowds on pavements and trams away from the stillness of the cemetery. It was the highest point in the city. The flood lapped around the base.

Leisure was reflected in three large pools left by the rain.

The people around were accountants or plumbers, and therefore had leisure on Saturdays for the dogs, or Rangers, or Johnny Fisher's rabbits, playing in the small square of green before their house.

On days like these David usually went to the pictures. They had 2d seats in the gallery, and they threw the paper wrappings of their caramels at the girls. If they giggled and looked around, they loved you. If they didn't, you cared as much as Hoot Gibson.

'Catch!' shouted Hughes again, and he looked up out of the window of his day-dream to see a ball, directly overhead, shooting down on him like a grey star.

Instead of waiting, he dived up to meet it and his knuckles struck against the rim.

'Yah!' screamed Hughes again, in his anger, running up to David and shoving him out of the way, so that he fell, and cuffing and swearing.

'Butterfingers!' he shouted, making a menacing gesture with the back of his hand.

David and Adam left the game. Hughes was bigger than either. His ears stuck out on either side of his head like enormous wings. They dandered tearfully up to the porch to wait for his father.

'Big swine,' said Adam. 'Damned bully.'

He couldn't understand why Hughes had done it.

The figure of his father came hurrying up the hill. Now, he thought, justice will be done, one way or the other. Ian Seymour's father had cuffed Willie Hemphill once in sight of the whole street for hitting Ian, and they were the same size. That was not right, but it was possible to talk to a fellow.

'Whit are ye cryin' aboot?'

'I'm not. Willie Hughes hit me.'

'He did? Listen here.'

He looked up. His father seized him by the nape of the neck.

'If ye don't go back now and give as good as ye got, so help me I'll gi'e ye a slugging.'

'But . . .'

'Nae arguments.'

He went. On the vacant lot, Hughes and Fagan and the others were still playing cricket. He gathered a clod – a dirty, big clod, they said, with worms hanging out of it – and leapt on Hughes' back, rubbing the clod over his face. It was the only way to get near him, he was so tall. Half-blinded and furious, Hughes lashed out with hands and feet, but David and Adam were gone by then, to the orchard up the street, which often served as a sanctuary.

It was full of apple trees and pear trees, and surrounded by a high wall. Entry lay through a small wooden door, like a trap-door, set in a large gateway. Up to the castle led a winding path. Though all overgrown with weeds and only partly inhabited, it had great prestige in the neighbourhood and was still referred to as The Castle. The Russells lived in it. Charles Russell was a slightly pompous boy – not quite a prig, but not far off – who went to the High School.

'What'll we dae noo?' asked Adam, as David was admiring this totally new country.

'Take the milk up and get some apples.'

Milk cans, with long shoulder handles, stood at the gate. Boys sometimes carried them up to the door. It was a good excuse for being inside.

They stuffed into their pockets a few wizened and shrunken pieces of fruit – the white hair on which imparted a sweetness, they thought – picked up the battered milkcans, and walked up to the house in trepidation. There was said to be a large dog in front of it.

Mrs Russell was in a laundry where one of the towers had been. Charles was playing with his sister on the lawn. That was sissy. He looked suspiciously at them as they dodged under the trees.

'Oh, thank you, boys,' sang out Mrs Russell. 'Give them an apple and some pears, Charles.'

'I've a good mind to set the dog on you,' whispered Charles as he did so.

David was furious, and disgusted. The castle was yet another of his ruined illusions. For two pins he would have knocked Charles through one of the windows.

'The castle,' he said. 'I've built better out of blocks.'

Out of the other gate they went over to Springburn Park. When it rained the frogs came out of the gorse under the flagstaff. There was always wind, and the waves in the pond lapped merrily over rudimentary piers.

Glasgow's parks were studded with yachting ponds, but they were not, properly speaking, children's yachting ponds at all. The City Fathers, always in over-evidence, had here thoughtfully provided boathouses for large and costly models, to enable other fathers to dominate their sons even at play, with an ample supply of keepers in uniform to damp down the ardour of children who might imagine the park was wholly theirs. The Art Galleries boasted one Rembrandt and the largest collection of model ships in the country, but here again it was less a question of Clyde tradition and love of adventure than an indication of the juvenile mentality of so many male Glaswegians, who in any case were unable to distinguish an early Rembrandt from an early George Stephenson.

It was heart-breaking for a boy to place a proud schooner in the water and watch it turn turtle on its first voyage. That did not happen ever with the yellow and black models marked 'Clyde Built' which you could buy in the Arcade for one-and-six. David had one of these. On its bows, stamped in tin from a machine on Gourock Pier, was the gleaming name *Elk*. He liked the *Elk* best when it was dripping with water after a race across the sea. He bet it was one of the fastest for its size in the whole of Springburn. Once he sailed it over with a frog tied on as captain, lashed to the tiller in case of a storm. Captain Frog arrived unhurt.

Today they had only a glass jam jar. They played for a while on the swings near the bandstand, but dusk was falling and it grew chilly. The pond, too, was stormy, and they dragged for a bit with their improvised nets – a cane and an old rag – without catching much. You could see, if you looked closely, thousands of baggies, little dark forms swarming under the surface in minute shoals. Adam caught one with the palm of his hand while David looked along the path toward the duck-pond. That was where she and Miss Cott walked on a Sunday, their coats and ribbons and haughty demeanour all part of the flying park, with a law against trespass that was even in the Lord's Prayer. Trespass to him meant only Mary then. That must be why she and Sally went to Sunday school before coming out on their flirtatious walk. It did not seem right.

It was cold when they returned, between the long beds of eternal flowers, red and yellow and blue, and they were tired and footsore. They had hunted frogs, fished for baggies, looked for birds' nests over the railings among the rhododendrons in spite of the keeper's whistles, and even looked for girls. They had trailed bubbles again through the tropic seas of the winter gardens and studied intently the stuffed fauna in the little Museum. Fauna was a large bird like a penguin.

The nicest thing you could see in the evening was the red railing surrounding the park, before you went down the quarry and home for a fish tea.

IV

'O-o-o-u-u-u. O-o-u-u. O-u, o-u. Ou, ou, ou. Le coup. E-e-e-u-u-u. E-e-u-u. E-u, e-u. Eu, eu, eu, il a eu.'

It was like listening to a gramophone record.

Beau Tibbs, the French master, was six feet tall, with a long, protruding nose like an ant-eater, delicate in his movements and sinuously furious when aroused. He wore a high stiff collar and a tie, the knot of which was bunched like a fist. All day he walked around holding up his book like a prayer-book and uttering strange sounds, like groans.

They learned to recite with mechanical regularity, not knowing a word of the sense, one or two pieces of verse:

> Enfin nous te tenons petit petit oiseau
> Enfin nous te tenons et nous te garderons.

The boys said:

> Ongfang nootitinong pitee pitee wazo
> Ongfang nootitinong ay nooti garderong.

'Now you, Macrae.'

Through the long summer afternoon they drawled. Even afterwards, there was no relief, for two periods of English followed, with Paddy Marshall. He wore an equally stiff collar, but turned out, as if it were a dicky, with a bow-tie or an artist's tie pinned on. This was the proper aesthetic touch required of an English scholar. When he was angry, which to do him justice was quite often, his face went purple and swelled up out of his collar like a frog's.

'Here are the exam results,' he said. 'McDougall, 54. Not bad, McDougall, not bad at all.'

McDougall was just backward enough to confirm Paddy in his idea of himself as a *teacher*. He didn't know just the very things that Paddy did, so they complemented each other. McDougall smiled his shy, wry smile, happy, not that he had done so well, that did not matter in the slightest, but that he had succeeded in pleasing Marshall and escaped the lash of his tongue, and even 'the tongs.'

'Low, 61. What's the matter with you, Low? You can do better than that. You're lazy, that's the whole trouble, bone lazy. You've thrown marks away right and left.'

Paddy bit his lips and showed great yellow fangs, lowering his bald head in anger. Low sat blinking; for a year he had been one of the brightest boys in the school, but of late never seemed to do anything right. He had to deliver milk in the mornings before coming to school, and could not concentrate afterwards, but the masters did not know that.

'Macrae?' Marshall stared at David, livid.

'So you've never read a dry book?'

'Nossir.'

'The question was "What is a dry book?" "Describe some dry books you have read." Macrae, who only gets 64 by the way, says "I have never read a dry book," and draws a bloody line! What do you mean by it, boy? What do you mean by this impertinence?'

'I don't know, sir.'

'Answer! You don't mean to say you like Scott?'

'Oh yessir!' The class tittered.

'Well, what about Thackeray? Wouldn't you say he was rather dry?'

'Oh nossir, not Thackeray, sir.'

'You're a liar. And so is your "essay." You'll stay in after school. Lord? Very good, Lord. Lord has 67, the highest mark in the class. *Vanity Fair* is rather dry, isn't it, Lord?'

'I thought so, sir.'

'Quite so, quite so.'

It was all a question of confirming people in their prejudices and characteristics.

'Poor old Mac!' they said. 'Never read a dry book. Do you read the Bible every night, Mac?'

'What if I do? There are good bits in it.'

'Haha, hear what he says? Dirty dog. He's a sly dog in'y? You're a sly dog, Mac!'

'Should I bark?'

'Yeah, bark, Mac! – Mac's going to bark!'

They went from one classroom to another, for each lesson. Science was the worst.

'What is the boiling point of water, Macrae?'

'The point at which water boils, sir!'

'Oh, is it?' smiled vicious Russell.

'What is heavier? A pound of lead or a pound of feathers?'

'Please sir a pound of lead!'

'You nit-wit! You numbskull! You're up the spout!'

'I'd rather be hit on the head by a pound of feathers, sir!'

And the birth of Kings in history was set out in a series of goal-posts. ⌐⌐ ⌐⌐ Why?

The whole tin building smelled of ink and rubber and rulers. Often they met Joshua the Head. He cut the end of his strap into strips and steeped them in vinegar to make them bite. He was always testing new leather, and had found a whopper he kept like a pistol in his hip-pocket. As he walked across the playground in his striped trousers and tails, his hands tucked under his coat, he looked always as if he were going to a wedding. He wore eye-glasses and his hair was cropped close, like a German's. His eyes were bright with merriment or sadism.

'Boys,' he said, 'when you are asked in after life which school you attended, I want you to say with pride "St Albert's." '

He was liable to break into this peroration in the morning after prayers, in rooms where he had no business to be, and, of course, at prize-givings; so often, in fact, that he almost seemed to be doing it for his own benefit, as a morale-restorer.

'There's Joshua,' said Sheriff, and picked up snow in his cupped hands. 'Let him have it.'

He threw the snowball, and aimed better than he knew. It hit the Head on the back of the neck. He had six of the best.

All the staff firmly believed in the virtues of the strap, all except Higgins, perhaps, although Higgins, the maths master, could use it when he liked. Higgie had a sense of humour. Somewhere he could see that David and maths did not go well together, and although the thought confounded and appalled him, so that his mouth repeatedly fell open with astonishment, he was still kindly, even when he shouted, and did not insist too much on the impossible.

He stared, eyes wide open like a child's: 'I can't understand how a boy like you, who can do so well in French, has to fail in mathematics! It just doesn't make sense!'

That was exactly what David thought of mathematics, though he did not like to say so.

The one class in which they all felt free was Maggie Scott's. Every Wednesday after 'the baths' she let them do what she called a 'Five Minute Essay' on any subject they cared to write about. David wrote on a film he had seen: Ibañez *The Enemies of Women*.

She had a long nose, and walked with long strides in a tweed skirt and Fair Isle jumper. She was a 'sport,' they all said, but she did not like his essay.

'Where did you get all this stuff?' she asked. 'Is it really what you think? Because, if it is, I'm going to give you the strap.'

'Yes,' said David, 'it is.'

'Come out to the floor.'

That was what you did with Maggie. You had to be fair. She gave him two.

'It's not fair!' they shouted. 'It's a free period!'

'All right, we'll have a vote,' she said, 'and if you think I was wrong you can strap me.'

The show of hands showed she was wrong. They picked 'Stork' Hughes to strap her because he was the biggest, and he hit her hard. She winced.

'You wait, Hughes,' she said. 'Next time it's your turn I'll belt you as hard as I know.'

They howled with delight.

In the second year, those of the pupils who 'were going on' were allowed to take German and the others Latin. David was offered choice of neither.

He immediately bought *Hauff's Grammar* and began making obscure noises to himself in an attempt to catch up with the others. Dass houz, dee frow, der man, were easy enough, but he said der nabe instead of der Knabe, and decided he had better not go on, except when they did prep in Muriel's German class, and he had a chance to listen to the reading of Storm's *Immensee*. He murmured to himself over and over again his introduction to the language: 'An einem Spätherbstnachmittage ging ein alter, wohl-gekleideter Mann langsam die Strasse hinab . . .' It was common-place enough, but for a long time he remained caught in the web of glittering words and sentiment thrown around him by this opaque language.

It was the story of a love-affair, and held him possibly because one of his own was just beginning, and it seemed a curious prophecy or anticipation of his own experience.

Mary lived at the end of their row of houses. She was to him the personification of the perfection he had begun to seek. Once his mother had given a party at Christmas and she came unexpectedly along the corridor at the back, which was piled high with snow. She wore a white dress shot with blue, and it sparkled with flame enveloped in ice against the glittering darkness. It was a picture he would never forget. He remem-bered his shyness as he opened the door, in case she should see the love in his face.

Adam Hamilton went to sleep on the couch in the room. They handed round little sweets with messages written on them. *You are sweet. I would like to kiss you. When can I see you again?* None of those he received were any good for passing on to Mary. He had only messages like: *A stitch in time saves nine*, or *Tell me the old old story*, or even *Keep a civil tongue in your head.*

It was like being given the wrong instrument if you were a musician, or a code you did not know if you were a wireless telegraphist.

He watched her coming up the road from the front room window for so long, that his mother wondered what he was doing, and called him away. He was full of vague longing, that began to plague his dreams. He watched her, too, as she walked along the road to and from school, sometimes with Johnny Fisher, who was in a different class. He was jealous of Fisher, for he was very handsome, with an air of easy assurance. He was going to be an accountant. Evidence of such familiarity with figures was breath-taking. He fully expected Mary and Fisher to get married almost any day.

They were fifteen.

His whole story, he felt, was in the book by Theodor Storm, the obscurantist German of which he could not dissolve quickly enough to allow him to follow the plot. It seemed that the hero, Reinhardt, was an old man, and that he had been in love in his youth. What had happened? Why had he not married the girl?

It was not only that there had been another fellow, like Fisher. This Reinhardt had gone away, and seen much; he was a kind of tragic figure, a romantic hero almost, and the tragedy was that he had grown away from the girl he loved. There could be no other explanation.

'Meine Mutter hat's gewollt' was the title of the chapter. 'My mother wanted me to marry the other man' was the explanation in the tale, but it was not the true one. The girl perhaps had not loved Reinhardt at the time, or had not known she loved him, but Reinhardt had grown away from her, attracted by the allure of a world he did not know, believing himself born to grapple with some problem involving humanity, and forgetting his deepest desire.

Mary left school and went to work with a firm in the town, returning by tram in the evening. David could see the drama unfolding before his eyes. He wanted to leave school to be with her, and yet he felt he must go on. He took to going down at 5 p.m. to buy a paper, so as to meet her coming up the hill.

They were mostly all leaving school, but David wasn't, though
his father wanted him to come into the shop. He had a talk with
him about it.

'You're growing up,' he said. 'One of these days you'll meet a
nice young girl and you'll want to marry her. You've nothing to
offer her. Have you thought of that?'

Had he thought of it, when the question was beginning to fill
his mind? He resented the knowledgeable way in which adults
talked, and the way in which his life was being mapped out for
him beforehand. He could not bring himself to mention Mary,
knowing only too well the consternation it would have caused,
especially in his mother.

'Yes,' he said.

'I need help onywey. Your great-grandfather was an engineer,
ye know, and a good one. He cut canals, built bridges and
lighthouses, like the Stevensons. In my way, I'm an engineer,
though tractors and engines are my line. I could have gone further
if I'd had had the time and the education, but I've learned the
value of practical work. Do you feel like it?'

'Not yet,' he said. 'Could I study for one more year and then
tell you?'

His father was surprised. He was not accustomed to being
crossed. He was a man of action, an engineer.

To David he was the symbol of the wrecking, crippling process,
which was destroying, not liberating, his country.

'All right,' he said, after a while, 'I'll give you a year. But you'll
have to make up your mind. Think about what I've said.'

If he went to work, he could pay for evenings out with Mary,
and even after a while offer to support her. The thought was
terrifying in its attractiveness. What was the price of this love of
his? Slavery. Corroboration of his father's errors in helping to
build the mechanical cackle called civilisation.

He thought about it, even in school.

He was thinking of it when he saw Howden, a cross-eyed
ragged urchin, cunning as a weasel, come up the street, dressed in
the resplendent garb of a telegraph-boy.

'Hello,' said Howden. 'Hoo d'yi like ma claes?'

'Hello,' said David, coolly. 'It's a marvellous uniform. Does it
mean you've left school for good?'

'You bet,' said Howden. 'I'm leavin' the morn. Gee, I'm gled.
Where iyi gon? Iyi gon a message?'

'Yes,' said David.

A message in Scotland is passive and intransitive. It is gone.

'Haud on a meenit and I'll show you something,' said Howden, disappearing. At the end of five minutes he was back in his ordinary clothes.

'The erse is oot ma troosers,' he said, 'bit it disny maitter.'

'You mustn't play with boys like Howden,' his mother said.

Why not? His eyes were bright with mischief like a magpie's. It did not matter in the least to David that he was as filthy as human ingenuity could make him. His feet were bare, his knees black, his trousers holed, his jersey in tatters, and his eyes, alternately horror-struck and filled with animal gloating, squinted through his hair.

'Iyi comin'?' he asked.

David followed him down the hill to a grocer's shop. Stalking in like an Indian, Howden said: 'Kin I hiv some o' thae pickles at the back?'

Fetching a small ladder, the grocer climbed up. As soon as he did so, Howden whipped a handful of biscuits into his pocket.

Astounded, David could not utter a word.

'This kind?' asked the unsuspecting grocer.

'Naw, that other kind,' said Howden, pointing to a bottle at least three feet along.

The grocer climbed down and moved along, during which time Howden stuffed more biscuits, chocolate ones this time, up his jersey.

'Is this whit ye're wantin'?' asked the grocer.

'Is there ony ingin in them?' asked Howden.

The grocer looked closely at the bottle.

'No,' he said, 'there's nane!'

'They're no' the right kind then,' said Howden. 'My mother likes ingin.'

'Whit wey?' asked the grocer. 'Did she ask for ingin?'

'Oh, aye,' said Howden. 'She says Napoleon aye ate ingins.'

In a sudden rage, the grocer climbed down.

'Ye bluidy wee deevil,' he shouted; 'ye've stolen ma biscuits!'

'Me?' said Howden the picture of injured innocence. 'Me? I never did! Did I pinch ony biscuits?' he asked David.

'How do I know?'

'Ye did; I saw you,' said the grocer.

Howden flew into a fierce temper.

'Whitna lie!' he screamed. 'Catch me snaffling biscuits. I widny eat them. It's the last time I'm comin' intae this shope,' he went on, holding up his hands. 'Come on, search me! Search me if ye're so sure!'

'Gae tae hell oot o' here,' shouted the grocer. 'Wait till I come roon' this coonter! Ye impident deevil!'

They ran outside, feet covered in sawdust, but once out: 'Hiv a biscuit,' said Howden; 'they're good yins. I bet ye never saw me!'

'No thanks,' said David.

'Whit wey? Jeez you're daft, they're the dodds,' he said, wiping his nose convulsively on the sleeve of his jersey.

'Iyi wantin' some chocolates? I'll get ye some!'

'No thanks,' said David; 'don't bother.'

'Are ye feart?'

'No.'

'Watch me.'

He was worse than 'Ingins.'

What appalled David was less the deed than the swift ruth-lessness, the resolution and decision it revealed, which he had been unable to read in Howden's face.

They went into R. S. McColl's together.

'Hoo much are thur sweeties up there?' asked Howden again.

'Where? There?' asked the girl, trying hard to help, and twisting her head round.

For no apparent reason he remembered a rhyme in *The Rain-bow*:

> What are little girls made of?
> Sugar and spice and all that's nice,
> That's what little girls are made of.

'Naw thur,' said Howden.

As she reached, David, hypnotised, saw the hand of Howden snake over a heap of chocolate cracknels.

'How many do you want?' she asked.

'I don't want nane,' said the incorruptible; 'I want to know how much they ur.'

'Sixpence a quarter,' replied the young lady, nettled.

'Too dear,' said Howden, and stalked out.

David was again amazed at the transformation. In school, Howden had been invariably either asleep or in a furious temper. His abnormal good humour was a revelation. Howden had solved his problem in a radical way. He was 'seeing life.' In time he would settle down, with luck, to the steady career of a respectable burglar, unless any victim was unwary enough to rouse that homicidal temper of his. David felt sure that, as an old Albert

boy, he would never rest content to plod through life as a pilfering
postman.

'Where iyi gon noo? Iyi comin' tae the Tally's for pea-brae?'

'No, I've to go and see Summers. So long.'

Bernard Summers was his best friend. His hair was blond and
curled over one eye. His eyes were blue and he had a long Roman
nose. He spoke with an English accent. He was best at drawing in
the whole school, and they both saved stamps. He lived on
Orange Terrace.

The light was beginning to fade, and he could see in the sky
the cloudy wisps of white and purplish smoke that spelt drops
of gathering rain. The Summers' house was one of a group of
three semi-detached dwellings of which there were four rows,
clinging to the side of the hill that straggled down to the
locomotive works. As he walked up the flight of stone stairs,
washed and combed with fantastic curlecues of chalk, and
knocked at the wooden varnished door, brass-plated like a
coffin, he felt both astonished and vexed. Summers had sworn
to be there. This was no way to treat a friend, after he had
walked all the way down from Balgray Hill and put off seeing
Al Jolson.

Disconsolately he knocked again. No reply. He remembered:
' "Is anyone there?" said the traveller, knocking on the moonlit
door.'

He hung about the close-mouth, watching the dripping ghosts
of clothes strung on the palings and railings and ropes and
crumbling dykes, or staring gloomily at the hordes of purple
and bright-blue men streaming uphill from the maze of steam and
hooters and pistons that was St Rollox.

He remembered one night on that moor when he had won a
coconut at a shy in the Shows. Gypsies, his mother called them, or
'tinkers.' Sometimes she called him a tinker. It was not a pleasant
word. It was like being a terrier and wild and doing things you
shouldn't, or being an incorrigible wanderer.

At last he saw Bernard coming up the street with his mother.
They were very jolly.

'What a pity,' she said. 'David has been here all the time,
Bernard. Come in. Come in.' When they went in, Bernard
showed him some drawings of a man called Ally Sloper, which,
privately, David thought very silly, though he assumed he must
laugh politely.

'My father did these.'

'Did he? He must have been very clever.'

'Oh, he was. He was killed in the war, you know. This is Ally Sloper's Cavalry. He was in it.'

'We're going away soon, you know, David,' his mother said.

Shocked, David went pale.

'Far?' he managed to say. 'Are you leaving the neighbourhood?'

'Yes,' said his friend, 'we are going to Stockton-on-Tees.'

Equally well might he have said Wurtemberg, or Ortisei.

'Look,' David said, 'I've brought my autograph book along. Will you draw something in it for me?'

'Certainly,' said Bernard, in his queer English way. With a ruler, which David considered brilliant, he proceeded to draw a toy soldier.

'You can have this stamp-album,' David said, 'I don't want it anyway. It's an old one. Have you one of these?'

He showed Bernard a triangular African, with a snake.

'Mar-vellous,' said Summers ingenuously, touched by the beauty and frankness of that smile.

'Keep it,' said David simply.

'For me?'

'Yes. And here are some transparent hinges.'

'Tomorrow is my last day at school,' he said.

'Albert won't be the same place without you,' David said.

Summers was supposed to be rather effeminate, but they were like David and Jonathan. The only love he admitted was for Summers.

In the morning as he went into school he saw Galt and Prigg standing looking down the gravelled hill past the church. They were watching a young girl. It was Ian Seymour's cousin.

'Could she take it?' Galt said.

'Could she!' agreed Prigg with a grin on his pimpled face like a scar. 'Look at these hips.'

He was a tall boy, almost six feet, and his pale face bore the embarrassed expression of a camel, perhaps because of the short trousers he was forced to wear.

He moved loftily among the other boys – like a giraffe, not looking down.

'Take what?' asked Summers, coming up.

They laughed.

'Take what he says,' sniggered Galt.

'You don't mean to say you don't even know how you were born?' asked Prigg with a sneer.

'He's a baby,' Galt said. 'He'll shave in about ten years. Do you know the difference between a man and a woman?'

'Have you ever watched dogs?' asked Prigg.

Summers slowly blushed.

'Git,' Prigg said viciously. ' This is a man's conversation. Some paps!' he said.

McDougall, Galt, Hughes, all the precocious, tall, tough ones, gathered admiringly round Prigg, the fount of wisdom.

Bernard turned away and began to kick a tennis ball.

'Did you hear, David?' he asked. 'What do you think?'

'About what?' asked David, miserably.

'Is it true? About men and women. Sleeping together and all that?'

'What they say isn't true,' said David.

What had it to do with them? He could not really understand Summers' embarrassment. He did not really know if it were true. He hadn't thought about it. He supposed something like that went on, but he thought more at the moment of Summers.

'Forget them,' he said. 'They're a lot of rogues.'

Prigg was shouting now.

'It's the bluidy miners,' he said. 'They should get a bluidy good thrashing.'

His father was a policeman.

'There'll be a bluidy riot tonight,' he said.

'Whit's up?' asked McDougall.

'The bastards are on strike.'

Workers in revolt were strange. He did not associate them with his grandfather or with the thousands in St Rollox. They were like men at the dogs, or drunk at the foot of the hill, full of strange power, determination and tension. You could not argue with them and it was wrong of them to starve their children.

'What has it to do with us?' asked David. Prigg looked at him.

'If there's nae coal in the school cellar, ye'll bloody soon know what it's aboot.'

David walked away.

At four o'clock they all ran down the hill to see what was going on. There were students driving trams in blazers and women in shawls shouting 'Blacklegs.' People lay on the tram-lines and had to be forced to rise. A procession passed, with red banners. The police tried to break it up.

'The mounties!' came a cry, as the horses bore down on the crowd. There was a scuffle and David saw a man fall through the window of the Balgray Arms. His leg smashed the glass. He was drunk, but unhurt. It was a wooden leg. Others were not so lucky, and there were many bleeding heads.

He was furious. He did not belong to the dice-capped, mounted and blue-clad, besotted, jigot-faced cavalry who rode down with criminal indiscrimination a crowd of workers complaining in the street. He did not belong to the yellow bell coptouts, or the gay young students who were making General Strike Day into a Carnival like their Charities Day. To him it was no prank, or jape, or chance to dress up and break the law and still be a hero. He saw the masks of violence hidden behind even Hallowe'en. He did not belong. He hated students and police alike.

Every year they went to Fairlie for their holidays, and met their Uncle David from Belfast.

Uncle David always believed in a good time when he came, he said. He always stood ice-cream all round, the expensive kind, in glasses, not just sliders, and putting for all on the golf course, and he always went for a row.

This time he went fishing as well and took David with him – nobody else – because he was his namesake.

'Where'll we get the boat?' he asked, and his moustache wagged, muffling his voice. 'Fraser's?'

Fraser was a real sailor. His chest grew out of his jersey like the roots of a tree in the ground, and he was burly as a bottle. His boats were well tarred, but before he let you have one he always looked up at the sky and his eyes fused.

'No,' said David, 'Knox White's!'

Together they ground down the sucked beach, crushing shells and crinkling shingle, striding the hungry tongues of red-reefed sandstone. Knox White was the only other boatman in the village and his boats were a by-word. So was he. He wore a tam o' shanter, even in bed, had a beard like a goat and a face all mottled like a sea-urchin. He rarely changed his clothes, and rarely washed. His boats were never repaired. Half of them had stove-in bottoms. He was mean, too. Even the tins he handed out for bailing were given grudgingly, yet everybody liked him, for he was a landmark. He gave the village character and made it feel superior.

His jetty lay just beyond the yacht-builders', a huge barn of corrugated iron like a granary, where the long, black trunks, shining with rain and fungus, were trimmed and shaved into knife-edge racing craft white as swans.

Knox did not speak, but nodded the nod of an old gray crow, and hobble-de-hoyed down his crazy landing-stage.

'You kin have this 'un!' he shouted, and cast off a small-boat. 'Goin' far out?'

'No,' said Uncle David. 'We'll fish a bit in the bay. Have you tackle and bait? A line will do.'

'Mhmh,' grunted the old man, meaning yes, and fetched the weighted line, bait and two tins.

'For bailin',' he said. 'You'll be needin' them,' and stood still till they were well out in the bay.

At first they did not go far, for Grandma in Fairlie was watching from her window, and she did not like them to go out far. She was a bad sailor, she said, and even made David sail his schooner on the green at the back with a piece of string in case he was drowned.

They paddled about a bit, and cast the line far out plump into the water a lot, so as to please her and make her think they only meant to bring back fish for tea. Then they drifted below the pier where the stakes were black and encrusted with limpets, and Uncle David caught three mackerel. Right out of the sea's maw, out of shell-stump teeth and an acid salt-bite!

'Grandma will be pleased,' he said. 'We can do what we like now, eh? It's mackerel weather all right. Look at the clouds! A mackerel sky! We could catch them all day, but we have enough for tonight. See over there,' he went on. 'That's the Big Cumbrae! D'ye think it's far?'

'No, it's quite close,' said David.

'Could we be over there and back, d'ye think, by tea time, and grandma would never know?'

'Yes,' said David. 'I'll take an oar.'

Even if they were late, they could always give her the fish.

David pulled and pulled and the water slapped away from the bows at a smacking pace, but the boat kept spinning round in the wrong direction.

'That's because I'm rowing harder than you,' said Uncle David. 'Put your back into it. Take that jacket off, and that cap!'

When he had done so. David pulled harder than ever, and the bow did not spin quite so much. He saw his uncle rest oftener on his oar, as if he were tired.

Still the water swirled and smacked away from the blade a merry pace, and every now and then he turned to see if the Big Cumbrae were any nearer, but, although it was plainer, it looked as far away as ever, for the distance was plainer too.

Once he caught a crab, Uncle David said, though David saw none in the water, and fell full length back in the boat with a creaking of timber.

'T-t-t-t-t!' went Uncle David. 'What if this was a race? Oxford and Cambridge? Eh? You'd have lost the race by one mistake. They'd tip you in the river! *Dip* the oar in the water, just below the surface, not too deep or you'll never get it up. At an angle! And turn the blade whenever it comes out, at the finish of the stroke.'

He said so much, David couldn't follow it all, especially as he was trying to think what Grandma would say if she saw him now, half-way across to Millport in a Knox White boat! It made him shiver. She'd have half screamed that tomahawk face off. And yet he couldn't help feeling superior to anyone who ever talked about the Boat Race now he'd such a coach.

'Feather it!' said Uncle David.

The Cumbrae they did not reach for half-an-hour.

'What about climbing that hill?' asked his uncle. 'We can get some heather to take back to Grandma along with the mackerel.'

When he looked at the hill again he saw it was a cliff.

'Can ye do it?' he asked.

'I think so.'

'Come on!'

The sky was mackerel coloured, with flaky clouds. It took them twenty minutes to reach the crest of the hill, and David was puffed. He could not even gather any heather.

Uncle David was tramping all over the moorland, into holes and burns that soaked his feet, and even though he was supposed to be Grandma's favourite son, David wondered what she'd say if she saw him.

He liked being there. It was so high you could see the Cloch Light and Largs across the bay, and a liner booming up the Firth for a pilot. It was like the roof of the world, and as if the heather extended right up into the clouds. If you kept on walking you came at last into the Plains of Heaven.

'Is this enough?' asked Uncle David, his little cheeks blown like a bulldog's.

'Let's wait a bit longer!'

'Remember the tea,' his uncle said. 'Grandma has to fry the mackerel, and I'm hungry. It's a long way back.'

He knew that. He was beginning to be a little afraid. He didn't know why, maybe because he didn't want the good time to end so quickly, and he knew it would.

If he had known what was coming, he would have waited for

Fraser's motor-boat to come and rescue him, then Grandma would have been glad to see him all right.

'Come on!' said his uncle. 'Race you down.'

He had been a harrier.

'The tide is with us this time,' his uncle said as they pushed out. 'When we came over at first we had to cross at an angle and row against the current part of the way.'

They had to be careful now and not drift too far, he said. You could stop drifting just by putting an oar into the water. When they were only half-way, however, the old tub sprang a leak, and then he began to shout.

'Quick! Stop rowing and bail! Bail like Old Nick!'

The wind sprang up and carried away breath and voices.

It blew the boat off its course and Uncle David had to row till the veins stood out on his head like knots and crosses.

Tin after tin of water David threw out, splash into the sea, and either the oar or the spray flung it in again, or it seeped through the floorboards lurching in drunken riot.

'Stuff your jacket in the hole!' shouted Uncle David again. He was breathing regularly now, like a pair of wheezing bellows.

'There isn't any hole,' said David. 'It's the floorbeams. They leak like old boots!'

One of them began to float as he spoke.

He was really scared now. They had no rockets and there were no coastguards or anything. He could not swim more than a length at the baths. He hoped Uncle David might take him on his back, but that generous figure had shrunk to less than human proportions with exertion.

The whole of the bottom was covered now and his uncle was trying to row and bail at the same time.

'Sit at the stern!' he ordered, and stood up in the boat. It wobbled.

'Never stand in a boat, even a paddle-steamer,' his grandmother said. 'It's dangerous.'

She knew everything.

Edging along the side, he sat at the bottom. His uncle followed.

'To keep half the keel out of the water,' he said. 'We're still a long way off.'

His hair was blown and curly, like bubbly fankled seaweed.

'How fast is it rising?'

'I don't know,' said David. 'I haven't a stop-watch.'

'It's a stop-cock you want, not a stop-watch,' his uncle said.

Soon there were four inches, then five.

'We'll start to sink when there are about six,' his uncle said. 'Jump for my neck then.'

It crept up to five and a half, five and three-quarters. It was at six!

Then David saved their lives by catching sight over his uncle's shoulder of a motor-boat heading straight for them.

'A motor-boat!' he screamed.

'Don't dance,' his uncle said, 'or we'll go down.'

He lifted the mackerel and they both stood in the stern so the boat was almost perpendicular.

The other approached, and David caught sight of the bottle-shape of Fraser.

'Third sinkin' this month, sir,' Fraser said when he was alongside.

'What'll Grandma say when she finds out?' David asked through chittering teeth.

'We still have the mackerel, haven't we? We can say we only did it to get her a tasty tea. She only worries in a storm. There's no storm now; can't be with a sky like that.' And he slapped the fish in David's face.

The house was right on the shore, up limestone steps all dotted with pebbles, chuckies and shells, like currants and icing in a gray dumpling. David pulled the bell.

'A present for your grandma,' his uncle said, wiping his walrus moustache when she opened the door, because she liked it.

'I've been watching!' she snapped. 'Through the glasses! A fine cairry-on!'

Sure enough, the binoculars lay on the hall table.

'What's this?' she said, unwrapping the paper. As soon as she saw the fish she ran screaming down the path to the breakwater and threw them far over, farther than he could have done, her face all blue with anger and fright, and one eye staring.

'Mackerel! Mackerel!' she screeched. 'An' the spots on their backs! They turn into maggots! Swarming maggots! Ugh!'

She twisted her face into one spot and let her scrawny hands dangle in the air like a dead bird's claws.

David saw the sky suddenly darken with gulls in a gathering shriek and swoop that made him shiver. A maggot swarm! It was a mackerel sky all right! They fell like bullets on their prey. He was afraid to look on the fish.

THREE

I

IN THE KITCHEN where his mother kept her special dishes there was a lead-rimmed cabinet. It was in its way a work of art. The sliding glass doors, of which there were three, bore on their surface elaborate designs inlaid in semi-precious stones. There were three shelves, and underneath, nine drawers, with a protruding ledge on which he had sat at times, though it was narrow and his mother discouraged the habit. Here she kept all her precious cups and saucers, with coats-of-arms from all over the country, and occasionally from other countries. Edinburgh, Ayr, Largs, Braemar, Goslar in Germany, figured among her treasures, but David was always fascinated in particular by the arms of Helensburgh, depicting a man clad in skins and bearing a huge club. Dimly he associated this figure with the seaweed on the shore at Helensburgh, and with Charlie Friel, who had once looked pretty much the same, except for the club, but its significance occasionally disturbed him. Was it an antique, or a portent?

He liked to sit and read over the mottoes when he had time. There was *dum spiro spero*. That was rather good. And the proud *nemo me impune lacessit*. He was proud of being able to read most of the Latin.

In one of the small cups – mostly the size of demi-tasses – lay a threepenny bank. It held twelve pieces, and when it was full the lid sprang open and a small fortune was at your disposal. This gave rise to a very unfortunate incident.

As he and his father were walking home one evening from the garage, which was in Sanny's Piggery, they found his mother in tears and terror. She had discovered the top of the bedroom window down. Someone had been in the house during their absence. His father set to work methodically to find out if there was anything missing. Opening the door of the cabinet, he found that the threepenny bank was gone.

'It's been a kid,' he said, 'after the bank.'

'Oh, my oh,' said his mother, 'I'm tellin' ye.'

Uncle Norman was standing behind her in contemptuous neutrality, working his jaws.

'The question is how did he know it was there? Had you anybody in here?' his father asked.

He hated his father just then. Why did he have to be so clever? How did he know these things?

'No,' he said.

'David wouldna do a thing like that,' his mother said. 'I'm surprised at you. And when could he do it onywey?'

'He must have had somebody in,' maintained his father, coughing through his nose in the way he did, which might have been because of asthma, 'but when? Try and think!'

The situation was desperate. He did not want to give anything away. He knew how jealous of the house his mother was. The penalty for having it overrun with tramps when she was out, he shuddered to contemplate.

'Come on, when?' said his father. 'I'm damned if I'm going to have Teenie frichtit in this wey!'

When he was angry his father always talked in Scots. It sounded so much more abominable, like swearing in German.

'Maybe on Saturday,' he said timidly.

'What happened on Saturday?'

'Well,' he said, terrified, 'I had some of the boys up in the attic in the forenoon. We ate a plate of ice-cream, then we had boxing.'

'Boxing?' – 'Yes.' 'With my horsehair gloves?' – 'Yes.'

He thought his father would be very angry, but he wasn't. He was quite pleased.

'That's when he must have seen it,' he said. 'Who had you in?'

'Alfie Fagin, Adam Hamilton and Malcolm Hemphill.'

'Hemphill, that wicked wee deevil! There ye are, ye see.'

'Oh, my oh,' said his mother, leaning over so as to miss nothing, but not understanding it all, looking to her husband's face to read his mood, in perturbation. 'I'm fair flabbergastit! It's an ill-win' . . .'

That was what he hated. Couldn't his father see that? Couldn't he read her face? What right had he not to reassure her immediately?

'I'm sorry,' he said. 'I didn't know.'

'I'll away to the polis,' said his father, putting on his jacket. 'Don't worry. It wisna your fault, David. Had ye a good scrap? That's the main thing!'

'Oh my, oh my oh,' said his mother. 'Nae sooner dae I turn my back! I tell ye!'

He awaited the inevitable storm.

'I feel as sick as a dog,' she said.

The police interrogation was a thrill. They had found the little bank outside, in the street, empty as a nest. He wondered whether, against his father's will, they would arrest him. In the small house, the uniforms looked absurd and somehow obscene. Were they human, or did they pretend to be? Why did people become, not inhuman, but unhuman because of the limited ridiculous activity in what they called their 'job'? They took themselves too seriously. They forgot that others in other 'jobs' also took themselves seriously, which meant elevating the Position of Responsibility into a Thing *per se*, in which humanity, and other people, might count for very little. They were cursed by the superstition of abstraction which makes a Government sacrifice a people in the name of the 'nation.'

Fortunately, it seemed that in the absence of proof they could do nothing even with Malcolm. David both could and did. He remembered his mother's face as they had come in that evening. He remembered his father's saying 'I'll no' hiv Teenie frichtit in this wey!' The idea that a malicious Hemphill could terrify his mother in that casual, bold way made him furious. Meeting him going a message, he took a vow in the street where the Seymours could hear that he would punch Malcolm's nose – hard – every time he met him, and thereupon proceeded to do so.

He himself, he felt, might well have been blamed for the theft, had he not been unjustly accused two Sundays before. His father had placed twelve pennies one on top of the other on the ledge of the cabinet. They fell off, scattering in all directions, under the table, below the bed, down wedges and cracks in the floor, and finally out through the door.

'Pick them up, David,' said his father.

He was unable to find a single one.

'They've all gone,' he said. It was a mystery.

'Don't be a stumer,' said his father. 'There must be one or two lying about where ye can see them.'

'No, there aren't,' he replied, crawling about on hands and knees, poking his head under the bed-vallance. He could not see there, so he crawled into the light, where seeing was easier.

His father lost his temper.

'Dae ye take me fur an eediot?' he shouted, jerking him to his feet.

'Gimme the money!'

'I haven't any money!' he said, appalled, not understanding.

'I'll gi'e ye a last chance and then ye're comin' up to the attic, wi *me!*'

'I can't help it,' he said, the water running down his legs. 'I haven't any money.'

His voice sounded very far away.

'Come on, you're fur it! Big as ye are!'

Upstairs, he was slapped and punched around like a drunken man. He could not see where the blows came from, and dared not look. His father had always been a good man. He did not keep a strap hanging up by the fire like so many other parents. He was enlightened, but now he seemed to have lost all sense of justice in the face of overwhelming if circumstantial evidence.

'Confess,' his father shouted. 'Tell me what you did wi' the money and it's finished. Come on! Spit it oot!'

More blows. There were so many now he didn't care.

'I didn't touch a penny,' he said, weeping. 'You can go on as long as you like, but I didn't touch a penny.'

It was the change in his father that appalled him, not the blows themselves. There was always a hidden reason, he believed, for these changes. It was his own stupidity kept him from seeing them.

At length his misery touched the man. The storm subsided, and David was led downstairs feeling drenched, and dazed.

'I believe he's tellin' the truth, Teenie,' he heard his father say. 'They're gone! Fancy! I never heard onything like it! The whole twelve!

Not one was ever found.

His father had lost face. He knew it. His attempts to remedy matters were as absurd as his accusations, and when he noticed this he covered it up by being very gruff and drawing down those brows of his.

'We'll hae the Bible reading noo,' he said.

'God made a Covenant with Abraham,' he went on sternly, as if not believing it himself.

There was not much to be said after that. David felt humble, like Abraham.

'So you have the word "Brith" again. "Brith Ish", "Covenant Man" in Hebrew. And God said unto Jacob, "In thy seed shall all the nations of the earth be blest."'

That was a nice thing to say to anybody. It had started quite a bit of trouble.

'Such was the Union with Jacob. Do you see? Union of Jacob. Union Jack.'

Once, he thought, his father forbade him to read the *Union Jack* because it was the name of a 'blood.'

'It's Gospel truth,' his father said.

'Oh yes, David,' put in his mother, head on one side and eyes rolling slightly. 'It's BI truth you know.'

The woman in her underlined the dreadful seriousness of purpose inherent in the race. Equally appalled and adoring had she been as a child at the thought of her father, whose affection she had craved.

'It's not scientific,' replied David defiantly.

'Are you one of those Modernists?' asked his father fiercely, his brows sewn together with thick black cotton. 'There's an article you should read this week in the *Banner of Israel!*'

'No, no,' he had to say. 'I know nothing about them. To me they are as mistaken as the others.'

'Mistaken! I'll show you who's mistaken!'

Outside, people fought to get on. In this house you had to fight to stand where you were. He picked up the *National Message* in a white passion.

On the cover, the world sat between the flags of the UK and the USA, while a scroll underneath said *Ephraim, Manasseh*, and *In Thy Seed*.

There were so many trumpets and pyramids and pillars and battleships and rising suns that it resembled rather an illustration of the Battle of Omdurman than a religious tract. Signed Paul Klee, it might have sold for 200 guineas.

'The ideology,' David said, 'is 1878. It's jazz and religious Kipling.'

'What's the matter with Kipling? *The Light that Failed* is a great book.'

'So is *No and Where to Say It*,' David said.

That was the name of a prize his father had been given for regular attendance at a Victorian Sunday School.

The veins on his father's temples were standing out. He took up the paper with obvious difficulty. ' "Some Symbols of Identity between Britain and Israel," by the Revd Pascoe Goard,' he read.

'Is that a name,' said David, 'or a title? It sounds like a kind of Rabbi, or a Ben.'

Such literature poured from his father's cornucopian pocket. There was, in addition to the *Banner of Israel* and the *National Message*, implying, of course, no Semitic ancestry in either case, a galaxy of pamphlets, all seeking to prove that Britain and America 'represented' the Lost Ten Tribes of Israel.

You could prove it easily between reading *The Mirror of Life* with Tancy Lee in tights on the cover, and the *Sunday Companion*, with a picture of the Queen Mother looking down the muzzle of a naval gun. For Brit-Ish meant Covenant-Man, or even 'Covenanter.' That was only the first step in what was really more fascinating than word-making and word-taking, acrostics, or any parlour-game so far invented.

There were countless variations of the one infallible proof. The Keltic tombs in the Crimea, the Scotii-Scythians, the Cymry-Cumbrae-Cambrian-Cimmerian-Sumerians; the Rivers Don in Russia, England and Scotland, named after the Tribe of Dan, with all their ramifications, Daniester, Danieper, Danube, Drava, Drina, Douro. There were the original megalithic civilisations of England, Scotland and Ireland and Egypt; the similarities of syntax between Celtic and Hebrew, the relation of Druid to Tibetan philosophy, or vice-versa, and of Gaelic to Hindu – Sgeind, Ind, Indus in Gaelic meaning 'swiftly-flowing.' There was the mysterious Basque 'Euskara' meaning 'Basque,' the 'B' being aspirated so that it was really 'Eusk,' the same word as in the Esk River.

It was a fact that the Celts had travelled across Europe from the cradle of civilisation in Asia Minor, leaving everywhere imperishable traces, even among the Mongols (a Celtic word) and the Georgians. There were even those who identified the Slav word 'Nemets' (meaning German, or foreign) with the Gaelic 'Naomades,' indicating links with Noah and the Nomads.

'I suppose you know the Stone of Destiny is Jacob's Pillow?' said his father.

'And his coat of many colours was tartan?' said his mother. 'What else could it be?'

'I always thought it was a patchwork quilt,' muttered David, 'like the one on the bed.'

'Now wouldn't he look silly going around in a quilt?' his father witheringly said, and, quick to follow up his advantage: 'Ye have only to turn to the Bible, Genesis 12, verse 2,' he said: ' "I will make of Thee a nation and a Company of Nations and I will bless Thee and make Thy Name Great." What does that mean? Tell me that? If the Bible is true it means this nation. No other nation is called Great, except "Great Britain." '

That was taking things very literally, he thought. To him it was a strange grotesque morality-play in which his grandfather was

Abraham, his father Isaac, and he himself expected to act the part
of Joseph.

'And the vines shall blossom and hang over the wall,' his father
said.

'Does that mean anything? The vines are in the four corners of
the Earth, "and the branches run over the wall."'

It was a nice picture, but David was thinking of the black-
currant bushes at the foot of the garden.

The lesson was ended. Although his mother liked the old
Scottish psalm Tunes, they did not sing hymns on Sunday
evenings like the Seymours next door.

II

'You can believe what you like,' said Easton, staring straight
ahead, to Jowett, 'but I believe in evolution, like Hardie.'

Hardie was the History master.

'Your soul will roast in hell-fire,' said Jowett, with indifference.
He wore glasses. They had thick lenses. His nose was thick too.
So were his lips. When he smiled, he bared his teeth in a cold
sneer. Something potentially vicious in him made David shrink.
Jowett was 'saved.'

For a long time he could not think what that meant. It was so final.
Jowett's parents, he decided, had made some private arrangement
with solicitors by means of which Jowett need not work so hard or
play so hard as other boys, or even make the effort towards
elementary kindliness in human relations required of others. He
was 'Saved.' He went on living in this parody of a world merely as an
act of grace on the part of the Ego of Master William Jowett.

'You will all roast in hell-fire,' he said, smiling like a fish in a
bowl.

'There is no Hell,' said Easton scornfully, still not looking at
Jowett.

'Oh yes there is,' said David quickly; 'what about Whitehall?'

Whitehall was the name of their school.

They laughed.

Once they had had to draw two circles and write underneath:
'Graphical Illustration of Spiritual and Temporal Power.' That
was the height of silliness.

It worried him, because he did not trust the pronouncements of
Hardie, the History master. There was something slightly smug
and wrapped-up about Hardie. His opinions were too glib and
two-a-penny to be taken off the premises. You felt, when he talked

to you of evolution and Genesis, playing billiards all the time in his pocket, that he was not so much concerned with your education as he was with his own nimbleness in scoring off people who were probably dead and who didn't matter anyway. He was a Rationalist. Not that evolution itself worried the boy. It was absurd if it meant a monkey for an uncle, while if the relationship were much more distant, it lost much of its urgency as an issue. It was a word to describe the process and not the purpose of Creation.

'Will you come along to the Bible Class tonight?' asked Jowett.

'Yes,' said David.

'There's a lecture against evolution,' said Jowett, 'illustrated by lantern-slides.'

'Will you come?' he asked Easton.

'OK,' said Easton, 'if Mac comes.'

'There's the Bell,' shouted Sheriff, 'run!' But as soon as he began to run the books fell out of his strap all over the muddy road, and he was late.

They had to wait in the School Hall to be seen by Baby King, the Maths master, a man who combined a furious temper with a complexion like a cherub and an expression of the most satanic pride and malevolence.

'Why are you late?' he barked at David.

Surprised at the absurd squeak in the man's voice, David stared at the spots on his bow-tie.

'Why are you late?'

'I had to come from the end of the Parade,' he stammered.

'Which end?'

'The other end.'

'Are you trying to be funny?'

He began to sweat, in a nightmare of injustice.

'Take a hundred lines!' cried Baby King.

The masters at the new school were as mixed as they had been at St Albert's. There was 'Charity,' or 'Stinks,' who whined through his nose when talking and wore a hat turned up at both ends which Easton at once dubbed 'The Show Boat.' Then there was the Maths teacher, who wore outstanding ears like those of an orang-outang, a forked sarcastic tongue, sinositis, and such an air of worldly content that David lost all interest in mathematics whatsoever. As the class was now approaching the calculus, this was a serious matter, and he never recovered. Always he was afraid of the lash of that tongue and the malice in those little eyes. It was:

'Macrae, can't you see the board?' because he was peering, and:

'Yes, sir, but I can't see what's on it!' Or:

'Macrae has been playing with the rope all afternoon. Why do you come to this class, Macrae?'

'Because the Education Authority lays it down that mathematics is a subject for study, sir.'

Often they were asked to buy a new copy-book for the class. These cost 3d. As David had no interest now in the man or in his subject, he failed to see why he should buy one, and steadily refused to do so all through term, borrowing pages or odd scraps of paper from the others, who were fast coming to regard him as a 'Clown.' It was:

'Macrae, you will buy a jotter for the next class.'

'Yessir.' or,

'Macrae; why have you no jotter?'

'No money, sir.'

'Haven't your parents any money?'

'No sir.'

'You boys will not lend Macrae any pages in future. Understand?'

'Yessir, yessir, nossir!'

It was:

'Macrae, what are you writing on now?'

'A brown paper-bag, sir.'

'Where on earth did you get that?'

'I brought my lunch in it, sir,' or 'I found it, sir, down the back of the pipes, sir.'

He began to write on the backs of desks in ink, and was given up as hopeless; yet not insolence, but nervousness, had inspired the entire episode, plus knowledge of and dislike of the Maths master himself.

At the first exam he received 5 per cent for maths and 10 per cent for general neatness. That made a total of 15 per cent. In other subjects he did better. English, for example, had begun to be English, instead of the mere naming of parts of speech, and a beginning was made with poetry, though 'Lycidas' sounded strangely excruciating between the lips of Mr Walsh, who tore at the lines:

> Yet once more, O ye laurels, and once more
> Ye myrtles brown, with ivy never sere . . .'

as though they were so many bones.

Yet 'English' was less remote than the History class of Mr Vey, who in a mincing tone, would talk for hours about the Ostrogoths

and Visigoths as if they were so many ladies in the chorus, and
even made jokes about them. This was to hide his own pronunciation. 'Ostrogofs,' he said, and 'Visigofs.'

David could not help wondering what he would have done if a
Visigoth had suddenly entered his classroom there and then,
complete with horns and spear. Vey, in spite of his interest in pre-
history, or perhaps because of it, was a pansy but he also sailed a
yacht, which raised him in the estimation of a class apt to judge
him solely by his profusion of silk handkerchiefs.

Nevertheless, it was a strange bias which in a wholly Celtic
country had steeped these children first in Scandinavian Mythology and then in an entirely irrelevant and alien 'Germanic'
history, dominated by the equally mythical Goths – with whom
they could feel no kinship, but only hostility. There was an
apparent conspiracy to separate them from their identity, and
the 'BI,' as his mother called the 'British Israel Association,' at
least informed and furnished their unconscious revolt with precisely those elements it needed, heralding the downfall of 'Ger-
manism.'

There, Keltic pre-history was admitted and recognised in the
place-names of Europe, and the Goths relegated to the barren
political barbarism from which they had never in fact finally
emerged.

Thus, again there was a division between what he learned at
school and his private life. More and more he distrusted the
glibness of the existing order.

Throughout the Fourth Year David worked as hard as the
others, since ambition was now beginning to enter the lives of all.
They were out for the Higher Leaving Certificate, the Highers,
they called it. *Altiora peto* was the motto of the school, which they
translated freely as *I seek my Highers*. He liked work but not play,
which was made into work.

Across from the main school buildings stood the gym. It had a
queer, brown, tiled exterior, which looked both cold and treacherously slippery. Inside, they wore gym-shoes and shorts, going
through the series of exercises from the buck to the ropes in the
greatest cold and inconvenience. Against the walls were parallel
bars. Down from the roofs slid beams for vaulting, and every form
of physical contortion. The mat and the rings were so many
instruments of torture unnaturally evolved from the torture
mechanism of the Middle Ages, just as so many blood-sports –
instead of being the spontaneous exercise the body demanded –
were so many excuses for the martyrdom of the spirit, like

hectoring and bullying in the army in the name of discipline – which is either organic or non-existent. He loathed the trotting up and down the gym. Still more he loathed the sandalled teacher who stood in one spot jumping up and down and shouting 'Look, I'm not tired! One, two, one, two, one, two!'

Hating this, he was bound in honour to hate its external manifestations such as rugger, in which again the scrums and tackles seemed devoid of purpose except the general one of throwing one's weight about.

'Give him the beef!' they shouted. 'Give him the beef!'

Day after day he stood on the gym field with Mackay. He was idle.

'Idle! That's what you are! Bone idle!' shouted the gym master. 'Come on now!' If he had had a whip, he would have cracked it, across the cinder field.

'Let them chase around if they want to,' said Mackay. 'I'm not playing rugger anyway. I'm going to stand here against the fence and read the *School for Scandal*.'

That was breaking a great taboo. Mackay was a dude. He was chi-chi. He wore light tweeds and a bow-tie. He had a very attractive manner, but he was not perfect, because he was too aesthetic. He was also practically a 'cad,' because he did not share in the myths the others recognised.

He organised the Dramatic Society and produced its plays. He was going to be a Dramatic Critic, he said. David liked to sit next to him in class, for he read unashamedly through *Androcles and the Lion* or *Outward Bound*, no matter the subject for study, and David therefore felt it safer to concentrate on *The Ancient Mariner* or the *Scottish Ballads*, to the exclusion of all else.

The two were heartily despised for having no interest in sports. Mackay was even said to be a ladies' man. Together they borrowed books from the library in the Great Hall. One was in French. It was called *Servitude et Grandeur Militaire*, by de Vigny. The style was sonorous and dignified.

It was his father who put a stop to all this.

'You're not getting enough exercise,' he said. 'I've arranged for you to go and have boxing lessons from Carswell's. He's a friend of mine. He has a private gym.'

In some ways that was not so bad. They had medicine-balls and punch-balls and they did Swedish drill. In other ways it was worse. They boxed for at least half-an-hour towards the end of the lesson. He hated the smell of the gloves, but at least the Ring was honest.

Once he ducked below a boy's left and hit him in the stomach.
'Good,' said Carswell. 'Now you must try that with my son!'

David had only been taught the straight left and ducking under
a straight left. Carswell's son knew all the answers. He was a
beautiful boxer. He knew what was coming and blocked David's
blow easily. Then he sailed in to the attack. David was driven
round the ring, and hit from all angles. Punches he had never
heard of gave him no time to recover, and he was supposed to use
only his left. Two wicked right hooks caught him on the point of
the chin and he almost fell. He felt jarred and dizzy, and had
barely enough presence of mind to shamble round the ring. Then
he saw Carswell's son coming at him again, with a grin on his face,
and found the prospect rather upsetting. His nose had begun to
bleed, but no one paid any attention, as once with 'Ingins,' so
instead of waiting, he leapt at the figure before him and threw out
his right suddenly, striking the chin and knocking Carswell
straight across the ring. He pounced forward, but they all became
very concerned suddenly and said that would be enough for today.

'What are you goin' to do now?' his father asked him again.
'When you were fourteen I asked ye that, and ye said could ye stay
just a wee while longer, as a favour. Well, it's long enough I think.'

'I'd like to study a bit more,' David said, 'and get to know
things.'

'Whit things? You're just wastin' your time.'

'No I'm not, really I'm not.'

'Well, what *are* you doing?'

'I don't know.'

'I wished I saw you settled down,' his father said, 'like other
boys. There's Fisher in an accountant's, and Willie Hughes a
draughtsman. You could be a mechanic.'

'I don't know what settling down is.'

'An' you don't know why you want to go on wi' this stuff either?
Is it a fad?'

'I know I like books. I'd like to go on to the sixth year, then I
might leave if I'm not clear about what I want to do.'

'Just another year then,' his father had said. 'We don't want any
faddists in this family!'

Now the year was up he had won two medals. It said so in the
School Magazine. They were not important medals, French and
German, and the Rosebery Burns Club. The dux of the school
and the second dux and the runner-up and most of the others,
prefects and captain of the school, looked on him rather pityingly,

as a popular wit and no more. It was not expected that he would appear anywhere on the bursary list. There would be Violet Smythe and Cameron and Kirk and a few dark horses. When the list appeared in the *Herald* one morning, however, there was a sensation. Kirk was 85th, Cameron and Smythe were nowhere. David, it seemed, was 52.

They could not understand it. Neither could he. He slunk around the school playground with his cronies, hiding from prefects and teachers alike, till the Maths master saw him on the stairs.

'Macrae!' he called. 'You've done well, haven't you? Congratulations!'

It was painful. It should never have happened.

'Where did you learn Spanish?' Miss Barr asked him.

'In the evenings.'

It was a dirty trick, learning Spanish in the evenings. Why couldn't they leave him alone? What business was it of theirs? He had no use whatsoever for their absurd conventions and pretensions and prejudices.

'You've certainly kept up the honour of the school,' she said.

That was how they put it. Having done everything possible to prevent him from learning anything, now they said he had kept up the honour of the school. He had kept up his own honour – at the cost of a lot of extra work at night – not the school's. The school could go to blazes.

Yet, if the school could go to blazes, why did he wait after four on that last day, at the foot of the stairs in the hall, listening to the marching feet that no longer came? Listening, and trying to remember the sound of the waterfall behind the stair, as boys, in countless classes, filed into school, their footsteps beating an iron music on the stone? Why did he stand and listen to that sudden silence, and softly move into the hall to gaze round at the books and up at the high glass roof over the welled stair, if not because of a sudden feeling that a part of life had ceased to move for him? He felt no different. What would he be found to have lost, apart from the quick friends who were so swiftly gone?

'David!' shouted Sheriff outside.

He left the deserted building and walked over to the corner they always stood at, outside the shed, and picked up his books.

Low was there, and Easton and Jowett as well, four lonely figures in a bewildered playground.

'Howdy! Are you going on?' he asked Low.

'Na, I'm leavin' the day,' he said, shifting his feet and looking across the road, so they should not see his mortification.

'Is that why you've a hooker on?' asked Easton with a laugh.

'He's a tough man,' he said to Jowett, and they both laughed unkindly, David felt, at Low's checked cap. He had never worn one before. It was the symbol of his sudden servitude.

David's face fell.

'Got a job?' he asked.

'Aye,' replied Low, 'Millar's.'

'A rotten shop,' said Easton as he walked away with Jowett. 'Terrible wages.' His father was a Labour man. None of that for him. In some ways he was not unlike his friend Jowett. They were both 'saved,' and had little use for folk beyond the pale.

It must be comforting, David thought, to be so exclusive. You could be exclusive in blood, politics or religion, all so many shawls to be wrapped round the chilled and flagellating ego.

Geordie smiled, hitched up his trousers and sniffed.

'It'll be fun,' he said.

David was overcome with sadness. He liked Low. He had been very brilliant at school, and in the third year was one of the hopes of his class. Now he seemed always to be tired, his life a constant fight against falling asleep and falling in people's estimation. As soon as he awoke his mother shouted: 'George! George! You've to deliver the rolls remember!'

His breakfast was cocoa and bread and dripping.

Nobody had known of the rolls at school in the old days, neither immaculate 'Stinkie,' the drawing master, whose pansy breath smelled, nor Felix, who told the boys so often never to be ashamed of the school, that they felt quite ashamed for the first time.

When George was really awake he was clever. In German he was one of the best, although he was a 'corryfister.' Muriel, the teacher, was quite certain he would get a bursary and go to the University.

He had worked only for that. Easton, always neat in his blue suit and skull-cap, as becomes the son of a respectable Co-op man, and Jowett, who walked sedately under his cap as though balancing a basket of rolls, and who would go far in insurance like his florid kirk-elder father, had made George woefully conscious of his own torn corduroys, missing handkerchief and comb. At the sight of them he would pass his hand through his hair. Only in study had he hoped to equal them.

At four he had been one of the little band who stayed behind for special instruction before the bursary exam. He left at five and then began the long swotting of isotherms; longitudes; Pitt, Peel and Gordon Pasha, date of birth, death and deed; potted biographies, geographies, and word derivations, as well as other subjects unenlightening because unrelated. It was difficult to swot in their little warm kitchen beneath the naked gas-mantle, with five human beings chattering around him and him tired. He kept falling asleep in the chair at the side of the grate.

Now he had to leave because he could not afford to go on any longer.

'I'll come and see you,' David said. 'We can go hiking together. Let me know how you get on.'

George smiled and said yes, but it was as though he knew something David didn't, and as though he did not really believe that they would continue to be friends. It was the parting of the ways.

It was strange. He wondered what his father would say now, on this day of the breaking-up of old associations.

He was not left long in doubt. Before he had a chance to explain things himself, his father came into the house. His face was white, his mouth hung open as he threw bags of sweets, comics and newspapers on the table, laid keys and heaps of small change on the mantelpiece, took off his cap and tossed it on to a hook, to hang swinging on the back of the door.

'This is a fine thing ye've din tae me!' he said.

'What?'

'In the *Herald*,' his father said, dropping his jacket round a chair and sitting down. 'A bursary to the Uni? A hundred quid? Was my money no' good enough for ye?'

'How did I know I would win anything?' asked David.

'Ye knew damned weel! Put it there!' said his father, rising impulsively and holding out his hand. 'You're a tryer!'

This was embarrassing. His father was jumping to all kinds of conclusions, as he often did.

'You make me feel that size!' his father said, holding his hand a foot above the floor. 'Will it buy your books and pay your fees?'

'Yes.'

'It's terrific, isn't it, Teenie?' he said, undoing his collar and bow-tie.

'I wanted to go on studying.'

'An' I was going to make you a mechanic! I could have put you through. It's a smack in the eye to me. You're sure you didnae mean tae insult me?' he asked again.

'Don't be silly.'

He was still apprehensive. Only yesterday he had read a bit of Hendrik van Loon aloud, because it struck him as funny, about a bird chipping away a piece of rock every second, taking one million years to wear away a mountain, and beginning then to take a fraction of eternity: 'Bloody rubbish!' his father had said. 'I don't want to hear any more of that tripe!'

'The money might not be enough,' he said, 'and then I won't have to go.'

'If ye need any help, jist say the word. But remember, keep shovin' yer ain barra. Helpin' other people is aw very well, but this socialist stuff is tripe. Ye hear me? Tripe!'

He thrust his face close to David's own, so he could see the brows drawn down and the jaw thrust out for all the world like a dog about to bite.

'Capitalism isn't tripe, of course,' said David. 'Two million out of work and living in hovels is quite normal. If it's economics to let all that labour rot, let alone humanity, all I can say is, let me out of here!'

'Ye bluidy eediot,' his father said. 'Is that whit I've spent my money on yer education for? I know what I'm talkin' aboot. My best pal, my best pal,' he repeated, the veins standing out on his forehead in an effort to be earnest, 'dipped ma pocket once when I bought yer mother a silk scarf! Naw, if ye shove somebody else's barra, dae ye know what happens tae yer ain? Eh? It slips back. Doon the hill.'

'A stoot hert tae a stey brae,' said his mother, sitting in patient resignation, her hands folded. He looked at her. She shook her head from side to side like a peasant woman in lament. There were tears in her eyes. She was 'keening.'

'I've seen the day,' she said, 'when ye wad hae seen that wi' yer ain e'en!'

He was mystified when they began to talk like that. The language he understood, but what lay behind it was incomprehensible. They seemed to be carrying on a performance which had only a partial reference to what went on in the world. They were living a past tragedy, the tragedy of a proud race that had lost its way. They were hating a cruel humanity, and scorning and fearing a future when the fight for survival might become more bitter than ever. Yet they said none of these things. They were Celts, and they acted it out in gesture and proverb.

'That's a' I hiv tae say,' said his father heavily. 'Hiv some common eighteen-pence. Look at what yer daein' tae yer mother. I mind o' a man, I mind o' a big man, a big man . . .'

'I'm not the only one,' said David, fatally interrupting the incantation of a tale.

'What do ye mean, ye swine!'

His father's temper was notoriously quick.

'I mean you.'

'Oh my, oh my,' said his mother again, tears standing out in her eyes like nails.

'There have been other rebels in this family,' he said, in a subtle effort at compromise and flattery. 'What about my great-great-grandfather?'

'That was different,' his father said vehemently. 'He was fighting against Romanism.'

'Nonsense,' said David. 'He was fighting against Episcopacy as existing in the English Church, and against Feudalism. He was fighting for freedom.'

'Weel, whatever it wis,' said his father, 'he wasnae a Communist.'

'Grandpa always says Christ was a Communist,' said his mother, eyes wide, as if pleading for clemency.

'Aye, an' he votes Tory.'

'There was John Maclean,' David said.

Silence fell. The name of John Maclean was not one to be lightly set aside. During the Great War he had died of starvation in Barlinnie Prison. He was said to have been highly regarded by Lenin. A Shaws man, he was the true Scottish revolutionary of the Muir type. His fight was the fight of the workers of the world, but no more welcomed by the English than the fight of James Connolly in Ireland. Something in his complete intractability appealed to the Scot everywhere.

'A madman,' his father said. 'A madman. One o' the wild men.'

'Les fauves,' said David.

'I've heard them a',' he said finally, dismissing everything and turning to his wife. 'Are ye fur the BI the nicht, Teenie?'

She looked at the clock.

'I'll jist mask the tea,' she said.

'Tim it oot, then,' his father said. That was a joke. 'Tim' was a funny word in the family. 'Tim it oot or we'll be late.'

They did not know it was the old word 'toom' they were using, as in John Balliol's nickname, 'Toom Tabard.'

His mother was treasurer. Meetings were held in the Christian Institute in Bothwell Street. To David, there was something wild about the name 'Bothwell Street,' but there was nothing remotely wild about the Christian Institute. Sometimes a mass meeting would be held in the Great Hall, complete with maps and dates, on the 'Great Pyramid of Ghizeh and its Significance in Prophecy.' The words always seemed put together with a trowel.

These lectures were conducted by an engineer called Haroldson, of whom his parents spoke in bated breath. The dates, corresponding to inches, indicated that the Great War began in 1914 – which few were likely to dispute or forget, or, even if they did, to construct a Great Pyramid as a mnemonic – and that another war would begin in 1928 or alternatively 1936.

The sands of time, it seemed, were again running out.

In retrospect, the prophet pointed out, there had been no war against Russia (which, note, was ASSUR spelt backwards, or nearly so) in 1928, but instead a drastic fall in world commodity-prices, doubtless the same thing as Soviet aggression to the affluent promoters of this new totemism.

The BIFW, with which was affiliated, as his mother used to say, the Scottish-Israel Identification Association, had been introduced to his father by a Freemason called Mr Finger. There was a photo of him at home, wearing an apron like Salome; white gloves like a conjuror, and a frockcoat. Standing before a table of trowels and maces and glasses of water, he was unquestionably the man who had just built the Pyramid.

His father and mother took it all most seriously, and indeed there was in it much that merited serious attention.

'You are an Israelite of the Tribe of Benjamin,' said his father.

'I thought I was a Scotsman!' he said.

'The Scots are all the Tribe of Benjamin!'

An old gentleman in striped trousers who constantly sucked his whiskers – adapted rather to tobacco and black-striped balls than to public speaking, insisted on giving a sermon that evening entitled *Cui Bono?* This led him into incredible predicaments of self-questioning which the small audience saw straightened out with considerable relief.

It occurred to David that he was talking to his own conscience. Congregations were really audiences, which accounted for the apathy in the kirk. They went only to be entertained to an exhibition of histrionics, or individual catharsis, much as they watched cripples dancing in the streets. When they 'caught' religion, as in some of the cults, where it came to resemble a bad cold, that was bad. They ought not to be 'religious.' Only sinners had the right to be religious, and they were by no means sinners. The sinner, with all due respect to him, stood in the pulpit, as the murderer strode the stage, and the Judge clung to the dock.

The Christian Institute was full of halls which were hired at least once a week by various sects of which there was a formidable list docketed downstairs, together with the number of the room, much as if it had all been a list of firms in some block of offices.

There were the:

Assemblies of God,
Associated Bible Students,
Anabaptists,
Bethel Hall,
Bible Students,
British Protestant League,
Canal Boatmen's Institute,
Christian Brethren,
Christian Scientists,
Church for the New Revolution,
Church of the New Jerusalem,
The Gaelic Free,
Elim Tabernacle,
Congregational,
Mains Street United Original Secession,
Railway Mission with Singer,
Reformed Presbyterian,
St Silas' English Episcopal,
Shiloh Hall,
The Church of God in Glasgow,
The Four Square Gospel,
Unitarian,

as well as the Wee Frees, the Quakers, the Parish Churches, the Methodists, and the Scottish Episcopalians, plus:

Adelphi Radiant,
Camphill Communion Healing Circle,
The Greater World,
The Rosicrucians,
The Good Shepherd,

and last but by no means least, the 'chapels' – which here meant the Roman Catholic Churches – the synagogues, and Mr Campbell, who gave trance addresses all by himself, every Friday, which seemed on the whole very sensible.

Each of these multitudinous churches vociferously complained of small audiences, and of the decline in religion in a country the size of London in population. All maintained that not only their particular religion but their sect, their parish, their district, and ultimately of course they themselves were more religious than any other, a defence and denunciation in itself most suspicious, reminding David of Howden protesting his innocence. It would indeed be curious if 'religion' should prove to be no more than a complex of unacted guilt.

They talked of everything from the expansion of life and the latest novel to the future of Europe and the coming struggle for power. Rarely if ever did they speak of the Saints. They were all wild exiles in their own perpetual conflict, as their fathers had been imperial exiles, transforming that conflict into geographical terms and building up domination abroad to cover an inner fission – more explosive than any atomic fission. They were all escapists from themselves and Scotland, though only Mr Campbell perhaps, speaking in a trance, might accidentally stumble on the fact.

They did not read St John of the Cross, nor the Bhagavadgita, nor the mystics. They had lost all knowledge of their own earliest Christian church, the Culdee Church, now extinct, and only by hearsay did they know the Druids, whom they regarded as a species of Ku Klux Klan. They did not consider spirit the greatest possible realisation of the potential in the actual, but a polite fiction. Yet they did love freedom without realising what it might involve, and they preferred the right of choice, though it had led them where they were.

Easily the best of the evening was his mother at the organ, slightly flushed at times when they sang the wrong note, or the wrong version, or even the wrong hymn, but always adjusting herself rapidly to the meeting, always playing and singing well 'The Old Hundred,' or 'By Cool Siloam's Shady Rill.' He loved to see her sitting there, head turned, watching the proceedings and intent on her 'cue.' She looked so helpless and embarrassed now and then, and it made her very attractive. It was a pity she always had to wait behind and count the money. It was a waste of her time and talent, which she regarded as sordid. He hated, too, to see her inward indignation and excitement as she marked up the various small sums, feeling as she did that the meeting was not really to be judged by the amount of alms collected.

David was most impressed by the BI but he could not help feeling strange when he saw, streaming out of the hall across the

way, a band of equally eager, equally convinced and dogged
Apostolics, who regarded others as being quite as lost as others
apparently regarded them.

It was most confusing.

The Christian Institute did not, however, exhaust by any
means the activity of the city. When you came out there was
The Evangelists' Association in the Tent Hall, Tron St, Saltmarket, with Miss Longshanks illustrating addresses with a story-
graph, and the singing of West African Choirs, including at 8 a.m.
a free breakfast for the Adult Poor.

That night at prayers they read together the 39th Chapter of
Ezekiel. It was an appalling chapter. The fury of the prophets
haunted the boy. They were filled with terror of Him. They
believed in Him, and yet, in an outburst of ·hysterical violent
oratory, they prophesied universal downfall.

It was the old Story of Father and Son. In prophesying Christ
they foretold their own ruin at the hands of that omnipotent
Father of theirs, who had no more to do with Jehovah, than with
the goats that gave their children milk. Tribal conflict, he felt sure,
lay at the root of it all, and if the clans had broken up, tribal spirit
among the Scots existed in plenty, with all its hates and unresolved violence and inhibition. He had not been entirely wrong in
developing a feeling for historical faces. These were so many
unresolved lives peeping through history. Aunt Bessie was one.

It seemed that whenever the Father motif in a society weak-
ened, terror broke loose which He had held concentrated on
Himself. This was the real reason for Fear of Freedom. God was
not the Father. He was the Trinity. He was all three, Father, Son
and Holy Ghost, the three phases of the human spirit on its
journey. Society made Him the Father, held Him prisoner in His
Fatherhood, because only thus could the very worldly fathers
maintain their tyranny. It was disgusting. Scottish society had
never recovered from Culloden. The defeat in battle of the
Scottish fathers then had left an ugly, festering sore. The defeat
of the German fathers had been worse. Neurosis had spread like a
weed where there ought to have been only happiness at relief from
tyranny.

The German solution had been to rivet terror of the father even
more tightly on to a leader who was at once new father and
scapegoat son of the Fatherland.

He heard his father and mother whispering about him as he was
reading by himself, imagining doubtless that he read only the
more salacious chapters of The Buik.

'When I came in the day he was on the fluir readin' it. Whit dae ye mak' o't?'

'Dae ye think he's all right?' asked his mother anxiously.

'Oh aye, but it's no' good for him, Teenie. It's no' good for him at a'!'

'Maybe we should ask him aboot it? Dae ye think he'll be a minister?'

The scholarship, of course, made no difference to David's attendance on Sunday evenings at the Institute. In time he knew the inside of the Pyramid as well as the inside of his own home. It seemed you entered high up on one face, as if the opening were a cave on a mountain side. Then you went down a long passage called the Grand Gallery. This was high and broad. At last you came to a small cavern, along which you had to crawl on hands and knees, and which was known as the Ante-Chamber to the Queen's Chamber. A similar cavern followed the Queen's Chamber, leading to the King's Chamber, inside of which you could at last stand upright.

The amazing thing about the King's Chamber was that there had never been a body there at all.

'Now,' said the orator, 'does that not prove that the Pyramid was built for a different purpose from the others? It is our contention that it provides an illustration in cross-section of human history, and especially the history of Israel.'

You started off with the Pyramid inch. It was only lightly different from the British inch, owing possibly to what in other spheres was called the Displacement Factor. This was a very variable constant. He found himself inprisoned in an expanding cage of mathematics, as at school, only this time it was not so easy to escape, for they had been given divine sanction. God, it seemed, was a Scientist, the first step in making the Scientist God.

The main point emerging from such deliberations was that counting the number of inches from the entrance to the final narrow corridor, and allowing an inch to equal a day (Gregorian Calendar) you arrived precisely at the date, August 4th, 1914. It was from there on that you had to crawl on your hands and knees, and when at last you emerged into the Queen's Chamber the date was said to be November 11th, 1918. 'Crawling,' of course, meant the War Years, known to the authorities as the Years of Tribulation.

The audience, as the speaker unrolled his maps and tapes and charts, sat enthralled in apocalyptic rapture. The man was a prophet. He forecast a new era of crawling to which everyone looked forward with morose glee, to begin on May 28th, 1928. Reading between the lines, and taking it all in conjunction with the 37th Chapter of Ezekiel, one sinister purpose revealed itself behind this gallimaufry of nonsense: war with Russia.

It was now April 1928 and the prophet was a little nervous. He emphasised that no man could foretell the future – though he omitted to mention that not a few mediums on the Stock Exchange actually sold it – and only afterwards would the actual event become known. May came and went, and the sun was as lovely as ever. The waves at the coast maintained their serene regularity. Golfers went by with unhurried swing. Apocalyptic urgency was seen to have its origin in deep-seated repression amounting to a hatred of nature in the highest degree Puritan, unhealthy, and even, paradoxically, irreligious. The Crucifixion itself had been just such a hatred of nature and the whole ridiculous mathematical scheme to imprison the nature of things in a formula – including even human nature – was bound to burst as it had before in the blind fury of human resistance called revolt of the unconscious.

'He may be all good and glorious within,' said his Aunt Bessie of the prophet.

'It's a pity you couldnae flipe him,' said his mother.

He didn't understand that at first. It seemed that after socks were washed you turned them outside in. They were then 'fliped.'

III

In the winter air, pictures froze his mind into visions of loveliness that already, he could see, were passing so swiftly that they ought to be cherished far more than they were. There was the picture of Mary Watson coming up the hill, her head lowered on account of the wind that wrapped her skirt around her figure with a loving hand. For a long time, he thought, she lowered her head when she saw him coming, out of shyness, and forgot about the wind. He still felt strangely unhappy when he saw her talking to other boys on Saturdays. That was her free day. She seemed rather brazen, somehow shameless then, and most certainly free and mature – a woman, in society, whereas he was condemned to remain a 'schoolboy.' When he passed, she smiled at him sweetly, but absently, and went on with her conversation. Yet he was exactly one year older than she, and coming to 'know' much more from books about ways of thinking and feeling and living that did not make him altogether happy because they were deliberate instead of being spontaneous – as she was.

For long he stared through the window at five in the evenings to see her coming up the street. Through his sister he sent her invitations to go to concerts with her niece. He knew he was in love. When he looked closely into her face and saw she had freckles, they seemed miraculous. There were large brown checks on her coat, too, and they seemed to match the patches of sunlight on leaves against the sky, and in her eyes, where hid such heaven, he was afraid and could not bring himself to kiss her as he wished. Was it that he no longer believed in heaven?

Sometimes he saw her come home late at night with someone else, and stand at the little gate under the lamp, parting from the man with a swift kiss; or he lay awake in the attic under a heap of old rugs and blankets, wearing headphones attached to an old crystal set, and taking them off every now and then to listen for the quick step and the bang of the door that meant she was home after an evening out. If for some time he heard voices in conversation it was worse, and worse still to hear her silvery laughter, and know she had been to a Palais de Danse. One day he hoped he might marry her, and she did not even know how he felt. She could not read what was in his face because of the rather bitter mask which hid it, and there was nothing to be done but lie and listen to the Savoy Orpheans from 2LO playing 'Valencia,' or 'The Waters of Minnetonka.'

He thought of asking her out himself, but something always seemed to crop up, a visit to his grandfather in the Shaws, or work at home. Now and then he managed to slip downhill to the tram-stop towards five o'clock, saying he was going to buy a paper. There he walked nervously up and down, watching every white car that came along, until he saw her, but then he strolled past the stop as though he did not see her.

Opening the paper, he walked on slowly up the hill, reading politics and expecting a war. There was a headline 'Japan Invades Manchuria,' which almost made him forget that she was coming up behind him. Closer she came, with long strides and her wide, attractive outward arm-swing.

'Hello,' she remarked. 'You're a stranger.'

He leapt at the words like a dog at a bone. What did they mean? Their conventionality distressed him, but he strove to find what they meant to her, if anything.

Together they walked on uphill talking and laughing for a few fugitive moments, and he noticed again, with a pang, that her eyes were as blue as cornflowers in wheat. He wanted more of her, yet he hated to have to plot in order to see her. In any case, when he did see her, he did not know what to say.

'Are you busy?' he asked.

'Fairly busy,' she said.

It made him angry, impulsive, impatient, in contrast with the wonderful sensation of looking at her, and of walking with her.

Soon he began to see her in the mornings too, as he rode in the tram. Climbing proudly upstairs, he would take out *Immensee* to read in German, and she would sit down beside him, admiringly he hoped. He opened the book. They were together, she and *Immensee* two of the things he loved.

'Look' he said, and began to read a passage to her.

> Heute, nur heute
> Bin ich so schön;
> Morgen, ach morgen
> Muss alles Vergehen!
> Nur diese Stunden
> Bist du noch mein;
> Sterben, ach sterben
> Soll ich allein.

'What does it mean?' she asked.

'It is a piece of poetry,' he said. 'Listen to this.

> Meine Mutter hat's gewollt,
> Den andern ich nehmen sollt;
> Was ich zuvor besessen,
> Mein Herz sollt es vergessen;
> Das hat es nicht gewollt.
>
> Für all mein Stolz und Freud
> Gewonnen hab ich Leid.
>   Ach, war das nicht geschehen,
> Ach konnt ich betteln gehen
> Über die braune Heid!

'You mean you understand all that?' In her face there was only a puzzled look, and a hidden distaste.

'Nearly all.'

'What does it mean?'

'It is the story of two lovers who have to separate, because one is a student. When he returns he finds his sweetheart married. She says it was her mother's wish, but she realises she has made a mistake. This is how they separate at the end: 'Upstairs in the house he heard a door close; steps came down the staircase, and when he looked up Elizabeth was standing before him. She laid her hand on his arm, and her lips moved, but no word came.

"You won't come back," she said at last. "I know. Don't lie to me. You will never come back."

"Never," he said. Her hand dropped. She said no more. He walked to the door; there he turned again. She was standing motionless in the same spot, looking at him with dead eyes. He stepped forward and held out his arms. Then he forced himself to turn away, and went out.'

'Silly,' she said. David was hurt.

'What's silly? I think it's wonderful. Only he wouldn't really step forward and hold out his arms. That *is* rather silly.'

'I think it's rather nice,' she said, glancing out of the window, almost casually.

'One day I'll come back and find you married, I expect,' he said.

'Oh no,' she laughed, 'not me. You'll have found some nice girl long before that I suppose.'

'Never.' The very idea shocked him.

'Oh yes you will!'

'It's time I left,' he said, putting the book away and rising.

'Cheerio!' she smiled, and the commonplace word at once became one of the loveliest words in the language, a red gem on her lips.

Three mornings before, he had seen a reporter waiting for her at the car-stop, a man he knew who had been out with her, and *they* went upstairs together in the tram. That filled him with a cold fury and yet with fear, because she seemed so talkative and merry. Either, he thought, she was doing it to make him jealous, or she considered him very dull, since he never went anywhere. He decided to ask her now.

'Are you doing anything on Saturday?'

'All right!'

'I'll meet you at 6.30 at the car-stop!'

It was done.

Was it imagination, or did her father, an elderly man with curling white moustache, eyeglasses and grim granite exterior, *really* begin to nod to him churlishly in the street? When he passed their house, where her mother sat at the window, did she really beam at him? He hoped they would not talk. He was not ready for that yet. All he knew was that he wanted to be with her.

They went to the Regal. He bought matches, and a box of chocolates for her.

'Here you are,' he said ungraciously. When they sat down to watch the film he found himself sitting behind a pillar, but it did not matter.

He could follow nothing. Mindless characters talked out of turn. Beams of flickering light and shadow were to him less than his cardboard theatre compared with the girl at his elbow, and yet he hardly dared glance at her in case his expression gave him away, so he sat in the dark, feeling how wonderful it was merely to be with her. The evening was expensive. He could not afford many of them. One and six each for the seats and one shilling for the chocolates made four shillings; a small bribe really to have her in his company, but a large sum for a student.

'Enjoying it?' he asked.

She looked at him and said 'Yes' in the low voice that always stirred him, and he was overcome by panic. He imagined he saw tears in her eyes.

Could there be? Of course not. She would not waste a single thought on him. Might there be? He did not know.

Perhaps he was a brute not to take her out more often, not to take her hand and not to kiss her, but how could he, till he was sure she cared for him at all? It was brutal to kiss her if she didn't care for him. Others did, he knew that, and it was none of his affair, but he loved her too much to do so, casually, though his whole being yearned for her.

He stole a glance at her and saw she was following the film intently. David tried to do so too, so that he could talk to her about it afterwards, but the pillar blocked his vision.

He must not be too late or his mother would ask him where he had been, and then it might all come out. He did not want Mrs Watson and his mother laughing over the two of them or saying knowingly: 'Yes, there's something in the wind all right!' He could not have borne that.

A comedy film came next, and he laughed uproariously, unashamedly, until he saw . . . no one else was laughing. It was her turn to look at him strangely, almost wistfully; but the moment was all too swiftly gone.

'We shall have to be going soon,' he said. He had not held her hand. Not once.

Outside, the Neon lights glared redly through the fog. David reckless at the thought of losing her for another week, or perhaps longer, said: 'Will you have a coffee?'

It had been a very pleasant evening, but there was a gulf between them. She seemed to think that being employed in the town made her a woman of the world, and he felt the tragedy of moving away from her into the dark forest of books. They were both friendly, but shy, and they could not compose this difference.

'How is school?' she asked.

He hated her for saying that. It made him feel so young. Girls matured sooner than boys, they said, and already she used scent.

'I'm at the University now.'

Couldn't she see the love in his eyes? Couldn't she see that he adored her? Couldn't she read his anguish? Then there was no use in anything. To her he was at school, and she longed for smart clothes, a car, cinemas, dances. They were still drifting apart. 'Education' was a wedge being driven between them, as between him and George Low. He wanted her to understand the things he read so that they could enjoy them together, poems of Mörike and Heine and Eichendorff, but she was not interested.

The restaurant they entered became luxurious with her presence. The carpets took on an added gleam and the flowers sprang up at her approach. Out of the radio a mechanical man made love for him because he did not dare.

'Did you like the film?' asked Mary.

'I'm afraid I didn't see much of it.'

'How do you like the University?'

'I like it, but I don't like moving away from my friends.'

'How do you mean?' He told her about Low.

'He's a friend of mine. We were at school together. Now he works in a leather shop, making soles for shoes out of compressed paper for 15/- a week. It's no job for him. He was very good, but he has to take what he can get.

'It won't last long, so he says. He can make the soles now so you don't feel the nails for months, but he'll get the sack. The firm is feeling the draught.'

'I don't understand. He's still a friend of yours.'

'He doesn't think so.'

He could say no more. He could not tell her how he had met George coming up from the library, and of the last talk they had had. George was on the dole now.

'The buroo's no' sae bad. Nuthin' tae dae bit go and sign on once a week. I've ta'en up wrestlin' noo. You should come to the classes. Last night, a fella, ye should a seen 'is muscles, caught anither man a beauty right on the chin wi' his fit!'

As he said it, George's eyes shone and his shoulders bunched. There was a smirr of rain.

'I'll tell ye what,' George had said in an embarrassed tone, 'come hikin' wi' us some week-end.'

He sniffed loos.

'Last weekend we wur away for four days, sleepin' in the open, lightin' fires. We got a lift as faur as Loch Lomond. Gee we hid a lot o' fun pinchin' totties an' tumshies. On Sunday we hid tae walk twinty miles hame!'

'I'd like to come,' said David. 'It must keep you fit.'

'Oh aye, I hid a wumman up there. One night we were sleepin' in a barn. I didnae know her. We had a bit o' a talk in the dark ye know, then I crawled ower.'

He braced himself, in a gesture of bravado.

'Well, what is it all about?' asked Mary, through the silence.

'It's hard to say,' he said.

('We're clubbin' thegither for an army tent,' George said.)

A wedge had been driven between them. They were pals. They wanted to remain so, but the old friendship was split asunder like a piece of wood.

'I might go abroad this summer,' said David.

'Oh?' Geordie put his head back as though politely inviting further news and his blue eyes tried to smile, but nothing came. There was only a glaze.

'I told him I was going abroad,' he said, 'and he thought it was swank.'

'Was it?'

'What do you think?' ('It must be great there,' George said: 'David's no' what he used to be,' he was thinking. And David was thinking 'Geordie's no' what he might have been.')

'People change,' she said.

'So now,' he thought, 'he'll live out his life in Wellfed Street, near Buggery Brae, next door to the Starvation Army.' That was what they had called Wellfield Street, and Balgray Hill and the Salvation Army.

She did not know what else to say. 'We'd better go,' he said.

As they rode home together on the tram, he tried to make her laugh by talking politics. Mary said she knew nothing about politics.

'How do you expect to get on,' he said, 'if you never read the papers? There's going to be a war, don't you know that?'

'I leave that to the men,' she said.

'Aren't *you* interested in going abroad, then?' he asked.

'Why should I be? I haven't a chance.' She looked squarely at him, and he felt a fool, felt as if she were looking through him and as if she knew very well that he watched her through the window coming up the hill and that their 'meetings' had not been accidents. It was too as if she might be saying, 'My only chance of anything like that is with you!'

'Well, you could now!' he said.

'How?'

'You could save up,' he concluded miserably, and she turned her head and looked out of the window again.

They stood at the top of the hill, watching a flurry of lights.

He frightened her, too late he realised it, as he said in a sudden access of hate: 'Are you going to go on living here?'

'Yes,' she said, with mild surprise, 'aren't you?'

'No,' he said, looking savagely across the sea of lovely dusk and moonlight that formed the city beneath them.

'I'm going to get out of it all.'

In a way it was only that he could not bear to be with her when she seemed even slightly indifferent.

'You *are* strange,' she said at last, rather sadly.

'Why?'

'The way you talk about getting away.'

'Do you blame me for wanting to get out of this?'

Dramatically he pointed to the factories, the smoke, and the red glare in the distance of the blast furnaces, called 'Dixon's Blazes.'

'It's all dead, a dead Inferno.'

She shamed him. He knew she would always live there and there too would always be his place, no matter where he might go. He had a vision, absurd, perhaps, of her beauty stifling in years of smoke, and he could not bear the thought.

Now they were standing outside of her home, beneath the lamp-post where he knew she had been kissed before.

'Well,' she was about to say, 'good-night,' when a sound at the head of the lane made her look round. A figure at the top appeared to draw back into the shade, peered and then slowly descended the hill. Softly she laughed.

'What is it?' he asked her, watching the golden face.

'That woman thought we were going to kiss or something,' she said, and looked at him.

They were standing very close, under the green lamp. He looked uphill, thinking it was a lie.

'Did she? She should have known we'd have told her first!' he said bitterly.

'You are a card!'

'What?'

'You are a cool one,' she said.

Yes, he was a cool one, standing there, wishing he could take her in his arms and yet mocking himself for the thought. He was more than a cool one, he was a futile one!

He wanted to tell her so much, that it was difficult to explain. She did not always speak his language. She might not understand. But need she understand? Was that not being futile too, to 'understand?'

'Goodnight then,' she said cheerfully. 'You must come in next time and meet Mum and Dad!'

Shocked, he looked up at the house. The room was comfortable and inviting, with the flames of the coal fire flicking the walls and shadows gesticulating through the windows. There was nothing he would have liked better; and yet – to meet Mum and Dad! It sounded terrifying. It would mean he was practically the chosen one. He'd seen it in the case of her sister.

'Goodnight,' he said to her sincerely, almost affectionately, as she ran off. He felt hopelessly in love, but how? In a different way from others? He adored her. She was the most significant thing in his life, but he was not ready to face at once that significance. He could not reconcile it with his image of the world. It would not be fair to go in there, until he could. That would take years.

There would not be a next time. He would never see her again. He would not even write. That was the kindest way. He would go, because he loved her too much to see her hurt in all this ugliness. He felt absurdly like Reinhardt, and could not get her out of his mind. For him the freckles round her limpid blue eyes were made of gold dust.

Along to the front of his own house he walked in an agony of remorse. Why had he not acted? He did not know. Always he was remaining mute and motionless at the wrong moment, as if his will were paralysed, or shrinking from decision, so deep was inhibition burned into him, and hatred of his prison. He did not realise how important a part in his life his father had played, how every decision paled into insignificance beside the decision of taking matters up with his father and opposing that iron will.

He would say he had no job! He spun in the shell of his own torment. He would not have his life determined by anyone! Or was he shrinking from the rebuff he feared, a rebuff more than once received from his mother, who naturally gave his father pride of place?

The hatred of machines he mentioned to Mary, was it not hatred of a father-projection? Would he always be afraid of doing anything which resembled stepping into his father's shoes? And afraid of power itself?

At cricket, rugger, football, he had always been picked last for the same reason, that he shrank from any form of self-assertion. He had an inferiority-complex. Why should a girl differ from a football captain?

Inside the house he ambled about with such an expression of unhappiness on his face that even his mother was affected by it.

'Whit's the matter wi' ye? Take yer tea.'

'I don't want any tea. Nothing's the matter.'

'I'll no' thole it,' she said. 'Look at him! If this is how he's going to behave when he comes back from the pictures on a Saturday he'll no' go at a'.'

'I'm damned if he will,' his father said. 'I'll slaughter him!'

He did not mean that. That was stupid 'British' heartiness because he did not know what was wrong. It was boring.

He remembered how she dropped her head when she saw him coming down the street. Why had he spoken as he did, or run away from her and himself, making himself a permanent exile even in his own country?

'Comfort me with apples and stay me with flagons, for I am sick of love.'

Now he knew the meaning of the Song of Solomon.

'He's been to the Shows. He's been to some coconut-shy,' his mother said.

'I don't know what's eating you,' said his father, 'but always remember this: Don't get het up. A wee bit pits ye right, and a wee bit pits ye wrang.'

IV

Now David had to study at home by bright gaslight, on a table covered by white waxcloth – the same chair he had once pretended was a racing car – an obscure drama of Hebbel, when there was in the little kitchen a far greater drama waged, the drama that his father wanting the light out and yet expecting results from his study, could not see, a drama of hidden guilt, a battle between 'work' and 'culture,' and love.

'I've tae be up the morn's morn' at the back o' six,' his father said. 'I've tae work!'

He never knew what was meant by that masterpiece of a phrase 'the back o' six,' but he resented the implication that no one else besides his father worked.

'I don't work, I suppose,' he replied. 'This is all a lot of stuff and nonsense!'

'You said it yoursel',' his father said.

He read for a little then, his mind full of the secret drama burning his life into the white incandescence of the fragile mantle that yet gave so much light. He knew he was hopelessly in love, yet, having gone so far in developing the intellectual approach to organic love, miscalled culture, he was forced to study further, and to derive such consolation as he could from the cold classicism of Racine's *Phèdre*. Its deadness sickened him. He turned to Marshall's 'Principles of Economics.' That was marvellous. It was a watertight system, but it postulated scarcity. Economics was defined as the science of the disposition of scarce means among unlimited ends. He read Henderson and Cole and Stamp and Keynes and Gregory and Beveridge, and, as the days went by, Cassel and Withers and Robbins and Jevons and Hobson and Smith. As the world-wide economic blizzard blew up outside, he read steadily through their theories of overproduction and under-consumption and even sunspots, with increasing bewilderment, and would not at all have been surprised had the Great Pyramid been brought in again to explain a sudden decrease in supply, as once he had heard it used to prophesy, or defend, a fall in commodity-prices.

What kind of 'science' was it, he thought, which explained the trade-cycle in terms of sunspots? What gave such scientists the right to laugh at superstition? The fact was they were all equally scared and superstitious men, with an equal interest in obscuring the truth. Their voluminous books were merely an attempt to put 1,000 pages between them and the reality that mended their taps.

It was gradually borne in on him that the immediate causes of what was now called The Crisis were the transference of financial control from the Bank of England to the Bank of France and the Federal Reserve Bank, and the consequent complete cessation of foreign lending on a pre-war scale. *The Waste Land* was an American export in more senses than one. Their financial wizards expected to hold all the gold in the world, without lending it to anyone for fear they lost it, and at the same time expected no effect either on capitalism or on international trade. It was the final proof that the whole legion of economists were 'liars and lickspits.'

A more fundamental cause, however, was simply that Smith's

insistence on labour as the real creator of wealth had been overlooked by the subjective philosophers, until wealth had come to mean gold as it had to the Mercantilists though that was merely the mechanism to which it was tied. The growth of vast urban populations had created an enormous potential wealth which gold was quite inadequate to measure at all. He read the Report of the Gold Delegation of the Financial Committee of the League of Nations.

'Britain was built on the Bible,' his father said; 'God, not Gold, that is what we believe in.'

It was wide open to cracks about missionaries and soldiers and capitalism, but perhaps in the final analysis it was true as most things, in that what counted was the faith of a man in himself, his motives, and in those of his country, his country being simply the way men such as he lived together. Again he came up against the sense of community he had lost on leaving school.

He remembered a text his sister had had to learn by heart when she was five. They all had a text to learn every Sunday, illustrated and in colour, and they were always happy if it were short. Hers read: *Thy faith hath made thee whole.*

Poor Meg. She could scarcely talk at all. She said: *The face has made the hole.*

He thought, too, of the ludicrous philology of the BI Christ was not a Jew, they said, He was an Israelite of the Tribe of Benjamin. He said so Himself. Ten Tribes had been lost, including Dan.

'Dan shall judge his people . . . Dan shall be a serpent by the way, an adder in the path that biteth the horse's heels so that the rider shall fall backwards . . . Dan is a lion's whelp. . . . And they called the name of the city Dan, after their father.'

It was incredible how many Dans there were in Europe. Dan-Mark – the boundary of Dan. And Don? And Dun? Most of them were Irish: Donaghadee, Dundalk, but also there were Dundee, Dunfermline, Dunedin, Dunoon. The sounds were the sounds of the river he rowed on: the Clyde, Caledonia, Caledon, Chalcydony – philology on holiday.

He drifted into an attitude of scepticism. Where the Gold Standard was kept, what was Vitamin B, or the Nature of Idealism, were things of which students had even less idea than he had once had of Santa Claus. Less, in fact, for they did not distil little lightnings of snow, nor did they wear a scarlet cloak. They were not sweet in the mouth, and they certainly had not been met with *in practice*, yet they thought themselves more

scientific than ever, hearing them in the words of their teachers.
They grew more gullible in fact as their scepticism grew. The gap,
the old hole in the chimney widened, and a stream of sooty words
blew down which they picked up and ate with the ashes, though
they constantly crumbled and made them filthy. Perhaps if they
had never grown sceptical they would have been a lot less gullible.
Perhaps the first myth was the best, the more organic, the living
poetry that would have given them freedom. Only most of them
had lost sight of it, and for each of them it differed.

Living, it appeared, was not enough for some of them. So
terrified were they of mere lives that they invented and willy-nilly
hunted down mythical enemies, heretics, scapegoats, witches,
with the entire paraphernalia of paranoiac finance. That grew to
be his name for the system: paranoiac finance. It was paranoiac
finance that caused wars, and lay at the root of greed. To his
professors, however, it was only a glib phrase, and not 'scientific.'

As a relief, David joined the Boat Club, situated on the banks of
the Clyde. He always regretted that the windings of the Kelvin
made boating on it impossible, otherwise it would have been an
ideal site.

As he walked through Glasgow Green to the river, the first day
he caught sight of Currie.

'Hello, whit are you daein' here?' Currie asked, tall and thin,
standing stiffly till David came up, as though he were on stilts.

'I'm joinin' the club.'

'Gee, so am I. How do you get in?'

'Here's the door, I think.'

Inside, the place was like a stables. The air was coated with
dust, and in an inner room they found a student with his coat still
on and his feet on the mantelpiece. David remembered the
student he had seen on the tram, when he was a child, wearing
the velvet-tasselled cap of an athlete. The comparison was odious.

'Can we join the Boat Club?' asked Currie.

'Set ye back ten and a tanner,' was the answer. 'What weight
are ye?'

'Nine-ten,' David said.

'A bit light. You might make bow. You?'

'Six stone,' said Currie.

'Good God!'

The man leapt to his feet and walked round Currie as though
he had discovered a phenomenon.

'What?' he asked. 'Jeez, are *you hollow?*'

'No,' said Currie; 'a clear case of malnutrition when an infant.'

'I don't care what it is. You're hired. You're cox in the first boat, starting right now. Get your clothes off!'

'I don't know anything about rowing,' said Currie. 'I came here to learn!'

'You'll learn! Here's a megaphone! Get going! We'll have to start you on a tub.' He turned to David. 'Bill will take you out. He's coach. Hey, Bill, freshman here.'

The tub was not so bad. It was like the boats young men took their girls on when he had been on the River Laggan, but it was hard work. He sweated and pulled.

'Come on,' the coach said. 'You're not trying. I can see that.'

Now and then there passed a skiff or shell in which there sat a crack oarsman pulling at the sculls. They went four times as fast as he did, but sometimes they overturned and had to be rescued.

The river, too winding to allow of eights, restricted their racing activities, and they had to have fours. Under the bridge the currents were swifter and below the middle span there was quite a whirlpool, which invariably cost ten minutes of valuable time. They called it 'The Tunnel.'

So David came to love the river and the rain, the walk along the towpath and even the speakers on the Green on a late afternoon, when yellow lights went on shimmering in the mist like tall crocus. Along the banks as they rowed upstream there rose against the evening sky the bare branches of poplars, shaped like feathers, and the river was silent and morose, murmuring only to itself as the oars plashed. It was his bed.

Far down towards the coast they could occasionally hear the sounds he had heard from childhood, and almost heard no longer; the sirens booming mournfully in the far distance, like great birds travelling over seas and continents. He used to ask his mother what that was.

'A ship in the Clyde,' she said, 'going to America, or India, or China.'

He watched them from Fairlie, steaming down the river, telling from the colours on their funnels the line they belonged to, and so whither they were bound. There was the *Anchor Line, White Star, Burns and Laird, Blue Funnel,* and countless others, steaming into the distance like incarnations of destiny. One day he hoped to take one of these ships. Meanwhile the river was a good substitute.

'Where does this river run to?' a stranger had once asked a Glaswegian.

'It runs to America, ye silly bugger,' was the answer. Down past the boathouse and the lights it ran, to America.

Eirich agus tiuginn o, he thought.

In the morning he awoke, stiff as an oar.

FOUR

I

EVERY TIME HE climbed to the top of Gilmorehill he stepped
into a dream. It was a dream in which there lay below him a wild
panorama of buildings, where thousands of people still lived in
the Victorian Age, out on the mudflats of civilisation, on drear
islands of English industrial towns untouched by any tide. Side by
side with these, the Middle Ages strangled like creepers the lives
of Balkan villages, though ghosts and dwarfs were more alive and
gentle there than the cold, inhuman horrors and shadows cast by
twentieth-century industry and inhumanity wearing the mask of
science, or the cones and triangles of factories and chimneys
building a geometry of trance.

The thing was to bring abreast of each other these contemporary centuries of the mind until they too were spread out and
visible as in the panorama below. It was very difficult. To those
who still lived in the Victorian Age that Age was very real. To
those who still thought of the summer of 1914, that summer
was a panacea. To those who still hoped for the return of the
good old days of golden sovereigns, there was no other criter-
ion of the normal. They felt no other history. One and all they
finally swarmed like flies around any one of the gigantic
buildings and institutions that still seemed to promise them
some thwarted form of salvation – the Bank, the Infirmary, the
Church – in them depositing their panic, their savings and their
wounds.

He stared down.

By Alexandra Parade, where his father worked, stood the giant
block of the Royal Infirmary, a strange Sing-Sing, redolent of
skyscrapers, courtyards, small doors and endless haunting corridors; frozen with mirrors, stiff with women in white, like secret
nuns, overflowing with fast cars and alarums and flowers and
knives and sudden, overpowering chloroform.

Once his father had had a weight fall on his head, cutting it
open, and had rushed round, clothed from head to foot in blood,

to the Casualty Ward, where a small staff fought off immediate disaster amid blood and repression.

They took it for granted he had been in a riot, or perhaps a fight with the police, who were not always scrupulous in their choice of heads.

At the entrance to this factory of devotion there stood a large clock which punched you a ticket saying when you came in. He had one of these every time he went round to the bacteriologist's with a parcel of piping, to watch by the laboratory-door through a haze of aprons and flames, the slow pickling of disease. It was a mysterious process, grim with ordered purpose, unlike the jungle peering through the small windows outside.

Beds lay out in the drowned sun. Patients coughed, and the sound was like paper softly blown over wide playgrounds. Out on verandahs old men, paler than primrose, lay back into breathless white cushions.

Once a year from its towers of mercy there started out through the imprisoned city a strange white chain, called the Children's Flower Procession. It had one small band, the BB (standing for Boys' Brigade), with pipes, flutes and drums. Long files of children in white, escorted by their parents, walked along the cavernous streets on a carnival of thankfulness, bearing collecting-boxes for the infirmary of wounds. The girls, dressed like brides, the boys like pages or clansmen, marched to George's Square, where they joined May Day processions of joyful horses, red banners from the ironworks, silken Masonic emblems hung with tassels, and the needle and thread of beflagged Church Orders, until, in waves that scattered into a thousand rivulets by the river, there swept over Glasgow Green one giant tide of mercy and revolution and temperance and labour and love and charity and fruitfulness.

Glasgow, from the hill, was always attempting in incoherence to free its own rude pagan vitality, and anything served to rouse the currents hidden in the recesses of these canyons.

Next door to the Infirmary lay the Cathedral, where the blood was dead, the Regimental, the Highland, the Covenanting blood, draped in the grapeshot of silken colours, and the receding waves of headstones in the Yaird. Next to that again stood the silence of sealed and turbulent Barlinnie, a feudal castle of broken hopes and criminal intentions, more feudal, more criminal than the blood and neglected death lying opposite. Farther down still, the North British Goods Station, releasing fleets of drays, wove steadily through this whole incomprehensible politic a python of horses swallowing carts, and a long rope of tails, mooring to the banks of the Clyde undesirable economies of dirt and abuse, until finally the city came to resemble a ship being boarded by pirates.

These were the activities going on around Whitehall School and Gilmorehill. They deafened the still tomes in the libraries. They drowned the ineffectual voices of the teachers. They made drunk with the illicit stills of romance the sober schoolboys with their books, in which the real pirates were symbols of Romance. The colossal plunder of Nature in the mining of one and a half million human beings was ignored. The pirates were in command. The defeated walked the plank of poverty and death.

There lay the Tron Steeple and the Tron Gate, dating from the days when the city had gates like floodgates, and down from Barlinnie, the Gallowgate – foundation of an orgy in the 'Killing Times.' By Langside lay the Battlefield where Mary Queen of Scots was utterly defeated in 1580 by the followers of Knox. That to Scotland he thought was the greatest defeat ever suffered, greater than Flodden, greater than Culloden. He could see the Queen poised on a white charger, awaiting the outcome of the battle, and her dogged, glib-tongued opponents tearing down her cavalry as at Drumclog, fighting down first all the love for women in their hearts to build the grim prison of Calvinism for their country. The ruin of that image, he felt, was the ruin of the Scottish matriarchy, as Culloden was used to discredit Scottish manhood.

It was why women could not rule and why men ruled too harshly; why his mother was unhappy, her father dour, and his own father a relentless fighter. It was why his mother said to the minister: 'We don't think enough of the Virgin Mary in the Kirk!' surely the most daring thing said since the time of Jenny Geddes.

It was why religion was the one vital thing left in an emasculated country, though he felt obliged to renounce it. Above all, it was his mother demanding the whole love of his father; Mary and Knox, Eros and Ananke. Yet her love too could turn to violence and tyranny, from the multiple poisons of disappointment.

England, they said, was a matriarchy still. In Scotland the matriarchy was dead. Women there were good housekeepers, not good mothers. At least, he thought, they had avoided that horrible concatenation of corrupt power which produced the doggy English female, the English matriarch, supreme in the riding-breeches, tweeds, bowlers and blotches of over indulgence in physical appetite for power, with all her absurd pretensions to agility of limb and potency inexhaustible.

'At least,' he said aloud, 'we were spared the pervert and the lesbian for rulers when our rulers were betrayed. Power may consist in the inhibition of conscience, as conscience is nothing but the inhibition of power, but women have no conscience and therefore can have no real power.'

'You're telling me,' said Rollo. 'They're pussy-folk. Ever notice them in the German tutorial? Men pool their sex. You know what I mean. They neutralise it, in a kind of comradeship. Women sit in isolation, like creatures of prey, doing nothing but growing their hair and painting their nails.'

It was true. Only motherhood matured them, yet in spite of that they remained largely immature. Even their cosmetics and their rouge, derived from days of blood and gunpowder, were stored against the cadaverous obedience of some future love.

'I hate them,' he said.

'I love them,' said Rollo.

'Well, the burgeois ones, those who have so inherited cadaverous obedience that they feel their very bones to be property brought to the marriage.'

Why? How could he? Did he hate his mother? Was it hatred of his mother that made him hate Mary, and hatred of Mary that made him hate his environment? Did he hate his environment because he hated women, or vice-versa?

'You must suffer from mother-fixation,' Rollo said.

'OK,' he said. 'I'm not an engineer, so I have a mother-fixation. There is no escaping industrial perdition is there. No escaping the conical sections of perversion!'

There lay the adult dream, where the figures were not the spontaneous emanations of his fancy, but animals, in various stages of rut or fetish. He could not stand aloof as with the cardboard-theatre. The vision was stereoscopic. The figures walked out of the screen and ran round him, claiming validity, infecting him with their own nameless excitement, demanding interest and approbation, participation in their schemes and ultimately even his servitude; after which he would cease to be of any interest.

First it had been violence in the fist-fight with Ingins.

Most, it seemed, never grew out of that stage. The strange fear of sex which had conceived these children in violence also embedded and rooted them in violence, so that they could never grow up, but lived out their lives in a wasteland, a class division, a mental age and country within the frontiers of the comic strip.

He, too, was ashamed of sex. It was sissy. Emotions were sissy.

It was sissy to cry and sissy to love and sissy to have anything but
hard muscles bunched for action like Buck Jones. None believed
violence derived from emotion, or that emotion was the mainspring of action. Accepting action and aggression as independent
phenomena they sought them everywhere – in the boxing booths
to which his father took him, at the markets, and on the battlefields, where they were confirmed and canonised, and condemned.

That was still a battlefield down there. He saw the OTC
coming back from a route march. Miners were a finer army.
Any man in the street with a cause and the average amount of
courage was a finer soldier than these dolls. Theirs was a ritual
mania, a khaki Hengler's, a form of ballet unrelated to any
conception of war. The rifle and the bayonet, the 36 grenade,
and tommy-gun, were not the important things in that secret
society, but the drill, the inculcation of a correct attitude of mind
they had the impudence to call character. Such leaders, he
thought, over-anxious to step into the harness of type and tradition, were less the embodiment of the social virtues than the
expression of the ruling social neurosis. Rulers wielded power,
and power, Lord Acton said, corrupts. Already they were the
corrupted. They had begun to imagine corruption a prime
necessity for the attainment of power. They had become a fount
of disease.

Like the great bell in the tower, its clapper silenced, the University
hung suspended over the city, a shell. Noticeboards in the empty
rain stood like shop windows with nothing to sell. Around the
quadrangles drifted black gowns and red, whispering of corporate
life and social events, but ultimately the students walked apart, so
many doctors intent on diagnosis of their own reasons for coming
thither.

This pile was indeed visited only by doctors and engineers. It
was one of the first martyrs to science. It had become a factory for
industrial design, a clinic for inventive practitioners, since vivi-
section on the social body was to be encouraged. More rarely, it
was a museum or grave for the Humanities.

From the front he looked across the drifting cloud and smoke
toward Glasgow. Tenements in the foreground loomed like
gigantic ships' hulls. Behind, lay Townhead of the royal-blue
lights and bleeding heads, light blue suits and red ties, with the
Cathedral and Barlinnie Prison, like Fort Bay. He always thought
of the Bastille as a kind of impudent Barlinnie. The horse-

droppings helped. Nearby stood the City Hall, amid dung and straw and houses like horse-boxes in the rain. Over them the clouds floated, like wraiths.

Nothing had happened between these walls since Adam Smith.

With Stott and Currie and Rollo, he walked through the tiny doorway and joined a group of medicals.

'Nice corpse this morning?' tittered one.

'Was she a virgin?' sang Stott.

'Tee-hee-hee!' smothered Currie. 'Anatomy, what crimes are committed in thy name!'

'You are discussing Glasgow and you don't know it,' he said.

'Glasgow,' said Currie, the wit, the Polonius. 'Let Glasgow flourish!'

He glanced round and saw Poole, a wizened, dark-haired individual with recessive eyes, blush and hug his bag tighter. All the best in his life was crammed into that bag, out of sight, so that he might earn a position as a mediocre preventer of the young.

'Swotting away, I see,' said Stott to him.

'I haven't even read yesterday's lectures yet,' said Poole, turning away and heading upstairs, his eyes screwed up behind his glasses in a girn of concentration.

The bell tolled. The quad filled with monastic and nun-like shapes fading again into the concrete. Rollo appeared mysteriously still at his side. He liked Rollo. Though he was unaccountably brilliant when the occasion arose, he was also aware of the uncomfortable panorama beyond. It was a pity his awareness had no issue except in calculations regarding engines, pistons and table-rapping. When he spoke, his voice was a monotone metallic as a low-pitched bell.

'We had a nice time last night,' he said. 'Quite spooky. The table answered three times. You ought to try it.'

He spoke without moving his lips, looking straight ahead. His eyes were of evanescent blue. He was strangely attractive. He was Banquo.

'Coming up to class?'

Class today was the weekly rambling lecture on Gothic architecture by Professor Gow, delivered in German and illustrated with lantern-slides. As it droned on, and the Roman arch was succeeded by the Norman arch and the final crown of the Gothic arch, David had plenty of time to think. He was tired of being dogged by the Goths. To the Professor every close in Glasgow had a Gothic arch, or should have. There must be some mistake.

He thought of the problem of value. It was the first attempt
David had ever heard at a rationale of things. Value, of course,
was purely economic. No attempt was made to link it up with
value in any other sense. That would not have been 'Pure
Economics.' It was strange how much vice and abuse and
debased living was connived at by 'Pure' Science and 'Pure'
Economics. They dealt with the skeleton in the cupboard –
Economic Man. Yet, one would think, there was a Political
Philosophy or there was not. It seemed no, there was not. Philosophy, too, was studied separately, as 'Pure' Philosophy, under
many guises, the latest of which was the 'greatest good of the
greatest number,' while the world outside was falling completely
apart. Nevertheless it must all have been relevant *once*, say during
the bourgeois revolution in Scotland, when Watt harnessed
steam, and the necks of millions of his fellow countrymen, born
and unborn. It all meant nothing whatsoever to Rollo, who could,
however, regurgitate it with a quiet efficiency. Lecture-room or
barrack-room? David was not quite sure which. What a pity there
was no Department of Social Psychiatry to give the old place a
good spring-clean! Already he could see large spider-webs forming on the ceiling and on the stairs; large wrinkles growing on the
forehead of the professor, and on his breast great silver fish, that
might be the Legion of Honour.

Once or twice, he had indeed caught a glimpse of vanished
splendours, even in German. During the capping ceremony in the
Great Hall, for example, the whole audience of students and
visitors had stood and sung 'Gaudeamus Igitur,' and other
student songs. They sang with such fervour, he felt he was
unknowingly attending a mysterious initiation, like those of which
his father had told him in the Masons. These graduates in robe
and gown acquired significance as part of a freemasonry hitherto
unsuspected. For a moment they gathered the force of Druids.
What could it mean but a survival of belief in the only community
worth having – the community of the intellect? What had he lost
in Whitehall but that same sense of community? Surely that was
why he had listened to the waterfall behind the stairs, trying to
remember and recapture that comradeship?

In the evenings, in the German club, they sang old drinking
songs and ballads of the 'Wandervogel' deriving from the days
when travel for a student or apprentice was a convention having
the weight of compulsion. Then there was all the vast community of European Humanism to be explored, with its craftsmen
and students. Now there were few craftsmen. Their tradition

was being ground underfoot by capitalist society. A gulf divided the 'intellectuals' and the 'workers,' as if students and apprentices had not belonged together from time immemorial in the only association ever known, the association of creation, and the only Republic worth having, the Republic of Work and Thought!

The Sorbonne, with its various colleges of the nations, lived on in the Nations of the University of Glasgow, though no one dared remind the Scots students of their ancient ties with Paris, and the 'Auld Alliance' was become part of the same drunken impotent sentiment attendant on 'Burns' Nicht.'

In those days, he felt, life was accepted as picaresque. Goethe wrote his 'Wilhelm Meister,' but the 'Sorrows of Werther' no longer convulsed a generation that had buried natural feeling with the impact of Freud. The world was imagined to be crumbling because perruques and back-scratchers were no longer *à la mode*.

He, too, would have his 'wanderjahre,' in which he broke with everything and everyone, and sought his own era among the friends of Ronsard.

'After all,' he said to Rollo, 'the English Universities destroyed Humanism. They moulded education around the growth of an Empire, and reduced the Universal to the Imperial. They and they alone are responsible for the mortal wounds inflicted on the modern world in the name of Physical Science and Imperial Government.'

'My foot,' said Rollo.

'What is the aim of education?' he asked. 'I say to produce free men and women, responsible for their actions and decisions, and of independent spirit and judgment. Instead, what do we find? A host of echoes of the imperial spirit. A set of clerks in the Imperial Civil Service. Education by the die-stamp.'

'Balls,' said Rollo. 'Balls.'

'All right, Milton, Newton, Smith, Shelley, Mill were all civil servants manqués. Scotland never had a court. There was no Fergusson, Burns, Dunbar or Henryson. English art and letters since 1800 have shown unparalleled development.'

'What are you talking about?'

'A nation of clerks,' he said. 'And a nation of office-boys to the North.'

'Remember,' he went on to Rollo, outside, 'the Renaissance was no divine accident. It was not discovered like America, by any Columbus of a monk. It was the expression of the rise to power of the bourgeoisie of Genoa and Venice and the Hanseatic towns.'

'The monks preserved the manuscripts,' said Rollo, 'in their cells, all through the Dark Ages.'

'In their body-cells?' slavered Stott.

'Yes,' said David. 'Yours are adapted for a different purpose.'

'What's that?'

'To serve as hogsheads for bearing whisky down to posterity.'

'Hurrah! Here's to the good old whisky, it makes ye feel so frisky!'

'In what did the Dark Ages consist?' asked David. 'In the fall of chivalry, or, shall we say, the decay of feudalism. It was the period when power was becoming centralised into the hands of princes who beat their rivals down. There is nothing sacrosanct about tradition and family or the age of murder. Absolute kingship, divine right, was the first blow at feudalism, not the invention of gunpowder, because it was the first blow at chivalry. It was the first manifestation of the future struggle for naked power, and the birth of power-politics.'

'Sure,' nodded Stott. 'What the hell did Edward want up here? The Hammer of the Scots? Well, he got a hammering all right! "See approach proud Edward's power, chains and slaverie!"'

'The bourgeoisie did not rise to power till after 1789,' said Rollo.

'They rose to world power then,' said David, 'but they had lost their *raison d'être*. The Renaissance was finished. Why do you think was there no renaissance as we know it, in Russia? There were Chronicles there, as old, if not older, than those of Froissart, those of Nestor and Avviakhim. Why?'

'The Russians were out of touch with Europe,' said Rollo.

'I'm out of touch with this,' said Stott, 'bugger this for an argy-bargy!'

'What Europe? Venice and Genoa. There was no bourgeoisie in Russia. None ever grew there. Theirs is the Twentieth Century Renaissance, the Era of the Common Man.'

'Bullocks,' said Rollo.

'If you say so, perhaps,' said David, 'but I think not.'

'Why doesn't Gow say all that?'

'You *are* a bastard, Davy,' said Stott. 'You'll get no marks for that high-flown tosh in June. You're nothing but a sucking bolshie.'

'Your mother must have been frightened by the Bogey-Man on the stairs,' said David. 'Besides being useful for holding up a hat and filling a fortuitous space between the ears, that portion of bone directly above your nose can be used for visualising sights and sounds and links unapparent to the naked eye. Did you know that?'

'You bleedin' pig!'

'Stick to the prescribed books,' said Rollo.

'No, they present the Renaissance as a sudden and unaccountable treasure-hunt. A vast Hunt the Slipper, an archaeological expedition into the deserts of history, and by God they *are* deserts!'

'Nothing of the kind.'

'It was less a time-discovery than a passing of the arts of culture into new and eager hands.'

'Ooh, I'm a fairy,' shouted Stott, gadding about and throwing his books in the air.

'I don't agree,' Lew said, coming up. 'The paintings, the writings were already there. All that was lacking was the will to explore them by those who had the power to sway men's destiny. Why should they? They had all they wanted. Their interest was in ignorance and superstition. That is what is meant by reaction.'

'What do you mean, all they wanted?'

'The power of initiation and decision. The bourgeoisie raised these to new heights, with the force of a revolution. You will never have your National Scotland,' he said to Rollo, 'as long as the bourgeoisie retain the power of initiation and decision. Growth of empires was incidental. Power had already passed to the middle classes. They created the civilisation of the Adriatic in the Middle Ages. They failed to create any in Sheffield or Pittsburg. There was more raw material there, for manipulation.'

'Bullocks,' said Rollo again.

'I suppose you think this bloody place is civilised because you can have a cup of coffee in the Union for 2d,' said David.

'You old Gow,' hissed Scott. 'I've a good mind to drop you one.'

He and Currie were invariably together. They hunted in pairs, Stott and Currie, the one with the long jaw of the kangaroo and the same height and slouch, looking for something to put in his pouch; the other the bright weasel, teaching his grandmother to suck eggs.

'What does your mother vote, Wullie?' asked Stott in a sing-song whine and whistle.

'Tory,' said Currie. 'She doesny know what she's daein', but I'm going down to the Corporation today to see Bailie Gie-muckle. There's a teachin' job goin', and tae hang wi' bein' put on a waitin' list!' he chuckled, slightly slavering.

It was cowardice that inspired his ambition. To Stott, on the other hand, the Varsity was a free bank where the blank cheque of a degree might be cashed, which by some incomprehensible miracle was at once exclusive and universal.

'Have you been to the Adviser on Careers yet?' he asked.

'I'm going now,' said David.

'For Pete's sake don't say you want to be a teacher!' gittered Currie.

'Why, is the profession overcrowded?'

'Overcrowded? It's worse than puttin' your name doon for a hoose, intit Harold?'

'Aye, that's right,' said Stott; 'honest,' and nodded his head in emphasis.

'Whit are ye gonny be anyway?'

'I think I'll try to find out what being a man is like for a start,' said Rollo.

'Dirty dog. He's a dirty dog, inty Mac?'

'You don't understand.'

Hundreds of students thronged the stairs, waiting to see the Adviser on Careers. Every now and then, in the irascible tone of the overworked doctor or psychiatrist, they could hear the scream of the Adviser: 'Get to bluidy hell out of here! Next!'

No doubt he was sick of interviewing the prospective leaders of a nation at 2d a time. No doubt he was appalled at these candidates for the world coming up in wide-eyed droves, but, felt David, he might occasionally have remembered that his tragically useless advice had been made compulsory.

He was also the Adviser of Studies, a post he filled equally well.

'What do *you* want?'

'Nothing.'

'What are you here for then?'

'On instructions.'

'Course?'

'Arts.'

'Honours?'

'I hope so.'

'What do you mean you hope so?'

'One never knows.'

'Subjects?'

'French, German, Economics.'

'What are you going in for?'

'The Civil Service, I hope.'

'You hope a lot, don't you? Come back next year.'

It was time he had a drink. They were just open.

'No more today,' he shouted through the open door.

Stott and Currie were waiting in the quadrangle.

'You ought to take Philosophy.' Stott said.

'The history of philosophy,' said Rollo. 'There's no philosophy in this place except the philosophy of bowdlerism.'

'I'll buy it,' said Stott.

'Hee-hee-hee,' Currie tittered.

'It is a racket,' David said. 'Rollo's right. It's not a question of believing in something or investigating something up here, but of being able to read the minds of lecturers and examiners and serve up in a palatable way what is wanted upstairs. With the proper kitchen-maid mentality there is no telling how far you will go.'

'Is that whit ye do in Economics?' asked Stott.

'Are youse two Malthusians?' lisped Currie.

'I believe in limiting population, but not by discouraging marriage,' Rollo answered.

'Surely ye know that marriage is only a fertility rite?' said Currie in surprise, laughing and baring his teeth like a horse.

'I can see you limiting population, you ram, you,' Stott said, jaw more pelican than ever. 'You would press on the means of subsistence all right you would.'

'We all press on the means of subsistence,' said David; 'that's what we're here for.'

'You don't quite get me, does he, Wullie?'

'I hope no'!' sneered Currie, convulsed.

'Malthus gives a static picture of a dynamic society,' said David. 'What is needed is a sociology of change.'

'Whee-whee, Stott, look,' said Currie, 'ain't she a nice bit?'

'She's certainly a hot momma,' Stott said. 'I wis an accident. Were you, Mac?'

'Do you use contraceptives, Mac?'

'You know, these airships?'

They gazed at each other and burst into desperate laughter, holding their sides like boxers punched in the stomach. Currie's teeth were clenched and his eyes stood out of the sockets as though he were being throttled.

'Jack-of-all-Trades,' said Stott.

'Master of One,' giggled Currie.

David gazed at them. Their attitudes were frozen compulsion, like the movements of a Javanese dancer.

'You should come into English Lit. with us, you really should, Mac,' sang Stott.

His lips pursed when he spoke, and his cheeks contracted as if he were sucking something delectable.

'We read the choicer bits of Chaucer and Burns, dain't we, Currie?'

'We sure do,' said Currie. 'It's all we do do.'

'You *are* a bastard, Currie; did yer mother no' tell ye?' laughed Stott, shaking his head, so that David could see he suffered from St Vitus dance.

'I suppose you're St Paul?' grinned Currie.

On they raved, in their happy communion of unacted guilt.

'Women to you are unpurged images, are they not?' he said.

'Listen!' squealed Currie. 'Who's talking!'

'You don't recognise the voice,' said David. 'English Lit. and you don't recognise the voice?'

'It's got a cold,' said Currie.

'As I said,' repeated Stott, 'I'm an accident. I used to swim about in a green bottle in a chemist's windy. I came into this world when the rubber tore.'

They rolled about the pavement, wrestling and grabbing at each other.

He knew what that meant. All along Buchanan Street where processions of carters in convoy marched proud horses, there were dark and furtive shops disguised as herbalists, and surgical stores, claiming to sell bird-seed and artificial limbs, but dispensing in reality rare books; cigarette-cases, with naked women on the front, containing four sheaths; as well as whirling-sprays, enemas, and other medical items to be sold only under the twin disguises of hypocrisy, and pornography.

'Are you taking a degree in French Letters?' sniggered Currie.

A crime was fastened on their hearts like a leech. How did they propose to assuage that crime? By the crime of the usurpation of power. Was there no end to the Hamlet sequence?

'He's the strong silent type,' Stott said. 'He doesny have tae answer that, do ye, Mac?'

'Hahahaha,' Currie staggered as if struck, holding his stomach.

Mary had marked him for life. He could not laugh, remembering the Christmas three years before when she had disappeared along the back in a shimmering white frock, like an apparition. It was then he had thrown an india-rubber into the gas-fire in the room for a bet. Sparking out, it had permanently marked his left hand. The white patch of skin was still there, under the last knuckle, like a weal. At the time he had not realised why he did such a stupid thing. He knew now, watching them caper like monkeys.

The thing seen against all lack of purpose and direction was its soul and inmost spirit. To a novel or a picture the same applied as to the individual life and will.

'Spit it out, Mac! Whit dae ye think?'

'Unless and until we are given full and final freedom we will not accept responsibility. Until State and external authority are dead – together with economic exploitation of one man by another – we shall not act, for we shall be incapable of true action. There will be no action, only reaction; no literature, but only the mouthings of fearful fools; no philosophy and no wisdom, but only the cunning thought that hides knowledge from the majority, to employ as an instrument of oppression. The ultimate power – the sanction of force – must be broken before this book or that book or any book can be given direction or purpose or form, or life itself brought to accept what we are pleased to call responsibility, but which is only awareness of action.

'Hurrah!' shouted Currie.

'Hip-hip-hooray!' screamed Stott, throwing his cap in the air. 'Whit a swot, eh Wullie? Where did that come fae, Mac? I know, Stevenson! Or was it Dr Johnson? God forbid it should sound like Johnsonese!'

'I was just practising,' said David.

'Well, ye'll get nae marks for that here, willie Wullie?' Stott bawled, and Currie slapped him as they ran off. 'The great lexicographer!' they shouted.

He turned and went into French.

It was a currycomb curriculum. The French Professor, precious and precise M. Prince, Chevalier de la Légion, not unfortunately Etrangère, possessed an exquisite accent owing largely to his habit of sucking his beard.

'*Balzac est le plus grand romancier!*' he said, kissing his hand in the air.

He hissed when he mentioned Flaubert. One did not read Madame Bovary among the prescribed books, but La Légend de St Julien, or was it the tobacco? To him in his gallic enthusiasm, there *was* no Tolstoy, no Dostoievsky, no Gogol, not even a Zola. Was he, could he be still, a dreyfusard? He conveyed the impression of being a piccolo pétain, with his head so full of flags and trumpets and slightly swashbuckling honneur that he could not hear the sub-machine of Louis-Ferdinand Céline in the sewers.

To David, fresh from the Russian class, where at any rate a sense of history was instilled, he represented the punctilious decadence of Tsarism, the satin-bearded, the satyr, exquis.

'*Victor Hugo est sans doute le plus grand des poètes français,*' he added.

French poetry stopped at de Musset. There was no Baudelaire, no Rimbaud; Ronsard here like Villon was a medieval aberration.

M. Prince was ably seconded by M. Gold, who carried a small Gladstone bag and cultivated a Latin moustache in memory of the Paris busses. Sweeping in on the eddies of his gown, he was greeted with cries of: 'Good morning, Dr MacPherson!'

Chief clown in this musical comedy was, however, jovial M. Leblanc, who ought to have been expounding de Maupassant and Paul de Kock instead of 17th century drama. He hoped one day to rise to the position of ringmaster.

If art was a stripping of motives, a search after truth, a process of historical indexing, a *prise sur le vif*, the place of these gentry, felt David, was surely the Empire Music Hall, not Gilmorehill.

He was therefore glad when the gong sounded and he could reach the comparative sobriety of the Economics Department, though there, too, nothing was up to date. The very walls exuded weariness in their damp, and the prof. lay across his chair like a tired Roman Emperor in his toga, unable to touch, far less digest, a morsel of the wondrous banquet lying around in profusion; sipping Godwin, putting a fork in J. S. Mill, parodying scripture with a bored gesture, yet the scripture was there.

He dealt with the problem of value at great length, in order to relate it to nothing in particular.

'Wrap up the affairs of State in my fish and chips!' said David to Rollo, but it was no laughing matter.

As the professor rambled on David dreamed an English lesson.

'Let us consider today,' the professor said, 'the extravaganzas of the word "shop." Probably the most important word in English or any other language. "Nation of shopkeepers," said Napoleon. Not, you will notice, shopwalkers or shoplifters, though a good case might be made out for the latter, but shopkeepers, "Keepers of the Privy Shop." The derivation of shop is not clear. "I'll shop you," says the army, which may or may not mean "I'll treat you as a piece of goods" – an empty threat in any case, for are not soldiers merely the goods sold up the river in the War Shop? Not that the War Shop is a knocking-shop. Heaven forbid. Knock – you may knock – but it shall not be opened unto you, is Holy Writ, or should be writ, but we must not get on to the subject of writs today.

'The shop is one of our most cherished institutions. It is mentioned in the Doomsday Book, wherein occurs the entry – Rent of Shoppe – Nil – Desperandum, telling us of the acute economic crisis of the period. One does not even need a shop in order to be able to shut up shop and go home. A shop is literally forced on every infant at its birth – the children's shop. No matter whether it call itself a church, an office, or a gallery of art, a shop by any other name would smell. Psychologically, etymologically, epistemologically, it is still a shop where goods are sold, and here we have the key to the entire symbiosis. The town is a shop. The whole country is a shop, and we had better sell out quick if we wish to make a living.

'Housing shortage? Mm, yes. But who ever heard of a shop shortage? We talk shop, we walk shop, we tuck shop. Home, Guards, and at 'em! Export or fly! As Chaucer skylarks in the Old Wives' Tale: "Honey, suet queue, mail ye pence!" '

It might have been said of the Professor that he had spent so much time learning how to think that he never actually thought. He was a sub-division of Hamlet. Moore on Logical Positivism he found so fascinating as a proposition that he sat for hours wrapped in the contemplation of mere ways, incipient channels of thought, angles which, however, never taught him tolerance. Like the spider, looking all ways, he rarely missed the chance of swallowing a passing victim.

'No, no, not fundamental!' he said with a dyspeptic look. 'The relation of methodology to metaphysic and to the biology of human conflict is much more cogent than apparently you realise!' Throwing aloft a frown, into the snows of his Tibetan thought, until he could smell the bacon and, in later years, the curtains, burning.

He was an unlaughing dwarf with a brow like a giant John Bull. His temples bulged like the dome of St Paul's, and he knew everything, for he had read all the books that ever gathered around him. He walked, if it is of any consequence, with long flat strides like a determined duck, quite *pregnant* with consequence, eyes huge and revolving, like the butterfly's eyes, imprisoned in a bottle. He rarely smiled. Such is not the habit of those to whom life is earnest, or who have discovered, little by little, that life is real and must be given a purpose, *their* purpose.

When once he did laugh, however, a revolution broke out and rapidly spread to every part of his face. This is not to say it required a revolution to make him laugh, or that laughter inevitably entailed a revolution in his nature. Those with an English love of compromise know how one can laugh without meaning it, so that the personal revolution is not really one, or revolt, laughing, so that the political laughter is real but not a revolution, if you follow. His pupils seemed to pop out of their sockets, and his head jerked forward as though he were being strangled, while his face grew purple. That was the moving into position, the strategy of his laughter. Then he half rose from his seat, propping himself up with stiff arms and a low rumbling came from the direction of his stomach like distant gunfire. By devious routes the rumbling reached the throat. The isosceles triangle of his face collapsed on its apex the chin. The eyes protruded more and more on to the cheeks. The cheek-bones stood out. The man seemed *hungry*! And blood-vessels filled with red made a blotch on the face. It looked like a retching fit, but no, no, no, he hee-hee-hee-heaved and *laughed*, shaking his body and filling with blood that egg of a head – a sack of tilting potato-delight!

'There will be war. It is absolutely certain,' he hissed from between his teeth, eyes poking forward in prophetic trance. Invariably in his later youth he dealt with 'absolutes' and 'fundamentals' and other cabers tossed from his gut.

In a way he was a symbol. His books were so many fallen leaves, authors in hibernation. Yesterday a summer-house of culture, a challenging tower of the intellect in the days when each ivory tower shone like a lighthouse, now withered at a breath of war and winter, tumbled into ruins, burned, if necessary, by the new-born pagan suckled in a creed out-worn at the merest hint of a trumpet blow.

He was one of the sects moving in a dream of their own making, a dream not even war or the dissolution of all they held dear could break, the dream that the exclusive ideal, the madness of each would overcome all the others. This was the Imperialism of Thought. Their only belief in democracy was as a vehicle to ensure the supremacy of their particular dream. Would they still cling to a democracy in which their own private dream had been defeated? Pacifism? Personalism? Anarchism? Would they attain that love? The pot and the kettle. The whole political set-up, he felt, as he read Muggs on Political Theory, was an elaborate camouflage for personalities and libidinous leanings. It was a crude struggle for power by men ignorant of conscience, and devoid of reality except the reality of a few small minds asserting their blindness over that of the others.

The one hard fact was a cliché: the means of production were not in the hands of the people. This had been said so often that no one listened any longer, but one day they would have to listen, when internecine conflict would so isolate and destroy the fabric of communal living that there would be nothing left for people to do but direct the machinery of production, much as a passenger on a bus might have to drive it, on finding the driver dead at the wheel.

The gong sounded again.

'Let's get out of here quick,' said Rollo.

Every day during break David walked with Lew and Rollo in the grounds of Kelvingrove, his mind caught by the classical lines of a church in Doric style, or the windings of the ardent Kelvin.

'You're so clever,' said Rollo to Lew, 'you're a chameleon.'

'How am I a chameleon?'

'Adaptation to a background of self-colouring is a feature of jungle life,' said David.

They walked along towards Keppochhill Road humming the Stein Song.

Keppochhill! – a name full of the sound and fury of the Western Isles, sea and soft rain and landing-stages constantly awash. There were plaids in it, too, and something altogether wild and tameless and immortal. Rollo, he felt, would understand that. Looking up, he remembered as a child going along this street on a tram one Saturday afternoon when the city was gradually growing into a vast revelation. There was a Symphony Concert for Schools in St Andrew's Halls.

The tram was full of boys. As it swayed and rattled, the long pole gave off red and blue sparks. They sang and whistled sitting upstairs in a crow's nest, even passing the loud cemetery with its pearls of lilies and white stones set within rusting red railings of fleur-de-lys that guarded the marshalled dead.

On the other side lay a steep cutting, a viaduct and then a mine. It was absurdly like hell and purgatory. To the boy, the compact ugly images of the town were wedged together so tightly that their associations were difficult to extricate. One had to be an archeologist to sift their significance. Most people ignored them and sailed about in trams and trains as in a dream not of their own making. They pretended this intensity was not there. They called themselves practical people, surrendering themselves to the blind and ruthless forces that had built up this environment.

Schools for crippled children, iron playgrounds for those not yet crippled, nursing-homes and public-houses, succeeded each other with bewildering swiftness as the blue car sped down its slipway like a yacht. A dizzy coma of whitewash and placards blossomed on a field of hoardings. They read: BEER IS BEST. Twelve hundred and fifty-two shops displayed a myriad of goods in small windows before they reached Charing Cross, and Charing Cross itself was one enormous bay-window of furs, home safes, gigantic castellated wedding-cakes and super undertakings through which these matchless goods might be owned for no less than quite a temporary slavery. No feudal village in the thrall of tyranny, no medieval city in mortal fear of hostile neighbours, nor buried ruins of Colosseum or Carchemish had ever thrown up such a monstrous brood of terrors, such a catalogue of idols of introspection as this modern city of whip and fetish.

The Halls themselves were grim and grey. They were like Barlinnie, or obstacles on a battlefield, imprisoning promise and tokens of thought. Children in a horde stood outside, like beggars, holding warm sixpences. Yet when the music began inside, it set everything dancing, the wires, the seats, flowers, trams, cemeteries and shops, and made the river speak.

On the way back they passed the Kelvin Hall. He remembered that too! All the winter it had been a raging sea of coloured lights and laughter, a vast, impersonal rushing noise, like the wind, filled it like a sail. That was the wind from the Whales.

Every year there were the Whip, the Hammer and the Whales, groaning up and down their green and red and purple turbulent mountains. There was the Hall of Mirrors, where your head was bigger than your body and your stomach bigger than your head and your legs two inches long. That made them all laugh. Different mirrors inside made you different shapes. Even in the same mirror you were a different shape if you walked up close from what you were if you walked away. How could you ever be sure what you were?

His mother was a different shape from his father – but she wasn't really.

They were all comical, spherical gnomes of no meaning but laughter. They were all gaunt, elongated lozenges with no desire but hymns of praise and emptiness. Or else they were bumpy, wart-like freaks, offspring of the illusion of sin. It all depended on the way you looked at folk.

He liked the Fishing Pond. It had real water, not a mirror. You paid 6d for a rod which worked by magnetism, and there were tin fish, of which he caught six. They were more magical than the prize, which was only a small box of chocolates, mostly ginger.

His father preferred the Hammer, where he always rang the

bell, or the punchball, which he always nearly burst with a powerful right you could 'see leaving the house.'

When at last they tired of walking among these vast acres of booths and incalculable enterprise, laden with coloured balloons and pogo-sticks and dolls and wally dugs, they met a smirr of rain outside, that melted the lights into liquid roses and crocus.

He loved Glasgow in that dark and mist just before Christmas when all the shops, like Trerons, contained a little Kelvin Hall of jollity and fun, with an office for Santa Claus.

In the tram again he sat back relaxed. It was a blue one, so there was a blue light behind the blue glass knob downstairs. The thing was a blob of swaying clanging light. And, once in the house, he went to bed dreaming of dwarfs and heads balanced on sword-blades on chairs, and of other near-perversions, preferring always the music of the Whales, whose voices were the vast organs of the deep.

'There's Mr Pan,' he said, pointing to Stott in the distance, 'the boy who laboriously grew himself up by adding to his stature every week until it was taken for granted that his mind was suitable for long trousers.'

'Let's avoid him,' Rollo said. 'We can go into the Mitchell.'

His friends were cultured in so far as they had risen above culture. Meeting them, talking to them, were so many parts he did not deliberately act, but was forced to act because of the theatre, the décor in which he found himself, not false, real enough, but not totally he, a scene in which he was being fitted into a jacket too small for him, like Professor Gori in Pirandello's story 'Marsina Stretta', part of a concatenation of circumstance to which he owed no allegiance but the allegiance of affection.

To them, Pirandello was of little interest. They were content with their triple catalogue of books, one for class-reading, one for general reading (the University Library) and one for private reading (the Mitchell).

In actual fact, private reading was both prescribed and pro-scribed.

'The whole place is for illiterates; no reading but public read-ing, no thinking but public thinking are encouraged. I can't stick it,' said David.

'I'm finished when they give me that degree,' said Rollo. 'I'll never open another bloody book.'

'Lucky you. I want to tear out the Hidden Index. I want to be an "Unqualified Reader" in some Museum.'

'You're a fathead. You'll only ruin your eyes.'

'The only department worth a damn is the Russian Department.'

'How?'

'In Russian literature you find an interest in people of all classes, merging always beautifully with organic feeling for nature and classical language. Read *A Sportsman's Sketches*, or *The Death of Ivan Ilyitch*, in the original. That interest was the tremendous motive power that shaped the Revolution of 1917, but there is no account of contemporary Russia here.'

'They're all Bolshies,' Rollo said, 'Are you?'

'The only vital force in the contemporary world is allowed to rot in a small corner of one quadrangle,' he went on, 'while vast new departments are built to house the eternal fantastic engineering by means of which Scotsmen try to build bridges to one another.'

II

'It gives me great pleasure . . .!'

'Yeah?'

'It gives me great pleasure . . . repeat . . . pleasure . . .'

'Liah!'

'I repeat,' said Sir John Suckling, 'it gives me the greatest pleasure . . .'

'YEAH?'

'Really!'

He was standing on the platform in the Debating Hall at lunchtime. The place was packed with students in search of a little colic, or bucolic, or alcoholic entertainment from the speakers in favour of the various candidates in the Rectorial Election.

'My purpose in coming here,' he said, glancing apprehensively at the gallery, 'is to speak . . .'

'Who's stopping you?' squeaked a voice. Two streamers floated gracefully down from the tiers. A long blower almost touched his nose.

'I do not propose to make a set speech and certainly not to outline the policy of HM Government . . .'

'HURRAH! HOORAY! Three cheers for Sucker!'

'But if I can answer any questions, or clarify any issues . . .'

They stood around watching him, smoking, eating pies, drinking tea, mostly with considerable scepticism. He fingered his tie nervously, Secretary of State for Scotland, not knowing what to expect from these barbarians.

'Does Sir John consider 15/- a week sufficient to keep an

unemployed man and his family?' shouted an undergraduate, leaping up.

'That raises an interesting question,' said Sir John. 'The view of the Government is . . .'

'Does Sir John consider 15/- a week sufficient?'

'You must take into account the price-level and the index figure for the cost of living,' shouted Sir John, losing control for a moment.

'ANSWER THE QUESTION! GO ON, ANSWER THE QUESTION!' they cried from all over the room.

'Then there is the point about Purchasing-Power Parity, known as PPP!'

'PPP,' they squeaked. 'PPP.'

It was the chief letter in their vocabulary.

'YES OR NO?' bawled the questioner.

'NO!' screamed an angry Sir John.

'HURRAH!'

'G.K.C. was better. He took all the sting out of the attack by demolishing himself.

'I am painfully aware that I am not one of your light Scottish riders,' he began; 'nevertheless, I think I may say that I attach a great deal of weight to any question. (Laughter.) Whether I am right or wrong, my view is bound to bulk large in any argument. (Renewed laughter.) In fact, I may be said often to dominate the proceedings by the mere preponderance of my presence . . .' (Applause.)

They liked this cheerful old man and would not permit him to debunk himself. What a pity he was a Distributist. He was the most brilliant of the speakers.

It was all a jape, of course, a 'rammy' like Charities Day. Now David remembered how he had envied as a child the gaily-dressed students on their Roman carnival. Here he did not care to join in. He could see the junketings were less gay than he had imagined, more reminiscent of the drill and mascara of some weary chorus than of Venetian nights. Instead of masks and palazzi and love under the moon, there were collecting-boxes rattling bones or dice and behind the gaunt Gothic shapes of the hospitals there lay the waxen masks of the dead, to quell his riot. For the others, however, it was still a sheer rammy, a riot of jollity and unlimited licence, although of the meaning of their Saturnalia they had no conception. Only a few sad-faced classicists perhaps, with gold and bronze medals in honour of a defunct empire, stood by and saw, not Donald Stott and Wullie Currie and Lily Weather wearing rumples, but a satyr and a goat and a Maenad, more alive than the gargoyles of George Square.

They walked out of the Union, leaving Stott and Currie, and along the dung- and straw-littered cart-track of Eglinton Street, past the Drill Hall of the Rover Scouts where he and his father had once seen the Scots boxers beat the Danes. Carl Hansen was there, the wizard of Rangers.

'The Pope is only infallible when he speaks *ex Cathedra*,' said Quinn.

'He's always infallible,' Rollo said.

'He isn't. That's a Protestant heresy.'

'Listen,' said Lew.

David looked up at the wires, thinking perhaps a bird was about to sing. Combined, their feet rang on the endless flagstones of nightmare. A city shrouded in a blanket of cobbles wept by his bed in his dreams.

'Listen,' said Lew's comforting deep voice, 'say the Pope says in private what he said *ex Cathedra?*'

'Ah, but he wouldn't!'

'But just say he did? For argument's sake?'

'Then he wouldn't be infallible in private!'

'That's illogical,' Lew said.

'I can't help that!'

Quinn laughed. He was a queer fellow, hungry and desperate-looking. His face was pale, the cheek-bones prominent, and his eyes bulged balefully behind the thick lenses of his glasses. Yet his hair, dried in wisps of innocence, and laughter, were as delicate as his voice. When he spoke, the rising and falling tones were unmistakably Scots, though he was of Irish origin.

'Stuff it,' said Rollo. 'You're always wrangling about the Pope. Why can't you talk about something decent for a change? I saw Lily today.'

'Lily who?'

'Lily who? Lily Weather!'

He thought of the day of the Orange Walk on Balgray Hill, when, all unsuspecting as you were, you would be seized by the shoulder and look up to see an upraised fist and hear the challenge:

'A Billy or a Dan?'

It was impossible to guess right. It was Bullies' Day.

'Tell us about her,' he said.

'I've asked her out next week.'

Rollo was a Son of the Manse, proud of his deceased father's library on witchcraft and warlocks.

'Better to marry than to burn, eh?' said Quinn.

Rollo was burning.

'Do you believe in free love?' asked Lew.

'If I can find it,' Rollo said, looking straight ahead, carrying his attaché-case, like some prim parson.

'Do you?' he asked David.

'I don't know. If free love means a rammy as public policy, no. Most people seem to take it that way. If it means the absence of marriage and the basing of cohabitation on sincerity of feeling, yes, but what does it mean?'

'If your wife wanted a man, could she have him?'

'She probably would. There would be something wrong with the marriage.'

'Not necessarily.'

'I'd decide that. Not you.'

'It's all in Ognyev's *Diary of a Communist Schoolboy*,' said David. 'In practice it doesn't seem to work.'

'You mean people are possessive?'

'Of course they are possessive! How the hell can you possess a woman if you aren't possessive?'

'Possessiveness has nothing to do with it. The trouble is in sticking to principles, revolutionary or otherwise. Love or marriage is a private affair. It must be free. You cannot impose freedom, like the Irish democrat who said "You are all free to vote as you like and if you don't we'll damned well make you!" ' Lew said.

'It's all a question of sex,' maintained Rollo. 'If the sexual attraction is strong enough . . .'

'French salaciousness,' said David.

'It's true,' put in Rollo. 'Now, take Lily Weather . . .'

'Is she like the weather?'

'I don't know. She agrees with me most of the time. She says it's because she loves me.'

'That's bad,' Lew said, 'bad, bad. If she loved you she'd be the opposite of you. She'd oppose you just for the fun of it even.'

'Sex and love,' said David, 'are like 2 and 4, the one contains the other; but if you go around thinking two *is* four, your measurements will be badly out.'

'The Puritan,' Lew said. 'Listen to the Puritan. Looking for the ideal woman.'

The writhing discontent of Glasgow coiled in their bones.

Lew and Rollo were doing well. So were Quinn and Poole. Rollo was outstanding, but careless of success. Lew was steadily brilliant with a tight-lipped brilliance. In the French library,

David, however, sat and read the wrong books for hours, Lar-
baud, Rimbaud, Verlaine, Baudelaire, Apollinaire, not the prescribed de Musset and Lamartine, resenting the establishment so
soon of alien criteria. In Economics, too, Godwin he found more
interesting than Mill, and Keynes than Stamp.

'You won't get your degree,' Stott said, nodding. He had taken
to wearing a cap, what they called in Glasgow 'a hooker,' or a
'skippit bunnet.'

'I don't care,' David said. 'I'm tired of traps and snares. If I
could start all over again I'd concentrate on philosophy, though
after Wittgenstein, it's hard to see what could be done except to
create a new organic philosophy. A degree is only the visa on the
passport of serfdom.'

'Serfs, eh? Did you hear that, Stott?' Currie said. 'That's a good
one, isn't it, Stott?'

'Are we serfs, Mac?'

'The most backward examples, for you do not yet realise the
fact of your serfdom.'

'He's a caution,' slavered Stott, 'in't 'e, Currie?'

He looked at David with menace, shoulders bowed, the long
tapir-face drooling.

'So we're serfs, eh? We ought to scrag him, Currie. Whit dae ye
say?'

'How long do you even devote to Scottish Literature?'

'Four weeks.'

'No Chair in a Scottish University. Shame!' he said.

'Listen to the serf,' Currie said. 'A Chair of Scottish Literature.
He wants us to study Rabbie Burns and Harry Lauder.'

'Dunbar,' David said, 'Henryson, the Makars, Fergusson,
Hogg, Drummond, Burns, Byron, Stevenson, Hume, Grassic
Gibbon, isn't that enough for you to be going on with?'

'There's nae dirty stories in them,' Stott said. 'We only read
dirty stories. That's why we like Chaucer. The Scottish Chaucer-
ians are only derivative, in't they, Currie? They lack Chaucer's
genius for the bawdy.'

'The body?' howled Currie.

'If that's what you like, why don't you take your degree in
pornography?' asked David. 'There's a nice list of prescribed
books at the Barrows: *Moll Flanders* and Maria Monk.'

He remembered the purple and crimson covers of books he had
seen, like deep-sea fauna. He had come on them one Saturday
afternoon, and all the way home, past the rattling trams and red-
brick factories, had tried to remember the posture on the cover. It

was lurid red and purple, with a girl lying in déshabillé on the bed, the flesh pale-cream above her stockings, under the title 'Damaged Goods.'

Arriving at the house, he found no one in, and stood looking at a puddle stretched half-away across the road. It was a soft yellow round the edges. Children with sailing boats of paper and matches for masts were kneeling by the side of it, pretending it was a pond. Standing there, he felt the liquidity and lability of everything – the sky brightening up after a shower of rain, like a tear-stained face; the chalked sandstone walls of the houses glistening like the hide of a beast, and the sliding ooze and worms lured up through the spongy ground by the sound of rain, coiling pale in the soiled water.

Even his memory of the picture faded fast. He could not hold it. The woman became floating and shadowy, but the conception of the picture remained. Did people think like that about women? Were women really like that?

His aunt came along the street with his mother and they went into the house together.

'I suppose I'll be seeing you here with your girl soon,' lisped his Aunt, with her red smile.

'No, you won't,' said David, angry and embarrassed, thinking of the one he liked and feared in case she should become one of those living mummies.

For a moment he saw the picture again clearly, and then his aunt's voice re-echoed in his ear, ancient in its 'harpy' wisdom: 'Oh, yes you will. Boys are all the same.'

She made him prefer the picture to the reality, the lurid to her, while children sat before the puddle pretending it was a pond although there was only the puddle. They had no pond of clear water.

'We don't know anything about Maria Monk, do we, Currie?' he heard Stott say.

'Na, tell us about it, Mac?'

'Yes, come on, tell us. What's she like?'

'She's a woman,' he said, 'not like Lily Weather. She doesn't care about agreeing with you or disagreeing with you, so as to attract you. She has no bait, except her appearance. She's honest.'

'Suits us, eh, Stott?' leered Currie.

'Her appearance is everything desirable. She has full breasts, well-rounded hips, just the right curves, and a lovely face, and she is content to be herself because she feels how real she is.'

'Where does she live, Mac?'

'She lives on the covers of a book on a barrow in Renfield Street,' he said, 'where you put her.'

III

'And how are you getting on with your lessons?' asked his uncle.

'I don't have lessons any longer. I have lectures.'

'Well, lectures then,' laughed his uncle, waving his hand as he sat himself on the window-bottom to watch the trams at the foot of the hill.

'I'm still learning.'

'What are you going to do?' asked his aunt, peering at him as though frightened or puzzled, wrapping her fur coat more tightly around her.

'I don't know.'

They were waiting for his father to finish tea.

'How's business, Johnnie?' asked his uncle, in quite a different tone, partly worried, partly patronising.

'OK, Norman; a bit slack.'

'Aye, it is that,' his uncle said, paring his nails with his fingers.

'What do you think of things?' he went on, turning to David, as if he had just remembered. 'You're studying economics aren't you?'

'Yes.'

'He's a Socialist,' his father said, as if secretly glad, though he himself was a true blue.

'What? No' a spouter?'

'There *is* an unemployment problem,' said David coldly.

'Socialism won't cure it,' his uncle said. 'You can't change human nature.'

'The gap in your argument is a chasm,' David said. 'You imply unemployment is in the nature of things; also that it is necessary to "change" human nature to cure it. Ergo, you can't change human nature. A large statement, coming from one who is said to believe in Christianity, and also a tragic one.'

He was quite white.

'Christianity is different.'

'What do you think your Christ would do,' said David, 'if He came into Glasgow now? Join the Kirk? Read *The Citizen*? The Scots have lost historical vision. They seem to have lost a sense of the eternal as well. A greater pack of money-grubbers and robbers would be hard to find. They are probably the one nation to *sell* their country, and later to hush up the deal and boast of it.'

'What do you mean?'

'Read Burns on the Union:

> We're bought and sold for English gold
> By a parcel of rogues in a nation.'

'That was a long time ago,' laughed his uncle.

'It's now a national custom. It would not be so obnoxious if it weren't wrapped in so much religion. Glasgow, according to an English parson, in tonight's paper, is a city of top-hats and churches. He thinks he is praising it! The Stock Exchange has taken over the Kirk!'

His uncle laughed uneasily. His aunt paled and bit her lip.

'It's right enough, Norman,' his father said. 'Religion and this money business don't mix. Not that I'm much of a one for religion.'

'God and Mammon,' said his mother.

'I'm neutral,' David said. 'You're the Christian. Or should it be Pauline? Christ, you know, did not want to be worshipped, but emulated.'

His uncle rose in a fury.

'Ye can't change human nature,' he shouted.

'Do you imagine that your career in usury has the remotest connection with Christianity? You are elevating your own faults into universal ones, like the capitalist everywhere. You may be right, but if you are, let's have no more platitudes about education and democracy.'

'My oh,' said his mother, 'these boys are on the wall again. I'll soon put a stop to that.'

She, too, was white with anger.

'I'll burn the balls that come over, I will.'

'They're *devils*,' she said.

'They're not,' said David. 'They're boys.'

'I was ten times worse than they are, Teenie,' said his father with a gust of sanity.

'They're your Socialist friends,' sneered his uncle. 'What's yours is mine and what's mine is ma ain! Eh?'

'If your creed is different,' said David, 'what are you belly-aching about?'

There was a sudden silence.

'It's sixes and saxes,' said his mother surprisingly.

'Norman,' said his aunt. 'We'd better go.' Her face was drawn.

'Eunice will be waiting.'

'Aye, O weel, good-bye Teenie.'

'By Heavens,' said his father, 'you certainly shut him up.'

'He's my brother,' said his mother, weeping.

'He asked me what I thought,' David said. 'I told him. You had a father as well, who lived in this same house, and had the very same trouble with your brother. He stood for something else than narrow-minded greed.'

'He widnae come and see us at a',' his father said, 'if it wasna to collect the drawings every week, for his bank.'

'How dare you!' his mother said. 'He comes to see me!'

'All right, all right, have it yer ain wey!'

'Oh dear, oh dear,' his mother whimpered, 'what I've tae stand! Some day I'll just run away, I know I will, some day!'

Her mouth began to work spasmodically, up and down, and no words came. She was drifting into a state approaching hysteria, in what he thought a subtle assertion of her own will. He saw his father pale and grow alarmed. Going up, he tapped his mother smartly on either cheek.

'Stop it,' he said. 'Don't frighten Dad like that.'

He had done it more for her than for him, but that was the way to say it.

'David,' she said, sobering at once, 'how dare you! I can look after myself, thank you. You are exceeding your competence.'

Afterwards his father thanked him.

'Ye're no' very fair to your uncle,' he said. 'He offered to put you through your studies if anything happened to me.'

'It was a nice thing to offer,' said David, 'but what makes him so sure I'd accept?'

'You shouldna say these things. You only hurt your mother.'

'I'm sorry, Dad.'

'I'd rather have seen you a boxer,' he said, 'or a mechanic, but I see you can do other things. Good luck to you, my lad. Don't be a wild man though.'

'I'm not as wild as I sound sometimes,' he said.

'And don't, ever, hurt your mother.'

'I'll try not to,' he said, 'but I think I know her sometimes as you don't.'

'Don't be too sure,' his father said, smiling. 'Now I want you to pay attention to this bit of lamb I bought today. It'll melt in your mouth.'

He held out his palm. On it lay a choice piece of meat, like a large red jewel.

'Ye'll no' find the spit o' that on a King's table,' he said.

Wrapping it up as if it were a gold nugget, and putting it away: 'Come awa' into the room,' he said, 'and we'll hae a crack.'

'How do ye like living in High Cartcraigs?'

'It's wonderful,' he said. 'Norman didn't want it, so I bought it. This is where your mother's family really belongs you know. The Laird has a "Quoich," and a model of Crookston Castle your great-great-grandfather made when he was a prisoner in the Covenanting days.'

'Why don't we ask for it?'

'Don't be silly,' said his mother. 'There's Ian Halley going up to the Life Boys!'

'I said why don't we ask for it?'

'Nancy said a wee loaf would be better to be eaten a day or two old,' she said.

'It's ours, isn't it?' I suppose he ought not to have been imprisoned in the first place.'

'The Finlays first came here to put down the Covenanters. Isn't it funny,' his father said.

'I didn't know that,' said David.

'I've a favour to ask ye,' his father said. 'I want you to come to Fairlie on Sunday. Will you?'

'Yes, of course.'

'I'm going out to Sanny's now. Are you coming?'

'I'll get my coat.'

He knew what to expect. His father still went to Sanny's Piggery, where he had once garaged his car. Sanny was a boyhood friend of his and they kept up the old association.

'You'll please him a lot if you come. Since you won that scholarship he thinks you're it. He'd like you to give Frank some tuition.'

'I'd rather not.'

It was more exciting to stand beside a large vat in which pig food was boiling, on a sunny morning, listening to the crack of Sanny and Bob Andrews and his cronies than to go to lectures in the University. These men meant what they said, most of the time. They lived in a dramatic world equally removed from the dilettante and the bureaucrat.

'So this is him!' Sanny said with a laugh. He was very small. 'This is the boy. Ye should be prood o' him.'

'I'm still a better man than he is,' grinned his father.

'That's what you think, Jock.' Sanny gave another giggling laugh. He was wearing old trousers and a belt and clogs. His shirt was open at the neck, and collarless. The sleeves were rolled up, and in his mouth, upside down, hung the stump of a discoloured clay pipe. Every now and then he punctuated his remarks with an eloquent spit. His voice was hoarse from much smoking, and husky too with concealed emotion.

'He's a good yin, Jock!'

'He'll have to be a good yin to be as gallus as his faither!'

They all laughed again and David felt embarrassed and miserable because they treated him as if he were somehow different. 'Gallus' was his father's word. His father was full of such words. He did not know where they came from, but they sounded good. 'Gallus,' he supposed, meant 'Gallic,' 'Gaulois,' like the garb of Old Gaul for kilt. It might be written 'Gallice.' It might be a French borrowing. His father would have been astounded to know.

They looked into the huge vat in which the pig food was simmering and bubbling. Sanny stirred it with a long pole. It was overpowering.

'Wad ye like tae see the pigs?' he asked.

They walked round the sties, where old boars and colossal sows wallowed and slept amid glorious filth.

'The dirtier they are, the healthier,' Sanny said. 'There's a mint o' money in dirt.'

He looked like a schoolboy overjoyed at an excuse to become as dirty as possible.

'How did ye make oot last year?' Mr Macrae asked.

'Bad, Jock, bad. The swine fever cleaned me oot,' he rasped, spitting quickly and heaving a sigh.

'I'll make a fortune next year though wi' a' they young yins comin' on.'

Sanny was always making a fortune. He never did.

They strolled over to the old railway carriage that served as quarters for the men and drank some tea.

'Hoo are ye gettin' on, David?' beamed Sanny.

It was rather a strain till Bob Andrews arrived, with pendent cheeks and a ruddy complexion formed into the jolliest expression imaginable. He was on the dole.

'He's a weel-read fellow,' his father said.

Bob was a Socialist.

'Whit dae ye think o' things?' he asked David, directly.

'Rotten,' David said. 'A pack of criminals in office set themselves up as saints.'

'Ha-ha-ha, hear that?' Bob asked Macrae, delighted, as if it were the best joke he had heard in years.

'Oh, he's red-hot,' his father said, not at all displeased now it seemed.

'Well, who's no'?' said Bob. 'We've had enough o' this for twenty bloody years.'

'Ye're no' a Socialist are ye, David?' asked Sanny, paling at the thought of losing his fortune before he had actually made it.

'He's a bit that way, I'm afraid, Sanny,' Mr Macrae said.

'Weel, he should ken,' said Sanny manfully. 'What's gonny happen tae us?'

'More and more crises, and then a war likely.'

'Jeez that's a fine way to cheer a man up.'

'If you don't alter things yourself,' David said, 'nobody will do it for you.'

Bob nodded cheerfully.

'Ye canna stop it,' he said, delighted. 'He has haud o' the richt end o' the stick!'

It was distressing that they believed not only in what he had to say but also in the 'learning' that was to be acquired at the University. The only learning worth the name was the learning realised in their arms and in their labour, but they persisted in imagining there was another.

'There's only one thing aboot him,' Mr Macrae laughed, 'he'll no' roll up his sleeves!'

'Ye canny blame him for that,' roared Bob. 'It hasnae brocht you hellish much!'

They screamed with laughter again.

'I work too,' David said. 'We all work.'

All three wore caps. Macrae had a rubber collar and a bow-tie. Bob wore a muffler and lived in a 'model.' They all remembered more of revolution and oratory and history than he had ever read. They had heard John Maclean and Guy Aldred and Robert Busby, who could sway thousands and might have been Prime Minister in a new revolutionary party, but for his sudden, never-explained disappearance. They spoke of men like those as they did of boxing champions who had finally lost their crowns, and now they were listening to him. He felt small and ridiculous. They only listened out of politeness, because his name was Macrae. They had faith in nothing but their own right arm, and perhaps a dim future in which rough justice would be done. Meanwhile it was best to be 'gallus,' to be cheerful and tough and self-reliant. Awkwardly David felt that he was by no means 'gallus' enough in his day and generation.

They had a tremendous respect for what they called scholarship, and yet their sons, the new generation, were betraying them. It was easier to betray them than to fight their errors and prejudice and lack of knowledge, easier to say 'yes' and then betray them. They asked for betrayal because they demanded confirming in their prejudices and hates, and thereby connived at the same deadly dangerous social system, and the same stupid errors of acceptance, they wanted to fight. Currie was betraying these men, and he was the most dangerous of traitors since he knew he was betraying. His china-mask of a face – the high cheek-bones and cunning eyes gave him the appearance of a Tibetan priest turned bandit – admitted his guilt and boldly laughed because there was no denunciation. His own father was a worker, but the sole idea of people like Stott and Currie was to rise out of that class and live in a cardboard bungalow full of paper hopes on some railed-off hill, secure in awareness of a fractional superiority. They were prepared for sacrifice, but it was the sacrifice of others. They were the new generation from which 'Scotland' hoped so much, and what they were becoming they did not care. Stott and Currie, identical in bullying egos.

Compared with such masterpieces of synthetic conscience as those 'products' of the educational system, David thought Sanny and Bob and his father wonderful people, but it was impossible to make them realise how wonderful they were. They regarded themselves as patient carthorses like the ones in the city, born for toil and sweat and worthy of no more. They talked of 'getting out of harness.' They were people of humility in that they had no desire for power and dominance. They left that to others, and here perhaps they showed awareness of true power.

'Oh, he's a worker all right,' he heard his father say. 'He'll read his brain into train-ile some day.'

'Hee-hee-hee,' laughed Sanny, without taking his clay pipe from his mouth, as if choking. His hands were thrust down into the forepockets of his trousers.

'Ye're an awfu' man Jock.'

IV

The people who lived at the top of the little hill differed from the people who lived at the foot, along the traffic-lined streets. It was not only that they had a little more money at their disposal daily. The houses at the top were often detached, or 'semi-detached,' whereas those at the foot were mainly in the form of tenements. Then the walking up and down the hill developed from a simple exercise into a kind of ritual. Unconsciously the hill began to symbolise effort and sacrifice merely by being there. The view from the top was said to 'reward' all one's efforts, as if it had not always been there but only appeared, like a magic vision, to those who had worked hard. Yet the sight of the smoking valleys lent a sense of detachment to David apart from any effort, except the effort to get out of the place altogether.

In winter the hill was covered with ice in treacherous webs, over which people gingerly stepped on their way to the chores they called 'work,' confusing toil with assignation. Sometimes a horse would fall down; and for hours make gallant attempts to rise, thrashing with its hooves on the cobbles and macadam, and striking fire among the sudden sightseers from the roots of flint. On these dark mornings when sparks leapt from the masts on the trams, emitting a blue flare, David felt its dim significance and was disturbed at his inability to put the scene into words. Sometimes then in a storm the slates would be ripped from the roofs to sail through the air like magic carpets, whilst the chimney-cans themselves spun merrily like boiling kettles on the hob.

At the very top lived richer folk, doctors and ministers, and Luke Sharp the accountant, whose daughter they said acted 'awful well-off' and had a hare-lip and eyes like two frogs, frozen full of laughter and mockery. Mid-way lay a row of semi-detached houses, starting with the Hendersons, whose son was apprenticed to a CA at half-a-crown a week and wore a bowler hat, and was tall and always clean, past the Pierces, prim, till fat, moustached Mr Pierce cut his throat in a lavatory, and ending with the Simsons, whose walrus father, a locomotive fitter on half-time, had been smashed up in his motor-bike without any compensation. Straggling downhill then to the bottom came a row of little cottages, once whitewashed, now peeled, with small windows and flagstone corridors that made every step a harbinger of doom.

He passed them on his way downhill to meet Maclean. They filled his mind: an absurd, ugly little world of irreconcilables. He was going to a meeting where they would be reconciled. It was upstairs in a tenement. Maclean said it would be good, and at least it was not connected with the luxurious pipe-dreams of the University.

There were two rooms, so small that seven people crowded the house. In the middle of one of them stood a short, plump figure with a coat on. It carried a stick which it kept banging up and down on the floor as it swore. The place was knee-deep in newsprint.

'Well, what do you think of it?' the figure rasped to David. It was obviously a great man.

'There's more intellectual activity here,' said David, 'than in the University.'

'What d'ye expect?' growled the irascible man.

The New Gael, 1d.; The Organ of Scottish Self-Government; Scotland the Milchcow of the Empire (Lord Derby) crashed the headlines on the sleek paper.

'I'm going to build this up till its circulation is in bloody thousands,' said the man, and you could almost see the circulation of his blood as he spoke.

'I've been addressing meetings in Edinburgh,' he said. 'The Fuller Life idea will sweep the country. Of course you are familiar with it?'

'The credit part, yes,' he said.

Maclean nudged him. He went on.

'Some people, though, say that there mustn't be enough currency in circulation to buy all the goods in the country, including capital goods, for that would lead to inflation.'

'Tripe,' said the man, 'bloody tripe.'

'I make no apology for the economics of scarcity,' David said, 'but I don't want to be forced to buy a steam-engine. I don't like steam-engines. Yet unless I take part in the process called making a living, and promise to work at making engines and wireless sets and cars and buy, eat and drink and sell engines, wireless sets and cars, I'm called an agitator, not only by the Government, but by everyone, including you and Fuller.'

'Bloody tripe,' repeated the man, the veins standing out on his forehead.

'Where am I wrong,' David said, 'granted I hate steam-engines?'

'Scotland and credit go together,' the man said, stamping his stick. 'You can't have one without the other. You are a clucking anarchist!'

'I am a man who likes to know the name of the street he lives in,' David said, 'and where he is going. I think James Watt was a bloody anarchist, and a dangerous one. His mental aberrations did in fact change society in the way he wanted it.'

'You must have vast credit,' the man said, 'for everyone.'

'Now you blackmail me,' David said. 'I can only be free, I can only be happy if I buy your bloody steam-engine. Is the country populated with teenage morons? What are you trying to do, hypnotise me?'

'Do you agree with the abolition of the price-level?' asked the man fiercely.

'As long as there are prices, how can anything be free?' asked David.

'Look,' the man said, 'if you have any difficulties, I wish you would write to me about them.'

He had now adopted the superior attitude of the missionary who does not H A V E to save souls for Heaven. His party was one of seven other national parties, though what was national about any of them was difficult to discover, considering that one and all of them had lost, almost irretrievably, every trace of national feeling and consciousness in the frightful greed and disordered chaos of the Industrial Revolution, for which their own ancestors had been at least partly responsible. They lived in the smoking ashes of a country more ruined and plundered than Europe at war. *Glasgow, Lanark, Barrhead, Motherwell,* were as Scottish as *Pittsburgh* or *Magnetogorsk* or *Chung-king.*

'Now what did ye want to go and do that for?' asked Maclean as they went sideways down the narrow whitewashed stairs – like those in a lighthouse or a dungeon.

'What Scottish architecture owes to the prison principle is better not investigated,' said David.

'He was going to help us!' said Maclean in the gas-lit close.

'He calls *me* the anarchist,' David said, 'while *he* helps *himself*.'

'Does that matter?' asked Maclean. 'Only Scotland matters.'

'Now there's where we differ,' said David. 'To you Scotland is something tangible, apart from the people. You are like the prophets abroad who oppress the people by talking of the nation, or the war-lords in London who even talk of the "British Nation" – which has as much reality as the American Nation. Did not an eminent English critic recently write that he would not trust the future of English Literature, or even an expression of English Literature, to a Scots-man? Why, then, should a Scotsman be expected to entrust the political destiny of his country to Englishmen?'

'I agree,' said Maclean. 'That's what I mean.'

'Why talk about the "Nation," anyway? The "Nation" is a dying fiction. You should go on talking of the people. There *is* a Scottish people.'

'We must recover a sense of nationhood,' said Maclean, 'like Ireland.'

'I think we must first recover a sense of identity,' said David. 'Until we know who we are, there's little use in finding out what we are.'

'That's too high-brow,' smiled Maclean.

Sometimes he looked like Stalin.

It was difficult to reconcile such living movements with the dead and moribund activities going on at Gilmorehill. At least they did not give doctors bodies to dissect which were composed of rotten and putrefying flesh. Nor did they instruct engineers by means of models of Roman and Greek engines. Only in literature and in the philosophies was it necessary to prevent anything remotely touching modern life from being discussed. The Classics, he suspected, were revered for the same reason as Christ or newly-deceased poets, that they were dead and their resurrection was not an immediate danger.

He tried to read as instructed, but finding it more and more impossible, looked forward with misgiving to the tutorial examinations.

On examination day, his nerves, uncontrollably on edge when he entered the room, crystallised into strained politeness at the sight of the examiners. He stood, he felt, too stiffly, behind a chair, until the Head motioned all four to be seated.

After an impressive pause, questions burst like bubbles from the pompous historian to be answered in a mechanical falsetto by the girl. It was obvious she had learnt her notes by heart. Her answers, he thought absently, resembled an after-dinner speech in all but the speed with which they were uttered.

Awaiting his turn, he watched the over-fed diplomat across the eminently suitable green baize table be now as agreeably surprised and now as unpleasantly startled as a diplomat ought. He heard, too, the clock before the bumptious chairman tick with maddening precision. It seemed as divorced from the proceedings as its maddeningly precise owner, who interrupted importantly now and then on catching some familiar name, but more often dozed.

He watched the chairman awake from a day-dream to dismiss the girl with one of his outworn platitudes: 'You must work steadily.'

It was not his turn yet. Playing the same game as the two fat little men, he outdid them in orthodox gravity. They had regulation falsefaces, he an expressionless mask, slightly darkened by the frown that passed over his features.

Catching it by chance, the chairman inwardly approved the results of academic training, while the youth was thinking how damned impertinent were these fatuities to have spent their time conniving at expenditure in blood and lives, while knowing themselves to be incompetent. He resented passionately their dogmatic impudence in teaching and requiring unformed youth to train in their movements and complexes of thought. He was amused at their smugness, sickened at their duplicity and afraid of the mysterious power whose tools they were, a power reducing to impotence by its silent and ubiquitous oppression, the power that lay in the hooves of stampeding herds. Who could restrain or direct this inhumanity? He suppressed an absurd desire to begin by stunning both of them with the clock and started up. It was his turn.

Stumblingly he answered the easy questions put to him. He felt now only contempt for the machinations of Metternich, and though he knew the answers well enough, lacked the desire to express them.

'What happened at the Congress of Troppau?'

He wanted to say: 'Austria desired the murder of blasphemous Italians demanding peace and freedom,' but instead he stuttered. The corpulent diplomat had a spasm of benevolence.

'The fellow knows, but he cannot express himself!'

The fellow did know. Intrigues by brainless wirepullers treating the earth as their preserve, and eternity as a stop-watch, had cost human puppets their slender lives. Tsars found inspiration for Holy Alliances in unholy mésalliances; honest men sacrificed their country's honour out of patriotism; the vicious circle spun ever quicker and wider.

The fellow could not express himself, other than by action.

He thought of a little yellow nation five thousand miles away which had learned such diplomacy and was blowing to the sky the culture of ages and the wisdom of the world. He wondered how its victim would react, and 'express itself?' The chairman awoke.

'Thank you,' he said ungraciously. 'Come back in a year's time. You will be better able to express yourself then.'

Outside, he met Lew and Rollo again.

'Hello,' said Rollo, 'how did you get on?'

'Horrible. Next year I ought to do better, he says. I doubt if I'll be here next year.'

'Why? What are you going to do? You have to justify your existence, you know!'

'For me it is enough I exist. What will you do when you leave?'

'Teach, I think.'

'You'll be good.'

'I'll teach them the opposite of Rollo's witchcraft in a rational Catholic school,' said Quinn with his speared smile.

'I'm going abroad,' David said.

Was it running away? From his city? From Mary? From himself? Or to find himself?

'Escapism,' said Lew.

'From what to what?' asked David. 'Go and paste up a poster if you want your words to stick. There are two ways of looking through every microscope. I'm tired of looking through one end only.'

No more sitting in sunlit trams in the mornings, rolling and swaying up to Gilmorehill to stop before the Union. No more gossip before morning lectures.

'I've been writing for G U M ,' Rollo said, 'but their punch-and-pseudo humour does not appeal to my taste.'

'Where will you go?' asked Quinn.

'America.'

'The new Pilgrim Father.'

'I'd only be doing what hundreds have done in the past.'

No more Mary Watson, no more evenings at the cinema, no more hope of renewing the friendship. He had a daemon that drove him on, whither he did not know.

Home he went on the rollicking tram to his attic in Cartcraigs, where they now lived, to the silence of the old house and to the tracery of the giant tree, like a wood-cut framed in the high cabined windows, home to the blackbird that sang every morning before his awakening.

How could he explain that he was not going to be a colonist, or an emigrant, or a refugee? Unless indeed he were a permanent refugee from the human filth and ignorance and depression and prejudice and cruelty of cities built by an Industrial Revolution which had made a mockery of man's liberties? How could he explain that he was leaving only as a gesture of war on these and their like? This monstrous perversion of Nature had begun to assume a life of its own – apart from the will of those who struggled in its mire and squalor.

To find a touchstone for the present age they must return not to the Middle Ages, not to the puny French Revolution, nor to any of the metrical measurements of former history, but to Stone Age Man, who by his discovery of fire conquered the animals, only to find them in his brain.

Ever since the Stone Age, man had walked, not upright, as confident scientists had depicted him, in distinction to the ape on all fours, but upon two crutches. One crutch was called Weapon, the other Self-Righteousness. These two were called into being to

balance the horrible creature that was first able to stumble about
outside its Cave of Terror.

The Atomic Age, or the Age of Space, had knocked away both
of these props. The Weapon, just at its most terrifying, was most
meaningless, for Self-Righteousness no longer held any justification. Yet was there ever such fear and yammering? Self-Righteousness had never been justified, except as the second crutch.
Yet now there was a mass fear, dark as the Dark Ages.

Man since the Stone Age had sought in the external world for
justification of himself. This process he called 'rationalism.' Now,
unleashing even the myriad caverns and corridors of the atom,
and still finding no justification of 'himself,' would he finally see
his story as one of growth and maturity? Would he, sooner or
later, cry out, throwing away his crutches: 'Away with palaces and
pomp and courts and finance and authority that bind me like so
many threads for Gulliver. I will Live; and for that any "justification" is both an insult and a mockery!'

Was a new Pre-History about to begin? Were the dinosaurs
revived in another form, endowed with power over life and death?

It would be said that the evil was not in the city but in the way the
city was run. It would be said that the evil was not the machine but
the way the machine was run. In a way it was true. Any improvement in control – especially workers' control – would help to tame
the gigantic animal. Only centuries, perhaps, of workers' government could disperse the monstrous creation of unbridled human
greed and superstructures on the Ego, into the depths of the
countryside where it belonged, so that its political power and
perversion would be of no more consequence than slugs on
cabbage-leaves. The destruction of this monster was the prime
task of all Government. That was the Disarmament of the Mind.

Communists said 'the withering away of the State,' and were
not always too explicit about it. Hobbes called it Leviathan.
Fascism was its ally. His mother would have said the 'Beast from
the Bottomless Pit.'

His exile was not escapism, for these tentacles were all over the
globe. It was an exploration, like the Joycean 'silence, exile and
cunning,' only this time preparatory to attack.

He thought of Mary, the Queen of his Elfland.

Perhaps he was going to find her country.

They were waiting for Mrs Macrae, to drive her down to Fairlie.

'Let me tell you a baur,' his father said. 'You know Big Jock,
eldest o' the family, and the most ignorant and unscrupulous as

well. The whole district knows him for a crooked fool. Well I went
to his faither's funeral yesterday, and he was a disgrace.

'He went to lengths in and out o' the business that no' even his
brothers would have credited, but the auld man knew it a',
Teenie.'

'Ach, I've heard a' this before,' she said. 'I'll away and get
dressed.'

'During the war every one of his machine-shops was making a
fortune, but when one of his assistants tried to buy a place of his
own, dae ye ken what he did? He did the dirty on him. Although
the man was honest and working for him eighteen hours a day, he
bribed the factor no' tae let him have it. Twenty years later, he
gave that same man a cheap gold watch, "For 25 Years' Faithful
Service." What a mockery! He wadna take it. I know. How dae I
know? I was that man.

'Huh, aye an' afore that even, when he knew his faither was
dying and went to see him to thank him, if you please, for leaving
him one of his shops, do you ken what the auld man said? "It's a'
richt, Jock," he said. "You were stealing it aff me onywey."

'The dirty swine was pilfering the till and wangling prices for
his ain benefit.

'He's no' happy though. That wife o' his is driving him
wrang in the mind. The money he made is in her name, and
she threatens tae pit him oot unless she has her ain wey. Maybe
she's right. He does mess things up, but whit a position for a
man to be in! He never gave his son a chance at school, but
took him away when he was fourteen for fear he would become
what he ca'd a "wide man"! Now he *is* a "wide man," dodging
work, smoking and drinking, and knowing less about the
business even than his faither. He'd have messed up you an'
a'. He says to me says he' – his father coughed – 'when I telt
him aboot ye wanting to go to the University, "Don't let him,
Jock. He'll turn oot a wide man. And then you'll be sorry." It's
him that's sorry noo, no' me.

'When you won that bursary, he tried to congratulate me, but I
just said: "Mebbe he's only a wide man, Jock!" '

He shook his head.

'Whit a stumer! Bob Andrews says he saw him one night in
Argyle Street at twelve o'clock. The rain was pouring doon, but
he didnae seem tae notice it. He was walking along like a man in a
nightmare, soaked, and his face drawn like somebody who's seen
the horror o' reality. His wife had pit him oot. Of course he goes
wi' other weemin, the dirty sod, but she *is* a tartar and the kids spy

on him for her. They tell her a' he does, and tell him what to do as
weel. Whit a midden! T-t-t-! Are ye ready, Teenie?'

'I'm just coming.'

'It was her, I bet you a pound to a hayseed, that made him mak'
sic a fule o' himsel' the ither day at the funeral, for she'll hardly let
him touch a penny, though she has her cars and fur-coats and a
maid and a' her orders. The auld man was a good yin. When he
was seventy he went into a tobacconist's for his usual ounce o'
thick black. The counterhand charged him three halfpence too
much, and he asked why and said it seemed a bit funny. Then the
youngster got cheeky and said something about his ignorance and
that it was his age that saved him. "It's my age that saves you, ye
bloody young pup," said the auld man, "frae dragging ye ower
the coonter and pulling ye ootside in!"

'He never ca'ed Jock's wife onything else but a bitch.'

David sat listening, miserably, wondering how his father would
take the idea of his going to America. Would he think he was
being a 'wide man' after all?

'Weel, as soon as the auld man deed, the seven brothers made
arrangements for the funeral. They were a lovely family really, a'
masons – and I wish I saw you a mason – seven is a mystic number
in masonry. One o' them's a vet, and one a Civil Servant. It was
one o' the finest initiations ye could see when they were made,
seven being the perfect number.

'Teenie!'

'Yes!'

'It's the hauf-oor!'

'I'm coming!'

'Well, six o' them turned up to pay their last respects to their
faither, complete wi' top-hats and frock-coats. It was touching to
see these six big men thegither, helpless, an' naebody wad hae
been mair touched, for a' his hardness, than their faither. But Big
Jock was late. The whole company had to stand roon' the open
grave, and the gravediggers blowing their hands and the minister
looking uncomfortable, as if his collar was too tight. They stood
aboot in groups, talking, but you can imagine what the conversation was like in the circumstances. Some o' them took a dauner
roon' the cemetery, peeping surreptitiously at their watches, and
the minister hid ablow a tree wi' a clump o' whispering weemin.
And a' the time the coffin lying itsel' near the grave wi' the win'
blowin' the flooers aff it. T-t-t-t.

'Some o' them began tae get angry, especially Wallace the vet,
and some o' the guests had left the place athegither, when in walks

Big Jock puffin' and blowin', his red face like a piece of roasting dough. I can see him yet, snivelling like a dog. Oh he was concerned, for once. He knew he had done something wrong.

' "Gee," he says, when he came up, looking pathetically at their faces, "I had to wait hauf an oor. I couldnae get a tram." '

'And he's a man worth thousands, mind ye, maistly left by his faither.

'They looked at each other and then at the coffin. This time the auld man was silent.

'Teenie!' he shouted again.

She appeared at last, buttoning up her coat and peering at him in bewilderment.

'That's a marvellous story,' said David.

'No' very nice though,' Macrae said. 'The car's ready for ye, Teenie.'

It was a Morris Oxford, 1926. Outside the sun was setting fire to buildings and metal. They had the whole day free, as it was Sunday.

'We'll just take a wee run doon tae Fairlie,' he said. 'Are ye ready?'

'I'm aye ready,' she said, rubbing Meg's face furiously with a wet cloth.

He looked out at the car. It was 14/28 horse-power, and a five-seater tourer. At the back was a luxurious windscreen where his mother and Meg sat peering and wrapped in draughts and blankets. He crouched in front with his father before the aluminium dashboard, remembering the first time they had all ridden together in the car.

'Should we take a run oot tae the Shaws first?' his father had shouted over the windscreen. 'We could go through Paisley?'

He coughed and sniffed. It was his habit; catarrh, he said.

'Dad! It's Sunday,' his mother said, and that was answer enough. 'T-t-t,' she went on.

'Whit's that got tae dae wi 'it?'

'Faither'll no' like it! Ye ken him yersel'. He's wild if I as much as make dinner on a Sunday.'

'He's annoyed if I study on Sundays,' said David.

'Whit tripe,' his father replied angrily, shaking his head like a terrier. 'There's mair real religion in taking a car oot and worshipping nature than in sitting in a stuffy kirk listening tae an auld blether!'

'It needna be a stuffy kirk,' his mother replied warmly, 'and it needna be an auld blether!'

'Think o' the pleesure we could gi'e him. We could take him a hurl before we gae doon.'

'He widnae thank ye for it.'

'Weel, damn him then! Are ye coming?'

'I've just this bit dustin' to do.'

'Dammit, the car's clean, Teenie,' he said.

'All right, all right,' she answered, frowning. 'I'm shair, it's an awfu' job!'

These remarks were quite untranslatable, being a form of speech peculiar to the person and not to anything else, language or dialect. On the verge of an outburst which invariably threatened to take away any pleasure they had, they started off. Not only were Willie Hughes and all the Hemphills walking admiringly around it, Malcolm slinkingly trying the electric horn, but the Seymours were all staring out of the window, and even Mrs Watson could not withhold a discreet glance. He remembered hoping that Mary saw it too. It was the machine drew their eyes, resplendent in gold and silver, for machines were something of a miracle and there was always a considerable amount of subdued excitement as to whether they would go at all.

After some fluttering with the gears they moved downhill in silent triumph.

'Is it to be the Shaws?' his father shouted back into the wind.

'All right, all right, I'm sure,' chorused his mother, gulping in the wind and biting her lips.

In the Shaws the whole family had come on to the front lawn to see the glittering land-yacht – grandfather, grandmother, and even Mr and Mrs Wood, still smoking her clay pipe.

'Whatsoever next?' chirruped Mr Wood, who was a poet of sorts. 'It's a wonderful invention, isn't it, Elizabeth?'

'It is that,' she sang, her voice old and reedy, pulling her tweed hat down over her ears.

'Would ye like a wee run roon' aboot?' asked his father. 'Just a spin?'

'A spin?' Mr Wood looked startled.

'We'll no' go far, Johnnie,' his grandfather said, with reluctance, 'seeing it's the Sabbath.'

He sat in the back with Mr Wood and his grandfather.

'Move up,' said Mr Wood crossly, 'and let your father in!'

'Oh no,' laughed his father. 'I have to sit in the front. You see I drive it.'

'You do? I thocht it went by itself for a meenit,' said Mr Wood.

'Not too fast now,' said his grandfather chidingly. 'Ten miles an hour will be quite ample, Johnnie!'

They did thirty all the way, and when they came back his grandfather said he thought they had been just a wee bittie slow coming hame.

They always went the same way to Fairlie: out through Paisley, past Coats' Mills, and the Abbey, on to the Waterworks, there to begin the long descent of the Hailey Brae. At the top of the Hailey they halted for ten minutes to cool the engine and admire the view. You could see clearly the Big Cumbrae, the Wee Cumbrae, Arran, and on a clear day, Paddy's Milestone, on one side; and on the other, the Gareloch, the Holy Loch, Loch Long and the Kyles of Bute. Below, as if in an aerial photograph, spread out the lovely crystal reaches of the Clyde.

He could see the red rocks and the rock-pools where he had hunted starfish and jellyfish of all colours, blue and maroon and yellow and brilliant gold, or newts and minute fish. He could see the jetty and the sea-wall and the scales under the old pier, and the church where they sang in an autumn of amber chrysanthemum 'Crossing the Bar.' Far down, along the shore road, he could see, too, the open bus with the broken springs hirpling into Largs, and Largs itself. There the paddle-steamer lay at anchor, on which his Aunt Nan came sometimes home in summer, though the distance was only two miles, purely for the sake of the sail. And he remembered the tragic run to Greenock by taxi one Sunday morning long ago, when his grandmother had to have radium-treatment for her eye; he remembered her pain, and the champagne she had to have when she came home. He remembered most of all, the long holidays he had spent in Fairlie, watching the hills of Arran covering themselves with snow, in silence, a bride with her veils, and at night, listening to the sea, as it cast in unceasing motion, its pale white beacons of light, on the shores of Ayrshire, and over all the shores of Scotland.

'We must get on to Nan's today,' his mother said. 'She'll ha'e tea a' ready.'

'It's ma faither I'm worried aboot. I wonder hoo he is the day.'

'It's a blessing *she's* awa' onywey,' his mother said.

He listened to their appalling comments on life and death as if not his mother were talking, but some arch-type of the race. When she huddled up her shoulders and sank her head between them, avoiding other people's eyes, she loosed searching if biting judgments on men and affairs like so many thunderbolts.

His grandmother, he knew, had died of a cancer eating its way, like an enormous rat, through the eye into her brain. For two years she had lived on champagne and cocaine, both provided by his father, at enormous expense.

The old man had rich white hair and blue eyes. He was always quiet and patient, unlike his wife.

When they arrived at the little gate, faces smarting, Nan rushed downstairs to meet them. She was small and thin, like Lilian Gish in looks, and took short, delicate steps, like a deer. She had not married so far because she had had her parents to look after.

'Teenie!' she said, leaning over the side of the car and kissing her. 'Oh my!' She smiled broadly into the air, and as she did so David could see that one of her teeth was silvered over. He liked Aunt Nan because she could always smile.

'Come away up,' she said. 'Tea's ready.'

The little table in her immaculate flat was laden with good things. Through the window at which you sat, you saw a row of pines, the smooth edge of the sea, and then the serrated outline of the snow-capped peaks of Arran. Nan loved Arran and Fairlie so much she seemed to own it all.

'How is he?' his father asked in his direct way.

Nan wept.

'No' sae weel, Jock.'

'Life's absurdly short, Nan,' said his father, in one of his pungent, if rare, pronouncements, and coughed and sniffed. 'Too short to mean hellish much.'

'That's true, Johnnie,' she said, sniffing too.

'Aye,' said his mother, looking away as if puzzled, her eyes puckered.

It was their tribute to philosophy.

Whenever his father was touched or moved, he thrust out his lip and his nose wrinkled at the nostrils. David liked that. It was a fierce denial of mere sentiment. Now he stole into the bedroom, looking very fierce indeed, in his stocking-soles.

David was not allowed to go in, 'unless he liked.' Death was a secret people hugged to their hearts instead of sharing it like the Irish or the Mexicans.

There was utter silence in the next room.

They began to eat – slowly.

At the back of the house – beyond the red wood railway station with its little paraffin lamps, the hills rose in broken, dark-blue bulges, almost sheer, with the fir stampeding across them, or, moving slowly, a clenching rainstorm. Now and then, for a few moments only, a train would stop, hissing a holocaust of steam. The whistle would scream like a shell, and then, gathering speed along the track, the long line of jangling steel and iron would sink into the distance like a stone thrown far out into the sea.

The old man, lying with his back to the window in the silent room, could see none of these things. When he opened his eyes, all that comforted him was pale-blue wallpaper, on which flowers in their thousands tumbled out of Greek vases. If he inclined his head a little to the right he could see the wardrobe, tall and dark-brown, like a coffin, and its ornate mirror, gathering ghosts in the darkness.

Carefully he listened as he lay, his white tam o' shantered head propped up on the pillow, to the wind, washing round the roof and seeping through the lathes in the attic, through the holes in the putty he had moulded between them. Then, deeper and more steadily, he heard the surfbeat on the shore, a never-ending hush-hush like a pulse, or a heart-beat, or like breath itself. The sound of trees. Branches. These were arms, flowing like pliant and patient strength, and never tiring. The sounds of the house. Springing floorboards, hoarding movement for sudden release, like a human body.

Someone, who, Nan, making tea. A voice. The voice would be Jock's. Trying to comfort Nan, his only daughter. Good Jock. A good son, always. Why comfort? If they only knew how easy life was and how peaceful when one was really adjusted to time and space. Then there was no brittleness. If only he could tell them what had always been his secret, he would be happy.

He had learned it early. When he began to be known as a diver, swimming in the current as silently and cleanly as Nan had entered the room in the semi-darkness there, thinking he didn't see, or was asleep.

One of the best in Scotland he had been. Adjustment to time and space is vital to a high diver. Once he had dived off the Forth Bridge for a wager. Timing was necessary then. His blue eyes, pale as the scallops cast up by the sea, dissolved at the thought into mischief. He seemed to hear his wife's voice saying: 'Ye auld deevil!'

Timing was necessary then, but it had been a wonderful sensation, first of all to take the bet and watch the amazement of the chaps in the work. To be drunk with resolution, ready to do anything and confound all who said he couldn't. To sneak away on a Saturday afternoon with a couple of Paisley buddies, saying nothing to the wife, though he knew she would say plenty to him. No' giving a damn.

They had had a drink first at Mally's Arms at the top of Parliamentary Road. They paid his fare. Footsteps. Jock coming in. Big feet. He smiled.

It was the first time he had seen Edinburgh, the capital of Scotland. One of the most lasting impressions of beauty he had ever received. A worker in the Cally had little to look at but nuts and bolts starving for grease, pistons thirsting for oil, rails new and rails derelict, engines on a practice shunt or disembowelled for scrap. He had been a man ministering to machines, and if he wanted to see anything else he must close his eyes, for he could not see through the wall of railway sleepers shaggy as wood-hair and caked with smoke.

If he would hear anything but train-shrieks, whistles, sirens and hoarse orders, he must cotton-wool his ears. His ears were full of cotton-wool now.

He had looked a long time at the outline of the Castle emerging grey from the morning mist, then light-blue, till finally the rock thrust green and a rich serrated brown, into the clear air. He took a walk down Princes Street then, before he went into a tram and away out of Edinburgh.

He couldn't remember if he had been tipsy. His wife, of course, said that he was a drukken rat and it was a peety he wasna droont to go and do a thing like that. Puir soul. Angry at him loving risk better than her, and loving timing and perfect precision in all things and not just in her.

Then they came to the bridge. And it was off with his things, taking a last look at the worried faces, and stripped, to stand arms outstretched, and the wind blowing through him as if he were a bird, taking flight, and the slow launch into space, with a last, quick kick-off.

Breast against wind to drop like a bullet aimed at the Silver Forth.

The air filled his lungs so swiftly, so cleanly, there was scarcely any breathing at all. Falling thousands of feet through space and time, he was never more uplifted, for his head was lifted back, his shoulders braced back and his arms like wings bent back in passionate surrender and burning quest.

In that first dreadful drop his mind was suddenly shot with memories. His wife leaning forward urging him on, not over the bridge, but from the river, where lay an image of her face. He could not believe it! She who so objected to all his escapades because she thought his first duty was to her, his family, the living, she was urging him faster to come, faster . . . and knowing he was coming, he felt, as the drop seemed to lessen, airily unreal, like a plane landing, meeting in the final moment of love or passionately defying with gravity all levity.

Would he never cease rise-falling? Would the wonderful rush of air never quench his breathing by its very richness? He did not care. Better perhaps if it did, and his questing body, filled with clean pure air, plunge into the restless gray of the Forth, forever to remain there.

'Faither! Faither!' came a scream. Oh horror, Nan! How could she be there? She had nothing to do with his plunge. She could not stop him now he was almost in the water. Terror-stricken, silly girl, would she follow out of fright? She mustn't. It wasn't to be. She wasn't ready. She wasn't born!

His mind reeled as though sick, away from the body, forgot its headlong ecstasy, and throbbed and said strangely: 'Why did you do it, Nan? Why did you do it? You've made it harder.'

'I couldn't bear to see you, faither, like my mither, dying,' she sobbed, head bowed.

He leaned weakly back on the pillows. The air was suffocating. If only they knew the delight of timing and how important it was – if only they knew!

'He's no' long for this world noo, Nan. Ye must be prepared for that,' his father said.

Afterwards, when they were driving home in the car, came the moment David was secretly dreading.

'Well,' he said, 'you are 21 now. There's £100 in your name in the bank on your coming of age. What are you going to do with it?'

'Go to America,' he said.

'America?'

Macrae turned and stared at his son, taking his eyes completely off the road. The car swung wildly, along the walls overgrown with shaggy red moss on the shore road.

'Why? Whit is there there for you?'

'I don't know. I want to find out. I may stay and I may not. You say the money is mine. If it is, I go to America. If it isn't, I stay here and don't touch it.'

'Oh, it's yours right enough. Only don't do anything hasty. There's George Aitchison went to America, and as soon as he landed he saw a hold-up. He caught the next boat back.'

'I won't do that,' David said. 'I'll stay a year at least.'

'You could go to an English University, Oxford say. I'd help.'

'I don't want to go to Oxford. I want to get out of the country.'

'For good?'

'For a bit anyway.'

'What will you do over there? Aitchison was going to make golf balls. He was good at that. What can *you* do?'

'The first people who went to America did not know what they were going to do.'

'No.'

'The main thing is to see this island from a distance first.'

'As you say, but I'd rather you didn't go.'

'I have to go. There's nothing for me here. It seems if you are not prepared to connive at the destruction of Scotland, there's no room in it.'

'Now you're talking tripe.'

'All right. Only I'm not the first to leave Scotland and those who left were by no means the worst.'

'If you want to go I can't stop you; but think it over, David, and think of your mother. She would like to see you settled down. I had such plans for you. You were going to join the Masons.'

'The Masons have always interested me. What are they all about?'

'I can't tell you "what they are all about," but I can tell you a few things. I wish you'd join. It would be a great help to you when you were abroad.'

'I don't want any help. How did it all start?'

'You're one of the "Illuminati," ' said his father. 'You've taken the oath.'

'What oath?'

'In the name of the crucified Son,

'Swear to break the fleshly bonds which still bind you to father, mother, brothers, sisters, husbands, wives, relations, friends, sweethearts, kings, superiors, well-doers, or anyone to whom you owe loyalty, obedience, gratitude, or service. Know God, Who saw you born, to live in another sphere, which you will reach when you have left this pestilential earth, the cast-out of Heaven. From this moment on you are freed of any oaths to your country or its laws. Swear to inform your new superior of all that you have done, taken, seen, heard or read, experienced or divined, and to seek and discover that which your eyes do not see.

'Live in the Name of the Father, and of the Son and of the Holy Ghost.'

'It sounds rather wonderful,' he said. 'Where did you learn that?'

'I know a thing or two,' his father said. 'Remember when we used to go to see Henry Baynton in *Hamlet*? I wish you could have seen *Oedipus Rex*. We could have done a lot together.'

'I think we could. We still might, one day. Who were these "Illuminati"?'

'An eighteenth-century sect, springing from the Templars. There were then the Freemasons, the Manicheans and the Templars. The original Masonic ceremony is said to have been that of Hiram Abi the Architect.

'The three sects originated among the builders of Egypt, who later went to Greece. They had a holy order, and regarded themselves as having a holy mission. In Greece, of course, the Egyptian names changed to Greek: Osiris became Bacchus, Isis became Ceres. They built theatres and played in dramas, after Thespis, the creator of the art of tragedy, had seen one of the builders holding a dialogue on a table at a Bacchic feast. They acquired the sole right of building temples, theatres and public buildings.

'Then three hundred years before Christ the King of Pergamo gave them Theos as a spot to live on, and there they organised groups, societies, colleges, synods or lodges.'

'I wouldn't mind being a theatrical mason. How did masonry start?'

'There are many stories. It seemed the Jews, too, practised this type of building, and were associated with the Phoenicians in the building of the Temple of Salomonis, under Hiram. The builders could not all speak the same language, some being Jews, some Egyptian, some Phoenician, so they had to recognise each other by means of signs and secret words. Hiram Abi divided them into three, craftsmen, apprentices and masters. Apprentices were paid at Column B, craftsmen at F, and masters in the middle room. No one was paid until he proved his rank. Three of the craftsmen, afraid that the temple would be finished before they reached the grade of Master, decided to wrest the secret from Hiram by force, so as to pass as masters in other countries. They were Jubelas, Jubelos and Jubelum, and they killed Hiram Abi by the East door, burying him on a mountain with an acacia on top.

'Before his death, however, Hiram had sent for the Cedars of Lebanon to use in building the temple at Jerusalem. No one knew what to do with these. The King despatched search parties to find the body, and told them to note the gesture they made when they did find it and the words they said among themselves, as these would have to replace the lost secret. They put on their leather aprons and their white gloves and when they found him, buried the master on Lebanon. They still try to find that word and sign.'

'It doesn't sound quite like my job,' he said.

'You don't know your job yet, do you?'

'No.'

'However, there is another story. Manes, founder of the Manicheans, was born in Persia about 220 years before Christ. At 17 he was bought by a rich widow in the town of Ctesiphon, who brought him up and gave him his freedom, making him her heir. He began to teach the creed of Soytienus, according to which there are two principles of creation, the good, spirit, light is God, and the bad, matter and darkness is the Devil. He was influenced by Zoroaster. He called himself an apostle and wrote an evangel dealing with the transmigration of souls, forbidding the killing of animals and the eating of meat. He attained fame under Harmuz I. of Persia and called himself Paracletus. Harmuz died, and the new King commanded Paracletus to perform a miracle. He did not. He was stripped, skinned and stuffed with straw.

'His followers then started a ceremony like that for Hiram Abi, and the higher ranks of freemasonry. They all stood round a coffin, the same number of steps down as the freemasons, but the figure was not that of Hiram whose secret they sought, but that of Manes, whose death they were to avenge. This was duplicated in another sect organised in honour of the death of Jacob von Molay. The only people on whom they could avenge themselves for the deaths of Manes and Jacob von Molay, the one executed at the end of the third century BC and the other at the end of the fourteenth century, were – the Kings. So Continental freemasonry became very political, unlike ours.'

'You haven't told me very much really, have you?'

'I can't. I've told you, you're one of the "Illuminati." That is why you are going away. Would you like to join before you go? There was another death. The death of Christ! On whom do we avenge ourselves for that?'

'I don't know,' he said. 'I can't join anything. Where is my blue shirt, mother? – At the laundry?'

His mother wept. His father put a brave face on it, trusting he said in his son's judgment.

'Ach, a cunny min', David,' his mother said with an expression of distaste.

'You're a helluva man, aren't ye?' his father said, as they arrived home.

'I got a tin of beans from Miss Sveso, wait till ye see the size o't. I says to her I says says I, "Miss Sveso?" Where are you going, David? This is a fine tapsalteerie!'

'Up to the attic.'

It was the only place where he could study, where he had once read Nansen. He could see right up Pollokshaws Road from there, and watch the green and red cars come lurching and swaying down from Dumbreck, Bishopbriggs, and Bellshill. As he moved through the house he loved, he felt he was moving in several dimensions at once. There was the bedroom as it had been in the time of his grandfather, with a small fire in the grate, littered with Victorian knick-knacks. He remembered being taken up-stairs to say goodbye to his grandfather, who was lying in bed. The old man was gentle, yet gruff. His beard prickled David's face. Afterwards it seemed that he had been dying, for he did not come downstairs any more. In the same room his Aunt Mary died. It was all brown then, as if the sun were concentrated inside the room and you could touch it. The coffin was brown too. Near it lay his aunt under veins of blue marble. It was all unreal, one of those conjuring tricks in which someone lies down in a box and then disappears because the hand is swifter than the eye. All the time you knew they had gone behind the scenes and it was only a trick, so you concentrated on the mystery of it, and pretended to be puzzled and even frightened at the mysterious power which had accomplished it all. Only, now he wanted to talk to his grandfather, he could not.

There was the library where he had worked for so long; the attics where he had read *Tom Finch's Monkey*, crawling up the steep stairs to a breakneck height. How different the house had looked with the various generations living in it! In his grand-father's time it had been severe, uncomfortable and very dusty, steeped in prayer and sanctity from which the only refuge was the attic.

When later his cousins had lived there it was a merry bedlam of shouting children, much as in the time of the original school. Aunt Bessie spent all her time making wonderful dessert-puddings. And through it all blazed the enormous fire on the hearth, that never seemed to go out, with the bells for the servants, smuggled away in cobwebs in the high corner.

They were all there still for him.

Why did they not claim the 'Quoich?' Why did his mother not

listen when people spoke to her. He read the chapter in Hume Brown called 'The Scottish Wars of Independence,' and went downstairs again. He had not read it since he was twelve, and even in school it had not been considered very important really. What was important?

'To play the game,' his father said.

'To live the Christian life,' his mother said. 'Oh yes, David.'

Surely what was important was to know what was going on in the world? No one ever mentioned that. The schools taught the past. To them the present was a controversial issue and the future a probable sin.

Entering the kitchen, he remembered his grandfather playing on the violin 'Rantin' Rovin' Robin,' and through the window saw again the dusty, hallowed hollytree wrapped in spiders' webs, and the prickly old bushes that were part of an older Scotland than he could grasp.

'If I can leave my son better off than I was, and he does the same, and that goes on for each generation,' his father was saying, 'to me that is progress . . .'

'You should at least have finished your degree,' his father said to him as he went in.

'Not if I'm one of the "Illuminati"!' he answered. 'When I went to see the Adviser of Studies I found there was no serious advice to be had. The University was a factory for teachers and scientists, not a place for learning, which is essentially disinterested. I might have taken a degree in Philosophy, or even in Economic Science but there are no opportunities for research there, as there are in Physical Science, and armaments and the weapons of power. Disinterested thought is not encouraged. I don't belong there.'

'Go to London,' his father said.

'That is no better,' he said. 'Scotland was the first nation in Europe to declare itself a nation. It gave the idea of nationhood to the world, but now it seems as if it will be the first nation to die. That does not mean that, like so many of my countrymen, I intend to become a form of Englishman.'

'It's beyond me,' his father said. 'I don't want you to be anything but what you are, but how will America help that?'

'All vision is a help,' said David. 'Neither nationalism nor religion nor any affiliation so far means anything to me because they are not wide enough. Only the world is wide enough.'

V

Everything was the same, yet not the same. The gray ruined walls and the dripping evergreen and the feathers of frost on ferns and rocks were the same, but leaving everything was different. He thought of the fall of lawns at Gilmorehill away into Kelvingrove Park, and of the strike of the wind in the small cloisters, and the beauty of the scene clung to him like a dream. The train moved on with increasing speed towards Greenock, but it was moving along the path through the rhododendrons behind Cartcraigs and it was whistling through afternoons among the ossified and undone history in the Art Galleries. As it screamed and hissed in anger, a woman opposite rose and put her head out of the window.

He was leaving Scotland, and not only Scotland but all of his previous life, perhaps for always. At the Tail o' the Bank stood a large ship, all ready to sail, her bunkers gritted with coal, her furnaces red with clinkers. Round her rose the mountains, rolling backward in motionless waves from Arran to Ben Lomond and Loch Long, the 'Loch of the Ships.' They were The Guardians.

Living, he thought, was always a stage cleared for action. He remembered the old man in the hardware shop, old Sneddon, selling the odds and ends of an existence he could no longer order or control, limping against fate.

'How are you, well?' an old dame simpered.

'Well, but poor,' tittered old Sneddon nervously, an eternal image.

Had he seen there a spirit, isolated against that background? What remained when he had nothing to cling to at all? Was that his soul, that bald radiance?

The decks were cleared for action. There was no other action than this final one in which he moved and had his being. There never was. Now he knew. The greatest things were space and the emptiness of space called time. The *Ding an Sich*. This was it, the thing seen against all lack of purpose and direction, was only to be loved, as a child is loved.

The whole world was a great empty stage on which the antagonist sought to create a final lack of purpose and direction so that creatures might be loved; a great empty stage on which no one had ever acted because no one had ever appreciated the stage, the audience, the act, the scene, the décor – or the nature of the play.

He saw a young Black Watch officer holding high his head, not knowing why, wearing his kilt like a bustle, quite divorced from war and the terrible knowledge of war.

He saw people in a passing train, girls looking out of a window, men smoking or reading, penned in space and time, again in the isolation that would be theirs always. To interfere, to help, was dangerous presumption. Their lives, their souls, were theirs. The responsibility was theirs. He had his own life and his own responsibility.

Living was a game of chess, or a vast design, a piece of music, a pattern of achievement. A sister was a sister and not a sister. She played her part and was a sister, having elected out of space to do so. 'Be sister to my tragedy.' There was in sisterhood a relationship like a geometrical design. So there was for a sweetheart who was and was not, in eternity.

'One of the "Illuminati,"' his father said. 'From this moment on you are free from any oaths to your country or its laws . . . Swear to break the fleshly bonds that bind you still to father, mother, brothers, sisters, husbands, wives, relations, friends, sweetheart.' Sweethearts – he remembered Mary – bless you, Mary – 'and to seek and discover what your eyes do not see . . .'

He stepped down into the pilot's cutter. His childhood was left standing on the pier, pulling chocolate out of slot-machines, hammering out the name TARANTULA for his yacht, waiting for the *Davaar* to come in from Campbeltown, standing by his father and mother. The cutter smelt of fish. That was Fairlie and the herring-boxes stacked for transport to London and Glasgow. Sidings of silvered scales like slippery sixpences. His aunt passing in the gray, old open-air bus. Goldfinches, mavies, gannets and heron like metal on the beach, in splendid chorus and incomparable ballet, dancing beyond the windows. The dot on the horizon was the *Queen Mary* coming up. It grew larger. Noon stood still. The sun swelled like a seed. You could see the silent bows of the ship, swollen now, cleaving the water without a sound. It was very mysterious and beautiful to be waiting for the *Queen Mary* that morning, arriving after the *Davaar,* and *The Marchioness of Breadalbane* to sail to Macrihanish Bay. How lovely the names were! The *Queen Mary* was faster than *The Viper* although *The Viper* was fastest in Ireland.

The slowest was *Eagle III*, but she was old.

Every widening ripple was a year. This ship was still larger, a floating generation. He strained his eyes through the light morning mist. There was no one to see him off except the hills and the river of his childhood. That was the best way to go. Now the liner was near; he could see a great hole in her side let down like a bunker for passengers to enter.

In he walked, and through a narrow corridor carpeted with silence, like a hospital, so ill for a moment he felt. On the deck the ship's band began to play 'In My Solitude' and the ship seemed an empty shell.

Only the gulls fluttered over the rain-swept decks.

A spotlight of sun touched the Cumbrae and it shone like amber.

The temples of the engines seemed to throb with music. The hills began their slow and solemn march past. He felt very moved. Now, for one wild moment, he would have liked to dash ashore with the pilot, and sit at the window in Gourock with Miss Gray, or in Helensburgh with the Friels, or in Fairlie with Nan, watching the waves, when a liner passed, coming in like cream-cruds. His country suddenly became very small and very beautiful, like a precious stone with a bloody history, lying in the outstretched palm of a dealer and a charlatan.

Fairlie and Millport and Dunoon, and Innellan and Rothesay and Kilcreggan and Arran, and Brodick and Lamlash, Lochranza and Lochgilphead stood up and bade him good-bye.

On the quays behind, a few stacks and chimneys still stood up like old women in grey shawls waving white handkerchiefs of smoke against a mournful background. He thought of his mother in the Shaws waving at the London train as his grandfather had waved from the old doorway. He thought again of Cartcraigs.

For him the family belonged to that house, and could not leave it altogether. It was not just a house, it was an experience, an assembly-point, a memory they all shared, uniting them no matter where. This was the meaning of 'living.' No wonder the Scots were called 'fey.' He would not have been surprised in the least to have seen his grandmother emerge from the cupboard below the stairs leading to the attic, holding in her hands a pair of ancient ladies' boots.

'Awa' wi' ye,' she would say, waving the boots at him. 'You an' yer fancies!'

That was because she did not want him to know too much, and because she was a very brave old lady.

A cold wind blew up in his face flakes of salt, cold as the water pouncing and worrying the rocks ashore.

Then the vast hand of the sea reached up and wiped away the inarticulate map of the fighting city, and, walking to the bows, he stood in the inscrutable future.

FROM SCENES LIKE THESE
Gordon M. Williams

From scenes like these old Scotia's grandeur springs,
That makes her lov'd at home, rever'd abroad;
Princes and Lords are but the breath of kings,
'An honest man's the noblest work of God';
And certes, in fair virtue's heavenly road,
The cottage leaves the palace far behind;
What is a lordling's pomp? a cumbrous load,
Disguising oft the wretch of human kind,
Studied in arts of hell, in wickedness refined.

O Scotia! my dear, my native soil!
For whom my warmest wish to Heaven is sent,
Long may thy hardy sons of rustic toil
Be blest with health, and peace, and sweet content!
And O! may Heaven their simple lives prevent
From luxury's contagion, weak and vile!
Then, howe'er crowns and coronets be rent,
A virtuous populace may rise the while,
And stand a wall of fire around their much-lov'd isle.

O thou! who pour'd the patriotic tide,
That stream'd thro' Wallace's undaunted heart,
Who dar'd to, nobly, stem tyrranic pride
Or nobly die, the second glorious part;
(The patriot's God, peculiar Thou art,
His friend, inspirer, guardian and reward!)
O never, never Scotia's realm desert;
But still the patriot, and the patriot bard
In bright succession raise, her ornament and guard!

Robert Burns (*The Cottar's Saturday Night*)

ONE

IT WAS STILL dark, that Monday in January, when the boy, Dunky Logan, and the man, Blackie McCann, came to feed and water the horses, quarter after seven on a cold Monday morning in January, damn near as chill as an Englishman's heart, said McCann, stamping his hobnail boots on the stable cobbles.

Dunky Logan rested his old bicycle against the stable wall, then hung the gas-mask case, containing his sandwiches and vacuum flask on a nail. The slack sleeves of his grimy fawn pullover hung down over his hands, stretching inches beyond the elastic cuffs of his green zip-jerkin. Even on a morning like this it would have been unthinkable to wear gloves. Only nancy boys wore gloves. He'd pulled down his pullover sleeves to protect his fingers from the freezing metal of his bicycle handlebars. Even in the stable the air was cold. It rasped on the back of his throat. His mother had got him out of his warm bed in the kitchen at half-past six. There was still a strong sensation of porridge at the back of his mouth, even although he'd been chewing bacon rind since he'd got up from the kitchen table and pedalled up the hill from the old tenement in Shuttle Place through the Darroch council house scheme, teeth working on the rubbery wad of rind, eyes on the frosty road for bricks or broken bottles, one hand on the handlebars, the other in his trouser pocket. At that time in the early morning the sloping streets of the Darroch scheme were almost empty. Men who worked in factories and engineering shops were only thinking about getting up. It made him feel tough and hard being a farmworker who had to be yoked by the time other men were only crawling out of their beds.

He'd cycled up the road which led from the edge of the sprawling scheme to the farm, along the edge of the field which lay between the back gardens of the houses and the railway embankment. The harsh blue sodium lights of the scheme streets ended at the railway bridge, a dank vault from whose iron rafters hung silvery icicles. It had to be very cold before the drips from the underside of the bridge froze up.

The farm steading stood on the left of the road past the bridge, its buildings low, black silhouettes against the faint light from the low moon. Dismounting, he could see from the yard somebody moving about in the farmhouse kitchen, Willie Craig, no doubt.

Once he and McCann had been inside the stable for a few moments it felt warmer, horse-dung warm, the three Clydesdales snorting and pulling at their ropes to see what was moving behind them in the darkness. McCann blew on his fingers and rubbed them in his armpits. He reached up for the paraffin lamp, striking two matches before he got a light. The black wick smoked into a ring of smelly flame. One of the horses blew steamy air out of flared nostrils, like a dragon in a story-book. Dunky rubbed his eyes with his knuckles. He could have slept for another two or three hours, no bother. Monday was always the worst day for getting up, especially in the winter. Monday was the worst day all round, the start of another five and a half days of work, back to the stable and its mess of sharn and straw and old harness and broken tools, a place that would be tidied up only when they'd finished lifting and pitting the potatoes, if it was ever tidied up at all.

McCann hung the lamp on an old saddle-post beside the small, cobweb-layered window.

'Come on then, Smallcock,' he said, his voice hoarse and impatient, not at all friendly. 'Get among they beasts, a bit of work'll soon warm ye up. In ye go, they won't eat you.'

McCann still didn't like him, even after three weeks' working at Craig's farm. Three weeks! It didn't seem more than a day or two since he'd been sitting in school waiting desperately for the Christmas holidays, to be finished at last with the daftness of lessons and homework, the whole silliness of being a schoolboy. Three weeks! He was still not used to the big horses, big brutes they were, only it wouldn't do to let McCann see him look nervous about going into the stalls. McCann could be very coarse. Some of them called him Blackie, or Black McCann, partly because he had jet-black hair and a blue chin, but more because of his moods. Nobody knew what caused his bad spells but when they came on two fields was a good distance to have between McCann and yourself. He was twenty-four, McCann, a fully-grown man. He had a funny sense of humour, too, even when he wasn't in a bad mood. He knew Dunky was scared of going into the stalls beside the horses and he took a great delight in rubbing it in.

'The weather forecast says it's going to rain by dinner-time,' Dunky remarked as he took the corn-pail to the big kist, trying to make McCann think he wasn't concerned about feeding the horses.

'More'n likely,' said McCann, standing against the end wall for a run-off. 'Ye'd better get a move on, Auld Craig'll be wanting to make an early start.'

He fed the mare first, the smallest of the three horses but still a good two inch taller at the rump than himself, a light brown horse with neat, white-mopped feet and a white nose. In the morning they got just enough corn to keep them going all day, just enough to stop them from starving for grass when they were yoked.

Her long, hard-boned head swung round to meet him, soft lips pulled back from old-yellow teeth as she tried to guzzle corn out of the pail. He tipped it into the earthenware trough. As he left the stall he gave her rump a friendly pat, partly because he liked her for being tame and partly to show McCann he was in control of the situation. She was a nice horse, female, soft, not dangerous. McCann leaned on the broom handle, dark eyes looking for signs of nervousness.

'Nothing to it, lad,' he said, grinning, sleep-puffed eyes giving him an air of added malice. Now for Big Dick, the middle horse, biggest of the three, a dark brown gelding who normally played up like a thoroughbred stallion. Big Dick stood across his stall diagonally, head in one corner, hindquarters blocking his entrance. As he approached the stall, hoping the horse would move over of its own accord, McCann lifted the broom handle and gave Big Dick a meaty smack on the haunch. The horse sidled abruptly, at the same time lashing out a hindleg in a bad-tempered swipe.

'There, that's how to treat the buggers,' said McCann, grinning.

It was a dirty trick to play, for Big Dick was bad-tempered enough without hitting him. McCann was trying to push him into a fight, he knew that well enough. Well, he was no mug. If they hadn't been alone he'd have taken his chance, probably swung the bucket into Blackie's face, hoping to crack him on the shebonk. If McCann kept this up they would have a fight, but he wasn't going to risk it when they were alone. For some reason he felt it would be embarrassing, just the two of them. Fighting was silly. It seemed more natural to fight when there were other men there, quite apart from the fact that the others would stop the fight before McCann could ruin him for life.

He could feel the great weight of Big Dick moving beside him in the stall. He kept his eyes on the horse's head, which was raised above its wooden hayrack, ears alert for trouble, eyes waiting for some excuse to swing over and flatten him against the solid, greasy boards of the stall partition, ready to bear down on his boots, metal-shod hooves bashing down with the force of a ton or more of Clydesdale. Big Dick was as chancy a bastard to deal with as McCann. On his very first day at the farm (not counting previous years when he'd worked there during school holidays and had only been the boy) he'd watched McCann going over Big Dick with the stiff wire brush and the horse had taken a casual side-kick at Blackie, casual in the way of a bad horse, a sort of half-interested gesture just to let you know peace has not been declared. Blackie had jumped away, feeling his shin, swearing something awful, although Dunky was sure he hadn't really been touched. Saying he'd worked horses all his life, he knew what to do with them, Blackie had hammered the toe of his boot into Big Dick's right hindleg, above the hoof, jumping clear at the same time. That was the good thing about industrial boots, McCann had said, viciously, they had fine steel-plated toe-caps for lashing into the evil bastard and showing him who was boss.

The horse breathed in steamy snorts, pent-up air released in abrupt, almost warning rushes. There was a slight suggestion of pawing the ground in the nervous movements of his forefeet. Even in the middle where his back slumped the brute was taller than he was. The great head swung down and round as he lifted the pail to the trough. He felt like dropping it and running, but sooner or later he *had* to get used to the bastard. The edge of the pail bumped against the bones of its head. He felt the power of it. A dribble of corn fell on the straw. He forced himself nearer the trough, feet tingling in anticipation of its hooves. Then the grains tipped out of the bucket and Big Dick fell to munching. He was out of the stall, safe, much to McCann's disappointment, no doubt.

'He's all right once he gets used to you,' he remarked.

'Don't kid me on, Smallcock,' said McCann. 'Ye're scared to death o' the beast, aren't ye, scared of a bluddy horse.'

'Is that a fact?' he said, as cheekily as was safe with McCann. He filled corn for the third horse, old Charlie, a tired old beast who hardly had the energy to lift his tail for a shite, let alone kick you. When he did try his hand with McCann he would definitely get a hammering, he wasn't near as strong as a man, but as long as Donald Telfer and Young Willie and Coll were there they'd stop Blackie before it got too bad. It was some kind of custom. In factories, they said, new apprentices always got some sort of roughing up from the men, like an initiation test. Until McCann had a chance to give him a hammering – or rub his face in cowshite – he wouldn't leave him alone. The very thought of it made him clench his teeth. His heart seemed to be beating against the skin of his chest. He'd had hundreds of fights but they were with boys his own age. McCann would try to knock his head off.

Mattha McPhail the knee-padder was next to arrive in the stable.

'Aye aye there,' was all he said to McPhail. He didn't like the wee dirty man with the fallen mouth where his teeth were missing (he kept his dentures for Saturdays) and the filthy white silk scarf knotted over his adam's apple. Mattha McPhail was actually quite pleased to be known as the knee-padder. Knee-padding was his game, he always said, as though it was much the same as being a Baptist or a greyhound fanatic. He did it in parks and woods and up on the Braes on Sundays in good weather, crawling about on his knees in bushes to watch courting couples on the job. Only once had he been caught, he always boasted; some guy had happened to look up at the least expected moment and lost his stroke as he saw Mattha's ferrety wee face peering at him from the whins. This guy had chased McPhail halfway to Kilmarnock, shouting the odds about kicking his features out of the back of his head, but McPhail was too fly to be caught. In any case, he said, he always had an answer if he *was* caught, the secret was to take your breeks down when you were slinking about in the bushes, then if you were nabbed you just said you'd crawled in for a quick shite.

'I know why you take your trousers down, you wee scunner,' Telfer would say. 'Ninety-nine change hands one hundred, ye mean, ye dirty old tosser.'

McPhail saw no insult in being called a masturbator, knee-padding was a great laugh all round, nothing to be ashamed of, why should it, it was his game, that was all.

Dunky felt glad he was no longer a casual and classed with McPhail, who was hired for the potatoes and the harvest, not much of a worker, always nipping off to go up to Kilcaddie Labour Exchange for his burroo money, hoarse-voiced and shifty, officially unemployed and still drawing dole money from the burroo, he said with pride, after seven whole years.

'Holy Mary mother of Jesus it's colder'n a nun's bum,' was McPhail's greeting.

'Ye're early this mornin',' said McCann, still playing about at sweeping the stable floor. 'Was something wrang wi' ye, couldn't ye sleep?'

Dunky took the other broom and swept horse shite and sharn

up the gutter which ran the length of the stable. Auld Craig, the farmer, hated anybody to look idle. It was Blackie's job to get the three horses yoked into the three carts, as long as he was shoving shite about the old man wouldn't shout at him. Auld Craig thought all townees (which meant anybody who didn't actually have dung on his boots) were idle scum out to rob him. Dunky liked to imagine the farm was under siege, what with the burgh housing scheme advancing up the hill towards the railway line and the new school taking up half the field on the other side of the embankment and talk of an annexe to the school to be built on the rest of the railway field, not to mention the factory going full blast on the west side of the farm; and there was talk that it would need to expand. Apart from all that, scallywag kids from the scheme were always burning down Craig's haystacks or chasing his cows or stealing his hens or playing in his corn.

He didn't consider himself a scheme kid and yet he lived in the town, so he wasn't one or the other. Like young Jim Hawkins, able to talk to both Long John Silver and Squire Trelawney, was one of his dafter notions. It was just as bloody well nobody knew how many daft notions he actually had. Sometimes he thought he might be a bit soft in the head. Ever since he could remember he'd had these funny ideas running about his brain, sort of play-acting; if he wasn't going to Hollywood and picking up Rhonda Fleming at a dance he was playing for Scotland at Hampden, the very first left-back who put the hems on Stanley Matthews. Or he was a *real* gangster who came back to Kilcaddie from Chicago and when the hard neds of the King Street gang came into a café he stood up, all silent and casual, telling them quietly to beat it . . . he'd noticed that the more he stayed at the silly school the dafter these notions had become. He'd wanted to get a job, be a hard case, a real working man, not a silly schoolboy whose brain was affected by too many pictures. He wanted Craig to treat him like one of the men, he wasn't really afraid of Craig, not the way he used to be afraid of his father before he'd been paralysed, no, not afraid. It was easier to do your work – more than your share if necessary – than be shouted at by Craig. One day he might be a hard enough case to laugh back at the old man, the way Telfer did when he got a telling off. One day . . . he couldn't risk it, he wasn't like Telfer, he was scared of the sack, really scared. Getting the sack would be a disgrace, something terrible, something you'd be ashamed to go home and tell your mother.

The stable sharn was solid and heavy against the stiff-bristled broom. McCann was gassing to McPhail when Young Willie came into the stable. He put his whole weight behind the brush, counting on Willie seeing that he was working.

'For God's sake, McCann, ye lazy hooring shite, ye've no' got they horse yokit yet, what the hell d'ye think this is, the civil service? Damn ye tae hell, McCann, ye idle shite.'

Young Willie they called him, although he was over fifty. The hardest-working man on the place, bar none. The Craigs were between housekeepers and he'd have been up for hours, feeding the beasts in the byre, feeding the hens, milking their two cows, making his own breakfast. The men said his roaring meant nothing, he only did it to show his old man he could run the farm.

McCann replied to Willie's bawling with his usual gesture of impudence, pivoting slightly on his toes to stick out his arse, making a farting noise with his lips. In a bad mood he was as likely to have gone into a sulk for the whole day. McCann could get away with it, he was young and strong and possessed all his wits, a rare combination for farm wages of seven pounds fourteen shillings a week. The factory paid a basic eleven with bags of overtime. Dunky imagined that Craig put up with McCann because he couldn't get any better, which McCann knew full well, saying in times of argy-bargy that if they didn't treat him decent he'd just as soon fuck off to the factory, or maybe join the police.

Young Willie went into Big Dick's stall and loosed the tether rope, holding his mane till he had the rope halter over him. Big Dick stamped a bit but young Willie could manage him. Dunky liked Young Willie. There was something comic about him, even the shape of his body, his short, bow legs and thick, squat trunk making him look short, when in fact he was as tall as McCann. He had big eyes which seemed to be trying to pop out of deep lined sockets. He cut his own red hair, cropping it short with kitchen shears. He hadn't shaved for a day or two, his shirt was near rotten under his filth-shiny waistcoat and his right eye was red with a weeping cold. His mouth had fallen – he said gums were just as good as Government teeth.

'Get out, ye brute!' Willie roared as Big Dick shied at the low stable door. Outside it was lighter, the highest part of the sky bright with a rosy glow. McPhail and McCann pulled the shafts of the high-backed, two-wheel cart down on either side of the horse and they yoked him in for the day's work. Dunky held the reins while they brought out the other horses.

The first tattie-howkers were coming into the yard for their eight o'clock start and he hoped they didn't think he was just the boy given the reins to hold because he wasn't fit for anything else.

Somebody had to hold Big Dick, especially in the morning when he felt frisky. As if he cared what that bunch thought, a raggle-taggle collection of women and girls and school-kids, some in woollen balaclava helmets, some in men's overcoats which hung down their shins, some in wellington boots with the tops turned down, some in ordinary street shoes. They were just casual labour, a scruffy lot taken on for the tattie-howking. They made him feel like one of the real men.

That was another daft notion which made him wonder if he was normal, the idea he had that all sorts of people, some he knew and some he didn't, were watching him wherever he was. Sometimes he talked to them, in his head. How would Craig's farm look to them, he wondered – *them* in this case being a vague conglomeration of town people, schoolteachers, girls who'd been in his class, guys he knew in football teams. Like an old dump, he had to admit it, a sharny old relic hanging on against the creep of the town, its steading here and there resembling an abandoned ruin, low stone walls sprouting weeds, the cartshed, the byre, the small barn, the big corrugated iron barn open on one side and one end, the tumbledy house in which there were stone floors and no carpets and three dogs and no hot water and two men who hadn't swept the floor since the last housekeeper left before Christmas and who wouldn't sweep a floor till the new housekeeper appeared, the black midden, the yard, all loose stones and puddles and frozen mud and bits of rotting wood and the mad black dog chained to an iron stake by a leaky kennel, chained there winter and summer, hail or snow, no wonder it was mad, poor brute, a blunt black dog which raced to the end of its chain when anybody walked across the yard, barking like a maniac, standing on hind legs, neck so calloused it no longer felt the choking pull of the chain, a dog that would tear your heart out if the chain ever broke. Out of all this Auld Craig had made, the men said, more money than the provost of Kilcaddie, and the provost owned three chemist's shops, so he was really rich.

Auld Craig reminded Dunky of the evil old uncle in *Kidnapped*, so mean and terrible he was; the corn in the loft above the small barn was typical, the old man happy to have it piled loose on the floor, not caring a tuppenny bun if his three horses had to eat as much rat shite as grain. The chances were, the men said, he was only hanging on until the factory or the council gee'd up their offering price for the rest of his land. Not a penny was ever spent on building repairs. Willie patched up the fences himself. If a window was broken the most that happened was a bit of sacking was nailed over the space. The old man, the men said, was stashing away his cash for his retirement. McCann's big joke was that on his ninetieth birthday (nor far away, they said) the old bastard would celebrate by lashing out two whole shillings for his first bus ride to Glasgow.

By eight they were ready to leave the yard for the tattie field, Donald Telfer leading the way with the Fordson tractor, the refugee-like howkers trailing behind the three carts. McCann led with Big Dick, Blackie McCann standing on the sloping floor of the high-walled cart, being carried above the black hedges of the unmade track road that led through Craig's hillside. Young Willie came next, walking at the head of the young mare, not interested in cutting a flash figure like McCann. He stood in the third cart with McPhail and Daftie Coll from Oban. Coll, the highland man, had a fat, open face which was always grinning away at something or another, looking back now at the stumbling pack behind them.

'Aye aye then,' he shouted, lifting off his cloth cap with thumb and index finger of his right hand and stroking grizzled hair with the three free fingers, his voice the high pitched sing-song of the highland cheuchter. 'It's a fine fresh day for you all, eh? Never mind, missus, the cold air will be killing all your wee bugs.'

A woman shouted something back at Coll, her voice the flat, abrasive accent of Kilcaddie, the kind of voice that came best out of the side of the mouth. There were about a dozen women and girls from the scheme, and twenty or so school-kids let off by the Education for tattie-howking – in the national interest. One and sixpence an hour! He had been a school-howker, he was glad he worked horse now, these kids actually thought it was better than school, grovelling about on their knees in cold, wet earth, hands so numb you'd think they'd been pulverised by a hammer.

Charlie's broad rump swung from side to side, his front hooves stamping down on frozen tracks, hind legs moving in a different way, the lower hocks coming forward uncertainly, shaking, almost like a cat picking a reluctant way through water. The iron-rimmed wheels trundled over stones and frozen mud ridges and crunched the ice on small puddles. The axle creaked. The hawthorne hedges were bare and black.

'D'ye hear their new housekeeper's comin' the day?' said McPhail.

'She won't last any longer than the last one,' said Coll. Dunky liked to hear Coll speak. Highlanders used a precise sort of English, they'd all been used to speaking the Gaelic and had learned English like a foreign language. Coll knew another high-lander who maintained the stretch of railway siding which ran past the farm to the factory. If Coll saw him walking by on the embankment he'd shout something to him in Gaelic. It sounded like gibberish.

'It's supposed to be raining later the day,' he said, wanting to join in the man's talk. The sky was now high and dull with just a streak of blue to the west, which might mean that the weather was breaking over the Atlantic, a wind getting up to bring rain clouds over the hills towards Kilcaddie. There were hills on all sides except the east, where even now he could see the black smoke hanging over Glasgow.

They turned into the field, the horse knowing the way so well he hardly had to use the reins at all. Old Charlie had been coming this way for eleven years and he wasn't a young horse when Craig had bought him, McCann said.

Telfer was yoking the mechanical digger shaft into the iron triangle-bar under the spring seat of the tractor. Coll and McPhail vaulted down from the cart. He stayed on board until he reached the far end of the field. Telfer the tractorman was as fair and open-faced and cheery as McCann was black. Just to watch Telfer swinging his leg over the tractor seat made him feel young and awkward and shabby. Telfer alone of the men didn't wear a cloth cap. He had curly yellow hair and instead of sharny old flannel shirts and greasy jackets and mouldy pullovers he wore a white undervest (back to front so that it showed white at the neck, the way the Canadians who played ice-hockey at Ayr wore their vests, or the way soldiers did in American films), a clean grey shirt and brown leather jerkin with no collar. He had blue denim trousers and working the tractor he could get away with wearing ordinary shoes. Dunky preferred the weight of his boots (an old pair of his father's) but there was no doubt that in boots your socks formed hard wrinkles under the foot, especially when they were a size too big.

'Look out, you people,' Telfer shouted as he swung the tractor and digger round towards the end of the drill, 'this machine's built for speed.'

He had a funny way of sitting on the sprung-seat, twisted round almost sideways, smoking a cigarette – which none of the other men did. The big tyre treads threw up small dollops of black earth. Telfer grinned at the howkers, no doubt looking for some bit that might be game for a ride one of these nights, creep back down to the hay-barn when the Craigs were in the house, that was

Telfer! Trying to look gruff and manly, Dunky jumped down
from the cart. It wasn't so easy if you were only fifteen and hardly
needing to shave. It was all right for Telfer, he seemed to think
work was all a great joke.

'Keep them at it, McCann,' Young Willie shouted as he and
Coll and McPhail headed off towards the tattie pits at the far end
of the next field. Telfer started up the drill. The whirling spokes of
the digger's wheel threw dirt and tatties and half-withered shaws
against a mesh-net hanging from a bar. The net let through the
earth but dropped the potatoes in a more or less straight line
about a yard wide.

The howkers had split up, two or three to each section of about
ten to fifteen yards. When the digger passed through their section
they either bent their backs over the line of potatoes, or got their
knees down on bits of sacking which they dragged along as they
threw tatties into their coracle-shaped wire baskets, each holding
about forty pounds of potatoes. Some of the women wore old
aprons over their coats. They were from the poor end of the
scheme and some of them probably had just the one coat.

He led Charlie to the first filled baskets. He was getting
hardened to it now, after more than a week among the tatties:
Bend, hands under either end of the basket, brace the stomach
muscles, up with it in one movement, shift the angle of the
elbows, push up, drop one end into the cart. Throw the empty
basket on the ground. Bend, both hands up, twist elbows, push,
and let the yellow potatoes rumble onto the wooden floor of the
cart. It was easy at the beginning, when the potatoes were below
the top of the cart walls, he could get a basket up onto the edge
and then let them drop in. He threw down the second basket and
walked to Charlie's head. His fingers were numb, but they'd
warm up by the end of the first drill. Two more baskets. The short
walk forward. Three baskets this time. Don't hurry, the secret was
to take it at a steady pace. Try to look flash now and you'll be
knackered by tea-break. A piece of earth fell onto his face. He
rubbed at it with the sleeve of his old jerkin. Halfway down, his
stomach muscles beginning to make themselves felt, he passed
Telfer on his way up to the head of the next drill.

'Aye, aye,' Telfer shouted, 'You still think it's better'n school?'

'Oh aye,' Dunky shouted back. Two more baskets. Up with the
bastards, throw the empties down, don't waste time, ten drills to
go before tea-break. The cart began to fill up. He had to throw
each new basket-load into the middle so that the potatoes would
be evenly distributed. The big iron-rimmed wheels sank into the

soft earth. Charlie had to jerk the cart forward after each stop. His arms began to ache. The secret was to swing them about a bit as you walked between the waiting pairs of howkers. Now the load was a yellow pyramid appearing above the walls of the cart. He had to push the last two baskets up to the top of the heap. The thing was to take it steady. Try to hurry and you'd let a load fall back on the ground – that would look very silly. By now McCann was leading Big Dick down the second drill. He put his hand on Charlie's nose strap and led him to the gate. If they worked it right there was always one cart out of the field, at the pits, one being filled, and one empty, ready to take up the next drill. McCann, being stronger, was supposed to do most of the loading, with him leading them to the pits. The cart rumbled up the slight bump at the gate and they were onto the track road. He kicked earth off his boots. At the pits the three other men were waiting by the long, low trench. They let him back Charlie towards the pit, and when it was in position they unyoked the cart shafts and got their shoulders under the shafts and held them steady as the cart tipped up and back. Then they pulled down the shafts and he left them to heap the yellow Golden Wonders into a continuous pyramid. They spread a layer of straw over the sloping pile and shovelled earth on top and banged it down with their spades, sealing the tatties off from the frost until it was time to open the pits and weigh them into bags for the potato merchant.

Back in the field McCann was already walking away from Big Dick's load towards the mare and the empty cart.

'Where've ye been, for Jesus' sake?' he shouted. 'Gie that lazy brute a kick on the arse if he'll no' get a move on.'

He went back to the pits with the second load, walking a good two feet clear of the horse's stamping fore-hooves, his own boots continually picking up an extra sole of black, cloying earth. With a full load even Big Dick had no chance of playing up, but on the way back with an empty cart, seeming to know that it was only a boy at his head, he decided to move along at a brisk rate, now and then throwing up his head when something unseen to Dunky excited him.

This time McCann was still loading. He took Dick to the end of the third drill, tying the rope reins tight to the shaft so that the horse wouldn't stand on them, which would cause more excite-ment. The short rest only made his arms ache more as he started to throw in the baskets, this time doing it with even more care, in case a potato flew up and startled the horse. He didn't joke with the howkers. He was too young to treat them the way McCann

did, like a lot of half-witted scum. The older women had terrible
sharp tongues. Bend, grip, up, twist, push, throw down the
empty, bend grip, up, twist, push . . . each time he took the
horse forward he felt the cold air rasping into his heaving lungs,
but his hands were getting warm. Black and warm.

On this trip he had a look at the factory, away down the hill
towards the railway line. It had two large hangar-type sheds, huge
buildings still painted with wartime camouflage, green and brown
in irregular blotches. Around the big sheds were smaller buildings, and at one end a mountain of scrap. They pounded this
down for melting with a huge iron ball dropped from a crane. And
the two-storey office block where, said Telfer, there was enough
talent to drain the balls of King Farouk. Telfer knew all about the
women in the factory office, don't worry, he'd rammed a few of
them, don't worry.

By nine o'clock the sky was streaky, smears of blue among high
drifting cloud. It seemed to be getting warmer, although that
might be just from working. At half-nine the factory hooter would
go for tea-break, vacuum flasks brought out of old gas-mask
cases, sandwiches eaten under a hedge, sitting on dry sacks. He
was famished already. He had bacon and cheese today. He was
coming back from the pits with old Charlie, standing on the
bumping cart floor, when he spotted Auld Craig's head moving
above the hedges.

'Girrup, Charlie,' he said, flicking the rope-reins on the horse's
sagging back. Charlie raised his head and pricked his ears, but his
step slowed back to normal in a matter of yards. He was willing
enough, but the muscle had gone. His head dropped again, his
great hindquarters rolling slowly, the cart creaking and jerking
along the slowly-melting ruts.

Auld Craig followed him into the field on his bike, boots
sticking out at right angles, his hodden grey suit hanging in loose
folds now that he was eighty-five or so and shrinking. Maybe he'd
be away to the far end of the field before the old man said
anything, he was a fearful man to speak to, a terrible bent old
man with light blue eyes that only occasionally allowed themselves to be seen through great grey eyebrows and heavily-
bearded cheekbones. He jumped off the cart to tie Charlie to a
post. From the horse's head he could watch the old man get off
his bike, a favourite performance among the men.

Auld Craig let the bike and himself fall to one side, making a
scrabbling sort of mad jump to free his old bowed legs from the
falling frame, at the same time waving his arms, getting his left

boot caught, half stumbling, finally jumping clear and taking a kick at the bike.

'MAAYYYAH!' was what his oath sounded like, the bellow of an old sheep. Dunky walked up the drill with the mare. Telfer was now at the far end, six drills dug now, little bursts of smoke pop-popping from the tractor's thin, upright exhaust pipe.

'MCCANN DAMN YE!' Auld Craig damned most people before he spoke to them.

'CRAIG!' McCann roared back, grinning at the boy from the shelter of the horse. McCann was very impudent, as long as the old man was a good distance away.

'COME HERE DAMN YE MAN!'

Dunky tied the mare's reins to the rear of Big Dick's cart and took over from McCann, who walked down the drill towards the old man. He took a firm hold on the rope so that it pressed hard on Dick's soft mouth. It was a good moment for Big Dick to be well under control. A bad horse was nothing compared to Auld Craig.

'You've got an easy time of it, huvn't ye?' said a woman howker, her face streaked with dirt, a balaclava helmet covering her hair, a woman who could have been anything from twenty to fifty.

'How's that, missus?' he said. Up with the basket, up to the top of the load, almost on tip-toe, arms and shoulders lead-filled.

'Ach, he's only a wean,' her mate said. 'He's no up to real toil.'

'A wean?' he said. Everybody thought everybody else's job was easier than their own. Howking was dirty and cold, but it wasn't heavy, just a bit sore on the back. 'Is that a fact?'

He'd thought he'd have time to give a bit of patter to the one or two good-looking girls, not a chance. He was breathing heavy again. What the hell would he do when the front cart was full? Bring the mare round in front? No, Big Dick wouldn't like that. He'd have to lead the horse forward and then walk back to the second cart. Wasting valuable time! Craig would notice that. Bend, grip, up, back sore, twist, hands raw against the wire, push, stay up you bastards. It must be giving him good muscles, what Baldy Campbell said he needed for football, more weight and strength. He took off his green zipper jerkin and tied its sleeves round the shaft. The elbows of his pullover were ragged holes. Under that he wore an old, collarless shirt of his father's. Crows and gulls were all about now, whirling in the sky, zooming down in flocks behind the tractor. The gulls were moving inland, they'd been told at school, more food. Watch out, birdies, he thought, ye cannae steal Auld Craig's valuable worms and expect to live.

'HEY YOU BOYYY, COME HERE!' Aye aye. Trouble. He hung the mare's reins over the shaft and led Big Dick's lead down towards the two men. Here and there was a Golden Wonder the howkers had missed. If Auld Craig saw them there would be ructions. Valuable tatties!

'We're not needin' the three horse,' the old man said, staring at his boots. 'Gin dinnertime take that old beast back to the stable. Two cairts is enough. And cut out that chatterin' to the girls, I'm no' peyin' ye to dae your winchin' here. Get a move on, damn ye, if it turns out wet we'll be buggert.'

'Aye, right, Craig,' he said. That was the proper way to address the farmer, although it sounded strange to call the old man by his surname. Willie had explained to him that his father was entitled to be called Craig – he was *the* Craig. Only men who didn't own land needed to be called Mister. Even Willie called his own father Craig.

'Hrrmmph.' The old man cleared his throat and spat a lump of catarrh the size of a penny. Then he squinted through his eyebrows. 'Is this suiting you better than being a scholar, Logan?'

'Oh aye,' he said, grinning. Craig must like him. He walked back to the two carts. It was very strange how the old man changed accents. Sometimes he spoke to you in broad Scots, sometimes in what the schoolteachers called proper English. They were very hot on proper English at the school. Once he'd got a right showing up in the class for accidentally pronouncing butter 'bu'er'. Miss Fitzgerald had gone on (him having to stand in front of the class) about the glottal stop being dead common and very low-class, something that would damn you if you wanted a decent job. A decent job – like a bank! His mother spoke proper English, but then she was hellish keen on proving they were respectable. His father spoke common Kilcaddie, which he knew his mother didn't like. When the Craigs spoke broad it wasn't quite the same as common Kilcaddie – some of their expressions sounded as though they came straight out of Rabbie Burns! Telfer had a Kilcaddie accent, but he pronounced all his words properly, no doubt from seeing too many pictures. McCann spoke very coarse and broad, but there was something false about him, as though he put it on deliberately.

He still spoke the school's idea of proper English, he knew that all right because every time he opened his mouth he could hear himself sounding like a real wee pan-loaf toff. (Maybe that was what annoyed McCann?) Why did Auld Craig and Willie change about? Did it depend on what they thought of you? He remembered Nicol the English teacher saying that broad Scots was pronounced very much like Anglo-Saxon or middle English or some such expression. If that was so why did they try and belt you into speaking like some English nancy boy on the wireless? He'd asked Nicol that and Nicol said right or wrong didn't come into it, proper English was what the school had to teach you if you weren't going to be a guttersnipe all your life. Was it being a guttersnipe to talk your own country's language? It would be a lot healthier if folk spoke one way. Sometimes you hear them say 'eight' and sometimes 'eicht', sometimes 'farm' and sometimes 'ferm'. Sometimes 'ye' and sometimes 'youse' and sometimes 'yese' and sometimes 'you'. Sometimes 'half' and sometimes 'hauf'. Was it your faither or your father? Your mither or your mother? He felt he was speaking to his audience again. You see, if school was any use it would teach you things like that, not just jump on you for not talking like a Kelvinside nancy boy. Why teach kids that Burns was the great national poet and then tell you his old Scots words were dead common? What sounds better – 'gie your face a dicht wi' a clootie' or 'give your face a wipe with a cloth'? One was Scottish and natural and the other was a lot of toffee-nosed English shite.

'See me, I'm Peter Cavanagh, the man with a million voices,' he said to Big Dick as they walked along the track road to the pits. 'Gi'es a len' o' yur pen, hen? What was that my good man? Sorry, lady, give us a wee loan of your fountain pen, madam. Otherwise Ah'll melt ye. And here is that ancient man of the moment, that crazy comic from Kilcaddie, Sir Crawly Craig, what song are you giving us the night, Sir Crawly – what's that, "gin lowsing ye'll ging for a wee donner doon the heather"? Very nice, I hope it isn't dirty.'

Coming back from the pits he passed old Charlie, now tied to the fence, head down looking for grass. Eleven years working for Craig, he deserved a rest. On the last time down the drill he'd had to kick him on the leg to get him moving. One of the howker women said it was disgraceful, kicking a dumb animal.

'It's him or me,' he'd said, trying to make her laugh. She didn't see the joke, ignorant old bag. Did she think he liked putting the boot on a horse – like McCann? He liked the old horse, he hadn't really tried to hurt him – just wake him up. Everybody had to work. Work or want. Kids got belted at school, horses got belted on a farm. But only if they wouldn't work.

Big Dick had lost a bit of steam now.

'Come on, you evil bugger,' he said, leading him forward down the drill, speaking softly so that the howkers wouldn't hear. 'Let's see how strong you think you are.'

They'd have to go faster now, with only the two carts and three men waiting at the pits. Still, it was a decent thought of the old man to let old Charlie stop working, his insides might have collapsed. Poor old devil, he'd earned his rest out on the grass. He hadn't really enjoyed kicking him. He wasn't like McCann.

As he came back into the field from his next trip to the pits he felt cheerful enough to bend down and pick up a stone. Once you'd got through the first hour or so of Monday morning you began to get used to it all again. He waited till he was within range of a bunch of strutting crows. They fluttered into the air but his savagely-thrown stone landed harmlessly on the ground.

Then the factory hooter went for half-past nine and tea-break. Only the tip of his nose was cold now.

TWO

ON THE BUS from Beith to Kilcaddie, Mary O'Donnell took the seat behind the driver's cab, downstairs at the front of the bus. There was a woman in the window seat. Mary O'Donnell sat on the outside, her stiff left leg sticking out into the gangway. She didn't care if people looked at it. She'd passed the girlish stage of being embarrassed by the wasted leg and its apparatus of metal rods which ran from a hip support down to a metal and leather knee grip and then down either side of shrivelled bone and flesh to turn at right angles into holes bored in the thick heel of her dumpy black shoes.

The red, double-decker bus was fairly full, wives going shopping in Kilcaddie or Ayr, a soldier in uniform, two men in soft hats, a few farmers on the way to Paisley market. The inside of the bus was warm, almost steamy. It was beginning to thaw outside, the black hedges looked damp and the fields cold and uninteresting. The road rolled over featureless hills, down through barren villages. She was looking forward to living near Kilcaddie. It was a real town, more than fifty thousand people, they said, with picture houses and big shops – a Woolworths *and* a Marks and Spencers. Her family back home in Sligo didn't understand why she preferred to live away in Scotland, working as housekeeper to dour Scots farmers. They thought it was all slaving away in cold old farmhouses. They didn't know the half of it, thank God.

As Kilcaddie drew near fields gave way to detached houses of dark red brick and then to semi-detached bungalows and then to good-class tenement houses, three and four storeys high, with shops on the ground floor. She'd been four and a half years with Stephenson, the Beith farmer. If it hadn't been for that stuck-up bitch who'd married Stephenson's son she'd be there yet, mistress of the house! When she'd left Sligo they'd all warned her how hard it was in Scotland, how mean the tight-fisted Protestants could be. Oh, sure, they were mean and dour all right – if you didn't know how to handle them. The old man Craig had come the mean trick at her interview.

'I cannae pay ye the full five pounds a week,' he'd said, hairy-faced old monument that he was. 'There's a lot o' jobs a limpy cannae do. I'll give ye four and your board.'

'And there's just yourself in the house?' she'd replied. There were more important things in life than a Scots pound note.

'No, there's Willie, my son,' he'd said. 'That's all, just the two of us.'

'Oh well, I'll take four pounds,' she'd said. 'But if I'm satisfactory you'll make it up?'

'Hrrmmph,' the old man had replied.

Buttoning up her heavy, meal-coloured coat, she watched as the bus came towards Kilcaddie Cross, a wide shopping street cutting across the main Glasgow road. As the bus drew in to the stop, she got up and limped along the gangway, ignoring the faces. The young conductor bent down to lift her suitcase out from the luggage space under the stairs. Mary O'Donnell didn't think much of a man who'd take a woman's job on the buses.

'I'll manage, thank you,' she said, not smiling, taking the case out of his hand. With one bad leg she was a better man than his sort.

On the four corners of the Cross stood small groups of idling men, no matter that it was Monday morning, a working day. She didn't like the looks of them, a scruffy lot, a lot of them fairly young, all with hard faces, eyes like rats. She knew what their type would be thinking and saying: *A good-looking piece, pity about the gamey leg, ach, who cares about their legs, she'd rattle good as anything. I'd do a turn with her any day, rather ride her than a tramcar.* She'd heard it all.

At the local bus stop she put down the case. Across the wide street she saw well-dressed women going in and out of a good class tearoom. Town women, fancy hats and high heels and nylon stockings. To her eye the solid greys and blacks of Kilcaddie's buildings seemed almost glamorous. Picture houses that weren't country fleapits. Here and there a shop with a newly-modernised front. From the bus stop she could see the town war memorial, two kilties with hanging heads on a granite plinth. Around the Cross, at least, Kilcaddie looked solid and well-off, real money in its granite-fronted banks.

The local bus turned away from the Cross through streets of shops and pubs and big stores, their windows bright against the grey gloom of the morning. In small shops heavily-laden women queued for butcher meat and bread and fish; dark-fronted pubs were already open at half-past ten, their shadowy interiors hidden behind swing doors and opaque glass, sometimes even stained glass; then it began to climb streets where older tenements stood side by side with brick sheds, timber yards, warehouses, small engineering works. In Sligo she'd always thought of Scotland as heather and mountains and shining lochs, but in these cold, windy streets people seemed to walk with their shoulders hunched, shabby people whose children had dirty faces, only the occasional young man walking with his head up.

The housing scheme marked an abrupt change from the old town, wider streets lined by three-storey blocks faced in grey roughcast and roofed with red tiles. Most of the garden spaces in front of the houses were unkept, rough grass criss-crossed by hard-tramped earth paths, battered privet hedges with gaps wide enough to take motor cars. Washing hung in balconies. Here and there a paling-fence lolled over onto the pavements; a motor-bike without wheels stood by one of the open block entrances. In Scotland, she knew, the working folk didn't care how their houses looked, inside or out. They talked about bog Irish, but they were rougher than any folk she'd known back home. These were good houses, but most of them didn't care.

The rain had started by the time the conductress told her they were at the stop for the farm road. With the case banging against the calf of her good leg, she pulled up her collar and crossed the road. Big drops fell from a low sky, a bitter wind getting up from the west. She walked with a roll, stiff left leg going forward, body leaning over as the iron took the weight, right leg forward in a long step. The sooner she was settled into the farm the better. Didn't even think of her having to change buses and walk nearly a mile. Hard. Well, they were making a mistake if they thought she wasn't just as hard as they were . . .

The rain came on heavier and after looking several times at the sky to the west, Willie decided it was going to be too wet to carry on working. It wasn't for the howkers he stopped – wet tatties were liable to go rotten in the pit. He and McPhail and Coll heaped earth over the last load. In the other field McCann threw a tarpaulin over the half-filled cart and he and Dunky led the three horses back to the farm, following behind the racing howkers. Rain, the curse of Scotland, Dunky thought, feeling quite cheery at the break they'd get. By the time they'd got the horses in the stable and rubbed them down with sacks it was hammering down in sheets. Young Willie went away to the house, walking at his normal pace, rain or no rain.

'Hey, Smallcock,' said McCann, 'you've to come over with us to the byre, we're to do a bit of muckin' out, keep ye from getting lazy.'

They ran through the bouncing rain, past the cartshed where the howkers sheltered in a rabble. Inside the byre door Telfer was lighting a cigarette, blond hair streaked and flattened, raindrops on his red face.

'This weather's lousy,' he remarked and McCann and he ran through the door. 'Ice in the morning, rain at dinnertime, snow by night no doubt. Just look at it, pishing down.'

'It's better in Canada, of course,' said McCann, banging his cap against his trousers legs. He pronounced it to rhyme with Granada, the way the more ignorant scheme folk did. Dunky knew this was McCann's way of taking the piss out of Telfer – who lived in the scheme and was never tired of talking about the great life overseas in Canada.

'Anywhere's better than rain like that,' Telfer said, bitterly. He drew on his fag. 'I'm tired of bloody rain all the time, sick and tired of it. One good week, that was all we had last summer, one stinking lousy week. Christ, it never stops in this place. I can't remember a bloody time in this town when it wasn't bloody raining. You get your shoes ruined and your suits ruined, ten to one if you walk out the door with the sun shining you'll be soaked before you reach the gate. You can't take a woman a walk but it comes down like buckets. It affects people, you know. That's why they're all such miserable gets in this dump. They've been rained on all their stupid lives, and they haven't got the imagination to get out of it. Rain, rain, rain – it gets in your brain.'

Neither of the men made a move towards the two lines of cattle. Dunky supposed they were to muck them out, fork out deep layers of manure, not the two milkers, Willie always did them, but the store bullocks, fat-backed black crosses brought into the byre for the worst of the winter, solid-flanked beasts who stood on a packed layer of their own skitter trodden into straw. Well, he wasn't going to start if the two men didn't, he wasn't that daft about work.

'Where wid we be without rain, eh, ever thought o' that?' asked McCann. 'Things wouldnae grow without it.'

'Who cares whether things grow or not? People, that's what matters. Give them one solid month of sunshine, you'd see the change. They'd be a different race altogether.' Telfer blew smoke towards the downpour. The blue cloud was slashed to nothing by the slanting drops. McCann stood behind him. He wouldn't be all that keen on mucking the byre either, he liked to think he was the horseman about the place. Daftie Coll did most of the mucking out. Cattle were beneath McCann.

'On ye go, Smallcock,' he said, turning on Dunky. 'Let's see ye do some fancy work with a fork, did they teach ye that in yur school, eh? Or would ye rather have a handful o' cowshite round yur balls?'

He had a funny look in his eyes. Once, when he'd been just a boy at the tatties, Dunky had seen McCann – who was then too important to notice him – take the trousers off some young bloke who'd been cheeky. After a lot of kicking and struggling he'd rubbed tractor oil on his arse. He wasn't going to have that. He pretended not to hear. He walked up the middle of the byre to where there was a four-pronged grape lying against a half-filled wheelbarrow. If McCann came near him he'd shove the tines into his throat. McCann walked a couple of steps after him. What he wanted was for Telfer to join in. One man roughing up a boy wasn't such good fun. With two of them it could be made to look like horseplay.

Dunky picked up the grape and made a move into the nearest stall, touching the shiny black back of a bullock with the grape handle. He saw McCann coming nearer. If the grape didn't work he'd break McCann's shinbone with the toe of his boot. That was one thing you learned playing football. In a way he was beginning to look forward to getting it over with, hammering or not. It had to come sometime.

'Hey, look what's coming into the yard,' Telfer shouted from the door of the byre. Dunky stood still, elbows pressed against solid, beef-covered ribs. McCann hesitated. 'It's the housekeeper woman,' Telfer said.

They stood in the doorway. Through rain which came up off the mud and stones in a fine white spray they saw the limping woman carry her suitcase, one strand of red hair falling from under her tight headscarf. Dunky stood on tip-toe to look over the men's shoulders. He'd kept hold of the grape, in case McCann wasn't interested in what Telfer had seen.

'She's a bloody limpy dan!' McCann looked astonished.

The woman came up the middle of the yard, alongside the midden.

Telfer put his hands to his mouth.

'Hey, watch the dog, missus,' he shouted. His voice didn't carry far through the bucketing rain. Dunky saw her look up to see where the voice had come from. She kept on walking. Telfer waved at her.

'Go over the other side,' he shouted, 'the dog's in the—'

She was almost at the end of the midden when the black dog came roaring out of its kennel. It was fly enough, Dunky realised, to stay inside till potential victims were in chain range. Its mad barking roared round the whole yard, frightening the steers who jumped and shook their chains, big eyes raised above the concrete stall partitions.

Mary O'Donnell tried to swing the case round to protect her from the dog. Telfer ran out of the byre, shouting, but the dog was on her, leaping up at her chest, ears flat back on its blunt head. The weight of its paws landed on the suitcase. Mary O'Donnell fell backwards, sitting on the mud with her left leg sticking out at a right angle, the case on her lap.

Telfer reached the dog before it could get at her.

'Gerrout, ya dirty brute!' he roared. Dunky watched him draw back his right boot and swing it into the dog's ribs. The kick sent the dog sprawling on its side. It started screaming with pain, an unnatural, high-pitched yelping. Telfer ran at it, boot poised again. The dog scrabbled away on its stomach and then scurried for its kennel, still howling like a mad thing. Telfer turned to the woman.

'Are you all right?' he asked. 'Come on, get up before you're soaked through.'

Her eyes staring, Mary O'Donnell was too shaken to move. Telfer bent down and pulled her to her feet.

'Can you manage to the house?' he asked, picking up her case.

'I'm not helpless,' she said. Telfer thought she was going to cry. He didn't like to take her arm. She started walking towards the yard-door of the house. He walked beside her, suitcase in one hand, the other hovering near her elbow in case she stumbled. He banged on the door.

'Hey, Willie, your housekeeper's here,' he shouted, giving her a smile, both of them standing under the shelter of the little porch. 'Welcome to Buckingham Palace.'

When Willie came to the door, he handed him the suitcase.

'She just about got killed by that brute dog,' Telfer said. 'You want that animal hung, it'll tear somebody's throat out.'

'I'm all right,' she said. 'It just caught me off my balance.'

'Ye'd better come in,' said Willie. 'You get on wi' the byre, Telfer.'

Telfer came slowly back through the rain, seemingly not caring.

'A bloody cripple, that's about Craig's mark,' McCann said, bitterly. 'I bet he's peyin' her half wages. What the hell's use is a limpy dan housekeeper?'

Dunky watched Telfer push back his hair. He wished he'd been the one who'd run out in the rain. Telfer had looked like a real hard man.

'She's Irish,' Telfer said. 'That black bugger would have had her throat out. I should've cracked its bloody neck for it. I will, one of they dark nights. Hey, Blackie, did you get a good look at her?'

'Ach,' said McCann, 'she's a limpy. Whut good's a fuck'n cripple?'

'She's a bloody smasher,' Telfer said. 'I felt the tits on her when I picked her up!' Without warning he picked up an armful of straw and rammed it into McCann's face. 'She's a bloody lovely bit of stuff, you miserable get. And I'm the brave boy that saved her life! Just watch me, you buggers.'

McCann cursed as he pulled straw out of his shirt. As Dunky began forking solid cow-shite he didn't know whether he was more jealous of Donald Telfer for having saved the woman or for having covered Blackie McCann in straw. It was all right if you were a man.

When it came to half-past twelve they left the byre and went across the yard to the stable. On Mondays he did not go home for dinner. His mother gave him two extra sandwiches so that she could get on with the washing. He remembered the smell of Mondays. Bleach, ammonia, worst of all on days when it rained and the shirts and pyjamas and towels and even sheets hung wet and cold from the pulley in the kitchen. Wet Mondays were the worst – the washing had to dry inside the house and he couldn't get out to play football in the street or catch newts in the ditch beside the railway embankment. Now he'd never have to worry about being in the house on washing day. He was a working man.

He gave each horse a twist of hay. Coll went home for his dinner, to the old cottages farther up the hill. So did McPhail, Christ knew what kind of mansion Mattha went home to, he had five or six full-grown sons, according to the knee-padder they were so rough they hardly let him inside his own house. The women howkers either walked home in the rain or stayed in the cartshed with their sandwiches – their 'pieces', jam and white bread. An Education bus took the schoolkids to the canteen at the scheme school. Craig should have given them hot soup, by regulation, but he was excused this because he had no house-keeper. Telfer was always asking Willie what kind of scoff he and the old man cooked up for themselves and Willie always said fried eggs and tatties, but none of the men ever went in for meals with the Craigs to find out. The house might be a bigger mess than the steading, but it was the farmer's house and they were just the men, and a few hesitant paces into the kitchen was as far as they penetrated. In one way Dunky resented this. Ever since he'd even thought about things like that he'd thought it wrong that some people should be better than others. That's what they were taught in the Sunday School – yet when he told his mother what he thought she said the Bible wasn't to be taken literally! Of course, she'd say they were as good as the Craigs and better than Telfer or McCann – and that made him glad he was one of the men to be kept out of the farmhouse. Maybe his family was a bit more – well, respectable, decent, whatever word his mother used, than the Telfers or the McCanns, but all he wanted was to be exactly like them. His mother was kidding herself on. Just because Grandpa Aitchison had owned his own shop! It reminded him of the Academy, having to wear a school tie, as if that dump was any better than ordinary schools. The first time he even remembered knowing about this sort of thing was coming home from the Sunday School, he must have been about four or five, he wasn't even going to school. To reach their church you had to go through one of the worst slum dumps in Kilcaddie, Bell's Place. The kids there never had shoes – they certainly didn't go to the same Sunday School as he did! One morning he'd been coming home on his own and a gang of boys from Bell's Place were playing football with a tin can – in bare feet. He'd wanted to play with them but one of them called him a toff. They'd pointed to his cap – a new one, he remembered it as clearly as anything, stupid bloody thing with a wee cloth button on the top and a skip, grey to match his suit. He'd taken it off and thrown it over a wall – to show them he hated it. He *thought* he could remember them letting him play after that, but maybe he'd invented that part later on to prove to Alec, his pal, that he'd always been a bit of a Communist. What he did remember was getting the belt from his father for losing the cap, a real belting with the old razor-strop.

McCann and Telfer and he ate their pieces in the dusty harness room at the end of the stable, sprawling on a wooden floor covered with white plaster dust and rat droppings, heads resting against rotten plaster walls which had disintegrated here and there to reveal the lathwork strips.

'No' be lang noo' fore we're finished the tatties,' said McCann. Telfer winked at Dunky.

'No' lang the noo, Jock, eh, hoots mon – where d'yah dig up all that Harry Lauder patter, eh?' McCann's face darkened, blushing under his heavy growth.

'I speak natural like,' he said. 'Better'n tryin' to sound like some yankee fly boy.'

McCann ripped into his sandwiches, not biting so much as tearing and cramming. Telfer had cheese on brown bread. His big thing about Canada was written all over him, one leg drawn up, white socks, even the way he held his bread. To Dunky, the Craigs seemed like something out of the past, even Young Willie, who'd been to the Academy. McCann was just plain, ordinary coarse. But Telfer was a big-timer, well-known in the scheme, notorious, almost. His father was away in England somewhere living with some fancy woman. Telfer's mother was a big dyed blonde, a fast piece, as they said. The Telfers had drinking parties in their house – which, said Dunky's mother, showed you what a fast crowd they were. She was always on the lookout for any sign that 'her wee boy' was getting too friendly with Telfer. He was Not A Good Influence.

'Ah talk normal,' McCann said. 'No' like you, Telfer, you're jist a picture fiend, yur heed's full o' fairy tales from Hollywood. Ah bet ye thought ye were right gallus, yah big-time idiot, out there in the yard wi' that limpy dan.'

'She's all right, that one,' Telfer said. 'What did you think of her, Dunky?'

'No' bad.' McCann made the inevitable sneering face.

'Him! He wouldnae ken whit tae dae wi' a wumman if she lay doon and pit her legs roon his neck.'

Dunky wanted to change the subject, knowing how long McCann could keep up that particular line of attack. Whatever the reason, he seemed to get on Blackie's nerves, just by being there.

What was it about guys like Blackie? Kilcaddie was full of them, tetchy bastards with hair-trigger tempers, guys who'd put a broken bottle in your face just for looking at them, guys who went to dances hoping for fights, guys who went on to a football pitch ready to break somebody's leg. He'd been a bit of a fighting cock himself, when he was younger. Once, when Shuttle Place had a lot more houses than it did now, they'd been playing football in the street with a composite rubber imitation cricket ball and some guys from the scheme had run away with it. Guys?

None of them could have been much more than five or six, including himself. The Shuttle Street boys had chased the Darroch scheme boys the length of Dalmount Drive before the scheme boys had stopped running. He could still feel the temper he was in at that moment when he grabbed one of them and dragged him to the pavement and sat on his chest and grabbed his hair and banged his head on the asphalt, banging and shouting, trying to kill him. Six years old! A man had dragged him off the other boy, a man in a boiler suit with dirty hands. He said he was going to get the police. They'd all run away and hidden in the coal yard, going home, eventually, in dread of a belting, only to find that the man hadn't called the bobbies and nobody knew anything about it.

So why had *he* stopped being like that? Was it because he'd gone to the Academy where, as his mother said, he mixed with a decent class of boy? Softies, to be exact. No, he'd had fights at the Academy. Was it the summer he'd been evacuated to Portpatrick, just after the Clydebank blitz when everybody thought the Germans were going to bomb the whole Glasgow area to smithereens? He'd gone to a village school there for a term. The country boys were bigger, they wore tackety boots, they had red faces . . . no, he couldn't remember having any fights down there. Was it because he was a coward? How did you know if you were a coward – it was natural to feel a bit scared before you went into a fight, that was half of the reason you tried to kill the other guy, in case he turned out to be stronger than you were.

Why, then? One part of him would have jumped like a shot at the chance of parting McCann's hair with a fifty-six pound weight, maybe he would have to some time, but the part of him that *considered* things found the idea disgusting. He didn't mind roughing up guys in a game of football, that was natural, the harder a player you were the more respect you got. But not fighting. Maybe it was from the same daftness that gave him his funny ideas? At school he could not remember any occasion when he'd been in agreement with the rest of the class. When everybody else wanted to be a Cavalier he'd found himself liking the idea of Cromwell and the Roundheads, because they seemed more like ordinary people. When they'd reached the '45 Rebellion he was on the side of the Lowlanders who'd more or less ignored Prince Charlie's army. Funny about that, he didn't care all that much for the Jacobites when he read about them operating in Scotland, but as soon as they were over the border into England he found himself wishing they'd gone on south from Derby and taken

London. It was the same with football. He'd never really *liked* Rangers, although he was a Protestant. Celtic had always seemed more friendly, somehow. Look at Charlie Tully. Rangers went in for strength, like granite. Charlie Tully had bowly legs and was bald and didn't look strong enough to beat carpets yet he had more personality in his little finger than Rangers had in their whole team. Charlie Tully would jink towards the Rangers defence – you'd need guts to take on big George Young and Willie Woodburn and Sammy Cox and Jock Tiger Shaw – and when they came at him, ready to hammer him into the ground, he'd bamboozle them, pointing the way he pretended to pass the ball, sending them chasing in the wrong direction, or running on without the ball but still pretending to dribble so cleverly they'd follow him, trying to make a tackle.

Yet despite all that, as soon as Scotland played England he thought of Waddell and Young and Woodburn as heroes – because they were Scottish then, not Rangers. Instead of being giants from Ibrox Park they became part of your own country taking on the might of England. That was the greatest thing he could imagine in the whole world, being picked against England – he'd *die* for Scotland.

It was just a pity that the Scottish selectors were blinded by Glasgow Rangers. Great players with small clubs didn't stand a chance of being picked for Scotland if there was some six-foot Tarzan at Ibrox Park. Rangers didn't even play like real Scots yet they dominated the whole game because they had the big money. Hibs played like Scots, tricky, clever, artistic – yet Gordon Smith, the great Gay Gordon who could do *anything* with a ball, hardly ever got capped for Scotland. Willie McNaught was the classiest left-back in the game, but because he played for Raith Rovers he never got a look in. Jimmy Mason of Third Lanark, small and round-shouldered and insignificant till he got on the ball, had helped Scotland beat England three-one at Wembley – but how many caps did he get after that?

So, he was chronically on the side of the small guy against the big guy. So what had that to do with not liking, or understanding, nature's hard cases? Was it just another of his silly-boy imaginings that he sometimes wondered if he belonged to a completely different race? Maybe aye, maybe hooch aye, as Grandpa Logan used to say. There was a man from another race, all right. According to his father, Grandpa Logan was such a nutcase he'd registered as a conchie in the First World War – knowing full bloody well they didn't take men whose right hands were carved out of wood and hidden under black leather gloves. Maybe he was a nutcase throwback to Grandpa Logan? That wasn't a very cheery prospect, all he wanted was to be like everybody else.

'Wasn't that funny, Auld Craig stopping Charlie working in the middle of the morning?' he said, hoping the other two could talk about horses without arguing.

'He's done,' said McCann. 'Craig was feart he couldnae walk to the knackers. He's about twenty year, that auld wreck.'

'I'd shoot the lot of them,' said Telfer. 'Machinery, that's what you need on farms these days. One tractor'll do the work of the three of them.'

'Bugger off,' said McCann. 'Given me a horse onytime. When does it break doon, eh?'

'It's the modern way,' said Telfer. 'Farmers with sense are getting machinery instead of horse. Craig's just too shiting miserable, that's his trouble.'

McCann spat. Dunky untied his bootlaces, finger nails picking painfully at the hard, wet knots.

'Horses are natural about a ferm,' said McCann. 'People are jist following a craze for machinery. Ye'll niver beat horse.'

Dunky took off his boots. He pulled at his stiff, woollen socks to straighten out wrinkles on the soles. His feet were cold and wet. He lay back, head on the wall, aches in the small of his back and his arms. His trousers were wet. McCann and Telfer weren't interested in anything he had to say. He stared round the harness room. It was festooned with old sets of harness hanging from saddle trees, black leather dry and cracked through years without oil, brass-work covered in green mould and white dust. Lying about on the floor were weights for filling potato bags, fifty-six pounders like four-sided, flat-topped pyramids, circular two-pounders like coins giants used in ancient days. The window was thick with spiders' webs, successive layers solidified in a dusty curtain (what did they catch?). On wet days the men had cut daft messages and drawings in the plaster . . . *The Pope's a Pape* . . . *D. Telfer, gentleman farmer* . . . *Oor Wullie pongs* . . . *Scotland the grave* . . . *Mrs Mcann hubba-hubba* . . . Blackie said he wouldn't lower himself to scratch that one out. His mother was twice married, her first man killed when a cattle float had crushed him against a byre wall. Blackie hated the second, a foreman at a big market garden out at the Brig, only a few years older than Blackie, they said, nobody ever getting McCann to tell them why he stayed on in the same house . . . *Women's knickers* . . . *Ride 'em cowboy* . . . there were swear words and scratchy drawings meant to be cocks and balls and women's fuds and doos, why men drew these on the wall he didn't know, unless it was just another form of madness.

'. . . you work Craig's horses all your natural for all I care,' Telfer was saying. 'Seven quid a week and all the shite you can eat – that's not my idea of living. Soon's I've got the cash I'm off, Canada, that's the place, work a tractor on a big wheat farm for a coupla years, save all you can, buy a place of your own, two hundred acres, that's just a croft over there, land's cheap, you go far enough into the wilds and the government gives you land for frees. They're desperate for skilled men, everybody knows that.'

'Skillt?' said McCann. 'Who's fuck'n skillt aboot here, eh?'

Telfer grinned at Dunky, who could just see him, perched on a big combine in a field as big as a shire. He agreed with everything Telfer said. He wanted to ask McCann why he kicked his horses if he liked them so much. Blackie threw the dregs of his tea across the dusty floor.

'Aye, it's all going tae hell now,' he said, a surprising touch of sadness in his voice. 'They used tae have six horse here and four hired men bar Willie and his brother George. Where the factory is they had three big fields, I remember ma Daddy takin' me roon by on a Sunday. They'll be nae ferming at a' soon, jist factories and corporation houses. All this fuck'n machinery, it's spoilin' everythin'.'

Telfer snorted.

'Sooner the better. That George was the clever one, away tobacco-farming in Rhodesia. Hey, I wonder what they cut at the harvest, Player's Full Strength?'

Telfer got up for a run-off down a hole in the floorboards. Dunky bent over his knees, tying his laces. He'd liked to have seen Telfer's weapon, just to find out how small his own really was by comparison. He could smell the piss and see its steam and spray, but he kept his eyes on the floor.

Young Willie came into the harness room five minutes before the half hour, his usual time. They wouldn't make a move till the factory hooter went at half-past one, gone were the days when Auld Craig's fob watch was the only timer on the farm and, as Willie told them when they complained, that old watch went hellish fast near yoking and hellish slow before lowsing.

'Hey, Willie, how's the housekeeper doing?' asked Telfer, grinning over his shoulder, the stream of water still spattering into the hole in the floor. That was another thing he didn't have in common with most blokes, all this pissing and spitting, pissing on the terraces at football matches (all they said was 'Hey, Jimmy, mind yur back' and got it out, even in a crowded ground), against walls and up closes – at school in Miss Peacock's class they used to crawl under desks and piss down a knothole. Spitting was another thing – when he was about four they'd had spitting matches in Shuttle Street and he'd gone home covered in the stuff. Everybody in Kilcaddie had catarrh and everybody spat, all the time, out of habit. A guy called Shanky had once spat in the High Street and said proudly, 'They'll skid on that all day.' Spitting and pissing were as common as breathing.

'Niver you mind about the housekeeper, Telfer,' said Willie. Dunky got to his feet. Willie was always good for a laugh, a mad bugger but good-natured. He got away with saying things that coming from anybody else would start a fight. Sometimes he'd go up to McCann and stare in his face, close-up, and shout so loud you could hear him two parks away, 'Ah hear ye're no good with wimmin, McCann, is that right what they tell me, ye're no' up to it?' His big eyes would open wide, white all round the pupils, roaring out his daft nonsense, staring into your face and then turning away and shrieking with glee. A mad bugger. Once he'd read in the papers about a Glasgow woman asking for a divorce because her man had run off with a fancy woman, described as 'pretty, dark-haired Irish Kitty Daly.' Something about this tickled Willie and for weeks afterwards he'd come up to you in the fields, eyes opening wide, staring into your face and roaring out 'pretty, dark-haired Irish Kitty Daly.' Nobody knew what he was getting at.

'It's a good job you're Craig's son, Willie,' Telfer would say. 'If you were just a common shite like the rest of us you'd be in a padded cell.'

It was still coming down in buckets when the hooter blew, a deep, hooting wail which was exactly like the sirens in the war, when they'd run down to the brick shelters in the street and spend the night drinking cocoa out of flasks, listening to the crump-crump of the big bombs and the lighter bangs of the ack-ack and the droning of the planes. Funny about those times in the shelter, looking back they were about as happy as any times he could remember. Everybody laughed and joked and shared their sand-wiches and cocoa. Grown-ups told funny stories and joked about for the benefit of the kids. James Mason hid in a shelter like theirs in the film *Odd Man Out*, when he was bleeding. Most of these families had gone away from Shuttle Place now that it was being demolished. Funny to think you remembered all these people and would probably never see them again.

'It'll be damn wet up the braes the night,' Telfer said, looking out. 'I'll need a tent and a groundsheet.'

This was his subtle way of letting them know he had a big date. If anybody was impressed they didn't show it.

'You are a ravishing scoundrel, Donald Telfer,' said Willie, speaking deliberately as though mimicking something he'd heard on the wireless. 'That's what you are, Telfer, a ravishing scoundrel. You tell the wimmin you're an agricultural student with a college degree, Donald Telfer, I'll tell you the only letters you'll ever have after your name, Donald Telfer – s.s. Shite Scraper, that's the only degree you've got, Telfer, ye dirty ravisher.'

'Women like a bit of fancy patter,' Telfer said. He fingered Willie's shirt. 'I'll tell you something, friend, you'll never get into bed with the housekeeper wearing a rotten old rag like that.'

'Niver you mind about the housekeeper, you ravishing scoundrel, you'll no' be getting up to any of your agricultural student tricks with her.'

'Oh,' said Telfer, winking heavily at the other two, 'I see, you fancy her yourself, eh? Willie's got a hard-on for her. That didn't take long. I suppose you and Auld Craig'll be mounting her in turns the night?'

Dunky noticed that McCann turned away as though angry about something.

'Hey, Willie,' Telfer went on, 'when *did* you last change that stinking shirt?'

It was a frequent question, a regular joke, Willie always having the same answer: 'Whit dae ah need tae change the bugger for, there's nuthin' wrang wi' it?'

'Most people change when they're dirty,' Telfer said. 'You're not supposed to keep a shirt on your back till it falls off in bits.'

'Ach, Telfer, we don't all want tae look like nancy boys,' said Young Willie. 'Hey, Blackie, tell they howkers we're feenished for the day. You, Logan, pit a halter on that old beast and tak' him doon the road tae Cairney's, ye know whaur they are, don't ye?'

'You want the boy to die of pneumonia?' Telfer said. 'Take him yourself, you lazy old fart, it's pishing down.'

'It'll dae his dandruff the world o' good,' said McCann.

Dunky ignored McCann's remark. He wanted to take the horse through the scheme, that would be something.

'I'll be all right,' he said. 'I'll take the oilskin.'

'There's an old bunnet o' mine in the kitchen,' Willie said. 'Ask the housekeeper for it.'

'Will I put a blanket over his back?' he asked Willie. It was said on impulse, without thinking how silly it would sound.

McCann laughed.

'What's he needin' a blanket fur?' he said. 'Ye think he's goin' tae the Royal Highland Show?'

Putting on the yellow oilskin cape, cracked along the lines of its folds, Dunky put a rope halter on old Charlie and led him out of the stable and round the small barn to the kitchen. A drain was choked and water was spreading across the yard.

Dunky led the horse up to the porch. He was excited – and a bit nervous – about having to speak to the crippled housekeeper. Telfer would have known what to say – all he could do was be serious, try not to give her the idea he was daft. When the door opened she looked out at the boy and the horse with a funny, almost bad-tempered expression on her face. She was wearing a brown cardigan. She had big tits. Her eyes were greenish, her hair red. Dunky tried to speak like a a man of the world.

'Hullo, Willie says you've to give me his old bunnet.'

She looked at him as though he might be trying to hide something from her.

'Wait here,' she said. What the hell did she think he was likely to do, walk Charlie into the kitchen? She came back to the door, the cap held out at arm's length. 'There you are,' she said, pushing it at him. He thought he could smell her. He'd felt the same way when he'd finally summoned up the courage to go up to girls and ask them to class parties. Like a criminal. His eyes couldn't help travelling down from her breasts to the gamey leg. 'Have a good look while you're at it,' she said. He blushed. He couldn't think what to say. She shut the door in his face.

The cap was far too big for him, never mind, so were his boots. Jesus Christ, he was a right galumph all right, he'd forgotten to bring his bike!

'Did ye get wet, poor wee bairn?' McCann sneered as he went into the stable. He ignored that.

'Face the oncoming traffic,' Telfer shouted after him as he walked away, horse rope in his right hand, fingers of the left hand splayed over the centre-piece of the handlebars. Telfer watched him from the door, a skinny lad in a daft cap down to his ears, walking with a decrepit old horse whose belly looked ready to sink to the ground. Telfer wondered if he'd ever looked as gormless as that. He lit a cigarette and wondered what repair job on the tractor he could invent to keep him out of the byre.

*

In the house Mary O'Donnell sat down again at the kitchen table, taking a piece of paper from the pocket of her apron. Checking that day's date from the newspaper, she counted on her fingers. Eleven days overdue now and still no period. Curse her bloody bad luck, four and half years with Stephenson and she'd been landed with it in her last month. Kicked her out just in time, that stuck-up bitch. Nothing like this would ever catch *her* out, not that hard-faced cow. Oh no, it never happened to women like her, they had brains like counting machines. They were all hard, hard as stone, the old ones and their sons and their women. Compared to them she was just trash, a nobody, a bedmat for as long as it suited the old devil then – out.

Maybe it was a punishment for her own sinful weakness, maybe she deserved to be treated like trash, maybe that's all she'd ever been good for, since the day she was born. But it wasn't going to happen to her child. It was going to get a fair chance, if she had to lie and cheat and murder for it. Nobody was going to treat it like trash. Her fists clenched on the table, she stared at the meaningless headlines of the newspaper. Her child was going to have a proper father and a proper home and a proper upbringing, she didn't care what she had to do, she'd give her child a proper life. They thought they were hard and mean, but she'd show them.

THREE

THE DOG BARKED at him from the door of its kennel as he led Charlie across the yard. Dunky kicked a stone at it, but its momentum was lost in a puddle. Craig knew what he was doing, having the brute in the yard, nobody could get near the steading without the dog making a din. (But how was Donald Telfer able to creep in at night to shag his big lumbers in the barn? Donald Telfer could do anything.) Rain drove down on the puddles, running off the peak of Willie's cap, cracking against the oilskin, washing down his face. They turned onto the road, Charlie walking with a sad attempt at a swing, clopping along in bucketing rain, poor old devil. Was the new housekeeper watching from one of the house windows? Why had she been so bad-tempered with him? Was she really thinking – *who is that hard-looking lad, I must get to know him better*? Rhonda Fleming – that's who she was like, with the red hair and the severe expression. Why did a lot of really beautiful women always have that bad-tempered look about them? He could imagine taking her up the town to the flicks and the neds at the Cross sneering at her out of the side of the mouth, *who's the geek with the limpy lumber*? and he'd go across to them, all calm and cold eyes, *you speaking to me, mac*?

The part of the scheme nearest the farm was known as The Jungle, the hard man's area. Here, it was well known, they kept coal or greyhounds in the bath. One family, the Sweeneys, had been kicked out by the Corporation housing factor because they'd taken big hammers and knocked down the wall between the kitchenette and the living-room, to save them the bother of walking through the lobby.

'They're just scruffs,' his mother said about the Jungle folk. 'It's a disgrace, there's plenty of money for drink and radiograms but the children don't even have shoes.'

The main scheme road ran for more than a mile between the big blocks, four storeys high, some with as many as five separate close-entrances. The biggest block, known as the Queen Mary, had six closes. Dalgetty's double-decker buses which ran from the scheme were called The Yellow Peril, their drivers being notorious speed merchants. He could vaguely remember them when they had open tops. There had been a murder once in the Jungle, an axe murder. McCann said he wouldn't live in the scheme, he called them razor-slashers and Irish scum, but this was just to get at Telfer, who always laughed it off saying the deadliest razor he'd seen was the one his mother used to shave her oxters.

He walked with the horse near the kerb, the rope hanging loosely in his right hand. He wouldn't have fancied walking Big Dick through the scheme, the very sight of a yellow peril bus made him turn side-on and kick out like hell. He talked to Charlie when there was nobody in sight, not that many folk were out in that weather, an occasional wifey hurrying home, a few school-dodgers playing headies up a close, occasionally a couple of men standing at a close-mouth, just smoking and gassing away the afternoon, their blue smoke rising into the rain, men who watched him go by, an event in their lives. Rainwater gurgled along the gutter, making triangular dams where a drain was choked, dammed by bricks and sludge and paper. Charlie's hair hung down his nose and neck, black wet plaits, natural oil being washed away. Now and then he lowered his head and gave it a great, spluttering shake. Poor old brute, done his eleven years' toil and all he got was a long walk in the rain to Cairney's. In England, he'd read, they did put old horses out to grass, but they could afford to be soft in England. Craig didn't have spare fields for old horses, even if he'd ever had such an idea, which was unlikely.

'Ach, you're probably better out of it anyway,' he said. 'Think of me, I'm just starting.'

White faces peered at them through the steamy windows of a bus, its inside lights already on at two in the afternoon. Aye, have a good look, people, he said to himself, it's just a daftie from the farm and a ruined nag. They'd be jealous underneath. Not many blokes of his age got to march a horse about the town, better than working in a stupid office. He should have got up on Charlie's back, ha ha, they'd have a right laugh at that, say he was playing cowboys and Injiens, just like a big saft wean.

At the far end the scheme street turned left into a cul-de-sac. He took Charlie and the bike between three stone pillars which stopped traffic from carrying through the narrow lane which led under a railway bridge to the Glasgow road. He stopped under the bridge, resting the bike against the wall, and pushed Charlie's hair back between his ears. The horse whinnied and rubbed its lower nose against the oilskin.

'If I knew a spare field I'd put you in it, old hoss,' he said. A man came towards the bridge, collar up, shoulders hunched. Dunky picked up the bike and started off again. People were very nosey. They'd wonder what he was doing.

They stopped at the main road, waiting for a break in the traffic. It was cobbled here, still inside the burgh boundary. Ayrshire County Council covered its roads with asphalt. Charlie might slip on the cobbles, he needed a good long break in the traffic to get across. A BRS lorry slowed up and the driver waved at him through the clear arc made by his windscreen wiper. He nodded his thanks and took a tighter hold on the rope, his fist against Charlie's mouth. He nodded again at the driver when he reached the other side. The real workers always took care of each other.

On that side there was a joinery behind a red-brick wall. It was darker now and he could hardly see the top of the braes for rain. The street lights were on, not the blue sodium of the scheme but orange lights on tall concrete pillars, a diseased orange which, in the dark, made people's faces seem all blotchy. Rain was getting down his back. Charlie kept snorting it out of his nostrils.

A girl called Mary Gibson lived up this road, a real smasher who'd been two classes higher than him in school. Her daddy was a policeman and she was a cracker, dark skin and jet black hair. The first time he'd really noticed her was at the school sports, she'd been in a relay race, big diddies bouncing up and down under her white shirt. He'd been too scared to ask her to any of the class parties, and he hadn't seen her since. She'd be working now, or at University or something. Pity she couldn't have seen him with Charlie, she'd have realised he was bigtime now, not just a stupid scholar. He'd have nodded to her, gruff like, big men with horses couldn't be wasting a lot of time with silly girls. Then they'd have met at the jigging at the Town Hall and she'd have asked him for a ladies' preference and said she'd seen him with the horse, wasn't it dangerous, and he'd have shrugged, all strong and silent . . .

'More likely she'd sniff the aroma of dung and go off with some gallus cunt from an office,' he said to Charlie.

The big notice, J. AND F. CAIRNEY LTD., yellow letters on green boards, stood above the main gateway of the knacker's. He led Charlie through into a red tarmacadam yard surrounded by sheds. He walked across to the small office building and propped the bike under a lighted window. The rain was slacking, easing off to a downpour as Telfer said. He rapped on the glass. A hand rubbed off condensation on the inside and a woman's face appeared. She opened the window an inch or two.

'Who are you from?' she asked.

'Craig's farm.' She looked like a married bit, weren't they supposed to be hellish experienced? Telfer said you could get it from practically any married woman.

'Oh aye, that's Mister Prentice you want, the last door on this side.'

'Thanks.' Thanks for nothing, you hee-haw office woman. He crossed railway lines sunk in the asphalt. It was a cutting off the same line that ran up to the hill from the town through the farm. Once, during the war, there had been a big outbreak of anthrax or some cattle disease and they'd brought dead cows to Cairney's by the wagonload, so many Cairney's couldn't keep pace with them. The wagons had piled up on the siding for days, the stiff legs of dead cows sticking into the air, a hellish stink of rotting carcasses blowing for miles. There were men who made a living nicking stuff out of parked railway wagons but they'd kept well clear of those cattle wagons, he remembered his father saying that, as though it proved something. What the hell could they have nicked from diseased cows?

It was chilly inside the big slide doors. He led Charlie into the shed out of the rain.

'Hullo?' The floor was of bare cement, with a pile of empty sacks in one corner. 'Hullo?'

A man appeared from the back of the shed, a hefty man in wellington boots that came up to his hips and a black rubber apron over blue dungarees. His bare arms were thick with gingery hair.

'Aye, it's a great day for the ducks,' he said.

'I'm looking for Mister Prentice.'

'That's me.'

'I'm from Craig's.'

'Oh aye, he tellt me he had a horse. An' how's Willie this weather, he's a terrible man that Willie, terrible.'

Prentice laughed. Terrible could mean all sorts of things. You could say a man was a terrible drinker or a terrible picture fiend or a terrible joker. You could even say a man was a terrible non-entity. Sometimes the word meant very and sometimes it meant terrible. From the way he laughed, Prentice seemed to be suggesting that Willie had done some terrible things in his time, which could mean anything from murder to letting down police-men's tyres.

Charlie stretched his neck, his mouth near the ground, and shook water off in a spray. Prentice put his hand on his shoulder and shook his head, eyeing the horse from head to tail.

'He's seen better days,' he said. 'Bring him through the back. Ye can leave the bike here, it's safe enough.'

Dunky kept hold of the rope and the bike, Kilcaddie was full of fly boys who'd nick anything, a bike, lead from a church roof, anything, quicker'n you could say Wee Willie Winkie.

They went through another slide door into a smaller area cut off by inside walls which didn't go all the way up to the corrugated glass roof. Prentice looked up and shouted.

'Hey, Ally!'

Through another door appeared a younger man, dressed like Prentice. Dunky thought it was funny he'd never seen either of them in the town. Maybe knackers' men didn't go about in public much. The young man took a chain off a hook on the wall and pulled it towards Charlie, the chain leading up to a pulley which ran above their heads. Prentice went to a metal locker on the wall and brought out a contraption which looked something like a revolver (not that he had ever actually seen a revolver, only in pictures). The young man took the rope from Dunky's hand. Water dripped from the horse's belly. Poor old Charlie, he seemed too big to be inside a place like this.

'The painless killer,' Prentice explained, holding the revolver contraption for Dunky's inspection. He nodded but didn't look at it properly. Prentice walked up to Charlie, the painless killer masked by his body. The young man put his hand on Charlie's nose. The horse swung his head in to the warmth of his body. Prentice put the killer against his head, near the ear. Charlie flicked water off his tail.

There was a noise like a hammer hitting a rotten post.

Charlie lurched once. Prentice stood back. Charlie lost his footing, then began to topple sideways, his rear legs buckling, his head drooping lifelessly even before his great body flopped onto the concrete floor. One of his hind legs straightened out in a slow kick. The young man dragged the chain across the floor and while Prentice lifted the head by an ear to free the rope halter, he whipped the chain in a loop round Charlie's rear right hoof.

Dunky stood back, left hand gripping the handlebars. The two men began pulling on another chain. Slowly Charlie began to rise off the ground, hind leg first. His body now seemed to have become pliable, as though death had turned his bones to rubber. When his nose was an inch or two off the cement floor the two men shoved him towards the sliding doors. These led into a long, darkish shed, where two other men were waiting, pink faces against shadows. Dunky put his bike against the wall and followed the rattling chains and the slowly swinging body of the horse. The other men had long knives. They were on to Charlie in seconds.

Dunky felt his stomach churning. Their knives worked so fast you couldn't follow the pattern of their cuts until the skin began to peel off. Under the skin was dark yellow fat, a slash of dark flesh where the knives had gone too deep. Then there was the slitting open of the great belly, the tumbling out of warm blood and steaming guts, the brown hide thrown to one side, the naked carcass looking like something that hadn't been born.

'He'll be gone in no time,' Prentice said. 'The blood's for artificial manure, the flesh for dog food, the rest boiled off in fat, nothing's wasted, the bones go for fertiliser. No, nothing's wasted here. Ye don't look well, son, is this the first ye've seen of knackers at work?'

'I'm all right,' Dunky said. Indecent, that was it, something you were never meant to see. He'd been working that hanging lump of red and yellow meat this morning.

'Of course, a lot of folk'll tell ye Cairney's meat goes into sausages and pies,' Prentice said, smiling. 'We boil the carcasses in these vats, they hang from the chains. Ye'll also hear that margarine comes out of here. Don't believe all ye hear, ha ha. In the war, maybe. Ha ha. See they pulley chains? The rats get along them at night when the carcasses are hanging – we wait till the oil's boiling and then lower them in, it boils the skeletons clean as a whistle. The rats are that desperate they come down the chains on to the carcasses, oh aye, a helluva lot of rats ye get in a place like this. The secret's to come up quiet like so's the rats don't hear ye, hundreds of them hotching about on the carcasses. Then ye pull the switch and shoot the carcass down into the oil, before they've time to get back up the chain. Man, I'll tell ye, the shriekin' would give ye nightmares. Ha ha. It's all put to good use, rats and all, I can tell ye.'

'You'll be well used to it?' Dunky asked, knowing somehow that this was what Prentice wanted him to say.

'Oh aye,' he laughed. 'Ye couldn't afford not to be, not if ye work here. Ach, rats are dirty brutes anyway. They add a bit of taste to the margarine. Ha ha, that's a joke, son, don't be goin' round the town telling people Prentice says the rats go into the marge. It's for axle grease and train oil, all that sort of thing. Nothing's wasted.'

Dunky felt cold and shivery. The smell was thick, like a bold, clammy cloth shoved in your face. He didn't look at what was left of Charlie.

Before he was halfway down the Jungle road the rain changed
to hail, icy drops stinging in his face as he pedalled the heavy-
frame bike. I bet McCann's never seen what goes on in the
knacker's, he thought. That would be something to tell them. It
was the speed of it all that amazed him. One minute old Charlie
shaking his tail . . . he felt curiously excited. It was only a horse,
wasn't it, what did horses know, they were just dumb animals. He
felt like laughing and telling jokes. This was the great thing about
being away from school, when you started real work you got to
know a lot of things they kept quiet from kids. Wait till the new
housekeeper heard he'd been to the knacker's. She'd be impressed all right.

They mucked among the bullocks in the byre for the rest of the
afternoon, Willie, McCann, Coll and Dunky, digging out the
solid sharn with the big grapes, filling the rubber-wheeled barrow,
which was heavy enough to give even Willie a bit of trouble as he
pushed it across the yard and up the single plank to the centre of
the midden. By four o'clock it was dark and the hail and rain had
stopped.

'It'll freeze the night,' McCann said. 'I'm glad I'm no' a
howker, they'll be frozen the morn's morn.'

'You don't call this cold, do you?' said Coll. 'It's chust a wee bit
nippy, that's all. Wait till it's so cold your piss freezes back up to
your cock and you have to be breaking an icicle to get free.'

'Ach, it gets colder here'n anywhere up in the hielands,'
McCann retorted. 'It's worse for us, anyway, we're no' a lot of
savages.'

'Savages, is it? There's more savages in that scheme than there
is in the whole of Africa. You won't catch a highland man fighting
with boots and razors.'

'No, ye cannae razor a man from the back.'

Willie said that McFarlane the bobby had told him a gang of
thieves had dug up forty feet of copper piping from one of the
scheme roads – just drove up in a van and got out the picks and
shovels and torn up the road in broad daylight. Willie thought this
was a great laugh.

'There's people aboot here who'd steal your eyes,' he said. If
Telfer had been there he'd have defended the scheme people.
Dunky pressed the grape into yielding straw and dung, the
smooth handle burning on his palms. He could never get as
much on his grape as the men, his body lacked the right rhythm,
or something. The secret of farm work was to get into the right
swing, to walk at a certain speed, to take a certain grip on a spade

or a fork, to go at things in a steady fashion. His trouble was that he tried too hard to do as much work as the men, with the result that he was either staggering under too heavy a load, or tripping over his feet in his eagerness to get the grape up from the floor. Yet the work must be doing him good, he could feel his arms and shoulders and back, a dull aching that made him want to groan every time he straightened up.

At five they went across to the stable. He took the broom and went to work on Charlie's stall, stiff bristles on lumpy cobbles, a light, dry sharn, horses not being as skittery as cattle.

'No more Charlie then?' he said to McCann.

Blackie stopped, leaning against the end of the partition.

'It's like a wee bit of history,' he said, 'this stable's about a hundert year old and I'll bet you that's the last horse that'll ever be in this stall. I'll tell you the truth, if they could get machines for us *we'd* be at the knacker's, I'm no jokin'.'

Wasn't that funny, McCann speaking to him in that sad, low voice, as though they were friends? And wasn't it even funnier, how he – and Willie – tended to speak almost proper English when they were on their own with you? No doubt there was some reason for it.

McCann shook his head and went into Big Dick's stall with the bucket of corn. He was in a good mood because tomorrow he'd have something to shake them up a bit. Tonight he was going over to the Brig to see a man there about buying his motor bike. Wait till Telfer saw him come charging into the yard with it the morn's morn, he'd do his nut with envy. He'd seen the bike once, a big powerful brute, do eighty or ninety no bother. He'd had a motor bike before, but this time he was getting one that wouldn't conk out every five miles. Great for taking women for rides into the country. If he played his cards right he might even get the limpy housekeeper interested, being a cripple she'd probably never travelled much, he'd say, like the bike? How about a wee spin, safe as houses? Next thing he'd have her away down to Troon, stop on the way, back of a hedge, riding the arse off her, that's what they all needed, easy as pie if you had a motor bike.

Yet the best part was thinking of Telfer when he saw the bike in the morning. It was time Telfer was shaken up a bit, he thought he was something great.

While McCann was in the stall, Dunky leaned down into the cornkist and shoved handfuls of grain into a paper bag. Willie let him take sacks of hay and straw home for his rabbits, but corn was different, it was safer just to knock it. He made a circular screw of the top of the bag and shoved it inside his jerkin.

Before they went home for the night the men always came into the stable. Coll and Telfer stood watching Blackie and the boy finish sweeping along the gutter, Telfer smoking, Coll looking on with what could have been a smile on his big, open face. Monday was his night for going to a pub in Kilcaddie with two other Oban men, getting a good bucket of whisky down him out of the proceeds of the five child allowances which his wife drew and he spent.

Willie came into the stable looking for his bicycle pump.

'What's for tea the night, Willie?' Telfer asked, winking at the other men. 'Two boiled eggs and a sausage up the housekeeper?'

Willie bared his teeth at Telfer.

'Ye ravishing scoundrel, Telfer,' he said. 'Ye're a sexual rogue.' He grinned at them all, as though they should be astonished that he knew such expressions.

In the farmhouse Mary O'Donnell limped across from the gas cooker to the big table, where Auld Craig sat staring at his hands, although she couldn't actually tell if his eyes were open or not.

'I hope you like black puddin' and fried potatoes,' she said, putting the plate in front of him. The three collie-crosses lay at his feet, eyes wide, chins on the floor, trained by dint of many kicks to lie still until the old man threw them whatever was left on his plate.

'Hrrmmmph.' He twisted his head to look at her. 'Don't be givin' us any fancy cookin', plain food's the best.'

She put down his blue-ring china mug of tea, watching the stiff movements of his arms. An old man like him would feel the cold, no wonder, in a house like this. When she'd arrived the first thing she'd noticed in the kitchen was the sink with dirty dishes piled almost as high as the taps. There was an old gas geyser for hot water, but it wasn't working. After taking her case into the ground-floor bedroom, she'd changed into her working clothes and got to work on the dishes. Willie Craig had promised her that a ton of coal would be delivered the next day, but until that there was nothing for fires. Already she'd sensed that the old man, ancient as he looked, was the real power in the house. It was him she had to pay attention to. Willie? He was a man and she knew what sort of attention he'd be after, no, the old fella was the one, too old to want to throw a leg over her, and a lot harder to get round because of it.

When he finished eating Auld Craig took his plate and swept the remains of his black pudding on to the bare stone floor. Mary O'Donnell's lips tightened; she had swept and washed the floor that afternoon, dragging the big table and the mahogany dresser and the heavy old chairs this way and that to get her broom into corners where crusts had gone green and dust gathered in thick rolls. Auld Craig stretched his hand to the centre of the table, to the white loaf. He tore several lumps of bread and crust, his ancient hands still wide and bony at the knuckles, the skin slack only round the purple veins on the back of his hand. As she watched him throw the fragments to the scrabbling dogs Mary O'Donnell controlled an impulse to shut her eyes and scream at him. Her chest was still heaving with rage as the old man pulled himself up out of the chair, his body jack-knifed over the table as he straightened his legs.

'Hrmmph.' He looked at her for a second, cold blue flints peering at her from under the great eyebrows. 'I'm awa' tae bed.' He took a bad-tempered kick at a dog which moved in front of him, the stiffness of his knee giving the dog ample time to escape the hobnail boot.

'Righto,' she said, watching him clump away to the lobby. She cleared his place, a familiar choking anger in her throat. Was the rest of her life to be spent watching men treat her like a servant, dropping their messes all over the house which she had to clean, the house in which she had all the duties of a wife with none of the rights of a wife? Sure as the fires of hell it was not. A house was a woman's place, to run as she thought fit, and she was a woman now, twenty-eight years of age, old enough to know many things about men, things that would have seemed dark and strange to a girl, things that would have stuck on her tongue in the shadows of the confessional, memories of words and faces frozen into her mind, a man's white back twisted away from her face, whisky-tainted air, not knowing what the unseen face was doing, not believing when she did know, not understanding – don't Andy, that's *dirty*!

Dirty? Of course, dirty, but the shock had gone by now, worn away by the years. There was power in the wasted leg and its ungainly apparatus. What she had learned was to see behind men's eyes, to see behind the first outward look of surprise and contempt. To see into the secret places where men had thoughts they themselves didn't know existed. And to use that power to gain her rights, to make her as good as any hard-eyed, nose-high, contemptuously sniffing *wife*.

Craig turned right on the upstairs landing, off which were two big bedrooms, one occupied by Willie and one by himself. Switching on the light he saw that his bed had been made, for the first time in a month or so.

'Damn and hell, it's cold,' he said. There was a single-bar electric fire in the empty grate. The girl had switched it on, electricity burning away all afternoon, damn the girl, did she think he was an old woman to need money burned for heat? He wheezed as he bent down to switch it off. He took off his jacket, arms stiff behind his back as his fingers pulled at the sleeves. He put the jacket on the chair, the heavy old rocking-chair his father had brought when they moved south from Aberdeenshire, 1891, his father's rocking-chair, they'd sawn off the rockers just before the great war – the right one had split at the front end; now it was a high-backed wooden chair with a ribbed back and arms honed shiny and yellow where paint and polish had been smoothed away by the elbows of the years.

He put his thumb against his nose and cleared one nostril into the cupped palm of the same hand, repeating the heavy snort with the left nostril. He wiped his hands on his trousers and sat down on the edge of the high double bed, bought by him for him and Jessie in 1917 at the auction rooms, two pounds six shillings, a good bed. He could feel the cold in his back, but these days his back was never quite right. He wheezed again as he bent down to unlace his boots.

'A dram's the best thing,' he said, turning to a walnut stand which stood by the bed, on it a small wooden barrel with a brass tap. Opening the door of the bedstand he took out a china mug, his father was given that mug when they opened the railway siding in 1894, the old Kilcaddie and District Railway and Traction Company, aye, the siding was to bring in cattle to the market, the big open mart, all football fields now, he could remember his father saying the mug was to be saved for special occasions as clearly as he could remember eating the new woman's black pudding. He held the mug under the brass tap, real malt whisky, a thin amber flow from the same barrel his father had kept by his bedside, must be near a hundred year old.

'Damn the lot of you,' he said, raising a slightly shaking hand to his mouth. He drank the whisky, a third of a pint or so, in three good gulps, the warmth spreading out from his belly almost as soon as he had coughed his usual cough, the same whisky and the same cough for near on fifty years now, just as his father had done, drinking is a fool's ploy, his father had told him, hiv yer ain whusky by the bed an' content yersel wi' a guid dram afore ye ging tae sleep.

Groaning inwardly with the stiffness in his back he levered himself backwards on to the bed and pulled up his legs, panting slightly, dragging the blankets up over his trousers and his thick shirt and his braces. Willie would put out the light, Willie who'd turned out not such a bad boy, better'n Jessie and him had expected, never a good boy when he was young, not like George, George was the bright one of the pair of them, but George was never happy about the place, always wanting to be off, desperate to be away from the day he left the school. Sons, ach, they wouldn't be told. The one you wanted to stay was far away and the other hung about the place and never got married or anything at all. A hundred and ninety acres then and now it was houses and the factory and scum from the town ruining the good land, aye, maybe George was bright enough to see it all coming, that's why he'd gone away to Africa, a letter and pictures of his bairns at Christmas, the one letter a year. George took after himself, he knew what was what. Left to Willie they'd have nothing left at all. The old man smiled. A hundred and forty-eight acres left, not counting the four rented fields from the old Campbell place, not bad for an old man that everybody thought was in his dotage, aye, he knew now how to handle these town boys, he'd hung on to his fields, seen the price go up from fifty pound an acre to fifteen hundred an acre and still he wouldn't let them buy him out, no, let the damnt factory boys hold their horses, land was going up all the time, damn the Corporation and their compulsory purchase orders, aye, Willie ye don't know the half of what your old father gets up to, you don't have the brains, didn't even have the wit to fake your own school report, signed my name like a hen scratching in a midden, had to leather you for that, always had to leather Willie for something, ten pounds wasn't a bad price for an old done horse, he remembered that land before Jackie Cairney started the knacker's, it was trees then, the cattle used to stand under the trees when it was raining, the old folk used to say the trees were in a round clump because that bit went back to the pagan people, he'd never had much time for that sort of history stuff and fairy tales, but at least he remembered what the old folk had said. Nowadays? Ach, the damnt people nowadays wouldn't spare the time of day, all they knew was their picture palaces and their chip shops, still, maybe the Logan loon would turn out all right – for a scheme boy. They'd finish the tatties this week, that meant he could give Coll his books, too

many damnt men about the place for all the size it was, that's
Willie on the stairs.

'WILLIE!'

Willie Craig came up the stairs in his stockinged feet. What did
the old bugger want now? He'd never liked going in that room,
not since his mother died.

'Ye're in bed then?' he said, standing in the doorway. The old
man turned his head on the pillow.

'Put off the light,' he said, 'I'm for sleep. We'll give Coll the bag
on pay-day. The boy's a fair worker.'

'Aye,' said Willie. 'Righto.'

He switched off the light and went across the landing to his own
room, which looked less now like an old bothy than it had done
since the last housekeeper, Mrs McNidder, had left to go south
and live with her widowed sister in Ipswich. They'd talked before
about sacking Coll once the main tattie crop was in the pits. He
put his boot on the rexine cover of the bedroom's only chair and
untied the lace from round the ankle. He'd heard a good joke that
day from Lapsley, the corn merchants' traveller. It was about Irish
women, he'd decided to tell it to Mary O'Donnell once he'd
changed out of his working gear. Tomorrow he'd get her to light a
coal fire in his grate, he was over fifty, he was entitled to a fire in
his bedroom. Rummaging in a drawer he pulled out a new flannel
shirt, cream with blue stripes, he'd been saving it for a special
occasion like Craig's funeral – his own would come first more
likely.

He put on the shirt and fastened its collarless neck with a brass
front-stud. Then he threw his wet socks into the fireplace, they
were rotten and could be used for rags. He changed his trousers
but not his long woollen combinations. The trousers were of the
same rough, hodden grey material as his father's, both suits made
out of the chest in his father's bedroom, the chest that contained
yards and yards of hodden grey, put there by Grandfather Craig
before the First World War, to be taken out every ten or fifteen
years when a new suit had to be made up, cloth that came out as
stiff and as greasy as it was when Grandfather Craig laid it down
fifty years ago, cloth that never seemed to run out.

He went downstairs in his bare feet, carrying a new pair of wool
socks and his number two boots.

She was at the sink, washing dishes. He ignored her, taking the
chipped enamel basin from under the sink and running hot water
from the geyser. She glanced at him, their elbows almost touching.

'I heard a good tale today about Irish people,' he said, taking the basin over to the table, where he laid it on the floor. He spoke properly to her, not because she was Lady Muck or anything, but because it was better for people you didn't know too well. He knew he didn't look like a man who'd once taken his Scottish Higher Leaving Certificate in five subjects (Latin, English, Maths, History and French, the last two at lower level, not nearly as good as George had done) – he liked to suprise people occasionally, show them there was more to him than common dirt. Not that he needed to care what they thought, there wasn't many had as much cash in the bank as his father.

She went on washing dishes, although he could tell she was waiting for the story.

'This woman moves to a new house a few miles outside o' Dublin and she comes back to see her friend next door and she says, d'you know what's happened, the corner shop's been taken by a Jew, a fella called Cohen. What's a Jew? says the other wife. You don't know, sure they're the dirty bastards who took Jesus Christ and kicked him about and nailed him to a cross and reviled him. Is that a fact, says the other wife, it just shows you, you move away for two weeks and you don't know half of what's going on at all.' He nodded, his big, staring eyes fixed, unblinking it seemed, on her face. Then his lips curled back and he shook with a soundless laugh.

'Very funny,' said Mary O'Donnell, wiping her hands on the dish towel, eyebrows raised in a haughty manner.

'Ye like a good joke?' said Willie, putting his feet into the basin. 'D'you know the one about the Glesca hoor who thought an endless belt was a weekend in bed wi' a black man?'

Again the searching eyes. Mary O'Donnell knew she was being sounded out. If she laughed she was fair game and he'd come clomping into her room that night. If she didn't he'd say she was high and mighty and he'd give her no peace until he'd rubbed her face in the dirt; she knew his type.

Reaching round to the table drawer, Willie took out a large pair of scissors and began cutting his toenails, parings sparking across the stone floor, grunting with the strain of the knee pressing into his chest.

'It's well seen ye haven't had a woman in the house for a long time,' she said. Willie went on cutting. He'd had a good look at her, fine, big arms, a good pair of paps, not a bad-looking wench, considering.

'Throw's over the dishtowel till I dry my feet,' he said, looking up.

'Ye'll do no such thing,' she said, taking care not to sound too bossy. 'Here, use this old thing, I'll have to wash it anyway.'

'Oh, I see, fancy notions,' he said. But he took the old towel and she knew she'd won something. She cleared the table while he shaved at the sink, the cut-throat blade rasping clean, pink swatches on the grizzled grime of his broad chin and heavy cheeks. Now he was cleaned up and fresh and ready to throw the leg over anything that was warm and moving. But not her, not as soon as this.

'You're a Roman Catholic, a Pape?' he said, turning so that she could see he was using the dishtowel to wipe the remains of soap off his face.

'I used to be,' she said. 'Wouldn't ye like a better towel than that for your face?'

'Ach, I'm no' bothered,' he said. 'We'll be having the priests sniffing round, I suppose, trying to get you back among the Papes.'

'Why should they?'

'Oh, they're hot on that, the Papish boys.'

'They can keep it for all I care. I got my blessing a long time since.'

He knew she meant the withered leg. For some reason he wasn't all that caring about her being a limpy dan. It made her easy to talk to, as though she had no right to be the equal of normal folk.

'I can aye give ye a hand wi' the milkin',' he said.

'Oh, that's all right. There's one thing ye could see to, get these dogs out of the house, they're just a mess.'

'Aye,' he said. 'It's time they were out anyway, I'd shoot them if I had my way.'

He went out then, not saying where he was going or when he'd be back. She made herself a cup of tea and sat at the big table. He'd wanted to see if she was game for dirty jokes, which meant was she game for him in her bed, and when he couldn't see that way clear he'd offered to help her with the milking, and then he'd admitted to her that his father had the say about the dogs. In time, she supposed, a wife could get him to have a bath . . . it was a hard thing to have to discuss in your own head, but she knew he'd be the best man she'd find to father her baby, the trouble being that these dour Scotsmen wouldn't marry a woman they thought was an easy ride, yet if she didn't do something quickly it would be too late and she'd never be able to make him believe he was the real father. She was a month gone by already. She might get away by saying it was two months premature, but not much more. And once she let him into her bed how did she know he'd ever consider marrying a crippled Irish Catholic? They were hard, the Scots, hard as granite. Him and his father might look and live like something out of a byre, but underneath they'd be as stiff and respectable in their ideas as only mean old Protestant bastards could be.

FOUR

TO BE QUITE honest, Telfer thought as he sat in the back row of the Granada cinema watching Burt Lancaster and Gary Cooper in *Vera Cruz*, he wasn't bothered if it was too cold or wet to get a quick shag with Agnes at the back of her house, he'd been up her three nights a week for four months, ever since he'd chatted her up at harvest-time, and he was getting a bit fed up with her. He had his right arm round her waist, the tips of his fingers gently prodding her breast.

'Mmmmm,' she mouthed into his ear, blowing hot air and letting her tongue touch it, wet and tantalising. He should've known he'd only to get his hands on her tits and she'd be wanting to climb all over him, when he was more interested in Burt Lancaster.

'Watch the picture,' he said, pulling her back to her seat with his right hand, his left arm on the back of the next seat. Agnes had been one of the dames he'd watched coming out of the office block at the factory, glamorous they looked then, him sitting on a tractor in working clothes, them in high heels, wearing make-up. Now she was just Agnes, familiar, you didn't buy the shop for a dab of sherbert.

They walked home through the Cross, Telfer keeping his hands in the pockets of his brown sports trousers, her hand on the inner elbow of his chocolate sports jacket, obviously well pleased to be seen about the town with a big handsome blond bloke. It was frosty and dry, ideal weather for a swift poke at the back of her parents' house in Barcraigie, a good-class area of detached bungalows where bankers and the like lived. He didn't even feel like making his usual joke, 'They always did say the knobs hang out in Barcraigie.' It was all too bastartin' obvious, start off looking for a new ride and end up being stopped at jewellers' windows 'just for a wee look at the engagement rings, oh, that's awfully nice, my friend Beth got one just like that, isn't it a *lovely* wee stone?'

He was different, he knew that. He wasn't like the men who were rolling out of the pubs after a good bucket, he wasn't interested in talking about football, he was—

'You're very quiet tonight, Don, is something the matter?'

Don! At the farm he was Big Telfer – everybody was either Big somebody or Wee somebody. He wasn't the same as the lads from the scheme, maybe because he was over six feet and curly blond, whereas they were all wee bauchly men with dark hair (one of Willie's favourite jokes – 'Ye hear aboot Erchie McEachern the dwarfie, he's suing the corporation, says they built the pavement too near his arse'), maybe because his mother and father were both what they called a bit fast. Maybe. Maybe aye, maybe hooch aye, as McCann would say, poor ignorant clown that he was. But he didn't like Don. Don was a nancy boy's name. Typical of Agnes!

At first it had been enough to give him a hard-on walking down the street, just thinking of him, a scheme fella, a midden-scraper, riding Agnes from Barcraigie, the floor manager's daughter, enough just to get into their toffs' living room on a Sunday night, when the pan-loaf McFarlanes had gone to bed, to get him steaming, enough to know they thought he was a scruff. Now he didn't give a fuck, she was just another girl wanting a ring on her finger. He wanted something different, he was different himself, he wanted something out of the ordinary. And when he thought of that he thought of his hands going under the strong arms of the new housekeeper, and the haughty look on her face and the cold look in her green eyes. That would be something out of the ordinary. To bang the cripple. He started singing. They were walking up a Barcraigie road, alongside neat privet, a good-class area where a car could be parked outside all night without having its windows kicked in.

> The village cripple he was there,
> He wasnae up tae much,
> He laid the virgins on the ground,
> And banged them wi' his crutch.

'Shoosh, Don.' He wanted to annoy her.

> Singing, balls to your partner,
> Arses tae the wall,
> If ye've never been shagged on a Setterday nicht,
> Ye've never been shagged at all.

'Shoosh, Don, people'll *hear* you.'

'I don't care about people.'

'You care about me, don't you?'

'Oh, yeah, sure.'

'That doesn't sound very enthusiastic.'

A squeeze on the elbow. A ring on the finger. A steady job. Kids to the Sunday School. Gran McFarlane's coming to tea tonight. Auntie Meg's asked us up for Sunday.

ALL THAT FOR A QUICK RATTLE?

'I'm thinking of emigrating to Canada, serious like '

No squeeze this time. Kilcaddie women! Sensible shoes and heavy tweed coats, just like their fatbag mothers, looking like wives the day after they left school.

'Oh! I thought we were, I mean, sort of—'

'You and me? Aw, look, Agnes, I'm just a common tractor driver, you're – different.'

Wheedling face at his shoulder, looking up.

'You don't think I'm different when I'm letting you do *that*?'

Tell me the old, old story. For men it was a game, for women some kind of favour they did you. God help you if you weren't grateful! They'd let you sin – now take your punishment – get married. In other countries it was different, he'd read things that would make a Kilcaddie woman's hair stand on end. America, Canada – over there women thought no more of a poke than lighting a cigarette.

'You like it as much as I do.'

She turned her head away. Embarrassed.

'Go on, admit it, you like it, don't you?'

'I do *not*.'

'You do sot.'

'I only did it because I loved you.'

Reproachful now. Tears on the horizon. He didn't give a rat's fart. She was just another on the list. Ticked off. He had it in him to roger every bloody woman in Kilcaddie. Thirty-four was the current tally. Not bad in seven years, considering all the time you wasted with prick-teasers and professional virgins.

'Did I ever tell you about the first time I got into a woman,' he said. He could feel she *hated* that. 'It was a bint called Aitken who lived in the next close to us. I used to deliver papers to her – she was married, had a baby, her man was working on the hydro-electric somewhere up north.' She pretended not to listen so he went on talking, knowing she'd blow up. 'One time I'm round collecting her paper money and she asks me in for a cup of tea, I was about fourteen. She was a right mawkit piece, I'll tell you, never got out of her nightie one week to the next. She gave me a biscuit and put her hand on my dick and says, "How d'ye fancy ridin' me?" Just like that. You should've smelt her, never washed except when it was raining.'

'That's *horrible*, I don't want to hear any more.'

'Aye, but that wasn't the worst part, every time I went with her paper she used to be waiting for me behind the door and pull me inside by the balls, I'll tell you, she was that desperate she couldn't wait to get on the bed, she used to grab me in the lobby and make me do it up against the wall. It's a wonder I ever reached fifteen.'

He felt her shudder. He laughed. People like Agnes were easy meat. All they had was their respectable front. As soon as you got through that you could walk all over them, they didn't have the guts of a jelly baby. It hadn't even been him that used to ride the Aitken piece, it was Sammy Campbell. What a laugh! Stupid Agnes, maybe she wasn't sickened properly yet. He began to sing again:

> The village postman he was there,
> He had a dose of pox,
> He couldn't stuff the wimmin
> So he stuffed the letter box.

'Please stop that, do you want to disgrace me?'

When they reached her gate she was still in an icy mood, but he didn't try to bring her round.

'Right then,' he said, 'where'll it be the night, the coal bunker or the garden shed? I'm easy.'

She stood at the gate. It was freezing now. Nice and quiet in Barcraigie, folks pulled their curtains here and put chains on their doors and sat round their big fires. Nobody kicking a wife through the wall, no nests of half-starved kids screaming into the night, no lurching boozers on the pavements. Agnes was the only one of them in the street, the only Barcraigie resident out in the night.

'I don't know what's got into you,' she said. He'd heard that quiet, brave voice before. It was trying to tell you something. He didn't want to know.

'Into me? All I said was where are we going to perform the night?'

'Is that all you're—'

Then, interrupting herself, she turned and fumbled for the gate latch and was up the path. He stood for a moment, then shrugged and walked away. It was a great feeling to rub their noses in it and make *them* break it off. Rub her toffee nose in it. Ram it into them and then shove their own dirt into their faces. He walked down the windy avenue, looking over solid privet hedges at the drawn blinds and curtains of Barcraigie's well-to-do. They had to hide themselves away in their big houses, the creepy bastards. Stuck-up load of shite, trying to pretend they were something, once the knickers were down they were all the same.

Big gloomy gardens always made him think of slipping quietly among bushes, tip-toeing up to windows, looking in, seeing some toff woman sitting high and mighty, then smashing in the window and climbing in, a dirty grin on his face, she'd start all haughty and then he'd make her grovel in front of him and beg for it and then he'd slash her face with a knife, take that, you stuck-up cow, think you're Lady Muck do you, cut her, cut her face and her body . . . he felt better when he reached the old tenements on the north side. He felt more at home in the real town, under proper lights. Anybody could have strange notions inside their heads, no need to worry, anybody could think what they liked, it didn't mean anything . . .

At the old slag heaps, ragged black dunce-hat shapes against the lights of the factory perimeter fence, Willie got off the bike and wheeled across rutted grass and slag, his path lit by the early moon, a frozen, green light that shimmered on the outlines of the old slag heaps and threw narrow shadows under big stones. He knew these black hills well, after nearly fifty years, their grass patches (one worn smooth as a bowling green from the feet of the Sunday morning pitch and toss school); their ridges and valleys, the stretch of water where he'd caught newts and tadpoles, forty-five years ago, where wee boys from the scheme still caught newts and tadpoles and sticklebacks. By day the black hills looked like a rubbish coup, a litter of broken McEwan's bottles and cans and flock-spewing mattresses and bits of bikes. By night the litter was hidden. Nobody had mined anything here since before the First World War. Turning round the base of one heap he saw the light from the fire, a brazier standing just inside the low opening of the Tink's wee house – half cave, half shale hut backing into a slag heap, its flat roof of railway sleepers and corrugated sheets long overgrown with grass and dockens.

'Aye aye there,' Willie called into the opening, unable to see past the white coals and the shimmering heat-rise of the brazier.

'Friend or foe?'

Willie put his bike against the wall of flat shale pieces.

'It's me,' he said, edging into the hut between the brazier and the railway sleeper doorpost, the door being a quilt of old grainbags stitched together by the Tink, pulled across only in storms.

Inside Willie saw that the Tink had been reading, sitting in his wrecked armchair (legs sawn off) with his feet on his bed, an arrangements of bricks walling in a well-packed grounding of straw, with two old blankets.

'Aye, it's a cauld wan,' he said.

'Have tea from glass, Willie my friend,' said the Tink, pouring from a billy can into a jam-jar. 'Your well-to-do folk, aristocrats and the like, they all drink tea from glass, they know that china imparts an oil to tea, glass is what your true gentry use, especially abroad, I believe the society folk in Russia and Germany regarded china as dead common.'

Willie felt the heat from the brazier on his legs and hands. He sat on the straw bed, legs straight out in front, size eight boots pointing roofwards. He never told any of them at the farm that he regularly dropped in on the Tink's wee house in the black hills, to them he was just the daft tink who lived like a rat in the slag heaps, a real looney who didn't even have a front door, just a hole. Willie knew everybody in the area, scheme folk, police, travellers, farmers and their men, the factory gate police, the ministers and even a priest or two, but the Tink was his friend. He wasn't really a tinker at all, his name was Archibald Stewart, he'd lived in the black hills for years, ever since Willie was a wee boy and terrified of him, running away from the hills when he appeared, running all the way home trying not to spill newts or tadpoles or stickey-backs, running away from the bogey man of the black hills.

Willie had first spoken to Archie Stewart during the war, when men were scarce and his father had said to ask the Tink if he'd turn out for the harvest.

'No, I won't work,' the Tinker had said, surprising Willie with his well-spoken accent, Willie who even at forty-odd was still a bit scared of going near the Tink's cave. 'Not that I wouldn't want to give you a hand, but I cannot break my rule, not after all these years.'

And while Willie stood by, changing feet, half-expecting the Tink to jiggle his eyes and scream bogey-man's lingo, Archie Stewart had told him why he lived in the black hills.

'I was training for the ministry when the great war broke out,' he'd said. 'They made me a lieutenant in the HLI, I thought it was our duty to fight for King and Country, I didn't want to be a padre. You know, I'd never mixed much with men before that. At first I thought they were terrible rough, the scum of the Glasgow slums, but I soon got to know them, not the way a minister knows people, no, not like that. And the more were killed the more I kept thinking, what has this English war got to do with us, English and Germans, I could hardly tell the difference, what had it to do with us, a lot of Scotsmen standing about in trenches full of water, our feet going gangrenous, rats as big as cats waiting to eat off your toes, a wee tot of rum before the whistle went? At first I kept praying to God to make me believe it was for civilisation, that's what they always tell you, no matter what war you're in or what side you're on. And I realised there was no God, we were only fighting for the rats, they were getting fatter and we were getting shot. Either the Bible was true and we were all God's people and the war was wrong, or the Bible was wrong and the English were right. But if we were shooting each other for the benefit of a shoal of French rats it didn't matter who was right, it was all wrong. The Jerries had ministers telling them the same things our ministers were telling us! I just lost the whole notion of God. I said to myself, if you ever get out of this, Archie Stewart, you're never going to have any more to do with them and their civilisation. I think it was all these wee men from Glasgow, men I wouldn't have hardly spoken to before, wee bowly legs from rickets and whatnot, hunger on their faces, even boys of eighteen. I kept asking in my prayers, what the hell has the King of England ever done for these wee men? Ship them out to France to feed a lot of rats? No, I came home and I left my family and I wandered the countryside till I found this place, the mines were spent by then, and I just built my wee house and here I'll stay.'

Willie hadn't been in sympathy with this line at all, at that time. 'It wouldnae do if we all jaked it in and lived in a rubbish dump,' he'd said. He was in a reserved occupation, nothing to be ashamed of it, just him and his father and mother and a mental defective to bring in the hearst, he was as much against Hitler as anyone else. Armies had to eat.

'It was Kaiser Bill in my day,' the Tink had said. 'He was a baby-eater as well. But I won't argue with you, I'm not interested. One day Scotland will wake up to itself, but I doubt it'll be after my time. You see that scheme over there, that's the civilisation the King gave all the wee men from Scotland. I'll tell you, I never go into the scheme, it makes me want to cry seeing the terrible old faces on the men and the children without shoes, I could cry in the street. A lot of wee men getting eaten by rats for that! I'll maybe believe in their civilisation the day I hear of God and the King of England sharing a two-apartment Corporation house.'

Willie had laughed then – and felt guilty at hearing such talk in wartime, he had heard tales of Scottish Nationalists being traitors

who made secret broadcasts to Hitler and listened to Haw-Haw
on the wireless. But over the years he'd come to accept Archie's
views as just a part of him, like his curious cave. Although it would
never do to tell the likes of Telfer or McCann that he came down
here, he often wished he could come out in the open and tell them
that Archie had a lot of brains. He never talked about football or
told jokes about the Pope or even mentioned women, the most
exciting thing in his life was the annual nesting of mavises under
his roof, year after year the same thrushes coming back to the
same place, living with Archie, only rising in a great chattering
when strangers came near. These days Archie was more or less
accepted and ignored, although there had been a time when the
neds had come down to smash up him and his hut, just out of
principle, the way they'd give a kicking to a man wearing a stiff
collar, or a Celtic scarf. After they'd pulled the place apart Willie
had expected Archie to be angry – or even scared – but there he'd
been, calmly rebuilding his walls.

'No, no, it's my fault,' he'd said. 'They know I'm free and they
aren't, it's only natural they resent me, I know how they feel. But
someday, Willie, they'll wake up to the truth and then they can
look out, they'll be kicking down the walls of Buckingham
Palace.'

Willie had never told Archie that he'd heard who these neds
were from people he knew in the scheme and had given the wire to
Big Watson, the bobby in those days, and that Big Watson had
bided his time till he got them, one by one when there was nobody
about, and that Big Watson had given all three of them a
hammering, three hard neds walking into a big Aberdonian fist
on dark nights, bang. Big Watson was dead now. He'd said the
Tink was a looney, but harmless, like a child, needed protection.
They didn't have bobbies like Big Watson nowadays.

'And how is the tea would you say, be honest now?' Archie
asked him, as serious as if he was asking the price of corn.

'Fine,' said Willie. It had neither milk nor sugar and didn't
taste like tea at all, but he drank it.

'It's made out of dandelion leaves,' Archie said, triumphantly,
nodding across the fire-lit hut. 'It's something the McGleishes
told me about.'

The McGleishes were real tinks, claimed to be descended from
Charles Edward Stuart, a roving band who lived wild and
mended pots. Since the scheme had grown they came less about
the farm, preferring to stay over towards the Brig. The story about
them was the day Sandy McNair, a farmworker, had met Old

Man McGleish on the road, the day after one of his daughters had married another tink. Old Man McGleish had said the couple were away on their honeymoon and Sandy, surprised, had asked where they'd gone. As far as the dam in Kilberrie Woods, McGleish had replied, quite serious. That was at least quarter of a mile away from the McGleish encampment in the Brig woods.

'We've got a new housekeeper,' Willie said, knowing that Archie liked to hear about the farm's goings-on. 'She's Irish, y'know, a gamey leg on her into the bargain.'

'That's nice,' said Archie. 'And how's your father?'

'Oh, no bad, his back's hurtin' him.'

'No wonder. It's amazing he still gets about, shows you the value of a good healthy life in the fresh air. I've watched him for forty years or more, a fine big man he was, too. Now he's like an old ghost walking the fields. I can imagine men like him on the moors when the Covenanters held their meetings, he's like the very granite. Wars will come and towns will spread and children will be brought up for slavery in the factories and kings will die and your father will go on, not giving a damn for any of it.'

'Aye, maybe,' Willie said. 'He's a ghost that won't lie down.'

They were both quiet, knowing that something had been said that should not have been said. Archie leaned back to throw some more anthracite on the fire, the glow shining through his fine grey hair, his head looking like a big egg covered in thin fuzz. There was something Willie wanted to talk about. Was Archie the man to discuss it with? Who else was there?

'Ehm, Archie, ye know how I've never got merriet?'

'Yes. A great pity, I always think – it's not for me, mind, but you'd like having a wife fine.'

'Aye. Ye're mebbe right.' He hesitated. Mother Craig had died when he was thirty-five, leaving him alone with Auld Craig; the old man had never been an easy man to talk to before but after that he'd kept himself very much to himself. It was difficult to come out in the open about things that affected yourself. 'D'ye think I'm past the age for it?'

Archie Stewart knew, by the abruptness of the question, that Willie wanted serious words from a friend. He put his head to one side.

'How old are you, Willie, fifty-three is it?'

'And a year.'

'Hmmm. Well, I would say it depended on what you wanted. Is

it love, or children, or just a wife to keep your feet warm and darn your socks?'

Aye, Willie thought, what is it I want?

'I'm thinkin' mebbe I should get merriet.'

'Well, at least you're a realist, Willie, just like your father. I remember saying to him when he sold those first thirty acres to the factory, what was it he got, twelve hundred an acre? I remember saying to him, you're a realist, Craig, it's a pity Scotland didn't have a few more dreamers and a few less realists.'

Suddenly embarrassed, Willie decided to make a move.

'Aye, well, I don't know about that, I think I'm for away.'

'I'd advise you to follow your heart and not your head, Willie. Life isn't all saving up cash to pay for a decent funeral.'

'So ye say. Well, I'm off. So long.'

'Bring your scissors next time, I'm needing a haircut now that we're into the New Year.'

His face flushed with the direct heat of the brazier, Willie went off round the shale heaps, frosty air nipping hot razor-raw skin. He rode slowly round the back of the factory, seeing lights and machinery working through a gap in the big slide doors. Plenty of overtime, nightshifts and such capers, that suited them fine at the factory. They were welcome to it. Having the woman in the house had put him in the notion. He hadn't intended to visit her, not after the old man saying he was going to give Coll the bag, but having the woman in the house had started him off and the heat of the brazier had done its work. He cycled about a mile round the back road.

The old miners' cottages stood in a single row, three of them empty and boarded up to keep out kids and tramps, old Mrs Graham living in the fourth and the Colls in the fifth. When they left the cottages were to be demolished. Ayrshire County Health said they were unsuitable for habitation.

He got off the bike on the grass at the rear and wheeled it towards the back door of the end house. He laid the bike against the wall and had a peek through the curtained window. He listened, then he knocked on the back door. It opened, showing a small kitchen lit by a paraffin lamp.

'Come on in then,' Morag Coll said, speaking her precise Highland tongue, 'are you wanting the whole world to see you?'

She bolted the door behind him, a small, bustling woman of about forty, with brown hair going grey. She took off her apron as Willie sat in the high-legged wooden chair by the black range.

'Do you want a cup of tea?' she asked. 'The bairns are all sound asleep.'

'I hud one wi' the Tink,' he said. 'By God it's a chill one. Coll'll need his dram the nicht.'

'Aye, but he hasn't got a lot of cash on him, he may be home early.'

'We'd better no' waste ony time then.'

She stood up and turned down the paraffin lamp, which stood on the mantelpiece above the range. She took a step towards him. He rose and began unbuttoning his flies. She got down on the smooth-worn carpet in front of the fire. He got down on one knee beside her, pulling at his long underpants. She pulled up her skirt and he came down on her, his full weight resting on her chest. He pushed himself up on his elbows to give his hand room to pull down her woollen knickers. Then he was into her, no bother, not after four years, he should know the road by now.

'You're desperate tonight,' she murmured, her plump face warm against his shaven cheeks, her arms around his back.

'Hmmmmph.'

Had Archie never had a single woman all these years? Love or children? Mary O'Donnell, would she be a good ride, iron leg and whatnot? He came and immediately felt better. He let his fourteen stocky stones flop down on her, crushing her against the floor.

'I'm finished, ye auld hoor,' he said, panting.

'You're flattening me,' she said.

'I'm a ravishing scoundrel.' His heavy body shook with laughter. He felt like rolling on his back and laughing out loud.

Then she was getting out from under him and he was on his knees, buttoning up his coms and his trouser flies.

'I'll away then,' he said, giving her backside a heavy pinch. 'Ye're an auld hoor, Morag Coll.'

She slapped at his hand, then let him out of the back door, not turning up the lamp till it was closed. She put the black kettle on the range fire and sat down in the big chair to read the *Women's Pictorial*. What a pity Willie had never found himself a wife, poor man, for all their money she felt sorry for him and his father, not that Willie saw a lot of the money. What she let him do was wrong, sinful, but she always thought of him living in that dirty old house, all alone, a man of his age, poor Willie, it was the least a woman could do.

Outside Willie got on his bike and headed back along the road he'd come, making for the factory gatehouse where he'd have a cup of cocoa and a gab with the nightman. When Coll moved away he wouldn't have his Monday rides with Morag. Maybe Archie had lost the notion of it altogether. *He* hadn't, he knew that. And now there was a young hole under his own roof he might not need to stravaig about the countryside on dark nights looking for an old hag who'd lift her skirt on the kitchen floor.

FIVE

IT WAS DARK when Dunky pushed his bike through the gas-lit tunnel of the close, dark and frosty with stars so bright they seemed nearer than the lights of the town. The Logans lived in a smallish, three-storey tenement building which stood isolated on a stretch of rubble-strewn ground, Shuttle Place, gradually demolished as folk were moved into the new Darroch scheme. Already one of the ground-floor flats was empty, its windows boarded up by Corporation workmen to keep out tramps and drunks and kids. There was some big row going on about delays in extending the scheme and finally clearing Shuttle Place, something about government grants and rates. In the meantime fifteen families lived on in the last tenement, living in two rooms with shared landing lavatories.

His mother would be putting out the tea upstairs but he'd work to do first. He padlocked the chain through the back wheel and put the bike in the wash-house at the back of the tenement, taking the front lamp off the handlebar bracket. His rabbit hut stood across the broken concrete yard against the railway sleeper fence of the coal-yard at the back of the railway. It had been old Mr McAllister's pigeon loft. When he died his wife said Dunky could have it for rabbits. As he knelt to feel for the key on a cross-beam under the hut he glanced up at the rear windows of the block. If only he never had to go up there again. Lights behind curtains, coal fires, windows closed, cramped and hot, no room to move, no place you could hide away on your own, away from *him*. His father and mother and Senga in the bedroom, Senga's bed behind the curtain, his bed in the kitchen, no room to move. Maybe that's why he remembered having such a good time in the air-raid shelter during the war.

They didn't know he kept the key under the floor of the hut, in case it fell out of his pocket at the farm. He didn't want them poking about the rabbits when he was at work. For one thing his mother didn't know how many he now had. She was against him having rabbits at all – 'just wasting your time when you should be at your homework' was what she'd always said. Against everything, she was. If she told his father the hut was fair packed he'd go wild and say they'd attract rats. Funny, even Alec, his best pal, was against the rabbits, said they were only silly pets for wee boys. Sometimes he thought Alec was right, but once the door was locked nobody knew the silly things he said to the rabbits.

He climbed up inside and slipped the bolt behind him. He put the bicycle lamp on the tea-chest so that it shone along the netting fronts of the hutches. The light made the rabbits thump and scurry. The buck's eye shone red as it stared at him, head to one side.

'It's only me, me bonny beasties,' he said. This was his place, his and his only. He'd built the hutches from old boxes and crates, some knocked from a joiner's yard, some from Laidlaw's vegetable shop. The door was shut behind him and he was the boss. Only he knew what went on in here. First he fed the nursing doe, a three-year-old bought from Findlay the big Chinchilla expert at Bridge of Kilmorchan, Findlay o' the Brig. He'd been three or four when a man called Murdoch or Murtagh or something like that had kept a few black and white rabbits at the back of the tenement. One day his daddy had taken him down to Murdoch or Murtagh's hutches and showed him a pair of young rabbits in an orange-box hutch.

'They're for you,' his daddy had said. 'Mr Murdoch says you can keep them here, but you've got to feed them and clean them out or he'll take them back.'

Of course he'd been too young. And then one day, he went down to feed them and he saw what looked like wee mice lying about on the straw, one of them was bleeding. He'd run to tell his father, and then had to stand by and watch while Murdoch or Murtagh and his father pulled out the babies and put them in the bin, Murdoch saying the father rabbit always killed the wee ones if you didn't get him out quick enough. Imagine keeping a buck in with a litter! They'd said he couldn't have them after that, they were too much bother, he remembered crying.

He'd almost forgotten those rabbits (Murdock fed his on dandelion leaves, silly bastard, anybody knew dandelion was an emetic!) until one Saturday he'd gone with Alec on the train from Ayr to Glasgow, to see the Dairy Show and then Rangers and Hibs in the semi-final of the League Cup. They'd gone to Kelvinhall in the morning, sitting in the upstairs front compartment of a tramcar, out past the Art Galleries. They had proper rabbits at the Dairy Show and as soon as he saw them he thought of Murdoch and the dead babies. He'd hung about until a man started speaking to him and told him the different breeds. Chinchillas were the best, a sort of bluey-grey with thick fur, solid, sensible somehow. This man gave him a book with breeders' names and addresses and it was there he'd found out about Findlay, whose rabbits won championships. About that time old McAllister died and next thing he was building hutches (using the old man's tools) and going out, rather nervously, to Findlay's. Fifteen bob for a mated doe! He'd brought the money (eleven and six in his biscuit tin and the rest from selling his football pictures to boys in the class) the next Saturday and Findlay gave him the big doe in a cardboard box. By the time he'd walked over the braes from Findlay's small-holding, which was at the back of beyond, to the Brig bus stop the doe had wet the bottom of the box and fallen out on the grass. He'd carried her under his arm, the people staring at him in the bus, the scheme kids following him as he walked down from the High Street.

Now he had that doe and three other full-grown does kept from her first litter, plus the buck (also bought from Findlay, for eleven and sixpence) and two half-grown does kept from Doe One's last summer litter. He'd only been at it a couple of years, Findlay said he wasn't producing show standards yet, but he could take all the young ones he produced to Ayr (in his mother's leather shopping bag) to sell to the pet stores for half a crown each. Findlay (a funny sort of man who liked to make a bit of mystery about rabbits) said that if he bred one with the correct fur density and markings he would help him to show it. Proper feeding, that was it, hay for bulk, corn for nourishment, a pinch of wheat for fur-gloss, just enough cauliflower leaves for liquid, water only for nursing does. Dandelion leaves!

He fed them corn from National Dried Milk tins and hay from the tea-chest. On Sunday he'd clean them out, good dry manure (if you fed them right the droppings were like soft, dry marbles) which Laidlaw the vegetable man dug into his allotments. At least it gave him something to do on Sundays, when you weren't allowed to play football on the Corporation pitches, or even listen to the Light Programme on the wireless. Imagine not being allowed to listen to comedies because your mother thought they were sinful on the Sabbath. Stupid old Dickens's serials were all right though!

When they were all fed he opened the door of the old doe's nesting compartment, while she munched corn from her thick clay Woolworth's dish, husks dribbling from her mouth. Placing his hand gently on the warm mound of downy white hair torn from her belly, he parted the nest and shone the lamp on the litter. They were the colour of a Gillette razor blade, blind little piggies with tiny furled ears and blunt snouts, fat little bodies already tinged with whitish hair. He moved them with his fingers, counting eleven. One was white-skinned, a throwback to the beginning of the Chinchilla breed when Angoras were crossed in to give the grey rabbits a thick coat. The whitey could go for a start. Four was plenty for a winter litter – Findlay didn't believe in winter litters at all, but the mating and counting the thirty-one days' gestation and watching the wee ones develop was the best part of it. It didn't do any harm, as long as she was fed right.

Two runts. They could go. The bucks were supposed to have square, blunt heads. He decided to keep one buck and three does. The other seven went into the cleaning-out pail. Before he'd left school he'd knocked two thick science books to use for breeding records, weight graphs and income and expenditure. You had to do it scientifically, grandfather and granddaughter but never brother and sister, grandmother and grandson, interbreeding the way they did with racehorses, to develop your own strain. It was something, Findlay said, you could only learn by years of experience, books were no good.

He shut the nesting compartment and took the pail to the far end of the hut. Once he had two or three does littering together he could kill all the poor ones and foster the remainder equally among the mothers, a delicate operation but nothing to a bright laddie with the right knack (and the knowledge that it's the smell that they notice, the secret being to rub your hands in the foster-mother's dirt pile before giving her the new babies).

'You see, you're all thinking this is cruelty,' he said out loud, thinking of his mother and the cripple woman and the girlfriend he didn't have, 'but it's just sensible stockmanship. Farmers can't afford all this sentimental blether, animals are only animals, these wee brutes don't even know they're alive yet. Women just don't understand what it's all about.'

He knocked their heads on the rim of the pail, one at a time, their warm, delicate bodies giving one long last pull against his palm, then going limp as the life went out of them. When they were all growing cold he shoved them down among the dirty straw in the pail. Laidlaw might get a shock – if he found he was digging in a heap of wee corpses! By now old Charlie would be lubricating trains, no doubt.

Only once in his life had he killed something for the hell of it, he'd never forget it, a dirty brute of a tomcat that kept hanging about their landing, yowling for their she-cat to come out, he'd got sick of that tom, especially one day he was in the house himself, in the afternoon, doing homework, they must have been let out early from school, anyway, the bastarding tomcat was up on their landing, yowling like a demented creature, he'd been about twelve at the time, his father had a hammer which he used to cobble their shoes, he'd stood behind the door with the hammer and let the tomcat into the lobby, slamming the door behind it, grabbing it by the tail and thumping its nut with the hammer, it'd gone out after two hits, but it wasn't dead, so he'd taken it downstairs to the lavvy on the landing and locked himself in and shoved the dirty great brute down the seat, head first, holding its head under the water by the scruff of its neck, it'd come round and tried to scrabble backwards up the seat, he'd had to belt it again with the hammer and hold it under, Christ it'd taken *hours*. He must have been dead callous then, he couldn't do anything like that now. You had to have a good reason to kill – even wee blind rabbits.

Before he left he gave them all a small hunk of turnip, something to chew on, to stop the ever-growing teeth from coming out and round in a circle, back into their own brains.

'Right then, now for the happy home.'

One day he'd have a big shed and keep enough Chinchillas to live off them, some for fur coats and gloves, some for showing, some for eating, some for selling to the young breeders who'd come around his place, aye, ye cannae dae better'n buy frae Logan, finest strain o' Chinchillas in Scotland . . .

He had already taken the worst of the mud off his boots in the stable but at the door on the first-floor landing he dragged the studded soles across the scraper, metal rasping on metal, twisting his ankles to make sure the heels were free of dubs. He then took off his boots and stood in his stocking soles, perspiration-soaked feet leaving wet marks on the clean stone, until his mother answered his knock. He placed his boots at the bottom of the small cupboard inside the door. He could smell kippers. Much and all as his mother didn't like Paps she certainly stuck to fish on Fridays. He hung his jerkin on the hallstand, lifting off the cloth cap his father would probably never wear again.

'You've been messing about with those rabbits, haven't you?' his mother said, accusingly, as he went into the kitchen, a brightly-lit room with pale blue wallpaper and shiny linoleum, with a brown rug in front of the black-range fireplace. She was at the kitchen sink, her stout back towards him, her apron strings tied tight into her green woollen cardigan, her brown skirt pulled up to show the backs of her knees, the way he always thought of her, bent over the sink, the back of a wet, red hand pushing away a loose strand of brown hair.

'Only for a wee while,' he said, 'we were late getting away.'

They'd get a bigger house in the scheme but for some reason his mother thought Shuttle Place was decent and Darroch wasn't. They needed a bigger house. As it was you could hardly turn round in the kitchen for furniture, his bed in the alcove, his chest of drawers, the heavy, dark sideboard, the sewing machine, another chest of drawers, the sink, the sink drying-board, the gas cooker, the big armchair where his father used to sit with his feet on the range fender, the small armchair with square wooden arms and slots for magazines and papers (the *Kilcaddie Advertiser*, the *Daily Record*, the Church of Scotland *Life and Work*, the *Women's Pictorial*, Senga's *Girls' Crystal*), the couch, brown rexine with antimacassar squares. He sat on the couch and turned to the *Record* football pages. For all he knew that there wasn't much she could do to him (just let her *try* to belt him!) and *nothing* that his father could do, he was still a bit scared of her. When they were alone, which was as seldom as he could help, his voice became hoarse and reluctant, short, gruff half-sentences dragging themselves out through awkward lips.

'Put on your slippers and don't sit about the house in your socks,' she said. 'It isn't nice.' Moving as slowly as he dared he pulled the worn cloth slippers from under the heavy sewing-machine pedal and pulled them over his thick, damp socks.

'Where's Senga?' he asked.

'She's away to Aunt Bessie's, she had to have her tea because you were messing about out there,' his mother replied, always the threat of irritable anger – or even tears – in her voice. In the kitchen press they had a cardboard shoe box full of old family pictures and in some of them she was young (hair short and bobbed, wearing a leather coat) and smiling. He'd hardly ever known her smile like that. Long ago he'd decided his father was a brute and that was why his mother was always snapping at him, but even now, when the old man was shut up in the bedroom, she was still the same. Not so much with Senga, though, just him. He didn't know why they hated him so much. Bobby Evans was back for Celtic, he read. He didn't care, either, they could hang themselves for all he cared, soon as he was over eighteen he was off out of it, away to England or even Canada, maybe go with Donald Telfer, two of them working on big wheat farms, moving about the country, doing what they wanted without being told off, picking up big women—

'Give me over the matches,' she said, always the same, do this, don't do that, never give you a moment's peace in your own house, hated to see you sitting still for two seconds in case you were doing something *you* wanted to do, run about like a wee boy going for the messages. Blackie would have spat in the fire and said get the bastards yourself. He got up slowly and looked along the mantelpiece, the china dog bought in Oban on *their* honeymoon, a chiming clock always kept half an hour fast because *she* said it gave her extra time in the morning, a brass tea-caddy embossed with a stag, never used for tea but kept on the mantelpiece as an ornament, holding matches and Kirbigrips and elastic bands and a spare hairnet and a thimble and needles and three French coins brought home from the First War by Grandpa Aitchison. He took out the matches and held them towards her, careful not to go close enough for them to touch each other.

'I wish you'd come in for your tea at the proper time,' she said, taking the matches, trying to fix him in the eyes. He looked at his feet and turned away.

'Any proper farmer feeds his beasts before he feeds himself,' he said, his voice falling away, knowing that nothing he said would make any impression on her. One day he would just tell her to shut her gob and get the bloody tea on the table.

'Farmer, farmer,' she hissed. 'It's a disgrace, you and your schooling, we worked hard to get you into the Academy, now look at you, wasting your whole life in that dead-end job.'

He stared at the picture of Bobby Evans, a burly guy, he wished he'd a chest like that.

'No more dead-end than getting your back broke in a stinking engineering shop,' he said. That would shake her up a bit.

'You're selfish through and through,' she said, eyes glaring, hands clenched at the side of her apron. He shrugged. 'Wash your face and hands, your tea's ready.'

About fuck'n time. Ignoring her closeness, her waiting face, he scrubbed his hands under the thin geyser flow, careful not to let dirty water splash onto the dishes drying on the zinc draining board, well-worn bristles not making much impression on the solid black dirt under his fingernails. Yet, he wanted to try to show her *he* didn't want to bicker all the time.

'I took the old horse to Cairney's the day,' he said, sitting down to his kipper and fried potato slices and greasy rings of black pudding. 'You shoulda seen the way they hacked him open, one minute he was standing there, the next his guts were all over the floor, fantastic to see it.'

'That's horrible,' she said, watching him begin to eat, then starting to dry the dishes. 'You're not going out tonight I hope?'

'Aye, I'm meeting Alec at the Cross at seven.'

Kippers, enough to give you dry boke. Telfer said his mother usually got in fish and chips from the mobile caravan that went round the scheme at nights, but his mother said bought fish and chips was only scruffs' food.

'Tsk, tsk, you've got no thought for anyone but yourself. You've been out this week already. Don't you ever think of your poor father lying in there day in day out?'

'Ach, all he wants to do is give me rows,' he said, eating fast so that he could get out as soon as possible.

'Duncan, you've not to speak about your father like that,' she snapped. Sometimes he found he had the courage to stare back at her, silently defying her to try and give him a belting. 'You're not a man yet, you'll show proper respect. And another thing, you've started speaking very coarse, it's that farm, you should never have left the school to work there, it's that Donald Telfer or whatever he calls himself, you shouldn't be mixing with people like that, they're *common*.'

This time he pretended to be very casual.

'Donald'n me are thinking of emigrating to Canada,' he said, washing down the last of the kipper with a noisy swallow of tea.

'You'll do no such thing!'

Aye, hare away into the old man, see if he can do anything. It'd taken him a couple of years to realise that his father was a permanent invalid, completely helpless, no fear of a thrashing. And being out at work was giving him the right idea of how to talk to her.

'You've to go in and see your father,' she announced, triumphantly, when she came back from the bedroom. Once that would have given him a dose of skitters in his pants, but now he felt the time was right to let her know things had changed.

'Why, is he going to give me my Saturday penny?' He looked at her coldly, trying not to let his face go red.

Beth Logan sensed that the boy might do something wild if she went on. She felt helpless . . .

Beth Logan's father, Robert Aitchison, had been a grocer, well set up for himself in the north end of Kilcaddie, lucky to have the kind of business that didn't suffer too much from the slump, owner of his own three-apartment house in the sort of good-class tenement where even the ground-floor close was always spotless and no wee boys chalked filth and no drunks wet the walls. Beth, his second girl, had gone to the Academy, Kilcaddie's best school, where parents had to pay fees of a guinea a quarter. The Aitchisons were furious when Beth started walking out with Duncan Logan, a boilermaker's apprentice, one of the black gang, they wanted her to marry somebody decent, like Norrie Spence who was in the Burgh Factor's office and who was sure of getting on in life.

They agreed to the wedding in the end only because Mrs Aitchison thought her daughter's continual state of depression must be due to pregnancy (they could never have spoken of such things out loud so Mrs Aitchison never found out that, far from being pregnant, Beth's depression was caused by Duncan's continual attempts to get her to let him go too far). After the wedding, at which Duncan's Uncle Archie had got drunk and sung dirty songs, thus ensuring that the two families never met again, she'd found herself living in a single-end, one room with a shared outside lavatory, in Garrashiel Road, the very *lowest* part of Kilcaddie. And Duncan had turned out for the worst, especially after wee Duncan was born and the doctor said she shouldn't have another child for at least three years, even knowing that he was still *incessant* in his demands and she'd found she hated *that* part of it, it was so horrible and disgusting, and after Senga was born, in nineteen-forty, she'd told him she wasn't going to do it, not ever again, and he'd tried to *force* her, in her own bed, it made her sick.

After a while he'd realised she wasn't ever going to let him do it to her again and he'd left her alone, but somehow he'd taken a dislike to wee Duncan, she loved the boy like a proper mother, of course, but as he grew up she'd seen his father coming out in him all over again, the same coarseness, the same nastiness (when he was only three and a half he'd come into the kitchen and smiled and said to her, 'Thepopesacunt, mammy', just as the workmen building the Darroch scheme had coached him to say).

And now, with Duncan stuck to his bed, with only the insurance and the interest on the compensation coming in, she was as poor as ever again and wee Duncan sounded more and more like his father, so much that at times she had to make herself remember it was her son and not her husband sitting across the kitchen table. Once, in her whole life, she'd been at a posh hotel, in Girvan, for the Fair Week. All her life she'd remembered that hotel, the clean tablecloths, the big bedrooms, cotton sheets that were stiff and white and cool, the waitresses taking away the dirty dishes, the soft carpets. For years she'd hoped that one day, when the children were older, they'd all go to a hotel for a holiday. Now they never would . . .

'You're not natural,' she sobbed. He shrugged, not knowing what to do. He felt helpless.

Standing with his back to her, Dunky changed into his clean socks (white, like Telfer's), black shoes, grey flannels (peg-topped, like the Ayr ice-hockey players'), brown shirt, no tie, light grey sports jacket (no pocket flaps, wide shoulder pads), throwing his farm clothes under the bed, careful not to let her see his prick, feeling guilty at having one at all when she was in the same room. At the sink he rubbed Brylcreem and water into his dark hair and combed it straight back, making a little wave at the front by pressing it with the palm of his right hand. He wished Senga hadn't gone out so early, it was always easier when she was there, her and her mother chattered away and he could pretend he didn't exist.

'All least you can say cheerio to your father,' she said, now the hard-done-by mother.

'All right,' he said. Funny how in the pictures you often saw kids give their mothers a kiss or a hug. He could no more have done that than shagged a horse.

Through the closed bedroom door he heard Jimmy Shand and his band on the Scottish country dancing programme. Too bad they couldn't have the wireless in the kitchen so that everybody could hear it. Hands stuck down in his trouser pockets he went into the bedroom. It, too, was crammed with old, dark furniture. He could hardly bear to look at his father, whose head was propped up on two pillows, arms resting on the quilt, his face pale and slack after three years in bed. The room, to him, meant the smell of his father, a big man's smell, hot pyjamas and sweatiness, the gruesome thought of his father and mother doing it in bed together.

'Hullo,' he said. He'd never called him Father or Daddy, not since he was too young to know they hated each other. He stood by the door, ready to escape. 'How're you feeling?'

He couldn't bear it, the smell, the look, the bed-clothes, the unnaturally clean hands, the eyes that seemed to be saying he was doing something wrong – as usual.

'Oh, jist marvellous,' his father replied. 'Ah've got the wireless and the *Advertiser*, whut more does a man want?'

IT'S NOT MY FUCK'N FAULT, IS IT?

'Whut's this aboot Canada?'

Dunky looked at his shoes, fists clenched in his pockets. Other people had bad things happen to them, didn't they, without making a profession out of it, like the limpy dan housekeeper? If *she'd* been his mother she'd have known that working men shouldn't be nagged at all the time like wee boys.

'Ach, I was just joking,' he said.

'Hmph. Funny kind o' jokes. Your mother's got enough to put up wi'. An' I suppose you're away oot, eh, away enjoyin' yersel'? God almighty, ye don't know the meanin' o' anythin'.'

Jimmy Shand in strict tempo, the best of the Scottish country bands, playing away regardless of what they were saying, somebody said the YMCA had tried to book him for a big dance at the Town Hall and his asking price for the one night was four hundred pounds!

'Aye well, I've got to meet Alec at the Cross at seven. I'm late already, I'd better be going.'

His father raised his head an inch or two from his pillows, one of the few movements he could make.

'Jist because ye're playin' aboot at bein' a workin' man disnae mean ye can dae whut ye like,' he said, his voice raised as though he wanted to let her in on the act.

'Cheerio.'

It didn't matter if the old man did bawl after him, there was nothing he could do.

Did everybody hate their own father?

The first two scheme buses roared past the stop, packed to the door with Monday-night jiggers and boozers and winchers from the scheme desperate to enjoy themselves after a grim Sunday shut in their houses. He decided to walk, although he was ten minutes late already. Alec would wait. Although it was the long way round he usually went up Brediland Street partly because it had more people, partly so that he could pass the school, now dark and quiet, thinking of it as an actual person who would see him pass by, a gallus lad, hello Patsy Fagin, a decent working boy, a working man, stick your rotten old school, I'm free of you now. He walked on the outside of his heels, toes turned inwards to give him a shorter, faster stride, like the professionals. Once when he'd been only eight or nine they'd gone to Kilmarnock to see Dundee and after the match they'd waited outside the stand to see the players leave. Dundee had just bought Billy Steel back from Derby County in England, the blond and dynamic Steel who'd formed one of Scotland's greatest inside-forward partnerships with wee Jimmy Mason of Third Lanark. Steel had walked like that. Although he actually modelled himself on Bobby Evans, the Celtic right-half, he often imagined he was Billy Steel, jinking up the pavement, dodging imaginary defenders, carving in on the English goal, hard as nails, beating tackle after tackle, small and blond and deadly . . . when he reached the brighter pavements of the High Street he quickened his walk and put his hands back in his pockets, guilty at having such secret notions . . .

Duncan Logan lay back, panting, staring at the wall. In the name of God what was wrong with the boy? God? Would a proper God let a man rot his life away in bed, helpless, finished at forty-one? He'd be better off dead, but there was no way he could even kill himself. Why did it have to be *him*?

At times he would wake up from a dream – nearly always a dream in which he and Beth were running to catch the boat at Millport Pier, in the sunshine – and for a moment or two he wouldn't remember what had happened to him. It was worst then, suddenly realising that his body was a half-dead thing lying between the blankets. He'd lie in the dark, while she slept beside him, happy no doubt that he was incapable of anything towards her, and think back to that day at Millport; they sat on the Crocodile Rock and took a pony-cart round the island, and bought ice-cream and watched the boys fishing off the pier and followed the black backs of the porpoises and paddled, with his trousers rolled up.

Other people still did that. But he didn't kid himself, they'd only gone to Millport once and then there never was time or money, always the baby to look after, the illnesses after the babies, the – oh Christ, his life had been a right ruination from the start.

No, there was nothing left for him here, a son who treated him like dirt, a wife who was just as happy to have him helpless on his back, a daughter who'd soon be wanting to be out every night. He was just a burden to them and to himself.

That's what Doctor Barr had said to him, a month or two before.

'Really you'd be much better off in Killearn, Mister Logan,' Barr had said. 'You'd be in a big ward with other men, lots of company, and your wife would have things a lot easier, think about it, they're doing marvels at Killearn these days, they wouldn't take you if they didn't think they could do something for you, it's a hospital not a home . . .'

These walls were driving him mad. Just suppose they did find a way of treating his spinal cord, oh God Almighty, take pity on me, for the love of Jesus Christ . . . when the sobbing started he was unable to control it and he turned his face into the pillow so that she wouldn't see the tears when she came in with his cocoa . . .

Up the town, that's what you said, I'm going up the town, up the town, see the people, eye the talent. Poor bastard, *he* would never get up the town again. Did *he* ever eye the talent when *he* was a young bloke? Maybe his mother had been talent? No, never, not her, it must have been different with them, parents were different, everything they did was – *official*, sort of. In all his life he could remember only one time when his father had really seemed to like him, one Ne'erday, Uncle Roddy was alive then and the three of them had gone to Ibrox to see Rangers and Celtic, the two men laughing when his mother said it was too dangerous for a boy, Uncle Roddy saying the bottle-throwing was only newspaper exaggeration. Uncle Roddy had a flat bottle of whisky, it smelled awful on their breaths, they'd stood at the Copeland Road end, the two of them lifting him onto the crush barrier, Uncle Roddy shouting back at two Celtic supporters, very nasty Glasgow scruffs they were, they seemed to suit what he saw of Glasgow above the shoulders of the crowd, the big shipyard cranes standing high above the docks, the bottles that were thrown onto the pitch, flying out from the packed terracings like black crows coming down on a field, him terrified in case they'd be hit.

At night they played *Monopoly* (which Uncle Roddy had brought for the big family gathering) on the kitchen table, he'd been too young to know what it was all about but Uncle Roddy had shown him what to do and when he'd bankrupted Aunt Jennie with his two hotels on Park Lane, Uncle Roddy had shouted out, 'The boy's got the makings of a capitalist.'

His father had smiled at him.

But his eyes were funny from drinking whisky, he remembered that all right. Pity the bastard hadn't got drunk more often. Jesus Christ, why in the name of hell did *he* have to have a father who lay on his back, paralysed, and looked at *him* and made him feel *he'd* done something wrong?

Alec was standing at the War Memorial, skinny and daft-looking in his big padded overcoat. His father had never liked Alec. He said he was a typical young spineless idiot, because he wore casual shoes with brass chains across the uppers.

'Hey,' said Alec, hands in his coat pockets (one thing about working on a farm, you got hardened to the cold), 'fancy going to a big Communist Party meeting in the Co-op Hall?'

The Cross always seemed exciting, plenty of talent about, always the chance of getting chatting to a big piece of stuff and making dates, but for some reason Alec was always wanting to go to political meetings and things instead of getting into the cafés and dances where there was a chance of a decent lumber.

'You thinking of becoming a Communist, eh?' he said.

'I would if I knew what it really meant,' said Alec. 'My father says they're the only party with guts.'

Alec had been in his class in the first and second senior years before he was kept back for being dead slow. Now he was an apprentice quantity surveyor, his father had made him go into that although Alec wanted to be a printer ('You can easily get a bigtime job on one of the Glasgow papers'). He shaved every day, to make his hairless chin develop a thick stubble, he said, although Dunky thought it was really because of his spots. He was a good enough guy for a pal, even if he was a bit naïve and stupid.

'Ach, come on,' he pleaded, 'it's only for an hour, then we can go to the Eldorado and chat up some big time wimmin.'

They went over the Cross and up Fergus Street. Dunky saw a big gallus-looking guy with his arm round a girl's waist. That's what he wanted to be, bigtime, gallus, a hard case. He wished he was older. Funny, he could still remember the very first Americans coming to Kilcaddie, soldiers, they walked about holding girls' hands openly, never seen in the town before, a disgrace, his mother said, the way scruff girls made an exhibition of themselves in public chasing Americans. When he got a steady he'd maybe just hold her hand in the street, but none of this smooching nonsense. Alec was going on about the men who worked on building sites.

'Ignorance isn't in it,' he said. 'All they want is a fag and the sports pages, they don't even read the real news. I thought they'd all be red-hot socialists and commies and bigtime political guys, but all they're interested in's the football and the racing. They don't even care if it's Labour or the Tories, imagine that!'

To Alec things were either bigtime or dead rotten. Lumbers were bigtime but girls who wouldn't let you see them home were dead rotten. Going to the pictures in Ayr was bigtime, much more bigtime than Kilcaddie's three cinemas. Owning a car was real bigtime.

They climbed two flights of stairs. There was a table at the entrance to the hall. The man behind it said it was sixpence to go in. Dunky wanted to turn away – sixpence got you a coffee in the Eldorado and for that you could sit for an hour – but Alec gave the man the money.

'The Communists have got to charge,' he whispered as they eased onto a bench at the back of the hall. 'They're all poor people, everybody's against them.'

Alec thought it was exciting and dangerous to be there, but it seemed more like school, with men instead of kids. Fancy grown men sitting through a boring meeting when they could be out enjoying themselves! His mother would have a fit if she knew. Communists – they looked more like a round-up of all the saddest men in Kilcaddie, sitting dreary-like in a draughty hall on a Monday night when anybody with any sense was giving the patter to some big piece of stuff. Alec was rattling on about what his father had told him about Karl Marx. He always called himself a true Communist, nothing to do with Russia. It was just another silly notion he'd picked up from his father and his two brothers, who were Communist daft.

'Hey, don't look now but d'you see who's sitting over there,' Dunky said, surprise in his voice at seeing Nicol, the English and History master, sitting by himself, four rows in front of them at the other side of the hall. Alec looked the way he always did when you told him not to look, straining round, gawking with his mouth open.

'It's Nicky,' Alec said, 'I bet nobody at the school knows he's a bigtime Communist.'

'He doesn't look very bigtime to me,' Dunky sneered. Nicol was an untidy man in a dark blue suit, his hair parted in the middle, too long at the back. He'd been in the Tank Corps in the army, an officer or something, he never talked about it much. Dunky had thought he was quite a decent guy for a teacher until one day in Free Discussion (Nicol had started them on Current Affairs and other subjects the older masters never bothered with) they'd had a debate on the Welfare State. Billy Aird had stood up and said the unemployed men who went to the burroo were just lazy. Dunky had already been working at Craig's farm in the holidays, he thought that Billy Aird was against working guys, his father being a cop.

'It's all right for a schoolboy who's never done a day's work to lay down the law about the unemployed,' he'd said, catching Nicol's eye when Billy Aird sat down. 'Especially when your father's been in the fortunate position of never being out of work in his life. If Fatty Aird had to live in the Darroch scheme he'd soon change his tune, he's got no business criticising people he doesn't know anything about.'

Nicol had stopped the discussion to use his speech as an illustration of the *ad hominem* argument, which they knew from Latin. Dunky resented being the object of the lecture and he'd never said another word in Nicol's Free Discussion period. It was typical of school, a lot of baloney.

A man stood up behind the trestle table on the platform and welcomed them to the meeting and then read out a list of future meetings. Dunky kept looking along at Nicol, but there was no particular expression on the teacher's face.

'. . . and now here is our speaker for this evening. Comrade MacLean, whose long career in the socialist movement is well known to us all . . .'

MacLean was *the* local Communist. His name was always in the *Kilcaddie Advertiser* in connection with some row or another. His father always called him a dirty red traitor who should be sent packing to Russia if he liked the place so much. He was an old man with red cheeks and white hair. He turned out to be quite funny at first, which surprised Dunky, who'd always thought of Communists as being nasty men, all bitter and anti-British. MacLean made jokes about the Labour Party and about Attlee, calling him Major Attlee, which Dunky didn't understand.

'. . . and so we had the ludicrous position that a so-called working-class party gave the boss class cheap coal, cheap railways and cheap steel and put their welfare responsibilities onto the state – in fact they made British capitalism work, something the Tories have never been able to do. Believe me, comrades, capitalism could have been sunk without trace in 1945. That's what the people voted for, wasn't it? And what did we get? Major Attlee and Ernest Bevin! Were they any better than what we've got now – Crofter Macmillan and Mister Butler? Would you rather be told to eat snoek or over-ripe pheasant?'

Everybody laughed. Dunky noted, however, that Nicol kept a straight face.

'We have no quarrel with the rank and file of the Labour Party,' MacLean went on. 'But we have to understand that the socialist movement cannot be allowed to remain in the hands of quislings and traitors . . .'

The main part of his speech followed. MacLean had just come back from a tour of Australia. He told the audience that the emigration scheme was not much better than the German slave-labour system. He said he'd seen with his own eyes the forced work camps ('No, they don't actually have dogs but they do have wire fences') into which the ten-pound emigrants were driven when they reached Australia. He said there was no housing and few good jobs. Dunky thought it was a lot of rubbish. Alec whispered that this was the benefit of coming to Communist meetings, you heard things the capitalist press wouldn't let you know about. Dunky wished he knew more about politics. They'd only reached the Chartists when he left school. MacLean mentioned Ramsay MacDonald, saying he was the man who taught Attlee how to betray the working class. This got a big handclap. Funny enough, his father had also once said that Ramsay McDonald was a traitor, but his father had said all politicians were crooks. History was interesting – as long as it didn't have anything to do with school.

Then there was a question period. To their surprise Nicol was first on his feet, his hands in his pockets, his scruffy head slightly to one side, the way it used to be in class.

'I would like to ask the speaker for his views on the preservation of Scottish culture,' he began, his voice dry and sarcastic, like all schoolteachers. 'If the Communist Party were to get into power what would their policy be towards the disappearing language and history and literature of Scotland?'

MacLean said that was a very good question. As everybody knew he was a staunch Scotsman and on his many trips to Moscow he'd always been more than welcome as a fellow-countryman of Rabbie Burns. Rabbie was favourite in Russia. In a socialistic society the preservation of folk cultures was of prime importance. This didn't mean the feudalistic, nationalistic and Catholic-fascist attempts by the Irish government to force a dead language on its people – that was a cold-blooded manoeuvre by Catholic land-owning interests to keep the working class of Ireland in ignorance and economic slavery. No, it wasn't to be like that, but whatever it was it would be good for Scotland. The audience murmured 'Hear hear.'

Nicol got to his feet again.

'Mister MacLean has made a great deal out of his belief that Scotland always has and still is being milked dry by English capitalists,' he said, as sarcastic as ever. 'To my mind this Scottish patriotism of his is a particularly hypocritical form of chauvinism, for all we know how much independence Scotland would have under a Communist central dictatorship based on London – less,

I imagine, than Mister MacLean's puppet-masters in Moscow allowed independent Hungary—'

Nicol went on trying to speak above a growing noise from the men in the hall. The chairman rose to his feet and said he couldn't allow provocateurs to disrupt the meeting with attacks on the speaker. Nicol kept on.

'You're using patriotism to kid these people into being Communists and when you get power you'll shoot them for wanting to be Scots,' he shouted. Then, as the uproar grew again, he walked down the gangway and out of the hall. MacLean said something to the chairman, who waved his arms for order. The meeting ended. As Dunky and Alec came to the head of the stairs they saw Nicol face to face with a man who was shouting at him. Dunky thought there was going to be a fight. As long as they weren't involved he couldn't care less, Nicol was old enough to know better. He managed to get Alec past the two men without Nicol seeing them, Alec, of course, wanting to get into the act. Bigtime. They were on the first floor landing when Nicol overtook them.

'Ah, Mathie and Logan, the two working men,' he said, his stubby face slightly red but otherwise sounding just as if he was in the classroom. 'Without actually seeming to run I should advise you to make haste, the mob seems thirsty for blood.'

They followed him down the stairs. He always spoke like that, Dunky thought, you could never tell what he really meant, even when he told you education was necessary for getting on in life you had the feeling he was being sarcastic about people who did get on in life. Schoolteachers were all namby pamby. Alec winked at him. Bigtime, escaping with a real teacher from a commie riot! Dunky looked down at Nicol's untidy hair and stooped shoulders. Shovel shite for a day and he'd break his back.

Alec fell into step with the teacher as they went down Fergus Street to the Cross. It was five to nine on the Town Hall clock. There was a cold breeze. The street was almost empty. Most people would be in the pictures or at the dancing or in cafés.

'Well, I trust you enjoyed the free flow of debate in a Communist ambience,' Nicol said, looking sideways at the two boys. For a man who'd shouted so much about Scotland he had a very English-sounding accent, Dunky thought. That was another thing, all teachers were snobs. 'Are you two interested in Communism?'

Dunky wouldn't have replied at all, but Alec couldn't hold his water.

'Eh, we just go to meetings, sir,' he said. 'It's very interesting to hear different speakers and so forth.'

'Aye, an' it's cheaper'n the pictures,' growled Dunky, looking straight ahead. Alec trying to suck up to a teacher was enough to make you sick.

'That's my Logan,' said Nicol, 'always the realist. And how are you enjoying your career in agriculture, eh?'

Nicol had given him a talk about staying on at school. Dunky was, at first, sneakingly pleased the man remembered him at all, but then he felt annoyed at even caring what a teacher thought.

'You don't get the belt from a lot of silly old women,' he said. Half of him was still frightened, he hadn't been out of school all that long and Nicol was still a figure of authority. But he was determined not to suck up to him. What did he care about schoolteachers any more?

'Spoken like a man with a thousand chips on his shoulder,' Nicol said. He allowed himself a thin laugh. Bitter and twisted, that's what he sounded like. No wonder, if you had to wear an attached collar and a stiff suit all the time.

'Are you a Scottish Nationalist, sir?' Alec asked. Dunky could have kicked him on the ankle. Sir!

'I believe we're being swamped by cheap commercialism and public ignorance,' Nicol replied. 'Scotland was the first nation in Europe to have a proper system of mass education, never forget that. This used to be one of the leading countries in European culture. But here we are at Kilcaddie Cross, gateway to the new darkness. Don't look so browned-off, Logan, it's not a complete social disgrace to be seen with a schoolteacher, not yet anyway.'

Christ, how did he know that's what he'd been thinking? Maybe his face wouldn't show red under the street lights. Nicol smiled briefly and went on his way, one shoulder slightly higher than the other, unworkmanlike shoulders. Thin and sarcastic, dry skin and dry hair.

'Come on to the Eldorado,' he said to Alec. 'Thank Christ we're out of school.'

'He's not a bad bloke when you get to know him, isn't he?' said Alec.

'Hrrmmph.' Real men didn't suck up to schoolteachers. Was Nicol always like that, even when he was a wee boy? All right, so he had brains and compared to him guys like Telfer and McCann and Coll were ignorant morons – but what good did his brains do him? Fine for lording over kids in the school, but outside he looked frightened, as though he knew he wasn't a real man. Still, he'd nerve, to get up like that at the commie meeting. Maybe it was because a meeting wasn't all that much different from the classroom, it was *safe* to speak your mind. Education was something you went in for if you weren't good at anything else – guys who played football well never bothered with school much, guys who could get off with women easily never came top of the class. Who did? The swots – and everybody knew that swots were always hopeless with women or football, or anything but their lessons. It wasn't quite the same with girls, in his class the four or five smashers all got good marks at exams. But it was different for girls – education suited them, they'd nothing else to do with themselves anyway.

In the *Wizard* and the *Adventure* and the *Rover* comics he'd never liked school stories – they were all about English boarding schools where they played cricket and went to tuckshops. In the best film he'd ever seen, *The Naked City*, the detective walked about the New York slums looking for a killer and he'd decided then he wanted a job where he worked outside. In fact, for a while he and Alec were going to be either plain-clothes detectives or film directors after seeing *The Naked City*!

The Eldorado was crowded and they had to stand by the counter until they got two seats. On the jukebox it was mostly Johnnie Ray (girls), Nat King Cole (boys) and Tennessee Ernie's *Shotgun Boogie* (hard cases).

'Not much talent about,' said Alec.

'How about that piece with the red coat?'

'Nah, rotten body.'

'How d'you know?'

'You can tell. Hey get a load of the new waitress, hubba hubba.'

She reminded him of the very first time he remembered noticing a woman's legs. It was on a scheme bus during the war. At that time nylons were scarce and some women used to dye their legs orange to look like stockings. The conductress had thick legs and he'd suddenly found himself wanting to lick the dye off.

Ian Nicol let himself into his four-apartment flat in the row of three-storey buildings (tenements in all but name, this part of the town being for respectable folk) in Polson Street, on the east side of the town.

'Is that you, Ian?' his wife called from the living room. He hung up his coat and jacket and went in, waistcoat over striped shirt. 'You look frozen,' she said, getting up from the armchair. 'Sit there by the fire while I make some tea.'

'Thanks, Bobs,' he said, kissing the side of her head as she passed. He had a nervous habit of rubbing his hands together, only he didn't quite understand why he should be nervous now. Logan had upset something inside him, Logan in a dark shirt and sports jacket, hard faced and tough, only out of school a matter of weeks and already changed. He looked at the open book on the fireside stool. Poor Roberta, she was becoming addicted to Francis Brett Young. He looked at himself in the concave mirror above the fire. The thin, contracted face, the lifeless hair, the stiff collar, the narrow shoulders, no, it was no wonder the Logans didn't find their hero figures in the classroom. He sat opposite Roberta while she poured tea.

'I met two of my former pupils at the meeting,' he said, the tip of his tongue slightly stiff, as though a dentist's injection was just wearing off. 'Remember I told you about Logan, the one who went to work on the farm? God, when I think of that boy I want to kick something.'

'Was he the one who was awfully good at English?' she said.

'Yes, remember I brought home his composition on Kilcaddie? You should've seen him, like a Hollywood gangster, hard as nails, I didn't know whether to laugh or cry, you know, brown shirt and lots of Brylcreem.'

'Don't let it upset you,' she said. 'You can't work miracles for them all.'

When he'd met Roberta – at a summer course in the big house at Abington in Lanarkshire – she'd been what he always thought of as the typical Edinburgh girl student, bright eyes and short hair and a conscious determination not to sound like the narrow-minded little Edinburgh *Hausfrau* that she was so obviously destined to become, taking a teacher's course because even a *Hausfrau*-to-be had to go through a respectable interim of outside activity until Mr Right came along and gave her the keys to her own kingdom.

'I wish I'd never seen a blackboard,' he said. It was true. Chalky hands, bleary eyes, beginning of a stoop, the studied sneer and, if that failed, the belt; parents who drove their children on *not* for the sake of educating them, oh no, that was the very last thing they cared about, no, to be able to show off their children's exam marks to other parents, like a new fur coat, the parental rat-race. Boys who thought of school as a punishment. A whole system of education designed to cater for the parental pride league.

'Oh, Ian, don't let it depress you so much,' Roberta said.

'You're already a senior master, it won't be long before you're made a head, then you can bring in some of your own ideas.'

Well, *was* he a man? Were the boys right, were you just the same as the spinster teachers who drank tea through pursed lips and complained about parents who didn't know how to bring up well-behaved children? He wanted to talk to Roberta honestly for once. She understood him, or so she always said, she encouraged him to go to meetings, to read as much as he wanted, never complaining when he brought home a case full of exercise books to be corrected . . . yet he was discontented, that part was only a small bit of him. She'd decided, however, it was all of him. She never seemed to realise that there might be more, a part of him that wanted to wear dark shirts and get out among the other kind of people. God, it was as well she didn't know all of him, least of all about the thoughts he often had about some of the older girls. That would test her powers of understanding. He half-listened to her description of Francis Brett Young's description of the Black Country.

'Bobs, there's something I—' he looked down at the thin china cup (tea-set wedding present from her Uncle Trevor, cold-nosed Edinburgh solicitor), 'I want to ask you something.' Better to get it out all at once. Learn to take the twist out of your sentences. 'Would you say I really satisfy you, *sexually*?'

I mean, how can I? Once a week, if that, generally on a Saturday evening? Be honest with yourself, man, what you're trying to say is – she doesn't satisfy you, sexually.

'Oh, you *are* in a bad way.' She smiled. He knew damn well she was putting on what, in her terminology, was a 'roguish' look. Still a bit naughty, to talk about sex with a man, out loud, even if he was your own husband. White breasts, long rather than full, fuzz of black hairs on her forearms. Oh yes, he knew everything about her, everything that was decent for a mere husband to know. Yet, maybe deep down, there might be something different. Some deeply-concealed desire to let *something* loose.

'No, I'm serious, I mean, you could hardly describe my lust as insatiable, could you?'

Still the same defensive sneer at himself. Too much time spent with children.

'Oh, Ian, you're being silly, you're a perfect husband, you ought to know that.'

'No children, though.'

'They'll come. You let the school worry you too much, that's all. That's why I fell in love with you, you were so angry about things and so serious, all the girls at that course were bonkers about you, the way you stood up and told that old gasbag from the Education Department that he was turning Scottish education into an apprenticeship for mindless robots.'

'Ah yes, my moment of heroism.'

In bed, her arms pulling his head close to her cotton-covered breasts, he made a conscious effort not to pursue a line of thought which led to the conclusion that he despised a woman who could be so fixated on a shrivelled apology for a man like himself. He started telling her what was wrong with everything about his work, he wasn't a teacher, he was stage one in the disciplinary process, knocking them into shape, a sergeant-major, belting them into memorising mere facts, into behaving themselves, above all into keeping quiet. Facts they didn't understand and would forget immediately exams were over, closing their minds instead of opening them.

'I pity Logan and envy him at the same time,' he said. 'I know his life's being wasted but he doesn't, he'll just sail along, sex, booze and football, thinking he's having a great time. Next year or the year after it'll be the pub. If they thought the teacher was a real man, like a footballer or an ice-hockey player, they might listen, that's the whole rotten thing about it, they *despise* us. And in ten years' time I'll be just like our beloved headmaster, dry as dust, not caring a damn about them as long as they keep quiet and pass their exams. The swots plough on towards their decent little jobs, and the dead-heads fall by the wayside and the one or two who might have a spark of something different see the whole thing is a fraud.'

'You're an idealist,' she said, pressing her mouth on his forehead. God, make her do *something* she couldn't tell her mother about. He made love with his eyes closed, knowing that he was only using her body as a masturbatory substitute for heavy-chested girls in white blouses, ripe girls with bottoms that strained against pleated hockey skirts and full, bare calves.

'There, darling, that was lovely, wasn't it?'

He held her tightly, as though to make up for everything. At least it was a lie that made *her* happy . . .

Dunky left Alec at the Cross, after standing there for twenty minutes or so, when it became obvious that it was another night when they weren't going to get a lumber. Two girls they knew had come into the Eldorado, but they'd sat at another table. What the hell, only four days to Saturday, pay-day, the game against

Glenryan Juveniles and at night a dance in the canteen at the Blackinch chemical factory. Football was the best. Not having to play in the mornings for the school team was a help, work didn't take it out of him as much as a match. He'd a secret idea that Baldy Campbell, the big boss of Cartneuk's four teams, might give him a trial in the first eleven, most of whom were seventeen. That would be fantastic. Cartneuk was famous in the West of Scotland, lots of their players had trials with big clubs, scouts watched them all the time. They said Baldy got so much money from English clubs he didn't have to work at all, just collect his divvy for every boy who signed professional. Who needed women if that happened?

At the top of Brediland Street there was a small gang being turfed out of the fish and chippers, a right load of scheme neds and hairies. He crossed the street lower down, it was easy to get mixed up with drunken blokes. In a dark close entrance two men tottered together, one pulling a bottle from the other, knees ready to buckle at any minute. Drunks were insane, anybody knew that. Yet . . . well, everything else his mother was dead against seemed to be enjoyable, so maybe drink was the same. The old man had only been really nice to him once – and that was because of drink. But drinking was poison if you played football.

Ahead, on the straight stretch of road past McCracken's coal yard he saw three girls walking arm in arm. He always felt embarrassed, passing girls at night. Kilcaddie people had a habit of turning round to see who was coming up behind them – with good reason at this time of night when gangs of neds roved the streets looking for fights. And girls from the scheme could have very coarse tongues, especially if they knew you weren't one of their mob. He walked as quickly as he could, whistling to let them know he was harmless. Be a hard man. Ignore them. Pretend you're deep in thought about serious matters. They were only girls who didn't have their own blokes.

'Well, hell-o there,' said one as he came abreast. He went on whistling, looking straight ahead, pretending not to hear. They giggled.

'All alone then, handsome?' More giggling. He kept on, hands sweaty in his pockets. They were just hairies. Ignore them.

'Here, it's that fella from Craig's farm,' he heard another one say. 'All high and mighty then, pal?'

'Get lost,' he said, half-turning his head.

'Ach, come on, pal, how don't you give us a bit o' your patter well?'

He walked on, trying not to make it obvious that he was quickening his step.

Then, what you always dreaded, the sound of someone running towards you from the back. If it had been blokes he would have run, straight away. He looked over his shoulder. A dark-haired girl, her pink coat flying out at her sides, was almost beside him. Brazen, that's what his mother called scheme girls. Watch your step with they hairies, McCann always said, they've all got big coal-heavers for brothers, they'll turn vicious as quick as look at you.

The girl was laughing. She got hold of his right arm with both hands, looking at him with a silly grin on her face, slightly breathless. So was he!

'Don't kid on you don't know me,' she said. 'I saw you looking at me when we were howking.'

Play it tough, don't let her know you're shaking. Maybe it was just a kids' game. She didn't look young enough for kids' games.

'I didn't recognise you with your face washed,' he said, hoping the sarcasm would put her off. She was close beside him, hands gripping his jacket sleeve. He felt terrified. What kind of girl would do this sort of thing?

'Oh,' she said, raising her eyebrows, 'coming the old vinegar, eh? Your own wasn't so hot either, y'know. Where d'you live when you're at home?'

'Shuttle Place,' he said. He did remember her, now that he could think again. Telfer had pointed her out at the beginning of the howking. 'I'll bet she rattles like a tin can tied to a tomcat's tail,' was what he had said. He said it about almost anything in skirts.

'That's being demolished,' she said. 'I bet you wish you had a decent house in the scheme?'

'No thanks.'

'Too common for you, I suppose you think you're the bee's knees just because you've got a horse to play with.'

'Hmph. Play with?' He looked round. The other two were following about twenty yards behind, arm in arm, heads together in a big giggle.

'What's your name?'

'Dunky Logan. What's yours?'

'Elsa Noble. You went to the Academy, didn't you, my pal Betty saw you at a dance, she thought you were smashing.'

He looked at her, ready to sneer like a hard man. He'd taken girls out before, from the school. Prick-teasers told lies and

buggered you about. The others were too shy to talk to you at all.
She was grinning.

'You've got a brass neck,' he said.

'My pal Betty dared me. Are you a pal of Donald Telfer's?'

'Yeah. We're thinking of emigrating to Canada together. How
you know him, do you?'

'Everybody knows Donald Telfer, he's a dreamboat.'

Wouldn't it be fantastic, walk into the stable in the morning
and drop the word to Telfer, all casual like, see yon blackhaired
piece, yeah the Noble woman, well I lumbered her last night, not
bad at all. FANTASTIC.

'Where d'you live?'

'Down the scheme.'

'I'll see you home then?'

No, he shouldn't have asked her, he should just have kept
on walking. Whenever you tried to get things straight with a
dame she got all funny. It would all end now. Too good to be
true.

'Just to the corner,' she said. 'My father's very strict. Here, I
hope you don't think I was picking you up or anything, it was just
a dare.'

She'd think he was another bigtime guy, like Telfer, because he
worked on the farm. Because it had all happened in such a daft
way he didn't feel nearly as shy as he would have if he'd tried to
chat her up at a dance. Her hands began to take a less firm grip of
his sleeve, her pals were out of sight now, the big dare was
beginning to wear off.

'Telfer said he fancied you at the howking,' he said, making it
sound as though he and Donald were big buddies when it came to
eyeing the talent.

'Pull my other leg it's got bells on,' she said. Funny, sometimes
she talked 'nice' and then the real scheme edge would come into
her voice.

'It's true, cut my throat and hope to die.'

'Did you think I was er, ehm, like bold, coming up to you in the
street and that?'

'It happens to me all the time. How old are you?'

'Seventeen. D'you go to the Town Hall dancing? Me and Betty
go every Saturday, it's smashing.'

'D'you ever see Cut the Lugs Reilly?'

'Who's that in the name of God?'

It was because Alec was scared of guys like Cut the Lugs Reilly
that he wouldn't be coaxed to go to the Town Hall. One night

they'd been passing when the dancing was coming out and they'd
gone up to a crowd at the main entrance. It made it easier to talk
to her, having a story to tell.

'The blood was all over them, one of them had his shirt torn
half off him,' he told her. 'It's this bloke from the Brig, he's always
miroculous on VP wine and wants to cut people's ears off with his
scissors. I'm not joking, he carries scissors about in his pocket,
that's what he's called Cut the Lugs Reilly for. You shoulda seen
this other fella, he was hammering him, like a madman he was, no
wonder if you were going to get your lugs cut off, and then, you
know what, this woman got out among them trying to separate
them and she got a whack on the jaw, you shoulda seen her, flying
she was.'

He felt breathless at having spoken so much. He wished she'd
take hold of his arm again. It made it feel as though they knew
each other. Maybe she was getting fed up with him already. Just
his luck. Same at school, the good-looking ones wouldn't go
steady with you, too much competition.

'I don't like men who fight,' she said. 'It's just crazy.'

Bet Nicol never got a seventeen-year-old lumber from the
scheme. *Him*, he'd be scared to walk down it in daylight.
Nicol always said that crowds came down to the lowest
common denominator. He'd have to kid her he was seventeen
as well.

Going down the main Darroch road, deserted except for two
blokes trying to drag their drunk pal out of a hedge, watched by an
old woman at an upstairs balcony, she told him she worked as a
folder in a printing works, and that her father had once caught her
with a boy at the back of their house and sworn at him something
awful and given her a belting.

He told her he was only working at the farm until he saved the
fare to Canada. He told her his father was permanently paralysed
through an accident, she said she was awfully sorry. Maybe when
you were older you got to know what to say to women the first
time you lumbered them.

'This is far enough,' she said. They were at the corner of
Barskiven Road. She was getting all shy now.

'Hey, you don't live here, do you?' he blurted.

She stared at him, cheeky dark eyes no longer smiling.

'What about it? We're not all scum, it doesn't matter what folk
say.'

Barskiven Road was The Undesirables. Bad Corporation ten-
ants (didn't pay their rents, didn't dig their gardens, let their kids

smash up windows) were transferred to The Undesirables until
they showed they'd improved. His mother called them scum.
Barskiven Road houses had all-metal fittings. Only the window
panes could be broken, unless you had a blow-torch. McCann
said they'd have them, soon. At the dancing blokes always made
jokes if they knew a dame was from The Undesirables. It was
supposed to be the worst street in the whole of Kilcaddie.

'I don't think you're scum,' he said, smiling at her nervously.
'You think we're all toffs in Shuttle Place?'

He stood with his back to the battered privet hedge, still
holding her hand. Her hair was very black. She was a smasher.
If he tried to kiss her now she might not like it. If he didn't she
might think he was dead slow. Girls made him panicky.

'I'd better go then,' she said, not taking her hand away. She
seemed shy, too, even if she *had* run up to him in the street. But
that was only a dare.

'Eh, I'm supposed to be going to this dance at Blackinch on
Saturday night,' he said. 'You wouldn't . . .?'

'I've promised Betty to go to the Town Hall,' she said. For a
moment he thought of suggesting Alec should pair up with Betty,
but Alec wouldn't go near an Undesirable.

'You've got to go with her, I suppose?'

'I promised. She's my pal.'

'Eh, you wouldn't like to go to the pictures, would you?' His
tongue felt as though it wanted to stick to his teeth. Please let
her . . .

She looked at her feet. Funny, he knew she was thinking it had
only been a dare and now it was more serious than she'd
bargained for.

'Okay,' she said, quietly. 'But I can't manage it till next
Monday, my father only lets me out once during the
week.'

'Great.' He moved nearer her, looking at her face for any sign of
what she felt. He put his hands round her waist. Her body felt soft
through the pink coat. He started to pull her close. She let her face
come up to his. He didn't connect properly with her lips, but he
could taste her skin. There was a sort of shock through his whole
body. Then she was pulling away.

'See you at the Cross then, next Monday, seven o'clock?'

'I'll try. Ta ta.'

She ran down into the gloom of Barskiven Road, where half the
street-lights had been smashed. He waited until she was out of
sight. He turned away. He started to run, weaving past defenders,

sprinting, wanting to throw his arms up in the air. A big date. A smasher! FANTASTIC . . .

When he'd crawled into bed, relieved that for once his mother hadn't shouted through how late it was, he kept thinking of her name. Elsa Noble. Dear God, please let her love me, please . . .

SIX

IT WAS JUST after half-past five on the following Saturday morning when Willie came down the stairs into the kitchen. As soon as he switched on the light he could see the evidence of Mary O'Donnell's first week's work, the shining window panes, the swept floor, the breakfast things already laid, their big blue-ringed mugs upside down on a clean white tablecloth, not a dirty dish in sight.

It made him feel cheery – the way holidays used to, or days when they dressed up to take cattle or pigs to the market. His heavy flannel shirt rolled up past his elbows, he ran hot water into the enamel basin and splashed his face with cold water, feeling it wash into the sleep in his eyes. Looking out through the shiny panes, he saw that it was cold and dry, the yellow sliver of moon still high above the cartshed. Normally he couldn't be bothered shaving one week to the next, but with the kitchen looking so clean he felt he should. It was Saturday anyway.

Mary O'Donnell came into the kitchen as he was drawing the open razor down his cheek, left hand holding his jaw to one side. He saw her briefly in the cracked mirror. Her hair was down but she was dressed.

'Aye aye,' he said, taking a fresh grip on his chin, hard fingers biting into slippy skin. 'Ye're up then?'

'I'll have your breakfast ready by the time you're back from the byre,' she said. Milking was supposed to be the housekeeper's job. Willie had said he'd keep on doing it her first week, to give her a chance to get settled in. It made no odds, he never slept well after five o'clock, he'd have risen anyway. He'd never been in bed later than seven o'clock in the morning in his whole life and that was when he was a schoolboy.

Splashing away soap traces with cold water he dried himself on the clean face-towel she'd hung by the sink. A woman's touch, he thought to himself, supposed to make you feel better.

She'd started frying when he put on his cap and went out into the yard, fastening the collar stud at his neck against the still, cold morning. Before he went to the byre he had a walk round the steading, checking that nobody had broken into the hen-house or set fire to the hay-ricks or stolen anything. The black dog came out of its kennel but one guttural grunt was enough to send it back inside. Was she just playing up, because she was new, trying to make a good impression? Bobby Kerr of Barrhill had married his housekeeper, thinking she was a good worker, and no sooner was she back in the house from the kirk than she announced she wasn't going to break her back about the place, he'd have to get *her* a housekeeper. You could throw a leg over any woman alive but you didn't marry them for that.

Switching on the light in the byre he took the three-legged stool from its hook on the whitewashed wall and the big galvanised bucket from under the wall tap. His feet trapping the base of the pail, he put his head against the first cow's flank and felt for her teats, massaging them downwards with his fingers before taking them in the palm and thumb grip for milking. The white jets spurted with a tinny noise on the bottom of the pail. Soon the squirts hissed into creamy milk. He'd have to know a bit more about her, too, the kind of woman who went about housekeeping from farm to farm might be any kind of rogue, might even have a couple of wee bastards hidden away somewhere. He'd only once before thought seriously about getting married, that was when Big Watson the bobby died. He'd been visiting them for years and was well used to the woman's ways. When she was a widow she'd occasionally come down past the farm for a walk on a Sunday afternoon, not a bad-looking figure of a woman for her age. He'd got into the habit of hanging about at the entrance to the yard when she might be passing – it wouldn't have done for him to keep on visiting her when she was a widow living on her own, that would have started the neighbours gossiping, sure as anything, but it was respectable enough for her to come into the farmhouse for a cup of tea, his father being there.

Once or twice he'd been on the point of telling her they should get wed, but something had stopped him. Although she came from Aberdeen herself, and had been a farmer's daughter before she married Watson (who'd been at school with her and had married her on leave from Kilcaddie police), there was too much of the town about her. She wore hats and silk stockings and her hands didn't look right for the kind of toil the farm needed. It was a different life from what she was used to in her Corporation house – no rugs or nice carpets, not even a wireless in those days; Auld Craig wouldn't have a wireless in the place, said it would just addle their brains and put them off the notion of work. They had one now, but that was mainly for the weather forecasts.

He took the other two teats and soon the big bucket was heavy with milk. When he'd emptied her udder he poured the milk into the urn and sat beside the other milker. He'd tried to tell his father that they'd be better off going onto dairy farming altogether, get a milking herd and a milking machine and forget all the tatties and whatnot, save on wages, but his father couldn't be bothered with all the business of getting a Tuberculin Tested herd. He'd always been a mixed farmer, dairy farming was a lazy man's idea, it wasn't real farming at all unless you had to work at it. Today McCann and the boy would be muck-spreading and Telfer ploughing with the tractor. Coll and himself would start putting up a new fence on the field by the factory, Coll due for a shock when it came to paying time. Mind you, a cripple woman wouldn't be wanting to be running away to the town all the time, she'd count herself lucky to get a place of her own.

The oats had been soaking in the big pot all night. When she had them on the boil, the big bubbles popping up through the thickening porridge, she put a dab of lard in the frying pan. When it was sizzling she cracked in two eggs. Beside them she laid two big beef sausages. It wasn't her place to take her breakfast with the Craigs, not yet. There hadn't been any sign from Willie Craig that he was thinking about her, but that wasn't surprising. Stephenson at Beith hadn't said a word to her for about six months and then one night, when she was darning his socks and he'd been reading the paper, he'd just stood up and said: 'Come awa' to bed, woman.'

Willie was as likely to come out with it just as sudden, but unless it happened in a day or two he'd never believe the baby was his. Yet if she made the first move and later on the baby came a lot earlier than was normal, he'd get to thinking back. Suspicious wasn't the word for them. She wished she could be as hard as they were, instead of being weak and sinful. Even now, when she knew what she had to do for her own good, she was still not able to stop thinking about the big blond fella. Why was there always some-body like him about, confusing her, never giving her a chance to concentrate on what was sensible? God had cursed her, sure enough. Even her own mother had said that and it was true and not all the priests in the world could change it.

Willie's boots scraped on the porch cobbles. She was tasting the porridge when he came in, leaning to one side against the weight of the narrow-necked urn.

'There's a few of them need extra milk at the weekend,' he said, putting the urn by the sink. Most mornings they sold about a gallon and a half to people from the scheme, but at the weekends, with the men all sitting about their houses swilling down tea, extra customers came for fresh milk from the farm. It was hardly worth the bother taking the money, but they'd always sold it and no doubt they always would. Just as they sold a few dozen eggs to people they knew, even during the war when all the eggs were supposed to be accounted for to the government.

'Do you let them all have it?' she asked.

'Oh aye, jist keep eneuch for oor tea and oor parritch.'

'Your porridge is ready,' she said.

'Aye, where wud we be withoot oor parritch, eh?'

She ladled it into the brown chipped bowl and put it in front of him. Her hands had seen a wheen of work, he thought. Her fingers looked as though they'd been scraped with wire wool. The Watson widow had very nice nails, too nice by far for a farm. Looking down at the dirty pores on the back of his neck she felt like taking a scrubbing brush to him. He'd be a smelly brute of a man to lie beside in a bed. She thought of the other man's yellow hair and slim, red neck. But good looks wouldn't keep a woman and child in the house and home . . .

Willie had already tended the beasts in the byre, turnips and hay, by the time the men were in the stable at half-past seven. Telfer was smoking, McCann was brushing behind the horses and the boy was carrying their water. Coll arrived just behind Willie, pushing his bike, his gas-mask case strap across his chest, his cloth cap on the back of his head. Coll wore his cap with the skip slightly off centre and the rest of it pulled back. He and Willie were the only ones to wear nicky tams, strings tied round their trousers below the knees to stop dirt rising up their legs. Telfer watched Coll shove his bike against the stable wall. What a galoot he was, a real highland hayseed.

'How's Bonnie Prince Charlie this morning then?' he said.

Coll grinned.

'How's yourself, you perfumed ponce-boy?'

If you went too far with Coll he could get really annoyed and then he'd throw his cap on the ground and stick up his fists like a bare-knuckle expert and ask you if you were wanting your ugly features altered. Telfer decided he couldn't be bothered.

'Aye, well I don't smell like something the cat dragged off the midden,' he said, nodding at Willie. The boy began brushing the mare. 'How's you and Mary getting on, Willie?' Telfer asked, winking at McCann. 'Is it true what I hear, she's fair daft about your father?'

'Ach you shut your big mouth, Telfer,' said Willie. 'If ye'd a decent pair of balls on ye mibbe ye'd get yersel' a grown woman instead o' all they wee hairies ye smell round.'

McCann swept the last horse sharn into the pile at the end of the gutter and threw the broom against the wall. When he'd gone to the Brig to buy the motor bike it wouldn't start and now he wouldn't be able to collect it till Monday night. It hadn't made him any cheerier, having to go back to his mother's house and hear his stepfather's cracks about people who wasted their money on second-hand trash. Nothing ever went right for him, he reckoned. Nobody liked him. They all knew he was a bastarding failure from start to finish. Here it was, Saturday, with no fancy piece to take out, no pals to go to the dancing with, nothing.

Dunky knew he and Blackie were to be carting dung from the midden all morning, on their own.

'Fancy coming to a big dance at Blackinch canteen?' he asked McCann, standing behind him with the empty water pail. 'Me and my pal are going, plenty of talent.'

Blackie McCann looked at him, sleepy blue eyes staring out of dark stubbled face.

'Nah, whut dae I want wi' a lot of kids?'

Dunky shrugged. He hadn't really wanted McCann to come. He'd asked him more out of cheek, just to show him he was bigtime enough to go to the dancing. What did he care about McCann? Let the bastard rot.

Telfer went to start up the tractor. Willie and Coll started off down the track road, Coll carrying the bale of wire. Willie with the mell hammer over his shoulder. McCann and Dunky yoked Big Dick into the four-wheeler and backed it against the midden. The hills were still dark, a deep purple. Overhead the first light of the hidden sun sprayed out through high clouds like fingers of water moving jerkily across a greasy surface.

Telfer whistled 'Oh What a Beautiful Morning' as he yoked the tractor to the plough. A nice steady morning's work on his own, nothing to think about except keeping the drills straight, just him and the tractor, time to think about things. Like Agnes. He was well out of that. For a while it had been enough just to know he was banging the arse off a toff's daughter – he laughed to himself, banging was the right word for it, first time in she'd squealed like a stuck rat. Most Kilcaddie women were the same, anything more than a quick necking session was some kind of big sin – until you got married and then you didn't want to anyway. Something unusual was the best. The trouble in Kilcaddie was they were all small-minded – unless they were like Agnes, falling over themselves to do anything that would make you marry them. You couldn't put up with a woman like that, it wasn't the same once you knew she'd let you do anything. Forcing them into it the first time was the only good part of it.

As he turned round at the end of the first drill he looked across the field at the factory. He'd been in it once, terrible dump, no wind or sun, the noise fit to split your skull, nothing to look at but iron walls and assembly belts and bits of aeroplanes hanging from chains, starved of fresh air. No wonder they had to pay them fourteen and fifteen pounds a week, cooped up in that joint.

He knew that would be different, now. A woman with an iron on her leg! What would it look like, up at the top where it joined on? What would she do with it when you were riding her? Had any other guys ever poked her? Christ, it was hellish interesting just thinking about it. But how the hell could he do anything about her? She'd been stuck in the house all week and he could hardly bowl over to the kitchen door and ask her if she fancied a wee walk on a dark night down the black hills. He'd have to be very fly to get in sniffing distance. Still, if anybody could, he could. Tits on her like turnips! Imagine getting her down in the hay and ripping the clothes off her!

Not many guys had interesting ideas like he had, he was sure of that. Most of them couldn't think further than a quick knee-trembler at the back of a close . . .

Willie decided to say nothing to Coll about his sacking. They talked about a farmer on the other side of the Brig whose two-year-old son died in a milk urn being scalded with boiling water. Only two weeks later his Ayrshire bull had got his wife against a henhouse and battered her unconscious, doing serious damage to her pelvis. Things like that happened in threes, said Coll. They tried to think of the worst things that could happen to the man himself. Willie said he'd once seen a collie bitch getting its back broke by an Ayrshire bull, chucked in the air and headed against a wall. Coll had a nephew who'd been ploughing on a slope and the tractor had fallen backwards and whipped off his head. They hammered in posts and stapled wire and racked their brains for other stories to pass the time.

Jabbing the four tines of his fork into the solidly packed dung, Dunky hoped he wasn't going to be dead tired for the game that afternoon. As it was he'd have a hell of a rush to get back home and changed and up to the Cross to meet the team at quarter past one. He'd still not been able to tell anybody about Elsa Noble, and he was gasping to hear what Telfer would say. His boots ploughed down into the yielding surface of the midden as he turned to throw each forkful onto the back of the flat cart. The further down they got into the layers of byre and stable dung the heavier it got, until, at the bottom, it was like peat. There was a rest during the short trip to the field, but then he and McCann had to get up on the top of the load and fork it out over last year's stubble for Telfer to plough into the ground on Monday. McCann didn't say much. He could have taken out his temper on the boy, but being asked to go to the dance left him no excuse. It was aggravating having nobody to lead the horse up and down the field, that would have speeded them up a lot. It would be better on Monday, when Willie and Coll would have finished fencing and the boy could lead the cart in the field and one of them could stay behind at the midden loading the second cart. The job had to be done, so the quicker the better.

Mary O'Donnell was peeling potatoes for their dinner when the old man came out of the front room, where he'd been making up the wages into envelopes, the money having been locked in there since Friday dinnertime when, as usual, Farquharson the lawyer had called for Auld Craig in his car and taken him up to the bank.

'Peel away, woman,' the old man said, then made a noise that could have been a laugh and stamped out of the kitchen, his bowed head narrowly passing under the door lintel. She followed him to the porch, standing back in case he looked round and saw her idling. Willie and Coll were the first back in the yard, Coll walking splay-footed, his back straight and the skip of his cap twisted round so that it was almost over his ear, Willie ploughing along on bowly legs, the pair of them looking like Mutt and Jeff. Then the boy and the other man came in leading the big horse, unyoking the flat cart beside the midden, ready for the first load on Monday. She didn't fancy the looks of the man McCann, he was a dour-looking creature. The boy meant nothing to her at all, he was just the boy, there was always one about a farm, either full of cheek or else so quiet you'd think he was wrong in the head.

A hen tried to peck its way past her into the kitchen. When they'd had no housekeeper the Craigs hadn't bothered to keep hens out of the kitchen. They cleaned up what the dogs didn't eat, Willie said.

'Whoosh.' She blew out her lips and waved her arms and it squawked away across the yard. The others were turning the stable corner when she heard the tractor. Telfer brought it past the midden at top speed, standing up behind the seat, bending over to put in the throttle and turn her in a spectacular curve towards the opening between the stable and the barn.

But he had a look towards the house before he passed the stable and she drew back from the door in case he saw her. He was like a film star, not like the others at all. Clean. Handsome. A fella like that would never look at a cripple, he'd have all the girls he wanted. Not that she would have anything to do with him anyway, he was just a common farm servant and she needed more than that.

As usual Auld Craig took his time about paying them. First he had a bit of a stand and a stare at the hills. Then he watched Telfer backing the tractor into the narrow cartshed. Then he had a bit of a peek at his boots, in case they were thinking of making a dash for it on their own.

'Look at him, the old goat,' said McCann, standing at the dusty stable window. 'He's shiting himsel' about givin' away his money.'

'You'll be doing well, boy, if you're half the man he is when you're that age,' said Coll.

'They can tak' me to the knacker's afore I get to that state,' said McCann.

Dunky gave Big Dick his hay and then stood by the cornkist waiting for the old man to decide it was time to part with his precious cash. They were finished work, there wasn't another bloody stroke that could be done about the place, but the old bugger would hang on till the factory hooter went at half-past twelve. That was lowsing time, pay time, not a minute before. Willie nodded to his father as he came into the stable and took the hammer through to the harness room. The hooter went as Telfer went into the empty stall – Charlie's stall – for a slash, a fag already hanging from his lips.

'McCann!' shouted the old man.

Blackie went out and took his envelope. He counted it as he walked to his bicycle, which was propped against the trough outside the stable. He shoved it into his hip pocket, got on the bike and pedalled out of the yard.

'Telfer!'

Donald sauntered out and they heard him speak to the old man as he took the envelope: 'It's all there, I hope, you wouldn't try to swindle me, Craig, I hope?'

Craig looked at Telfer, and made a short braying noise. The fair-haired man went across to the cartshed and leaned with his back against the wall, one foot drawn up under him. Coll should have come next but Dunky heard Craig shout, 'Logan.'

As he walked the couple of yards from the stable door to where Auld Craig stood beside a melting puddle, he tried hard to look as casual as Telfer had done. It was time he stopped being afraid of the old man – not everybody was the way his father had been, ready to thump you one as quick as look at you.

'Here's your siller, boy,' said Craig, putting a fold of notes and some silver in Dunky's hand. Only the men got it in envelopes. Inhumanly pale blue eyes squinted at him from under heavy eyebrows. 'You'll be throwing it away in your picture palaces I suppose?'

'No, I'm saving up for a motor car,' said Dunky, grinning cheekily at the farmer.

'Hrrmph. Get away tae hell out of it.'

Dunky grinned at Telfer as he walked over to the cartshed, where he counted his five pounds twelve and sixpence, his back to Craig in case the old man saw him and thought he didn't trust him. That wouldn't do.

'One thing about Craig, he doesn't pay you much but it's regular,' said Telfer. He spat, not the way the others spat, wet and noisy, but in the American way, a smooth jet. Dunky wondered if Telfer did all these things naturally, or was he deliberately copying the films?

'Coll,' cried the old man.

The moon-faced highlander walked with his hand out, open, like a big schoolboy. Was he pretending, too, just acting the idiot to give everybody a laugh?

'I'll no' be needing you after next week, Coll. There's your money. Too damnt many men about the place. You can pick up your books on Friday. Plenty of jobs about.'

The old man looked at his boots for a moment, then turned and walked away round the stable. Coll stared after him, mouth open.

'Are you giving me the bag?' he shouted after Craig. The old man stopped, half-turning.

'Aye. So don't be throwing the siller over the bar counter, you'll be needin' it.'

And he was gone. Dunky felt frightened.

'He's joking,' Coll said to Willie, surprise giving his voice a squeaky tone. Willie stood in the stable door and shook his head.

'Craig never jokes,' he said. 'Ach, what're ye worryin' aboot, Coll, ye're a lazy bugger anyway, ye'll suit them fine in the factory.'

'Factory? I've been here eight year!'

Dunky wished he'd gone straight home. Coll looked ready to cry.

'You're well out of it,' Telfer said, putting his foot on the ground. 'You'll easy get another job.'

Not looking at the slack-jawed Coll, Dunky fetched his bike from the stable, hoping they'd have gone when he came out. Craig had given Coll the bag because *he'd* come to work there – at less wages. He waited as long as he could but when he wheeled the bike outside Coll was still there. Telfer and Willie were walking into the yard.

'Eight year,' Coll said to Dunky, looking at him with a frown. 'Eight years working for that man and now I'm bagged, just like that?'

Oh Christ, Dunky thought, Coll was going to cry. The first big tear ran down his red face. He didn't even try to hide it. Dunky put his leg over the bike, balancing himself on one foot. It was the worst thing in the world, to see another man crying. There was something daft and soft and silly about Coll, the stupid way he wore his cap ('More like a barrage balloon than a bunnet,' McCann said), his splayed feet, his idiotic back straighter than a fence post.

'You'll get another job in no time,' he said. Hmph, fancy a boy trying to mother a grown man!

'Oh aye,' said Coll, bitterly. 'Get a new job, just like that! And a new house! They treat you just like dirt.' He had stopped crying now that he'd got over the shock. 'You be as cheery as you like, sonny, someday it'll happen to you and you'll know what it's like.'

'I must go, I'm playing football,' said Dunky. 'Cheerio.'

Pedalling furiously, he rode away from the farm towards the scheme houses. He'd be late for the team meeting. Imagine a grown man crying in public just because he'd got the sack from an old goat like Craig! Some people were too soft.

Late as he was, he still decided to go home via Barskiven Road, but there was no sign of Elsa Noble. A gang of wee boys threw a stone at him. He stood up on the pedals to get up speed, not caring if they thought he was frightened. Coll had got the bullet because Craig thought he could do a man's work. Maybe he'd get a rise! That would show his bloody father!

From the way Telfer dawdled about in the yard, not in his usual hurry to be away home, Willie guessed that Mary O'Donnell was the attraction. When the black dog looked out at them Telfer bent and chucked a stone at its kennel. The dog shot back inside.

'Black bastard, it could've torn the throat out of her,' Telfer said. Willie stared at him, eyes wide open, the slightly insane face he put on when he was going to make one of his dafter pronouncements.

'There's more than the dog wants to get his teeth into the O'Donnell woman,' he said.

'You fancy her, do you?' Telfer asked, glancing towards the kitchen door. 'I suppose you think she's easy meat for you, living in the same house?'

Willie's eyes didn't blink as he spoke.

'You mind your own business, Telfer, none of your monkey tricks with her.'

Telfer grinned. Imagine smelly Willie thinking he could do better with a woman than him!

'You'll be short of a bit now, I suppose – with Morag moving?'

Willie's eyes were still wide open, but any suggestion of humour left his face.

'What's that supposed to mean?'

Telfer made a knowing face, lower jaw pulled down but mouth closed, right eye closing in a big, slow wink.

'Certain parties have seen certain goings on,' he said.

'Certain parties might get their faces massaged wi' my boots if I catch them spreading their dirty lies.'

Telfer laughed. No sign yet of Mary O'Donnell at the kitchen door. He hadn't quite made up his mind whether sacking Coll had been Willie's idea, to get Morag Coll well out of it so that he'd have elbow room to work the oracle on the housekeeper. Willie wasn't as green as he was cabbage-looking.

'Maybe I'll drop by for a cup of tea this afternoon,' Telfer suggested, eyes slightly narrowed. 'Saturday afternoon's often the best time about a farm, I sometimes think.'

This time there was no mistaking Willie's seriousness.

'You keep out of it, Telfer,' he said. 'She doesn't want anything to do with a common tyke like you. Stick to your wee hairies from the scheme, they're more your level.'

With that he went away into the house.

'You big-headed bastard,' Telfer muttered. 'Just you bloody wait.'

As he walked up the road to the scheme he thought of various ways in which he could get Mary O'Donnell on her own. If there was one thing calculated to make him deadly serious about the woman it was Willie laying down the law. What the hell was Willie anyway, a man of fifty still bossed around by his father? I'll fuck'n show you bastards, he thought, think you're the be all and end all, eh? Common tyke!

'Well, hallow there, if it isn't the queen of the howkers,' he said, overtaking the dark-haired girl who'd got off the bus at the stop in the main scheme road. She turned and as she didn't have a scowl on her face he took it she was willing for a bit of patter. 'Fine day for a walk up the Braes!'

Elsa Noble hoped her father didn't see her walking beside Donald Telfer. He had a bad reputation, supposed to be very fast.

'I've got a date with a friend of yours,' she said.

'Who's that, McPhail the knee-padder?'

'None of your business. I hope you enjoyed the walk.'

She crossed the road away from him. Not bad legs. His mother would know her name, she knew almost every family at this end of the scheme, she'd certainly know which Undesirable family had a girl like that, hot little eyes and all. Who did she mean she was dating? Somebody at the farm? No, Blackie was the only remote possibility and he messed his breeks whenever he got within two yards of a woman. He'd note that girl for future use, his main aim was to get at the housekeeper. Apart from fancying her anyway, it would be as good as rubbing Willie's nose in the midden, to rattle the Craigs' own housekeeper! On his way up Dalmelly Drive, where half of one large block was still a ruin from the bombing, the open end now a tatty mess of peeling wallpaper and rusty fireplaces, he overtook old Mrs Docherty.

'Carry your bags for you, sweetheart,' he said, giving the fat wee woman the eye. She had fourteen of a family, most of them lazy great brutes who wouldn't work, but she still had to do her own shopping.

'Oh, that's awfy nice of ye, Donal', right enough but,' she said, sighing as she let his hands slip through the leather handles. 'Ma varicose veins is fair killin' me, so an' they are.'

'Good job bread's off the ration,' he said, looking at the eight or nine big unwrapped loaves packed on top of the other messages in her two bags.

'Ye're no' kiddin', Donal',' she said, wheezing a bit, her voice

like gravel. 'If we didnae hiv bread tae full them up whut wud we
dae, that's whut Ah aye say, right enough but.'

He had always had nerves before a game, worse if there were
people watching. Glenryan was a village halfway between Kilcaddie and the smaller town of Bridge of Kilmorchan – the Brig.
Twenty or so men and boys were on the touchline of Glenryan's
cinder and grass pitch. They'd been known to attack visiting
teams.

Baldy Campbell made him even more nervous. The great fat
man in the belted gaberdine raincoat and flat checked cap was
watching the second eleven for only one reason – to see if any of
them were fit to move up into the big team. One silly mistake
could ruin his chance. He put the rest of the chewing gum packet
in his jacket pocket. The new chiclet slipped about between his
teeth and tongue until he'd bitten through to the gum. He always
felt the same way before a game, nervous, half-thinking he wasn't
good enough for the team, wondering if he'd play a stinker. He'd
been playing almost every Saturday, morning and afternoon,
since he was about twelve or thirteen and he was still nervous.
Nobody else knew just how seriously you took it, how much you
hoped that one day you'd play a blinder and a strange man would
come up to you after the game and write your name down in a wee
book and ask you if you wanted a trial with Rangers or Aston Villa
or Leicester City. Or even Ayr United – he wasn't fussy. Nobody
else knew that you thought of each game as a tightrope along
which you walked hoping you wouldn't fall off. You had a feeling
that the rest of the guys in the team didn't think you were good
enough to be playing, so you couldn't really think of them as pals.

You ran out onto the pitch wondering whether your studs were
hammered in properly, would a nail come up through your sole,
were your laces tied tight enough. Your thighs seemed darker and
hairier than usual against white shorts. During the kickabout you
didn't exert yourself, you took the odd shot at goal, you jumped
up and down feet together, you rubbed your hands against the
cold, you sneaked a look at the other team – who always seemed
bigger and stronger and more sure of themselves. You wondered
which one you were marking, was he a hard case or a fantastic
sprinter or a tremendous dribbler? Did you really need to go to
the lavvy again, or was it just nerves?

The first ball you got was the vital one, if you bungled it you'd
probably have a stinker. You saw the houses and the trees and the
people but you didn't think about them. After ten minutes you'd

know what kind of a game it was, hard and fast, a kicking match, a walkover, a hopeless defeat? Once you knew that you could fit yourself into it, play as well as possible. But the beginning was the worst, waiting for your first ball.

As they lined up for the kick-off he saw Baldy talking to his crony, Joe Overend. Were they talking about him? All Joe had said was that Baldy would be coming to their game, he never told you who Baldy was supposed to be interested in.

His first kick came after a few minutes running up and down behind the forwards. He saw it hit somebody's shin and run loose. He was able to trap it and look up before Glenryan blokes came at him. At this stage in the game everybody was full of wind, there was no time to hang about.

He hit it up the left-wing, wishing there had been time to make sure it went to one of their forwards. It landed near enough to Sammy Muir to make it look intentional, so maybe he was going to have a good game. As he ran about there seemed to be two parts of his brain. One followed the ball, deciding when to tackle and when to fall back. The other seemed to talk back to him, as though he was really two people, one making a speech to the other.

Go in hard. No time for fancy-work in juvenile football. Go in hard and don't waste time. One day play like Bobby Evans. Not really fond of playing wing-half. Centre-forward best position. Be Billy Houliston. Rummle 'em up.

One thing you've got – iron determination. Hard as nails. Don't care about being hurt. Only get hurt if you go in half-hearted. Do or die.

After half an hour the pattern was there. Glenryan's inside-right, the man he was marking, did most of the dribbling in their team. He was a nifty dribbler, fancy with it, too. Hands splayed out at his sides, palms towards the ground, copying Willie Woodburn of the Rangers, the spread-out hands.

Just before half-time Glenryan got the first goal. A long ball came up from their defence and by the time Dunky saw that he was nearest to it he was caught in two minds whether to go for it in the air or wait to collect it after the first bounce. On the greasy, melting surface, his feet slipped as he first went forward and then decided to run back. The ball bounced over his head. Big Colin Thompson, their right-back, tried a sliding tackle on the fancy inside-right, but he flicked the ball forward and did a neat little hurdling jump over Colin's scything legs. Swaying his head from side to side to confuse the goalkeeper he ran forward into the penalty area and shot it into the net just as Bobby Black, Cartneuk's centre-half, crashed him to the ground.

Cartneuk's goalie, Billy Forsyth, sat on one leg, the other stuck out in the mud, looking accusingly at his defenders.

Dunky spat. It was his fault. He made a tight mouth and shook his head.

'What was the fuck'n matter wi' you?' demanded Bobby Black, glowering at Dunky.

'Piss off.'

Bobby Black was fond of shouting the odds about other players' mistakes. Dunky thought Bobby didn't like him because he was the only one in the team who'd gone to the Academy, which a lot of the guys called a toffs' school.

The whistle went and they walked over to the dressing-room hut, where Baldy Campbell stood with Overend. Dunky went inside for a new bit of gum. The sun was shining, although it was cold. Overend had oranges for those who felt thirsty. Dunky didn't bother. What did Baldy have to say? Men who ran football teams were funny buggers. They never saw the game the same way as you did. Some of the guys always made a point of buttering up Baldy, getting in their versions of what'd gone wrong, trying to put the blame on somebody else. He didn't. He was lucky to be in the team at all, he supposed, yet he wasn't going to smarm up to anybody. If Baldy didn't like the way he played too bloody bad.

'You're not covering each other enough,' was Baldy's pronouncement. He spoke quietly, not annoyed that they'd lost the first goal. Although he was big he had very small eyes. Funny eyes. Different from the rest of him. His mouth said one thing, but his eyes seemed to be watching you listening to him, as though his eyes were separate from the rest of him. Dunky blew his nose, thumb against one nostril, snort, head bent forward so that it would miss his legs, middle finger against the other nostril, snort. Spit. It could be a bad sign, Baldy not being annoyed. Hundreds of guys wanted to play for Cartneuk. He didn't have to persevere with players. If he didn't think you were any good he just let you go. You had to fight to get a game, let alone become a regular.

'That inside-right's the danger man,' said Joe Overend. Normally he was in charge of the second team, a scruffy wee man who was very friendly towards everyone – and who told tales to Baldy all the time. You had to be careful what you said to Overend.

'I want the full-backs to play closer together,' Baldy said. 'Concentrate on the middle, their wingers is nothing hot.'

Dunky bent down and touched the dried blood on his knee, thinking that it would nip later on when he had to scrub the embedded cinders out of the skin.

'And Logan,' went on Baldy, 'don't be scared to take your man, if he thinks you're scared of him he'll do what he wants.'

Dunky nodded. Who the hell was *scared?*

A slight stiffness after the half-time rest. Get stuck in, that's what Baldy wanted. All right, I'll show you who can get stuck in.

At school it was all sportsmanship. You didn't play to win, oh no, you were told off for fouling. The referees were all schoolteachers, you couldn't play it hard or they'd give you a dressing-down, as though you'd been caught wanking in class. But once you were out in real football it was different. The ref could only give fouls against you, not treat you like a wee boy. And Baldy was only interested in playing to win. As long as you didn't give away penalties or get sent off Baldy didn't care what you did. He didn't care what the other team said, either. He said there was only one way to play the game. Hard – to win. He believed in real football, not a lot of namby-pamby schools' stuff. If you got in trouble he was on your side. As long as you were one of his players he would stick up for you.

The hand-waver trapped the ball near the touchline. Go in – hard as nails. Dunky leaned back as his left leg swept round from behind, knocking the inside-right to the ground, forcing the ball over the line. He shot up his hands and shouted 'Our ball' but the referee gave the throw-in to Glenryan. It was a short one to the outside-right. Dunky took a kick at it through the outside-right's legs.

'Hey watch it,' shouted a man on the touchline. The outside-right looked over his shoulder at Dunky. The ref gave another throw-in to Glenryan. This time it went into the middle. Dunky moved forward, taking up position to cover any breakaway attacks, aligning himself with Bobby Black and the full-backs. Another ball to the inside-right, who'd taken up position at the touchline, near halfway, giving him room to trap and move forward. Run out to block him. Body jack-knifed, eyes on the ball, never take your eyes off the ball. Go in – hard as nails. The inside-right put his foot on the ball and dragged it back out of range of Dunky's jabbing boot. Then he pushed it forward, past Dunky.

Up and after him. The wing-half must never stop running. Keep harassing him, don't give him a moment to get control. Thought so, like all fancy guys he wanted to hold on to the ball, work it a bit, show off. Dunky came up, cold air rasping on his throat. As the inside-right swung back his right leg to cross he went in, left foot first, knees together, throwing himself at the ball, seeing only the ball.

The swinging boot caught him on the knee. The ball skidded a yard. Bobby Black cleared it. Dunky drew in a gasping breath and bit his lower lip. His knee was in agony. Teeth clenched, he went on swearing until the pain faded. Limp a couple of steps, nothing wrong with it, bite your lip, all right. That was deliberate, pretending he couldn't stop his kick. Well, he'd asked for it now, the dirty rat.

The next time the inside-right came running up with the ball Dunky went in from the side, right hip thumping into the guy's side. At that speed he had no chance. Up you go, fancy pants.

'You dirty bastard!' roared a man on the touchline, his face red with anger, shaking his right fist. Dunky ignored him. Spectators meant nothing. Fancy pants made a great show of standing up in pain, rubbing his back, stretching, agony on his face.

They fell back for the free-kick. The ball was scrambled away. Overend was shouting them on. Glenryan didn't look so hot now. Like all village teams they were stronger than they were skilful. You had to have years of playing in the streets, a tennis ball on cobbles with twenty a side, sometimes under the streetlights, a tin can if there wasn't a ball – that's what you needed. Village boys were never nippy enough.

Go in hard. Their outside-right with the ball, dribbling up the wing, Glenryan's supporters stepping back to give him room. Sammy Muir was out there with him, but Sammy wasn't so hot at tackling. Go out to the wing, cover Sammy. The outside-right coming past Sammy on the outside, pushing the ball forward with the outside of his right foot. Choose your moment, then go in hard. Get the ball or man, both if possible, either will do, a free-kick out here won't do any damage.

He took the outside-right and the ball and himself over the line, crashing through the spectators, putting up his hands to protect his face, falling. Men shouting at him, a face looking down, an angry face.

As he got up a bare-headed man kicked his leg.

'Take that ye wee pig!'

Dunky spat at the man's feet and trotted, not too quickly, back on to the pitch. The outside-right knelt to replace his shin-pad. No foul! The ref must be blind. Still, you took what you could get. From the throw-in he muscled in on their right-half and came away with the ball. You had to try and *feel* them coming at you from behind, keep running forward, make ground. About now.

He jumped as he ran and the boot that came from behind only scraped his ankles, not enough force to trip him. Pretending to make for the wing he pushed it inside to Sammy Muir, stroking it with the inside of his right foot.

Sammy to Joe McNenemy. Joe going across the field, small and left-footed, he'll have to turn back again to cross it, his right foot's only for standing on. Move up for the cross. Light not so good, difficult to see the ball against the mud and cinders. Watch Joe's body, that'll tell when it's coming. Joe's cross. Coming from the right, kicked with the left foot, ball curling in towards the goal. Don't chase in after it, enough forwards in there already. Hover on the edge of the box, move this way and that following the scramble. Here it comes, high ball. One of their guys going to jump. Go up with him, push yourself up, elbow out in his chest, go in hard. Full strength header, back into the goalmouth.

Glenryan's centre-half took a mighty swing at the dropping ball, trying to volley it a mile. He misconnected. The ball hit the outside of his ankle. Before their goalkeeper could move across to cover the deflection the ball had spun, quite gently, in a series of bounces, into their net, a full-back entangling himself in the rigging as he tried to rush back and hook it clear.

After that they seemed to play for only a few more minutes and then the whistle went. Ah well, a draw wasn't bad, Glenryan were a strong bunch on their own ground.

As they ran towards the dressing-hut the Glenryan supporters were waiting for them, in a small bunch, directly between him and the door of the hut. He kept up with the rest. They ran through the men, ignoring their shouts.

There was a bucket of cold water in the dressing room. He wiped the worst of the mud off his torn knee, dipping one of his socks in the bucket. Baldy didn't say much till they were dressed and out of the hut again, having shaken hands with the Glenryan team, fouls seemingly forgotten.

Carrying his boots and socks, dirty strip and pants, shinguards and spare laces in his small brown case, Dunky walked with the team to the bus stop, listening to what Baldy was saying. Funny how much some guys talked about a game once it was over.

'You'll get your postcards about next Saturday during the week,' Baldy said as some of them left to get the bus to the Brig. It was almost dark now. Upstairs on the bus, Sammy Muir dragging on a fag like a grown man, Baldy sat next to Overend, the guys in the seat in front twisting round to speak to him, the same guys who always smarmed up to the big man. Dunky sat with wee Joe McNenemy. His knee was getting stiff. He'd have to scrub it with hot water and iodine or it might go septic. At

Kilcaddie Cross Baldy at last spoke to him, just before he left to catch the scheme bus.

'No' a bad second half, Logan,' he said. 'We'll mibbe see about trying you out in the first team.'

'Oh, great.'

Baldy looked at him, big face under the flat cap.

'Aye, just a bit more weight and you'd do fine.'

On the way down in the scheme bus he thought of all the balls he'd had during the match and how he could have done better. Christ, wouldn't it be great if Elsa Noble could come and see him playing for Cartneuk first eleven! That would impress her, dead right it would. Or maybe Baldy would mention him in the report he put into the paper. His father would have to read that. Then he might admit that he *could* play football . . .

Tonight would do for a start, Willie thought. He felt like it tonight. Nearly a week since he'd rammed it into Morag Coll and he felt like it again. As Mary dished out their tea he felt like shoving his hand up her skirt and getting hold of her arse and giving it a good twist. He got a hard-on just looking at her move about the kitchen. Once the old man had gone to bed he'd have a chat with her. He hadn't waited all week on account of her maybe not wanting to let him into bed, he'd never even thought that she might not be willing. He'd waited out of common sense, to see what she was like about the house. He had a feeling she'd have to be married – if he started at all. Something else had been keeping him back. Other men might laugh at him for wedding a cripple, an Irish Pape at that. But the moment he'd realised that Telfer was after her as well he knew he wanted her, married if it had to be that. He knew that Archie Stewart would say to marry her regardless of what she was. Archie always said to pay no heed to other people's small minds.

'Hrrmmph, I'm away to my bed,' said Auld Craig, dragging his tackety boots across the stone floor.

'I'm putting they dogs out in the old pighouse,' Willie said, elbows on the table, not looking at his father. 'They're no good in here.'

She'd wondered if he'd do anything about that. She carried dirty dishes to the sink, running her teeth over her bottom lip. He hadn't forgotten, so he must have been thinking about it all week. It being Saturday he'd be thinking he wanted a bit of fun and games tonight. All right, you smelly brute, I'm ready for you. Once you've enjoyed yourself you're as good as its father.

She would do it, because it was the best way to get what she needed.

'Aye,' said Craig. 'They're better off out of it.'

So that was that, the dogs would go out. Willie kept his elbows on the table as she finished clearing up.

'Another cup of tea?' she asked.

'Oh aye,' he said.

She poured the tea. He poked his nose with his thumb, howking into it as though he was delving for tatties.

'I'll be feeding the hens then,' she said.

'Aye, right.'

She limped across the yard, shining the torch on the ground. Inside the door of the hay-barn she found the bucket by the door, already filled with corn. Willie had done that, she knew. Oh, he was keen enough, sure enough. She smiled to herself. It wasn't much to have to do for a home of your own, give yourself to a smelly brute a couple of times. She limped round the corner, by the stable and the cartshed. The henhouse was just beyond the haystacks. She put down the bucket and shone the torch at the padlock. She'd never been on a place so near a town they had to lock henhouses against thieves. She turned the key and took out the padlock, opening the door, bending down for the bucket.

'Fancy meeting you here.'

She jerked round, swinging the torch. A man's hand caught her wrist and forced the torch down.

'Who's that?' she said, fear catching in her throat.

'Don't panic, it's only me.'

He took the torch from her and she found herself being pushed into the low-roofed henhouse. All she could see were a pair of trousers and light brown casual shoes. Then he shone the torch towards the roof, lighting the inside of the hut. He was grinning.

'Do you come here often?' he asked. 'The band's not bad but the floor's very sticky.'

When she saw it was Telfer she tried not to look frightened. If she pretended she wasn't frightened it might pass over as a joke. She knew it wasn't a joke.

'What're you doin' here?'

'Just out for a walk, you know. It's nice and quiet at night don't you think?'

He was grinning, his back slumped against the dusty wall, his head low.

'You gave me an awful fright.'

It'd been risky but as soon as she didn't start yelling and screaming he knew he'd be all right. Hens perched on rows on the sharny poles. They were used to night-feeding.

'Sorry.'

When a man grinned at you in that way you tried to tell yourself he was only guessing, but you knew all the time that he knew what you were really like. She noticed his flat, hard chest under his shirt. She tried to put on a severe face.

'If you'll let me move I've got to feed these hens,' she said, hearing the crack in her own voice.

'If it was up to me I wouldn't let you do all this dirty work,' he said. But he moved back and made no attempt to touch her as she tipped the bucket into the v-shaped trough. They bent down to leave through the low door, behind them two rows of hens picking away at shiny corn. She waited for it, her whole body seeming to jolt with each thumping heartbeat.

He walked slowly, keeping pace with her dragging walk. Past the haystacks. Make a joke, see how she feels. He touched her elbow.

'Nice night for a wee walk,' he said.

She knew what to say. She knew what would send him away like a scared rabbit, *wait till I tell Willie you were hanging about the henhouse, he'll die laughing.*

'Sure so it is.'

'Fancy it?'

Go on, tell him, make out you don't understand why he's here.

'What? Oh sure, I know what kind of walk that would be.' She tried to laugh out loud, as though she was far too fly to fall for that old bit of blarney, as though it was harmless.

Once they made a joke of it you were halfway there. It meant you could go on with it the next time you met her, a safe wee joke. The main thing was, she hadn't squawked. She knew what he was after but she hadn't squawked. His fingers felt for a grip on her arm, a good strong arm it was, too.

'Ach, come on,' he said. 'You don't want to sit in there on a Saturday night. You should be out enjoying yourself, a fine-looking wench like you.'

'Oh I enjoy myself, don't worry. There's better things to do than tramping about in the dark on a cold night like this.'

Don't rush it. Pretend you're just having a bit of nonsense. Nothing put them off quicker than letting them see you were desperate. As they turned the corner into the yard, stepping into the light from the kitchen window, he put his arm round her waist and gave it a pat: 'Maybe I'll take you out on the town some night, you never know your luck. Don't let Willie inveigle you into any wild orgies.'

She hadn't expected him to leave so easily. At the very least she'd been waiting for him to grab hold of her for a kiss.

She spoke before she thought: 'Is that all you wanted?'

Telfer turned back. It was like tickling trout, your fingertips waited for a touch, you never rushed it – and when you got very good at it you showed them who was boss by playing them along for a bit – as though you were sure you could land them any time you chose.

'Who me? What did you think I wanted?'

'I'm sure I've no idea,' she said, trying to cover her confusion with a sort of uppity indifference. 'You tell me why a grown man hangs about a henhouse late at night.'

'I'm a good employee, I don't want anybody knocking Craig's property.'

She knew he was grinning, although she couldn't see his face. Damn him, she shouldn't have stopped him leaving.

'I'm glad that's all you had in mind.'

'Oh yeah, what did you think I had in mind?'

'I've no idea, I'm sure.'

'I'll bet.'

He was pretty sure he could get a hold of her now and she'd let him take her over the haybarn, but there was still a chance she'd squawk. No, he'd wait till she came to him. She was keen enough, all right. It would help to get her steamed up if he left now.

'Ta ta,' he said. 'If you need any more help let me know.'

As she limped across the yard she felt flushed and confused. She wouldn't have let him do anything, it was too near the house even if she'd been of a mind. Yet she'd expected him to try a bit harder. Was he having a joke with her? Didn't he think she was worth the effort? Cheeky devil, who did he think he was? Donald Telfer! Just a common-as-muck farm servant.

She'd been ready to fight him off and now she'd been left, just like that! Somehow she felt insulted. When she came into the kitchen Willie was sitting beside the fire, head bent over the Kilcaddie paper.

'There's mibbe something on the wireless,' he said, not looking up. Yes, Saturday night, sitting with a smelly brute of a man listening to daft rubbish on the wireless. She breathed in between clenched teeth as she turned the knobs of the set, a tall old Bush with a round canvas front. She tuned the band to the Light

Programme. It was an old set and unless you concentrated it was
hard to tell what the voices said. She sat opposite Willie and
picked up her darning.

'D'ye ever wish ye could go dancing at all?' Willie asked,
looking over the paper. 'It'll be kinda dull for ye, no' bein' able
to jink about so much.'

She could see he was trying to be friendly.

'You never miss what you never had,' she said, fingers picking
at his sock. 'There's other things to do with yourself.'

'Aye, there's aye something to be getting up to.'

She let the mushroom-shaped darning stool rest on her lap.

'Just because I've got a bad leg doesn't mean I'm some kind of
freak,' she said. He liked her accent. Compared to the way
everybody else spoke it had a sort of a fancy touch to it. She
watched his face.

'I never said ye were.'

'No, you were thinking it.'

'Ach, don't be silly, woman.' He spat into the fire, a solid
gobbet of yellow-green catarrh and saliva which hissed on red
coals. 'Ye're as good-looking as any of them. How come ye've
never merriet?'

She shrugged, at the same time raising her brow and blinking
slowly.

'Maybe I've never met a man I liked well enough.'

'Ye've been beddet, I suppose?'

She blushed. His face was hard. He still hadn't made up his
mind. It depended on what she said, how she reacted to his chat.

'It's none of anybody's business,' she replied, but there was a
kind of weakness in her voice.

'Mibbe no'. How would ye fancy bein' beddet by me?'

She could tell he wasn't asking her out of desperate need. He
was trying to find out about her, testing her.

'Just like that?' She snorted. 'Scotsmen are all the same, you
think everyone else is cheap whores. Me being a housekeeper
makes me just a bed mat, does it, something for you to pass the
time on?'

Willie shook his head, eyes not leaving hers.

'I never said that.' His voice was quiet. 'Ye're a fine-looking
woman, it's natural, isn't it, bedding a woman? Ye'd bed the
Queen o' England if she gave you the chance, wouldn't ye? Ye
think I'm some kinda nancy-boy homo?'

'I'm sure I've no idea—'

'Oh!' Willie grinned. 'Ye want me to prove it? Ye think I wear corsets and things? Ye talk a lot o' havers, woman. I'll tell ye one thing, it's high time I got merriet mysel'.'

'I daresay it is. In the meantime I suppose you think I'll do you fine for the odd night or two?'

'Ach, I could do worse than you,' he said. He kept the grin on his face as he watched her. It was more than he'd meant to say. If she'd said yes straight off he'd have gone to bed with her and left it at that, handy to have a good steady ride under your own roof. If she wanted to hear wedding bells first – it made no odds, at his age he wasn't likely to find anybody better. Craig would have a fit, that was dead certain. Craig had never liked the idea of him marrying at all. To him any wife would be an outsider and the thought of somebody bar himself, the old bastard, getting a hand on the money made him mad. Craig had once told him to go up to Abderdeenshire and find himself a proper wife, a farm woman who knew how to work and look after money, not some fancy bag from the town who'd throw it all away on lipstick and nylon stockings and enjoying herself.

She didn't think he'd said enough in that direction.

'That's a nice way of putting it, you could do worse than me. You sound as though you're hiring a skivvy.'

He spat into the fire. He stropped his nose on his knuckle.

'Ach, I'm not a great one for fancy talk,' he said. 'If we were to get on all right, you know, we could easily get married. It's not all that different from housekeeping anyway. I've been thinking about it, I'm game if you are.'

She looked at the darning stool. This was important, serious. Why was she still thinking about the other man!

'I don't know whether to laugh or cry,' she said. 'Is that supposed to be a proposal? We hardly know each other. You're just having me on.'

'No I'm not.' Talking out loud had made up his mind. 'I'm serious, woman. I'm game if you are. Will you have me?'

'Your father wouldn't agree for a start, it's ridiculous, you don't know anything about me.'

'There's only one way to find out.' He grinned. 'Craig can do what he damn well likes, he can't run the place without me. What d'ye say?'

She had him now. It was too easy. She had what she wanted. It was her moment of triumph. She wanted to enjoy it. She'd show that big-headed Donald Telfer!

'It's ridiculous,' she said, shaking her head, smiling weakly. 'I've only been here a week. It's not me you want, it's just a wife, any woman would do, you'd have married whoever was the housekeeper. Anyway, I'm only twenty-eight, you're twice as old as me, I mean, I'm sure you're a good man but you're just saying you want to marry me, you'll change your tune as soon as you get what you want.'

He snorted. Once a woman started talking like that you knew you had her.

'Wheesht your havers, wumman, an' come tae bed. If we're getting merriet the sooner the better.'

They looked at each other for a moment.

'I hope you're not having me on,' she said. He laughed.

She made him wait while she went to her room and undressed. He went out into the yard and had a run-off against the byre wall. You've done it now, he said to himself. When he went into her room he was disappointed to find the light off. Still, it didn't matter, he'd get a look at her stump soon enough. He was curious about it. Maybe it would scunner him of the notion altogether, maybe not.

'You're a heavy brute,' she said as he came down on her.

'Ach, don't worry, I'll only flatten you a wee bit.'

Dunky stood on his own at the men's side of the hall, watching for Alec and his woman in the eerie light thrown on to the dancers by the revolving globe in the middle of the canteen, reds and greens and purples and blues, the kind of light they had in a lot of dance-halls, moving rays of light flickering across the walls and the people. It was supposed to make the joint glamorous. Diseased, more like it. He had to keep thinking of his date with Elsa Noble to stop himself becoming depressed. Dances were all the same, no matter how much you looked forward to them thinking *this* time it would be different. You shaved and your collar burned against your raw neck. You wiped Brylcreem and water into your hair and combed it and combed again in the lavatory mirror. You tried not to let your hands get dirty or sweaty in your trouser pockets. Your shoes were shining and your best trousers creased.

You didn't come too early, when there were only a few guys there and the lights were still up and everybody could see you. But you came before the pubs closed and the boozers had fights with the men at the door. About half-past eight was a good time. You paid your six shillings (at private dances there was a ticket, stiff cardboard with curly edging and a pink border) to the two men sitting at the trestle table in the entrance and then you went to the lavatory and had a run-off and a last comb at your hair.

Then you went inside, trying to look as casual as possible, hands in your trouser pockets. Private dances were better because there weren't so many hard men as there were at the Town Hall jigging and also because there were a lot of olde-tyme dances, Pride of Erin, St Bernard's Waltz, Gay Gordons, Military Two Step – they were easy to do, easier than quicksteps. The band always looked the same, three or four men in red jackets and evening-dress trousers and bow-ties, a pianist, a drummer, an accordion player and a saxophone player. They always sounded the same, not like a real band on the wireless, thinner and more harsh, loud and a bit squeaky.

You stood with all the other blokes at one side of the hall, looking across the empty floor at the dames. You looked for girls you knew, because you weren't so embarrassed at the start if you got a dance with a girl you knew from school or from some other dance. You discussed the talent with your mate, trying to make it sound as though you were a couple of bigtime guys who'd been to bigtime places and thought this was smalltime jigging for kids. You felt you'd never have the nerve to walk across the floor, all the way across, and ask a girl to dance with you.

There was always an MC – 'Ladies and gentlemen, take your partners for a slow tango' – and you decided you'd wait this one out, saying to your mate that you wanted to eye up the talent a bit more. Maybe a guy you knew from school or the football would come up and have a chat with you. You'd tell him about your game that afternoon, he'd interrupt you to tell you about his game. He'd say he was winching steady, a smashing piece who'd had to stay at home that night with her sick mother. You'd say you'd been winching steady but you'd chucked her in, going steady was a mug's game. You knew you were lying so you took it for granted he was lying.

The first dance was the worst. As soon as the MC said what it was all the blokes started across the slippy floor, walking fast in case some other guy got in first, not so fast so that you actually broke into a run. She always looked away when the rush started, pretending not to notice, chatting desperately casual to her pal. You touched her elbow and said 'May I have the next dance, please?' or just 'May I?' If you knew the girl or if you were a hard case, you might say something else, a joke, like 'Lend us your body for the next struggle' or maybe just nod your head towards the floor.

If the girl you headed for was grabbed by some other guy you kept on walking hoping to see something good-looking. You might be unlucky and be left with only the horrors, the wall-flowers, and then you had to turn away and move round the hall, back to the men's side. She might even say 'No thank you' and everybody would see you getting the brush-off, that was the worst thing of all.

You felt tense, most of the time, except when your mate and you were standing together between dances. Twice or three times at every dance the MC would announce a ladies' preference. That could be worse than ever. You'd no idea what girls thought of you but this was when you found out. You might not be asked at all – quite a lot of girls didn't get up for ladies' preference. Or you might find your elbow being touched by a tremendous horror. You couldn't refuse, that would be too difficult. You had to go round and round the floor with her, all the other guys knowing she was the best you could manage. You could take the easy way out at a ladies' preference and nip out to the lavvy – but you could get tired of going to the lavatory.

Older guys had it easy, they knew what to say to dames and some really bigtime guys would actually stand *at the ladies' side*, chatting up the dames they were going to dance with.

Once you'd danced a few times you had to start thinking about getting a lumber, the only reason you went to a dance, a girl who'd let you take her home. By about ten o'clock you had to have some idea, maybe danced with her twice. You asked her where she lived. Sometimes it might be the first thing you actually said to her. Maybe on a good night you'd have two possible lumbers lined up. You had to make up your mind which was the best-looking, which would let you go farther, which lived at the end of a long bus journey (meaning a seven- or eight-mile walk back home, probably for ten minutes' necking and a quick hand down her diddies), which was known (if you could believe what other guys told you about how far they'd got) to be game for as much as a grope.

You generally asked her during the last two or three dances.

'Eh, can I see you home?'

If she said 'all right' you thought you were bigtime and in the crowded lavatory you made sure the other blokes heard you telling your mate that you were lumbering Big Moira or whatever her name was.

But if she shook her head ('I'm sorry, I go home with my friend Betty', or 'No, I couldn't, I've got a boyfriend') you'd had it –

unless for the very odd occasion in which you and your pal bumped into two dames at the exit and were able to work the oracle with a quick bit of patter.

Dunky kept thinking to himself that the greatest thing in the world would be for him and Elsa Noble to go steady, so that he'd never have to go to a single dance again in his whole life.

When Alec came back from his dance with Katie Semple, a girl who, Dunky thought, looked like a camel, he shook his head.

'She's a waste of time,' Alec said, 'no use.'

'You could do worse.'

That was true enough. Alec had no idea at all about getting off with women. Once Dunky had asked him what he actually said to them during a dance.

'Just the usual things.'

'What, exactly?'

'Well, I start off saying it's not a bad dance, the band's all right, the floor's a bit slippy, then I say, "It's your turn to talk, my patter's finished".'

'You mean you actually tell them that, "my patter's finished"?'

'Yeah, sure. Why not? What the hell do you talk to wimmin about anyway? They're a waste of time.'

He saw a girl called Magda Gemmell from the school. He went across and asked her for a slow foxtrot. She was a dark-haired girl who wore glasses, shortish but she had a good pair on her. At school they always said she had everything – except a good face. Close-up it wasn't all that bad. It was the glasses that put guys off. One thing about her, she was easy to talk to.

'What's it like to be working?' she asked him.

'Not bad. Better'n school.'

A slow foxtrot was easy, you just slipped round and round, right hand on the small of her back, left holding her hand somewhere near your left ear.

He could smell her perfume or shampoo or something. At school he'd never fancied her much, she talked all the time, even to boys – as though you were her pals. You didn't fancy a dame like that. Especially with specs. It wasn't so much what you thought of her that mattered but what the other guys would think of you for going out with her.

'Why didn't you like the school, Dunky?'

That was typical of her, calling him by his name. Not many girls would have done that.

'I dunno, I just didn't like it. They think you're a wee boy. Working's better.'

Actually she wasn't bad-looking, not close-up. Guys didn't fancy her because she was sort of – *pally*. The dames you fancied were the good-looking ones who kept their noses in the air. What was it McCann said – who cares what they look like when their legs are round your neck? He couldn't imagine why you'd want a woman's legs round your *neck*. What would Telfer think of Magda Gemmell?

'What class are you in now?'

'Four B. I'm taking domestic science instead of Latin, that's why I went into the B class.'

Then the foxtrot was over. He walked her to the edge of the crowd of girls.

'Thanks very much,' he said. He walked back towards Alec. Another thing he hated – being looked at by a crowd.

'You should try her,' he told him, 'she's got enough patter for both of you.'

At the other side of the hall Magda's friend, Joyce, waited to hear Magda's verdict on Dunky Logan.

'He hasn't half changed an *awful* lot,' Magda said. 'I don't think he likes me but.'

'How not?' asked Joyce.

'Oh, I just know.'

Magda Gemmell knew that boys didn't like you if you weren't afraid of them. Sometimes she wished she didn't like boys so much. They were lots better company than girls. Duncan Logan had never paid much attention to her at school. He was one of the wilder boys in the class, always fighting and playing football, scruffy, his school tie never in place, his hair all tousled, dirt marks on his face, his socks round his ankles. Now he was all grown up. It made him even more interesting.

At the interval there was a barney in the gents. Behind him and Alec as they stood on the ledge facing the wall was a guy called Hunter Rennie, a bloke who thought he was really bigtime because his old man was a coal merchant. He was half-drunk – or pretending to be half-drunk, to impress the blokes crowding into the small lavatory. He had a quarter-bottle of whisky in his hand. Once he'd told his mother that Rennie the coalman's son got drunk at dances and she'd said it was a disgrace that a family with that amount of money should let their boy go round the town making an exhibition of himself. He was about twenty. He wasn't in the army because he was still at Glasgow University.

The fight started when Rennie began singing.

'Shut your fuck'n row,' said a guy standing along the ledge.

Rennie went on singing, waving his free arm in the air. He always wore a dark suit, something that Dunky associated with having a well-off father.

The other guy – who looked as though he might work at the chemical factory – turned his head and spoke out of the side of his mouth.

'Shut up, yah big-mouthed cunt.'

Rennie smiled, eyelids droopy, swaying slightly. He reached out his free hand and patted him on the head.

'Do I bother you, little man?' he said.

The other guy jumped round, left hand pushing away the hand on his head. Alec backed away quickly, bumping into Dunky. The other guy hit Rennie on the face. Close-up it made a soft, pulpy noise. Rennie staggered back. The other guy jumped at him, right elbow pulled back. Dunky and Alec fought to get out of the narrow doorway, pushing against other blokes queuing to get inside, Dunky trying to button his flies.

'He'll murder him,' Alec said on the stairs.

'Too bad. He thinks he's something special.'

'I hate violence,' said Alec.

'Ah shut up, you always try to make things sound dramatic. Why didn't you go to his rescue?'

They were schoolboys on the edge of a man's world. He wished he was eighteen.

Magda Gemmell asked Dunky for the next ladies' preference.

'You know Rennie, the coalman's son? He was getting his face smashed in downstairs.'

She was impressed, as though his having seen the fight made him part of a bigtime man's world. When she asked him if he ever got into fights he shrugged and didn't say much, making her think he did it all the time. He liked that. Alec said Magda was a no-gooder. Your mates always said things like that if they didn't have a lumber of their own. Another good thing about going steady with Elsa Noble would be seeing less of Alec. At the age of sixteen (almost sixteen) you were too old to be playing silly boys. By half-past ten the hall was packed. Alec went off to try his luck with a black-haired girl called Ethel Carruthers, who was almost six feet tall and wore flat-heeled shoes so that she wouldn't tower too much above the heads of her dancing partners.

'You can always put a bucket over her head and swing on the handle,' Dunky said.

Dunky went downstairs to the gents. By now there were several guys drinking from bottles. There was no sign of Hunter Rennie or the guy who'd bashed him. Stepping on to the ledge in front of the stalls Dunky bumped the raised elbow of a bloke swigging from a bottle of VP wine.

'Who d'you think you're pushing?' the guy said. His two mates looked hard at Dunky.

'Sorry, pal,' he said, deciding he didn't really need the lavatory.

'Don't say fuck'n sorry to me.'

He turned his back on them and squeezed through the door.

'He thinks he's a hard case, I'll show the bastard,' shouted the guy.

Dunky ran up the stairs, trying not to panic. Guys like that would give you a kicking just for looking at them the wrong way. And Alec wouldn't be a great help if they came after him to put the leather in. He moved through the crowd of blokes. Christ, he'd get a real hammering if they caught him.

He saw Magda Gemmell standing with her mate. He asked for a dance. What he should have done was make a bolt for it, to hell with worrying if you were a coward. As they danced he watched the entrance over her shoulder. They didn't appear. They'd stay in the lavvy drinking till the last dance. They'd wait for him at the door. He'd seen enough of it to know that's just what they'd like, they couldn't get women so they'd make up for it by bashing him.

'Would you like me to see you home?' he asked Magda.

'It's too far, all the way to Barskeddie,' she said. Unlike a lot of girls she took a good firm grip when she was dancing.

'That's not far,' he said. 'D'you think we could go now, there's some guys wanting a fight, it'd be better if we left before the end.'

'I'll get my coat and handbag,' she said. Dunky stood on the edge of the floor until Alec and Ethel came round. He nodded for Alec to come over.

'I'm pushing off,' he said. 'There's three guys in the lavvy want to bash me.'

Big Ethel was impressed. A lot of girls liked to hear blokes talking about having a rammy.

'You should just have thumped him one,' Alec said.

'What, with three of them? I detest violence, especially against me.'

He and Magda had to run to catch the eleven o'clock Barskeddie bus at the Cross. They sat upstairs, Magda doing most of the talking.

'You were very good at English and history,' she said. 'You could get a better job than just working on a farm.'

'Oh aye, like working in a stuffy office all day?'

Halfway to Barskeddie, at a scheme stop on the south side of the town, the driver had to get out of his cabin and come round to help the conductress chuck a drunk on to the pavement. He leaned across Magda to see what was happening down below on the pavement. The drunk fell backwards into a hedge, shouting and cursing. Dunky laughed.

'I think it's terrible the way those men get drunk so much,' said Magda. She was wearing an Academy scarf. Dunky felt rough and hard, like one of his heroes, the sailor in *USA* by John Dos Passos, the one who kept coming back to see his respectable sister. Magda was his sister, refined. He was a working bum. Nice people stayed on at school and went to university or got jobs with a future in offices. They wore collars and ties and spoke with pan-loaf, Kelvinside accents, the kind of stumers who went to school reunions and lived in bungalows outside the town, like Magda Gemmell, who live in a semi-detached bungalow in a dead-end road just before the small town of Barskeddie.

Nothing was said as they walked round the back of the house. He'd lumbered her and she knew he hadn't come all this way for a handshake. Magda turned round at the coal-bunker, stepping back against the wall. He stood in front of her, left leg forward so that it touched her knee. He put his hands round her waist. She started wriggling as soon as he kissed her. When he put his tongue in her mouth she pressed her tongue against it, her arms holding him tight. Gradually he let his hand drop till it was touching her bottom. She didn't push it away. Their mouths were wide open. She played with the back of his neck, making his scalp tingle. He put his right hand on her shoulder and worked it down. She kept wriggling. He pressed the palm of his hand on her breast. She didn't push it away. He pressed again and then let his fingers pull at the top button of her coat. Her tongue ran round his teeth. He undid three buttons and slowly slipped his hand down until it was under her dancing frock, touching the taut brassière. You nearly always got this far with most girls you lumbered.

Her hand moved across his stomach. He'd never imagined she was as fast as this. It just showed you! She let her hand drop quickly over his flies, touching his hard-on. He forced the tips of his fingers under the brassière. Her breast felt warm and fragile. She took off her spectacles with her left hand and put them on the coal-bunker, their mouths still locked. She breathed hot air into his ear.

'You don't think I'm fast, do you?' she murmured.

He thought of Elsa Noble. She'd made him feel – well, good.

Excited. Nervous. Just holding her hand. It was different with her. He was nervous in his stomach just thinking about his date on Monday. He didn't feel nervous with Magda. Funny, his mother would never believe – not that he'd tell her, not in a month of Sundays – that a girl from The Undesirables was not nearly as fast as an Academy girl.

'You're not fast,' he said, now leaning his whole weight on her, his knee jammed between her thighs. His right hand was aching from twisting round to feel her breast. Slowly she began to massage him through his trousers. Oh Christ, don't stop, don't let her stop. He had her coat unbuttoned the whole way down. He pressed her thighs, feeling the hard suspender. She kept rubbing his front. He began lifting her skirt. She shook her head but he pressed harder with his mouth and she didn't stop him when he ran his hand up her stocking and felt the bare skin. Girls were warm and soft and perfumed. They drove you mad.

Then his finger was into her wet fud and she was wriggling more and more. He didn't even like touching her wet part, it felt all sweaty and slimy, yet he didn't want to stop. Her fingers took hold of him through his trousers. He made to unfasten his flies but she pulled his hand away. He didn't risk it again. Don't let her stop now.

Then he was shooting his load into his pants.

'Oh Magda, Magda,' he moaned. She let him jerk his body against her.

He felt wet and dirty. He wanted to get away. He couldn't bear to kiss her, let alone go on groping.

'I love doing that,' she breathed in his ear. 'It's awful of me, isn't it?'

He'd never do anything like this with Elsa Noble. Never! They'd love each other and be real sweethearts. This business was all sweaty and hot and clammy. He wanted away.

'Will you be going to the cricket club dance next Saturday?' she asked. He stood back now, his hands round her back, looking down at her, wanting to make jokes.

'Maybe,' he said. 'Alec'll have to get the tickets.'

'I hope so. I'd better go in now, my father might come out looking for me, he's very narrow-minded.'

So that was that. He set off on the six miles back to Kilcaddie, his legs stiff from football, the wetness in his pants cold and nasty against his skin. Frost shone on the road. Occasionally he was dazzled by oncoming headlights. Six mile for a grope and a wank! Still, he was away from it all now. What would it be like if you were actually in a bed with a big woman, like Mary O'Donnell? Would you feel the same once you'd ridden her, sort of disgusted? Women looked great in the pictures, all lovely and cool like Rhonda Fleming and Virginia Mayo. But when you actually got near them they were hot and smelly. In a dirty book Alec had nicked from his big brother there was something about learning the art of making love so that the woman came to a climax at the same time as you did. What the hell did that mean?

He whistled *Leezie Lindsay* and walked on in the moonlight, imagining the marvellous things he and Elsa Noble would do, nice things, when they were really courting. It would never be dirty and sweaty with her. Never . . .

SEVEN

FOR FEBRUARY THE weather wasn't bad, a dry wind and high cloud, and that Sunday Dunky rushed through cleaning out the hutches, wanting to be away in good time to meet Elsa at the Cross. The winter litter should have been weaned at eight weeks old, but he'd never seemed to have the time to knock up the new hutch. They were good youngsters, a buck and three does, good coats and upright ears, very lively. He'd definitely spend two or three nights during the week to build the extra hutch. Then he'd have to think about taking them out to Findlay for his inspection. Maybe he and Elsa could go together next Sunday. She'd come to see him playing for Cartneuk, the Saturday he got his first team trial, they were winching seriously enough now to do things like that, even if she had come with her pal Betty and had been too shy to wait around for him after the game but had gone on back to Kilcaddie with Betty. Luckily she didn't know anything about football, she'd said he was very good. Baldy had said he'd need a bit more weight before he was ready for the first team. Be honest, he'd had a stinking game, too nervous to do anything brilliant with the ball when he did get it and too slow to make many good tackles.

He rushed away after Sunday lunch, telling his mother he was meeting Alec.

When he'd gone, Duncan Logan shouted through to his wife. She came into the bedroom, untying her apron.

'Have you finished with the *Sunday Post*?' she asked. For Duncan they also took the *News of the World*, but it embarrassed her to have it in the house.

'Aye,' he said. 'Eh, Beth, I've been thinking . . .'

'What about?' She sat on the edge of the bed.

'What Doctor Barr was saying I should dae, go to Killearn.' He looked at her, his face expressionless, his eyes heavy, as though he was trying to say something else. 'I've decidet it's the best thing. I want ye to get him ower here and tell him.'

She shook her head. Poor Duncan, he didn't know what he was saying, his mind was wandering, being cooped up in the bedroom.

'Don't shake your head at me!' he said. 'I've decidet. It's the only thing to dae. I'm no good to you here, jist a lot of extra work. Beth, I'm goin' out of my mind lyin' here all the time. Doctor Barr says they're good company at Killearn, they might even find a way that I can walk again. It's no use arguin', I've decidet.'

'Don't talk daft,' she said. 'You think I'd let you go into a *home*! You'll stay here where I can look after you, with your own family.'

'Family! Don't make me laugh. The boy hates me and Senga's too young tae care and you – well, it's killin' ye, woman, runnin' back and forth for me.'

'I don't want to hear any more about it,' she said, rising to go back to the kitchen. There were set times when she sat with Duncan, talking to him. This wasn't one of them. She wanted to sit by the fire and read the *Post* and put her feet up on the stool.

'Aye, well ye've got to hear about it, because I've decidet and I'm the man and I make the decisions.'

He must have guessed that she'd been secretly wondering what it would be like if he was off her hands! She felt angry at having had such evil notions.

'You may be the man but I'm the one that does the work,' she said. 'You just lie back and rest yourself. I'll bring in a cup of tea in a wee while. I'll take Senga to church tonight. Isn't there anything good on the wireless?'

'To hell wi' the wireless! I've made up my mind, woman!'

She walked out of the room. His clenched fists thumped the bedclothes. Jesus Christ, if he could just get on his feet for two minutes he'd bash some sense into her. He was the man in the house and he'd decide what happened. His mind was made up.

'Aye,' he said, 'an' before I go I'll tell that young bugger a thing or two.'

He could imagine them once he'd gone away, they'd start to realise the truth. Their own father – in a home, permanently. They'd realise then how little attention they'd paid to him. He could even see Beth sitting beside his bed in the ward, her lips trembling the way they always did when she was going to cry. And one day he'd be dead and they'd feel even worse. Thinking about his decision made him feel good. Running round the back of his mind was a thought that he knew he shouldn't have: *What if they did find a way of getting him on his feet again?*

No, don't even think about it – or it won't happen.

But what would you do – if . . .?

Be a man in my house again. Show that boy who's boss. Walk up the town and go into a pub and have eight halfs and eight pints and come back home and when she started moaning about him drinking, belt her one. Right across the chops. BANG! There, you bitch, I should've done that twenty years ago. Now shut up your whining, you know what I want. Don't talk back to me. BANG!

Try to remember what it actually *felt* like. Tight, he could remember it being tight. Up and down. Tight . . .

WHY IN THE NAME OF GOD DID IT HAVE TO BE ME!

When Willie heard the old man coming down the stairs, tackety boots banging on bare boards even though it was a Sunday, he picked up a paper and pretended to read. Aye well, he thought, here it comes, don't be scared, he's only a done old man, he can't touch you.

'Hrrmmph,' grunted Craig as he looked at the kitchen table where the woman had put a small bunch of dried flowers in a little blue jug. 'Flooers now, is it?' he growled.

'Aye, ye're up then,' said Willie, glancing up from the paper. Of late the old man had taken to staying in his bed till after noon on a Sunday. It was the first sign he'd given of feeling his age.

Craig looked round for the housekeeper.

'Nae tea, is there?' he asked, not looking at Willie.

'She's got somebody wants milk,' said Willie. He could hear her moving about in the dairy. 'Her and me's goin' to get merriet.'

'What's that ye say?' Craig turned to look at him, eyebrows raised, his voice an old man's squeak. Willie thumbed into his nostril, eyes on the paper.

'Her an' me's goin' to get merriet,' he said.

'Ye are, are ye?'

'Aye.'

'Can ye afford it?'

'I'll need mair wages from ye.'

'Oh, ye will, will ye?'

The farm and the money was all going to be his anyway, when the old man died, that was why he'd never bothered about money, ten pounds a week in his pocket had always been more than enough for him, it wasn't as if he was a drinker or a smoker, he'd never even had a single day's holiday to his life, not since he'd left school. And out of the ten pound a week he'd saved near enough a thousand pound, something the old man didn't know about.

'We can sleep in her room,' he said. 'It'll make no odds to you.'

'It won't, will it?'

By Jove, it was just like Willie, never found a wife all these years and now her, a useless cripple bugger and an Irish Pape into the bargain! Just after the money, that was all there was to it.

'An' will the bairns be Papes or what?'

Willie delved at the other nostril. He'd expected Craig to take it like this, not saying much at first, giving himself time to make up his mind.

'She's a lapsed Pape,' he said. 'It'll be at oor kirk.'

'Them, they never lapse.'

Mary O'Donnell came back into the kitchen. Craig's bowed head turned to stare at her. No wonder she'd stuck flowers on the table, she thought it was her house already.

'I've just telt my faither we're gettin' merriet,' Willie said.

'And does he approve?'

'Hrrmph, I've to *approve*, have I?'

'Oh yes, it wouldn't be proper unless you gave us your blessing.' She went across to the sink and ran hot water into the basin. Willie had said his father wouldn't like it, not with her being an Irish Catholic, but Willie had never had a woman to sleep with every night before and he'd stand up to his father to make sure of keeping it that way. She smiled to herself as she bent over the basin, rinsing out the two cups.

'I'll have a cup of tea,' Craig said. He pulled a chair from under the table and sat down stiffly. He looked down at the tablecloth. She looked over his head at Willie, who bared his teeth at her in one of his mad grins.

Back home men didn't marry till late and she was used to grown men who behaved like boys until they were old, when they started behaving like tyrants. Willie would be no trouble to handle at all. Craig said nothing.

Willie looked at her backside, solid under the dark tweed skirt. I'm riding a young woman, he said to himself, feeling like laughing in Craig's face. I may be daft but I'm not stupid. A fine young piece that Telfer would've liked to get his leg over. Hard lines, Donald Telfer!'

'Go outside, woman,' Craig said, 'I want to talk to Willie.'

It was on the tip of her tongue to tell him she wasn't the housekeeper any more to be ordered out of the house like that, but Willie nodded at the door. She limped out into the yard. It was a clear, sunny day, quite warm for February. She rubbed her bare forearms. If she got this she would be happy. She'd always felt like an intruder in the more important lives of other people, a useless cripple who had nothing of her own, a single woman who was lucky to get a bed in somebody else's house.

She walked down the length of the emptied midden, now a
drying bed of tarry-looking mud. The black dog knew her step
and didn't come out. She'd get Willie to do something about its
kennel, poor brute, nobody cared if it was wet or cold the whole
winter through. It had taken less than two weeks to make sure she
had Willie where she wanted him. She hoped her luck would
hold.

As she stood at the end of the yard she saw a column of boys
coming up the outside road. On Sundays they took them for a
walk in the country, the boys from the James Lyle Approved
School. They marched in threes, led by a master, a long column
of boys who wore boots and long grey stockings, grey suits with
short trousers and navy blue school caps. The oldest ones didn't
look much more than sixteen or seventeen. They had pale faces,
or so they always seemed to her, as though they could do with a
good while in the open air and some proper nourishment.
Whenever there was any noise from the column the master at
the front would look over his shoulder. When she'd first seen the
James Lyle boys on their Sunday walk she'd said to Willie she
didn't think it was fair, making them march around the countryside in full view of everybody, as though they were criminals.

'Whut d'ye mean?' Willie had said, surprised. 'That's whut
they are, criminals, a lot o' hooligans from the town. They don't
get sent to the James Lyle for nothin', ye ken.'

To Willie and his father they were just scum, the dregs of
Glasgow and all the other towns round about. She'd even heard
Craig say that shooting was too good for them, the criminals, but
Willie had afterwards said that Craig's remedy for practically
everything was to shoot folk, it was just an expression.

'Ye'll have got her in the family way no doubt,' said the old
man.

'More'n likely,' Willie replied.

'Damn and hell. Ach, you've got no more sense than a
dementit heifer,' growled the old man. He hawked and coughed
and spat into the fire, retching and wheezing for a bit before he got
his breath back. 'Marry her then and be damnt to ye.'

'I'll be needin' mair money,' Willie said.

'Aye, I don't doubt it. Ye can have twenty pound a week, I'll tell
Farquharson to see the bank. I suppose ye'll be askin' me next for
a cheque for the wedding present?'

'Oh aye,' said Willie, 'I've worked a few year for it.'

'Ye got your wages. I made the siller with my brains. When I'm
gone ye can do what the hell ye like wi' it but I'm no' gone yet, tell

her that, I'm no' gone yet. An' don't let her get any fancy notions she's too grand to do the housework. There's no room for idlers on this place.'

'Oh aye, she'll do the work all right.'

Nothing was said about the will. Craig had that much power over them. When he announced just after tea that he was away to his bed they both knew what he meant. He couldn't bear the sight of her, not now that he knew she was getting her hands in amongst *his* money. To him she was just common Irish trash, no more and no less, no better than a tink, just fly enough to have inveigled Willie into marrying her.

'Well?' she said, looking over her shoulder from the sink.

'I tellt ye he'd be all right.'

'He didn't seem very sociable.'

'It's jist his way.'

'How much is he going to pay you?'

'Twenty pound the week. An' a cheque for the wedding present.'

'And how about the will?'

'Don't you bother yer heid aboot the will, jist treat the auld man proper an' he'll see us a' right.'

She'd known there would be a snag and the will was it. Even Willie didn't know how much money the old man had tucked away in the bank and in shares. His own son! Never mind, if she had to keep in the old man's good books she would, no matter what he thought of her. In any case, it wouldn't be for very long, and while he lasted she'd be a match for the old devil. He wasn't just dealing with Willie now.

Upstairs, sitting in his armchair, Craig stared at the unlit coal and sticks and paper in the grate. He could see through that woman as clear as glass. The money, that's what she was after. Well, she didn't have it yet. He'd just see how she behaved and then he'd decide what to do. She might be able to trick Willie but not him. The money would go to somebody who appreciated it, he hadn't worked his whole life to hand it over to some fly-by-night. He snorted with amusement. Maybe it would do Willie the world of good having to hold the reins on a wife who was only after him for what she could get. It might be the making of the boy. He'd just bide his time and see how things turned out and if it was all for the worst there was always George out in Rhodesia, *he'd* know the proper value of the money. George was like himself, hard-headed and canny. And he hadn't been content to hang about all his life waiting to be handed siller on his lap. George had

said be damn to you, I'll make my own way. That was a real man
for you . . .

It had always been Dunky's ambition to have a steady girl and
here he was, sitting with her on the coarse grass near the top of the
Braes, sitting on his jacket with his arm round her waist, looking
out over the flat land that ran to the sea, Kilcaddie stretched out
below them, the new schemes in reds and browns, the old town
black and grey.

'It looks all right from up here, doesn't it?' he said. 'If you fancy
scenery that is. I'd rather gaze deep into your mysterious eyes.'
He tried to make her laugh, but there was something wrong.
She'd been in a funny mood since they'd met at the Cross and
walked the four or five miles to near the top of the hills.

She turned her face away from him with an irritable sort of
movement.

'You must think I came up the Clyde on a bicycle,' she said.

'What's wrong, come on, tell us or I'll bite your ear off.'

Under her black coat Elsa wore a blue blouse and a navy blue
cardigan. He was in his best clothes, dark shirt, sports jacket and
flannels. Her nylons were the kind that didn't let you see the skin.
He guessed she wore that kind because the skin was a wee bit
reddish above her ankles. The only thing he didn't like about her
were her shoes, black with fairly high heels, all right for the
dancing but a bit daft for climbing hills. He'd once seen a film
in which the girl went out with her bloke wearing a cardigan and
skirt and bare legs with brown brogues. Dressing like that meant
she was really *friendly* with her bloke, not just going out on a date.

'It's nothing,' she said.

He couldn't think what he'd done wrong. In the time they'd
been going steady he hadn't tried anything fast with her, they
hadn't had one row, today he'd been on time and managed to be
cheery enough, even if it was bloody Sunday. Sunday! Even up
here, miles away from the town, it was impossible to get away
from Sunday. It was something you felt in your brain and your
stomach. Dull and hellish. Dead. You've not to listen to the
wireless on a Sunday. It's time for Sunday School. Dressing up,
getting your ears washed, sitting on dark wooden benches,
listening to Mr Lockhart, the Sunday School superintendent,
talk about rotten dull things from the Bible, always the big picture
of Jesus with the children round his feet, then splitting up into
classes with the Sunday School teachers, Miss Robb, who also
sang in the church choir, reading to them from some kids'

magazine, different from school yet just as bad in some ways, dry as dust, your legs itching from the elastic garters which held up your long stockings, your new shoes cutting into your ankles. No football on a Sunday, no playing in the street, no wireless, nothing but being dressed in your best and thinking of school in the morning and the homework you'd been putting off till the last moment, mummy sitting reading the papers, all dull and stuffy, no fun on a Sunday at all, the shops all closed. He *hated* being a wee boy, and Sundays were the worst of all.

'Did you hear about the big negro who gave a woman a cross-bar on his bike for ten miles and when she got off she saw it was a ladies' bike?' he said. Going steady meant you could tell your girl dirty jokes.

'Tell us another,' she said, bitterly.

He felt sick. She was working up her courage to tell him she didn't want to see him any more!

He took her hand and squeezed it.

'Can't you tell me?' he said, his voice quiet and anxious.

'I've got my periods,' she said, suddenly, staring at him.

'What's that?'

'Don't give us that, you know what they are.'

He shook his head.

'No, I don't.'

He did and he didn't. He'd heard the word before, blokes made jokes about girls' periods – 'having the rags up' – but he didn't really know what they were. Something to do with girls' troubles.

'Didn't any of your other girlfriends tell you?'

He made a daft, vacant face.

'No. Ma mammy said Ah wasnae tae talk tae girls.'

'Don't make jokes about it.'

'Sorry. You're the first girl I ever really talked to at all, you know that?'

She made a little unbelieving face. He leaned against her, his nose into her black hair.

'It's menstruation. Girls get it every month. It means you bleed between your legs. My mammy says it's a curse for being bad.'

'What d'you mean, *bad*?'

'It's to do with having babies. It makes you feel sick.'

'Oh.'

'If you don't have it every month it means you're pregnant.'

Most of all he loved her face. It was better than other girls' faces. Her eyes were light blue, no, more like very light-coloured slate. Her hair was smooth, parted in the middle and combed smooth to a page-boy sort of business below her ears. Her mouth wasn't like other girls' mouths either, she had very thin lips and smooth teeth, unusual teeth, they had almost no gaps between them at all, not like most people's teeth, they were all the same length. He had two long milk teeth in front, too long they were, he hated them, silly boy's teeth he had.

Best of all she was all warm and she smelled nice. Not sickly perfume-smelling, no, just nice. When she kissed him he liked the taste from her mouth, it wasn't like some girls whose lipstick came off on your face in greasy dollops, it was like the taste you'd imagine you'd get if you chewed a rose. He'd always wanted to chew a rose, which just proved he was a bit soft in the head, if only folk knew.

'If everybody gets it it can't have anything to do with being bad.'

'My mammy says it's God's punishment.'

'Oh shut up. People's mothers are all the same, a lot of old henwives.'

It was her father who'd got them transferred to The Undesirables. He had an awful temper and he drank heavily and when he came home drunk he generally smashed up the house and threw things out of the window and two or three times he'd put her mother out on the landing in her nightdress and she'd had to knock up neighbours because she was freezing to death, people called him Noble the Wife-beater. Elsa was always ashamed in case people in the street recognised her.

'Oh Dunky, I'm that miserable, I don't know what to do' it's awful, you don't know what it's like.'

She turned towards him and hung on to him, beginning to cry. He stroked her hair and held her tightly. I'll soon be sixteen. I'll make her happy. I love her.

'Oh Dunky,' she went on, sobbing away into his chest, making him feel all manly and protective, 'you don't know what it's like, I don't want to get pregnant and be married like that, you get old and fat, they're always fighting and shouting at each other, I don't want to be like that, will I be like that, Dunky, tell me I won't.'

'No, of course you won't get like that,' he said. He was supporting them on his left elbow. He eased it free and they lay facing each other, her face against his chest, his arms round her, her nose sniffing as she tried to stop crying. 'When we get married we'll be different, we'll save as much as we can and get a house of our own and we won't have any babies till we've enjoyed ourselves a bit and I'll give you all my pay—'

'And we won't *ever* start calling each other Mum and Dad, will we?'

'No, never. And we'll go to dances just like now and you'll be a right smasher—'

'And I won't get my legs burned from sitting in front of the fire, will I?'

'No, if I catch you sitting in front of the fire with your legs splayed out I'll smack your bum for you.'

'And you won't go out and get drunk and leave me in the house and let me become just a fat wife, will you?'

'No, we'll go places on the bus, like Girvan and Edinburgh. It'll be different from them, don't worry.'

'Oh Dunky, I hate it at home, I wish we could run away, just the two of us.'

'Elsa, there's something I lied to you about.'

She looked up, her eyes wet and her face red with wiping away her tears. He looked at the sky.

'I'm not seventeen yet, I just told you that in case you thought I was too young for you.'

'How old *are* you?'

'Eh, sixteen – just about. My birthday's in May. I left the school early.'

'Gosh, you're old for your age,' she said. She still loved him. He hugged her and kissed her hair. With Elsa he'd never once felt like doing anything *dirty*.

'You don't think I'm too young for you?'

'No,' she said. He knew she got embarrassed when she wanted to say anything affectionate. Even girls weren't supposed to say soppy things, not in Kilcaddie. Never mind, he was daft enough for both of them.

'We could emigrate to Canada,' he said. 'It's different there, you get a lot better wages and there's lots of things to do. Not like dead-end Kilcaddie!'

When it became too cold to go on kissing and talking they stood up and brushed the grass and burrs from their clothes.

'You're the best-looking girl I've ever seen,' he said, kissing her once more before they set off down to the hill. 'Being married to you would be fantastic.'

She smiled shyly and wiped her cheeks with the back of her hand.

'Do I look awful?' she asked.

'Lovely.'

It was getting darker and colder by the time they were back in the town. They went for a coffee in the Eldorado, which was almost empty at that time in the late afternoon.

That was about all you could do on a Sunday in Kilcaddie. There was a tea-room halfway up the hill called The Croft. When he was still with the gang at school they'd often gone up there on Sunday afternoons, eyeing up the talent, sitting with their Coca-Colas, talking about women and football and other guys, finding out how to cause a riot by pouring a teaspoon of sugar into a Coke and letting it spray up to the ceiling, watching for certain girls to leave so that you could pay your bill and follow them down the road, trying to chat them up by shouting things after them. Or you could do what a lot of them did, spend most of Sunday evening parading up and down the High Street, just walking from one end to the other and back again, eyeing up the talent, pretending you were having a great time with your gang, all the time wishing you were winching instead. Telfer had been winching a big piece from the factory office and her parents had always gone out visiting on a Sunday afternoon so that Donald and his bit could have a necking session on the living-room couch, but that was more like something out of the pictures. Imagine his mother going out so that he could neck Elsa in the kitchen! Imagine going up to Noble the Wife-beater and asking him, dead gallus like, 'Hey, Mister Noble, you mind pissing off for a couple of hours so's me and your Elsa can get snogging in peace?' Imagine!

No, you could sit in the café and drink coffee or you could walk up and down. Elsa had to be in by ten o'clock on a Sunday, her father might be fond of wrecking the house and administering the leather to his wife but he was dead strict about Elsa being home in time. They'd walked far enough for one day, his legs were quite stiff, especially the left one where he'd been kicked during Saturday's game. It was ten past five. Also, he was hungry.

'What d'you fancy doing now?' he asked her. 'I'm starving. All you can get here is biscuits. If we had our own house you could be getting the tea ready, I love mutton pies and fried tomatoes and chips.'

'When I've got a house of my own I'm never going to have a single thing out of a tin,' she said. 'My mammy's tin daft.'

'And your father's canned all the time.'

It was all right to make jokes like that now they were both looking forward to being married and being totally different from their own parents. She wasn't annoyed.

'Maybe I should come down to your house and ask for your hand,' he said. She liked him making daft jokes about things, like pretending that her father would clap him on the back and send the butler for the whisky and ask him what were his prospects. Imagine Noble the Wife-beater's reaction to the arrival of Dunky Logan, boy farmer and general hard case!

'No, I'll go and see your mother and tell her I'm marrying you so's I can feed you properly.'

'She'd think that was hilarity unbounded,' he said. His mother would go wild if she knew he was going out with any girl. He couldn't imagine himself ever having the guts to take a girl back to the house and telling his mother they were getting married, but if the girl was an Undesirable . . .

The only thing he wanted to tell *her* was goodbye the day he got on the boat for Canada. He asked Elsa if she thought it was evil to have thoughts like that about your own family.

'It's no wonder,' she said. 'Parents just think you're there to be bossed about.'

Ian Nicol and his wife were walking along the High Street on their way home after Sunday tea with Ian's cousin when he saw the boy with the dark shirt walking towards them, holding a girl's hand, not a bad-looking girl, either, heels a bit high for that age, trust Logan.

'That's my *bête noire* Duncan Logan coming towards us now,' he murmured to Roberta. 'The brown shirt. He'll hate this.'

Dunky saw Nicol and thought for a second about trying to cross the road before they met, but decided not to lower himself. Anyway, he didn't care about schoolteachers any more, not now that he and Elsa were in love.

'There's one of my old teachers coming along,' he said out of the side of his mouth. 'The one with the suit. I wonder if that's his wife or his Girl Guide captain.'

Then the enquiring looks, turning to nervous smiles as they decided to recognise each other. Dunky wouldn't have embarrassed Elsa by introducing her, but Nicol made a point of saying this was his wife, and Dunky felt cheeky enough to describe Elsa as his fiancée. She made a little face. She'd only been to King Street junior secondary, she thought Academy boys were snooty enough never mind actually talking to an Academy school teacher in the middle of the High Street! Dunky knew he was blushing and felt more determined than ever to show Nicol he wasn't just a silly scholar any more.

'I don't suppose there's a lot to do around here on a Sunday, is there?' Nicol asked. His wife kept her hand through his arm as they talked, but Dunky had let go of Elsa's hand. Nicol's wife wasn't a bad piece – for a teacher's wife. Her skin wasn't as smooth as Elsa's.

'No,' Dunky said, looking at Elsa, beginning to grin. 'We just go up the Braes and admire the view, don't we?'

Elsa grinned and said nothing.

Nicol felt something daring stir in his mind. He'd felt something unusual would happen, right from the moment he'd woken up in the morning. *Make* it happen, he told himself.

'I know you think teachers are on a social level with pariah dogs,' he began, 'but how would you and your fiancée like to come home and have a coffee with us?' He looked to see how Roberta reacted. She seemed a bit surprised. It was certainly not the done thing – to have social intercourse with pupils. People might talk!

'Yes, would you like to?' she said to Elsa, who went a little red and looked at Dunky. He looked back at her, clearing his throat. He'd never heard of such a thing.

'Eh, well, we were sort of . . .'

Nicol knew the agonies that Kilcaddie adolescents went through, he always told himself. At that moment he felt he represented the new force in education, teachers who'd been in the army, seen real life, not one of the superannuation prunes of the blackboard.

'Don't worry about us, we're quite normal really,' he said, smiling encouragingly at the girl. There was something very delicate about her, the black hair against the pale forehead and the red cheeks. Not an Academy girl, though.

'Well, if it's all right . . .' Dunky said, hesitatingly.

'Fine.'

There were several awkward moments as they walked the High Street, Mrs Nicol on the inside, then Nicol, then Elsa and himself on the outside. At the front of the Playhouse cinema a gang of blokes were horsing about on the pavement and they had to move outside to pass them, Mrs Nicol almost getting bumped. A policeman passed them, his face hard set. Dunky looked back and saw him stop before the small mob, who moved off, reluctantly. What was it like to be a bobby? Willie was always telling them of the time when Big Watson was taking in a ned from the King Street gang when a mob tried to rescue their mate. Big Watson, whom Dunky remembered vaguely, had drawn his baton and stood with his back to the wall, one arm round the throat of the guy he was running in, the other bashing at the gang with the baton. By the time other bobbies arrived he'd laid out three of them and still had his prisoner. One guy had tried a knife on him and Big Watson had broken his wrist with the truncheon. What Willie liked best about the story was how the three guys couldn't be taken to court for weeks because they were too badly bashed up. And when Sheriff Long saw them in the dock, with bandages over their skulls, he'd made some crack about the need to protect Kilcaddie policemen from violent mobs!

Kilcaddie bobbies were a hard lot. They needed to be. They lived in the real world, something a guy like Nicol knew nothing about. What did a guy like Nicol know anything about? You'd think with all his brains he'd know all sorts of interesing things, yet on their way to his house at the East End of the town, a better-class area which Dunky associated with women in fur coats and dentists' brass plates, he didn't say much at all. Dunky felt embarrassed on behalf of the four of them.

'You know that meeting you were at, Mister Nicol?' he began, looking across Elsa at the teacher. 'Er, I was wondering why you went to it?'

Nicol let out a nervous sort of self-conscious laugh.

'You could hardly call it a love of free debate,' he said. Elsa didn't understand. Dunky winked at her. They were holding hands again. The hell if anyone saw them. 'No, I occasionally stir out of my lethargy to try and find out what's happening in our beloved Kilcaddie. I suppose I was a trifle foolish attacking the great Comrade MacLean. Almost as dangerous as Free Discussion with the third year at the Academy!'

Logan would probably be uncomfortable with too many school references. He could hear the false note in his own voice. Many older teachers suffered from insecurity outside the classroom, now it was happening to him. Already he'd given up the habit of changing into a wool shirt when he got home in the late afternoon, finding it less trouble to sit in his school attire, striped shirt, attached white collar, waistcoat and suit trousers. There was a sort of ready, functional *voluptuousness* about Logan's tieless brown shirt. Had he ever belted Logan? No – perhaps in the first year, when the new twelve- and thirteen-year-olds were still anonymous faces. The boys laughed at the belt, he knew that. But was the laughter real – or a necessary sign of bravado? How deep did the strap reach? How deep did he *want* it to reach?

'Sit wherever you like,' he said as they entered, in their varying degrees of shyness, the living room. Dunky associated bookcases with public libraries. He'd been in houses like this before, more space than he was used to, a carpet that wasn't worn smooth to

the cord fibres. Nicol switched on a standard lamp while his wife
knelt at the fireplace, removing a printed screen to turn on the two
bars of an imitation coal fire. It had a warm red light which
waltzed slowly through the translucent mould of simulated coal.

'I'm sorry we don't have the fire set,' Mrs Nicol said, smiling at
Elsa. 'We didn't bother today.'

'It's a lovely fire,' said Elsa. Mrs Nicol took her coat and left
them with her husband. Ian Nicol had often thought of moments
like this and to that end he'd collected various items, curios, a
ram's-horn snuff-mill dating back to the eighteenth century, old
maps of Ayrshire with Kilcaddie spelled Kilcawdey, an ostrich-
egg, early photographs of the old town, showing men in leather
aprons standing by low-roofed cottage-type buildings, bits and
pieces that visitors might be interested in. They rarely were, not
their usual visitors.

'You might be interested in this,' he said to Dunky, handing
him a newspaper cutting which he kept between the pages of
Lewis Grassic Gibbon's *A Scots Quair*. 'My mother sent it to me,
she still lives in Aberdeen, one of the old generation, y'know.'

An awkward moment, Dunky half-rising from the armchair to
save Nicol the bother of coming right across the room to hand
him the cutting, Nicol hurrying his step to save Dunky the trouble
of getting up.

'I thought you might like to compare agricultural *mores*,' Nicol
said, standing back, smiling self-consciously at Elsa. Dunky took
the delicately-folded cutting, reading the headline:

SO BOTHY LIFE IS

STILL LIKE THIS!

Enforcement of hygiene has been the battle-cry of sanitary
inspectors for years, but the lads who live in the bothy make
a mockery of their plea.

Bothies have changed little over the years, but perhaps a
few of the smells have changed, diesel oil and paraffin
prevailing over the pungent horsy odour that made the
townsman's nostril twitch and curl.

A look at one of these farmyard hostels the other day
made me wonder how civilisation even managed to get a
foothold in this world, writes a *Journal* man. And yet these
bothy lads have survived and they must be one of the
hardiest races.

This particular bothy, which one it was I cannot divulge lest the society for prevention of cruelty to oneself should catch up with the characters, was perhaps a more de luxe version than some.

The lads were fortunate that one of the cottar women took a motherly interest in them.

They had real soup, none of these tinned varieties that other farm loons thrive on, a varied meat course, a drop of pudding, and tea.

But here the difference ended.

Each of the men ate every course out of the one white clay bowl – including tea!

'It gangs the same wey onywey,' was one of the tractormen's earthy comment. 'You should'a' seen this afore the wifie cam' in every day. Man, the dishes were never washed, and I jist washed my bowl wance in a six-month.'

One who had been spreading manure sat down at the table without washing his hands. Another was like a snowman. He had been spreading lime and was covered in the dust.

Both assured me they had never had a serious illness in their lives, and their rosy cheeks and clear eyes convinced me.

'Pit the tatties on then, Wull,' shouted the senior. The tatties were for the evening meal, which is not prepared by the cottar woman.

Wull got up from the table, his boots leaving a muddy trail to the door. He picked up a pot with custard sticking to its side, filled it with water, and threw in a few potatoes from a bag.

'They taste better when they're done in their jaickets,' he said.

Shaving brushes and razors adorned the window sill and single beds crammed one corner.

'We're better aff than some,' said Wull. 'The last farm I was at they had double beds and ye jist jumped intae the first ane that wis empty.

'The sheets are changed here aince a fortnight, but in some places they're jist changed when they wear oot. Bothy life's changin' richt enough.'

Mrs Nicol brought in a tray with china coffee cups and saucers and a plate of sultana cake and another plate of assorted biscuits.

'I don't suppose you'd like farming so much if you lived like that,' Nicol said.

Dunky gave the cutting to Elsa, who looked at it and then laid it carefully beside her on the couch while Mrs Nicol gave her a cup and saucer.

'The farmer's son at our place says he never changes his shirt till it starts falling off his back,' he said. 'Did you come from a farm, Mister Nicol?'

'Oh no, my father was a minister. He had a church up near Fraserburgh and then he moved down to Largs. My mother went back when he died. I consider myself true West of Scotland. But my wife's from Edinburgh, aren't you dear?'

Look dutifully at Mrs Nicol. Hope Elsa isn't fed up. Doesn't look very comfortable, perched on the edge of the couch. Don't look at her legs. How about telling Nicol her father's Noble the Wife-beater!

'I'm not ashamed of it,' Mrs Nicol said. She had cold hands, nice nails. Women like her always had tea and coffee on trays round a wee low table. Lot of fuss and bother. Why not just sit up at the table and get it down you and cut out all this perching cups on your knees?

'I went to Edinburgh once with my auntie,' Elsa said. 'We went to the Zoo. All I can remember's a big golden eagle and a tiger.'

'You've left school, I take it?' Nicol asked her. Elsa was uncomfortable at being asked a direct question. It had taken her a bit of nerve to tell them about the Zoo! Dunky must have been awfully clever to be asked to a school-teacher's house.

'Yes, I'm a folder at McKechnie's printing works,' she said.

'And how long have you been engaged?' asked Mrs Nicol. Elsa looked at Dunky, making a funny mouth. He didn't smile in case she got a fit of the giggles.

'Not long,' he said. 'We've not actually bought a ring or anything.'

He wanted to giggle himself. It reminded him of a joke Telfer had told them in the stable. A young bloke and his girl get on a Glasgow tramcar. There's no seats. The bloke says to a grown man, 'Hey, Chief, how's about givin' your seat to a lady?' 'A lady?' says the man. 'She's only a girl.' 'Aye, but she's pregnant.' 'Pregnant! She doesnae look very pregnant to me. How long's she been pregnant?' 'Forty-five minutes, but her knees are still trembling.'

Nicol wanted to say something to Dunky without offending him – or sounding like the man at the blackboard.

'And tell me, Duncan, is there much future in farming as a career today, would you say?'

Future? What was he going to get, a Careers' Council lecture?

'I think there's courses you can take for farm managers' jobs,' he said. Aye, imagine telling Auld Craig you'd a diploma in farm management. 'I don't know much about it.' Craig would tell you to go and manage the midden.

There was a bit of chat, but Dunky could see that Nicol was working up to some serious gab. When it came he put on his classroom face, eyes on the teacher, mouth neither yawning nor smiling, head shaking slightly to let him know you were still listening, mind wandering through football matches, rabbit hutches, necking sessions, looking up his wife's legs, grown-ups talking at, at, at you, from a different life, boring, going on and on and on . . .

'. . . it may suit you now but d'you think you'll still be happy when you're over twenty? The money seems good enough now when you haven't any responsibilities, it's the curse of our society, big wages for school-leavers in dead-end jobs, you grow up but the money stays the same . . .'

Dunky didn't feel any need to put his side of the case. Nicol wasn't really asking him questions, not really interested in *him*, just giving him a lecture in class.

Before they left Nicol made a last attempt to get through to the boy.

'Duncan,' he said, and they both recognised the strained attempt to knock down barriers with the use of his Christian name, 'would you tell me one thing, as honestly as you can? Forget I'm a schoolmaster, I'm asking you man to man. Why did you really want to leave school so much? Really.'

Because I felt silly. Because I hated it. Because I got the belt from Miss Colquhoun and Miss Peacock and Mr Sinclair and Mr Everybastard. Because I hated exams. Exams and more exams. Because I hated being treated like a wee boy. Because you got an hour's homework every night and two hours after the third year. Because it was *official*.

He coughed. He knew Elsa was fed up, too. He didn't know what to say to Nicol.

'Er, well, I didn't want to work in an office and staying on another two years would just have been a waste of time, I dunno, I just wanted to leave.'

I didn't want to get like you, I mean, snobbish, peely-wally, pan-loaf, stiff-collar, useless hands.

'Well, if you ever change your mind you can always come and see me,' Nicol said. 'You can do a lot in night-classes these days.'

'Thanks very much. Eh, I think actually we should be going now.' He didn't know what made him come out with the next bit, but suddenly he was saying it, straight to Nicol's face. 'Elsa lives in The Undesirables, her daddy doesn't like her out too late in case something happens to her.'

'What did you have to tell him that for?' she asked, angrily, in the street. 'That was a dirty trick.'

'I didn't mean to,' he said. She wouldn't let him take her hand. 'You don't care about people like them, do you?'

'You'd no right to tell them. People say you're scruffs if you come from Barskiven Road. I didn't know where to put my face, so I didn't.'

'You're as bad as they are,' he said. 'Ach, forget it, we never died o' winter yet. Hey, didn't they have *wee* cups?'

There was a scheme for getting your passage paid to Canada if you were a farm-worker. In Canada all the guys would live in a bunkhouse, not a sharny old bothy. Now that they were engaged Elsa and he could probably start doing it. Engaged? Telfer always said that you'd only to walk by a church with a Kilcaddie woman and she had the rope round your neck. Telfer was just a big-mouth and a smart aleck. He didn't know anything about real love.

Still, they'd had something to eat now, they could go to the Thomson Park and sit on a bench till it was time for Elsa to go home. Their necking sessions always left him shaken. It must be a great relief to be a man and not be frightened of sex.

EIGHT

IT WAS APRIL now. When the trailer lorry came into the yard there was only him and the boy about the place. Willie knew the straw bales would be a bit heavy for the boy, but McCann and Telfer were sowing and that job couldn't wait. Logan would just have to do as best as he could, the trailer had to be loaded and turned round before night. The driver said he'd help once he'd been to the phone box at the end of the scheme road to phone his boss, but Willie knew how long that errand would be spun out. Drivers didn't go much on toil.

'You get up on top, Logan,' he said. He climbed on the back of the trailer, which was backed against the open-side barn. Dunky climbed the square bales of straw to the top, high enough to be able to touch the rounded corrugated roof with his hay-fork. Willie looked up at him. He dug the hayfork into a bale, the tines taking it in the middle, under the tight string. It was a helluva weight. He had to hold it out from the side and then lower it so that Willie could catch the bottom end and pull it off the fork. The bales were about two foot high and three foot long, solid packed. On the end of the fork they seemed to weigh about a hundred-weight.

'Chuck them down,' Willie sang out. Back and forward he went under the big iron roof, jerking bales out of their close-packed layers, stumbling across other bales, knees bent to give him balance under the weight, arms and hands and wrists threatening to give out on him as he stood at the edge, keeping the bale on the fork until Willie had a hold of it, slipping out the tines at the right moment so that Willie could swing into position as it was dropping, clambering back for another while Willie heaved it into position, Willie always ready for another, waiting, his stomach taking most of the strain, the shiny hayfork handle burning into his palms.

When the driver came back he got on the trailer with Willie. Building the load so that it would stay on the trailer was skilled men's work – *anybody* could do the heavy lifting. On and on they went, bale after bale going down to the two men, the level on the back of the long trailer hardly rising at all. Once he stumbled and a bale almost fell over on to them.

'Don't kill us, Jimmy,' shouted the driver. He hated that, showing he wasn't as strong as a man. He went faster, the lead creeping down from his shoulders into his forearms. Muscle, that's what you needed. There wasn't time to stop and take off his shirt and pullover, whenever he was slow in appearing above them with another bale they'd shout up 'Don't go to sleep' or 'Only five ton more'. One layer from the great block of bales in the barn made two layers on the trailer. It would have been easier to load them all from the front of the barn, but Willie wanted the bales taken off evenly. He had to walk to the far wall, delve into a bale, pull it away from the others, lever the hayfork handle across his thigh, stagger back to the open edge, swing it out, careful, keep a grip on the fork so that it didn't fly away still stuck in the bale, perhaps belting one of them on the face. Between bales there was just time to stretch back your shoulders and arch the small of your back and blow out air in a silent groan.

Then the full ten tons was loaded and the two men lifted the great canvas hap and they threw it up and over the load, lashing its ropes to hooks under the trailer. They threw the big ropes over the canvas-wrapped load, the driver in charge now, working quickly, pushing him out of the way, snatching a loose rope-end, breathing so hard you'd think *he'd* been working, Willie getting loose ends of rope and pulling them tight, his own hands too raw with opened blisters to exert much pull on the thick rough rope, his back feeling as though somebody had tied a knot in it.

In the stable at five o'clock he moved stiffly as he fed the two horses. Telfer and McCann filled a bucket of water from the horse trough and splashed the white dust off their faces. Dunky had told them about the bothy in Nicol's cutting and 'decent table manners' had become a joke, with Telfer and McCann trying to catch each other out with dirty nails at tea-break. Willie getting married to Mary O'Donnell was still too much of a surprise to be joked about. When Dunky had quietly asked Telfer if he thought she was up the stick Donald had turned quite sharply on him and told him to watch his tongue. He'd given up bothering about McCann. Now that Coll was gone he was getting a lot more heavy work about the place. As he swept behind the horses, holding the brush as gingerly as possible in his raw palms, he told himself McCann wouldn't have forked ten tons of straw bales in that time without making a song and dance about it.

That night he went home and had his tea and then went out to the rabbit hut, to clean them out for the first time in two weeks. The evenings were becoming lighter now that it was into April, but he had to switch on the bicycle lamp before he'd finished. By half-past eight he had mucked out the hutches and given them new bedding. The rabbits were going to pot. There never seemed to be enough time, what with seeing Elsa two and three nights a week, her pretending to her father she was at her pal's house, and playing football on Saturday and going up the town with Alec on midweek nights when he wasn't seeing Elsa. Jesus Christ, he still hadn't made the new hutch for the four half-grown ones. The buck would be serving his sisters in a month or two if they weren't separated. Rabbits were a lot of work. It would be much easier if he got rid of them. His back was still sore as he walked across the yard. There was a slight taste of fog in the air. He felt heavy, all over, good job it wasn't a Friday or he'd be ruined for playing football. They were only three points behind the leaders of the Ayr and District Juvenile 'B' League and they had to win every game if they were going to catch up.

He closed his eyes as he leaned against the landing wall to take off his boots. On Saturday, on the way home from the game, he'd call in at McKillop the butcher's and ask him if he'd buy two or three rabbits. His mother wouldn't take them for eating in the house. Or maybe he'd bike out to the Brig and see if Findlay would buy the whole lot back. They were getting too much for him.

'You look exhausted,' his mother said. 'Wash your hands and face, your father wants to see you.'

For once Senga wasn't out at the Girl Guides. He'd tried to interest her in the rabbits so that she could do some of the work, but she was always going out to her pals' houses or the Brownies or some bloody thing. Girls had it easy. Senga was in the 'C' class at school and she didn't even get much homework. As he dried his hands and wrists he looked at her and wondered if other guys thought she was good-looking. You couldn't tell with your own sister. At home all she did was sit in the corner and read her stupid girls' magazines and grunt when you spoke to her. His mother said it was 'just a stage she was going through'. He couldn't remember her ever giving him the benefit of 'a stage'. It must be great being a girl. No bloody worries at all.

'What's my father want?' he asked his mother, putting as much tired complaint into his voice as possible. 'I'm tired out. I wish I had a bedroom to myself!'

Imagine having to go to bed in the kitchen, with your mother and wee sister still sitting by the fire! And she wondered why he stayed out late every night!

'Go in and see him,' she said.

He went into the bedroom, rolling down his shirt sleeves. Once you'd washed yourself the tiredness seemed to go, normally, but tonight was different.

'Tell your mother I want her as well,' his father said. It sounded serious. He'd even put off the wireless, that was pretty drastic.

'He wants you, too,' he said to his mother. Senga looked up. 'Not you, hen, you sit and read your wee girl's comics.'

She made a face at him, sticking out her tongue. Once she'd been quite good fun but now she seemed to be in huffs all the time. She had light brown hair, like her father. On the odd nights she did stay at home she was always playing at it, putting in rollers and washing it and whatnot. He wondered if she was winching. At thirteen? You could never imagine another bloke fancying your sister.

'I've got something to tell ye,' his father said when they were both in the bedroom, his mother sitting at the foot of the bed, Dunky standing by the window, hands in his pockets, glancing out at the lights of the coalyard. 'Doctor Barr's arranged for me to go to Killearn.'

His mother obviously knew all about it from the way she looked at him.

'What for?' Dunky asked. He supposed he had to say something.

'For proper treatment,' his father said. He seemed well pleased with himself. 'I'm jist a burden on ye all here so I've decidet I'll be better off in a hospital.'

He didn't know what to say.

'I think it's terrible you going away from your own home,' his mother said. She seemed to be talking to *him*.

'What, can they do anything about your back?' Dunky asked. That would mean more room in the house, God strike you down for thinking evil thoughts.

'Ach, I don't suppose so,' his father said. 'I don't care, I'm fed up lying here bein' treatet like some useless *thing*. I maybe wouldnae be goin' if I'd ever had a single civil word out of you.'

The room seemed very small. Tense.

'Speak for yourself,' he said.

'Dunky!'

'Oh aye, the big man can cheek his father, I'm only a helpless invalid.'

'At least you're no' able to kick my arse now, are you?' He glowered at his father, thinking of the heavy bales and the ache in his back.

'I niver kicked ye near offen enough.' His father raised his head, trying to get up on one elbow. It was the most energetic he'd looked since he'd been laid out. 'There's bad blood in you, sonny.'

'Mibbe but I'm workin' like a cunt an' you're lying there, ye're happy enough with the money.'

Deep down you weren't really sorry for cripples at all. Not really. They'd got out of it somehow. People were *supposed* to feel sorry for them. They could be the most evil bastards in the world but if they lost a leg people would immediately feel sorry for them.

Duncan Logan shook his head. His own son, speaking to him like *that*. Unnatural. In front of his own mother. Not an ounce of respect in him.

Her face was white and empty. To hear your own son use a word like that, in his own home. Wasn't there anybody who could do anything with him? She started crying.

'There's whut ye've done to your mother,' Duncan Logan said. 'I hope ye feel proud of yourself.'

They were crowded together in the small room, too close together. Christ, he'd often imagined leading Big Dick up the stairs and into this stinking wee house and let him kick at it, smash it to pieces, pound the stinking furniture to bits, bash down the walls, great horse hooves wrecking *everything*.

'I'm sorry, mum,' he said, hanging his head. He wanted to cry, too. 'I'm sorry.'

She went on weeping.

'Stop your greetin', woman,' said his father. 'Things is bad enough without you bawlin' your eyes out.'

'I can't help it,' she sobbed, lifting the end of her apron to her eyes, dabbing at them, her chin quivering out of control as each new burst of sobbing made her shoulders shake. 'I don't want you to go away.'

Did that mean his mother really *loved* his father?

'Come on now, Beth,' Duncan Logan reached a hand towards her shoulder. 'They don't take incurable cases at Killearn. The only reason Barr's gettin' me in there's to see if they can sort my back. They're doing wonders up there.'

Was his father just pretending to be nice? Why couldn't they have been nicer to each other before? In some way all this crying and sadness was *his* fault. He'd been enjoying himself playing

football and breeding rabbits and going to dances and courting
Elsa, and they'd been suffering. But why couldn't they have been
nicer to *him*? Maybe he didn't deserve it, maybe it was true what
his father said, he had bad blood. Other people didn't like him
much, either, did they? It was a fluke that he was going out with
Elsa. His only pal was a bit of a half-wit. It *was* unnatural, for a
bloke his age to be mad about rabbits. He didn't like people and
people didn't like him, that's what Jim Querns had said about him
one day in the Croft tea-room. It was true. Even when he was a
wee boy Grandpa Logan had called him a thrawn wee devil, the
time he'd hit Neilly Graham from the next close with a half brick
during a row about a marbles game in the gutter. If only he could
say something nice to them. His own father was going away,
maybe for good, and he was such a thrawn, unnatural person he
couldn't think of anything nice to say. God had given him bad
blood. He felt like being sick, anything to get out of the bedroom.

His mother dried her eyes. His father patted her arm. When he
looked up his eyes were wet, too. His voice was squeaky.

'Ye're goin' to have to act like a man now,' he said. He didn't
sound angry. 'It's your responsibility. I'm jist a useless wreck. If
there's any heart in ye at all ye'll no' let your mother down.'

Instinctively Dunky glanced in the rusty-edged wardrobe mirror, wondering what he looked like at that moment. He'd always
been too fond of looking at himself in mirrors, he knew that.

'Don't worry, we'll be all right,' he said. For some reason he felt
he should shake his father's hand, but he couldn't. There was
something unnatural about him. God was punishing him all the
time for that dream, the one where he'd been in bed with his
mother, the one that made him sweat just to think about. Jesus
Christ, why didn't you make me just like other people?

'Right then, I'm away for a wee donner,' said Willie.

'Off to see your pal the Tink?' laughed Mrs Mary Craig, née
O'Donnell. 'Don't pick up any fleas.'

'He's cleaner nor me,' said Willie.

'That wouldn't take much, you smelly old billy-goat.'

As he passed the sink he gave her buttock a hard pinch. She
jumped forward, twisting round to push his hand away.

She watched him out of the window until she saw his dark
shape in the light at the end of the yard. She felt like clapping her
hands and letting out little squeals. She had her own husband
now and her own home, set up as well as any woman in the land.
Sure and a lot better than most, for how many women had
managed to get what she'd got – *and* a bit of fun as well?

She was waiting at the kitchen door when she heard the quiet footsteps and the gentle knock. She opened it just wide enough for Donald Telfer to slip through, sideways.

'He's away down the back road,' Donald said.

'You're sure?'

'Sure I'm sure. There's no flies on me, Missus.'

Holy Mary forgive her for a mortal sin but Donald was a lovely man. The very sight of him made her itch to get her hands on him. Nodding for him to follow she limped slowly to the door to the rest of the house. She cocked an ear at the foot of the stairs. There was no sound from Craig's room. He'd be dead to the world, the old brute. Putting her fingers to her lips she beckoned him to follow her into the bedroom.

'Are you sure the back door's snibbed?' he whispered, his long, clean hands already at his shirt buttons.

She nodded, closing the bedroom door. It was as safe as houses. Willie would be away for a couple of hours and Craig could sleep through an earthquake. The only light in the room came from the window, its curtains drawn back, the April moon and stars throwing a misty glow over the buildings outside. Even in the half-darkness Telfer's hair was bright, the brightest thing in the room. She ran strong fingers through the yellow hair as he knelt before her, pulling down her skirt, kissing the hard front of her, smoothing his hands up her nylon slip, then rising to press his tall, hard body against her while he felt round her back to unloosen the row of brassière hooks. She pulled at his trouser buttons while he ran his hands down her back and pressed the palms against her buttocks.

He was so hard and slim and long. When he lay on top of her there was no weight to him at all, just the long body hard in her arms, his rock-hard thing going into her, deeper and deeper, filling her up, never ending, her hands kneading at the hardness of his ribs. It couldn't be wrong to want a man who could make you feel like this! Even his bum was hard, smooth and hard. There was a smell of soap off him, everything was hard and smooth and warm.

'Into you, into you,' he hissed, now lifting himself on his palms, looking down at her, his body like a length of smooth steel.

Then he lay on her, one hand flat under her buttocks, the other feeling the outlines of her breasts, his face pressed against the muscle of her upper arm. Only the cold touch of the metal supports on his knees reminded him that she was a cripple, the rest of her was strong and warm and muscly.

'Is that better than Willie?' he asked her, his voice a murmur that she could feel vibrating from his chest.

'Wouldn't you like to know,' she said.

It was the one thing he wanted to hear her say, but she never would. Some daft idea about being loyal, he supposed. It was all right to let another guy ride you, in your husband's bed, but not to tell you what *he* was like.

'You're a devil, making me do this,' she whispered.

He snorted. It'd been as much her doing as his. He ran his hand down her belly.

'Crivvens, you're putting on weight,' he said. 'Anybody would think you'd a bun in the oven.'

'Would they now? And whose doing would that be, I wonder?'

She was a sonsy bitch all right, she knew what she wanted and she didn't care how she got it.

'Come on,' she said, digging her fingers into it, 'we haven't got all night.' She knew how to get him going again, too, pinching the tight skin over his ribs, biting his ears, jabbing her good heel down the back of his leg, squirming under him like an itchy pig.

'I'll tear you in two,' he said, his hands pinning her arms back on the pillows. 'I'll gie you a baby all right, see what they say when it's a wee yellow bastard like me!'

She laughed up at him.

'You think you're man enough?'

He hissed at her and then he was forcing the smile off her face, making her shut her eyes and roll her head from side to side, her master, her real thing, knowing what she needed and giving it to her, hot and strong . . . look at me now, Willie Craig, who's the man and who's the common tyke?

'Well, it sounds as if you've done all right for yourself,' said Archie Stewart. 'You're lucky it's all worked out so well, Willie. Have some tea. Isn't it grand when the nights get lighter and you know summer's coming? Summer's the time I enjoy best. The rain's even enjoyable in the summer.'

It made Willie feel better to hear Archie say he'd done the right thing getting married. He had a notion other people – the men, some of the scheme folk, his father to be sure – were laughing at him behind his back for marrying the cripple woman. He guessed they'd say things like 'Nae fool like an auld fool' or 'She got her hooks intae him quick enough' . . . or even 'Is that the best he could dae for hisself?' Of course Archie didn't get about the place much, he wouldn't know what folk were saying.

'What would ye dae if ye had to leave here?' he asked, the hand holding the jam jar resting on his thigh, his back against the wall, his legs stretched out towards the glowing brazier, his feet crossed.

'Leave here!' Archie the Tink put his head to one side. At times he acted like a wee boy. 'I wouldn't fancy that, Willie, not at my age. No, I want to die here, in my wee cave. Where would I go anyway? The McGleishes tell me it's getting harder for them every year to find a place to put their tents. If it's not the councils it's the farmers. I hear they're talking of building a whole new scheme at the back of the Brig, right up to the Kilberrie Woods, acres and acres of council houses! Have you heard anything about that?'

'Aye, I believe there wis something in the papers aboot it. Don't worry your head aboot the McGleishes, they'll aye find some neuk to nest down in.'

'Oh aye, they're canny folk for all they're supposed to be ignorant tinks.'

'But what aboot yerself, Archie, ye're a fair age, would ye no' be better aff somewheres they'd take care o' ye?'

'What, a home you mean, an institution for old folk? No, no, Willie, you'll never find me in one of those places. I'm my own man down here in the Black Hills. Can you see me in a bed in an institution, a toothless old haverer getting fed on pap and having my bum wiped for me?' He laughed at the very idea. 'I'll go to a place like that the day your father does.'

'Aye, that would be the day all right.'

He only half-listened while Archie talked away about the countryside and how it was gradually being swamped by the towns. The day before his father had told him Kilcaddie Burgh Corporation were talking about using the Black Hills as a site for an industrial estate. Ayrshire Country Council owned the land. Kilcaddie Corporation wanted the new factories because of the jobs they'd bring to the town, but they'd need more than just the Black Hills. They also wanted the two low fields between the Black Hills and the road.

'We'd have less nor a hundert acres,' Willie had said to Craig. The rented fields didn't count. You didn't depend on land you didn't own, that was Craig's motto.

'Aye,' his father had replied. 'Hardly worth the bother farming at all. An' they say they'll want more land once they've levellet it up.'

Willie had seen them preparing a factory site before. First they carted away the topsoil. For a year or so they'd drive in lorry-loads of rubbish from the Corporation destructor, tipping it on to the fields, bulldozing it flat, the dirty rubbish from the town, ash and cans and muck. They'd bulldoze the hedges. While the coup was being laid the sky would be dark with crows and seagulls. Packs of rats would swarm over the rubbish. The fields round about would be covered in dust and the roads littered with papers and cans and cardboard boxes off the lorries. Combustible waste would smoulder under the surface, its dirty, stinking smoke reeking the whole countryside. The whole place would become an eyesore. Then one day they'd have levelled it up to their requirements and they'd begin to lay the foundations for the factories.

And in two or three years you'd never even know that land had once been a farm.

He knew his father was as much against this as anybody, but he was a funny old bugger, Craig. Maybe he'd rather let the land go to hell in factories than die knowing Mary and him had taken his place. A lot of old farmers were like that. They'd rather see a thing destroyed than lose it to somebody else. He decided not to say anything to Archie. His father might decide not to sell them the two low fields and without access the Black Hills site wasn't much good to them. They'd probably go for a compulsory purchase order, but that took a fair while to go through. Maybe Archie would be dead by then.

He left the hut with Archie walking him to the dirt road.

'Aren't the stars just glorious?' said the Tink.

'If ye keep lookin' up ye'll fall down a hole.'

Mary was already in bed when he went into the house, after a walk round the buildings and a look in at the horses. He put his clothes on the chair and sat on the bed to take off his socks. His body was white, his neck burned red, his forearms hairy and dark with engrained dirt. She didn't look up from the pillow as he went across to switch off the light. She didn't want to look at his waistless body and his thickening gut. Not after the slim hardness of the other man.

'I'm tired,' she said, irritably, when he climbed between the sheets and put a hard hand on her backside. It was like feeling a sack of coal sliding over you. As soon as was safe she'd tell him she was pregnant and couldn't be bothered with sex.

'Ye'll be mair tiret when I'm through,' he said, panting as he laid his chest on hers and got his knees between her legs.

One thing at least, he didn't seem to care if she moved about or just lay back and let him get on with it. When Willie got going he snorted away like a horse pulling uphill. He wouldn't have cared then if she was his wife or a bag of chaff with a hole cut in the middle . . .

Of course it wasn't serious, only a bit of an ache from moving all those bales. Or could it be something more? Whatever, Dunky couldn't get to sleep. The fire was a dull glow of red coals under a thickening spread of soft ash. He got out of bed and opened the bottom of the window. Fresh air, that's what the house needed. Windows open, cold draughts blowing out the heat and the staleness. He made water into the sink, standing on tiptoe so that it would flow down the side and not make a splashing noise. His mother expected him to go down to the landing lavvy, in his bare feet in the middle of the night!

He tried thinking about women, Mrs Nicol letting him undress her on their soft carpet, Mary the cripple crawling into a pile of hay, Miss Peacock the maths teacher keeping him in late after school and telling him to run his hands up her nylons, then taking him home and ordering him to take off her clothes with his teeth . . . he couldn't concentrate on any of his usual bed-pictures. What he needed to do was to *think*, about real things, about Elsa and the rabbits and Canada. About the future. There was bound to be even less money coming into the house when his father went to Killearn. He was already giving his mother four pounds ten shillings a week, only keeping eighteen shillings for himself. He'd have to ask Willie if the old man would give him a rise. He could always chuck in his job at Craig's farm and go into the factory – at his age he might get eight or nine pounds there. But as long as he worked on the farm he was exempt from National Service. Having to go into the army was about the worst thing he could imagine, just as bad as two years in prison. What was it like to work in a factory anyway? Shut in all day, the noise of screaming machines, having to work with *metal* – hellish.

Telfer said there was an assisted passage scheme to Canada for farm workers, but Telfer didn't think it applied if you were under eighteen, or if it did you have to have your parents' written consent, they'd never give it, they'd say he was leaving them in the lurch. Bad blood. Where did it start? He remembered sleeping in this bed with his father when Senga was being born in the bedroom. Hated that, sleeping close to *him*, still felt funny thinking of that, remember the time you saw his cock and felt ill, terrifying, horrible. Getting belted for throwing his brand new Sunday School cap over a wall on the way home, hated that stupid thing, *must* have been a thrawn wee devil to be chucking away a good cap . . . never really *liked* the other blokes at school, they always seemed to be laughing behind your back, most of their fathers were better off, not common boilermakers! He'd much rather have gone to King Street than the Academy, the only boy from Shuttle Place among a nest of smalltime toffs' kids. He'd never fitted in at the Academy with its silly school tie and its mammy's boy football teams, frightened to get their knees dirty, scared to death of teams from 'scruff' schools . . .

Wee Ernie Lavelle's father had given him a new rubber ball a half-size imitation of a real leather football. It was the best ball they'd ever had for football on the lower school playground, where the surface was fine gravel on hard earth. Billy Aird, the bobby's son, kicked the ball over the high wall at one end of the playground. He said he wouldn't go round to the tenements to fetch it because playtime was almost over. He said he didn't care about Wee Ernie's ball. Ernie was a hopeless wee gnaff who wore specs and cried if the teacher was nasty to him. He was crying at the thought of having to go home and tell his father the ball was lost. I'll go, he'd said, and he ran all the way out of the other end of the playground, along Clark Lane and up Brediland Street and through the tenement close, panting, running about in the backyard of the high black tenements until he found it wedged between some dustbins and a wash-house wall, running all the way back, seeing the empty playground, trying to walk to his desk before Miss Walker saw him, where do you think you're going, Duncan Logan? Three of the best, hands crossed, palms upwards, her face twisted as she shook her right elbow clear of her black gown, shutting your eyes as the thick leather belt whammed on your outstretched hand. He waited for Billy Aird at dinnertime, he could remember every bit of that fight, he'd rushed at Billy Aird as he came down the steps, walloping him on the nose before he knew what was happening, hitting at Billy Aird the big fat policeman's son, funny you didn't feel any pain when you were actually in a fight. Billy Aird ran away and he'd chased him to the lavvy, Billy Aird trying to hide his face and kick him at the same time, the crowd followed them, then somebody shouting that Miss Bell, the head primary teacher, had seen them out of the staff room window, running to the main gate, thumping Billy Aird on the back of his neck, Billy Aird's fingers poking in his eyes, wanting to murder him, grabbing his blazer lapels and hitting him on the face with his forehead. An eleven-year-old Academy using his noddle to butt somebody! Putting the head in was a scheme scruffs' trick, even if the other guy was a rat and a cheat and bigger than you.

Being dragged into the school by Mister Mason, the only man teacher

in primary, Miss Bell sending him to see the headmaster in the big
school, walking on his own up the hill while everybody else was at
school, waiting outside the head's office, senior scholars staring at his
bleeding lip and torn button, frightened out of his wits, Zorro Sinclair
the headmaster, called Zorro because he was supposed to have a Z
carved on his belt and it left Z cut in your hands after he'd belted you,
the Mark of Zorro, a thin creep of a man with glasses and flat grey hair,
a terror, the man who never smiled, six of the best from Zorro Sinclair,
stingers, being embarrassed more than hurt, that should have been it
but Zorro made him wait outside and then gave him an envelope
addressed to his father and sent him home early. The sneaky rat!
Telling his mother the truth, her not even listening when he said it
wasn't his fault, waiting hours for his old man to come home from the
works, praying to Jesus and God, lot of good that was wanting to be
sick, red sweat line where the cap had pressed on his father's forehead,
face grim as he opened the white envelope, then rolling up his sleeves
and taking down the shiny black razor strop which hung beside the fire,
the real belting then, round his legs, across his hands when he tried to
push it away, embarrassed, *them being nearly as big as each other,*
two of them alone in the kitchen, the strap cutting into the back of his
legs, trying to move away without running, that would make it worse,
his father growling, not actual words, all he could think was of being
ashamed, *getting a leathering in your own house, his father not*
interested in his side of the story, then the last and worst, his father
lifting his boot to him, kicking him on the bottom of the spine, right on
the bone, bawling like a big baby, his mother coming in to stop it,
having to undress in front of them in the same room, nobody speaking,
pulling the covers over his head, lying there in the dark with them sitting
beside the fire, one day I'll be bigger and stronger and harder than him
and I'll come in the house and grab him by the throat and ram him up
against the wall and hammer him in the guts, holding him up by the
adam's apple, battering into his belly, I'll kill you, don't worry, I'll
never forgive you, you'll be sorry, dead sorry . . .

Even thinking about that had made him breathe faster. Naturally his old man had forgotten all about it, now he needed to be
loved by his family. He'd never forgotten, though. Never would.
Nor the guys at school. That still puzzled him. Next day when
he'd gone back they'd taken Billy Aird's side. They wouldn't
speak to him, none of them. Even Norrie Cochrane, whose gang
he'd been in, wouldn't speak to him or let him play football with
them. God, when he thought of all those days he spent hanging
about at playtime, pretending he didn't want to play football
anyway, hearing Billy Aird's sneaky laughing behind his back,

desperately wanting them to ask him to play again, being pathetically happy and smarmy when one day they didn't ignore him any more . . .

Was it silly to remember things like that? When Nicol asked him why he didn't like the school he would have felt like a big gawkit schoolgirl telling him *that*. But it was the start, no doubt about it. He'd never forgiven them, not even when they reached the second and third year in the senior school, Billy Aird, Norrie Cochrane, Ian McInnes, Bobby Young, Dovat Shand, Tom Cadenhead, Peter Fleming, Hugh Gilchrist, Hammy Alston, Ian Barclay, Jimmy Barr, Jimmy McDonald, Rhonach Kennedy . . . that was why he'd made big pals with Alec, he'd come to the Academy in the first year in the senior school and hadn't been one of them.

If he lived till he was ninety and he met any of them in Kilcaddie High Street he'd still want to kick the ballocks off them. And if ever Cartneuk were against a team in which one of them was playing that's exactly what he would do. Bad blood, maybe they were right. Too bad. Better to have bad blood than be a big mummy's boy and have to suck to keep in the gang . . .

'SO AH SAYS tae him, listen here, mister, ah says, if ye think ye kin talk tae me like that ye've got anuther think coming, so ye huv. I wis fair livid, so I wis, richt enough. A big strappin' fella like *him* tellin' me whut fur! I felt like cloutin' him ower the heid wi' ma message bag.'

Telfer had intended to stay in the house that night, read the paper or *Wide World* magazine, listen to the radio or play some gramophone records, but Mrs Sneddon had come across the landing to borrow a shilling for her meter and now her daughter Bertha had come in as well and they looked set for the night, gassing away to his mother like houses on fire. His mother was too soft with them. He tried to make it obvious he wanted them out by swinging his feet up on to the arm-rest of the shiny rexine couch, lying back with his hands under his head. The very sight of Bertha's newly-washed hair, combed flat back and still wet, and her pale pink lips with their chapped edges, and her bare feet in tatty slippers and the leg veins burned brown from sitting too near the fire, made him want to boke. Years ago, when he was a wee boy about ten or eleven, he'd stuffed her among the Black Hills. Even though she was now married to a bloke serving with the army in Germany she often tried to give him the eye. Boooogh!

'Don't mind our Donald,' said his mother. 'He always puts his feet up when there's folk in.'

'I'll leave you in peace in a minute,' he said. 'I can tell when I'm not wanted.'

'Och, don't be gaun' oot jist because of us, Donal',' said Mrs Sneddon. 'Me'n Bertha's gaun' tae the flicks, she's peyin' me in.'

'Ah am not,' said the girl.

'Ye are sot,' said her mother. 'Here, Donal', ye couldnae lend us a fag, could ye, Bertha's been smokin' like a linty a' day and I've run out so I huv.'

He watched his mother rising to get her packet from the sideboard. How she put up with an old bauchle like Mrs Sneddon and her mawkit daughter he didn't understand. His mother had class, blonde hair in a fancy style, a tight white pullover, fuzzy, black slacks and high-heeled shoes, long red nails – not cracked and chipped like Bertha's.

The Sneddons took the hint and left, or maybe they'd just been hanging on to borrow the fags.

'I'd lock the door to that lot,' he said.

His mother shrugged. Only when you saw her face, close-up, the hard lines not quite hidden by make-up, would you have known she was forty-six. From the back she looked like a thirty-year-old. 'You stayin' in the night then?'

He scratched his hair.

'Suppose so, nothin' better to do.'

'Your fancy woman's got pregnant on ye, I hear.'

'Oh aye. You hear a lot, don't you.'

'Word gets round.'

Just once, that was all, one time and never again. Ne'er-day, the first after his father ran away, even his straitlaced brother Davie got drunk, Davie was just demobbed from Korea, people dropping in, bottles of whisky, bottles of VP wine, screwtops by the dozen, drinking and dancing, wild 'hoochs' and the floorboards jumping, the front door open, records on full blast, windows rattling, Bobby McCaffery and his three mates wanting a fight, him and Davie throwing them down the stairs, drinking and dancing and shouting, then about four or five in the morning the people going away, Davie flat on his back behind the couch, dead to the world, just him and his mother, her wanting to go on dancing, his own mother, just the once, an accident, too drunk to know what they were doing, his mother crying and holding on to him, big brother Davie unconscious on the floor behind the touch, thinking he was a big man helping his own mother to bed, her too drunk to stand properly, just the once, her fault, she was his mother, she was old enough to have known better, could never forget it, neither of them ever forgot it, never daring to talk about it, remembering all right, see it in her eyes when they looked at you, try never to look at her too much, just like other women, not how you were supposed to look at your own mother, not like other women, try never to be alone with her too much, not to let her touch you, once was bad enough, happen again you might want to cut your throat, like a disease, Davie never even guessed, Davie very cold and straitlaced, big noise in the Boys' Brigade, Davie would be shocked out of his mind, not even like somebody from the same family, never got drunk again after that Ne'er-day, him and her not like Davie, too much alike, knew what each other thought before they spoke, never forgetting that once, remembering it every time he had a woman, nobody could say you were abnormal if you had other women, lots of them, prove it, normal, just the once and too drunk to know what they were doing . . .

'George not coming round the night?'

'No, it's his wife's birthday.'

George was his mother's fancy man, unhappily married to a real shrew, not a bad bloke for a fancy man, at least with him hanging around her he knew she was getting her ration. As long as there were other people about, his women and her fancy man, they weren't sitting around looking at each other.

'I think I'll away out for a ride round on the bike,' he said.

'I thought you were going to stay in.'

'No, I think I'll away out for a bit. Get some fresh air.'

Other people had families that meant something to them. Not us Telfers! A father who'd run away. Two brothers who might have been strangers. Him, always having to remind himself that she wasn't just another woman, but his mother. What was it all supposed to be about, anyway? From the moment you knew anything you knew it was supposed to be wrong. Yet it happened all the time. Joyner the coal-heaver got seven years for fathering bairns on both his daughters. Reid the farmer at Cauldrum was fined fifty pounds for letting his own kids sleep together until they were fourteen or more – one of the girls getting up the stick by her own brother. You knew it was wrong all right – but nobody ever told you *why*.

He cycled down their road and round the corner into Crags Avenue. No point in going near the farm, not that he minded Mary being pregnant but she said it was too risky, if Willie caught them he'd say the baby wasn't his and kick her out. Of course it wasn't Willie's baby! It stood to reason it must be his. As men there was no comparison between them. It was just his rotten luck, most women gave him the screaming habjabs as soon as he'd won the battle to get the knickers off them, the only one who could keep him on the boil was married to somebody else. Just his rotten luck, to have to think of her and Willie, himself and his mother. Was that why it was wrong? Did it affect you with other women? Spoil you? What, just that once, all that time ago? Never. Yet why the attraction for the kind of women he went with? For a cripple? Was it like a *disease*?

It made you think of yourself as some kind of stranger, a man alone, cycling about the dark scheme streets, looking in other folks' windows . . .

*

'Och well, it's just that nothing ever seems to happen about us,'
Elsa said. 'It'll be years before we get married.'

'Stop your moaning,' Dunky said, bear-hugging her head into
his chest. He'd felt sick after getting out of his father's bedroom,
but being with Elsa made him all right again. They couldn't get
married quick enough. She was marvellous! Now that it was April
and the nights were warmer they'd got into a habit of spending
their midweek nights on a wooden bench seat on the edge of the
Corporation football pitches, holding hands, necking, talking and
thinking about the great days ahead. Only on Saturday nights did
they spend any money, five and sixpence on back stalls seats at the
pictures.

'I'm fed up never enjoying ourselves,' she said.

'Don't you enjoy yourself with me?'

'Oh yes, but it's always the same, a wee walk down here and
then home again.' For some reason she *wanted* to make trouble,
no, that wasn't it, she didn't *want* to fight, it was something inside
her, a wee devil voice egging her on. Her mother kept telling her
she was far too young to be running about with a serious
boyfriend but her mother was against all men because she thought
they were all like her father. Something her pal Betty had said was
in her mind as she lay against his chest, his arm round her
shoulder, his right hand on her lap.

'When I get engaged it's goin' to be with some fella who's got
bags of money, I want to enjoy mysel' while I can,' was what Betty
had said. At first Betty had thought it was 'awfy romantic' for Elsa
to be courting seriously, but it didn't look as though they could
even afford a ring for *years* and there was no fun in being
unofficially engaged, you were supposed to save your money
and you didn't even have a ring to show to the girls at work. That
was the exciting part, first showing them the engagement ring,
then planning the wedding, people regarding you as *important* . . .
other people had fathers who gave them the money to get
married. Her father put all his money over the pub counter
and Dunky's father was permanently paralysed and even if they
did have any money they'd never let them get married, not at their
age.

'We agreed we wouldn't waste our money on daft things,'
Dunky said. 'Didn't we?'

'Yes but it'll be *ages* before we can get married.'

It came over him in a rush, as though he'd jumped into water
and was kicking to get to the surface, then gasping in air and
shaking his head.

'All we ever seem to do is argue,' he said. He could hear the change in his voice, hard and abrupt. 'If you want to enjoy yourself go ahead.' He had a sudden picture of his rabbits being killed, all the work he'd put into them going to waste. It made him want to cry. He'd been prepared to kill them all for her. He'd really loved her, never even asked her to go farther than kissing! The hell with it.

'One of the girls at our work was engaged and she and her boyfriend had a trial separation, to see if they still loved each other after two months.'

'All right, if that's what you want. I'll tell you now but, I'm not going to go out with other girls.'

'Me neither.'

He could go home and start work on the hutch straightaway! It felt great. And he wouldn't have to go on worrying in case his mother found out about Elsa.

'What, you're not going out with other girls?'

'No, silly. I won't go out with other boys. Just dance with them.'

There was no reason to go on necking so they got up from the bench and walked, hand in hand, across the football pitches towards the street-lights.

'Don't bother coming all the way down to my place, I'll be all right on my own,' she said as they reached the top of the street.

'Okay.'

They both knew it was probably over. Their last kiss was against the roll-down door of the Co-operative butcher's shop in Balloch Road.

'We'll know if we're really serious,' she said, as if it was a promise of good things to come. When they parted he waited behind the corner for a second and then looked round after her. It was a funny thing about girls, when they were strangers you thought it would be the greatest thing in the world to get to know them, and when you'd been going out with them for a while you didn't even notice that they were good-looking. He could never tell guys like Alec or Telfer that he'd never stuffed her, they'd say he must be a homo or something. They didn't understand real love. What do you know about real love, you cold-blooded bastard, you're not even sorry it's over.

As she walked along the pavement in Dalmount Drive, which ran from the shops and two-storey houses at one end into the Darroch Scheme at the other, Elsa thought of all the things she would do in the next two months. Betty had started going to the dancing in Ayr, she said it was fantastic compared to Kilcaddie Town Hall, the fellas were dead fast and experienced, you had to watch yourself in Ayr all right. And even if she met a really smashing bloke, rich, with a *car*, she'd never forget Dunky.

At first she ignored the man on the bike, pedalling slowly to keep pace with her, hoping he'd go away.

'Getting too high and mighty to recognise your old friends then?' said Telfer. Recognising the voice she looked at him for the first time.

'Oh hallo, it's you,' she said. 'I thought it was a strange man.'

'I'm a very strange man,' he said, sitting back on the saddle, steering with one hand. 'Where's lover boy tonight?'

'I've just left him. We've decided to have a trial separation.'

'Just like film stars, eh? What's wrong, would he no' give ye half of his dolly mixtures?'

It made you feel *very* important, to tell people you were having a trial separation.

'Very funny I don't think. If we still love each other after two months we're going to get married.'

'Where, in your cradles?'

'You think you're awfully smart, don't you? I never see you with a girlfriend, how's that?'

'It depends where you go. I don't fancy kids' dances in Kilcaddie. What're you doing on Saturday?'

'Wouldn't you like to know.'

'Fancy going to the pictures in Ayr?'

'We've promised not to go out with other people.'

'He'll no' know. How about it, eh?'

Betty would be dead jealous. She thought Donald Telfer was better looking than Dirk Bogarde – and he was her dream-boat film star!

'You're very fast, aren't you?'

'Who, me? I'm very shy if you want to know the truth.'

'Pull the other leg, it's got bells on.'

'I'll meet you at the bus stop in Ayr, all right. Nobody'll know.'

'But I have to get home on time or my father'll melt me.'

'Do I look like the kind of bloke who'd lead young girls astray?'

'Definitely, I wouldn't trust you with boxing gloves on.'

'Tuts tuts, you've got a very suspicious mind for your age, what kind of fellas have you been going out with?'

'I don't go out with fellas.'

'What's young Logan then, bit of a nancy boy is he?'

'That's different.'

'Come on, what d'you say?'

'Oh all right if it means that much to you. I hope you haven't got any funny ideas but. You'll be disappointed.'

'Funny ideas! I'm only asking you to the *pictures*, kid. I'll wear handcuffs if it makes you any happier.'

'Ta ta then.'

'See you at six o'clock at the bus station?'

'If I can.'

'You'd better.'

She ran across the road and round the corner into The Undesirables. Funny how you could see a bint knocking around and not even begin to fancy her until some other bloke was taking her out. Now that he thought about it, she looked just like one of those film star women, what was her name, the dark-haired piece. Whistling 'High Noon', he cycled along the main scheme road. For once they'd had two whole days without a drop of rain. Hard lines on young Logan, ha ha, wee boys shouldn't get big ideas before their time . . .

TEN

'HERE, LOGAN, AWAY an' get the big horse from the school field,' said Willie. 'Hey, Blackie, whaur's a rope for the boy?'

'I'll better go wi' him,' said Blackie, giving Dunky a cocky look, one cheek twisted in a sneering grin. 'We want tae get startet the day.'

'I can manage fine,' Dunky growled, but McCann took the rope halter off the hook and didn't offer to hand it over. Telfer was filling water and paraffin into the tractor. He ignored them.

'Doesn't the year go by quick?' he said to McCann as they walked across the yard and out into the road. 'It's hardly like yesterday we were at the hay last year.'

He liked to think that nowadays he was above McCann's sarcastic remarks. On the three or four occasions Blackie had looked like having a real go at him something had always happened before they got to fighting and now it was only now and then that Blackie would drop the odd insult.

'Last year!' said McCann as they walked under the railway bridge and up the metalled road in the early July sunshine. 'That's nothin', I can remember this field stretchin' all the way tae the scheme.'

High red metal fencing separated the asphalt playground from Craig's grass. Big Dick was grazed in this part, he was enough of a menace to keep the scheme kids off Craig's land. It was too near the houses for anything but grazing a bad-tempered horse. Craig liked his crops and his cattle on the other side of the railway line, protected to some extent from gangs of marauding brats and rubbish-dumpers and neds who thought nothing of a game of football on spring corn. They went into the field and shut the rusty iron gate behind them. The mare was already in the stable, brought in by Telfer on his way down to work. It was as well McCann had come, Dunky thought, for Big Dick was a fly devil who knew very well what the rope halter meant – back to work after two or three months' loose grazing.

As they approached the big horse, Dunky scuffed the toes of his boots into the darker circles of long grass which still grew thicker than the rest although no cows had dropped pancakes there for two or three year. There was no dew on his boots. Summer was here and the grass was dry by half-past eight. For almost a month they'd been at turnips, hoeing and thinning, monotonous, earthy work, day after day in the long drills, your neck muscles feeling it most of all. Starting among the hay was the sign that the summer was really here.

'Hullo, Dickie, Dickie,' said McCann, gently, walking steady towards the horse, the halter in his right hand behind his back. The horse took a final bite at the grass and then raised his head, cocking it just enough to see them come up from his rear. Dunky stopped. McCann had to get the rope over him first go, before he realised he was being yoked.

The horse took a sideways step as McCann lifted his hand. McCann murmured something, patting at the great neck. He worked himself nearer its head, one hand among its black mane, the other slowly bringing up the halter. Then the rope was being lifted up round its mouth. Dick shook his head in the air and walked away from McCann, stopping with his back to him. McCann moved forward. He had on creased blue dungaree trousers whereas Dick's legs were brown and hard and smooth. There was more power to one of his towering hindlegs than there was to McCann's whole body. He knew he didn't want to work, to have the rope round his neck. Why the hell should he?

Maybe he knew what had happened to old Charlie. If he was bright enough to know what a rope meant why shouldn't he wonder where the old, done horse had gone?

On McCann's second attempt Dick reared more energetically, front hooves leaving the ground, dropping down, a casual gesture as though he was trying to show them what he might do if he took them seriously. Then he trotted away, four legs moving evenly, head up, mane flying, an easy disciplined canter like practice for trotting in a circus.

'Come on,' said McCann. 'He's jist playin' up.'

Laughing to himself, he followed McCann across the grass. Perhaps people were watching them from the windows of the scheme houses. Two men chasing a big horse, silly men in silly trousers and jackets, fragile wee bodies. Pursuing the noble beast. Man came down from the trees and only his superior brain kept him alive among the predatory creatures of far greater strength. What superior brain?

At that side the field was fenced with wire, three strands through thin metal shafts. This time he made a wider circle and stood about ten yards in front of the horse, McCann again approaching it from the rear, talking to it in the quiet voice that was supposed to keep him calm. This time Big Dick kicked up in earnest. McCann ran a yard to the side and then tried to throw the halter noose over its head. The rope flicked Big Dick's neck. McCann half-fell. The horse trotted towards Dunky. He raised his arms, meaning to turn its head back to the fence. It came straight at him. He jumped for the wire. The horse went trotting past him, the earth vibrating under its drumming hooves.

McCann's face was flushed under his stubble.

'Get a hold o' him, for God's sake,' he said.

They walked twenty yards.

In *The Dog Crusoe* the man caught his wild mount by creasing its neck with a bullet, great marksman that fella! Or maybe, if it wasn't okay to try shooting it unconscious, they could try tiring it out! Your cinema cowboys went right up under their front feet and threw the rope over their heads. He wasn't going in for any fancy tricks like that and by the looks of him neither was McCann. A fine pair of Neanderthal men we'd make!

This time Dick was waiting for them. As soon as McCann slowed his walk, the halter rope across his chest, right hand holding the loop at the running-knot, it turned on them. They saw its ears up and its teeth bared. They sprinted for the fence, scrambling over the three wire strands.

Dunky floundered on the grass verge of the track road, laughing as soon as he saw the horse wasn't coming over after them but had veered away, hair flying, towards the middle of the field.

'Whut's so funny?'

'Nothing.'

McCann would get the blame. Ha ha.

'You take the rope then if ye think it's that funny.'

'I'm too young to die.'

'Come on, Craig's no' goin' to be laughin'.'

All right, we've got the brains, what do we do now? Kids in the school playground, they'd have a great laugh. They climbed the wire fence and set off on a pincer movement. It wasn't so funny, not really, not when you came nearer the brute. Here's your domesticated work-horse, gentlemen, bred to work and obey. But something's wrong. It wants to be free and we've forgotten how we tamed it in the first place. All right, Big Dick, you've had your fun, how's about getting on with the hay?

'That way!' roared McCann as the horse jerked to life, pointing to the corner near the gate. Dunky raised his hands in a wave, shouting. Big Dick came round in a heavy semi-circle, straight for him. He was too far from the fence. For a split second he watched its high-flying head, its great rolling shoulder joints, the hooves flat-pounding the grass. He ran to the left, looking over his shoulder, studded boot soles slipping on grass, McCann shouting.

Dick chased him all the way to the tall school fence. In jokes men chased by wild bulls were able to vault hedges in their stride, but he could see no grip on the smooth red fencing. He was going to be kicked, would it be painful? He slipped, one knee touching the ground, floundering to get up, glancing wildly over his shoulder at the horse, still coming at him, run along the fence, kids on the other side, only a joke to them, no joke to me, horse isn't giving up, don't worry about looking scared, get moving, just run now, don't look back.

Between the scheme and the field, the boundary of the farm, was another wire fence and a continuous hump of clay soil overgrown by hawthorns and wild roses. He ran at the fence, one sliding boot on the slack bottom wire, hands pulling on thin metal, right boot catching on the top wire, sprawling into a mess of grass and tin cans and bottles. He looked round. The horse had given up the chase and had turned on McCann, who was running like a madman from a silent film, knees going up and down like pistons, stiff elbows, his cap flying off.

Behind the fence the kids were yelling at them.

Dunky climbed back into the field and walked round its edge to the gate, always ready to leap to safety if Dick turned towards him. McCann reached the big gate.

The horse, hair streaming dramatically, careered back to the centre of the field, where it halted and began to graze.

Willie was there, on the road, with Telfer.

'Whut's wrang wi' ye, McCann?' Willie was roaring. Dunky climbed the metal gate.

'The brute's gone mad,' said McCann.

'Ach, ye stupit eejit, can ye no' even fetch a bloody horse when ye're asked?'

Willie climbed the gate and held out his hand for the rope. He walked straight for the horse. They leaned on the gate, Telfer smirking like a schoolgirl. Dunky saw it in a flash, smoking cigarettes, liking tractors better than horses, wearing ordinary shoes – Telfer was a *town* man, through and through, and town men were no good. Yellow bellies. Safety first. Clean hands.

'We'd better give Willie a hand,' he said to McCann.

'Suit yourself,' said Blackie. Dunky climbed the gate and walked out towards Willie and the horse. He could hear McCann's voice behind him, the very sound of it suggesting a man covering sneaky fear behind a know-all sneer.

Then the horse was chasing Willie and when he saw him making for the gate Dunky turned and climbed, not too quickly, out of the field.

With three men beaten it was suddenly a matter for a big joke. Willie was just saying they'd have to coax him over to the gate with a pail of corn when Auld Craig came stumping across the road towards them, in a fine state judging by the unusually high angle of his head.

'Get out of it ye lazy hoors,' he shouted at them, snatching the rope from Willie. Dunky stood back. Craig pushed the heavy gate open, nobody giving him a hand. Should he follow the old man, prove he wasn't yellow, get in Craig's good books? Why not, he could out-run the horse.

'This'll be worth watching,' said Telfer.

Craig was bawling at the horse as he stumped over the grass, right hand holding up the rope. Big Dick waited, ears cocked. Craig walked straight for his head. Dick stamped one forefoot. Craig roared at him. He reached the horse just as it began to draw back into the air. Dunky followed behind, already thinking of the advantage this would give him over McCann. The old man drew back his right arm and slashed the halter rope across the horse's face. Still bawling. For a moment it looked as though Dick would rear up and pound him into the grass. Craig kept slashing at its face. Then it was on four feet, only its head raised. The old man, neck now inclined at its usual position, grabbed a handful of its forelock, then its ear.

'Here, pit the halter on him,' he said to Dunky.

It took an effort to go that close, but he wasn't a cheap townee hiding behind a gate.

'Take him in,' said the old man. 'Call yerselves men?' he roared at the other three. If the horse should buck now he'd let the rope go and the hell with caring what it looked like, but Dick walked quietly out of the gate and across the road and down into the yard . . .

Later, in the afternoon, he was walking behind the hay-mower, pulling the greenish hay over the churning teeth with the wooden hay rake, McCann sitting on the cantilever bucket seat with the reins loose in his hand. Telfer and Willie were cutting with the tractor in the low field. McCann was still in a temper with the big horse and when the dragging rein ends – which a good horseman should have kept off the ground – caught in the mower axle he lost his head completely. The saw stopped chattering between the iron teeth, which skated across uncut hay, scarring into black earth.

'Jesus Christ,' shouted McCann, hauling the reins tight. As he came round the back of the mower he gave Dunky a push in the chest. Always the same moment – did you go in? Was he bigger than you? Were you keyed up to beat his brains out – for once you went in that's what you had to do.

Dunky let himself sit down heavily on the swathe of mown hay.

'Temper, temper,' he grinned.

McCann growled, head into the machinery. The rope was twisted tight, dragged into the cog wheel that drove the saw. They backed the horse but the rein would not come free. McCann had to cut it out with his pocket-knife. Dunky thought of the bothy men he'd read about at Nicol's house. They sounded like real farmers, even though they lived in an Abderdonian midden. The idea was coming to him that Craig's men weren't real farming people at all. Too near the town. Who was he like? Who did he want to be like? Telfer? McCann? No, they were nothing. Didn't amount to anything. Auld Craig was a real man, maybe the only one he knew.

They started mowing again, round and round the ever-decreasing area of hay, McCann holding the reins, turning Big Dick, working the mower-lever at the corners, swathe after swathe lying behind them, the sweet, natural smell of bruised grass strong in his nose, almost able to taste it. He kept his eyes on the mower blade, watching the dancing stalks stiffen as the blade took them, then fall like millions of miniature tree-trunks, his rake making sure they fell the right way, over the mower arm. A mouse ran under the swathe, his eye catching the dark movement, his heel on it almost without breaking stride, a second downward hack crushing it. Dark blood mixed with earth.

Why did I do that?

Because you always killed mice, or rats, or rabbits. Wee sleekit cowrin timorous vermin.

It wasn't a bad life, out in the open air, the sun on your face, dodging along behind the rattling mower, free to think of any-thing that came into your head, watching the field being laid low, your bare arms and chest going red, the muscles toughening, whistle a bit of this and a bit of that, imagine daft things, have a laugh to yourself at the thought of Dick chasing them over the field, wonder if *next time* you'd be ready to open McCann's skull for him, a great life if you didn't weaken.

On days when it was going to be hot the mornings were cool and slightly misty, the men's clothes dark against the pink and grey smear of medium-height cloud, their voices taking on a suggestion of echo through the damp air. Real farmers knew all about the weather and he was beginning to pick it up.

It stayed dry for a week and by that time the cut hay had been turned and dried and built into bowl-shaped coles a couple of feet higher than a man. Raising the great pole for the horse-fork in the yard was, to Dunky, another signal that summer had really come. The year before, in the school holidays, he'd been taken on the day the pole was raised. Then he'd led the mare, pulling the rope which lifted the grab-fork up to the men who built the haystacks. That was a boy's job, nothing to do all day but stand at the horse's head, take him forward again, back and forward, ten yards worn into a dark earth scar on the patchy grass of the stackyard.

This year he was one of the men and when they went to the stackyard, in the small field adjoining the steading, Craig put him at the end of one of the pole's four ropes. The pole looked as thick and long as a ship's mast. Willie and McCann had the other holding ropes, and the fourth was tied to the tractor's tow-bar.

First Willie and McCann lifted the far end of the pole off the ground, bending with knees splayed out like men picking up a caber at the Highland Games, straightening up like Samson bracing against the pillars, hands above their heads, then walking, stiff-legged, under the pole, lifting its head farther from the ground. As soon as it reached the right height Telfer opened the tractor throttle, taking the weight on the tractor rope. The pole started to rise. McCann ran to his rope end and slipped it round the spike. Willie took the rope on the opposite side to the tractor. Craig stood to one side, waving and shouting instructions.

He never liked this bit. He put his left boot on the spike, his back to the pole, the rope hard against his left side, running round the shiny spike and held by his right hand. If the pole began to fall to McCann's side he was supposed to take its full weight, heels dug in, hands holding on no matter how the hard, rasping rope burned his palms, trying to make out what Craig was shouting – too much pull on his rope and the pole would swing towards him and McCann would have to hold it from falling, too much slack and it might fall towards McCann.

Daftie Coll had once misheard Craig's shouting and let his rope go when he should have pulled. The pole had fallen and split and the hay had been held up for a day and a half until a new one was delivered. He looked over his shoulder. Craig was waving at Telfer, Willie was jack-knifed over his spike, heels into the ground like a one-man tug-of-war team.

Then it was up and all he had to do was put a double loop round the spike and hold the rope until Willie came over and tied the proper knot. This year Telfer and McCann were bringing the coles from the fields, on low, rubber-wheeled trolleys, Telfer on the tractor, McCann driving Big Dick. Willie and McPhail the knee-padder were to build the stacks. He was to work the hay-fork.

There was a boy to work the horse, a thin-faced scheme boy wearing the shiny, back-pleated jacket of an old chalk-stripe suit and narrow-legged light blue trousers and crêpe soled shoes. In the stable in the morning he hadn't said much and Willie hadn't told them his name, although Telfer seemed to know him.

When Telfer and McCann went off to the field Willie and McPhail and the boy and himself sat on the first stack's straw foundation to eat their pieces and drink their vacuum-flask tea. The boy had nothing to eat.

'Your mither doesnae believe in spoilin' you then?' Willie remarked. Boys were fair game to take the rise out of. Dunky chewed on white bread and Cheddar cheese. McPhail brought an unwrapped sandwich of white bread and jam out of his jacket pocket, blowing off hairs and bits of pocket-grit before munching into it with the kind of thin, deliberate bites of a man adrift on a raft eking out his day's share of hardtack.

'I don't need it,' said the boy, sniffing a slow balloon of catarrh back up into his nostrils.

'What do they call you then?' Dunky asked him.

'That's a Rafferty frae Kilmairns Avenue,' said Willie. 'He's a car-wrecker, aren't ye, Rafferty?'

The boy sniffed. Dunky knew who he was now. The summer before a gang of scheme boys had taken big stones up on the railway bridge and dropped them on the roofs of passing cars. Willie had helped the bobbies catch them and they'd been taken to the Juvenile Court and given probation.

'Ye've got three sisters a' brides o' Christ, haven't ye, Rafferty?' Willie went on.

'Yeah, so whut?'

'What's that, brides of Christ?' Dunky asked.

'They marry Jesus when they get to be nuns,' said McPhail.

Rafferty wiped at his nose with the sleeve of his jacket. He didn't seem to care what they said. Dunky had never heard of brides of Christ. Apart from the fact that the Pope kidded them on he was better than Jesus and they weren't allowed to read the Bible in English, he didn't know much about Catholics. They had their own school in Kilcaddie and apart from playing football against them there was hardly any contact. It interested him, to think that in a small town like Kilcaddie, where in the street everybody looked the same, different religions meant that some kids went to one school and some to another. He'd once asked about this in class and Mr Mason had said it was the Catholics who wouldn't come to the Academy, not the other way round. All the people he knew were Protestants – bar his mother none of them gave a fart for God, although most of them, even Alec, went to church fairly regularly. Why did Catholics, wee scheme rats like this Rafferty, take their religion so seriously? Didn't that mean it must be better than Protestantism? Even his mother said that Catholics were much more sincere in their worship, going to mass early on Sunday mornings while they were still in bed. They could go to chapel in working-clothes, too, whereas their church was the height of respectability – his mother had once given him a belting for going to Sunday School without garters.

He knew the usual things about Catholics: they supported Glasgow Celtic, the priests told them what to do and took away their money, they confessed their sins in a wee box, they had beads, they preferred Eire to the Union Jack, they worshipped Holy Mary instead of Jesus, they bred like rabbits, their priests weren't allowed to marry but had fancy women and children, they would let you marry a Catholic girl only if you promised the kids would be brought up as Papes. From the day you were born people told you Catholics were the enemy – they'd take away your freedom if they got the chance. Every year there was a big Orange Walk with banners and men in fancy clothes singing songs from Ulster about King Billy slaying the Papish crew at the battle of Boyne Water and hanging the Pope with a northern rope. Was it just another of his daft ideas, secretly thinking that Catholics couldn't be all that bad? In the school debating society he'd argued against the idea of the masons – lot of nonsense, grown men dressing up in aprons and gabbling on about Solomon's Temple and giving each other the best jobs. Billy Aird had said his father was a freemason, it was the only way to get promotion in Kilcaddie police. The teacher had interrupted Billy and told him he shouldn't say things like that. If Billy Aird said it it must be nonsense, yet even his mother always said her father got on well at business because he was a mason. In Eire, they said, books were banned and priests ordered the folk how to vote. McCann was fond of telling everybody that. Some day he'd tell McCann that shouldn't bother him, he'd never voted or read a book in his life. Folk were funny about it – you'd hear them shouting the odds about Mary, Queen of Scots, how John Knox terrorised her and how Queen Elizabeth murdered her, but when you asked them if Mary, Queen of Scots, wasn't a Catholic anyway, they didn't know what to say. Same with Bonnie Prince Charlie – they all thought he was the greatest yet if he'd beaten the English they would have had a Catholic king. Very strange, folk, most of the time they didn't know if they were coming or going.

He had to show Rafferty how to work the horse. Looking at the sniffing wee gnaff he wondered if *he* believed in God, he didn't look as though he knew the difference between God and a poke of chips. He tried to be friendly.

'D'you hear the joke about the Two Proddestants who went to Parkhead and saw a priest and one says, "Hey, Alex, I'm going to take a rise out of that priest" and he goes down and says, "Hullo, Father, is it true what they're saying, your new Pope's a big drunkard and a homo and on the drugs and steals all the Vatican cash and fancies wee boys and behaves like a big animal?" The priest says, all polite like, "Is that so, my son, my my," and the man goes back to his pal and says he can't get a rise out of the priest at all, so his mate says he'll have a go, so he goes down and says, "Hullo, Father, is this true what they're saying, your new Pope's a freemason?" and the priest says, "Aye, so your friend was just telling me."'

Rafferty shrugged and sniffed.

'I don't know nuthin' about the Pope,' he said.

'It's a joke. It's supposed to be against the masons.'

'You can fuck off any day.'

'Oh, coming the big hard man, eh?'

'Fit for you anyway.'

'Ach, don't be daft.'

Telfer backed the trolley into place beside the big pole. He helped Telfer push the cole towards the back, then heave up the front of the trolley, holding the rope round the cole while Telfer started the tractor and dragged the trolley from under the hay. He whipped off the ropes which held the cole together.

'Right, take her forward till I shout,' he said to Rafferty. The boy obviously knew nothing about horses. He walked beside him, hand on the bit ring, until the fork was dangling just above the rounded top of the cole.

'That's all you've got to do,' he said. 'Don't jerk it about, just take it up steady and down fast.'

He clambered up the smooth side of hay and guided the four fork prongs down until they had a good grip. Then he stood back, the thin release-rope in his hand.

'Go forward, slowly but,' he said. Rafferty pulled on the mare's bit-rope. She'd done this so often she probably didn't need anybody at her head, but you could never rely on a horse not to take the notion to do something daft. The fork lifted a foot into the air.

'That's enough,' he shouted. As it swung out over their heads he pulled the release rope and the hay fell between Willie and McPhail. Moving about like men in a snowdrift they forked the hay evenly over the straw. 'Back now,' he shouted at Rafferty. The boy was too slow and the fork swung back again, making Willie and McPhail dive to avoid it.

'Start her back's soon as she's dropped her load,' Willie shouted at the boy. Dunky felt sorry for him. It had taken him days and days to get the right rhythm at the horse's lead – when you were new to it you were half-scared all the time in case you did something wrong.

He guided the fork into the top of the cole.

'I'll show you,' he said, going to the horse's head. The boy sniffed.

'As soon as I've got the teeth into the hay and raise my hand you take her forward, steady like,' he told Rafferty. 'Then as soon as I pull my rope and the hay falls start her back, fast as you can. I can pull her clear of the stack on the way down. I can't guide her on the way up or I'll pull the catch. You get me?'

'If you're so smart you work the fuck'n thing,' said the boy. Dunky sucked air through clenched teeth.

'Just do what I tell you,' he said.

Rafferty started the horse too early the next time and the fork sailed up into the air clutching only a few whisps of hay, knocking Dunky off the top of the cole.

'For fuck's sake wait till I tell ye,' he shouted. The boy shrugged and spat a thin gobbet out of his curved tongue. The next thing he did wrong was to start backing the horse before the trip-rope was pulled. The forkful of hay landed on McPhail's shoulder, knock-ing him onto his knees.

They were only halfway down the first cole when McCann led Big Dick into the yard with the second.

'Never let boys dae men's work,' he shouted up to Willie.

'Ah ballocks,' Dunky shouted back. 'Come on, Rafferty, get a bloody move on.'

For the rest of that day they were behind, either Telfer or McCann having to stand about waiting for the previous cole to be lifted up on the stack. Dunky found he could only keep Rafferty working properly if he ran back and forth from the horse's head to the coles, snatching the halter-rope out of the boy's hands, pulling the trip-wire then starting the horse back, running to meet the fork and shove its teeth into the hay.

In the afternoon when they had their break, he tried to explain the whole business again to the boy. Rafferty didn't seem to give a bugger either way.

'Look, I'm no' going to run myself to death doing your work as well,' he said. 'If ye don't brighten yourself up they'll sack ye. Aren't ye wanting the money?'

'I can get plenny money,' the boy said. 'I can make more'n this nickin' stuff. This kinna work's for mugs.'

'Aye, but it's better'n goin' to jail.'

'Who goes to jail?'

Dunky didn't know what to say. All he'd ever stolen was small stuff from Woolworths, pencils and notebooks and packets of envelopes, just for dares during school dinner-time – and even then they were so scared of being caught they used to drop everything they'd knocked off into letter-boxes.

'What's your father do?' he asked.

Rafferty sniffed and spat and turned his head away. Where his dirty, fair hair met his neck there were blackheads and small pimples.

'Casual labourin',' said the boy.

Willie must have been listening, above them on the top of the stack.

'Aye, casual labourin' in Barlinnie jail,' he shouted.

'Fuck you,' the boy shouted back.

Dunky expected Willie to slide down and give the boy a hammering, but instead he laughed his mad laugh and repeated what he had said: 'Casual labourin' in Barlinnie jail, Rafferty. Nae wonder yer sisters got merriet to Christ, naebody else would huv them.'

Thanks to the boy they had to work till after six to get the first stack finished and the canvas hap put over its top and the hap's brown ropes weighted down with bricks. As he brushed hayseeds out of the horses' coats Dunky waited to hear if Craig had paid the boy off – casuals got their cash at the end of each day. As he cycled home he wondered why on earth Craig had kept him on. It was hard to get boys to do the work, everybody knew that, but it wasn't that hard, surely? Rafferty wasn't right for a farm. What kind of people were his kind, to talk about mugs working and nicking stuff for a living? People in Shuttle Place were no better off than people in the scheme, yet he felt completely different from them. As though your family was older and more respect-able – *decent*. At school it had been easy to think about things like that – feudalism had given way to the industrial revolution and eventually the working classes had fought for votes and rights and whatnot. By working class you thought of men in overalls in factories, tending machines, big, grown-up men with families to keep – honest working guys as Alec called them.

'What class would you say we were?' he asked his mother at tea. It was easier to talk to her now that the old man was out of the house. *He* felt like the man of the house now, all tough and hard after a day's toil.

'We're middle class,' his mother said. 'D'you want some more mince?'

'Aye, but how can we be middle class, I mean my father only worked in a foundry, didn't he?'

'Your father's job has got nothing to do with it. We're middle class.'

'I'm working class,' he said. 'I work for a wage, don't I, and get my hands dirty? What's middle class about that?'

His mother tut-tutted as she ladled more mince onto his plate.

'It's not what you work at, it's what you are,' she said, 'Your grandfather had his own business, don't forget that.'

'Aye, but we don't have any business.'

'It doesn't matter. It's just something you *know*.'

'What class are you, wee Senga?' His sister was fiddling with her hair in front of the mantelpiece mirror.

'I'm not wee Senga,' she replied.

'Big Senga then. What class would you say you were, Big Senga – cookery class?'

'Very funny I don't think.'

Out in the hut he gave the rabbits new hay and, while the light lasted, cut wire-netting with pincers for the front of the next new hutch. It was a pity they didn't get more sunshine. Soon he'd be seeing Elsa again, the rabbits were thriving on good summer feeding, he'd built two new hutches and sold a couple of duds to the butcher, he was dead lucky not to have been born a Rafferty, on Saturday they had a good chance of winning their semi-final against Darroch Youth Club, even the house didn't seem so bad – now.

Back inside he decided to clean out his shelf of books and rubbish. His mother was listening to the *McFlannel* family on the wireless. She always said they were very, very common and shouldn't be allowed on the wireless, not that coarse Glasgow talk, but she always listened to the programme. She knitted, occasionally shaking her head and making little tsk-tsk noises as Paw McFlannel came out with his real Glesca sayings. He carried an armful of old exercise books from the kitchen press to the couch.

'You don't go out so much these days,' she said.

'No?'

No, I'm saving up to get married!

'Senga goes out more than you do.'

'Why don't you stop her?'

'It's only to the Guides or her pals' houses.' On the wireless Paw McFlannel was saying, 'Crivvens, wumman, ah always cuts ma coarns oan the livin'-room cairpit' and his mother shook her head in agreement with Mrs McFlannel, who said, 'I don't care, you clear up this mess, I'm not having you disgrace us in front of Mrs Cotton.'

If his mother thought Paw McFlannel cutting his corns on the living-room carpet was 'common' what would she think of the way they talked at the farm? Funny, how you could speak one way at work and another way at home, without too much effort. Did you put in the swear words artificially at the farm or take them out artificially at home? That reminded him of Gillespie the science teacher – or Wee Sammy as he was known – saying there was no such thing as cold, just absence of heat. And ice broke natural laws by floating instead of sinking with its denser gravity. If ice did the normal thing whole oceans would freeze up. What good did it do you knowing stuff like that?

He decided to throw out his books of pasted-in football pictures. Kids' stuff. He tore out each page in turn and put it on the range fire. The flour-and-water paste had gone green with age, giving some of the pictures a funny tint . . . then the best pictures, England 1, Scotland 3, 1949 at Wembley . . . first Jimmy Cowan of Morton put up a fantastic display in goal, saving point-blank, time after time, from Mortensen . . . then Reilly crossed to

Jimmy Mason, there he was, stabbing the ball with his right foot, past big Frank Swift, the ball going in off the post . . . number two for Scotland, Billy Houliston of Queen of the South going into Swift and Aston, hard man Billy Houliston, toughest guy in the game, the ball hitting Swift and running to Billy Steel, head down, blond, picture number three from the *Sunday Express* showing him left-footing it into the net and turning already, hands going up, the great Billy Steel . . . and number three, Willie Waddell crossing from the right, the great Deedle-Doddle, Lawrie Reilly, Hibs, body parallel to the ground, heading it past the falling Swift . . . that was *the* team, Jimmy Cowan, Morton; George Young, Rangers; Sammy Cox, Rangers; Bobby Evans, Celtic; Willie Woodburn, Rangers; George Aitken, East Fife; Willie Waddell, Rangers; Jimmy Mason, Third Lanark; Billy Houliston, Queen of the South; Billy Steel, Derby County; Lawrie Reilly, Hibernian. He'd only been a wee boy then, but ever since almost every man he knew had gone on talking about that game. Christ, what would it be like to play for Scotland? Must be fantastic. He decided to keep the pictures. One day he'd have a wee boy of his own and he'd show them to him and say, 'That's what I call a great Scottish team, son.' Ha ha. Everybody thought the teams they saw when they were young were the world's best. The hell with keeping a lot of silly pictures. They went into the fire. The last one he burned was of Jock Tiger Shaw with the Scottish Cup, being carried on the shoulders of Willie Thornton and Sammy Cox. Jock Shaw had no teeth in front, his hair was shorn up the sides of his head – Tiger right enough. He threw the covers of the exercise book into the fire. There was a knock at the front door.

'I wonder who that can be?' said his mother, looking worried, gripping the arms of her chair.

'I'll see.' He shoved the other books into the press, not wanting visitors to think he was still a wee boy playing with football pictures.

Alec was on the landing, the gas-light reflected on the shiny red skin of his cheeks, which had been shaved clean of spots and rubbed with Valderma.

'Hullo there,' he said. 'How's the lad?'

'Come in,' said Dunky. 'It's Alec,' he told his mother as he led the way into the kitchen.

'Hullo Mrs Logan,' said Alec, who could be awfully polite to grown-ups. Little did they know. For some reason his mother always seemed to be apologising to visitors. She stood up and moved a cushion and looked embarrassed, as though Alec was the minister!

'I'll just make a cup of tea,' she said.

'Don't bother for me, Mrs Logan,' said Alec.

'Oh, it's no bother.'

'No, don't bother, mum. I'm going to show Alec the rabbits.'

'Will you be out long?'

'No, not very long.'

He put on his shoes in the lobby. Alec watched him. He'd never come much to the house when his father was there. It was an awful thing to say, even to yourself, but everything was a lot freer and easier nowadays.

'I've got something to tell you,' Alec said as they went down the stairs and into the close. 'Guess who I saw up the town last night?'

'Who?'

'Guess.'

'Charlie Tully?'

'No, guess, go on, somebody you know.'

He unlocked the hut door and they climbed inside. Like most people Alec glanced at the rabbits without real interest.

'Come on, tell us.'

'Guess.'

'Come on, cut the cackle.'

'Elsa!'

'Oh yeah? So what? She's allowed to go up the town, isn't she?'

'Ah yea, but who with?'

'Whaddye mean, who with?'

There were moments when your brain seemed to leap about inside your head, thinking all sorts of thoughts, working so fast you touched on hundreds of things in a second. He felt a shock coming, even before Alec said it: 'That big blond guy from your farm.'

'What, Donald Telfer?'

'That's the one.'

'Maybe she was just walking up the road with him.'

'Oh aye, sure, at half-past ten at night with his arm round her? They were winchin', definite.'

Alec was pleased, he knew that. Telfer knew she was his woman, so he'd done the dirt on him deliberately. She'd done the dirt on him, too. Telfer was older than him. He'd treat her just like another stray shag. Why did she want that? He'd been in love with her. Saved seventeen pounds fifteen shillings up till last pay day, to get married on.

'Oh,' he said. Alec was waiting to hear him go wild. He

wouldn't. She'd betrayed him. Bugger her. He was finished with women, permanently. 'Just as well I wasn't serious.'

'Tell us another, you were dead serious.'

'Was I hell! She was just a good shag, that's all.'

'You were actually – ehm – poking her then?'

'What do you think? What else d'you go with women *for*?'

He forced Alec to look in all the hutches, explaining how old they were and which was the buck and pulling the nest apart to show him the latest litter, six babies about nine days old, eyes open, ears just unfurling, all the time thinking about his so-called pal Donald Telfer. For some reason he decided it had been a shame to burn his football pictures.

ELEVEN

DUNKY DIDN'T SPEAK to Telfer all day, ignoring him when he drove into the stack-yard with each new load, walking away when he tried to talk. He didn't want to speak to any of them. Maybe it isn't true, he kept saying to himself. Telfer eventually realised that he was sulking.

'What's wrong with Smallcock then?' he shouted up to Willie and McPhail.

'You call me that once again an' I'll bloody do you,' he shouted to Telfer.

'What's wrong with you for God's sake? Getting one of Blackie's moods are you?'

'Never you bloody mind.'

He knew he'd made a mistake letting them know he was in a temper when Telfer started singing 'Ghost Riders in the Sky', substituting Smallcock for Ghost Riders. He kept his teeth clenched. Telfer must have said something to McCann as they passed on the road for when he came into the yard he, too, made a point of calling him Smallcock. It was like telling somebody you hated the sound of two knife edges being rubbed together, soon as you told them they got out two knives and kept rubbing them until you went mad.

'A lone Smallcock went riding out one dark and windy day,' sang Telfer. Just you wait, you dirty rat, I'll fix you.

They put the hap on the new stack just before six. In the stable Telfer again tried to speak to him.

'What's got your goat then, kid?' he asked.

Dunky spat on the stable floor. He wanted to fight Telfer, he wasn't afraid, he knew he might get a battering, he could take it. To *start* it was the worst thing. His stomach churned, just the way it did when he was necking with Elsa and they were getting more and more excited. He wanted Telfer to start it. Just as he wanted Elsa to tell him when she decided he could go the whole way with her.

But Telfer wasn't interested enough to make it into a fight. Dunky felt cheated. Telfer should have started it.

He fed and watered the horse and then got his bike and left them without saying cheerio. He cycled up to the scheme and along to Barskiven Road. On summer nights The Undesirables was like a nest of tinks. Wirelesses blared out of open windows. Children threw stones at each other, chased up and down in howling packs, climbed into living-room windows. He sat on his bike, left foot on the pavement kerb, hands in his jerkin pockets, lips tightening whenever he thought of her. If it was true she was just a dirty wee Undesirable hoor.

Eventually she came out of her house, walking down the path to the open gate. He stared at her, face as grim as he could make it.

'Hullo,' she said. He glanced at the ground floor kitchen window. Maybe Noble the Wife-beater was watching. So what? He couldn't care less.

'I want to speak to you,' he said. She came across the pavement. She had bare legs in fluffy slippers. She looked guilty.

'My tea's ready,' she said.

'Are you goin' out wi' Donald Telfer?'

'What?'

'You heard.'

Somebody hammered at the kitchen window.

'That's my daddy, I've to go in for my tea.'

'Just tell us, yes or no. Are you goin' out wi' Donald Telfer?'

He saw two boys rolling about the pavement, one bigger than the other, the smaller one crying in agony as his arm was twisted up his back. She wouldn't look at him properly.

'Are you?'

There was a face at the kitchen window. Big Noble doing his nut because she was out on the pavement, talking to a lad. Disgracing the decent family!

'I just went out with him, that was all, it wasn't serious.'

'No' much.'

He looked at her.

'I've got to go in,' she said, looking back at the house.

'So that's it then?'

'We're too young to be serious,' she said. Maybe she did still love him. If she didn't she'd probably have sent her father out to him.

'I would've waited.'

'I've got to go in.'

'On ye go.'

'Cheerio then . . .'

'Cheerio.'

He cycled off down Barskiven Road thinking of all the things he could do to Telfer. He'd get that rat, one way or another. Maybe he couldn't smash his face in but he'd do something. At tea his mother said he was to go and visit his father in Killearn the following Sunday. He didn't care, he'd nothing else to do, now. After tea he biked through the town to Alec's house in the Meiklepark scheme. With Alec's big brothers both married and out of the house Alec had a bedroom to himself. They sat and listened to Alec's records on his wind-up gramophone.

'I went to see Elsa the night,' he said. Alec's best record was 'Down the Road Apiece' by the Will Bradley Trio, Ray MacKinlay's Orchestra playing 'Chicken Gumboogie' on the other side. 'I've chucked her in.'

'Good riddance if you ask me,' said Alec. 'Wimmin just give you a pain in the neck. Hey, it's our YM's bus outing to Portpatrick on Saturday, you fancy coming, your friend the big Magda woman's going?'

'I'm playing football.'

'Can't you skip it for once?'

'Are you kidding? I've a good chance of getting into the first team. Give up football for a stupid bus run? What'll they do at Portpatrick anyway, play rounders and have a picnic, just like the Sunday School?'

'Not on your nelly. Big Shanky's going. He goes in pubs, y'know that?'

'Bigtime eh? You wouldn't go in a pub, would you?'

'Try anything once, that's my motto. Anyway, who's going to see you in Portpatrick?'

'You won't get me in pubs, it's a mug's game.'

Who would he go out with on Saturday night? Being on your own was hellish. He didn't want Alec to go on the bus run. Alec was supposed to be his pal – okay, so he'd ditched him when he was winching Elsa but that was different, you expected your pals to ditch you when they had a steady woman. He could always go to the YMCA and see if there were any guys he knew in the snooker room. Yeah, a right lot of bigtime bastards they were. Why didn't he have more pals? He looked down at Alec as he wound the gramophone. The playing-arm was held in place by one rusty screw and the mainspring was broken. Alec had bought it for five bob in a junk shop. When he played a record he had to keep the arm in place with his left hand, fingers pressing down on its base, and keep winding it with the right hand. Alec had soft hair without a proper parting. It was a nondescript brown colour, combed straight back. He never used Brylcreem or water. He had clean, *office* hands. When he was with Alec he felt hard and grown-up – was that why he liked him as a pal? In the snooker room he always felt young and shy compared to the bigtime characters who went there on Saturday nights. Tomorrow he'd walk into the stable in the morning and be faced with Telfer! Everything was lousy.

Alec went through his own records – Glenn Miller, Woody Herman's 'Hail Caledonia' ('What makes your big head so HARD?'), Tennessee Ernie's 'Shotgun Boogie', Spike Jones and the City Slickers ('Leave the dishes in the sink, Ma'), Jimmy Shand's 'The Laird of Cockpen'. It was still light outside. Through the gauze over the bottom half of the window he could see wooden palings, green clothes' poles, the tops of concrete coal bunkers, high stakes for Alec's father's sweet peas, a garden hut. Jumbled, that's what it looked like. Small gardens, tidy lawns – cramped and jumbled. Compared to the farm it was all too small – unnatural, somehow. The only time you'd feel you weren't being watched from the windows of the houses opposite was in the dark. Meiklepark was one of the older schemes. Instead of big blocks it had grey roughcast houses, two families upstairs and two on the ground floor. Paths were gravelled and front doorsteps were always newly step-stoned. They even had greenhouses!

'D'you want to hear my old man's records?' Alec asked.

'Yeah, sure.'

They were in a black box with a hinged lid. Thick old records marked with grey scratches, edges chipped with little half-moon shapes . . . Count John MacCormack singing 'The Kerry Dancing', Harry Gordon's monologue about the sweetshop, accordions playing 'The Blackthorn Stick Quadrille', 'The Punishment fit the Crime' from *The Mikado*, an orchestral selection from *The Maid of the Mountains*. Alec had a little tin box of steel needles, his clean office fingers fiddling with the tiny screw as he changed the needles after every six records.

Dunky felt daft, sitting there in the gloomy bedroom listening to the scratchy old nonsense, thinking about the terrible things that were happening to him, watching Alec on his knees beside the mawkit old gramophone, wondering what the hell was going to happen to him.

'You're dead cheery I must say,' said Alec, stretching over the gramophone to put records back in the black box. 'It's all this love rubbish. You're lucky you're finished with that Elsa piece. I'm going to have nothing to do with wimmin till I've seen some real life. Know what I'd like to do?'

'What?' Dunky asked, knowing he'd heard all this a thousand times.

'Join the merchant navy and see the world.'

'You could get a job on the McBrayne boats.'

'Ha ha very funny I don't think. I mean the real navy, bigtime, bags of spending money, big nights out in foreign ports, what a life, eh?'

'Big nights out in Rothesay you mean. Nobody ever does the things they say they'll do.'

Elsa was the only person in his whole life he'd really *talked* to. Imagine that, a dirty little traitor knowing all your secrets! She'd tell Telfer all the daft things he'd said! It made him sweat, just to think about that. Telfer was a big gallus smart-aleck rat, he'd tell everybody else. They'd all laugh at him.

'Will we go to the Eldorado tomorrow night?' he asked Alec when they went round the back of the house to his bike. He was actually nervous in case Alec said no!

'I've got my evening classes,' Alec said. 'I'll be out by nine o'clock but.'

'See you at the Cross then, about nine?'

'Okay. Pity you can't come on the bus outing.'

'Ta ta.'

Why the hell couldn't they have had their bus outing after the football season was finished? The YMCA league finished in June but the Juveniles went on into July. Another two weeks and he'd have been able to go with them. Football was great but once the game was over you still had the rest of Saturday to get through. And on Sunday he was going to see the old man in Killearn!

He cycled through the town, looking for people he might know, pedalling slowly in case he might see Elsa – or somebody. At Shuttle Place he locked the bike in the wash-house. He didn't feel like bothering with the rabbits again. They were just a stupid hobby. People would be laughing and saying, 'Look at that geek, he's unsuccessful with wimmin, all he's got is his stupid rabbits.' He even talked to them!

When he got into the lobby, a key now kept for him on the end of a string which hung through the letterbox, his mother came out of the bedroom in her cotton nightdress, her hair in curlers, her face white and smeary with cream.

'You should've been here,' she said, 'there was a man looking for you about the football, I didn't know where you were.'

'I was at Alec's house. What did he want?'

'It was Mr Overend, at least that's what he said. You've to go to his house tomorrow night, it's important.'

'Didn't he say what it was about?'

Trust her to let Overend go away without even asking.

'Just that it's to do with Saturday. You shouldn't have been out so late, he waited till ten o'clock. I had to sit with him in the kitchen, I didn't know what to say to him.'

'Oh all right. Night night.'

In bed he wondered what it could be. Maybe the game was off. Maybe he was dropped. He was just a failure. God was punishing him for everything he'd done. God knew every single thing that happened. Maybe Jesus would forgive him if he prayed for forgiveness . . . *Dear Jesus I didn't really mean it when I said God didn't exist it was just talk I'm sorry. As I lie down to sleep tonight I pray the Lord my soul to keep. If I should die before I wake I pray the Lord my soul to take, I'm sorry I don't pray every night, Jesus, I do believe in you, honest, it was just smart-aleck talk, you understand, please help me to be happy and I'll never let you down again make Elsa love me, I'm sorry I don't know any real prayers I'm so lonely and miserable, if you'd just make Elsa give me another chance I promise I'll never do it to myself again and I'll never swear again and I'll love my mummy and daddy and I'll go to church on Sundays and say my prayers, please Jesus help me I'm sorry, really I am . . .*

'Ah come on, what's wrong with you?'

'Nothin's wrong with me, I just don't believe in doing that. You think I'm one of your fast pieces, don't you, a right doxy? Well I'm not.'

'Ah come on, what's the harm in it?'

Telfer and Elsa Noble were in the bottom field at the back of the factory, hidden from the back road behind a cole of hay, sitting on his jacket with their backs against the hay. It had been hard enough getting her to come for the walk and even harder coaxing her into the field, but he'd thought once she'd agreed to that she'd be game for anything.

'What's the *harm* in it? You think I came up the Clyde on a bicycle or something? You're just like all the others, Donald Telfer, you're just out for what you can get.'

The trouble was he really fancied her like mad. Since he'd been going out with her the most he'd managed was the hand in her blouse yet here he was, after more than a month, still steamed up if not foaming at the mouth. It wasn't like him – to let a stupid wee virgin keep him on the hook. Christ, he'd banged some really class dames after one night at the pictures!

'Well what are you going out with me for then?' he asked, pulling a length of hay from the cole and chewing it between his front teeth, chin sunk on the cheot. He could see her knees and about an inch of thigh. Young and firm and smooth. That was part of the trouble, she *was* young and he wanted her more than he'd ever wanted any of the others. There was a big difference with a young thing like Elsa, she wasn't only attractive on the surface, he knew she'd be sweet and juicy under her clothes. With older pieces you got steamed up looking at them dressed and then, when it was all over, you noticed they were a bit flabby or had a touch of varicose veins or smelled or some bloody thing.

'Oh you're all right to go out with,' she said, 'but if you think I'm the kind that'll let you go too far you've got another think coming.'

'Too far! Jesus Christ, you're like an iceberg.'

'Why d'you want to go out with me then?'

'Because I want to, that's all.'

'Aye but it's no' me you want, it's what you can get. I don't believe in that.'

'What d'you believe in then, if you don't mind me asking?'

She'd told him she'd been fed up because Dunky Logan had got too serious and they'd never had any fun. He'd thought the way to get round her was to keep her laughing. Make jokes all the time. That was fine while it lasted, she was good enough company which you couldn't say for a lot of women, not like Big Agnes, for instance, *her* brains were all in her knickers. But now he was serious, he wanted a bit.

'I believe in lots of things,' she said. She seemed quite cheery about it all. 'You wouldn't understand.'

'Oh no? I suppose I'm just a big thick tractor-driver, eh?'

'Don't kid us on, you think you're real smart, don't you? Can I test your brains?'

She rapped his head with her knuckles.

'Ow.' He put up his arms as a shield. She dug her fingers into his ribs, pinching and poking, raising herself onto her knees, tickling him and chapping on his head. He rolled about trying to dodge her hands. Then she stood up.

'Christ, you're *vicious*,' he complained, looking up at her.

She smiled.

'Only dirty old men look up girls' skirts,' she said. 'Come on, I've got to go home.'

He sat up and pulled hay off his neck.

'What's your hurry? The night's young yet.'

'Come on,' she said, buttoning her pink, three-quarter length coat. He took as long about getting to his feet as he could, hoping she might change her mind. Once again she'd got him steaming and once again she'd made up *her* mind to push off. She had a bloody nerve. Maybe he'd just grab her and—

'Crivvens, there's a man watching us,' she said.

His first thought was that it would be McPhail. The dirty wee bastard, spying on *him*. But when he got up and looked round the side of the cole he saw that it was Willie, standing by the gate, the bike at his side. He'd seen them all right, Willie had eyes like a hawk, nothing could move within five miles of the farm but Willie spotted it.

'It's Willie Craig,' he said. 'Give him a wave.'

'I will not. You said there wouldn't be anybody about down here.'

'Willie doesn't matter. We might as well go and talk to him, he'll wait all night if we don't.'

They walked across the field.

'I hope my father doesnae get to know I was here,' she said.

As they approached the gate she wished there was some way she could prove nothing had happened. From a distance Willie Craig had looked very stern, staring at them from under his cap, but close up she saw that he was grinning.

'On overtime then, Telfer?' he said. She sneaked a look at Donald. He was trying to hide the fact that he was blushing!

'Nice night for a wee walk,' he replied. 'How come you're no' at home, the wife drives you out, does she?'

When Willie looked at her he had very big, round eyes. They made her want to laugh. Donald would never live it down, being caught with her in the field. He opened the gate and they stood on the grass verge.

Telfer knew that anything he said would come out first thing in the morning. Young Logan wouldn't like it.

'Looks like being a clear day the morn's morn,' he said, looking up at the sky.

'Red at night's a shepherd's delight,' said Willie, big eyes peering at her as though he was about to jump in the air and scream. She knew what he was thinking, yet for some reason she didn't really care. It was a funny sort of feeling, to be with grown men who joked with each other. Her father made her feel like a wee schoolgirl, yet here she was a real grown-up, old enough to suit herself whether she went into a hayfield with a man.

'Willie's wife's expecting,' Donald said. She nodded. Willie nodded.

'Aye, she's like a prostitute in an institute wi' a belly like a parachute,' he said. 'I hope ye werenae smokin' in among they coles, Telfer, there's enough fires a'ready aboot this place.'

'Do I look that daft?'

'He's a very heavy smoker,' Willie said to Elsa, nodding, as though telling her a big secret. 'He smokes like a wee lum.'

'I know,' she said.

'There's no smoke without fire,' Willie said, winking. She knew he was getting at something else. She looked at Donald.

'Willie's father doesnae let him smoke yet,' Telfer said to her, making a sly face. 'Isn't that right, Willie?'

'Craig says if we'd been meant tae smoke we'd huv chimneys in our heads.' Willie gave her his daft stare again. 'It's good money puffed away up the sky.'

'You must get some pleasure out of life.'

'He's a pleasure fanatic, Donal' Telfer, that's what he is. Pictures and smokin' an' what else, eh?'

'It wouldnae do if we were all like you Craigs – he thinks a wee run round on his bike's a great event, don't you, Willie?'

They were both talking to her. She liked it. She knew a lot about Willie Craig from Dunky and Donald. She suspected from things they'd both hinted at that Donald had fancied the farm housekeeper before she got married to Willie Craig. She liked the idea of that, it must make you important, more than just a wee girl, to be going out with a bloke who'd fancied a grown woman. Donald had had lots of girlfriends, she'd have known that anyway, he was so *experienced* when he tried to do things to you.

'Tell the missus I was asking after her,' Telfer said as they began to move away. 'Tell her she wants to keep you in the house at night, dirty old man knee-padding down the back fields.'

'I'll tell her all right,' said Willie, getting on his bike. 'I'll tell her what she's missin'.'

'He's halfways round the bend,' Telfer told her as they walked up the back road.

'He'll tell people he saw us but,' she said.

'There's nothing to tell, more's the pity.'

'Hard cheese. You'd better get yourself another girlfriend who doesn't mind what you do to her.'

It was still quite light when they reached the corner of Barski-

ven Road. He decided to walk her to her gate, the hell with Noble
the Wife-beater, he might be a big man when it came to bashing
his wife but he'd take him on any day.

'When'll I see you again?'

'I didn't think you'd be bothered.'

'Don't talk daft. Wednesday night, eh, we could go to the
pictures?'

'Does that mean you still fancy me a wee bit?'

'Don't ask silly questions. If I didn't I wouldn't ask you, would
I?'

'How do I know?'

'Oh, you want me to tell you a lot of guff, like "I love you, my
darling" and all that?'

'Suit yourself.'

'You're very sure of yourself, aren't you?'

'Just careful. I've got to go in now.'

'I'll see you on Wednesday at the Cross, seven o'clock?'

'Okay, I'll tell my Dad I'm going out with Betty. You'd better
wipe the grass off your back, folk might think *you've* been lying in
a field.'

She went up the path. He looked at her kitchen window but
there was no light on and he couldn't see if Noble was watching.

When he got home Mrs Sneddon and her Bertha and his
mother were all at the entrance to the close, with Mrs Docherty
leaning out of her front-room window.

'Oh hallo, Donald,' said Mrs Sneddon, 'isn't it a right pity aboot
Eileen Graham's wee baby, did ye no' hear whut happened tae it, oh,
you tell him, Mrs Telfer, Ah'm fair wobbly jist thinkin' aboot it.'

'What happened?' he asked, thinking to himself that they were a
right load of old tea-wives, standing there with the latest gossip
and scandal, just dying to tell anybody who came along.

'A cat got in the pram and suffocated the baby,' his mother
said. 'She was only up in the house for a wee while and when she
went to get the baby in for its tea it was dead.'

'Christ. She should've had a net on the pram.'

'Aye, that's jist whut Ah tellt her,' said Mrs Docherty, voice
loud enough to let the whole of Darroch scheme know her views.

'It's they cats, they're a right scunner,' said Mrs Sneddon.
'Somewan should destroy them, so'n they should.'

'Come on up the house,' he said to his mother. The other three
women went on discussing the baby's death. Halfway up the stairs
he told his mother she ought to think more of herself than stand at
the close-mouth with a lot of old bauchles.

'It helps to pass the time,' she said.

When they went into the living room his brother Davie was sitting at the table, writing his Boys' Brigade reports, wearing his spectacles. He was going to get married and out of it, the sight of Davie in his spectacles had made up his mind. When a bint had class enough to hold out on you like Elsa you knew you were meant to marry her. Willie had been impressed with her, that made a lot of difference. If she'd been just another hairy Willie would jeer at him for even thinking of marrying her. He'd do it, too. Better than wakening up one morning and find you'd nothing better to do than put on spectacles and write reports.

There were times now when he'd suddenly look up and see the walls of the bedroom or the kitchen and he'd be unsure what year it was, then or now, or whether he'd been dreaming. It was important to keep a grip on your wits, all about you were the scavengers and the rascals and the smooth lads, smiling to your face and ready to rook you to the last bawbee.

He found himself looking at the woman. He must have drowsed off. She was well kindled now, her belly sticking out like a cow with milk fever. Willie's wife. But no' Willie's bairn inside her, she might have kidded Willie on but she couldn't fool him, a man of Willie's age didn't take in a woman's belly the first time he mounted her.

'An' ye say that's Willie's bairn ye're carrying?' he said.

He spoke so seldom your ears weren't used to picking up his gruff old voice, and he usually spoke so fast you couldn't make out what he was saying. She put her knitting in her lap, fingers pressing on the half-finished stitch.

'What's that?'

'Willie's never the faither,' he said. 'It was too damnt quick.'

'Sure'n that's a nasty sort of thing to be saying.'

'Hrrmmph.'

'Would you like a wee cup of tea if I get you one?'

Oh aye, they could be gey smarmy when they wanted to butter you up. He knew what she was after, dam' right he did.

'No. I'm no' wanting tea.'

'What makes you say awful things like that?'

She'd found the best way to deal with Craig was to speak to him the way you would a wild wee boy. He detested the idea of her being married to Willie, but his brain was going, half the time he couldn't remember what he'd started saying. As long as she kept humouring the old devil he'd go to his grave without giving them any bother – provided he could remember to go to his own funeral.

Why bother wasting breath on her? He could hear his father speaking to him in the byre in Aberdeenshire, the time he'd taken his breeks down and given him laldy with his walking stick on the bum for fathering a bairn on the dairy-maid from the laird's farm: 'If he hiv tae mount a damnt servint ye'll tak' guid care na tae gie her yer bastarts.'

His backside had been black with bruises for a month but he'd learned his lesson. He should've taken a stick to Willie and driven the idea of marrying an Irish tink out of his head. You were never too old to learn a lesson from your father.

'Ye can tell Willie what ye want but ye're no deceivin' me,' he said. 'Who's the faither?'

She shook her head. His jacket hung in folds from his shoulders. He was shrinking away every day.

'You should know better than to say things like that at your age,' she said. 'You've a dirty tongue on you, Craig.'

'It wasnae always like this,' he said. She didn't understand him. Was he trying to say sorry?

His father met the laird's factor at the door of the house and he'd sat in the kitchen, eating his brose, with his mother, while the two men went out into the yard. His father came back into the house and told him to go out into the byre and wait for him. He was listening in the wee porch when his father was saying to his mother: 'He's given wan o' the maids at the big hoose a bastart. Ah've tellt the factor Ah'll hanle him.'

'Ye're no' tae tak' the stick to him, he's a grown loon o' siventeen.' His mother aye stuck up for him.

'Ah dinna care if he's forty-siven, he'll learn better'n get queans in trouble.'

Put your hands on the kist and bend down. He never cried once. Twenty times, the walking stick across his bare backside, just the noise of his father's breathing and the swish of the stick and the whack and the grunts of pain in his own throat.

'I learnt my lesson,' he said. Mary O'Donnell made a face to herself and went across to put on the kettle. The old man was havering now, in his dotage. It must have come on him very quick. There was one thing Willie had to do, see Farquharson the lawyer about the will. The old devil might try and change it, put them out of it altogether. She'd *make* Willie see Farquharson, whether he wanted to or not. Willie was weak, through and through. He didn't even know how much money there was, imagine that, a grown man treated like a baby. He was lucky he had married her, left on his own he'd have been hopeless. Craig dragged his boots across the hearth and went to the stairs, grunting heavily.

'Night night,' she said after him.

'Hrrmmph.'

He went upstairs to where she couldn't follow. Jessie wasn't there, no, she'd been gone a long time. He still talked to her at times. He puffed and wheezed as he unlaced his boots, a terrible business getting old. You remember when we first came here, not a house for miles, they said father was daft buying a wasted old place like this, three fields near enough bogs and the land all sour. By Jove we worked to make this place right, worked, my father and my mother and then you and me, just one orra loon to help, folk laughing at us and saying we were soft in the head, it was like a ruin, land's too low they said, soil's gone bad. They'd never seen folk working like us, not about here, not round about the town. It wasn't so much of a town in those days, was it, a horse-bus once a day to Ayr. Two farms where they built that Darroch scheme. Remember on market days we'd put on our Sunday best and walk the beasts down the hill to the old mert, right up the High Street? The great war was a help, oh aye, they all like the farmers when there's one of their wars on, nothing's too good for you then, soon as it's over you can rot, we don't need the farmers now, not enough money to buy decent clothes for wee George, they didn't care, not them in the towns, we were good enough for them in the war, they don't like the farmer because he knows how to work and he doesn't want dole money and charity, oh aye, but when that other war came, oh aye, we're great folks again, remember that, Labour in, subsidies for this and subsidies for that, George aye made jokes about the subsidies cheques, he said we got subsidies for ploughing land and sub-sidies for planting this and that, and all the time we'd have done it anyway, Labour had no idea, they didn't have the brains, why did George really want to get away to Africa, eh, can you tell me that, Jessie? Och I know what you say, I'm too hard on Willie, maybe I am, he was never much good at the school, you remember that, if I'd ever had half his chance of schooling nobody knows what I might have been today, I never wanted to work on a farm, there was nothing else for me, my father had me out of school when I was eleven, two horse of my own to work, remember how we tied our boots round our necks to save them from wearing out when we walked to the school, winter and summer, och your feet soon got used to it, they had to, travelling five miles there and five back, now they've got wirelesses and gramophones and fancy clothes and picture houses, never been in a picture house in my life, nor to the dentist, remember the dances we had up north, just the fiddle and the squeezebox, my they were *real* dances, Jessie. That was how I got the laird's maid in trouble, after a dance, walked her home from Mains of Dalgety, eleven mile, and mounted her at the end of it, just the one serving and she took. It could never be Willie's bairn that woman's carrying. Willie wouldn't take in one go, it's some damnt tink's bastart she's carrying. No, Jessie, I'm no' being ower hard on the boy, I'm jist damnt if some tink's bastart is going to get the money we worked for all these years. I'll see Farquharson first thing the morn's morn, he'll tell me how to do it. It'll do Willie the world of good, he can't depend on his father all his life. No, I winna be too hard on him, it's for his own good. She's only a common Irish tink, Jessie, she doesn't deserve anything from us. I'll see Farquharson in the morning . . .

Willie tried to tell Archie Stewart what he thought about Telfer, but Archie was in a funny sort of mood, as though he wanted to disagree on principle.

'You can't go round calling people rubbish, Willie,' he said. 'We're all human beings, it's just a lucky dip that some have land and money and some haven't. The rank is but the guinea stamp – remember? Poor old Rabbie, the same folk that hounded him all his life are now the very ones that get up Burns' suppers in his honour. Can you imagine what would happen, Willie, if Rabbie came to live near some of they masons and whatnot that make such a song and dance about him? They'd go off their heads. We Scots are that warped we can only admire our great men when they're safely dead and buried.'

He didn't stay long in the Tink's house in the Black Hills. He felt annoyed. There was something wrong with the fact that a scheme tyke like Telfer should be having all the women he wanted and he was stuck with a wife who was too pregnant to let him on her. He'd thought he'd got the better of Telfer by marrying her – now he didn't even have her *or* Morag Coll, while Telfer went on regardless. The hell with her, he'd get it the night whether she liked it or not. It wasn't a good feeling, to know another man was doing better than you.

Mary was still in the kitchen when he got back to the steading. At first he thought she was just having another moaning session about the old man and he didn't pay much attention, but she kept on and on at him.

'You'll have to see Farquharson,' she said, 'the old devil hates me for some reason, are you going to let him say things like that to me in my own house?'

'It's his house,' he growled. 'Come on tae bed.'

'I'm telling you, he's old enough and dottled enough to do the dirty on us just out of spite. He could make a will and leave you out altogether, d'you know that?'

'Ach don't talk daft. Come on tae bed, I'm feelin' like ye know what.'

'You know you can't, will you—'

'I know nothin' o' the sort. There's nothin' stoppin' ye, it doesnae dae any harm tae the baby.'

'Will you listen to me? You've a duty to me and your child.'

'AN' YOU'VE A DUTY TO ME!'

So violent was the anger that flooded his head he hit her before he knew what he was doing, the back of his hand smacking her on the ear. She stood her ground, glaring at him.

'You're scared of him, aren't you, scared of him? You're not a real man—'

He hit her again, a real thump. Tears came into her eyes but still she was in at him.

'Go on, hit me, does it make you feel big? Go on.'

As he went for her he could hear shouting in his brain about his father and Telfer and her all laughing at him, all taking him for a mug. She cowered her head, scrabbling round the table to escape. She found a china-handled knife near her hand and lifted it to him. He punched her arm and grabbed her wrist and held it between his big hard fingers until she thought it was breaking. The knife fell on the floor. He grabbed her by the hair and forced her towards the bedroom, thwacking her ear, her scalp in agony.

'Get your clothes off an' get intae bed, go on, hurry up, I'll kill ye if ye don't.'

She was still crying when he came on top of her, the weight of him pushing down on the baby, his fingers digging into her shoulders. When he finished she lay with her eyes closed, moaning and sobbing.

'Shut your whinin',' he said, lying on his back beside her. He felt sorry for having lost his temper. She shouldn't have gone on at him like that. It was her fault. But he shouldn't have battered her. 'Come on,' he said, 'it'll no' do the bairn any harm.'

She said nothing.

'Ach, come on, I'm sorry. I'll go and see Farquharson the morn's morn if it'll make ye happy.'

He thought he could get round her that easily. He'd bruised her whole body, her head was ringing with his blows, he'd just about torn her hair out by the roots – and he thought it was that easy, just say sorry and make a few promises? She was just a useless cripple woman, something he could thrash like a dog. She'd show him! And his father! She'd show them both.

After he'd got up and put on his pyjamas he tried to get her to say something, but she lay so still and quiet he began to think he might have done her an injury. It worried him so much he couldn't sleep. He kept saying he was sorry but she wouldn't answer. He began to feel panicky, if he'd hurt the baby he'd never live it down. At last she decided to speak to him.

'Will you promise me you'll see Farquharson?'

'I tellt ye I would.'

'Then you'll have it out with your father once and for all, you'll *make* him leave all the money to us?'

'Aye, I will, I promise.'

'You swear you will?'

'Don't be daft, I said I would.'

'All right then.'

'Ye don't think I—'

'I don't know. We'll just have to wait and see, won't we?'

'I'm sorry.'

'All right, you're sorry. It's time you faced up to the fact you've got a wife and a baby on the way. You're a man, act like one, your father's kept you down all your life.'

'Aye, I know.'

'All right then. Don't lean on me so hard, I'm sore all over.'

TWELVE

TELFER CAME INTO the stable while Dunky was watering the
horse. He'd felt scared before but never like this. His hands
shook. His chin quivered. His breath seemed to go down only as
far as his throat. His heart thumped. Blackie was feeding Big
Dick, McPhail was at the stable door, Rafferty hadn't arrived.

He came out of the stall, the empty bucket in his hand. This
was it. Telfer looked about seven feet tall. Run at him and sink the
boot in his balls. Bang the bucket into his skull. Get your hands
round his throat and choke him to death.

'Hullo, Dunky,' said Telfer.

He could *feel* himself killing the big blond bastard yet—

Admit it, you're scared to death.

'Don't talk tae me,' he said, pushing past Telfer to the cornkist.

'Oh don't say we're goin' to get all that again?' said Telfer.
'You're getting as bad as Blackie. What's the matter with you, for
Christ's sake?'

'Ye know bloody well what's the matter.'

He hung the bucket up on the nail. You could call it self-
control or common sense or whatever you liked. You were a
coward and you knew it.

'Look, I'm sick of all this,' Telfer said. Dunky tried to push past
him, but Telfer grabbed his upper arm. He tried to pull himself
free but Telfer's hand was like iron. Grinning at him, big and
strong, too big and too strong. 'Tell us what's eating you or I'll
dump you in the horse trough.'

'Leggoa me! I'm no' frightent o' you, Telfer.'

Telfer had white teeth. He was still smiling, but there was a sign
of bad temper in his eyes. Close to he could feel the size and the
strength of him. He tried to wrestle clear. Telfer held on, easily.

'Look, kid, nobody buggers me about. If you've got something
on your mind get out with it. Come on, I'm no' jokin' about the
trough.'

He spat in Telfer's face.

'*I* was goin' out wi' Elsa Noble, yah rat!'

He half-closed his eyes, waiting for the first blow.

Telfer looked at him sideways on, his eyes half-closed, his face beginning to open into a wide smile. Then he shoved him away.

'So that's it. I stole your woman, eh? Christ Almighty, act your age. *I stole your woman?*'

Blackie and McPhail were watching. He stood back, hands clenched. Telfer was just laughing while he made up his mind what to do to him. All right, so he'd get a battering but he'd fight till he dropped.

Telfer shook his head, pityingly. The boy looked wild enough for anything. Poor young cunt, he didn't know what it was all about.

'I met her in the street and asked her if she'd go to the pictures with me,' he said. 'I didn't even know you were winchin' her. Then she told me you used to go out with her but you'd chucked it in. That's all there is to it.'

It didn't sound so bad, put that way.

Dunky wanted to scream at him. Dirty big rat, he'd do the dirty on her and then leave her. He'd loved her, Telfer was just out for another ride. *His* Elsa.

But he knew how that would sound.

'Pinched your woman, did he?' McCann said, winking at Telfer behind Dunky's back. 'Ah'd slaughter any bastart that pinched *ma* woman.'

'You keep out of it,' Dunky snapped. McCann shook his head and picked up the brush.

'All's fair in love an' war,' he said, 'that's whut they say.'

Dunky stood, fists clenched, waiting for one of the men to come at him. Telfer looked amused, McCann went on brushing. They thought he was too young to bother with. He wanted to scream at them. He felt stupid. He wanted to run away.

They yoked Big Dick into the hay trolley and he took the mare to the stackyard. Now they'd all be laughing at him. Cowardy cowardy Logan, all wind and water, big mouth and no guts. When McPhail tried to speak to him in a friendly sort of way he walked away. He didn't need to be friends with a dirty knee-padder. Or with anyone else.

By the time the hooter went at half-past nine he thought he could hear them talking behind his back. Every time he looked up at the two men on the stack they seemed to be wiping smiles off their faces. He took his piece and his vacuum flask and sat on the half-lifted cole, his back to the others. One day he'd get his revenge. He could hear what they were saying all right, behind his back, pretending to talk about Daftie Coll and his new job on a farm at Kilberrie, winking and grinning at each other about him, whispering about him.

He worked with his teeth clenched, ramming the hay fork into the cole, nodding sullenly at Rafferty to take the horse forward, pulling the trip-rope as hard as he could, hoping it would hit Willie or McPhail, not even looking at Telfer and McCann when they brought in each new load.

'Come on, ya Papish bastard,' he shouted when Rafferty was slow in backing the horse.

The scheme boy stood still.

'Whadye call me?' he shouted back, his eyebrows lowered, his mouth open. The hard man's expression. So Rafferty wanted a fight?

'Ah called ye a Papish bastard, d'ye want tae make something of it?'

He could feel satisfaction come over him as he saw Rafferty leave the horse and come towards him. He waited. Fighting was easy – if you knew in advance you could beat the other guy.

'You don't call me that,' said Rafferty. Then he started running.

As they punched and kicked and kneed each other he kept thinking of something Willie had said: Townees think they're tough guys but they don't have the belly for it. They're fast enough lads till they get a fist in their guts.

Rafferty was slippery and vicious. They rolled in the hay. He tried to get his thumbs into Rafferty's eyes. Rafferty kept jabbing his knee up, biting as well. He grabbed Rafferty's ears and tried to pull Rafferty's face onto his forehead. Then he had him, knees across Rafferty's chest, hands pinning down his wrists. Rafferty jerked and wriggled. He lifted his left knee off the ground and rammed it into Rafferty's chest. If he could get Rafferty's wrists together in one hand he could smash his dirty face in for him.

Rafferty spat up into his face. He'd spat in Telfer's face. Telfer hadn't battered him. He was bigger than Rafferty. He didn't need to show off by hammering the wee rat.

He stood up quickly.

'Had enough?' he said.

Rafferty scrambled to his feet. They faced each other, panting, Rafferty's face swollen under the right eye.

'Shake?'

He put out his hand.

Rafferty tried to kick him. He jumped to avoid the shoe and then caught the boy in a bear-hug.

'Come on, chuck it in,' he said. 'I didn't mean to call you that.
If I say I'm sorry will ye chuck it in?'

'Don't call me names again.'

'Awright.'

Willie and McPhail had been watching over the edge of the stack.
They'd seen what he'd done. They would let everybody know. You
didn't have to prove you were a hard man. Hammering guys was
what animals did. He'd handled Rafferty the way Telfer had
handled him. That made him equals with Telfer. The next time
Willie made a joke he joined in the laughing. Telfer seemed quite
keen to be pals again. By dinnertime it was all forgotten.

At least they'd forgotten. Oh yeah, all big pals, now.

But he knew he was a coward, a *real* coward. Rafferty wasn't a
coward. He was a coward. When Telfer had got hold of him he'd
known he was a coward. Why else had he wanted to run home to
his mummy?

By Friday the hay was in and stacked and the canvas hap put
over the last stack. In the afternoon, with the sun quite warm and
only a few small, white clouds in the sky, the four of them, Willie,
Telfer, McCann and himself, went with two scythes to open roads
round the corn in the field beside the road.

Willie and McCann worked the scythes, swinging from right to
left, the big, chipped blades cutting down thin swathes of the
shorter, not-quite-ripe stalks growing beside the ditch at the side
of the field. He and Telfer came behind, bending to gather up the
stalks until they had enough in an armful to make a sheaf, tying it
in the middle with a twist of longer stalks.

'Lot of thistles this year,' said Telfer, shaking his head.

'Hey, Willie, are we supposed to be working tomorrow afternoon?' he asked. 'I'm playing for Cartneuk first team, it'll be
awright, will it?'

'You're a football fanatic, Logan,' said Willie in his BBC voice.
'You've got football on the brain.'

'Aye, but can I get off to play if we're workin'?'

'Seen as how ye're no' everybody.'

'What's the game?' asked Telfer.

'It's the final of the East Ayrshire Cup,' he said. 'I've got to play
because two of the first team are too old, they're ineligible.'

'Good for you,' said Telfer.

Were they all really friends? Even McCann? It seemed like it as
they worked their way round the first field, just the four of them,
Willie and McCann scything, him and Telfer gathering, joking
away to each and telling daft stories.

He wanted to be friends with them. Why was it that things always happened to muck you up?

When they'd scythed roads in the five fields of corn and wheat it was time to get the binder out and start cutting. Telfer drove the tractor with Willie on the binder seat, his hand on the lever that raised the mowing arm when they turned round on the corners, his eyes on the teeth that whipped twine round the sheaves, on the lookout for a break in the string. Corn fell forwards over the mower teeth on to an endless canvas belt that carried it to the middle of the binder. It was carried up one side of the triangle-shaped machinery and down the other, tied sheaves dropping out every yard or so.

It took a while to get into the way of stooking again. Dunky remembered how stiff he'd been the summer before. The weather forecast said it would be fine for most of August, not that you could rely on the forecast, but if it was they wouldn't have to rush the whole harvest through in a panic in case it rained. The year before had been wet and when there was a couple of fine days Craig had them working in the fields till it was dark.

Stooking was a plodding job. You picked up a sheaf by grabbing the corn just above the string round its middle. The sheaf didn't weigh much. You walked forward to the next one and picked it up with your right hand. One of you would start the stook by propping the heads of two sheaves together, like a Red Indian wigwam, short stalks on the inside so that it would stand in the wind. You bunged your two sheaves down in line with the first two, the ears at the top of each sheaf pushed together, the base close to the first two. When there were five pairs of sheaves leaning against each other the stook was finished. You walked on and picked up more sheaves and began another stook. The new stubble cracked under your boots. In some places there was thick green grass and clover shoving up among the stubble, in others, where it was drier, you walked on earth. Sometimes you came on a sheaf the binder had dropped without twine, then you had to take a handful of stalks and knot them round the sheaf, a job that needed a strong hand.

McCann and McPhail and Rafferty and himself stooked until Telfer and Willie had cut the whole field. Then they'd join in till all the sheaves were up, you didn't want to cut another field ahead of the stookers in case it turned to rain and sheaves went rotten lying on their sides. Corn was easier than wheat, it was soft and you could stook with your bare arms, even stripped to the waist, the sweat running off your brow, the sun on your back. They started about eight, having to walk or bike to the field. They had their break at half-nine, then the dew had gone and Willie and Telfer could start cutting again. He biked home for his dinner at half-twelve and was back again by half-one, his afternoon piece in the gas-mask case. It was harder bending down after dinner, with your belly full and your eyes wanting to go to sleep. By afternoon break you were starving again. They'd sit against a stook and grunt with stiffness as they ate their pieces. Then it would be up again, going round and round the field, never-ending rows of lying sheaves, your back so sore you couldn't think of anything but the next sheaf, the tips of your fingers beginning to smart from the hard straws. Around five o'clock Craig would come down to the field – God knew where he spent the rest of his time – and have a look at the sky and a look at his boots and a squint at his workers and then tell Willie whether you were doing overtime or not. If you were you went on at it till eight or nine o'clock, still going round the field, the six of you bending and picking up, banging sheaves together, walking forward, bending and picking up, another stook finished, another to start, each man with a different style of working, some always doing a wee bit more than others, Willie liking to place the first two sheaves, keeping his hands buried in the ears of corn till the next two were placed at their side, making sure the stook was steady, eye on the sky when there was a moment to look up, would it rain by morning, were they well ahead, had they fallen behind?

On the second morning you were so stiff you swore you wouldn't be able to bend to lift a sheaf to save your life. Your back was raw with sunburn. You felt giddy and sick and ruptured but nobody told you to have a rest, you started with the others and panted with the stiffness in your back and your shoulders and your legs and soon you didn't notice the stiffness any more.

People came up the road to watch the harvest, it always attracted them, women with prams, men on the panel, men on the burroo. That made it more enjoyable, somehow, as though you had an audience. By the second day you were used to it again.

'One time me and Coll and the man we had then, McAndrew, were stooking on the field where the factory office is now,' Willie told them at morning break on the second day. 'There wus two wifeys lived in a house across the road, it's demolisht now. Everytime ye lookt up ye could see the two o' them peerin' at ye through the curtains. McAndrew says, "I'll gie ye somethin' tae luk at, ye auld hoors," and he whips his breeks down and

bends over and points his arse at them, the three of us did it, great
muckle arses winkin at them, I'll bet they got the fright o' their
lives.'

'D'ye want to hear a good joke?' said McCann. 'Well, there's
this wee girl and this wee boy coming home from school and she
says, "Hey John, I'm bleedin' in my knickers" and the boy says,
"Come ahint this hedge an' let's see" and he gets down and has a
look and then he says, "By jings, Mary, nae wonder ye're
bleedin', somebody's cut the knackers off ye."'

Then they were up on their feet, hands on their backs as they
stretched and groaned. He tried to remember a joke to tell at the
afternoon break. The great thing about this kind of work was
being able to think. About anything that came into your head. It
was something he'd never been able to do, think, not if it meant
sitting down and concentrating. Too impatient, he supposed.
Once his mother had taken him and Senga to Troon for a week in
the summer, Aunt Bessie had looked after his father. There was
nothing to read in their room, nothing at all, not even an old
newspaper lining one of the drawers, nothing, not even a piece of
paper and a pencil to see how many words he could make out of a
big word, like perambulate or metamorphosis. His mother and
Senga were in their big bed by nine o'clock and there he was,
stuck with nothing to read – the only time in his life he'd been in a
bed with a small light of his own above the headboard. He'd
decided he would have to *think*, something interesting. Huh, he
couldn't even think of anything to think about! Thinking like that
was dead boring. How could a person be interested in something
they thought up in their own heads? You needed something to do,
or something to read, your own life was boring because you knew
all about it already. Alec said he often liked to go for walks on his
own and think about the real meaning of things. He could never
tell you what it was he'd been thinking about, or what he'd
decided, maybe he knew but was too shy to tell somebody else.
People like them, all the people he knew in Kilcaddie, never
talked to each other about what they *really* thought. Football, the
pictures, gossip, the weather, he'd heard all they had to say.
Voices he'd been hearing all his life. All saying the same things
. . . I think it'll rain the day. Where ye workin' noo then? How
d'ya like ma new boots? Rangers is the greatest. Rangers is a lot of
gorillas. Rangers bribes the refs. Rangers doesnae need tae bribe
the refs. Celtic's a lot of Fenian bastards. Celtic's more fair-
mindet than Rangers, Celtic'll play a Proddestant, Rangers'll no'
even huv a Catholic on the turnstiles. Big Frank Brennan's miles

better'n Willie Woodburn. Don't talk soft, Woodburn's the greatest. Is it true what I hear aboot your Nellie, she's winchin' one of they Yanks? Our Bob's back's fair killin' him, so'n it is. Ma certes! The priest came to the McGrorys' and took away their last ten bob, an' no' a bit of bread in the house. That McCandless fella, drinks like a fish and his wife's got awfy bad asthma, so she has. Jings aye, oor Jeanie in America's got a car and a refrigerator, imagine that! They GI war brides should be ashamet o' thersels, so they should. Ma John says Churchill was only good in wars. Ma daddy's bigger'n your daddy, so there. How come Meiklepark gets more buses than Darroch, that's what I want to know. Oor Nessie's been on the housin' list for eight years and the factor says they've got no hope, is that no' scandalous? Oor minister takes a good drop, you can't deny it.

When you were young and didn't know any better, you asked people idiotic questions, like 'How does the wireless work, daddy?' or 'Is the king a good man, mammy?' or 'How can God listen to everybody praying at once, Miss?'

You grew up and learned not to talk daft. People laughed at you if you told them what you really thought, so you kept it in your own head. People laughed at you for almost everything. Like Uncle Charlie laughing at his diary, that time he found it under a cushion on the couch. Oh aye, big laugh, reading out all the things he made lists of . . . Books I have Read . . . Opera Seen ('*Carmen* and *La Bohème* at the Picture House, oh you're an opera hand, are you?') . . . Places I have Visited ('Listen to this, King George V Playing Fields, bus, twopence, to Porterfield Road, Ayr – my, you've travelled widely, Dunky') . . . Scottish Country Dance Bands Heard . . . Films I have Seen . . . International Teams . . . Modern Dance Bands Heard . . . Catches I have Made ('Oh, Bessie, listen to this, Species, sticklebacks, number, twenty-one, result, put into bowls, the ones in the glass bowl lived but the rest conked out, oh Dunky, you're a scream so you are') . . . Plays Heard . . . Neutral Matches I have Seen . . . Classmates . . . Pals . . . Film Star Favourites ('Who's this Broderick Crawford, Dunky, I've never heard of the man, you've got him down here as *excellent*, have you heard of him, Bessie?') . . . Dances I have Attended . . . Cafés Visited ('Oh Beth, your boy's a rerr terr so he is, listen to this, The Rainbow, Ayr, food no bad, service grim, dames rotten, oh Dunky, my sides'll burst from laughing') . . . and worst of all he could have *died*, when Uncle Charlie came to the last page where he kept a list of all the girls he'd dated or lumbered, with comments on them in French! And his mother wondered why he never went near Aunt Bessie or Uncle Charlie! How would anybody like to hear their uncle reading out what was written on the front of the book, 'This is the chronicle of the life of Duncan Aitchison Logan, plus some information appertaining to his interests'?

They made a song and dance about sending you to school and then they laughed their heads off because you learned words like appertaining! His mother should think of *that* next time she complained about him working at the farm. They *wanted* you to be as thick and dim as they were, so he'd show them he could win the Scottish Cup for ignorance. He'd grow up into a real moronic working-man and balls to them. What did Uncle Charlie know about anything, a bloody clerk, that's all he was.

At dinnertime he was surprised to see Willie Craig standing at the scheme bus stop, obviously heading up the town. Willie didn't see him pass on the bike and he didn't shout out. That was one of the things you learned on a farm, keep quiet and watch and learn wee things you weren't supposed to know. Keep it in your head, everything was safer if you kept it secret. Willie hardly ever went down into Kilcaddie, he couldn't tolerate the town. What would he be going now for, in the middle of a harvest day?

Farquharson the lawyer was more than surprised when Willie Craig came into his office above the bank in Fergus Street. Auld Craig had left only an hour or two before, wanting to change his will. He was just going to say 'My my, two Craigs in one morning' when he stopped himself. The old man wouldn't be wanting Willie to know he'd been in, especially if he knew what the old man had come to see him about.

'This is a bit off your usual track,' he said to Willie, noting that the man's only concession to the town was that he'd put on clean boots. He hoped too many folk hadn't seen him come into the office dressed like that, not even a collar or a tie.

Willie sat in front of Farquharson's desk, his cap in his hands, his knees splayed wide, holding on to his cap with both hands so that he wouldn't absent-mindedly start picking his nose, which Mary told him was one of his worst habits. He didn't like coming into the town and he didn't like being in the office, not with Farquharson looking like Lord Muck in his fancy clothes and the silly bits of girls giving him queer looks in the front office. Still, he was worth more than Farquharson and his fancy kind put together, or at least his father was.

'My father's gone a bit funny,' he said, not really knowing how to start, speaking carefully to let Farquharson know he might look a bit rough but he'd had as good an education as anybody. 'I'm thinking he's taken a scunner to the wife and eh, well, it's difficult like, but how do I stand? That's what I want to know. I mean, he's no' got all that long to go, what happens to me and the wife when he dies?'

Farquharson put the tips of his fingers together. This was a tricky one. He'd just been looking forward to his lunch in Semple's Tea Rooms, too.

'Haven't you spoken to him about it?'

They must have had some kind of row. Otherwise why would the old man come in at one moment, demanding to change his will so that his other son, George, the one in Rhodesia, got all the money and then Willie come in the next moment asking about the will?

'Och, you can't get through to him these days, he just humphs and jumphs and pretends he doesn't hear you. I'm worried he's thinking of doing something daft with his money, I mean, I've worked for him all these years, I should know what's what, shouldn't I? Has he *made* a will, for instance?'

'Aye well, Willie, it's not just as simple as that, you see, I'm actually his solicitor, not yours, d'you follow me? It puts me in a wee bit of an awkward situation, doesn't it? I wouldn't really be acting properly if I told anybody else a client's business, would I?'

'Aye but he's my father, I'm entitled to know.'

It was really a bit much, people like the Craigs with more money than they had the brains to know what to do with. Farmers were all the same, peculiar folk.

'I can tell you the law, that's easy enough,' he said. 'Your father's entitled to leave everything he has to anybody he likes. He could leave the farm and the land to *anybody*, it doesn't matter if they're family or not, you couldn't do anything about that. However, under the law you can claim a quarter of the residue of the estate, that means all moneys and stocks and shares. That's as his son. Of course, if you felt you were being treated unjustly you could bring an action to have the will altered, you might even try and show he was of unsound mind when he made it, or that you were entitled to a large share by reason of the years you worked for him. Mind you, that's just hypothetical, you under-stand.'

Try as he could Willie wasn't able to get anything but hums and havers out of Farquharson. He saw by the clock on the wall it was ten after one, time to be getting back for yoking again.

'Will you just tell me one thing?' he said, getting up. '*Is* there a will?'

'I think I can tell you that, yes, there is a will, and legal.'

'And you can't tell me what's in it?'

'No, I'm terribly sorry, you must see my position.'

'Aye. So if he's turned against me all I'll get is a quarter of what's in the bank, not the land?'

'*If* he's turned against you. Why don't you have a quiet word with him, Willie? I mean, he is your father, surely you can ask him outright? Old people can be a bit peculiar about wills, you know, one day they think one thing and one day the next.'

Willie felt like picking Farquharson up by his scrawny neck and choking it out of him.

'Aye, I'll ask him,' he said. 'Do I pay you for this talk?'

Farquharson smiled.

'Oh no, no charge for a friendly wee chat with an old friend. You're thinking of that story of the man who left his umbrella in a lawyer's office and when he went back inside for it the lawyer told him the second visit would be another six and eightpence. Ha ha, folk think the worst of lawyers, don't they?'

With good reason. He was glad to get back on the scheme bus and watch the town sail by. Farquharson was a real townee, shifty and devious. They were all the same, look at them, daft creatures in daft clothes fancying themselves as something important. Too much money and not enough work, that was their trouble. All he knew was that there was a will. He'd always expected the old man would leave the farm and the land to him and give George a half of the money, that was fair enough. Suppose he left the lot to George, what would George do? All these years in Rhodesia and not so much as a letter, just the usual wee scribble at Christmas. Not much of a brother even when he was here, either. His father's favourite, nothing was ever too good for George, George this and George that, no thanks to him for having stayed at home all these years, oh no.

'On ye go, McCann can sit on the binder,' he said to the men. He went into the house.

'Where is he?' he asked Mary.

'Out in the garden, I don't know what he's doing,' she said. 'What happened with Farquharson?'

'Ach him, he wouldnae tell me anything. I'm goin' tae have it out wi' him.'

She went through into their bedroom and stood behind the curtain, her hands clasped on her belly. She could see the old man jinking about in the long grass. He had three crab-apple trees out there, he was so mean he thought everybody was always trying to steal them.

Willie swung his leg over the low wire fence and walked between the trees towards his father.

'Settin' traps are ye?' he shouted.

The old man looked up, jerked his head in a sniffing sort of way and bent down again. Willie watched where he put his feet, the old bastard might easily have put down gin traps to catch wee boys.

'There's somethin' I want tae talk tae ye about,' he said.

'I'm busy.'

'Aye, busy wi' a lot of sour wee apples that's nae good tae anybody ye mean?' Craig was stringing wire between the trunks of the three trees, about a foot off the ground.

'This'll stop their thieving,' he said. 'They'll mibbe trip and break their ankles.'

Willie shook his head. It was a pity Craig hadn't kicked the bucket before his brains went. It wasn't very nice to see a strong man turned into an old dotard.

'I've been tae see Farquharson,' he said. 'He tells me ye've made a will, is that right?'

Craig's big claw hands fiddled with the wire. That woman had been putting Willie up to this.

'Is that all he tellt ye?' he said.

Willie remembered being in this garden with his father forty-odd year ago when he was about twelve. They'd caught a boy from the town stealing apples. His father had grabbed the boy's collar and told him to run and fetch the police. Get the polis for a pickle of crab-apples, even at that age he knew it wasn't right. The boy had squirmed and cried and then shouted out, in desperation, 'I've kieched in ma breeks.' He had, too. There had been a terrible guff off the boy. He'd pretended to be too frightened to go for the police and his father had let the boy go after giving him a good cuffing round the lugs. Then he'd got a few on his own ears for not doing what he was told.

'Aye, he says he's your lawyer, no' mine. I want to know what's in the will.'

'I've no doubt,' said the old man. 'She'll be putting you up to this, I suppose?'

'Never mind her, it's me that wants to know.'

'Aye, no doubt. Well, you'll just have to want, won't you?'

'I've a right to know.'

'Have you now?'

'Aye.'

'I wouldnae count on it.'

He'd made his own choice, he'd sided with her against his own father, now he could rot in hell for all he cared. He'd go back to Farquharson tomorrow morning and make him change the will. He should never have let the lawyer get away with his impudence, telling *him* to think it over for a few days!

'Are ye goin' tae tell me?'

He stood up, the wire at last knotted round the foot of the tree. Man, it was a rare day for the hearst. One year it rained that much the corn was flat and they'd lost it all. When was that now? He saw Willie standing beside him. What was he wanting?

'Ye should be yoked,' he said. 'It's by dinnertime.'

'I want to know about the will.'

'The will? My will ye mean? Is George been putting ye up to this? Aye well, ye can tell him he gets nothing, nothing at all. An' tell his mother, it's no use arguin', if he wants to be away let him go but he's no' gettin' any of it. Tell them that.'

'Ye're haverin',' Willie said. 'Come awa' in the house, ye need to rest.'

'Aye, I'm tiret right eneuch. It's a' this business wi' George.'

No, it was with Willie, not George. He tried to remember what had been happening. As Willie helped him into the house he saw the woman staring at him from the kitchen door. It was her that was the cause of it all. Damn the woman, Jessie should never have let her in the house.

'Damn ye,' he roared at her. Willie tried to hold his arm, but the old man got away. His fist was up, clenched, as he tried to run at her. Willie knew he was only waving it at her, he knew it then. He let Craig go on. He wasn't as daft as everybody thought. Let him go for her. They'd all know he was mad then. He thought his mother was still alive! Unsound mind, Farquharson had called it.

The old man slipped and half-fell, his legs scrabbling stiffly for support. His mouth hung open, but his breath came in urgent, rasping pants through his nose.

Willie watched. He felt nothing for his father. All his life he'd done what the old man had told him. Now Craig was flopping about like a hen in its death dance. To the end, just before he fell on his chest, Auld Craig kept staring at Mary, saliva slopping between his lips. Only when he was still did Willie move. Nobody but Mary would ever know how he'd stood back and watched his father thresh about.

'We'll need the doctor,' he said to Mary as he carried him, moaning and raving and muttering, up the stairs. 'Go over tae the phone box and get him down here.'

He waited by his father's bed till the doctor arrived and then he left him, the old man lying on his back, eyes closed, the doctor poking about with the stethoscope round his neck. Telfer stopped the tractor so that he could take McCann's place on the binder seat. It was a fine day for the hearst. Too good a day to waste sitting in the house. He'd know soon enough what the doctor said. No, he wouldn't have the old man put away in a home, there was no real harm in him. Poor old bugger, he'd just lived too long, that was his trouble. Well, maybe his time had come now so there was no point in thinking about any of it.

As they cut into the middle of the field a hare sprung from the small square of standing corn. The two dogs were after it in a flash. Telfer stopped the tractor. They chased it, waving and shouting, their caps in their hands. The hare darted up and down among the stooks, doubling back, the dogs barking like the clappers of hell. It was a big one. If it didn't see a way through the hedges it would run about in the stooks till its lungs burst. They always did.

'Keep it runnin',' he shouted.

Eventually it gave up and the boy Rafferty jumped on it, trapping it in his shirt which he'd pulled off as he ran. Not that it needed trapping, it was fair done.

He wrung its neck across his knee and carried it by the hind legs to the tractor, where he wrapped it in his jacket and laid it in the tool box.

'It's a buck, make a good bite or two,' he said to Telfer.

'Bags I the next one,' said Telfer.

'Fun's over you lot,' Willie shouted to the stookers.

It made a nice wee break in the monotony, he thought.

'Get tore into these Victoria people,' said Baldy. He patted each player on the shoulder as they passed him and clattered down the tunnel. 'Don't let us down,' he shouted after them.

Bigtime! Running out of a proper dressing-room and down a wee tunnel and out into the sunshine. A real football stadium – only a junior ground, of course, but it looked bigtime, with the wee wall round the pitch and the folk standing on the little terracing. The first-team strip was the same as Hearts, maroon shirts with white collars and white pants, black stockings with white bands. All sorts of people were watching, Baldy had said.

Scouts from big clubs. He'd told them how he'd been given this strip by Hearts when they took one of last year's first team on to the groundstaff. That was to make them feel bigtime. Baldy knew what he was doing, all right. It was guff but you wanted to believe it.

He and Sammy Muir were the only two from the second team. Sammy was a wee terror, smoked like a demon and yet could run like wildfire. He hardly knew the rest of the first team. Bigtime guys. He didn't run about too much in the kickabout, it was a hot day and they'd need all their wind for later on. This was his big chance. Keep the heid, that's what Joe Overend had said. Keep the heid. There was nobody in the crowd he knew. He trapped the ball and set it up for a cross. Have to impress them, show I'm good enough. Right foot. Not bad. Norrie Picken, their goalie, caught it and rolled it out to the forwards. He ran round to the corner of the penalty box, chewing hard, sleeves still rolled down to his wrists. Nice white cuffs. Made you feel neat and sharp. Like Willie Bauld, neat and deadly.

They lost the toss and changed ends, running through the oncoming Victoria team. The goalies shook hands, nobody else did. They looked a hard lot, sort of scruffy, too, they had Airdrie strips, white with the big red V down their chests. This way they'd face into the sun. In the second half it would be lower, better angle for dazzling them.

The ref looked round the two teams. People shouted. He watched the centre-forward's feet. The ref raised his whistle. Wait for it – the centre-forward had jumped the gun. The new ball, round and *lovely*, as bright as a Belisha beacon, was replaced on the spot. Then the whistle. God make me play a good game.

No wonder the first team hadn't lost since Christmas. They were fantastic. He hardly had any work to do. Victoria didn't have a hope. He took the ball off one of them easily, tackling the way you were taught, boot jammed in hard, knee over your boot, body over your knee, hit ball and man hard, bring it away, don't hold it too long, look for a man. Going up the left side of the field he saw Sammy and another of their forwards, but they were marked. A man came to tackle him. He cut in, switching to his right foot. Then he crossed it to the right wing. Had the scouts seen that? It went to their outside-right, McLatchie, all smooth and elusive. Nothing came of the cross. He fell back. Victoria must be *some* good or they wouldn't have reached the final. Most of the players had new laces on their boots, white on dark leather, the whole *thing* was neat and bright.

Victoria had a good inside-left, a very solid guy who could dribble like mad. Strong, too. After they'd seen two or three of his runs they began to tackle him in pairs, trying to crowd him off the ball.

In from the side, hook the ball away with the right foot. Missed! Going down on his left knee he curled his right leg round the guy's shins and hooked the feet from him. The ref shook his head when the Victoria guy raised his arms for a foul. Somebody else got the ball down field. The Victoria guy rubbed his knees.

'You try that again an' I'll kick yur face in,' he said.

'You and what army?'

'Jist watch it.'

Some guys thought they were very bigtime. Big mouths was more like it.

They scored the first from a corner, a header, easy as winky. While they all ran to clap their centre-forward on the back the Victoria defenders argued among themselves. Their goalie should have got it. That made you feel great. You were going to murder them. He could hardly believe it when the next came, a couple of minutes later. It was the first real thing Sammy Muir had done, flicking the ball over the right-back's head, running round him, belting it from just inside the penalty box. When you saw it hitting the net you felt like screaming, as though a bright light had flashed in your head. They mobbed Sammy, hugging and kissing him. He wasn't nervous at all now. Then it was three, McLatchie dribbling right to the line and then cutting it back for Archie Kennedy to bang it in. Three up at half-time! Look at us, people! They ran into the wee tunnel, their studs clattering on concrete.

'No' bad, lads, you're doin' okay,' said Baldy.

He sat on the bench that ran round the room, his head resting on somebody's jacket, panting slightly.

'Score another three and show these people,' said Joe. 'They're a load of rubbish.'

Some guys shouted the odds and some combed their hair and some scratched their balls with both hands and some horsed about and some sat still and looked on. Baldy moved about, chatting quietly, a huge man in a pair of trousers that would've fitted an elephant. He made you feel you were somebody. You wanted him to speak to you, to give some sign he thought you were playing well. The lads said that if Cartneuk won the Scottish Cup Baldy would say 'No' bad, lads' and then tell you off for not scoring another ten goals. McLatchie had once scored four goals for the first team and all Baldy had said was, 'Pass it about more, lad, you're gettin' a bit selfish.' It made you want to laugh. Or to do the impossible and see what Baldy said then.

'Don't get carried away,' he said as they stood up to go out again. 'Ye havenae won till the final whistle, remember that.'

'What does he want, jam on it?' said somebody. They got a fair roar as they went out again.

This is what it would be like playing for Rangers, knowing you were in a *real* team, too good for anybody else, bigtime. He watched the inside-left. He thought he was a real hard man. Cheek of the rat, threatening *him*!

Up they came, Victoria must have had a real telling-off in their dressing-room. They looked angry. How about that then, he thought, as Jimmy Clark, their centre-half, shouldered the inside-left to the ground and cleared half the length of the pitch. He was near enough to hear the Victoria inside-left have a go at Jimmy.

'I'll do you,' he was saying.

Jimmy spat and sniffed.

So that's what he was, a tough guy? Right then, let's get tore into them.

He went for the inside-left's ankles the next time he was near him, tapping the right heel so that his toe went on the wrong side of his left foot, sending him flying face first.

The ref gave a foul for that, although he put on an innocent face and held up his hands as though he couldn't believe it. The other Victoria forwards seemed like weak nonentities, not worth bothering about. Jimmy Clark had the same idea as he had. They both got near the inside-left and when the foul was taken they rammed him in the back as the ball came down.

The ref didn't give a foul. He was weak!

Victoria were getting bad-tempered. Their backs began to take fly-kicks at people. Faces were pushed together and fists clenched. Great fun. Beat them hollow then finish them off.

One of them got Sammy Muir in a two-footed tackle. Sammy went down so heavily they thought he was really injured. Joe Overend came running on to the field with his dripping sponge, his jacket flying at his side.

'Fuck me,' said Sammy, lying on the grass, the rest of them looking down at him. 'Is ma ankle broke?'

'They're asking for what they get,' said Jimmy Clark. Joe gave Sammy a last rub and then walked back to the wee stand.

So they wanted a kicking match? Right. Let's get tore in properly. Next time he'd tramp on the bastard's hands. All the people who watched him thought he was a coward. They all remembered him being frightened of the horses, of Blackie McCann, of guys at the dancing, of Telfer. There was only one way to show them.

It was the only way to play. To hate the other team. To want to destroy them. Jimmy Clark tripped a guy when the ball was at the other end of the park. Two of their forwards charged the Victoria goalie so hard he was actually crying. Two Victoria guys sandwiched McLatchie, almost breaking his ribs. The ref was hopeless, he ponced about and hardly saw anything. The crowd was going mad, especially the Victoria supporters. They were well beaten so they had to shout about something.

He hated the bloody lot of them.

The inside-left started another of his runs, this time moving out into the shadow of the stand, a thick-necked guy he was, very sure of himself, a hard man, thought he was Torry Gillick or somebody.

He beat one man, then hit the ball down the wing and started after it, quite fast. There wasn't much point in tackling him, the idea was to fall back and let him come to you, but what the hell, they were three up, he could take a chance.

He started out for the ball, body leaning forward, sprinting as hard as he knew how. The inside-left had his speed up now, going to make a dash down the wing.

Hit him, go on, hit the bastard.

There was a blinding sickness in his face and head. Everything went black. His stomach tried to heave up. The pain in his face made him want to vomit. He saw things but didn't understand what they were. People had a hold of his arms. He tried to say something, but they were miles away. He heaved up again. Shocks of agony went through his head. He couldn't hear what the voices were shouting. It was a dream. A dream . . .

He woke up in a bed and thought for a moment it was still Saturday morning. A white bed, white blankets? Not at home. A big window. Where was he?

Then Joe Overend and his mother were coming towards him. They were looking at his face. He put up his hands. There was a bandage over half of his face. The game!

'How're ye feelin', Dunky?' Joe asked.

His mother looked as though she'd been crying.

'What happened?'

As he spoke he felt his mouth funny. His tongue was thick and sore. He ran it tenderly along his teeth. At the front he could only feel soft stuff. His mother leaned over him. Looking away from her he saw other men in white beds.

'Your nose is broken and you've lost two front teeth, oh Dunky, thank God you're all right.'

'What happened?'

Joe patted his mother's back.

'You'll be all right, son,' he said. 'You should see the other guy. Huh, he'll no' be out of plaster for months.'

He couldn't believe it at first. He didn't remember a thing about it. Joe said he'd charged the inside-left like a tank and sent him flying on to the wee wall, breaking his arm and two fingers. He must have broken his nose when he hit the guy, Joe said. Before anybody could get near enough one of the other Victoria guys had run up and booted him in the face, knocking out his front teeth. They'd run him to the Ayr hospital in Joe's van and then fetched his mother.

'The ref says he was sendin' you off anyway,' said Joe. 'You and the geezer that kickt you. Och, don't bother your head aboot it, Dunky, we'll claim proveycation, he was threatenin' quite a few o' the lads.'

'Did we win?'

'Of course we did. We are the people, eh?'

They X-rayed him and found nothing worse and his mother came to collect him later that night. They got a bus from Ayr to Kilcaddie, folk looking at his bandaged face, his mother acting as if he'd broken his skull.

'I'm all right,' he kept telling her.

When they got home he was still feeling chirpy, but suddenly he had another attack of vomiting and she put him to bed.

'I'll be all right, I'll be at my work on Monday no bother,' he said.

At least it had saved him from having to decide what to do with himself. A great way to spend a Saturday night.

But it was his own fault, he knew that. He'd behaved like an animal and he'd got what he deserved. The big day all ruined, just because of sheer animalistic hate. He'd wear false teeth for the rest of his life, serve him right. And what about the other guy? Maybe his arm wouldn't set properly, or his fingers. What kind of job did he have? Christ, he'd behaved no better than a criminal. His father had always been right, he *was* unnatural.

No, that was soft, to think like that. The other guy had asked for all he got. Bad luck, that's all it was. Or bad timing. He should've been more clever. If you were going to put the mockers on another player you had to do it the canny way. Learn to get away with murder, that was the motto. He'd been carried away. It was a lesson learned. Know better the next time.

Thinking about the next time made his stomach rise. The same sickening shock echoed through his brain, the breath-catching, heart-constricting shock you always got from a bang on the nose. He lay completely still, hands holding the blanket, eyes closed, trying to hold it down.

They thought he was finished. Aye, he knew. They weren't sorry. They wanted him out of the way. It would be theirs then, they thought. His land. His farm. No, damn ye, it's mine. I am Craig, the only Craig who counts.

Whatever they said was lies. They said he was to stay in bed. All of them, the woman, Willie, the doctor. Hangers-on. It is mine.

What was he doing on the floor?

Trousers.

Damn. He was weak.

Bed's for dying in. He wasn't dying.

Gey clever of them to keep him in bed. Weakening his legs.

Lying on his chest, face on the blankets, he pulled the trousers up and eased his arms into the braces. He pushed himself to his feet.

Boots.

Dam' it, he was that weak he could hardly stand. That was what they wanted. My memory's good as any, better than most. What do they know?

Jacket.

I'm coming, ye're gey clever laddies but have no fear, I'm coming. It's mine still. I'll shake ye.

Mary saw him as she came round the corner into the yard, the empty corn pail in her hand. He was at the end of the yard, walking like a man trying to cover ground before he fell, head down, back bent, arms at his sides, feet rushing to keep up with the forward fall of his body.

'Craig! Come back here!'

He was off down the track road. She let the pail fall on stones. She felt frightened. It was like something supernatural. Dying people were supposed to do strange things. She hurried to the stack-yard to tell Telfer.

They were forking on to carts now, forking wheat, great brutes of sheaves, your gut tight with the strain of throwing them up on to the top of the load, working like demons to get it in before the forecast rain. Two prongs into the sheaf, brace yourself, take the weight, right hand at the bottom of the fork, left hand level with your chest. Up the side of straw, push it up, hold it up, feel Willie's fork jabbing in, got it, pull it away, bringing down your lead arms, into the next sheaf, get them two at a time, stagger under the weight, try to balance, shove them up, come on Willie, take the bloody things, arms bursting, take one next time, throw it up, bring it up to your hips, the fork held like a rifle with a bayonet, heave it up, watch it sail up, chaff flying about like snow, dust in your eyes, was it up? Another one, the cart going forward, another stook, hurry up, we havenae got all day down there, Logan, hurry it up, how much more? Want to eat something, shaking with hunger, stomach quivering, weakness in his arms, sickness in his throat, another two up to the top, arms stretched as high as they would go, take them, Willie, for Christ's sake, head feels like I'm going to faint, hot and sweaty, like a fever, starving of hunger, caught you suddenly sometimes, forehead sweaty, black spots before the eyes, shoulders wet, waves of fever, keep going, another sheaf, don't be a mammy's boy throw it up to the top, make it rain, hot and cold at the same time, my arms won't take it, isn't this load on yet, it's rolling forward like a great bloody sailing ship, Willie and McPhail on top, can hardly see them, they can't build it much higher, I'm shaking all over, Christ it's only half-past three, five hours yet at least, I'll never manage it, I'm sure the blood's lashing out of my nose, maybe the bandage has cut off the blood to the brain, I could pretend to pass out, they wouldn't laugh, they'd blame it on the nose . . .

He saw McCann pointing across to the hedge. They were well into the middle of the wheatfield and he had to rub his eyes to spot what McCann was seeing. 'It's Craig,' McCann shouted, looking up the outward-sloping side of the load.

It was the face he remembered afterwards, the white, mysterious face peering out between gaps in the hedges moving up the track road on the other side of the grassy bank, a strange white face much larger than it should have been, somehow, at that distance.

Willie let his feet dangle over the back of the load, layers of sheaves sagging under his weight. Then he let himself fall forward and down, a dark winged shape against the faded orange of the wheat stalks. He hit the ground with a thud and sprawled forward.

Picking up his cap he ran across the field towards his father. Dunky lay down on his back. He didn't understand it. Craig was supposed to be ready to kick the bucket. The white face had looked mad, somehow. He shut his eyes. Dazzling circles of light moved across his eyelids. Your eyes and your stomach seemed to go together. The moving lights were making him sick again. He opened his eyes and looked away from the sun. The whole sky was covered by grey cloud, except to the west where the sun came through a clear patch, making a strange, watery brilliance of light. Away to the east, over the hills, the sky was dark, gloomy, thunderous. He was a little bug lying all by himself in the middle of a huge field under a lightning sky. A stubble stalk cracked as he moved his head. It was the only sound he could hear. Everybody else was dead. He listened. Nothing.

He realised the fainting sensation had gone. Sitting up he looked for the others. McCann had been forking sheaves on the other side of the cart, but he was gone. Willie was gone. Was McPhail still up on top?

He stood up. For a moment he felt faint again, as the blood ran out of his head, but the giddiness passed.

'Hey, where are they all?' he shouted up the side of the load.

'At the gate,' shouted back the unseen McPhail. 'They've got the auld fella.'

He waited at the horse's head, watching the small figures moving at the far end of the field.

'Ye'd better take this lot in,' McPhail said.

The great load lurched across the field, cart wheels creaking and rumbling over the stubbly ground. Big Dick stamping his hooves, body straining forward against the weight, top sheaves bouncing as they crossed a rut.

Craig was still on his feet when they drew near to the gate. Willie had hold of one arm. McCann was at his other side, not too sure of whether he was supposed to grab hold, too. Craig didn't seem to notice them. He was staring across the field at something they couldn't see.

It was downhill going out of the gate and there was no stopping Big Dick there, not with that load pushing at his back. He tried to slow him down, both hands pulling on the reins, but the horse was no match for the weight of wheat on the cart. He jammed his back hooves into the ground, body leaning backwards, but the horse-shoes skidded forward on the grass and he had to keep going forward or fall between the shafts.

'Look out for fuck's sake!' Dunky shouted.

McCann and Willie pulled at the old man's arms but he stood his ground. They looked like two men holding on to a bull's horns. Dunky had to run to keep at the horse's head. Everybody was shouting.

Then McCann dived against the old man, knocking him out of the road of the horse, scrabbling to get clear of the wheels.

Dunky was still in front of the horse, running backwards, both hands on the reins, glancing over his shoulder to see the gate-posts, the horse snorting in his face, the load lurching from side to side.

The front right wheel hit the gate-post, which gave way with a rotten crack.

The load stayed on. He wheeled round and into the road and then he was able to bring the horse to a stop. He hung the reins on the shaft. At his back he heard the tractor. He saw Telfer standing behind the red bonnet, Willie's wife sitting on the empty cart.

He walked round the load, keeping as far into the ditch as possible in case it slipped off.

Willie was kneeling beside the old man, McCann standing over him.

'I couldnae stop at all,' he said.

Willie looked up.

'We'll get him on the empty cart,' he said. 'We were lucky it didnae coup over on him.'

They made a bed of sheaves for the old man, whose eyes were closed, and laid him on the back of the empty cart.

'I went to feed the chickens and he was away out the house before I knew anything about it,' Willie's wife kept saying, as though she was being accused of something.

Telfer took it slowly along the back road, with Willie and his wife and McCann holding the bed of sheaves steady against the bumps, the soles of the old man's boots forming a right angle, the patterns made by metal segs on the soles seeming to Dunky like dull bracelets.

He followed them leading Big Dick, with a tight grip on the bit-rope, left thumb stuck in the shoulder of his cotton vest. If you listened long enough to the tractor engine you thought you could hear voices speaking to you through the noise.

When they brought the two carts into the yard the grey clouds had blown over and in the sunshine the old farm looked as though it had been sleeping.

THIRTEEN

THIS WAS WHAT it felt like to be a man!

Carrying the small leather cases with their football gear, Dunky and Billy Forsyth, the second-team goalkeeper, walked through the loosely-swinging doors of the public bar. There were men there already, lots of men, pressing against the chest-high bar counter, smoking, talking, drinking, ordering.

He put his case down beside the wall and loosened the belt of his gabardine raincoat. Billy went for the drinks. They always had the same to start with, a half of whisky and a dump.

'Cheers,' said Billy, handing him the two glasses.

'Here's to Ne'erday,' he said.

Whisky was for men. It went down inside you like a burning blow-lamp. Billy put his beer glass on the little shelf and got out his fags.

'Thanks,' he said, taking a Capstan from the packet of ten. Fags were for men. They came out of the packet white and crisp between the nicotine stains of the first two fingers. It felt like a man, being a man, rolling the whiteness between the fingers. His nose looked horrible, his tongue never stopped licking round the sickening shape of his dental plate. He was repulsive, no use thinking of real love now. This was best, drinking with the real men.

The beer was cold. It was only half-past eleven in the morning and the beer seemed to make your stomach roll about inside you.

'Got your bottle for tonight?' asked Billy.

'I got a bottle awright, it's stuff called Old Maclean,' he said. 'You ever heard of it?'

'Nah,' said Billy. 'They sell anything at Ne'erday. You've got to order months in advance if you want a proprietary brand. Takes the enamel off your teeth a lot of what they give you at Ne'erday.'

Men knew about whisky.

He unbuttoned his coat and put his left hand in his trouser-pockets, his yellow wool scarf hanging down his shirt-front.

'I was lucky I wasn't working the day,' he said. 'The gaffer wanted us in this morning. We tellt him to go and boil his heid.'

McCann had told Willie. Work on Hogmanay? Get lost, McCann had said. Telfer had joined in. Willie eventually said they could take the whole day off then and damn the lot of them. He'd sounded exactly the way Auld Craig used to sound. He'd changed, Willie. He was getting very miserable. McCann said it was because Mary was spending the Craig money as fast as the banker could cash the cheques. Or because their bairn had black hair. Ach, to hell with work. What good was Auld Craig's money doing him now he was rotting away in Kilcaddie Cemetery?

'I don't fancy this game at all,' he said to Billy.

'Me neither. Is your mates coming?'

His new mates, Big Shanky and Jakie Reid – Springheel Jake. It was like a man to have mates like them. Big drinking mates.

'See me,' said Billy. 'I play better wi' a good bucket in me, so I do. Whisky makes you frisky!'

It was like a man to stand at the bar, nodding cheerily to the wee drinking fellas who let you up to the counter, giving your order to the barman in the white jacket, dropping your fag end on the floor and looking down as you wiped it flat with your toe, handing over the pound note, taking your change in an open palm, shoving it straight in your pocket without counting it, fingers knowing how to lift four glasses at once.

He had to laugh when he thought of the first time. Him and Alec on a Saturday night before the dancing just after the harvest. They'd walked up and down past the pub four times because Alec was scared one of his relatives might be passing, or somebody who knew him and would tell his father. But they'd been determined to do it, regardless. They'd walked into the crowded noise, Alec pretending to be blowing his nose into his hankie so that he could cover his face till they reached the far end of the bar and could stand with their faces to the wall. Then they didn't even know the names of any drinks! Luckily the man next to them had ordered. Two dumps. They'd ordered two dumps too, not knowing what dumps were, relieved to buggery when they turned out to be small bottled ales. A right pair they must have been!

Shanky and Jakie came in looking very gallus. They were both eighteen. Shanky had been a bigtime guy at the Academy, a right bad lot he was called because he nicked off school in the afternoons to play snooker in the billiard hall. Jakie was an electrician, a hard wee guy with red hair and fingernails chewed almost to the knuckles. Wee Springheel Jakie and Big Shanky, his gallus mates. He'd met them in a pub. Alec had stopped coming. He didn't like them.

'What's in the cases then, chief?' asked Jakie. 'A cairy-oot for this afternoon?'

'Football boots,' said Billy.

'Who're ye playing for, Alcoholics Unanimous?' said Shanky.

It was like a man to stand in a jam-packed pub on Hogmanay morning and tell dirty jokes with your gallus pals and drink whisky and beer and feel cheery. Wee Jakie always had new jokes.

'This bloke's wife is always having a kip in front of the fire when he comes home for his tea . . .' *Uncle Charlie saying the boy's got the makings of a capitalist and his father, daddy, smiling* . . . 'he belts her across the chops and says if she's sleeping in front of the fire the next night he'll kick her teeth in . . .' *it was for money you worked, not to show you were decent and steady, nobody thanked you for working till you almost dropped, they laughed at you* . . . 'so he comes home and there she is, snoozing away in front of the fire, her legs wide open . . .' *it was women who told you to be respectable, women didn't know anything, what life had his mother seen, what did she know about pubs and men?* . . . 'so he says, you know what'll happen, you'll melt your guts sitting like that wi' your legs open . . .' *the first time it tasted terrible but after that you began to like it, an acquired taste they called it, but it didn't matter about the taste, it made you feel better* . . . 'she's doing the same again, so he runs back down the stairs and goes to the butcher's shop and says give us a pound of offal . . .' *it made you forget all the things you'd ever worried about, school, the belt, exam results, getting a job, getting a girlfriend, speaking to your father, being called up to the army* . . . 'so he goes in quiet like and drops the raw bloody, stinking offal on the carpet between her feet and nips out again, she's still sleeping . . .' *nobody else knew how much you worried, nobody else knew anything about you with a drink or two inside you it didn't matter* . . . 'and when he comes in again she's crying and his tea's on the table and she's begging him to forgive her and he says what happened? . . .' *they were just nobodies, a family of nobodies, no better than anybody else, she had nothing to be snooty about, pubs or anything else* . . . 'she says, oh John, you were right, my guts did melt and they fell out on the floor and I'd a helluva job getting them back in again . . .' *you could laugh with your pals and put your hand on their shoulders and forget the whole bloody lot of it. Men didn't care if you were ugly.*

He and Billy Forsyth chewed gum on the way to the Corporation pitches but he was pretty sure, as they ran out of the dressing-room and across the mud, that Joe Overend knew they'd been in the pub.

The first half felt like a game played in a dream, where everything he did was perfect, where he ran quicker than anybody else and tackled harder than anyone else. He had a broken nose, he was a hard case, he could smash the lot of them. He even tried Charlie Tully's trick, raising his left arm and pointing to the wing as he dribbled the other way. It came off, the other team's right-half running the way he was pointing, chasing an imaginary ball.

At half-time his stomach felt full of gas. He sat on his hunkers and tried to belch the wind up. Maybe he'd got over his bad spell now. Maybe Joe had been right, he could play himself out of it.

'Awright, Dunky?' Joe asked, standing above him.

'Oh aye,' he said, 'I've got fuck'n indigestion or something.'

'Ye could call it that.'

He looked up at Joe, grinning. Joe grinned back. Joe didn't care if you had to be carried on to the pitch, as long as you got tore into them. The old Celtic stars, they always said, used to have a dram or two before the game.

But in the second half he knew it was no good. The drink had worn off and whenever he went for the ball he felt himself wincing, ready to cover his face with his arms in case he got a knock on the nose. His tackles were too late and too clumsy. If you had to screw up your courage before each tackle you might as well not bother. Why? He didn't feel afraid. Yet every time it was the same, as though his *face* remembered what had happened in the final, and was scared it would happen again. Reflexes, he supposed.

By the end of the game he was too winded to chase butterflies. Even off mud the ball seemed to bounce faster than he'd ever known a ball bounce before. A wee guy he should have tramped on gave him a right run-around and there was nothing he could do about it. His legs were weary. He could hear Joe calling from the touchline. Joe would tell Baldy and Baldy would want to speak to him and he'd have to give Baldy some yarn and Baldy might give him another chance . . . ach, tae hell with it! It was only a bloody game. It wasn't worth the effort. Drinking was better.

He waited till they were dressed and some of the lads had already gone. Joe was putting the ball into a string-net.

'Eh, Joe,' he said, nodding for Billy to wait on him outside. 'I don't think it's going to be any good, I'm chucking it in.'

Joe put his shoe on the ball, rolling it backwards and forwards under the ball of his foot, the way all players always did.

'Och, I don't know, son, you'd quite a good first half.'

Aye, I had a brilliant first half, but I was too drunk to care if I got my head knocked off.

'No, my mind's made up. I get sick when I go to head it. Here's my strip. Tell Baldy I'm sorry.'

'All right, son, if that's how ye feel. Maybe if we're short some day ye'll give us a game? Pity to be giving it up altogether when you're only sixteen.'

'Aye, maybe. See you then, Joe.'

So that was that. A premature end to a promising career, as *Waverley* would say in the *Daily Record*. Ach, tae hell with it, he had a medal, he could always blow about that. It was only a rotten, stupid, stinking, lousy game.

'Come on,' he said to Billy, 'they'll be open afore we get to the Cross.'

They drank beer till six o'clock, then he went home on the scheme bus for his tea. He washed his feet and legs in the sink basin, seeing his face in his mother's wee cracked mirror. Getting used to the twisted, flattened nose now. Not so much like a freak. He pushed out his dental plate on the end of his tongue. Two false teeth, two more medals to add to the list. He rubbed his tongue on the underside of the plate, tracing the rough stain left by cigarettes. Outside it was dark, the street-lights shining clear with haloes round the lamps in that way which told you it was freezing up.

Eating made you feel better. Warm tea.

'Your father'll think it's rotten you not going to see him on New Year's Day,' said his mother. 'If Senga can give up her friends for one day so can you.'

'I'll go on Sunday,' he said. She'd been moaning on about the Ne'erday visit the whole week. 'Tell him I'll see him on Sunday.'

'Yes but it's Ne'erday, you should think of your father.'

'I think of practically nothing else,' he said, sticking his chin out at her. 'The sooner he's walking again the better, I can get on wi' my own life.'

His mother shook her head. Senga, as usual, had nothing to say. She'd put her hair up recently and had taken to wearing make-up. Not a bad-looking dish, for a sister. Sister? For all they ever said to each other they might as well be strangers.

'Will you be late?' his mother asked as he put on his good shoes, his sore feet crushing into the new, stiff leather.

'We're goin' first-footin', I dunno how late I'll be.'

He had the half bottle hidden under his clothes in the chest of drawers. He stood close to the drawer and slipped it into his raincoat pocket, leaving his coat unbelted so that she wouldn't see the bulge.

'Ta ta, Senga, darling,' he said, 'have a nice Hogmanay.'

'I will if I don't see you,' she said.

He blew her a big fart and left. As he closed the front door he could hear his mother talking, telling Senga to show respect to her big brother, no doubt. In the army, Shanky said, you could drink all you bloody wanted to, nobody gave a fuck. The army sounded good at times and hellish at others. Maybe it would be better to get in early and get the two years over with. It couldn't be any worse than working for Willie Craig now that he was the gaffer. Changed, just like that, snap, soon as his father was dead, snap, one day he was as daft as they make them, the next day shouting and bawling just like his father. The commies were right, it was a bloody swindle, you got seven quid a week and miserable bastards like the Craigs made a fortune.

He met Shanky and Jakie in the public bar of the Black Angus at half-past six. It was like something out of the Yukon gold-rush, Hogmanay and all the guys in Kilcaddie getting it down them as fast as it would come out of the bottles.

'So what's the big plans?' he asked.

Shanky had it all worked out. They'd stay in the Angus till closing at nine o'clock, making sure they bought the carry-out screwtops before they stopped serving in the wee off-sales cubicle. First they were going to the dance at the Caledonia ballroom, they could park the carry-out in Jakie's auntie's house in Tarbert Street. Then they were meeting a few other guys, Archie Hunter and his brother John, and their gang, and they were going to Chick Roy's house at Barskeddie.

'I'd like to call in at my pal Alec's house on the way to Barskeddie,' he said. 'He can't get out because he's getting engaged, poor mug. Let's drop in on the family gathering, eh?'

'You can but don't stay long,' said Shanky. 'It'll be hell on wheels at Chick's house, his folks are away. It'll be a riot, you know what Chick's like.'

By half-past eight the men were six and seven deep at the bar and the six counterhands were practically running to keep pace with the orders. A wee drunk wandered up and down behind the tightly jammed backs, waving an empty glass. Shanky poured him a drop of beer from his pint.

'Ye're a gentleman, pal,' said the drunk, his eyes like those of a dead fish, a dirty wee claw hand clutching Shanky's beltless blue raincoat, the shorty kind the Canadian ice-hockey players wore.

'Aye right, Jock,' said Shanky. The wee man wouldn't leave them.

'Ye're a Chrustyin an' a gentleman, pal. Ah'll no' ferget yese, don't worry.'

He put a finger to his lips and nodded.

Two young blokes started a fight, the crowd parting as their wild, wet faces glared at each other. Dunky shoved into the bar, holding up their glasses. If you didn't have your own glasses by now you'd had it.

'Three haufs an' three pints o' heavy,' he shouted at the barman. It was so crowded everybody seemed to be leaning on everybody else. Men raised small glasses in neat finger holds and tossed back their whiskies. Some eyes were bright, some half-closed. Hands gripped shoulders, lips shouted into ears. The barman grabbed his pound note. Jakie was behind him and he ferried the glasses over the heads of the men, bumping a guy in the face with his elbow.

'Sorry, pal,' he said.

' 'Sawright, Jimmy, 'sawright.'

Big grins, thumbs raised. It could have been a fight. They gave Shanky ten bob each and he went for the screw-tops.

'It'll take him hours to get served,' he said to Jakie.

'No' him, he's a fly boy, big Shanky.'

Sure enough, he was back in no time with three carrier bags full of pint bottles.

'We're drinkin' my rabbits now,' Dunky said, lifting his pint. Shanky grinned, unbelievingly. 'It's true, I got shot o' the lot o' them to some guy's brother. Five quid. No' bad, eh, for a bunch o' bloody rabbits.'

He'd sold the lot to Laidlaw the greengrocer's brother. Now he had no rabbits, no ties, no responsibilities. Free to wander.

On the pavement men stood in groups, shaking hands, gripping biceps, swearing undying friendship. Everybody carried brown paper bags. Men. He felt like singing. His mates.

As they walked to Jakie's auntie's house he told Shanky why he'd given up the game. Shanky didn't believe him. He told him again. Shanky said he was showing the effects of the drink. He felt angry. Jakie stopped to shake hands with four or five men. They stopped. A man passed round a half bottle. The streets seemed packed with people, mostly men rushing from pubs to houses. He could hear shouts and singing.

'Jist keep quiet till we're in the house, okay pals?' said Jakie. 'She's fed up wi' me fallin' at her feet when she opens the door.'

It was up a tenement close. Shanky asked Jakie if there would be any decent wimmin. Jakie said his auntie went like a rattlesnake. He sounded a bit gone himself. They went into a living room. The men looked like uncles, cheery uncles, all with a good drop in them. They offered to give everybody a drink from their bottles, but the men said they ought to keep it, the night had a long way to go Jakie's auntie gave them big whiskies.

'Here's tae us an' wha's like us,' said the uncle-men. 'Dam' few an' they're a' deid.' He found himself talking to a man about football. A woman asked him if he'd like a sherry, he said sure, it tasted sweet but went down fine.

Shanky dragged them away to the dancing. The pavement was slippy with frost, unless you walked close to the tenement walls. They met some more people and shook hands. Gangs of guys shouted across the street. A man sat in a close entrance, ear pressed on the wall, his feet crossed cosily as though he was at his own fire, eyes half-closed, singing to himself.

There was a crowd at the entrance to the hall, it was an all-ticket do and scores of folk had turned up in hope of slipping in. Shanky had their tickets. One guy wasn't going to let them through.

'We've got tickets, chief,' said Shanky. He could look very menacing when he wanted to. Bigtime.

'You lookin' for trouble, friend?' Jakie asked.

'Ach come on, Jakie, don't waste your energy.'

There were girls outside, some of them carrying dancing shoes, wearing silk headscarves. It was like having a ticket for Scotland against England at Hampden Park, maybe somebody would jump you and grab the tickets, maybe they'd lock the gates . . . in the cloakroom they gave their coats to a man. Boxing dead clever, he'd already transferred his half bottle to his inside jacket pocket.

He tapped it and winked as they went into the hall.

'We're awright for a wee drappie, don't worry,' he said.

'Keep it for later,' said Shanky. 'Let's view the talent first, I fancy lumbering a big piece to take to Chick's.'

Dances were great if you had a good drink in you. Women. Bigtime. Easy meat. He danced a couple of times in the half-light, not hearing what they said, trying to shout against the noise of the band. It was hellish hot. He shoved about in the men's side till he saw Shanky talking to John Hunter. They were talking about where they'd meet before walking out to Barskeddie. It sounded hellish boring.

'Fancy a drop in the lavvy?' he said.

They got in a stall and snibbed the door behind them, knees jammed against the lavatory seat.

'Just one,' said Shanky. 'We want at least one bottle for the game the morra.'

You needed a pal who could think ahead. They'd need a drink at the Rangers–Celtic game. He screwed the top on. Back in the dance he decided the hell with it he'd take a walk up the women's side and see what was going. Everybody was doing it. Every night should be Hogmanay, nobody cared what you did. He saw Magda Gemmell.

'Ye dancing, hen?' he asked her.

'Oh hallo, Duncan! My, you're a stranger.'

Between dances he kept his arm round her waist, why bother splitting up? She was fast, dirty-minded. The ideal woman for a horror like himself.

'Hey, we're goin' to Chick Roy's house later on, you fancy comin'?'

She said she would try to slip away from her father and mother. She was his sure thing. Bigtime. They were dancing cheek to cheek by eleven, when it was time to push off, her to get the Barskeddie bus, them off God knows where. They had a quick necking session in the corridor. She could get him steamed up any time.

'You'll be there, won't you? I'm countin' on it, Magda, you're the only decent woman I've ever known.'

Honest. Cross my heart. They stood shouting after her and her pal, waving and whistling, then they went back to Jakie's auntie's house. He felt better after an hour or so without a drink. What the hell had he ever seen in bloody Elsa? It made him angry, just thinking about that love rubbish, keeping themselves pure! She was just a frigid wee bitch. Real women let you do *anything*. To get it from miserable hairies like Elsa you had to buy a ring and stick your head right into the noose. He'd escaped just in time. Poor bloody Telfer! He started laughing. He wanted to jump in the air and wave his arms about. To get Telfer annoyed these days all you had to do was ask him how the furniture-buying was going. Bigtime Donald Telfer, buying furniture! Talking about the rents of two-apartment houses! The nearest he'd ever get to Canada was at the pictures!

It was like a man, to have a good laugh about other people's hard luck. Hard lines, pal, as they said in Kilcaddie, eyes grinning, hard cheese, kid, hard cheddar, Jock, fuck your horrible luck bud. Guys like Shanky, laugh like a drain as they told you of some bloke's grim luck. Well, that's how it was, a hard world, laugh while you can.

Back at Jakie's auntie's house it all seemed a bit too grown-up. Men with red faces put their arms round each other. Women in corsets giggled as they took another drink, 'Well, jist a wee wan mind, ye're no' tryin' tae get me merry, are ye?' Shanky gave Jakie's auntie a bit of patter, trust Shanky, how could anybody's *auntie* be game for a rattle? They turned up the wireless, Jimmy Shand, just before twelve, the accordion band blaring through the room, big rush to get glasses filled before the clock started chiming. He found it was easier just to grin at the people. Sooner they were away on their travels the better. Then a voice on the radio, some gabble, then silence, a woman telling her Bob to hold his wheesh, then the chimes, one, two, the end of the year. Like standing to attention for the National Anthem at the pictures. Then the last chime and the radio giving out the great roar from the crowds at Glasgow Trongate and the people turning on each other, shaking hands, kissing, 'A guid new year tae yin an' a',' they sounded like people imitating Scots people, they always did at New Year.

They were away up the road shortly afterwards, him and Shanky and Jakie. More groups on the streets now, the first-footers making fast time to the next house, shaking strangers' hands in the street, everybody was everybody's friend.

Great. So why did he suddenly feel peculiar? Alone and not really part of it.

On the way they passed St Andrew's Church. The entrance was lit and people were coming out, shaking the elders' hands, the minister on the steps, the religious mob, decent folk, the men pulling on their heavy nap coats, women in furs and hats.

'Look at that lot,' said Jakie. 'Give ye the dry boke jist lookin' at them.'

They stood across the road and had a pass round of Shanky's half-bottle, putting down the carrier bags. It seemed like a bit of fun, to show the toffs a bit of scruff carry-on. In the light of the church porch, his wife helping him on with his coat, he saw Nicol, the school-teacher.

'That's my old teacher,' he said.

'Which one?'

'Him putting on his coat.'

'Him wi' the kilt on?'

'The kilt?' He screwed up his eyes. He could see thin legs below the coat. 'So it is. Jesus Christ.'

'Ah know whut to do wi' guys wearin' the kilt,' said Jakie. 'Chuck stones at them, stupid buggers.'

'Come on,' said Shanky. 'We've to meet the Hunter mob at Meiklepark.'

They meandered uphill towards the scheme. Shanky even *walked* bigtime, shoulders swinging, back straight, collar turned up, like Sterling Hayden in *The Asphalt Jungle*. Funny about him, parents dead respectable, yet he was snooker king of the Academy. Funny.

The Hunters had a small gang waiting at the corner which led into Meiklepark. They stood under a tall, concrete lamp post. They had a few women with them, too. Bigtime. He hoped Magda would turn up at Chick Roy's.

'I want to go to Alec's,' he said. Jakie didn't want to go. Shanky said they'd wait for him. He said he would only be five minutes. He ran along the pavement, close to the hedge, eyes on the sparkling ground, right hand holding the half-bottle close to his chest.

'Welcome, happy New Year, you're our first-foot,' said Alec's father. 'Got a piece of coal, have you?'

'Eh, no.'

Alec's father took him round the back of the house and delved into the bunker.

'The first foot must have a lump of coal and a bottle,' said Alec's father. He held it out as they went into the brightly lit lobby. Alec came through a mob of aunts and uncles and whatnot, looking hellish glad to see him. Ethel Carruthers was there, too, banana legs! His cheeks burned after the chill outside. He had a couple of big drams. Neat. Down in a oncer.

'That's my big mate,' said Alec, approvingly. 'You can neck Ethel if you like, seein' how it's Ne'erday.'

'Yippee,' he heard himself shout. He got his arms round Big Ethel. She felt thin and cool and weak. No body at all. Hard lines, Alec. She didn't seem enthusiastic, either. A family party suited her. She looked like an auntie already. She didn't smile when he slashed a good drop from his own bottle into Alec's glass. Getting away was difficult, Alec couldn't come to Chick Roy's but he wanted him to stay, keep him company.

He ran down the sparkling pavement, the duty business over, let's get on with the big night! Yippee. Most of them had gone on, but Shanky and Jakie were still under the lamp post.

'Lead on MacDuff,' Jakie yelled and they started on the five miles to Barskeddie. Along the road they met a gang of blokes. Jakie knew some of them.

'Come wi' us,' he said, 'Chick Roy's folks are away.'

While they talked he sat down on the kerb and had a drag at one of the screwtops. Some guy in the other gang was miroculous. Suddenly he was shouting at Jakie and Jakie was lifting his fists to him. The other guy had a pint bottle in his hand. He ran across the road at Jakie, the bottle raised. Halfway across he slipped and sat down hard. The bottle broke. His mates seemed to think this was Jakie's fault.

'Ye fuck'n mug!' one of them roared.

'Come on,' said Shanky, grabbing Jakie's elbow, dragging him away. 'They're just a lot of shit.'

They walked away, leaving the other mob to pick up their pal, who was lying on the road, crying. They walked to the next lamp post.

'I'll get them,' Jakie kept saying.

Dunky hated them for being ignorant fighting animals. He had almost finished one screwtop. He swallowed what was left, turned back and hurled it at the other gang. They heard it breaking with a hard plop. Glass tinkled. They ran from the shouts. He was laughing. Shanky kept pulling him.

Walking five miles drunk was no bother at all. Like magic. He wanted to tell Shanky everything. Shanky was a bigtime guy, a real pal. Jakie fell into the hedge at the side of the road. They pulled him out, dragging him by the coat collar, forcing him to keep walking. People liked you when you were drunk.

'You like me, don't you, Shanky? Nobody likes me, Shanky. You like me, Shanky, don't you?'

'Yeah, sure,' said Shanky.

'No, *really* like me?'

Jakie sat down between them. They dragged him up by the coat sleeves.

'Nobody likes me, Shanky, nobody in the whole world. They hate me.'

He was sick. He stood for a few moments, head leaning forward, trying to keep it off his trousers. It came again, erupting out of his throat. Jakie sat down. He stepped round the vomit, shaking his head, blinking tears out of his eyes.

'That's better,' he said. He made himself belch but there was nothing more to come up. 'I'm awright now. Come on, Jakie, we'll never get there.'

'People hate you,' Shanky said. 'And you hate people. Thank Christ you've stopped all that snivelling.'

'I wasn't snivelling.'

'I don't care what you call it. Let's get this drunken bastard moving again. Look, Jakie, I'm telling you for the last time, I'm getting to Chick Roy's whether you come or not. You want us to leave you in the ditch?'

'Leggoa me,' said Jakie. He dug his heels in and shook their hands off his arms. Shanky took hold of him again. Jakie tried to punch him. Dunky got a fistful of Jakie's shoulder. Jakie, bent almost double, twisted round and tried to butt him in the stomach. Jakie always got a bit stupid when he was drunk. He couldn't tell his pals from his enemies. He called them a lot of dirty bastards.

'Awright,' said Shanky, 'if that's how you want it.'

Jakie sat down in the middle of the road. His carrier bag of screwtops lay across his leg. 'Leave the bugger right there,' said Shanky.

'What if a car comes? He'll get killed.'

'Too bad.'

'We'll put him on the grass.'

'On you go. I'm off.'

'Ach, it's his own fault.' He did, however, stop a few yards away and shout back for Jakie to get up. Jakie shouted something back. 'Get killt then for all I care.'

So it was just him and Shanky, walking like big hard men, under the moon, along the dark, icy road, trees on one side, a hedge on the other. The idea of Jake sitting there till a car's headlights lit him up suddenly seemed the height of hilarity. Shanky thought it was funny, too, although he wasn't the type to laugh out loud.

'We'll know what happened to him on the way back,' he said. 'If there's no big flat blob on the road we'll know he's awright.'

'You're a cruel bastard, aren't you?'

'I've no time for nutters.'

'But he's supposed to be your pal, you bastard.'

'Ballocks to him. Look out for number one, that's the big motto. I'll tell you a story, kid. This English bloke's a Bevin boy down a mine in Fife, a right softy. He's shovelling for this big hard case of a miner who's on his back with his pick. The English bloke hears a rumbling up the tunnel but the big miner says nothing. It gets nearer. The miner keeps digging away into the seam. Then the English bloke looks up and sees a runaway bogie, weighing about a ton, crashing towards him down the line. He jumps for the side, it goes past like a rocket, it's so narrow in the tunnel it touches his back and whips the clothes off him and the skin off his shoulder blades. He's about ready to faint but he says to the miner, "Christ, you musta known what that noise was, why the hell didn't you warn me?" The miner bloke looks up. "Why shouldn't I?" he says. "I'm no' your mammy," he says.'

'Is that what you believe in?'

'Yeah.'

The detached bungalow had a little white wooden paling round its garden. They jumped the paling and ran across the grass. The door was open. Inside it was like VE night. He and Shanky did a tour of the various rooms, seeing what was what. They put their beer into the kitty but kept the half bottles in their pockets. Chick Roy and the two Hunters and the main crowd were in the living room, guys sprawled on the floor, a couple necking on the couch, some drunk kneeling beside the gramophone, a girl trying to calm down her sobbing mate, some guy unconscious in an armchair. The drunk kept putting on Elvis Presley at the wrong speed, 'Blue Suede Shoes' sounding like Mickey Mouse. Another guy kept shoving the drunk away and changing the gramophone to the normal speed.

'Hey come on an' I'll show you something,' said Archie Hunter, thumbing them towards the door with big winks. 'Chick's too far gone to care, they're wrecking the joint.'

They followed him into the kitchen, drinking from screwtops. In the deeper of the two sinks, the big one used for steeping the washing, there was a bloke! Pissed to the world, his face on his knees, which were doubled up to his chest. The water was up to his elbows, the tap still running.

'That's Tommy Patterson,' said Archie. 'He's got gastric ulcers or something, he shouldnae drink at all. We put him in the sink for a laugh.'

They roared. It was hilarious. Shanky passed round his half-bottle.

'That's no' half of it,' said Archie. 'The place is a wreck, Chick'll get murdered when his folks come back. Come on through the bedroom, hey, it's worse!'

It was one of those fancy bedrooms, the kind with a white rug and a brown silk bedcover and wee lace mats on the dressing-table. Archie pulled off the silk bedcover. There were two guys in the bed, wearing all their clothes, both unconscious.

'This one's just drunk,' said Archie, pulling the guy's ear so that his face turned up, showing where he'd vomited on the pillow. He let him drop back into it. 'This one hit his head falling off the dressing-table, he was dancing on it.'

The second guy had dried blood on his forehead.

Other guys came in to inspect them. They rolled back to the living-room and joined in the hilarity. There was wine, too, bottles of VP. He tried that but it was too sweet to drink on its own. He poured some into his beer. There was dancing and jumping about. Some guy started shouting the odds about his whisky having been knocked. He wanted a fight, but Shanky and John Hunter got his arms up behind his back and shoved him face first out of the window, his legs slipping out of view.

He got up and went back through the kitchen, whisky in one hand, beer and wine in the other. The guy with ulcers was still unconscious in the sink. Water was now pouring onto the kitchen floor. He went through to the bedroom, singing. There were some dames in there being shown the two guys in bed. Holding the glasses above his head he tried to show them the sword dance. The rug slipped and he sat down on his spine. He lay on his back and laughed, the beer and wine pouring on his chest. A girl said something nasty about him.

He scrambled to his feet.

'I'm no' drunk, I havenae even startet yet,' he shouted. 'Yippee.'

Magda was in the living-room. Nobody would listen when he said she was his big steady. He sat on the floor beside her and tried to hold her hand. People kept walking in and out in crowds. He had a whole bottle of VP beside him, and his whisky in his breast pocket and a screwtop between his feet. Magda loved him. Singing. Magda talking. Magda on his lap. Laughing about Jakie. Laughing when a guy threw a bottle at the big mirror. Something about walking with Magda. Going to get married. Falling in a garden. Back in the house. Big rammy in the living-room. Shanky's my mate, he'll look after me. Falling down. Where's the bloody booze gone? I want a drink, thieving bastards, I want a drink . . .

It was daylight. One of his eyes was closed up. His left leg had gone to sleep. It was over the arm of the chair. His neck had a crick. He tried to move and his head tried to burst through his skull. This was it, his first big hangover. It was worse than what they said it would be. He remembered all sorts of trouble. It was morning and he was still at Chick Roy's house. His mother would do her nut. He was a disgrace. She'd tell his father! His father was going to walk again and come back to the house. No, he couldn't stand all that again. Where would he go? Canada? No, that was just a big dream, a fancy notion for boys with their heads full of nonsense. There was no place for him at home. He was a

disgrace. A drunkard. An ugly mug. Jesus would never help him
now, God had given him plenty of chances. Maybe if he made it
his New Year resolution, never again, not another drop . . . the
hell with it, he was a disgrace, a bad lot. Maybe he'd been cursed.

What did it all mean? What were men, anyway? Why wasn't he
a man himself? He was a nothing, a collection of poses. Easily
led, his mother called it. Nobody knew anything about you. You
didn't know anything about anybody else. Telfer was getting
married. McCann was talking about joining the police. Willie
had become like his old man. Elsa had betrayed him. He hadn't
cared, now he wanted to cry when he thought of her. You
couldn't depend on other people, you couldn't depend on
yourself.

If grown men could change so quickly how could you be sure of
yourself? You wanted to be like other people but they did the dirty
on you, one way or the other. You started off trying to be
different, trying not to turn out like all the others. You ended
up worse than them. You ended up knowing you were a disgrace,
full of all the things you hated in other people.

He could never face them again, none of them. He wanted to
run away. In the army they didn't care what you did. It was a hard
life in the army. It was what he deserved. It would be his
punishment. He wasn't fit for anything else. He was a waster.
He might as well sign on for life. Never come back to Kilcaddie
again, not ever.

Shanky came into Chick Roy's living-room, whistling, buttoning his shirt, his raincoat over his shoulder.

'Awright?' he said. 'You look lousy. Come on, kid, on your
feet, we don't want to be late for the train, let's beat it before
Chick's folk come back, they'll go wild when they see this
joint.'

On the bus to Ayr and in the Glasgow train he kept wanting to
be sick. It was madness to go all the way to Glasgow, but Shanky
was determined to have his big day out.

They carried seven screwtops and an almost untouched half-
bottle into Ibrox Park. He thought of his mother. She'd always
said, since he was a tot, that the Rangers–Celtic crowd were the
lowest of the low, drunken animals. A disgrace to Scotland. Who
cared? He knew he was doing the wrong thing but he started
drinking again all the same. What the hell did it all matter? Soon
they were talking to some other men and bottles were being
passed round. Rangers scored and they yelled themselves hoarse,
banging each other on the back.

Somebody chucked a bottle on the pitch. They all laughed and had another drink.

'Kill they Fenian bastards,' shouted one of their new pals.

'We are the people,' shouted another.

He held his hands high above his head and roared and roared until his throat was sore.

APPRENTICE
Tom Gallacher

Contents

Preface

IT WAS THE shipyard labourer, a man known to all as Lord Sweatrag, who advised me to keep a notebook which would record my progress to becoming a marine engineer. In the event, I found it did nothing of the kind. Instead of the Strength of Materials, the Theory of Machines, the Calculus and Steam Entropy, the notebook is full of people. Five years serving my time serves instead those spirited, funny, maddening people to whom I was an outsider. They criss-cross and collide through every entry; appearing, disappearing, re-appearing – governed by reasons which were rarely apparent to me. And that, probably, is how they should be presented – as a continuous roll of inter-mingled lives. But I was a young man when I made the notes, and therefore possessed of the fallacy that these vivid, individual people somehow existed only for my benefit. So what was true of them outside my personal intervention and knowledge is missing. Unfortunately, I do not have the ability to invent it. That being the case, it seemed that the best thing to do was *un*wind the intermingling threads and present the people in separate stories; one for each year of my apprenticeship.

Even so, there are some characters who insist on intruding at times and in circumstances where the matter does not concern them. I've let them do it because I could not, for example, deny them the use of public transport or access to the pubs, the river, or the grimy precipitous streets of Greenock in the 1950s; particularly since I've kept them waiting for close on thirty years. The delay is due to a fundamental mistake of mine. I thought that having qualified as an engineer it followed that my life should be devoted to engineering. Until recently that is how, and why, I have wasted my time. But I kept the notebooks safe, cherishing the delusion that some day I'd try to make proper use of them. I was over forty before that day arrived. It was at a funeral and I decided I would quit engineering altogether. I don't know why it took me so long to realise that, when I was in Greenock, it was not my true function to be an apprentice engineer but an apprentice human being. My teachers were the people in this book. I wish they'd had more success.

W.T.

Portrait of Isa Mulvenny

FOR ME, THE Past begins at Euston. That is, Euston in the mid-Fifties at about ten o'clock in the evening. In summer months it was still clear enough to sit out in that little front garden with a good view of the splendid archway which, eventually, could not be saved. Winter and summer I arrived in plenty of time for the journey back to my apprenticeship on the Clyde after Fair holidays, Christmas holidays and at the end of strikes. Each time I walked under that arch I felt a little less English than the time before; each time more convinced that my separate Scottish identity was the real one. They should have a Customs Post at Euston.

Now – again – I am going down the ramp to that interminable platform which curves out into the dark. The train is in place and already crowded with people who will keep their vigil sitting up all night, confronting each other with stoic resentment. In the past I did that, but now I walk on, beyond their carriages, and they glance at me as though a threat has passed. Somewhere, if I can find it, my name is posted on a window as a first-class sleeper to Glasgow. I wish I could believe it.

'Good evening, sir,' says the sleeping-car attendant, genially hovering at the door.

'Thompson.'

'Aye, Mr Thompson. That's er . . . number eleven. Is that all the luggage ye've got?'

'Yes. I'll be coming back tomorrow.'

He effaces himself in a corner to allow me to squeeze past him and move down the corridor. But apparently he is still short of information. 'Jist a wee business trip, eh?'

'No.'

'Ah, well . . . there you are, sir. Number eleven. I'll take your ticket the now and no' disturb ye later.' I take off my raincoat to get at the ticket, and thereby give him another clue. 'Oh, I didnae notice the uniform outside there. Merchant Navy, eh? Engineer?'

'That's right. Here you are.'

The train starts. 'Thank you, sir. That's us off now. You're jist in time, Mr Thompson.'

'I hope so. Good night.'

'Er . . . will you wish tea in the mornin'?'

'Yes, please. About half an hour before we get in.'

'Certainly, sir. Good night. Sleep tight.'

That's what Isa said. I heard her voice echo it as she, smiling, withdrew from the room. 'Good night, sleep tight, don't let the bugs bite. If they bite, squeeze them tight. Well . . .' she shrugged with great good humour, 'there's no' much else ye can dae wi' bugs, is there?' She laughed heartily and closed the door. That was the first night I slept at the Mulvennys'. Isa's new lodger, aged sixteen. I thought she was joking about the bed-bugs and what to do with them. But she wasn't. In the morning I complained to her about the marks they left on me. 'Tut, tut, tut. You must have a very sensitive skin, son.' I thought that, on the other hand, it could be she bred ferocious bugs. 'But don't you worry, son. I'll get rid of them.' Very sympathetic, Isa. Made me wish I hadn't mentioned it. Maybe I could get used to being covered in angry red blotches – like all her previous lodgers; probably. However, Isa did know an antidote. When I came back from my first day at the shipyard, she was out on the stairhead landing.

She was on her knees, hammer in hand, smashing camphor balls. She peered down through the cast-iron railings when she heard my feet on the stair. 'Is that you back already? Your tea'll no' be long.'

'What are you doing, Mrs Mulvenny?'

'Camphor . . .' Smash. 'Best thing for bugs.' Smash. 'But ye cannae lie on lumps of it, so I have tae . . .' – smash – '. . . crush the stuff. Feel it. Quite fine powder that, eh?'

I rubbed some of the violent-smelling powder between my fingers. 'Yes, it is. But can't you buy it as a powder?'

'I don't think so. Anyway, I always get the balls and smash them. And it's better out here on the landing where there's a stone floor. D'ye think that'll be enough?'

'Yes, I should think so. Do you just sprinkle it on the bed?'

She laughed. 'Oh, no! Under the sheet. You'll hardly notice it. Except for the smell.' She gathered the sheets of newspaper together, making a pile of the white crystalline powder. 'There. I'll let you by. Young Andy's in, and ma man should be back shortly. Watch yer feet! I'll clean that mess the morra. It's my turn for the stairs.'

She followed me into the dark lobby which was much restricted by the huge coal-box behind the front door. An ornate sideboard ran the full length of the other wall. She called to her schoolboy son. 'Andy! Here's Bill now.' A dark-haired, truculent youth emerged from the kitchen.

'You got a start in the yard,' he said.

'Yes, I started today.'

'My father's a charge-hand there. In the plate shop.'

'Oh.'

My limited response must have meant that I did not understand the significance of this, so he went on, 'That's like a foreman . . . ye know. One of the gaffers. What's your father do?'

'He's an engineer.'

'At a desk or at the tools?' he challenged me. From the front room, where she was dealing death to the bugs in my bed, came the sound – and the very sweet sound – of Isa singing 'The Rose of Tralee'.

'He's a consultant,' I said.

'Huh. That's like a Doctor.'

'He's a doctor of Science.'

'And he's put you in a shipyard!' There was an even mixture of scorn and disbelief in his voice, so that I could take either – depending on whether or not I was lying about this odd arrangement.

'*He* started in a shipyard,' I explained.

Andy swivelled slightly, so that his back rested flat and easy against the wall. 'I'm studying to be an accountant,' he said.

'Oh.' The subject did not interest me. I had but one pressing idea in mind. 'Could I wash before we eat?' It seemed that now would be the time when I'd discover where the bathroom was. The previous night I had been shown the lavatory on the half-landing of the outer stair, but no bathroom.

Andy called to his mother, who was now in the kitchen. 'Ma! He wants to wash!'

She called back. 'Certainly. I'll let him in here at the sink as soon as I've strained these potatoes.'

There was no bathroom. And Andy was not yet finished with my briefing. 'My father's a runner. Cross country. That's all his medals and cups and plaques there on the sideboard.'

'Really.' I was tired of standing, oily-handed, in the lobby.

'He won them. Does your father go in for any sport?'

'No. He's, er . . . too fat.'

Andy had clearly gained the advantage at last. He smiled and went on in a much more pleasant tone, 'Ma Da' won all them. Outright. Wi' the Harriers, mainly. This year he's sure tae get the Levi-Allen Shield.'

Isa clashed a pot lid in place and called to me, 'There you are, Billy. In you get and give yer hands a rub.'

The table was set in the kitchen for the evening meal. Isa had cleared a place for me at the sink which was banked with pots and pans, with piles of vegetable peelings stacked neatly in the corners. As I tucked my elbows close to my sides and sluiced my hands under the tap, I remarked to her, 'Mr Mulvenny has won a lot of trophies.'

'What, son?'

'I was admiring the trophies.'

'He means the silver,' shouted Andy from the lobby. The Mulvennys preferred calling to each other from separate rooms rather than conversing in the same room.

'Aw, aye! The silver.' Isa accepted the translation without looking up. 'Next week he runs in the Leafy Allan. We'll put that in the middle.'

'If he wins.'

Isa tucked her chin and gave me a tolerant glance. 'He'll win all right. Nae fear aboot that. There's nobody can touch Andrew at the runnin'.' We heard the front door open then slam shut. 'That'll be him noo.'

'Hello, Da',' Andy greeted his father.

'Andy,' observed Mr Mulvenny's voice, completing the ritual. He was a man who expected to be met, however laconically, and Andy was certainly the person he expected to meet him.

'I'm in here, Andrew,' called Mrs Mulvenny.

'Where the hell else would ye be?' her husband shouted back. Isa laughed, delightedly. 'Aye! Where else, indeed!'

Mr Mulvenny appeared in the kitchen doorway and everything about him defied even the suspicion that he had just returned from the grimy plate-shop of a shipyard. 'Well, how's our new apprentice?' he asked me.

'Jist gettin' ready to eat,' Isa told him.

'It wasn't too bad,' I admitted.

'Dirty work, though.'

'Yes.'

Mr Mulvenny sucked a deep breath through his teeth and drily smacked his lips at the end of it. 'Well, them that can't do better have to show the signs o' it. And I've done my share, eh. But I'm grateful my son'll never have to get his hands dirty.'

'It washes off,' I said.

'Sure. At first. After a while, though, nothing'll shift it. Aye. Them that can't do better have to show the signs o' it.' He took off his jacket, and folded it over the back of his chair. When he sat at the table he sat with a perfectly straight, unsupported spine.

'That's your place, Billy,' said Isa, hovering, pot in hand. 'Sit there.' Young Andy was already seated and I realised, with surprise, that the table was set for only three people. Mrs Mulvenny stayed on her feet, tending and serving, until we were finished. This was necessary, apparently, because they did not use serving dishes on the table. The food was served straight from the pots, kept warm and in need of stirring, on the stove. Only when Mr Mulvenny was settled with his evening paper at the fire and Andy had gone to his bedroom would Mrs Mulvenny sit down to eat. We had almost finished our meal when Mr Mulvenny spoke to his wife again. 'Did you tell him about the room?'

She was immediately contrite. 'Oooh! I did not.'

'Isa!' his voice grated with instant irritation.

'I would have remembered, though. Before next week.' Then, less sure, 'I expect.'

Switching on his reasonable tone, Andrew turned to me. 'Well, you see, Bobby . . .'

' "Billy",' his wife corrected.

'Billy. You've got the front room and that's where we have . . .'

Isa babbled, unsuppressed, 'Because the piana's there and wi' the . . .'

'Isa!' She stopped. He continued. 'Because it's the biggest room, we have our wee celebrations there. I don't suppose . . .'

'You'll enjoy yourself.'

'. . . you'll mind. They never go on very late. You'll be able to join in the sing-song.'

'When?' I asked.

Andrew smiled modestly. 'Well, whenever I win another lump o' silver. Just a few neighbours, ye know. And friends.' Clearly, these were separate groups.

'Joe Harper's a great man on the keyboard and Isa gives us a song.'

'The same song,' said Andy.

'Well, they like it,' retorted his mother.

'They've nae choice,' said Andrew. 'And she usually manages tae break a few dishes into the bargain.'

'I do not!'

'Of course, there have been times when things got a bit rowdy. I remember one time . . . now, when was it? The Western Division Challenge Cup, I think it was . . .'

'That's right,' confirmed Andy.

'When I won that for the third time. A field of over a hundred, mind you . . . and some well-trained opposition.'

Whatever the opposition Andrew had to face running across fields, he never had to face any opposition at home. And, of course, he won the Levi-Allen Shield – outright. It joined the Western Division Challenge Cup on the gleaming altar of silver piled along the lobby sideboard.

Meanwhile, I had to get used to conditions at work and to learn as quickly as possible the shop-floor hierarchy. To begin with I was preoccupied in getting used to the sheer height and length of those glass-roofed, aircraft-hangar spaces which are so cosily called 'shops'; the row on row of different machines set into the concrete floor and each provided with its wood-spar foot-board; the 'clear' alleys inviolately defined by fresh painted lines; the piles of metal and neat stacks of finished pieces; and strad-dling all this, overhead, the heavy cranes patrolling to and fro, controlled by unseen drivers who themselves could see the smallest gesture which might summon them. Compared with all that, the men were insignificant and identical, except that the foreman wore a suit – and a soft hat which, apparently, he never removed in public. He ruled his department from a little wooden hut. It was like a small garden shed set indoors, leaning against the soaring whitewashed wall which rose sixty or seventy feet to the glass roof.

Immediately outside 'the box' was a long trestle table in front of a bank of filing cabinets. That was the domain of the foreman's chief assistant, the charge-hand. He was responsible for all the working drawings that came to the department. The charge-hand had no real power but was an invaluable intermediary and was a great retailer of information in both directions. Then there were senior journeymen who all wore caps and junior journeymen who rarely did until they were thirty, or were blessed with premature baldness. Then came the apprentices in strict order of their year, from fifth to first. Last were the servants of all these – the labourers. I never discovered if they had their own pecking-order because if there was anything that the youngest apprentice wanted done, even the oldest labourer would have to do it.

Frank Fogel and I were the youngest apprentices that week in March, 1955. We had our medical together and received our Works Number together. Frank was 874, I was 875. These numbers were die-stamped on brass discs called 'tickets' and were used as a check of our arrival and departure from work by the Gatehouse keeper and also our bowel movements in the works lavatories by the Shithouse keeper. The urinals could be used without handing over the 'ticket'.

Frank explained. 'That's because a piss takes less than three minutes an' ye don't sit doon for it.' He gave me a suspicious glance. 'At least, *A* don't.'

'Do you think we have to memorise the number?' I asked him.

'Not at all!' he scoffed. 'Jist get it branded on yer arm, there. The important thing is, *they* don't hiv tae remember yer name.' He laughed. 'An' I know ye've memorised that.'

I wished that I felt as self-assured as he sounded. Of course, he'd already worked for a year outside. While waiting for his sixteenth birthday he'd taken a job as a van-boy with a bakery roundsman. I was grateful that he seemed disposed to be my general guide; also, my interpreter of the foreign language spoken in that part of Scotland. His first words to me were, 'Siv us a li', i' ye fulla?' which turned out to mean, 'Would you give me a light?' Even in that first week he started the habit of adding a translation to anything he said which, by my expression, he saw I had not understood. He was bilingual and understood everything I said, though my accent seemed to him fanciful.

'A hiv tae laugh at the English,' he said. 'They wull miss oot the R's when there is an R, but when there *isnae* wan they put it in.'

'Do we?'

'Aye!' To illustrate the point he invited me, 'Say, "the warmest girl in the world".' I did so and he pointed victoriously at my mouth. 'D'ye see whi' A mean? Noo say, "Law and Order".' Again I complied and, delighted at my manifest failure with the R, he delivered the whole damning sentence in my voice, ' "The wa'mist gel in the wo'ld is Lauren Auda." A'm tellin' ye – if ye wrote doon English as *you* speak, it wid look ridiculous.'

For the party, my bed, still smelling richly of camphor, was disguised as a divan and Isa, gawky and exuberant, prepared to entertain. Her long, beautiful hair was elaborately braided and coiled. Since it was a special occasion, she wore make-up. The effect betrayed lack of practice. She also wore her 'costume'. That is, a matching jacket and skirt; a tailored suit, in fact. She thought it made her look 'not so tall'. But really it did nothing for her height and only added to the impression that she was a gate-crasher at this assembly; an enthusiastic guest who'd escaped from a seedy wedding-reception somewhere else.

On this and many similar occasions, Mr Mulvenny held court, dressed in a neat dark suit, glowing with health and obvious fitness. His button-bright eyes darted in and out of the conversa-

tion, finding every lull that could be stretched to accommodate
reference to his sporting achievement. His guests, aware of who
was providing the drink, were apt at wrenching any subject
instantly off-course to ensure that the object would be Andrew.

Isa was very proud of him. So was Andy. Usually, I was more
preoccupied in praying that everyone would just go away and let
me get to bed. That never happened until they had all done a
'turn', which usually involved singing. Joe Harper, a spry, prematurely old-looking man, was glued to the piano stool. Though
undoubtedly 'shachly' – as they said in those parts – he had the
jaunty assurance of a relentless entertainer. Perfectly willing as he
was to accompany others, he had his own repertoire to get
through. One item was always 'South of the Border':

> South of the border, I rode back one day,
> There in a veil of white, by candlelight, she knelt to pray,
> The Mission Bells told me that I must not stay,
> South of the border, down Mexico way . . .

Then we all joined in, 'Ay, Ay, Ay, Ay . . .' Big finish, 'Ay, Ay,
Ay, Ay-ya-yay!' And everyone applauded.

'Lovely, Joe,' said Andrew. 'Very nice indeed.'

But Isa went on singing, unaccompanied. '. . . I lied as I
whispered, "Mañana" – for our tomorrow never came. South
of the . . .'

'We've finished it, Isa!' her husband shouted, and we all
laughed.

She stopped singing, but added, 'I think it's very sad, that.'

'What?' asked Joe.

' "Mañana".'

'Eh?'

'Forget it, Isa,' her husband instructed. 'Fill up Joe's glass. It's
thirsty work playin' the piana.'

The pianist eagerly agreed. 'It is that! Especially down Mexico
way.' He accepted the refilled glass. 'Aw, ye're a good lassie, Isa.'

Joe's wife, Ella, a plump, tightly-bunched little woman, now
turned to me. 'What's your name again, son?'

'Bill Thompson.'

'That's right. Well, it's time you did your turn.'

'I can't sing.'

'Even so, you'll have tae dae somethin' tae oblige the company.'

'Thank you, I'd rather not.'

She drew back, affronted, and mimicked my accent. 'Oh,

really!' Then, overwhelmed by the insult, called to her husband, 'D'ye hear that, Joe?'

'Whiss-a'?'

'The boy here doesnae think much o' the entertainment.'

He swivelled round on the piano stool and squinted at me in a mock-humorous way through his cigarette smoke. 'Aw, that's a peety. We do our best.'

This seemed to me grossly unfair and I protested, 'No! I didn't say that.'

Isa, on the other side of the room, must have heard the concern in my raised voice and hurried over. 'What is it?'

But Ella was not willing to have the matter smoothed out by Isa just yet. 'Andrew!' she called. 'You'll hiv tae watch yer step as well, now ye've got such a choosey ludger.'

'I really didn't mean to . . .'

'Listen tae 'im!' cried Ella. It was my accent which annoyed her much more than my refusal to perform.

'What is the matter, Billy?' Isa asked me, very softly.

'I just said that I can't sing.'

'Never mind. Maybe ye can do a wee recitation.'

Blessedly, this possibility was interrupted by Joe who was concerned that attention had been too long off the champion. 'Andrew, I've meant tae ask you . . .'

'What's that, Joe?'

'Are there any exercises I could do tae . . . Oh, I know I could never be as fit as you, but I'd like to . . .'

'I know what you mean.' He sprang up, prepared to demonstrate. 'Well, here's one. See how my feet are placed. Then ye just . . .'

His wife, who knew exactly what was coming next, felt she could afford to pursue her suggestion to me. 'Jist a wee recitation, that ye learned at school, maybe.'

'I don't know if I can remember anything.'

Ella sighed noisily. 'Ahhh, leave him alane, Isa. It disnae bother me. It's jist I never expected tae meet a stuck-up youngster in *your* hoose.' This meant that, now, Isa was somewhat to blame. Then attention was switched again to the acrobatic Andrew as he completed his very stylish exercise.

Joe was stunned. 'Och, I could never do that!'

'All it needs is a bit o' practice. See! Here's another wan.'

Ella halted him in mid-swing. 'I'd think you might have somethin' tae say about that, Andrew.'

'What? About what?'

'Just watchin' you gives me an awful drouth,' said Joe, un-willing to abandon, or prolong, his preparatory work.

The good hostess took over. 'Hand me yer glass.'

'You're the girl for me, Isa. Ooops!' She fumbled the change-over and the glass smashed on the edge of the piano stool. She flicked the fragments under the stool and got another.

'Stuck-up youngsters,' muttered the tenacious Ella.

'He's remembered something,' said Isa, pouring for Joe. 'Ha-ven't ye, son?'

'Yes, I think so.'

'That's the boy.'

'Order! Order!' cried the pianist and played a portentous chord.

' "Abou Ben Adam",' I announced and began:

Abou Ben Adam, may his tribe increase,
Awoke one night from a deep dream of peace,
And saw . . .
And saw in the moonlight of his room,
Making it rich like a lily in bloom –
An angel, writing in a book of gold . . .

I paused. The next line refused to drop into my memory. Mentally I did a quick re-run of the opening, racing up to the blockage as though I might hurdle it with sheer speed. That didn't work and I repeated aloud, ' ". . . rich . . . like a lily in bloom . . . An angel . . ." '

'Another angel,' hissed Ella sceptically.

'Shhh!' cautioned Isa. But silence was no help. I was finished.

'That's a very short poem,' my tormentor observed.

'But very nice,' said Isa, leading a round of applause that nobody followed. 'And now it's time tae do my turn. Joe?' He at once launched into a florid introduction to 'The Rose of Tralee'.

'What's that tune called?' Andrew, heavily waggish, asked of the company.

'Och, you!' She aimed a playful swipe at him and he leapt nimbly away. Then she sang. She sang quite beautifully. Her sweet, light voice was transportingly clear and confident. But she seemed surprised, as surprised as anyone hearing her for the first time that she possessed so obviously fine a talent. There she stood, ungainly at the piano, badly made-up, the willing butt of so many jokes – singing with a pure spirit that held all of us enthralled. Even Andrew, I noticed, was gazing raptly towards her. And on that instant I knew intuitively why she always sang that song. It was his favourite. She sang for him. And he was affected by it. Indeed, *only* when she sang could one detect any outward sign of Mr Mulvenny's fondness for his wife. His habitual expression to her of impatient condescension changed to that of wonder. And while such moments lasted, both of them looked curiously young and vulnerable.

Apart from celebrating his victories, it was our duty to watch Andrew achieving them. Since he was a cross-country runner, this always had to be done at a distance and, apparently, through heavy rain. Sometimes – when there was a roadway close to the route – Mrs Mulvenny was an observer, but usually it was Andy and I who trudged from one vantage point to another then waited for the straggling line of runners to go piston-squelching past. Most of them looked as though they'd rather be doing *anything* else rather than what they were doing. Andrew, though, looked as though he was enjoying it. He also managed to look *cleaner* than any of the others when, as was usually the case, he came in first. And there, waiting for him on a bare little trestle-table, was the latest trophy. He was the only athlete I'd ever seen bow when he was given the prize. And whatever it was – cup or shield or plaque – when his name had been added to it, he would hand the prize to Mrs Mulvenny when he got home. It was *she* who'd place it on the lobby sideboard. To my relief, it was only for genuine silver trophies that parties were held.

Even so, my undisputed right to sole possession of the front room was steadily eroded. Andrew just could not imagine that anyone, other than himself, had a right to privacy. Often when I came back in the evening or on a week-end afternoon I'd find him there. Evidently he could see nothing wrong in that, but it annoyed me a great deal.

'Were you looking for something, Mr Mulvenny?'

'What's that, Billy!?' He turned in a leisurely fashion from the window.

'I wondered if you were looking for something.'

'No. I was just looking across the park, there. They're thinkin' of buildin' a sports centre, I believe.'

'Are they!'

He nodded and gave his attention once more to the wide and overgrown field which stretched from the back fence to steep rise of the hill. 'It's time they had some facilities in this area,' he said.

'Mr Mulvenny, did you have any lodgers before me?'

'No. Why'd you ask?'

'Because it seems you can't get used to the idea that this is my room.'

I had all his attention now. He crinkled his eyes. '*Your* room?'

'Yes.' For such a small man he was very intimidating but I'd made up my mind that this was something which had to be cleared up. 'While I am paying you rent it is my room.'

'So? Who says it's not?'

'Well . . . you seem to use it quite a lot.'

'The parties, you mean? Now, Billy, we explained at the outset that . . .'

'No. I don't mean the . . .'

'Don't you interrupt me!' He started rocking to and fro on the balls of his feet and his eyes glittered.

'I'm sorry.'

'It'll get ye nowhere comin' the high and mighty here, m'boy. We explained about the parties the first night you were here and you agreed it would be all right.'

I allowed a couple of beats of silence before I replied, 'Yes. That is all right. I didn't mean the parties.'

'When dae A use it any other time?'

'You are often in here. Like you are here now.'

He gasped with incredulity. 'Is that what you call "using" your room?'

'Aren't you?'

'I was lookin' out the window. I walked into an empty room and looked out the window. How does that interfere wi' you? Don't be daft.' He shook his head and padded away from me. 'Hah! Ye'll be wantin' a lock on the door next.'

'Yes. I do want a lock on the door.'

He came swinging back to poise himself directly in front of me and almost hissed, 'Well, you can want all you like, boy, but I'll have no locks on the doors inside my own house.' The full force of such a bizarre request struck him. 'What a cheek!'

'It's quite usual, Mr Mulvenny.'

'It's no' usual for me.'

'I'm sure if you had another lodger, he'd expect the same.'

'There won't be another. There wouldn't be you if it wasnae for young Andy.'

'What?'

'You were supposed tae have *his* room – when he went tae college.'

'But he still had a year at school when I arrived.'

'Aye, well. That's because he had tae repeat his last year at school to get the certificate for the college.'

'I see.'

'Oh, he got it all right. Be startin' at the Accountancy College in the Autumn. That'll mean *he* has tae go into digs in Glasgow – so, *your* money was tae pay for that.' He gave me a sharp admonitory nod. 'Ye can be sure it's only for his sake I'd put up wi' a lodger.'

'In that case, could I make a suggestion?'

'Okay. What is it?'

'When Andy's looking at digs, could you tell him to make sure there's a lock on the door.'

Andrew gave the slightest grimace of discomfiture. 'I'll tell him,' he said. 'And maybe, in the Autumn, you could move intae the wee room.'

'No. I'm sorry, I won't.'

'In that case, Billy, you'd better put up wi' things the way they are – or get out altogether.' I thought he would leave me to think about it but he wanted an answer there and then. 'Fair enough?' he prodded, waiting for surrender.

'I'll stay.'

At the door he gave me a tight little smile. 'I thought ye would.'

The moment he'd gone I discovered that I was holding myself tense and feeling suddenly tired. Other people, too, remarked that Andrew had a draining effect upon them. He seemed so packed with controlled energy. It was as though any antagonism to him induced a dangerously high voltage and if you stood close enough you became either a fuse wire or an earthing device. At seventeen, I was a rather thin fuse wire. After that interview my integrity was blown as far as Mr Mulvenny was concerned. For me it seemed enough that, whereas I hadn't won my point, I had at least made my point. Less reassuring was the discovery that I amounted to no more than away-from-home expenses for Andy.

In the year I'd spent at the Mulvennys I had noted the faith that Andrew had in his son but could find no possible justification for it. And perhaps it was because Andy himself had difficulty finding justification for it that he tried so hard to please his father in matters where neither intelligence nor ability were required.

One afternoon, when we were out to watch a race that never reached us, we were caught in a downpour that couldn't be ignored and took shelter in a linesman's hut by the railway. 'Why do we do this?' I wondered aloud as I peered out at the water bouncing off the sleepers.

'A don't know why *you* do it,' said Andy, with unusual candour.

'Doesn't he expect us to?'

'He expects me tae watch 'im.'

'But you're interested in running, aren't you?'

'No' in the least! But my faither thinks A am.'

We were, necessarily, standing very close together. That, the heady smell of creosote, the confessional-box dimensions of the hut and an utterly miserable and wasted afternoon had apparently broken down Andy's normally defensive attitude. I couldn't let the opportunity slip, but started lightly enough. 'Maybe that's because you tell him you're interested. And you remember where and when he won everything he's ever won.'

'A don't remember them. A memorise them. It's jist a matter o' studyin' all thae trophies on the lobby table.'

I was amazed. 'Do you?'

He nodded sadly. 'Oh, aye. That an' the club records, and any wee bits in the newspapers. A memorise a' that.'

'What on earth for?'

'It's quite inter*est*in'.'

'But you said you weren't interested.'

He gave me a worried glance, as though resentful that I wouldn't allow him to mix truth and lies on the same subject. He opted for the truth. 'That's right. Well, the thing is, if A know a' that stuff, it keeps his mind aff the fact that A cannae run, or jump, or be an athlete like him.'

'Have you tried?'

'A've tried. A wis hardly able tae *walk* when he had me tryin'.' He scuffed one foot through the gravel inside the hut. 'It wis nae use. A'm jist no' made for it. Even he had tae admit that A'd never make a success o' it.'

'But you can succeed in other things.'

'Oh, aye! Wance A'm qualified as an accountant he'll be happy.'

'You *do* want to be an accountant?'

'Dae you want tae be an engineer? A mean, really? Is that whit you've always wantit tae be? Or is that whit's wantit fur ye?'

'I didn't think about it much. It's my father's occupation and I expect I'll go into my father's business.'

'Sure.'

'But your father isn't an accountant.'

'Naw. My father's an athlete. No' jist that – he's a good athlete. He wins prizes at it. That's whit makes him so sure o' himsel'. That's whit he was gonnae pass on tae me.'

For several minutes there was only the sound of the rain drumming on the tarred roof as we considered the obligations of only sons to the hopes of their fathers. More pertinently I tried to imagine how irascible my father might have become if I'd turned out to be dull and stupid with no aptitude for engineering when he'd devoted his life to it, largely on my behalf. I began to appreciate Mr Mulvenny's fortitude and spirit when the only possible success in the future depended upon Andy. It was not, after all, that he had unfounded faith in his son. It was more fragile and more tenacious than that. He had unfounded hope. I asked Andy, 'Couldn't your father go in for promotion in the shipyard?'

'Instead, you mean?'

That was what I meant, but said, 'No. As well.'

'That wid be like admittin' that his job wis more important than his runnin'.'

'And isn't it?'

Andy shook his head. 'He knows the job's nothin' special.'

And that, of course, was the motive force of everything in Mr Mulvenny's life. He *was* someone special. There were many charge-hands and foremen and managers in the shipyard. There was only one champion runner. He could do with ease what few men could do at all; and out there, through the downpour, defying the weight of the sodden turf and the hazards of treacherous mud, he was proving it, again. To me, in the snug dry hut, it now seemed less objectionable that at home he was a haughty and irritating despot. His home was just where he kept the emblems of his real identity; and his family.

At the shipyard I very rarely saw him at all, since the engine side was quite a distance from the shipbuilding side. And it was there, in the department which stored and worked all the plating, that Mr Mulvenny was a charge-hand. On one occasion, though, I was sent across there by my foreman with the secret plans of a kitchen wall-cabinet he wanted to have constructed.

'Ask for Andrew Mulvenny,' my foreman said. 'Anybody there will point him out tae ye.'

'I know him.'

'Oh? Well, jist hand him this sketch and tell him it's fae me. He'll know what it is.'

This seemed superfluous since, even at a glance, a child would know what it was. It was a small kitchen cabinet made of aluminium planishing sheets. But what my foreman meant was that he had a confidential arrangement with Andrew to have the

'home-job' done, and have the time and materials costed to a
legitimate customer – probably the Admiralty, which bore the
cost of most unexplained expenditure in that and every yard
where they were philanthropic enough to place a contract.

The plate shop was vast and very noisy. Sprawled all over the
sanded floor were gargantuan machines which rolled thick cold
steel as though it were papier-mâché. There were huge presses,
bending machines, and punches which could bite gaping holes in
anything that was fed to them. Overhead, hanging from slings or
magnets, the cranes bore plates as slender-looking as guillotine
blades or as unwieldy as the whole bow section of a ship. Through
this giant's playground-in-pandemonium the small figure of Mr
Mulvenny strode with purposeful calm and authority. He wore a
brown 'smeeky', or dust-coat, which looked as though it was
tailor-made. As he approached me I started shouting the message
I'd been given. Without pausing he shook his head at me and
walked past. Without looking back he beckoned, indicating that I
should follow him to a little office which had been sound-proofed
by the simple means of covering it with sandbags. There were no
windows. It looked exactly like a wartime command-post. Andrew sat at his desk and extended his hand for the sketch.

After a moment he said, 'That seems clear enough. When does
he want it?'

'He didn't say.'

'You can tell him it'll be after the week-end.'

'I don't think he wants me to know.'

Andrew leaned back and raised his eyebrows. 'Why's that?'

'Well, I got the impression it was a . . . private arrangement.'

'I don't think he'll care what impression you got, Billy. And I
think he'll want to know it'll be ready by Tuesday. So, tell him
that. Okay?'

I nodded, then suddenly he sprang up at me; or so I thought
as I stumbled back. He lunged out of the door, allowing me to
hear what he had already identified. The clamour had increased
to include a violent screeching sound. Mr Mulvenny was running towards a group of shouting men gathered at one of the
massive rolling mills. A long sheet of thick steel plate which was
being drawn into the machine had slipped out of the guides
which fed it squarely into the rollers. It was buckling and
grinding. The machine operator had jumped clear of his perch
as the free edge of the plate reared up at him, blocking the
machine controls. There was no way of stopping the machine
and the great jaws went on pulling and folding and tearing the

plate. The noise was incredible and the mindless violence of it was frightening.

Andrew, alert and on his toes like a boxer squaring up to the inhuman giant opponent, circled round assessing the dangers and the damage. The free edge of the plate was scraping over the control position and crumpling the little handrail which surrounded it. The access ladder had already been chewed into the machine. Andrew took off his dust-coat and lay down on the sand. He wriggled carefully under the plate as it continued to move slowly forward. All we could see was his forearm and his hand gripping the edge of the plate as it started to drag him as well. Only then, when it was too late to stop him, did we realise his intention. Clinging to the back of the plate, he hoped it would pull him near enough to reach the Stop button. If the plate folded inward he would be crushed. If the Stop button was damaged or its effect delayed, he would be too near to avoid falling under the roller. His men watched his progress open-mouthed and one was weeping at the sheer bravery of it.

As he edged nearer to the control-box which we could not see, we *could* see blood running down his exposed forearm. He was supporting practically all of his weight with one hand and the edge of the plate was cutting into his palm. Meanwhile, electricians were in a frenzy of activity trying to find the main power point which fed that particular machine. One after another the wrong machines fell silent while the one we were all watching screeched and thundered. Andrew held on and inch by inch the plate continued to buckle outward. Then the roaring stopped. He'd reached the button and it worked. Suddenly deprived of power, the rollers violently regurgitated several feet of twisted plate. It loosened Andrew's grip and threw him clear. Whether he was unconscious or just exhausted I didn't know but he was carried into the little sandbagged office. His trousers were wet and soiled but the men who lifted him cared nothing for that.

I waited around until he recovered. They told me he wanted to see me and when I went into the box he was dressed in dungarees and his hand was bandaged. He beckoned me close so that the others wouldn't hear. 'Billy, ye'll say nothing aboot this at home.'

'But your . . .'

His voice was soft but peremptory. 'Nothing! Okay?'

I nodded and went back to the machine-shop, marvelling that anyone could take such a risk to save a machine. Admittedly, it was a machine worth tens of thousands of pounds but I think Andrew had taken that risk because it was his responsibility; and because he was sure he could do anything he set his mind to. Nor did he ever mention the incident. Though willing to boast about his prowess as a runner, he said not a word about his astonishing courage. But it was saving the machine which got him promotion, whether he wanted it or not. The firm jumped him over the position of foreman to make him a manager.

As soon as he got the much higher wage in his first *monthly* pay cheque he wanted to throw me out. In his view it was bad enough that a charge-hand should take in a lodger. The thought that a *manager* should have one was insufferable. By then I was settled and unwilling to leave. Also, Mrs Mulvenny had got used to me and with Andy only home at week-ends she liked having my company. It was she who suggested a quite subtle formula. 'Tell him you'll move as soon as ye find another place jist as good.' That's what I told Andrew. And occasionally I reported hearing of a vacancy but it did not surprise either of us that such finds never came up to the standard of *his* accommodation.

Young Andy was more fortunate. He'd found lodgings with a saintly old couple in a lane off the Broomielaw. As he told it on his week-end visits, they had to be forced to take the rent and were obsessive about privacy. Not only did they give him a key to *his* room, but securely locked themselves away in their own. Everything was done for him, though he never saw them do it. He was less happy about his studies, however. The Glasgow School of Accountancy was a grimly efficient task-master with a reputation for producing winners. They did this partly by excellence of training but more by their ability to spot losers at a very early stage – and get rid of them. Their students faced a half-term test and a full-term exam in each of the three years of the course. Andy lasted a year.

I knew what news he had brought as soon as he came into the kitchen that Saturday afternoon at lunchtime. His parents, not knowing that such news was possible, were deluded until we had eaten the meal which had been kept waiting for him. I think that was the only time I felt sorry for Andy. As we ate he replied in the usual way to the usual questions about what was happening in Glasgow and if there had been any sightings of the saintly hermits. Mrs Mulvenny had detailed questions on the serviceability of his socks and underwear. Also, the state of his health. Constant study had made him pale and Mr Mulvenny always wanted a report on the quantity of fresh air taken during the previous week. All these questions were answered and Mr Mulvenny seemed well pleased. 'I think ye've got a bit more colour in yer face,' he said.

'Well . . . I've had a few days away from the College,' Andy began – trying to get to the point as gently as possible.

'Oh, aye? That's the end of term break, I suppose.'

'In a way, yes.' Andy followed his father in rising from the table.

Mrs Mulvenny was about to eat her meal and I remained seated, sipping my tea very slowly so that she wouldn't be eating alone; though she did not notice that I did so.

'If you had a few days off ye should have come home,' said Andrew.

Andy let that pass and I vividly saw how he had spent those days, walking along the river bank, wandering through the impervious Victorian city, wondering how he was going to tell his father the truth. He caught my eye and his expression was utterly wretched.

'I used to hate end of term,' I said, uselessly.

'So, you'll have had your Exam, then?'

'Yes. We had the Exam last week.'

'*Last* week?'

Andy nodded. 'This week we got the results.'

'I see.' And Mr Mulvenny was just beginning to see.

'They hiv an awful lot o' exams in that place,' Isa observed, her mouth full and her knife busily scraping the plate. She enjoyed her own cooking.

'Well?' asked Mr Mulvenny, ignoring the interruption.

'I didnae . . . pass . . . the Exam.'

'Oh! I'm sorry tae hear that. So, this'll mean another extra year, eh?'

'No.'

'I mean, like ye did your last year at school again. Ye got through fine the second time.'

'No, Da', it's not like that.' His voice had taken on that soft, ingratiating, tone I'd so often heard him use to his father – as though he was holding up a cushion to muffle the force of expected anger. 'On Thursday, there, they gave me a letter.' He drew it quickly from the inside pocket of his jacket and gave it to Andrew. But while it was being read he reported on the contents, trying to make the blunt rejection more acceptable. 'They have an awful lot of people wanting tae get intae the College, so they cannae really keep other people on if they don't pass the Exams. It's jist that they don't have the space, y'know, or the staff tae cope wi' . . .'

' "Quite unsuitable",' quoted Mr Mulvenny. 'Did it take them a year tae find out ye were quite unsuitable?'

'Whit's that?' asked Isa, now tuning in to the conversation. And, to my astonishment, they did not tell her. They just ignored her question and she did not find that surprising. There was a silence while Mr Mulvenny folded the letter and put it in *his* pocket. 'Whit dae they say?' Isa persisted.

Andrew brushed the question aside. 'It's jist a . . . it's an end of term report. A statement on the curriculum for next term.' He knew his wife would not pursue a word as difficult as 'curriculum'. And he was right. She gave a little grunt of impatience and set about clearing up the table. Andrew then looked directly at his son and promised, 'You're goin' tae be busy next term. And in Glasgow.'

At the time I assumed he meant another accountancy college. Certainly Isa would have no preference between one such establishment or another, and if that could be managed there was no point in alarming her.

'Thanks, Da',' said Andy, clearly amazed at the resilience of his father and no doubt ashamed that he'd been so fearful of breaking the news. What he, and I, had not realised was that the College had slighted not Andy but Andrew by the rejection he now carried. The son was now wholly an extension of his father, and his father – no matter what evidence might be presented – could never be a loser. It was too late for that.

' "Unsuitable"!' Mr Mulvenny repeated the word that rankled. 'How can ye be unsuitable when ye were good enough tae get in tae their College?' None of us could answer that and he went on. 'They found the fees suitable all right.'

'It's jist a matter o' the space. That's how they cannae let students do a year a second time,' Andy repeated to make it more true.

Mr Mulvenny puffed disdainfully. 'For all they've done ye'd have been as well at night-school like Billy, there.'

'How often dae ye go?' Andy asked me, as one unfamiliar with a plebeian ritual.

'Tuesdays and Thursdays here and Fridays at the Tech. in Glasgow.'

He was amazed. 'Ye go up tae Glasgow and back every Friday!'

'Yes.'

Mr Mulvenny shook his head dolefully. 'He's up tae his elbows in grease all day then back and forward on trains all night.'

'That's one reason why I'm going to buy a car,' I told them.

'A *car*!' They exclaimed the words in disbelieving unison. There was no one on that street, or for several streets around, who had a car of their own. There were one or two vans with holes cut in the sides for windows but no real cars. The idea that an apprentice should own a car was indecent.

'I'll be getting it in the spring.'

'What do you want a car for?' asked Mr Mulvenny. 'Ye go nowhere.'

'I will when I have it.'

'Maybe we could go over tae Largs in the summer,' Isa suggested.

'Of course! I'll be able to take you out wherever you want to go.'

'Wherever *we* want to go,' her husband decided, 'we can manage perfectly well on our own.'

'He could take us out to the field events,' Andy offered and I could see his father had difficulty rejecting that out of hand. But really I didn't care whether or not they found a suitable use for my car. What was important was that, at last, I would be able to insulate myself from strangers.

In the train, I stare up at the blue ceiling-light. It seems to gyrate and recede from me. It brings to mind the blue, flashing light on the roof of the police car.

That came on a stickily warm sunny morning. I was off work because a deep cut in my hand had become infected with lubricating oil. This did not prevent my habitual spare-time activity of repainting the coal box in the lobby. Shortly before lunch-time Mrs Harper called in on Isa before she went on to do some shopping. They were talking in the kitchen about Andy.

Isa told her, 'He comes home at week-ends, of course, but it's no' worth his while travellin' up and down tae Glasgow during the week.'

'How long will he be at this er . . .'

'Secretarial College.'

'Aye.'

'Another two years, if he passes the exams, that is.' She felt it wise to add this rider because young Andy had been 'unlucky' a few times by now.

'I expect he will,' said Ella. 'They're sure tae be easier than them he had for the accountants.' She eased the straps of her brassière off the red patches of her shoulders. 'How can ye stick the heat in here, Isa? And the smell o' that paint! Will ye no' open the winda?'

'Oh, certainly.' She leaned over the cluttered sink and hefted the frame up as far as it would go. 'But I think the air's warmer outside than it is in.'

'Ooooph! That's better. Just as long as there's some movement.' Ella unbuttoned her blouse and flapped it a few times. 'Still, it must be funny, not havin' Andy in the house, I mean.'

'Aye. And even though it's best for him, still, it's a worry.'

'A'm sure. Knowin' what Glasgow's like.'

'It's no' that so much. It's just . . . I'm that used tae doin' for them, y'know? Sometimes I just forget, like . . . he'll no' be in for his tea – and I make it. Then Andrew thinks I'm complainin'.'

Ella had her own views on how Isa should deal with Andrew's complaining but from years of fruitless advice and example knew there was no use in mentioning them. She changed the subject and lowered her voice – though not enough. 'Ye've still got yer ludger, though?'

'Oh, aye!' Isa stage-whispered. 'An' he's awful considerate. That's a change, tae. Aye, Billy's a big help tae me wi' Andrew out so much.'

The sound of the ambulance passing at speed, bell jangling, cut through the other traffic sounds which rose from the street through the open window.

'I thought he'd stopped the runnin',' said Ella.

'That's right. For over a year now. But he's out practically every night coachin' – trainin' the younger ones, y'know.'

'He's a right go-ahead man, your Andrew,' Ella had to concede.

'He is that!'

'I could have done wi' somebody like him, instead-a Joe.'

Isa shook a spoon at her in friendly reproval. 'Now, Ella, that's not right. Joe's very . . . cheery.'

'Aye, wi' a bucket in 'im.'

'He's a good turn.'

'On the piana – that's aboot a'.' She wriggled uncomfortably. 'And we havenae even got a piana.'

They lapsed into silence for several long moments, considering the merits of their respective husbands and gradually it occurred to Isa that in all the time she'd known the Harpers, one obvious question had never been answered.

'Ella? What does Joe *do*, exactly?'

'Do? How d'ye mean, "do"?' Any irritation in her voice was more due to the heat than the question.

'What does he do for work, I mean.'

'He does withoot, maist o' the time,' said Ella. 'When we got married, he was a welder – or, so he claimed. Since then I have no idea, but whatever it is, he gets money for it. I believe he helps bookies a lot.'

'Andrew doesnae approve o' gamblin',' Isa reported.

'Naw. There's a helluva lot Andrew doesnae approve o',' her friend observed, unabashed. She writhed in a struggle with her underclothes. 'Holy God! These things are stickin' tae me. I'd better go the messages before A melt. An' it'll be worse goin' oot in the efternoon.'

'I don't think I'll bother today wi' messages.'

'Well,' said Ella, sensing evasion, 'if you're no' goin' oot, is there anything I can get ye?'

'I don't think so, Ella. I think I'll just . . . er . . .'

'Make do?'

Isa laughed at being so easily caught out. 'That's it! Must do's a good master, and make do's his wife.'

'Aye, but first ye should make sure – what there is,' retorted Ella. 'You're a soft-mark, Isa. I've told ye that before. It's wan thing I'll say for Joe – when he's got it I always get the most of it.'

'I'm sure ye do.'

'Damn right!'

'It's no' that I don't get enough money,' Isa said, and believed it. 'The thing is A'm no' a very good manager. Time and again Andrew's showed me how A could've managed better.'

'Oh, aye?'

'He's awful good at figures, Andrew.'

'Figures, tae!' said Ella, but tempered the sarcasm in her voice just enough to avoid bringing it to Isa's attention.

'A think that's how young Andy got interested in accountancy – hearin' us talkin' aboot money.'

'He'd be able tae hear that well enough in his room, I expect.'

I went out carrying the can of waste turpentine to empty it in the wash-house drain. At the bottom of the stair I almost ran into a policeman and beyond him, framed in the close-mouth, I saw the police car with its flashing blue light. The policeman asked me which landing the Mulvennys lived on, then told me why he wanted to know. He was a young constable and obviously glad to find somebody else who could break the news.

The women turned at the sound of the front door slamming and were startled to see me burst into the kitchen. Several details imprinted themselves on my mind. Mrs Mulvenny standing in front of the sink at the window, looking over her shoulder at me;

like a tall, ungainly bird alarmed by a predator. And Mrs Harper, half sprawled on a chair, her legs stretched out and her blouse unbuttoned all down the front. I was glad she was there. Unskilled in the niceties of social occasions, she was a woman of resilience in a crisis.

Having caught my breath, I began, 'Mrs Mulvenny . . .'

'Billy! What is it?' Her voice was maddeningly far from suiting what I knew to be the occasion.

Ella focused much more accurately. 'What's up, son? Ye're as white as a sheet.'

'There's a police car . . .'

'Police!' Isa turned right round, but slowly, and took a step towards me.

Ella scrambled to her feet. 'Whit dae they want ye fur?' Then, coming immediately to my defence, 'I'll talk tae them.'

'No. Not me. They've come to take Mrs Mulvenny to the hospital.'

Ella knew at once why. 'Aw, Isa! It's Andrew.'

'My Andrew? Oh.'

I forced myself to go on. 'An accident in the plate-shop. They asked me to tell you and they . . . the police are waiting to take you to the hospital.'

'Oh, God! Is he bad?'

'They said he . . . I don't know. Car's waiting . . . now! They'll take you.'

'No.'

Ella, for whom time had not come to a halt, tried to reason with her. 'They've got Andrew in the hospital, Isa. You'll have to go. He'll want to see you.'

'Go? Like this?' With an attitude of wonder she gazed down at the floral, and stained, wrap-around pinafore she was wearing.

'Please, Mrs Mulvenny!'

She tried, yet again, to assimilate the separate factors which should not be any of her business. 'The police. Andrew in hospital. Car waitin'.' Then she came to me and stared close into my face – as though, after all, she would see I was lying. She saw I was not lying and said, 'Will you come?'

'Do you want me wi' ye, Isa?' asked Ella.

Mrs Mulvenny shook her head, still staring at me. 'Billy, will you come? I cannae go ma'sel. You come wi' me.' Then she picked her way out of the room and down the stairs, exactly as she was, and without looking back.

I didn't know what to do. And, at eighteen, that incompetence bothered me a lot. Later, I realised the main thing I had to do was – be there.

Andrew had been crushed under a steel plate when a crane-sling broke. It was several days before we knew whether or not he would live. Isa spent those days waiting in hospital corridors. She refused to eat. It was when they told her Andrew had started to recover that she collapsed – a result of delayed shock, relief and fatigue. What they did not tell her was that Andrew's legs would remain paralysed. He had been told but, with that maddening composure which was close to arrogance, this was something else he kept from his wife when we were able to visit him for the first time. The healthy colour and shine on his skin were gone from his face but his eyes were as sharp and bright as ever.

'Hello, Isa! Billy!'

Mrs Mulvenny bumped heavily against the corner of the foot of the bed in her eagerness to reach him. 'Andrew!' She was smiling and weeping at once. 'A've been here all the time but they wouldnae let me in till now.'

'Aye. They told me.' His voice was very weak. 'What have ye brought me?'

'Oh, not much. Billy's got it in the bag there.'

I laid out the usual array of fruit juice, fruit and magazines, then retired to a position notionally out of range of whatever private conversation they might wish to have.

'That's very nice,' said Andrew. 'Next time ye come ye could bring the local paper. I want tae keep up tae date wi' what the club's doin'.'

'When'll they let ye oot?'

'That'll no' be for a while yet.'

'A'll come an' visit ye whenever they'll let me,' Isa promised.

'No, no. Once a week will be fine,' Andrew decided firmly. 'One o' the firm's directors is comin' tae see me the morra. His secretary phoned them.'

'Fancy that! Still, it wis a terrible thing tae happen and A suppose they feel a wee bit responsible.' She was uncertain of that, but repeated, 'A terrible business altogether.'

Andrew shook his head impatiently and smiled. 'Not so terrible. One thing's sure, Andy's goin' tae be all right now.'

Mrs Mulvenny could see no connection in these remarks but I saw the clear line to financial compensation. When he said that, his voice had something of its old assurance. He knew that, even if he was going to be a cripple for the rest of his life, he would win.

It was the ward sister who told Isa about the paralysis; in a whispered conversation as we were leaving after a visit. On the bus going home she was very quiet and, suspecting why, I did not prompt her. As we were nearing the playing-fields she voiced the end of what must have been a commentary she'd been running in her mind.

'We'll have more time th'gither, that's wan thing,' she said.

'What?'

'Wi' him no' able tae get out at all, we'll have more time th'gither than we've ever had before. I'll be glad o' *that*, at least.' She turned to me. 'And if we have that, nothin' else can go wrong, can it?'

'No. I'm sure everything will be all right.'

Finding herself without the strict day-to-day guidance of her husband, Mrs Mulvenny cautiously, then wholeheartedly, expanded her interests. She took a job. Working with other people gave her a jaunty assurance she'd never had before. Now she and I sat down to the table at the same time and she'd tell me about her day.

'They lassies at the shop have me in stitches! And the things they don't know wid fill a book.'

'What sort of things?'

'Never mind. Things you've nae right to know.' She laughed. 'But I keep them right – or thin, at least!'

'Oh!' I was embarrassed. How was it, I wondered, that whenever one joked with women they always seemed to think it was a joke about sex.

'They're awful nice lassies, though,' Isa went on. 'Y'know, it's the first time I've thought it would have been fine tae have a daughter instead o' a son. Of course, Mr Mulvenny was quite set on havin' a son – tae be good at the sort o' thing he likes.'

'Yes.'

She at once purged this faintly disloyal thought, 'I'm just mentionin' that the lassies make me think o' that. Everybody really wants a son and Andy's a fine boy. He'll make a good husband for some lucky lassie.'

'Yes.'

'So wid you! You're such a great help in the hoose. When are you gonnae start coortin'?'

She smiled across the table at me. This was a theme to which she'd returned time and again during the winter that Andrew was in hospital. It seemed to worry her that I didn't have any 'dates' and occasionally, when I took *her* to the pictures, she behaved with uncharacteristic and wholly misplaced tact, thinking that I'd been stood up by some girl and that she was filling a painful breach. I made it as plain as I could that she wasn't standing in for anybody but she interpreted my insistence as evidence of hurt and tried harder than ever to make me enjoy myself. In April, though, I did have something encouraging to report to her.

'I shall be having my tea early on Thursday, Mrs Mulvenny.'

'Oh, yes?'

'I'm going to see *The Inn of the Sixth Happiness*.'

'Is that a picture?'

'Yes. It's based on a book called *The Small Woman* but they got a very tall woman to play it.'

She sensed some disapproval in this and rather sharply observed, 'Well, we cannae all be small and neat.'

'Or Ingrid Bergman, for that matter.'

Isa let that pass and fastened on the more important aspect. 'Ye're no goin' by yersel again, are ye?'

'No. I'm taking a girl called Elsie.'

'Oh, ho!'

'Yes. And we have some things to discuss first, so I'd like to have my tea early.'

'Things tae discuss?' To her that meant one of two things; an unwanted pregnancy or an imminent engagement. She had to tread warily. 'Ye never let on there was somethin' serious in the wind.'

'I only met her a couple of weeks ago.'

That was disappointing. Nothing serious could be obvious or arrived at in a couple of weeks, so she went on to relate the latest hilarious happenings at the wool shop.

The money she made at the shop was needed. For though the shipyard eventually paid Andrew a lump sum in compensation, it all went to Andy. He was to be set up in business. That meant he didn't really have to continue slogging at the Secretarial College. There was no need. He became a sort of Insurance Broker. He'd opened an office by the time Andrew was ready to leave hospital and drew himself away from the city long enough to accompany his father home in the ambulance.

In the sleeping compartment, once more in motion, I switch on the bunk-light and open the new pack of cigarettes provided by the attendant. I know I'll need them. The lighter flame is startlingly yellow against the neon glow. And I leave the light on. If I'm going to face that homecoming again, I can't do it in the dark.

★

I waited with Isa in a sparkling, spring-clean atmosphere that Saturday morning. In the lobby, the brand new wheel-chair, glinting with chrome, reflected the gleam of silver trophies on the sideboard. Even the coal-box, covered with a length of bright curtain material, was passing disguised as a hall-table. And, of course, Isa herself was wearing a new frock. It was deep cream-coloured in jersey material with long puffed sleeves gathered tightly at the wrist. Yes, everything was ready; over ready. It had been for days, during which her excitement and gauche high spirits had grown to a hectic pitch of expectation.

Then, about half an hour before Andrew was due, she decided to cut her hair.

'Why?' I asked her, more than a little irritated because I, as chief helper in all the preparations, had decided that positively nothing else could be done. She was in my room bending down to look in the triple mirrors of the dressing-table.

She sighed, 'Well, I've had it this way for ages. And ma face's got thinner. You don't mind if I cut it in here? You've got the mirrors where I can see the back.'

'I like it the way it is.'

'Aye, but you don't hiv tae sort it up every mornin'. Look! See the length of it! He must be sick of the sight o' me like this. I've had my hair the same way since we got married. Of course, it was all the "go" then – plaited and coiled, y'know. Like Mrs Simpson.'

'Who?'

'Mrs Simpson.'

'I don't know a Mrs Simpson.'

'Aye, ye *dae*. Her that married the King.' Isa began shearing off long strands of glossy auburn hair. 'Of course, she changed it after a while. But I kept it the same. Made me look no' sa tall, ye know, drawn down on my ears.' She chuckled as she peered into the mirrors to see what havoc she was causing at the back. 'Andrew made me wear flat shoes for the weddin' photographs. Quite right. It's that silly lookin' if the woman's bigger than the man – in a photograph, anyway. That ye're gonnae keep!' The strict logic of this line of thought defies explanation, but it made sense to me then, the way Isa said it. And she went on, 'I must say I always liked him – the Prince a' Wales. And they had a very happy marriage. Like us, in a way.' She surveyed the effect, so far, and sighed with satisfaction – whether at her skill as a hairdresser or at the continuing success of the Windsors, I didn't know.

Having rid herself of the sheer length of hair she now set about the idea of styling and vigorously wielded a comb. 'That's a chuggy bit,' she said, wrenching the comb free, then returned to Edward VIII and his lady. 'Pity they never had any weans, though. I'd have liked tae have more, but after the bother I had wi' Andy they gave me a big operation. If we'd had a few more sons, wan o' them might have went in for sports. Andrew would have liked that.' She ducked forward to catch my eye in the mirror. 'Have I got that straight? These scissors are no' much use. It wastes them, cuttin' up the cardboard tae light the fire. Still, bein' an only son means he has a' the better chance. He'll do well, the same boy. Just you wait!'

This meant that whereas she and Mr Mulvenny never had any doubts about Andy's prospects she was acknowledging that I may have been puzzled by his several choices of career when, for some reason, he didn't pass particular exams. That was all changed by the compensation money and now everything was clear ahead.

'Gi'es ye somethin' tae look forward tae in yer old age,' she said. 'Nothing should be spared for yer own.' There was a pause filled by the sound of random snipping, then she concluded, 'You know, I think she was bigger than him, tae – that Mrs Simpson.'

We were interrupted by the slamming of car doors in the street and I ran to the open kitchen window. Having caught the Mulvenny habit I turned back into the room and shouted, 'That's the ambulance now!'

Isa's excited voice called, 'Well, shut the winda in case he looks up!'

When I rejoined her in my room she had bundled all the shorn hair into a newspaper and was heading for the kitchen fire to burn it. 'Shall I go down?'

'Naw, you wait here. The ambulance men'll carry him up and there's no' much room on the stair. Oh, I'd better move these rugs so he can wheel the chair in. Is that everything, noo?'

'Everything's fine.'

'Are ye sure the chair's handy in the lobby, there?'

'Yes, I've . . .'

Suddenly, consternation smote her. 'Whit's that smell? Oh, my God – the stew.' She ran into the kitchen wailing, 'I knew there was something. Did ye no' see that smoke?'

'Maybe it's your hair,' I shouted.

'Is it Hell! It's the stew.'

I waited for her to return from the kitchen but before she could complete her salvage operation we heard the front door open and the ambulance party bumping against things in the lobby. Andy's voice asked, 'Is that all right, Dad?' I went to help them.

Andy looked beyond me. 'Is the place on fire?'

'No,' his father grunted. 'It's the dinner burned, I expect.'

'Can you manage through to the front room?' asked Andy. He meant my room. And he totally ignored the two ambulance men who'd carried his father up six flights of stairs. They turned and left without a word.

'I can manage fine,' said Mr Mulvenny. 'Fine. Don't shove me. Where's your mother?'

'She's in the kitchen,' I told them.

'Isa!' he shouted, and wheeled himself unerringly into my room. Obviously he'd done a lot of practice in chair-manoeuvring at the hospital.

Mrs Mulvenny called back, gurgling slightly with pleasure. 'Here, Andrew. I'm just putting the water in the pot.' Then she appeared, flushed and happy, in the doorway. Mr Mulvenny wheeled the chair in a neat arc to face her. 'Andrew! It's great tae have ye back,' she said.

'What have you done with your hair?' he asked in a voice that was contracted like a tight fist.

'Do you like it? I thought I needed a change.'

Andrew gathered himself and spat venomously, 'You look like a bloody clown!'

In the train, at a heart-mended distance of time and miles from that scene, I still find it necessary to reach for my handkerchief and mop up. An express rushing in the opposite direction seems to rake our train with heavy machine-gun fire as it passes and I rock on my feet. I slide open the silencing shutter then put out the light so that I can watch the amorphous shapes of the scenery whip past under a cloudy sky. There is something ridiculous about sleeping coaches, as Norman MacCaig said; about stretching yourself on a shelf to be carried sideways through the night. Increasingly, my shelf this night is becoming something of a rack. I try to recall the really happy times, for me at the Mulvennys', and realise – with dismay – that they'd all been when Andrew was in hospital and Andy was living in Glasgow. They were when Isa was working in the wool shop. She was such a cheerful woman and had an intricate way of thinking which I found fascinating. Other people, too, found her cheerful, but also muddled and vague. They did not take the trouble to follow her line of thought or, perhaps, were certain that their own line of thought was the only one to follow. They, of course, were much older than I and had the experience to confirm such a time-saving prejudice. Isa's conversation delighted me.

During that 'free' period she did not feel guilty of thinking primarily of herself, or of enjoying it, Andrew was being cared for in hospital – which was as it should be. Young Andy was full of plans and busy in Glasgow – which was as they'd always hoped. And there she was – gossiping with willing customers at the wool shop, sharing hilarious secrets with the sales-girls and earning 'good money' on her own account. At home her only duty was looking after a young English lodger who enjoyed a strange lapse of pride in thinking it natural that he should do many of the household chores. Isa could hardly wait for Andrew to come home so that he could see how much she had improved herself in assurance and capability.

In the event, he was not impressed. Indeed, he found her remarkable growth in assurance extremely irritating, since it seemed designed to emphasise his sudden lack of use as an athlete and as a worker. If the Harpers had remained in the neighbourhood Ella may have seen to it that Mrs Mulvenny did not give up any of her gains. But Ella and Joe had been among the first to be rehoused, away from the steadily deteriorating area where the Mulvennys lived. And Isa had to give in – without being really aware of what she was losing.

Joe Harper did make very occasional visits to the invalid, if only to keep his hand in at the piano in my room. One day I came back and, before I'd reached the second landing, heard the familiar Charlie Kunz style with the tune 'It Happened In Monterey'. I opened the front door softly and waited in the lobby, feeling that I couldn't very well barge in on my landord and his guest – even though they were occupying the room I rented.

Andrew was saying, 'I can rely on you for all the old favourites, Joe. And all the old times.'

'The old times were the best times,' replied the pianist, strumming. 'I always mind the parties we used tae have here. For you.'

'For all of us. Those were the days. You and Ella and . . .'

Joe interrupted eagerly. 'And another bit o' champion silver on the sideboard.'

'Aye, aye. Now all I can do is sit here at the window and watch them playin' bloody cricket across in the park, there.'

'Cricket, eh?'

'In the summer, nothing else. In the winter, nothing at all.'

'Heh, heh, heh,' chuckled Joe tactically. His attention remained fixed on the missing silver. I was sitting on the bare top of the sideboard. It had been bare for many months. 'Cricket, eh? Ye'll no' win many trophies for that.'

'Still, this is better than the kitchen window, lookin' onto the street.'

Joe tried again. 'I notice ye've moved the trophies.' There was a pause. He continued, 'I mean, off the lobby sideboard, er . . .'

'What?'

'Your cups and shields and that. Have ye got them stored away somewhere?'

'I got rid of them. Oh, aye. Too many memories.'

'Of course. I can understand that.'

'Got rid of the lot.'

'Uh huh.' Joe tried another ploy. 'Young Andy wid take them, I expect. Eh? Now that he's got a house of his own. He was always very proud of his old man.'

'It's very nice, I believe,' said Andrew, modestly restrained. 'We havenae seen it yet, but his wife and him seem to be pleased wi' it.'

'Oh, it's a nice area, that. Ella was sayin', they'll be expectin' us for a visit. Now they've settled.'

'I'm sure they'd like to see you.'

'We'll hiv tae get the address . . .' He paused. His friend did not respond. 'The exact address . . . ye know.'

'Aye.'

But Mr Mulvenny had no intention of giving him any address, exact or fanciful, and I decided I'd spent enough time hovering in the lobby. I pushed open the door and marched in. 'Oh, I'm sorry. I didn't know you were here, Mr Harper.'

Joe welcomed me. 'Come in, son. Come in. Nice tae see ye. You been tae the library?'

'No. These are my text books. I'm studying for the HNC.'

'We'll no' disturb you,' said Mr Mulvenny without turning his chair which was set at the window. 'We're just havin' a quiet chat. There's plenty of space.'

I moved to a corner of the room, dumped my books noisily on a table and gave the impression of setting immediately to work. Mr Mulvenny was dressed as fully and neatly as he was always dressed. He wore a clean shirt with a suitable tie and a well-pressed suit with a waistcoat. He dressed himself. His shoes were polished and his chair was polished. He did those himself, too. Every morning he emerged like that from what had been Andy's room and wheeled himself around all day, like a coiled spring.

The change in sleeping arrangements was made as soon as he came back from hospital. Mrs Mulvenny now had the 'set-in' kitchen bed to herself, Mr Mulvenny had Andy's room as impregnable home-base and I, it seemed, shared the front room with anyone who was passing

'What was I sayin'?' asked Mr Mulvenny, when the sounds of my intrusion had subsided.

Joe still had Andy's address in mind. 'You were sayin' about the boy's . . .'

'That's right. The boys' club I used to train. Folded up. Another season finished wi' no coachin' whatsoever . . . and they came nowhere. So – they've had tae pack it in. Saw that in the paper.'

Joe saw that the conversation needed extra lubrication. He stated boldly, 'Andrew, I'm not surprised. Ever since you had tae stop they've been headin' nowhere. They've got nobody wi' your experience – that's the point.' That, indeed, was Andrew's point and his old crony came to it more readily than most. 'Nobody near as good.'

'Maybe so.'

'No "maybe" about it! That club depended on you.'

'There might be something in that. I mean, there's got to be somebody the young lads can trust . . .'

'. . . look up to . . .'

'Somebody who's proved he knows what it takes.'

Scribbling in my corner I, reluctantly, had to concede the truth of that situation, however artfully presented. Mr Mulvenny had been an excellent coach, as he'd been an excellent athlete. Also, to most strangers outside his home, he was firm, equable and trustworthy. Yes, yes, I thought impatiently, 'outside'. But for a long time now he had not been outside; and I knew the inside target on which he let loose the strain that imposed. Lying in bed at nights I heard his shouting and her sobbing. I heard the doors bang and worse, the silences followed by what had become a dreadful sound – the sucking of the rubber wheels on the polished floor of the lobby before the foot-rest of his chair bumped against my door. Then he would wheel himself in and start on his addictive recall of past triumphs. Many, many, many evenings I had to sit there trying feverishly to study while he repeated long, rambling stories; many passages of which I knew by heart. Like the one he was telling Joe:

'I mind the time . . . now . . . when was it? The second season, I think. Aye. The second season I ran for them . . . and this is a very good example of the experience ye come tae rely on. Of course, I'd been runnin' for a top outfit on the other side o' the city for years before that . . . and they werenae very pleased when I left them . . . but just the second season after I came here . . .'

'They were very lucky tae get you,' said Joe in an alert, but I knew futile, effort to stem the tide.

'Well – it was handy, y'know. And this race that second season . . .'

'What time is that?' asked Joe, looking sharply at the clock on the mantlepiece.

'Aw, ye've plenty of time, Joe. They don't open for another half-hour. I'd offer ye somethin' tae eat, but I don't know what she's doin'.'

Joe was genuinely surprised. 'Isa! Is she no' at work?'

'Certainly not!' Andrew coiled even tighter. 'I soon put a stop tae that caper. No wife o' mine is gonnae be servin' in a shop.'

'Oh! Well, then, if she's in I must have a word wi' Isa.'

From my corner, I spoke up to forestall this. 'I think she's busy at the moment. Would you like me to make you some tea?'

'Busy?' hissed Andrew. 'What d'ye mean, "busy"? What the hell is there for her tae be "busy" at? Sit where ye are!'

'It's no trouble, I'll just . . .'

His voice was suddenly throaty with anger. 'Sit on yer arse! This is still my house, remember. And we don't want tae interfere wi' your studies.' He shouted, 'Isa!' And I could picture her in the kitchen, jerking sharply with fear.

'Mrs Mulvenny isn't very well,' I said.

Andrew's lips apparently smiled as he stared at me, 'Oh, that's news. She can still walk, I suppose?'

Joe tried to mediate. 'Now, Andrew, if she's no' feelin' well I don't want to . . .'

'Isa! Come here!' shouted Andrew, much louder.

'I'll see if she's any better,' I said, and strode out of the room.

Andrew continued to shout, 'It's none o' your bloody business!' Then he confided loudly to Joe, 'Honest tae God! Sometimes I think I'm the lodger.'

'The lad means well, Andrew.'

'He doesnae mean well by me. It's always her side he takes.'

I urged Isa toward the front room. Her voice was slurred and mumbling. 'I'ss all right, son. I'ss all right, I can manage fine. You put on the kettle.' She went in to face the men. 'Joe! I thought I heard the piana, but it was . . . but then I thought . . . maybe I was just dreamin'. Nice tae see you.'

Joe spread his arms theatrically. 'Hello, Isa!'

'Is, er . . .' she focused, with effort, to recall the name, 'Ella. Did Ella come wi' ye? Havenae seen Ella for . . . oooh . . . for a long time. Awful kind woman, Ella.'

Naw, she didnae come. This is her day for the Bingo.'

'Oh, aye. Never tried the Bingo. Crowds frequent them, though.' She sighed. 'Terrible crowded . . . places, I believe.'

'I was just leavin', Isa. Got tae get back, ye know.'

Isa adjusted her stance to take in his standing up. 'Aw, wha' a' shame. Ye could have played us a wee tune . . .'

'I'll see ye again before long, I expect.'

'. . . played us "The Rose a' Tralee", maybe.'

'Sure.' Joe headed for the door. 'Sure. I'll drop in again. See you again, Andrew. Cheerio, for now.'

Isa was having trouble keeping pace with the movement. 'Thought I was dreamin' when I heard the . . . Cheerio! Say to Ella that I was . . .'

The front door slammed.

'. . . askin' for her.'

Andrew, who had contained his fury until Joe was out of range now ran his chair forward as though he might run it into his wife where she stood, swaying slightly. His strong, packed voice lashed at her. 'You're a disgrace! Look at the state you're in. Get out of my sight you . . .'

'Andrew! What's wrong?'

' "What's wrong?" ' He aped her soft, slurred speech then went on in his own outraged tones. 'Ye're drunk ya gawky bitch, that's what's wrong. And that shifty wee bastard, Joe Harper, will see that everybody knows it. You don't care about that. Drunk, at this time o' day, and where ye got the money, God only knows! When I've had tae sell all ma silver, and pinch and scrape for no more than decency, you can afford tae buy drink.'

'Naw, Andrew. It was a present. It was money I got as a present.' He snorted in disbelief. 'Who'd gi'e *you* a present?'

'The boy.'

'Andy?'

'Naw, Billy. He gave me thirty shillin's. That's where I got it. That's true. That's where I got it, Andrew. A wee present.'

'For what?'

'For ma birthday.'

'And you throw it away on drink!'

The enormity of this seemed to affect Isa too. She slumped on a chair and tested the truth to see if it still made a

reasonable excuse. 'Well, Andy's away, y'see and I don't . . . I
don't get out that much, now. It makes ye feel a bit cheerier,
for a wee while.'

'That's enough. We'll have no more o' that. Don't you ever let
me see you in that state again.'

'I'm all right.'

'You're a disgrace. Nae wonder yer son cannae stand the sight
o' ye.' He'd known from the outset he was going to say that. It was
just a matter of choosing the right moment. And he chose well.
The woman crumpled completely.

'Naw, Andrew. That's no' true.'

'It is true. Why else d'ye think we've never been asked to their
new house? And I don't blame them.'

I pushed open the door and came into the room carrying a tray
with the tea things. Andrew turned on me. 'And you're as bad,
encouraging her. Well, I hope ye're satisfied wi' the result.' He
wheeled the chair smartly about to the open door. 'I'm goin' tae
ma bed, and I don't want to hear another word.'

'I'll come an' help ye,' Isa offered, starting to rise.

'You! Help me? When have you ever been a help tae me?'

When he'd gone, I asked her, 'Do you want some tea?'

'What? Oh, tea! That's very nice.'

I poured the tea, put in milk and sugar and stretched to hand
her the cup. But she was preoccupied and, raising her hand to her
head, knocked the cup on the floor. 'Oooh, sorry. My goodness,
look at that! I'm sorry.'

'It's all right. I'll clean it up.'

'Sorry . . . I didnae notice the . . . sorry. But that is not true.
No.'

'What?'

'It's not Andy's fault. Not ma Andy. I'm sure he wants tae see
me.'

'Oh?' I started mopping up the tea with my handkerchief.

'It's his wife.' But even then, allowances had to be made. 'Of
course, she's used tae a better class o' people altogether.'

'Is she?'

'Stands tae reason, that. People want people they're used to. I
widnae know whit tae say tae her.'

'I could think of a few things.'

'Ah, but you're different. You're her kind, y'see.' She forgot
about the tea and got up to wander back into the kitchen,
murmuring, 'Education's the thing.'

★

As the months went on, things became more and more tense at the Mulvennys'. Finally, I decided I would have to see Andy. I called him at his office and could hardly believe it was him when he came on the line. His voice was much deeper, of course, but his accent had 'improved' quite remarkably. 'Ah, Bill! Yes. You really must come out and see us some afternoon,' He gave me the address which Joe had coveted in vain. This was, indeed, a 'select area' and his modern bungalow was set in a fairly large, well cultivated garden. As it happened, only Andy was there to greet me. He led me out to a table on a small patio so that we could enjoy the sun.

'I hoped I'd have the chance to meet your wife,' I said.

'Yes. She should be back around five. Just having her routine check-up at the clinic.'

'Is she unwell?'

'The natal clinic,' he smiled modestly. 'She does want to meet you.'

'I don't think I can wait until five,' I said.

'That's a pity.'

'Yes. But it'll take me more than an hour to get back to Greenock and I told your mother to expect me at six.'

He shrugged. 'I don't suppose it'll matter much to her when you get back.'

'Yes, it does. And it matters to me, even more.'

'Oh!' He was surprised at my tone. 'I just meant that she was always a bit careless about time.'

'Not about the time to have a meal ready,' I reminded him.

Both of us looked away for a moment over the tidy green suburb and listened to the birds in the trees which lined this 'young executive' avenue. Then I glanced covertly at the expression of relaxed satisfaction on Andy's face. He had turned into a lean, handsome young man and his black hair was trimmed in the most fashionable cut.

'Would you like a drink?' he asked.

'No, thank you.' I was holding myself in decent check, waiting for a chance to pour out my grievances. But what if there was no chance? In this calm, civilised conversation, how could I force the matter on his attention? Again, and for a longer period, we gazed over the gardens.

'You know,' Andy said, 'I've often wondered why you went on living in that house. Especially since she's become so . . .'

'Your mother, you mean?'

He gave me a sharp, puzzled look. 'What's the matter with you? It seems there's nothing I can say but you jump on it.'

'Maybe because you don't say what I expect to hear. It seems to me you don't know what's going on in that house.'

'My father writes to me regularly,' he stated. Then added admiringly, 'Isn't it marvellous the way he's managed to keep his spirit – trapped like that in a wheel-chair?'

'Yes.'

'And on top of that, having to cope with h . . . – my mother. Well . . . you must know that she's started drinking.'

'I know nothing of the kind. She drank too much – once, eight months ago, on her birthday. And he's never let her forget it.'

'She may hide it from you, but it's my father has to put up with her ways.'

'What?' I asked very quietly, and felt like hitting him.

'I mean, she was always very slovenly – but now! If it hadn't been for Dad, God knows where I would have ended up.'

'Listen, Andy, if you don't do something about your – "Dad" – I know where *she'll* end up. In a lunatic asylum. That man is driving your mother to desperation.'

It was impossible for him to believe me. 'My father is an invalid.'

I gathered my breath and stood up; then began pacing round him, and the colourful sunshade, and the white table. 'Sure. Your father is an invalid and I'm sorry for that. But everything he has lost, he's taking out on her. Invalid or not, he has a vicious tongue and he can make her life a misery because . . . she still thinks the world of him. *And* you. She thinks there's nobody like you, either. That's why I came. To ask you . . . Invite your mother here. For a holiday. She needs a break. You owe her that, surely. And I . . . I'm sick to my gut of seeing her hiding behind doors and scared to make a sound, unless he speaks to her first.'

Andy stared up at me, and the light filtering through the sunshade glowed as bars of colour on his crisp white shirt. 'This is none of your business,' he said.

'My business?' I asked incredulously and leaned forward, resting my hands on the table. 'I live there. I've lived there for nearly five years and watched that woman . . . Christ Almighty!' I swung wildly away from him. 'If it's not my business tell me whose business it is; for – somebody – must do something!'

'Well, it's not your place, for a start. And I resent . . .'

I interrupted him, but softly – very softly now, because I dare not alienate him, for Isa's sake. I sat beside him. 'Andy . . . Andy, she is scared to lift a tea-cup with one hand, in case she drops it and the whole day is ruined.'

*

I close the silencing shutter on the train window again and, for a
few moments, it does seem to be effective. And there is nothing to
see anyway, or guess at, for we have reached the high hills of
Cumbria and the line runs through long sections of deep cuttings
which are no more diverting than tunnels. Staring at the strict
confines of the sleeping-compartment, I think it must surely have
expanded to accommodate the rooms and spaces I knew as an
apprentice. Surely my memory has seeped out and filled this
impersonal swaying box. Uncharitably, I hope that the next
person who occupies it will have as little sleep as I've had; and
be haunted by insistent images of perfect strangers. My eyes
retain the blur of coloured light on the stark whiteness of Andy's
shirt.

Soon afterwards I started my final year by moving into the
drawing office. About the only person who was glad of my
elevation was Mr Mulvenny. It impressed him that I'd joined
the ranks of those who never need to get their hands dirty. And he
was glad the neighbours could see his lodger going to work in suit,
collar and tie. Mrs Mulvenny worried about the sharp increase in
clean shirts to be provided and suggested that maybe if she just
washed the collars it would save ironing the entire shirt again.
She'd become very nervous of ironing because of the tremor
which had developed in her hands; and because of her husband's
complaints about *his* shirts. It was an issue that became inflated
out of all proportion to its significance and led to a bitter weekly
shouting-match. After one such bout I waited until Isa was alone,
trying to improve her ironing in the kitchen.

I interrupted her very softly. 'Mrs Mulvenny!'

'What's wrong, son?' Nowadays all her conversations seemed
to start with something that was wrong. She hastily placed the
iron on its rest.

'Nothing. Nothing's wrong. It's just that I've been thinking it
might be more . . . convenient . . . for you if I sent some of my
clothes to a laundry.'

'A *laundry*!' She'd never sent anything to a laundry in her
life.

'Just to save time, you know.'

'I see.' Her tone indicated that she was not offended or hurt,
just resigned to yet another of the large and small changes that
kept intruding on her life.

'I'll take a bundle in each week and then collect them.'

'Jist as ye like, Billy.'

'You can make up the bundle for me and maybe you could put in Mr Mulvenny's shirts as well.'

She leaned back, tilted her head to the side and gave me a slow smile. Now she saw what I was doing and why; and was grateful. 'Get the laundry tae dae them as well?'

'I'll pay for the lot,' I assured her.

'Right ye are,' she said, accepting this secret pact. Then, to my surprise, she managed a broad wink. 'Mr Mulvenny will think A've fairly improved.'

I nodded. 'Yes, he will.' But if he did he never mentioned it.

There was no holiday for Isa that summer and in the autumn I left the shipyard to start my time at sea. I gave her the itinerary for the trip and she promised to write. To my astonishment, she did. One day, about six months after my departure, she must have settled down with a dictionary and a few biros of different colours – all on the point of expiring – and wrote to me. I could imagine the trouble she'd had finding the writing-pad, and saw her setting it squarely on the oil-cloth of the kitchen table before she braced herself and sat down.

'Dear Billy – Thank you for all them lovely post cards of all them lovely places . . .' (the second 'them' was scored out and she substituted 'the') '. . . the lovely places your boat goes to. I hope you are feeling well and not getting sick with all that forn food they . . .' (clearly, that didn't look right. The word 'forn' was scored out provisionally while she turned to the dictionary for the spelling of 'foreign'. She looked it up under 'forn', though, and ran into all those variations on 'fornication'. 'Hah,' I imagined her chuckling with disbelief, 'this dictionary's got a wan track mind! An' the word A want's no' in it.' She resumed the letter, leaving 'forn' as an option for the reader which wasn't quite right but couldn't be proved wrong) '. . . its nice that you miss my cooking. Its very quiet in the house now that its empty that Mr Mulvenny is away as well. This is because I was . . .' (the word was so effectively scored out that I couldn't read it) '. . . I was stupid to get into some bother with the polis and Mr Mulvenny moved to Andys house. Maybe its best because there are no stairs and he can get into the garden. On Sunday there Andy came down for a visit to let me see the baby and he says Mr Mulvenny likes the change. Hope you are all right. Yours sincerely, Isa Mulvenny.'

On the face of it, that seemed to me good news. With Mr Mulvenny out of the way perhaps she would recover some of her old ebullience, and drop as many cups as she had a mind to. And she could go back to work. I was sure her old employers would be delighted to have the services of an assistant so popular with the customers. I wrote urging her to apply and suggesting, too, that she should take in another lodger. 'But,' I warned her, 'ask him first if he likes the smell of camphor. Nowadays I can scarcely get to sleep without it.'

As I sat writing in the oven that was my cabin on the Gulf, the pungent smell did come vividly back to me and at once it seemed that an idyllic existence could be enjoyed at the Mulvennys' in cool, rainy Greenock. In fact, whenever I thought of my three months off when this long trip was over, I saw myself, rapturously drenched, climbing the hills above the town. So when my first trip was over I did not go home immediately. I went to Greenock and I hired a car because I had a plan – a surprise. My car at the close-mouth excited the interest of neighbours and before I'd reached the first landing I knew all the facts about Isa's 'bother' with the police. It was a charge of 'drunk and disorderly' – a common enough charge on that street, but more scandal than Andrew could bear. It upset him particularly since Andy had to come down from the city to bail her out. It happened the day after I left. The sudden panic of being alone in the house with that man drove her out on the street to spend my going-away present. On the day I came back, that incident – and a great deal more – had gone from her mind. I'd sent her a note, of course, to tell her I'd be dropping by. It gave me an odd feeling to stand in front of so familiar a door, and to knock.

'Hello, Mrs Mulvenny!'

'Good afternoon, Billy. Come in. It's nice to see you again.' The greeting was cool, and very carefully enunciated. I crossed the threshold with some unease. 'Just go right through. You know the way.'

'Were you just going out?'

She seemed taken aback. 'No. Not immediately, no. If you clear away those books you'll find a place to sit down.'

'Do you have another lodger?'

Now she was offended. 'Lodger! No, I have not.'

'I wondered who was reading all the books,' I laughed.

'I am reading them,' she replied severely.

'Oh!'

'I was expecting you off the next train but . . .'

I broke in excitedly, 'Well, you see I came by car and . . .'

Her voice went right on, mechanically, '. . . I've got the tea things ready. Excuse me.' She turned and walked out of the room, repeating those words in exactly the same tone, 'I've got the tea things. I've got the tea things ready. Excuse me.'

It was as though she had rehearsed exactly those words and no others, but doubted if the information would carry conviction to a second person. And she was quite changed. She'd let her hair grow again, and it was plaited and coiled, just as it used to be. And dyed very near the colour it used to be. She wore her 'costume' – the same matching jacket and skirt – which had not been cleaned but had been pressed under a damp cloth so often that the material now hung unnaturally rigid on her much thinner body. I looked around. The house had a prematurely abandoned air. All the ornaments had been cleared away and there were bags and packages and parcels stacked against the wall – ready for departure. For a moment I thought she'd guessed that I planned to take her on the first holiday of her life. Or maybe she wanted me to take her away from that dingy street, for good.

The rattle of the tea tray approached and she came in, carrying it very high. 'I'm sorry there's not much to eat, but you won't be staying long, will you?'

'I don't want anything to eat, thank you.' I reached in my bag. 'And I've brought you something to drink.'

'Something to drink?' she asked, frostily.

'Yes. Look. Whisky! I thought we'd have a little celebration.'

'Just put it back in your bag, please. You know I don't approve of strong drink, especially at this time of day. What if somebody should come in?'

'Who?'

'Here's your tea.'

I was dismayed by how she sounded and her manner. It was as though I was talking to a woman I'd never met before. Still, I had an ace that would bring back all the old warmth and affection. 'Mrs Mulvenny! How would you like to come home with me for a holiday? To my parents' house. I've told them to expect you and I've got the car outside. We could go now. Right away!'

Then, I swear, she stared at me exactly as she'd stared at me when I brought news of Andrew's accident. The words I'd used then and now seemed to connect. 'Go now!' she repeated. 'Car waiting. Is he hurt bad?'

'What?' I asked, and tried to rouse her to the present. 'Mrs Mulvenny! Will you come with me for a holiday?'

She rose and retreated to the position she'd held when I arrived. And the mechanical words came out again. 'I'm sorry there's not much to eat, but you won't be staying long, will you?' Or maybe she was just ashamed that she couldn't prepare a full meal for me. I took a sip of tea and then I tried again.

'As you know, we live in Sussex. You'd like it there. I've got three months until I start my next trip. I could take you round all the places and you could visit my . . .'

'No.'

'Why not?'

'Well, as you see, I'm ready to move. To Andy's house. Any day now. Any day now. It would never do if he came to collect me and I was away for a holiday.'

'I see. I'm sorry. I didn't know you were going to move.'

'You surely didn't think I'd stay in this empty house on my own?'

'No, of course not. I'm sorry. I didn't know the . . . situation.'

'Why should you? I mean, it's not as if you were one of the family. Everything's quite different now. Quite different.'

'Yes.'

'More tea?'

'No, thank you. I, er . . . brought you this, too.' From my bag I took a small, flat package.

'What is it?'

'Open it and see.'

'Tell me what it is, please.' The absurd notion occurred to me that she feared it might be an odd, very flat, bottle of liquor.

'Just a little present from Hong Kong. A silk scarf. Turquoise.'

She took the package. 'Thank you. That's a nice word.'

' "Turquoise"? It's a bluish-green colour.'

'Yes,' she said. 'Turquoise. That's a *very* nice word.'

There was nothing else for me to do but go. She saw me to the door but closed it before I'd taken one step down. When I reached the half-landing I looked back. But no, the door was closed. My shoes clacked loud on each of those stone steps and I noted that whoever's turn it was for the stairs must have declared open-roster. It wasn't surprising. Many of the front doors I passed on the way down were covered by sealing sheets of corrugated iron, heavily sprayed with graffiti. I got into the hired car and set out for England, and Sussex and – undeniable now – home.

That was the last I heard of the Mulvennys for a long time. Isa was right. Why should I think of myself as one of the family? Perhaps I

had interfered too much. The changes and the progress of the
Mulvenny family were really not any of my business now. And
there was my own life to consider as, year by year, I edged up the
promotion scale. Still, I kept Isa up to date with itinerary sheets
and occasionally I sent postcards to her at Andy's house. But she
never wrote to me again.

When I'd qualified for all the necessary endorsements to my
Chief's Ticket, I applied to become an Engineering Surveyor
ashore with Det Norske Veritas. One of my early postings was
Clydebank, on the other side of the river from Greenock. I was
reluctant to cross over even to visit my former home. When I did
it was to discover that the old street was deserted. Most of the
close-mouths were bricked up and a lot of the windows were
boarded over. It didn't seem worth while getting out of the taxi to
trudge around a demolition site. The whole town was so depressing that I kept away from Greenock for the next two years. Only
when I had the comfort of a confirmed posting to London did I go
back across the Clyde. It was a rainy night and to brace myself for
a farewell tour of the familiar places I went into a dockside pub.
The air was thick with smoke and packed to the door. I ordered a
double whisky and, while I waited for it, my ears became tuned to
some variety in the cacophony of sounds which surrounded me.
In particular I detected the sound of a piano being played. When I
got my drink I started bull-dozing my way in the direction of a yet
unseen pianist, who was playing 'The Rose of Tralee'. When I
saw him I knew him instantly. 'Joe. Joe Harper!'

'Yessir, that's me. An' if ye want a tune it'll cost ye a drink.'

'I've brought you a drink.'

He didn't look up. 'Put it where I can see it. Whit dae ye fancy?'

I shouted to make myself heard above the clamour. 'Just play
"The Rose of Tralee".'

He squinted up at me pugnaciously. 'Whit sa gemm, Jimmy?
That's wha-a-am playin'.' But he stopped playing and craned
round to look at me more closely. 'Dae A know you?' he shouted.

'Or "Down Mexico Way",' I suggested.

'Fur God's sake, make up yer mind. Wan drink, wan tune.'

'We met at the Mulvennys'.'

'Mulvennys?' Then he gave the top of the piano an open
handed slap. 'Aye! Ye mind me o' . . . You were the boy.'

'Why don't you take your drink over here? It's quieter.'

He poured the drains of the drink he'd been drinking into the
drink I'd bought for myself and followed me to a less noisy

corner. When we were seated he inspected me more closely and nodded. 'You were the boy – the ludger they had – afore she went daft.'

'What?'

'Daft! Mad, ye know. Stupit wumman! Hiv ye seen her?'

'I saw her just before she moved away, to her son's house.'

He gave the table a thump, but made sure he was holding the glass with his other hand. 'Christ Almighty! Are you daft as well? Moved?' He shook his head vehemently. 'She hasnae moved. She's still there in that rat-hole o' a tenement. They'll knock it flat roon aboot her.'

'No!'

'Oh, but aye! She's no' right in the heid, I'm tellin' ye. Never has been since the "champeen runner" dumped her for his fancy son. And that's twelve year ago.'

I felt a stabbing pain of guilt in my chest. 'She's still there! Are you sure?'

'Certainly, I'm sure. Ella goes up noo an' then. She says the place is thick wi' muck and maist o' the furniture's been broken up for the fire. But Isa's still got all her belongings packed and ready tae move.' He tilted his chair back on two legs and gave a scornful grunt. 'Huh!' He lurched forward again, thrusting his finger at me across the table. 'Where could they move her? And who'd have her?' I didn't answer him. I couldn't wait a moment longer, but I heard him calling after me as I fought my way out of the bar, 'Hey! Hey, wait a minute. How's about another drink?'

I ran all the way. I ran along street after rain-slicked street, through deep puddles around blocked drains and over broken paving. As I got nearer, the street lights which still worked were fewer, but I knew my way. Solitary pedestrians backed against the walls in suspicion or fear at the sound of my pounding footsteps, and cursed me as soon as what they'd thought was a danger had passed. And all the time my feeling of guilt was tightening with the tightness of my breath. Finally, I staggered up to the close and stopped to gasp for a while before I climbed the stairs.

I knocked loudly on the door and waited. There was no reply. I knocked again, even louder. The echo of the sound came drumming back and filled the stairwell. When that had faded, I thought I heard a faint scratching behind the door. I glanced up at the fanlight and convinced myself there was a dim glow. Then I heard the voice, soft and hopeful. 'Andy? Is that you, Andy?'

She opened the door slowly, edging it open, and I slapped my hand to my mouth to muffle the exclamation, 'Oh, God!'

Her hair was white and it hung, disordered, in long greasy
strands round her face. And – at last – she was 'not so tall'. She
was stooped and leaning heavily on the door-handle as she peered
out from the dim lobby to the comparative brightness of the
landing. If I was not Andy, she had no idea who I was.

'I'm a friend of Andy's,' I said.

'Aw, that's nice. It was him A wis expectin', but you come in
anyway.' Her voice, though broken and distant, had resumed her
old accent and a ghost of its former warmth. 'In ye come an' sit
doon for a minute.'

There were no chairs; just a few wooden boxes. 'It's all right.
I'll stand,' I told her.

'What does Andy say?'

I had the answer to that implacably fixed in my mind. 'He's
coming to see you tomorrow morning.' I did not add that the
promise would be kept even if I had to drag Andy bodily to that
room.

'Tut, tut, tut,' she shook her head, apparently at her own
foolishness in forgetting. 'It's tomorrow it is. I've got everything
ready, y'see, but I couldnae mind exactly . . . when.' She smiled,
and again – for a moment – I saw the person I'd known through
the distressing mask of what she had become. 'D'you work in
Andy's office, Mr, er . . .?' she asked sociably.

'Yes.'

'That's nice.'

'Mrs Mulvenny, are you cold?'

'Naw. It's rainin', is it no'? It cannae be very cold if it's rainin'.'
Damp, though. Sometimes I feel the dampness.' But she brushed
that aside. 'Tomorrow. You tell Andy I'll be ready – as early as he
likes.'

'I certainly will.'

She sat on one of the boxes and rehearsed the scene. 'I'll put on
my costume and I'll sort my hair . . . and I'll wear that lovely scarf
he gave me.'

'Scarf?'

She took on her old exaggerated pose of incredulity. 'Did I not
show you that?' she exclaimed and pushed herself to her feet with
vigour. She knew precisely where to find it in piles of cartons and
packages and brought it to me. 'There! Still in the box.' The box
still had the ornate label of the Hong Kong gift shop. She took out
the scarf and draped it over her arm. 'Finest silk, that. Andy gave
me it for my birthday. And a lovely shade. It's what they call
"turquoise".'

Next morning I was on Andy's doorstep at seven o'clock. I waited in the tiled hallway until he got dressed. The most prominent piece of furniture there was a long table burdened with silver trophies. Everything Mr Mulvenny had ever won, and sold, had been reclaimed or refashioned. In the centre was the Levi-Allen Shield – and it bore only Andrew's name. Andrew himself I glimpsed as we were leaving. He was alone in the dining room eating breakfast, impeccably dressed as ever and not looking a day older than the last time I'd seen him. He glanced up as we passed the open door. Obviously, he did not recognise me but was in the habit of acknowledging Andy's business associates.

To be quite fair to Andy – or as fair as it's possible for me to be – he did not hesitate in coming back to Greenock with me and he was obviously shocked when he saw his mother. Nor did he raise any objection when I insisted that I should be consulted about a suitable nursing home. Evidently his neglect of it had made his business my business, too. It would have been wrong to keep her in his house for I knew, and he realised, that nothing would drive her further from sanity than having to live with her husband once more.

When a suitable place had been found and regular visits arranged Isa seemed willing enough to move in. I arranged with the Matron, in confidence, that regular reports of her health and progress were to be sent to me at our London headquarters. The following week I left for a five-year posting. Once there I sent her occasional gifts and greetings cards. At first, she thought they were from that assistant in Andy's office. Eventually, she knew they were from me; and knew who I had been. That small gain cheered me a lot.

There is a soft double tap on the door of the sleeping compartment and the attendant thrusts himself in, tray first.

'Good mornin', sir. Here's your tea. I'll just put on the . . . Is there anything wrong, sir?'

'No, no. It's just the light makes my eyes water.'

'We'll be in in half an hour.'

'Can I still get a connection to Greenock from Central?'

'Platform eleven. It's electric now. Do ye know Greenock?'

'Aye, very well. Or what it used to be, anyway.'

'Hasnae changed much,' said the attendant, rather grimly. 'You're going home, then?'

'No. I'm going to a funeral.'

★

The cemetery is exposed to a strong, rain-laden wind blowing up from the Clyde. I check with the gate-man and find the plot before anyone else arrives. And when they come they aren't many. I stand some distance away and watch the ceremony. When it is over, I walk away. There is nobody I want to talk to. It is Andy who runs after me, calling, 'Bill? Bill Thompson!' I turn to face him and see that Mr Mulvenny, too, is wheeling himself towards me.

'Hello, Andy.'

'Hello.' He catches at the arm of the wheel-chair. 'Dad, you remember Billy Thompson?'

'Yes, indeed I do,' says Andrew. He is perfectly composed. 'Will you come home with us, Mr Thompson, and have some refreshment?'

'No, thank you. I'm going straight back to London.'

'I was sure it was you,' Andy says. 'How did you hear about it?'

'From the Matron at the nursing home.'

Andrew nods. 'Ah, yes. A very officious lady. She's put you to a great deal of trouble. Maybe she thought you were a relative.'

'I know you were fond of my mother,' says Andy. 'And it was very good of you to make the journey. You're sure you won't come back with us?'

'Quite sure. But what a pity you didn't invite *her*, before it was too late.'

Andrew's bright eyes don't flicker. 'Mr Thompson, I think we've got to face it – the woman was no use to herself.' The chair wheels skid on the gravel as he returns to those who think that is true.

A Friend of Dosser Farr

LIKE ALL CLOSED societies, the world of engineering has its own initiation ceremony. Before he is fully admitted, the apprentice has to be 'greased'. What horrified me was *where* he had to be greased. In the shipyard where I served my time, there was an adamant preference for the genitals. Since I'd come directly from a minor English public school, that should not have surprised me. And, given the mechanical parallels of piston-rod and regulator-valve, it might even have seemed apt. Nevertheless, I was determined that nobody was going to do *that* to *me*. Thinking of it now, the whole business is fairly amusing, but then, when I was seventeen the prospect of such abject humiliation was terrifying. For a few months I was successful in avoiding any group of my fellows which wore that menacing, collective smirk and as I got used to the place I persuaded myself that they'd forgotten I hadn't been 'done'. I'd reckoned without the lack of supervision when, during roof repairs, we had to work on the night-shift.

Bent at my lathe in the Light Machine Shop, I realised that Frank, my only reliable friend, was smiling over my head.

I looked around but could see nothing unusual. 'What is it?'

'Nothin'!' But he smiled even more broadly.

The distraction was fatal to the gunmetal valve I was turning. The tool dug under the centre-line and the whole piece rocketed out of the chuck, smashed the machine-lamp and fell with a denouncing clang in the sump. I fished it out and revealed the deep gash in the valve face.

'What shall I do?'

'Whi' everybody else does,' said Frank, unperturbed. 'Dump it in the Dock Burn an' steal another yin fae the store.'

'I'd better wrap it up in something.'

'Wait tae ye finish the shift. The wey you're gaun, there's likely tae be mair.' But again, he was looking behind me and this time I turned quickly enough to see the advance of four or five older apprentices – one of them carrying a large can of axle-tallow.

Frank said, 'Ye cannae dodge it this time, Billy. Ye're gonnae get greased.'

'I won't let them.'

'Ye cannae stop them.'

'Will you help me?'

'Naw. But I'll no' help them.'

The long gallery of the machine shop was lit only by the individual machine lights and, since the light on mine had just been shattered, the area around me was practically dark. Frank, who had undergone the business with perfect composure more than six months before, moved away. I gripped the damaged valve tight in my hand and waited. I heard Jock Turnbull's deep laugh and I turned to face that way, but immediately I heard from the opposite direction the creak of the long footboard as someone stepped from the concrete floor onto it. Then they were all on top of me. My wrist was caught and banged against the tail-stock so that the valve again dropped loudly in the sump. I struggled as hard as I could – trying to wrestle my way *under* the machine. They gripped my legs and pulled me back on the footboard. Staring up I saw the repair tarpaulin on the roof flapping against the dark sky before faces and shoulders and arms blotted that out. And I could smell the sickly, thick tallow. My head was pulled up by the hair so that they could start stripping off the one-piece suit of dungarees under which I was wearing shirt and trousers. Between their legs I caught a glimpse of the labourer, Lord Sweatrag, moving sedately towards us. Suddenly I stopped struggling and was immediately commended. 'That's it, son,' said one voice. 'Lie back an' enjoy it!' said another. They were so intent in getting the dungarees off, they had stopped holding *me*. When they'd dragged the overalls down to my waist somebody undid my belt. I wriggled free; under the machine and up the other side. The apprentice who was fielding there reached out to grab me but Lord Sweatrag – as though unaware of what he was doing – blocked the tackle and I slipped away. I ran the whole length of the machine bay towards the foreman's box, then out onto the dockside. The foreman had had his feet up reading the paper but stirred himself to see me disappearing towards the river.

They did not pursue me immediately. Probably because such a concerted movement would have brought the foreman out of his box. I edged my way into a nest of empty oil drums, then lay back to recover my breath. The sky was overcast and everything was quiet. Only gradually did I become aware of the river lapping in the disused dock. This was the Dock Burn that Frank had mentioned where, traditionally, apprentice mistakes were consigned to the not-so-deep. I also realised why the greasers hadn't bothered to pursue me. This short stretch of dock was completely blocked at each end. The only way out was through the door by which I had escaped. They could come out and get me any time they felt like it. Tonight, they would not give up. With a stabbing pain of fear in my stomach I tried to think of how I could possibly escape the trap. If they came out, the pile of oil drums would be the first place they'd look. I started moving away from them, sliding my back along the wall.

My progress was blocked by an upright steel girder set into the wall. Looking up I discovered it was the support for an old loading gantry which jutted out, like a fixed crane, high over the dock. It was a feature I had not noticed, even in daylight; my pursuers would never think of it in the dim spillage of light from the lamps on the far corners of the building. I started to climb the warped and rusted access ladder which rasped at my fingers as I pulled myself higher. My arms were aching when I reached the top platform of the gantry and a position clear of the dockside, high over the water. For some irrational reason I felt safe there, but I also began to feel cold. It was now after eleven o'clock on a raw October night and I didn't even have the protection of my dungarees. There was no sign of the greasers. All they had to do was wait in the warm for my inevitable return.

About an hour later, when my misery had increased to such an extent that I felt like drowning myself to teach *them* a lesson, I saw – however incredibly – a boat directly below me. It was a small rowing boat; and there was a man in it – fishing! 'Hello,' I called softly. He reacted as though God had called softly. He jerked round and fell on his back, almost swamping his craft. 'It's all right,' I said, but that didn't seem to reassure him. He blessed himself with a pale, urgent hand. When he realised it was neither God nor the angel of death perched above, he rowed into the dockside and I climbed down to talk to him.

'Can you get me out of here?'

'That depends. Who the hell are ye?' He had a light little voice with a strong Irish accent.

'I'm an apprentice. There are people after me.'

'The polis?'

'No,' I said, and at once realised I should have said yes. 'Who are you?'

'James Farr,' he said proudly. 'But they call me "Dosser" Farr.'

'Mr Farr, may I come into the boat? I want to get clear of the shipyard. Now! Do you know how to do that?'

'Of course I know. We get out the way I got in. Under the wire when the tide is low. Put your foot there, lad, and I'll hold steady.'

I lowered myself into the dinghy and Dosser started pulling for the dock entrance and its insecure barrier. Evidently the tide wasn't quite low enough. The jagged ends of the wire tore my shirt as we scraped under. It seemed Dosser knew his way around those backwaters and he soon beached the boat at the rear of a disused factory. Then we began a long trail through back streets.

There were two men on the demolition site of a ruined tenement. The old man – a night watchman – sat at his brazier against a wall. The young, smartly dressed man stood staring into the fuming charcoal. Neither of them seemed surprised when Dosser squeezed through the protecting fence but the old man's expression changed when I quickly followed.

'Peter, my friend,' called my guide, 'I have brought you this young visitor.'

'And ye can take him right back,' his friend replied.

Dosser's finger tips pinched my elbow. 'The man doesn't mean it,' he murmured, leading me towards the warmth.

'A mean it, Dosser. It's bad enough puttin' up wi' you, never mind yer waifs an' strays.'

'He is neither waif nor stray – *and* he is not wanted by the polis!'

'Huh!' the watchman grunted at the novelty of this.

My rescuer went extravagantly on. 'No! His name is Bill Thompson and he's a refugee from persecution that I plucked from the very dockside not half an hour ago. He was perched upon a girder and he's cold.'

'Get in there at the fire,' said the younger man.

I moved closer to the brazier.

'So, I told him to jump down into me boat . . .'

'Is that right, son?' asked the watchman.

'Yes. I was hiding on the dock and I saw Mr Farr fishing.'

'Fishin', b'God! Where wis this?'

'The Dock Burn.'

'Ah!' He nodded with satisfaction and turned to Dosser. 'And whi' did ye catch this time?'

'Enough to make it worth me while,' announced the wizened little man. He undid his long ragged coat and from its many deep interior pockets produced a gleaming haul of gunmetal valves, small brass flanges and white-metal facings.

The watchman was impressed. 'Things are lookin' up, eh?'

'Oh, they are surely,' Dosser agreed. 'As apprentice quality in that place is going down. I'm glad to say.'

I laughed. 'If you'd waited you could have had one of mine.'

The scrap-fisherman was alert to my potential. He beckoned me to sit down beside him. 'So! Are ye on the brass-work, then? I have a great interest in the non-ferrous range; whether it's made into anything or not. I mean, why should you go to the bother of working on a piece, scrapping it and throwing it in the Burn where I have to trawl for it – when ye could jist give me it?'

'Don't listen tae him, son, or ye *will* be wantit by the polis.'

Dosser was offended. 'Am I not tryin' to save that shipyard money.'

'*Save* them money?'

'Certainly – on labour costs.' The young man laughed and Dosser, nodding at the appreciation, went on, 'They have to pay these boys, y'know, for the *time* they spend on the work they scrap.' He turned earnestly to me. 'You see that, don'cha, Billy?'

I nodded. The steady glow of the brazier had restored a lot of my self-confidence and at this secluded encampment in the middle of the night, my real initiation – into adoptive Scottishness – began.

'Where are ye from, son?' the young man asked me.

Before I could answer, Dosser leaned protectively in front of me and whispered, 'He's English!' His tone suggested the sympathetic acknowledgement of a rather messy disease.

'We *know* he's English,' Peter retorted. 'We kin *hear* that. But where in England?'

'I don't see that matters a bit,' said Dosser huffily.

'Sussex,' I revealed. 'On the coast. A town called Lancing.'

'And whi' made ye prefer Greenock?'

'Now, don't embarrass the lad. Here! I've brought ye some soup.' Dosser produced a can from yet another pocket.

'Did ye pull that outa' the Dock Burn as well?'

'I did not! I stole it from a very clean grocery.'

'Is there anything you don't steal, Dosser?' his host wondered as he opened the can and poured the soup into a blackened pot.

'Certainly. I don't steal what I can't steal. And what I can't steal – I can do without.'

While Dosser took off and *folded* his ragged coat, the old man made further enquiries. 'Sussex, eh? And where are ye livin' here?'

'I'm lodging with a family called Mulvenny.'

'No' Andrew Mulvenny?'

'Yes.'

'The runner!'

'Yes. Do you know him?'

'Know *of* 'im. An' his picture's always in the local paper – winnin' somethin'. So! He's takin' in ludgers, is he?'

'Only me.'

The man snorted. 'Oh, a good quality, right enough. But still, it's no' quite the thing fur a gaffer.'

The young man spoke to me. 'So, you're in the Light Machine Shop, eh?'

'Yes. At the moment. I shall be moving about, though, getting experience in different departments.'

'Sure. More of a *visitor* than a real apprentice.'

Peter said, 'This is my son, Michael.'

'Your son, Michael, of course,' Dosser exclaimed. 'I thought his name was Martin.'

'No, Michael,' the son insisted.

Dosser advanced with an extravagant flourish of his hand. 'I'm glad to see you again. I'm a great friend of your father's. And your mother's, too. Oh, yes, Maisie knows me well.'

'I've heard her mention you.'

'Michael, eh?' Dosser stroked his chin as though aware he was being conned but good-naturedly willing to play along. 'Back from the sea for a while, Peter says. Going to give the old town another chance. Settle down?'

'No. Just a short break. I'm going back on Wednesday.'

'Going back!'

'Yeah. Signing on again at Southampton first thing on Thursday morning.'

'Of course,' murmured Dosser the world-traveller, 'signing on. Again. For how long would that be?'

'Well, on the tankers that's another three years, at least. I've been standing-by for Chief – and the chance has come up.'

'"Standing by",' Dosser repeated. He loved such knowing expressions and hoarded them. 'But you could get an engineering job ashore, could you not?'

'Easy!' said the young man's father, but did not raise his head.

'Aye!' Michael retorted with a vehemence which implied that this was a standing argument between them.

'Easy enough,' the old man repeated.

'As what, though? I'm damned if I'll go back to the tools. The only place to get promotion is in the South.'

'Things'll change,' said Peter.

Dosser mediated. 'Oh, surely! Things are changin'.'

'Not in this place.' Michael moved away from further argument and encountered me. 'Scotland's for the hard graft, eh boy?' He turned to the others to offer proof. 'That's why they sent him up here to learn his trade. But you can be damned sure they don't expect *him* to stay here.' He looked down at me. 'Do they?'

'No.'

'No! You'll go back South.'

'Ah!' Dosser sighed. 'But for him, poor lad, that's just going home. It's a different thing altogether for you, Martin. You are home.'

'Michael!'

'Whatever you say.'

It was exactly there in the conversation that for the first time I felt a sudden distancing of myself from where I was actually sitting. As they went on talking, it seemed I was looking down at them. It happened several times while Michael was there.

Peter adopted a reasonable, disinterested tone through which I sensed hurt and disappointment. 'We thought, when ye did decide to come ashore, ye'd settle here. You did say as much.'

'That was in a letter. Now I've seen it again, things are different. Aye, now I've seen it – and *smelt* it again! The air's thick wi' dampness and rot.'

'Lately, the weather's been wet.'

'Huh! If the weather was all!' Michael moved away to pace the perimeter of the lighted space, so that he seemed to be moving against a circular void. 'It's a feeling. Like a clammy hand on your chest that ye have to push against every step ye take. It's always tryin' to push ye back where ye came from. And that hand is the hand in the glove of every bugger ye meet. They're all at it. Anxious. Holdin' back. Pressin' down. Makin' sure that you're still in the grip.' He paused and threw back his head in a bitter laugh. 'On Saturday, there, a man stopped me in the street. He'd read in the papers they were demolishin' this place. He wanted to know . . . Holy God! He wanted tae know what street we were *hopin'* tae move intae. Yeah! Though we left this dump twenty years ago, though I've been round the world seven or eight times, though I didn't even know the bastard's name – he was worried in case we might get one up on him.'

'Did he say his name?'

'He thought I *knew* his name!'

'What did he look like?'

'He looked like a frightened wee man whose only chance of keepin' his place is to keep everybody else back.'

'Oh, I know the sort well,' said Dosser. 'They're usually Special Constables, too.' The others laughed. 'Or at the very least, paid informers.'

Again I was watching them from a distance, but now from a different angle. Michael shivered. 'Well,' he told his father, 'now you've got better company I'll away home to bed.'

I saw him gather up his coat and start to move out of the lighted area.

Dosser called after him, 'Will I be seeing you again . . . Michael?'

'I don't think so. Unless you're here on Wednesday.'

'He'll be here,' Peter said. 'He's here every night. Cannae get rid o' the bugger.'

'Okay.' Michael waved and squeezed out through the fence.

When he'd gone I realised that I was drowsing quite close to the brazier and the talk was not nearly as clear as it had been.

Peter was saying, 'He'll drive down overnight on Wednesday.'

'Is that so?' Dosser marvelled. 'I suppose he knows the way to England all right?'

'He's done it often enough.'

'I doubt if I could manage it at all.' He took out his mouth-organ and blew a few exploratory chords. 'To any particular place, I mean. No, no. That is another country altogether.'

'He jist has tae stick tae the road.'

'Of course, there will be only one road going, and none at all coming back.'

Peter seemed to agree with that, for I did not hear him answer as Dosser played 'There's A New Moon Over My Shoulder'.

What with the hot soup and the fire and Dosser playing his mouth-organ and Peter Duncan reciting at length from the works of Robert Service, between dozing and listening, I spent a very enjoyable night at the demolition site. It was after five o'clock in the morning when I wandered back to my digs. Wearing an enormous unclaimed duffle-coat that Peter had lent me I strolled through the sleeping town. It worried me that Martin . . . I mean, Michael – Dosser's confusion began to confuse me. I wondered why Michael was so bitter. He was a fully trained engineer; as I hoped to be. But not here. The outrage of the attempted greasing had convinced me that I must get out of Scotland and away from the barbarous training that my father had imposed on me. I knew it was no good writing home asking him to reconsider and to send money for my return trip. I must get home in person and decline to be sent back. Nothing was worth the humiliation and fear I'd gone through that night. I must simply run away. When I reached my digs I waited in the street until the blind was raised on the kitchen window then went up to bed. It was with some difficulty that I was wakened to hear reports that I'd been drowned. And I was delighted.

The apprentices had kept guard, waiting in vain to complete the greasing. At daylight they searched the narrow stretch of dockside, found nothing and told the foreman. He recalled my panic the last time I was seen. In the plating-shop, Mr Mulvenny was informed and he came straight home to wake me.

Naturally, I took advantage of the situation and recalled that I had indeed *almost* drowned but was sucked out of the Dock Burn by the tide and cast ashore outside the yard. This story preserved Dosser's fishing trips and, more importantly, put the fear of God in the greasers. *And* I got the rest of the week off work – to recover. Little did they guess that I would not come back at all. If only I'd started hitching my way south that night I could have had them dragging the Dock Burn for my body. The very thought of that revenge cheered me. And I had thought of how I would escape. Michael was driving South on Wednesday. I would simply go with him.

In the afternoon, as soon as I thought everyone would be back at work, I was out and down the hill to see if I could find either Michael or his father at the enchanted ruin where I'd found shelter. The demolition team was going full blast, forcing monstrous entry upon tiny rooms. The variety and colours of their wall-paper seemed absurd, yet oddly touching; probably because the decoration which should only be seen indoors was now thrown open to the sky. So, the people who had put it there to adorn their lives were rudely made vulnerable, without their permission.

As I passed the filthy window of a small stand-up snack-bar, I caught sight of Dosser and went in to talk to him.

'Mr Thompson, again!' He bowed, flourishing a thick sandwich.

'Do you live near here, Mr Farr?'

'I live in two places, only,' he said. 'On me feet and on me back. That's the extent of my social position. Let others make a mark on the world – I'll jist make a dent in a dry tarpaulin.'

'And where is your tarpaulin?'

'Nearby. I prefer to be near one of my investments.' He nodded proprietorially across the street to the demolition site. 'That old tenement, now, is bulgin' wi' non-ferrous materials. When that was built there was none of yer plastic rubbish for pipes and fittings. No! It was lead, solid copper and brass from top to bottom. And it's worth a damn sight more this day than the day it was new.' He sighed. 'The very best of stuff.'

Both of us peered through the steamed-up window as though a quinquereme of Nineveh had just berthed by the far pavement.

'I suppose that's why they need a night watchman,' I said.

'Just so. But the night watchman likes company.' He gave me a consciously sly smile and wink, by which I understood that there was no duplicity. Peter Duncan knew why Dosser was always hanging about. And Dosser knew that he knew.

'But you've known Mr Duncan a long time, haven't you?'

'Indeed I have! Since he used to live there.' He leaned closer, allowing me an intimate close-up of the sauce dribble on his stubbled chin, and whispered, 'That man is keepin' watch on his own ruin.'

'What did he work at before he retired?'

'He did no work a long time before he retired. When he did work, though, he was a tool-maker. Till his hand got unsteady through drink.'

I was impressed. 'Tool-makers earn a lot of money.'

'Oh, they do that. And he spent even more. A terrible waste.'

'His son seems to have done very well.'

Dosser nodded vehemently as he emptied the remnants on his plate into the palm of his hand. 'That's Maisie's doin'. Mrs Duncan. She's the little woman held everything together when there was nothin' to hold. And she's workin' still.' He applied the loaded palm to his mouth with a gesture which could have been mistaken for covering a languid yawn. 'Now!' he said, 'you can oblige *me* with some information.'

But the Duncans were still nagging at my attention. 'I suppose they really don't want Michael to go away.'

'They do not. In fact, havin' their son home to stay is what they've been countin' on for the rest of their lives. Maisie, anyway. Havin' him in the town, a successful man, would have made everything worth it, d'ye see?'

I nodded. 'You mean, she could stop working?'

'No,' said Dosser. 'That's not what I mean at all.' And he had no intention of enlightening me. He went on, 'You were sayin' the metal store, in that yard of yours, runs right back to the river.'

'No. I didn't say that.'

'Did you not?' He was all alert surprise. 'Well, somebody told me that's where it was.'

'No, it's beside the gate-house; so they can unload from the street.'

He slapped the counter. 'Ach, to be sure! And how often would that be . . . they unload the material?'

'I don't know.'

'I could make it worth your while.'

I laughed at him. 'I really don't know!'

'You could find out, though.'

'Yes.' I did not tell him that there was now no possibility of my gaining any further information about the shipyard.

'And would ya do that for me, Billy?'

'Why do you want to know?'

He put his arm round my shoulder. 'I'm thinkin' of retiring, d'y'see, and nothin' would suit me better than to make off wi' a full bloody lorry-load of gunmetal forgings.'

'Can you drive?'

'Drive what?'

'A lorry. Can you drive a lorry?'

He brushed this aside. 'Well, I've never *drove* a lorry, if that's what you mean. Or anything else, for that matter. But there can't be much to it. Look at them ignorant yobbos that's to be seen in lorries day and daily. You don't think they could do it before they did it, do ya?' I stared at him incredulously and he took my silence as a proof of his point. 'Not at all. Drivin' the thing's the least part of it – if I only knew *which* lorry; and when.'

'Will you have another sandwich?'

His weathered little face folded into a delighted smile as he misinterpreted the offer. 'I will.' He patted my arm. 'It's a pleasure doin' business with you, Billy.'

'But . . .' I protested.

'I know! But don't you worry about that side of it. I have a friend with a little furnace that could soon melt a lorry-load – and the lorry as well, if we're pushed.'

Leaving Dosser in the snack-bar, I walked across the street and peered through the fence just to make sure that the magical space we'd occupied around the brazier was still there. Everything looked quite different. I stared around me wondering if this was the same site. I walked hesitantly beside the fence, then stopped and looked up at a jutting piece of what had been a second-floor flat. For no visible reason, but instantly, I was reassured.

On Wednesday morning I sorted out what few possessions I could take with me and still give the impression that I was only going to be away for the week-end. Nothing and nobody was going to stop me. Late in the evening, carrying a small bag, I went down the hill to the site. I got through the fence but was shy of emerging too suddenly into the light since only Michael and his father were there and they were talking amiably together.

Michael moved the bench nearer the brazier. 'Are the kids still goin' out as guizers?'

'Sure,' his father said. 'Battalions o' them.'

'I wouldn't have thought there were many kids left in this part.'

'Not now. But I've seen the day.'

'Oh, aye!' Michael smiled at the recollection. 'It was great fun.'

'Aye,' Peter sighed, 'I remember when you use' tae go oot for ye're Hallowe'en.'

'Always as a pirate wi' the . . .'

'Naw! Pirate? Naw, I remember the wee face wi' the . . . white . . . and big eyes. A mask. An *elf* or somethin' it was.'

Michael looked at his father briefly with pained perplexity then insisted, 'I was the pirate, always the pirate. The elf was Martin.'

'Oh!' said Peter and nodded quickly. 'But was he old enough tae go oot on Hallowe'en?'

'Well, if I was old enough he was old enough.'

'Aye, I suppose so,' the old man laughed uneasily. 'But I never think o' you two bein' twins.'

'I do.'

'Still?'

'Still.'

'I'm surprised you remember him clear at all. Martin died before you were . . .'

'I know well enough when he died. And why.' There was a callousness in his voice he hadn't intended and he watched anxiously as his father abruptly stood up, faced away, then started swinging his arms, as though to repel a sudden chill. 'Are ye cold?' the son asked.

'No. It's jist the change. The heat'll soon build up.' He turned back again to face the brazier. 'There's more warmth here in the open than we ever had in that house.'

'Maybe because you don't have to pay for the coal.'

Peter leapt from sadness to anger. 'What! It was me tae blame, ye mean?'

'No, I just meant that . . .'

'If we'd had the money I'd have kept him warm. An' well fed. If I'd been in work we could've moved fae this damp hole. But it wisnae jist lack o' warmth. Holy God! I would have burned the whole bloody street if it could have kept him alive.' He stared wildly at his surviving son who hunched deeper in the coat.

'Sure,' Michael grunted.

'There were families better placed than me that lost children in times like that.'

'I know.'

'We did everything we could for that boy. But he was frail. No' like you. Delicate. No' a bit like you.'

'No. I was always a sturdy bugger. Luckily.'

'You should be thankful for it, instead o' . . .'

'I'm thankful. But I wish there'd only been one of us.'

'You?'

'Or him. But one. And it would've been cheaper.'

'That's a rotten thing tae say!'

'I hate like hell to feel there's a gap at my side.'

'A gap?'

'When I'm away it's a gap. Whenever I come back here, though, it's more than that. Martin's beside me, or watchin' me. I wish to Christ I knew what he *expects!*'

For me, hidden in the shadow, that strange distancing again occurred. I was looking down on the two men. But now I knew beyond any doubt that what I'd been aware of above and around that place was Martin. I felt it had been with his eyes I'd watched them before I knew of his existence.

'What d'ye mean, expects?' Peter asked.

'I've been trying to think if I ever made him a promise.' The young man glanced, almost apologetically, at his father. 'When we were weans, y'know – maybe I promised him somethin' and . . . I didnae do it.'

'Weans make a lot o' promises.'

'But did he ever say anything aboot that? Can you remember?'

'Aboot you?'

'Aye.'

The old man thought for a few moments, anxious to be of use in this odd – it seemed to him pointless – conversation. 'He was awful fond o' you.'

Michael gave a sob that carried intimately across the whole clearing. 'Oh, my good Christ, I know that!'

Suddenly I felt ashamed to be eavesdropping upon them and, to suggest that I was arriving now, I rattled the fence then walked boldly towards them.

'Hello, Mr Duncan. I've brought back your coat.'

He took it absent-mindedly. 'Thanks, son.'

Michael was quicker to regain his composure. 'Well, er . . . Billy, you're all dressed up tonight, eh?'

'Yes.'

'Where have you been?'

'No – I'm *going.*'

'At this time! Where?'

'If you don't mind, I'd like you to give me a lift home.'

'Ye're not afraid o' the dark are ye?'

'No,' I said, then struggled to work out why he'd ask that.

'He means home, tae England,' Peter guessed.

'If you're going to Southampton I can get a bus from there, home.'

'Sure,' Michael said. 'But I'm not leavin' right away.'

'No. I'd like to wait here until you're ready.'

'Are your people expectin' ye?' Peter wanted to know.

I shook my head. 'No. I've been given a few days off work and I thought I'd spend the time at home. It'll be a pleasant surprise.'

'It will,' the old man said. 'A son that wants to come home is a pleasant surprise all right.'

'Oh, God!' Michael groaned under his breath.

From the darkness, a cracked but still lyrical tenor voice sang, ' "Trumpeter, What are you sounding now?" ' Dosser advanced upon us. He carried two bulging carrier bags. 'I tell you,' he said, 'I've had a busy day of it.'

'What's that ye've got?'

'Provisions!' the thief replied and started unpacking various groceries and fancy-goods that he'd stolen for the event. 'Seein' as how Martin will be drivin' a fair distance, I have brought various kinds of sustenance.'

'A'm payin' ye nothing for any of that,' Peter warned him.

'Would I expect payment?' Dosser invited our derision.

'Yes!' said his friend.

'No payment. Jist a wee favour, maybe.' He turned to Michael. 'Since ye've got yer car out there, I wondered if you'd learn me to drive before ye go.'

'But I'm going *tonight*,' Michael protested.

'I know that. Sure it's tonight I mean.' Dosser gave me – his fellow conspirator – a mock-despairing look that people could be so obtuse.

'Dosser, there's no time for that.'

The little man was hurt. 'Oh?' He looked around him for signs of activity. 'What's goin' on then? What am I missin' that's takin' up all your time?'

'I mean, it would take you longer than that,' Michael said.

'Why? D'ye think I'm stupid?'

'Mr Farr, it takes months to learn to drive,' I said.

'Can you drive?' he challenged me.

'No. But I'm saving up for a car. I'm too young to drive yet.'

'Exactly. Too young to know anything about it.' He turned magnanimously to the others. 'Still, never mind me. We can make a night of it anyhow.' He made a comprehensive gesture at the loot piled by his feet. 'What we can't use I'll take back tomorrow for a refund.'

'Don't be daft!' Peter told him. 'This has all been stolen.'

'Of course it has. That's the work in it. The refund is a bonus.' He explained to Michael, who might not know his system, 'I never steal money, y'see, but there are times when I do need ready cash.'

'I see.'

'That's what these women's blouses and girdles and what-not are for – takin' back.'

'What!'

'Shops are used to that.' He sighed, sharing the resignation of shopkeepers. 'Sure, if women don't know their *own* sizes why should I?'

'Aren't they suspicious in the women's department?' I asked.

He shook his head. 'They think I have a very fussy bedridden wife, or that myself is one o' them funny fellas.'

'But what about the receipts?' Michael asked.

Dosser gave him a patient smile. 'What makes ye think I can't steal them as well? I have a whole selection of receipt-books, and quite a few date-stamps, too. Oh, yes. I'm a great believer in havin' things legal.'

We all poked about among the bric-a-brac, food and fancy-goods that Dosser had provided. Peter put aside the bottles, the biscuits and the meat-pies. Dosser himself made sure that his items for return were safely repacked. Michael selected choco-lates and a small pack of thin cigars for the journey. That left me with two packs of bunting and a few crêpe-paper lanterns; with which, presumably, Dosser had intended decorating the demoli-tion-site. While the men were drinking I did my best to add this seasonal touch to the lighted space. I strung out the bunting between the posts on the drying-green which had lain behind the tenement but was now a desert of rubble. Where the strings crossed I hung paper lanterns. Michael helped me in this absurd decoration of his former home.

'I don't know what the foreman's goin' tae say in the mornin',' he said.

'He can say what he likes,' I replied, thinking of my own foreman. 'We'll be away and out of reach.'

'Funny, we never thought o' doin' this when we lived here.'

Beyond the space of the drying-green, I could just make out a
small, ruined, stone structure. I asked Michael, 'Why does that
coal cellar have chimneys?'

He laughed. 'That's not a coal cellar. That's the wash-house.'

'Out there!'

'Where else? Each of the families in this close would have the
use of it one day in the week. That was the day we had soup for
breakfast, dinner and tea.'

'Why?'

'My mother had no time tae make anything else. Washday was
a major operation and she was out here from morning till night.
We helped her.'

'Martin and you?' I gulped, thinking I'd trapped myself by
knowing about Martin. But if I had, Michael didn't notice.

He smiled. 'We could just manage tae carry an empty bucket
between us – or a clothes-peg bag on our own.'

'Did you stay off school?'

'This was before we were old enough for school. Martin loved
gatherin' up the clothes-pegs. He saw them as wee wooden
horsemen ridin' the clothes line in single-file.'

I couldn't imagine it, but then, probably, I had never seen the
right clothes-pegs. 'Like soldiers?'

'Aye. Then, when the washin' was done we'd all have our bath
in the boiler.'

I was amazed. 'In a boiler?'

'Sure. It was a big wide copper tub surrounded wi' concrete
and wi' a fire under it. Martin and me used tae love that. B'God, it
was big enough for us tae *swim* in. All that warm, sappley, water!'

'And was the fire still going, under it?'

'No, no. Your mother let the fire out as soon as the whites were
boiled.'

'And the whole family used it, one after another?'

He nodded. 'Good hot water was hard tae come by in those
days. But when ye came out of there ye warenae just clean, ye
were bleached!'

His face was illuminated by an orange glow as he tried to make
a lantern hang straight. He was smiling and I realised that far from
resenting the conditions in which he'd once lived, he remembered them with affection. As we picked our way back to the circle
of light around the brazier I marvelled at the image of those two
little boys *swimming* in a copper cauldron. We rested a while, then
Dosser brought out his mouth-organ and played a few songs to
which only Peter seemed to know the words.

Before long, it was time for Michael to go. 'Are you ready for the off, Billy?' he asked me.

'Yes, whenever you like.'

Dosser protested, 'Must ye go, Martin? So soon!' The words seemed to bear more weight than he could have intended.

Michael stared at him almost angrily for a moment, was about to correct the name again, but instead asked, 'Did you know my brother, Martin?'

'Your brother? I didn't know ye had a brother.'

'You mean, you didn't know Martin had a brother.'

Dosser was confused. 'That must be it,' he said, doubtfully.

Michael persisted, 'You remember Martin?'

'Oh, surely! As a tiny sliver of a boy. He used to follow me around. Always wanted to help.'

Peter, seeing his son's distress, tried to dismiss the subject. 'You're all mixed up, Dosser. Forget it!'

'Mixed up I may be, but I'm not likely to forget your lad. Nor will he forget me. Didn't he tell everyone he met, in his wee piping voice, "I'm a friend of Dosser Farr"'!'

Michael sat down abruptly, as though pulled down.

'Are ye goin' or not?' his father asked him.

'Sure. Sure! I'm going.' He pushed himself to his feet again and I waited politely at the fence as the men shook hands. 'I'll be *back*,' Michael promised.

'Visitin',' Peter said blankly.

'Aye.'

Dosser, the experienced driver, added some advice. 'Watch yer speed, now. And keep to the signs!'

Walking towards me, Michael laughed and called back, 'What signs?'

Martin's friend was less sure of specifics. 'Whatever signs there are. Dangers and warning. There's more than you on the road; even through the night.'

'I'll let you know how I get on,' Michael called and waved to the two men standing by the glowing brazier. Again the duality intervened. I saw me at his side as he waved and looked down on the heads of Dosser and Peter from above and behind them.

As we drove through Greenock and on into Port Glasgow, the headlights shone on several roving bands of 'guizers', all aged between five and twelve and many of them wearing full beards as part of their elaborate costume. They trudged along in business-like fashion from one housing scheme to another, like a greatly increased band of Snow White's dwarfs. 'Were you never out as a guizer?' Michael asked me.

'No. We don't do much for Hallowe'en,' I said. 'But this is the time we were all preparing for Bonfire Night.'

'That's right. It's Guy Fox night you hold.'

'Maybe that's where you get the name "guizer".'

Michael chuckled. ' "Guizer Fox"? No. I think it's more from "disguise".'

I wanted him to tell me about Martin and so – although I knew the answer – I asked him, 'What were you disguised as?'

'A pirate. And the water always got under the eye-patch when I dooked for apples. Always ended up wi' a soggy eye-patch.'

This was incomprehensible. 'Water?'

'What else would ye dook in?'

'That depends on what dook *is*.'

'It means, "ducking". Ducking for the apples, floating in the water.'

Evidently he thought he'd made the whole bizarre ritual quite clear and I didn't want to test his patience with such outstanding questions as – what water, and how did the apples get in the water, and why must they be removed without using your hands? We drove on in silence up the bank of the Clyde towards Renfrew, before skirting the south of Glasgow to join the A74 at Hamilton. The flashing beacons which mark the deep channel of the river traced a dotted line over the black surface of the water curving far ahead of us. Before we'd cleared the other side of the city I was asleep in the car – but, somehow, awake at the demolition site. Through the presence there of Martin I saw and heard all that occurred, or dreamt that I did.

Peter – as so often in his earlier days – was drowning his sense of loss in whisky. Dosser, too, had given up a fishing trip for that evening. They were excellent company for each other; one providing sentimental music and the other dramatic recitation.

The most effective of these was 'The Shooting of Dan McGrew' and for his audience of one – doubling as the kid that handled the music-box – Peter spared nothing in recreating the atmosphere of that hectic night in the Malamute Saloon. They were resting on the glow of a fine performance when they were unexpectedly joined by the woman who was known as Maisie. Peter's wife. She was a small, thin woman who – even over rough ground – moved with quick decisive steps. Her lips were pressed firmly together giving a stoic, though rather sad, expression to her lined face. She looked older than her husband; and probably felt it.

'What the hell are *you* daein' here?' he asked.

'Hello Maisie!' Dosser greeted her. 'You just missed "The Shooting of Dan McGrew".'

'Oh, A heard it. A heard it. I was jist pickin' ma wey across the shincut, there, when two guns blazed in the dark.'

'Did you duck?'

'Damn nae fear o' it! They guns hiv been blazin' in the dark ever since A kin remember.'

Peter was annoyed. 'What are ye *here* for, Missus?'

'Because I'm fed up wi' weans chappin' the door. Ye don't get a minute's peace.'

'Ye could put oot the light an' kid-on ye're no' in.'

'The hoose is empty enough without sittin' in the dark. Especially th'night, efter he left. But it's they weans . . . they keep chappin' anyway – tae find *out* if ye're no' in. And look through the letter box.' From under her coat she produced a bundle wrapped in a shopping bag that she'd been keeping warm against her stomach. 'So I boiled these spuds in case ye were hungry. Is the can on?'

Dosser rose in courtly fashion to receive the offering. 'You're a thoughtful woman, Maisie. And a few boiled spuds is about the only thing we're short of.'

Her husband was not so easily won. He said, 'You'd better get back or you'll miss the last bus.'

'I came on the last bus,' replied Maisie.

'This is a work-place, no' a bloody home-fae-home.'

'Oh? Ye're forgettin' it wis ma home, long enough. We knew and liked mair people here than we ever met again.'

'Bloody nonsense,' Peter growled.

She ignored the interruption. 'Ye know, comin' in that bus A wis used tae, and risin' tae get aff at the same old stop made me feel ower twenty years younger.'

'Is that a fact?' said Peter with heavy sarcasm. 'And what dae ye think of it, noo ye are home?'

Maisie surveyed the wide, desolate, gap among the ruins. 'They must have took back the furniture – *again*,' she said, tartly. 'I'd recognise this anywhere.'

'D'ye want a drink?' Peter asked, avoiding well-contested ground.

'Where did ye get drink?' The question packed accusation and disapproval in equal measure.

'Oh, it's just a wee something I stole,' Dosser modestly confessed. 'For Martin's goin' away.'

'He means, Michael,' said Peter wearily.

'I should think so.' Maisie drew her coat tightly around her. 'For Martin's been away a long while.'

Dosser shook his head dubiously and murmured as though to himself, 'Not away from here, surely.'

Peter tried the same diversion again. 'Well, Missus, dae ye want a drink or no'?'

'I thought it was Dosser's bottle,' she countered.

'Holy God! All right. Wid ye take a drink if *he* asked ye?'

'I would not!' She turned to the drowsy gift-bringer. 'Thanks all the same Dosser.' But she did sit down. 'So, Michael got away all right?'

Peter nodded, 'Oh, he got away. He got away fast.' He pushed the poker into the depths of the charcoal and jerked it upward, causing a flare of sparks. 'Did ye lock the door?'

'What's there tae steal?' the woman scoffed.

'Did you?'

'I locked the door! D'ye want the key?'

'Whit wid A dae wi' the key?'

'Lose it!'

Dosser had now divided the potatoes in three portions and was preparing to serve them on pieces of wrapping paper. 'Did ye bring any salt?' he asked.

Maisie reached into a pocket of her coat and produced a screwed up corner of a brown paper bag. 'There ye are. But don't give *him* much. It's bad for his heart.'

'You leave ma heart tae me,' said Peter.

'That's where it's always been,' his wife retorted. She could not resist scoring points against him; whether or not they were deserved, or even apt. Her whole attitude seemed bent on levelling an enormous score that her husband had unfairly gained many years before. Now, whatever he did, he could only lose. Apparently Peter understood this and offered only token resistance.

Maisie glanced around to find that Dosser was asleep. Then she looked beyond her husband to the black outline of the ruined tenement. 'They havenae far tae go now,' she said. 'Is that Mrs Chalmers' close they're at?'

'Naw, further up. They'll be at number thirty-seven the morra.'

'Miss Nisbit!'

'Aye.'

'Widnae surprise me if she comes round tae see they dae it right!'

'They know whit they're doin'.'

'And what'll you be doin', when they're finished?'

'Nothin'.'

'Oh, I thought ye might be lookin' for anither job as a watch-man '

'Maybe.'

'Suits you fine, doesn't it? Out all night – just like your younger days.'

'Whit the hell wis there tae stay in for?'

'Ye could have taken pleasure in your home.'

'I wis tellin' Michael, it's warmer here now than it was then.'

'We could have made it cheery,' said Maisie grimly.

'Aye, we could have. If you could have changed. Back tae whit ye were before ye lost that boy.'

'Me? I lost him! If you'd spent more . . .'

'When Martin died the life went out o' you!' Peter's voice overrode her protest. He was sure of his ground because she had confessed as much before now. 'Since then ye've put a cold hand on every chance we might have had. Maybe that's why Michael skinned out.'

'That's got nothing tae dae wi' me!'

'It has!' Peter gained strength from her defensive tone. 'He mentioned that – the cold hand.'

'That's a lie! Oh, you'd say anything tae shift the blame.'

'Is it a lie that you blame me? That the kiddie died? And at every turn since then ye've done everything tae make sure I'd never forget it. Or that Michael would never forget it and that's why . . .'

'Peter! No.' The oddness of Maisie calling him by his first name quite deflated Peter. He stared at her and she went on, 'That's not what I blame ye for. If there's blame for that it *is* mine. For that, I blame only myself.'

'But it spreads out, woman. It spreads out over me. Over the three of us. And you've no right to blame yourself at all.'

'It's no' somethin' I'd claim as a right,' said Maisie softly.

Peter, finding his opponent so quickly vulnerable, was at a loss and added with surprising gentleness, 'That's not what I meant.'

'I know. Ye say more than ye mean. Always have.'

'What I meant was that Michael feels guilty aboot Martin. That's how he had tae get away.'

'How can that be?'

'He thinks Martin's holdin' him responsible, or somethin'. He cannae get it oot his system that he's failed Martin over the years.'

'We a' fail somehow, over the years,' Maisie was prepared to confess.

'And the older ye get, the mair ye regret it,' said Peter. His wife knew this was the nearest he could come to an apology and, for the moment, she was content.

They were interrupted by the sound of drumming and I woke in the car driving south. We'd run into a rain storm at Abington. It grew heavier as we climbed towards Beattock Summit. The windscreen-wiper on my side swept maddeningly from side to side without *touching* the windscreen at all. Michael offered to stop and try to fix it but I told him not to bother. 'There's nothing to see, anyway.'

'We'll stop for something to eat at the border,' he said. 'I'll have a go at it then.'

'When do you think you'll get to Southampton?'

'Six or seven o'clock.'

'And when do you have to sign on?'

'I don't *have* to sign on. It's a matter of choice.'

'Oh, I thought they were expecting you.'

'No, no. It's just that I know what ships are crewing-up.'

'So, nobody's employing you at the moment?'

'Nobody's employing me till I sign on for the trip.'

'I don't think I'd like not being sure.'

'It gives ye freedom.'

'When I qualify I'm going to have a long-term contract.'

'Quite right. You'll be just the kind o' man the owners want, long term. In fact, I think you'll be the kind of seagoing engineer they'll want to keep ashore.'

I laughed. 'Does that mean a good engineer or a bad one?'

'It means, a man wi' good connections in the front office – that happens tae be an engineer. Great for impressin' the customers.'

'Do you think I could do that?'

'Certain. They'll be your kind o' people.'

I thought that what had started as a compliment was deteriorating into rather snide and unfair carping. 'What do you mean, my kind of people?'

'Oh, people you'd like.'

'I like Dosser Farr.'

'He's good for a laugh.'

'No, as a friend. Is that the sort of person I'd be dealing with?'

'Hardly! There are very few people like Dosser hiring oil-tankers.'

'Just as well, or they'd be scuttled for scrap.'

'Aye,' Michael laughed. 'Or run aground. Dosser wid want ye tae run it aground tae collect the scrap.'

'And he'd only take the "non-ferrous", at that!'

As we drove between the forests of Ae and O'er it seemed as though the car was attempting to part an unbroken curtain of water.

Shouting above the demented drumming on the roof, I suggested, 'Maybe you should stop until it eases off a bit.'

'If I stop we might start floatin',' Michael shouted back. He crouched over the wheel, lips parted, teeth clamped tight, as he tried to pick out what lay ahead of us. All I could see was a constantly shifting barrage of needle-pointed lights as our headlamp beams were flung back at us. The pounding of the rain had buckled the wiper arm on my side and it lay twitching across the bonnet. Perhaps, if Michael had stopped to fix it before we ran into the worst of the storm, the accident could have been avoided.

It happened at the roundabout south of Lockerbie. A truck loaded with steel rods was immediately ahead of us and as it moved onto the roundabout, Michael cautiously followed – assuming that the truck would take the main exit. He could not see that it was turning more sharply at an earlier exit to the left. It was as though a steel spear was suddenly thrown between Michael and me. The weight of shattered windscreen dumped in my lap made me twist round and I saw the look of stupefied wonder on Michael's face. There, not more than six inches from his eyes, hung a white elfin mask. It hung from the longest rod protruding over the tail-gate of the truck. It had been tied there as one would tie a piece of rag, to mark the length of the load. On this particular night, though, the driver had light-heartedly substituted a Hallowe'en mask.

Obviously the truck-driver had no idea what had happened behind him and, finding his way clear, he continued off to the left. The steel rod was drawn from our windscreen with a rasping sound and the mask dropped, grinning, on top of the instrument panel. Michael could not take his eyes off it. Of course he had been shocked by the collision, but now I realised that his shock was deepening when the danger was over. To him it must have seemed that he'd been forcibly stopped by Martin. That mask at which he was staring was identical to the one in which his twin brother always went disguised at Hallowe'en. I dared not say anything. We waited what seemed a long time, with traffic moving past us in the downpour.

Fatigue and shock made my head swim. I stared at the mask and it seemed to recede from me. Then, through the curtain of gleaming rain, I thought I saw the tenement. It was that same jutting corner of the second floor flat I'd noted, but now a small white face peered hopefully over the jagged edge of bricks. The image was soon blurred by the spray from a passing truck. Yet it lasted long enough to bestow on me the same curious afflatus I'd felt, looking up at the real building.

Gradually Michael eased his frozen posture and began to sob as though gusts of breath were forcing their way out of him against his will. And the rain was now pouring through the gaping windscreen. At last, my companion spared me the trouble of deciding what we should do. He'd made up his mind what *he* must do. Slowly, he jerked ahead on the roundabout. He swung past the exit to the south, then the exit to the west. With the mask staring at him from blank wide eyes, he completed the full circle and headed back from where we had come. I remembered Dosser's voice. Signs . . . Dangers and warnings, he'd said . . . there are more on the road than you. Michael could not lightly deny the most potent sign he'd ever been given. Nor, really, did he want to.

When we got back to the demolition site – soaked, cold and starving – it was almost daylight. Peter must have been off completing his round before the end of his shift for, at first, we could see only Mrs Duncan. She was dozing huddled in her husband's coat. The brazier was almost out because there was no point in refuelling it. As we drew closer, Dosser rose from the ground behind her, stretching himself.

'Ah, Michael!' he said. 'Did ye forget something?'

'No,' said Michael, 'I've changed my mind.'

Maisie shook herself awake. 'What was that?' She half rose from the bench then, fully appreciating that it was really Michael who stood there, slumped back on the bench.

'I said, I've changed my mind.'

'What happened to your suit?' his mother asked.

Michael shrugged. 'We got caught in a shower.'

'Dosser, get some more coke on that fire! They're soaked through.' He scuttled to obey and Maisie, with considerable self-control, remarked to her son, 'Yer father'll be pleased you're back.'

'And you?'

'Depends. Are ye home for good?'

'Yes.'

'I'm pleased,' said Maisie.

Michael nodded. 'Good.' He looked around at the debris of the night watch. 'Is there any whisky left in that bottle? We need something for the chill.'

'Surely!' his mother said. She lifted the bottle. 'I think I could go a wee nip, masel. Quick, before your Da' finishes his round.' But she wasn't quick enough. Peter walked into the clearing as the three of us were downing a jolt. He advanced slowly, keeping his eyes on Michael, determined not to give anything away. Maisie reassured him. 'Michael's decided to stay.'

'That's good news.' Then his voice leapt out of all restrictions. 'That's bloody good news.' He suddenly grabbed Maisie and whirled her round.

'Peter! Don't be silly!'

'I'll be silly if I feel like it. An' I've never felt mair like it.' Still holding her, he swayed happily from side to side and sang, ' "After the ball is over, After the break of day . . ." '

Dosser immediately took up the tune on his mouth-organ and as Michael and I dried ourselves at the revived brazier, Peter waltzed Maisie around us. They scuffed through discarded paper wrapping, over the powdered mortar and fragments of brick. Maisie began to enjoy the dance and she sang too.

Michael, while still smiling at them, turned to me. 'I'm sorry ye didnae get home for your Hallowe'en.'

I confessed. 'I wasn't just going for Hallowe'en. I was running away.'

'Were you?' he said, as though it didn't surprise him. 'That made two of us.'

'Yes. But you were running away from home. I was running back to it.'

'Aye.' He nodded but he was not really interested in what I was doing, or why and I wondered if, now, the gap at his side would close; if his being home 'for good' was what Martin expected of him. Quite involuntarily, but aloud, I said, 'Yes!' He jerked his head round to face me, as though I had answered exactly the question he'd been asking himself at that moment. The sound of his parents singing, the scuffing of their feet and the plaintive, reedy sound of Dosser's mouth-organ wrapped around us. Michael stared into the revitalised brazier then, very deliberately, pulled from his pocket the mask and dropped it onto the glowing coals.

When I went back to work there were no further attempts at greasing. Apparently it had been decided that anyone who was recklessly prone to suicide would just have to do without lubrication round the genitals. But they made it plain they were disappointed in me. That lasted until I was about to depart from 'the shops' into the drawing office. That's when the axle-tallow caught up with me. And it was from the drawing office that I caught up with the Duncans.

On one of my infrequent visits down the shops I met Michael Duncan working there. He'd been appointed to lead the Works engine-test team. It was a highly technical position requiring a great deal of experience. Michael was quite evidently enjoying the job.

'I know what I'm doing,' he said. 'And the money's good. On top of that there's the odd "jolly" as guest of Gebrüder Sulzer in Switzerland.'

The diesels we built were Sulzer design, manufactured under licence from the Swiss company. I smiled. 'Very nice! How are Gebrüder Sulzer?'

'Flourishing.'

'And how are your parents?'

'My mother's fine, but my father died a couple of years ago.'

'I'm sorry.'

Michael shrugged. 'His heart. He wasnae up to all that night watchin'.'

I nodded sympathetically but I was thinking that 'night watching' was a very imaginative expression. 'Do you ever see Dosser Farr?' I asked him.

'Occasionally.'

'I wonder if he ever learned to drive.'

'Drive?' Michael stared at me blankly. Obviously he'd forgotten about that. It may have been that he had purposefully put out of his mind all the events of the night we both tried to escape into England, but more likely he was the same as others I met who, perversely it seemed, forgot exactly the things I'd chosen to remember.

'I'd better get back to the office,' I said, suddenly aware that perhaps Michael couldn't remember who *I* was.

As for Dosser, he certainly postponed his retirement. For a long time after that he continued to hang around the yard gates, no doubt logging the time and nature of deliveries to the metal store. Occasionally, I saw him in shops disdainfully fingering the most unlikely items of merchandise. He nodded civilly enough but I could tell that he was disappointed in me, too. Clearly it was my loss that I had not gone into business partnership with him. Anyone so lacking in enterprise as that deserved to work for a living.

Store Quarter

SOME PEOPLE ARE 'car' people, whether they can afford a car or not. They are those who are not charmed by their fellow men in the mass, in the crush, or in the queue. They can be seen, sitting or swaying in public transport, fervently pretending they are alone. And I've always been one of them although I did not realise it until I left school, home and England at sixteen. Deprived of the parent-chauffeur service, I immediately began to save up to buy a car of my own. On my wages as a Clydeside apprentice that took some time and, while I saved, the weekly trip from Greenock to Glasgow Tech. was done by train. It was possible to be alone on the journey *to* the college, but coming back there were always some of my classmates.

'Hey, Billy!'

I didn't respond and held the tutorial notes firmly in front of me as a barrier. The four of us occupied the four window seats in the 'empty' I'd chased at Glasgow Central. Strictly speaking, they had invaded *my* compartment.

Archie Hemple was not to be ignored. He shouted to the youth sitting opposite me, 'Pull that bloody book aff 'im, Deanie.' This was done and I immediately turned to stare at my reflection in the dark window. Archie tried again. 'Hey, Billy!'

'Yes?'

'Is it right, you're gonnae buy a car?'

'Yes.'

'Whi' kinna car?' asked the note-snatcher, throwing the book back in my lap; thus scattering all the loose sheets of graph-paper.

'An A35. A Baby Austin.'

'That's awful *wee*. A wee Austin'll hardly haud the four o' us!'

'It will hold *me*,' I announced firmly.

'An' it's only got *two doors*. I hate getting' oot tae let somebody else in.'

'True enough,' Archie Hemple agreed with Deanie. 'Ye'll hiv' tae get somethin' bigger than that. Look at the length a' ma legs!' And he showed us one of them by stretching it into the crotch of the quiet little boy who sat opposite him.

'Get yer fuckin' feet aff me!' said the quiet little boy and big Archie did so – immediately.

'Oh, helluva sorry!' Archie saved face with effusive apology.

'A'd've thought,' Deanie told me, 'your old man wis rich enough tae buy ye somethin' *com*fortable.'

'His old man rich?' asked Archie.

Deanie gave an effete wave of his hand and imitated my accent. 'Can you not tell? Oh dear, yes!' Then resuming his own voice reported, 'Consultin' engineer. Heid o' a big firm, an' that. Makes a packet, dis'nae, Billy?'

'Christ! An' a' he's layin' oot fur is a pokey wee Austin?'

'My father has nothing to do with it. I'm buying the car for myself.'

'When are ye gettin' it?' the quiet boy asked. I tried to remember his name. It was Tommy or Terry or something.

'March.'

'Next month, eh?' He seemed to consider this with more care than it warranted. 'Hiv ye paid the deposit?'

'No. I'm buying it outright. It's cheaper that way.'

He nodded with what looked like worried approval, but Archie was less acute. 'Don't be daft! How can it be cheaper tae pay the full price when you could put doon a third o' that an' still get it?' He appealed to the quiet boy for common sense. 'Use the heid, Tony!'

'He means he'll no' hiv tae pay the interest,' said Tony.

Both Archie and Deanie were amazed, but it was Deanie who expressed their offended credulity. 'You mean, you've actually saved up the *whole* amount?'

'Yes.'

'An' ye've got that ready tae lay doon?'

'Yes.'

'An' ye never though' a the never-never as soon as ye had enough fur a deposit?'

'At that time I wasn't old enough to sit the driving test.'

Archie thought some retribution was in order, 'Well, A hope ye get landit wi' a clapped oot banger that bloody well explodes on ye.'

This puzzled me for a moment before I was able to inform them. 'I'm not buying a second-hand car. I'm buying a new one.'

Their astonishment turned to deep irritation, if not anger, and they held silence until we reached Port Glasgow where both Archie and Deanie got off. Not for the first time I was made aware of a crucial difference between my upbringing and theirs when it came to the use of money. We use it like soap. They use it like water.

Tony and I were alone in the compartment for the remainder of the journey into Greenock. Because he was so small and compact, with a pinched, sharp little face, he gave the impression of being much younger than the others. But he must have been at least the same age as me, and probably a good deal wiser. He put aside whatever was worrying him and – though I'd never talked to him before – seemed willing to be friendly.

'They clowns,' he said, shaking his head, 'they've nae idea.'

'About money?'

'Aboot anything!'

'Do you work in the yard?'

'No' in your yard. Further up. In Lamonts.'

'Oh.' They were small ship-repairers and their workers therefore lacked the kudos of new-building. Tony apparently read my reaction and gave a bitter little grin.

'It's no' everybody can buy everything new,' he said. 'Is this a college course you're on?'

'It will be after my third year.'

'Aye, A thought ye must be wan o' the college boys.'

'After my third year,' I insisted.

'Sure. But ye know it's there waitin' fur ye, don't ye?'

'Yes. If I pass everything before then.'

'You'll pass all right,' he assured me bleakly. 'You were reared tae pass.'

'I failed my driving test first time,' I offered.

But that was not enough to grant us equality. 'Ye can take that as often as ye can afford it, though.' The train slowed and he looked wearily out at the first of the platform lights. He got up. 'See ye next Friday,' he said, 'if no' before.'

'Yes. Good night!'

As it happened, I saw him the very next evening. The Fol De Rols were doing their season at the King's Theatre in Glasgow and I went there for the first house. He was sitting in the middle of an evidently well-fortified coach-party. They were led in every rowdy response by a fat middle-aged woman with an enormous bust and an equally outsized hair-pad supporting what was then the fashionable coiffure. Her constant rocking and tossing with laughter had shaken the pad well off-centre and must soon dislodge it altogether. I mentioned this distraction to Tony when I met him in the foyer during the interval.

'I've been spending more time watching that than watching the stage.'

'Ye're jist as well,' he said glumly.

'Don't you like the show?'

'It's all right. But it's always the same.'

'Pity you had to get stuck in the middle of that awful coach-party.'

'Aye.'

'Look! There she is now. She must have done some repairs.'

'Who?'

'That fat, vulgar woman with the hair-piece. She must be looking for the . . .'

'She's lookin' fur me,' said Tony. 'That's ma mother.'

His mother came towards us and now that she was on her feet I noted that her feet were crammed into delicate little shoes with absurdly high heels. She seemed to be tethered like a balloon between the fine tension points of her top-knot and her toes. It was difficult to see how she was able to remain upright.

'Here, Tony!' she called as she approached. 'Whit did ye dae wi' the bliddy raffle-tickets?' He started searching in his pockets but she did not await their discovery. 'Who's this?' she wanted to know.

'A mate o' mine fae the Tech. He's no' wi' us.'

She examined me. 'I should think no'! Be a while before *he's* in the club. Eh, son?' She gave me a playful dig in the stomach and laughed.

'Here's the tickets,' said Tony.

She snatched the book from him while still looking at me and asked, 'Wid ye like tae buy a few? It's in a good cause.'

'Twenty per cent commission, she means.'

She turned to her son. 'How'd ye like me tae shove these doon your throat, smart-arse?' she enquired.

'He disnae want tae buy any,' Tony unblinkingly insisted.

'Suit yersel'!' Her attention moved in the direction of the bar. 'Surely tae God somebody's got me a drink b'noo.' And she crunched off to find out, continuing to address Tony without looking back. 'Ask the boy if he wants tae come on the bus!'

'Dae ye?' he asked me. 'Ye'll get a free run back if ye like.'

'Yes. Thank you,' I lied. It was a small sacrifice to make for my mortifying clanger. 'Does your mother run a lot of these outings?'

'She runs every bloody thing she can get intae.'

'It must be very tiring for her.'

His chuckle remained entirely within his chest. 'Tiring?'

'Yes. Unless she's very fond of people.'

'You're no'?'

'Not in groups.'

'Don't care fur them much masel',' he said. 'In groups or otherwise.'

'Then why did you come?'

'She goto them tae hire me – as a kinda steward.'

'Oh! Do you enjoy it?'

'It's a' right, tae somebody vomits on yer suit. She claims them fur that as well, of course. An' runs the raffle on commission. Oh, aye. If there's a back-hander gaun, naebody can beat Big Delia.'

'Oh! Is that your . . .?'

'Ye've heard'ae'er!'

'Yes, I've heard my landlady mention her.'

'She in the Store?'

'Pardon?' Even after two years I had moments of difficulty with the foreign language of industrial Scotland.

'Is your landlady a member of the Co-op?'

'I don't know.'

Again he was looking at me in that worried, rather furtive, way. Then he seemed to reassure himself. 'Anyway, I expect she'll hiv' her ain number.'

'I'll ask her,' I said, since he thought it a matter of such importance.

'Y'see, ma mother deals in the Store for people that hivnae got their ain numbers.'

'Like . . . buying wholesale?' I hazarded.

'Only fur weddins,' Tony murmured, giving no inkling that this was a joke. He saw my confusion and smiled. 'You don't understan' this at a', dae ye?'

'No,' I said. Also, I saw no reason to try and understand it. 'I think I'll go in now,' I said. I'd seen Big Delia returning, drink in hand. She stopped me.

'Here, son! We've got a spare seat if ye want tae sit beside Tony.'

'No, thank you. I'm fine where I am.'

'But ye're all on yer own. That's no' right. Fine-lookin' young fella like you.' She winked at me then turned briskly to her son. 'Ye'd better start gettin' them oot the bar an' intae the right *row*.'

'They'll no' move tae the bell rings.'

'So, next time bring a bliddy bell wi' ye – an' ring it.'

Tony laughed and his mother threw her free arm around his neck. 'Away ye go an' tell them the bell rang while they were havin' a piss.'

'But whi' if they've no' . . .'

'Christ, son, they've a' had a *piss*. If they hivnae, the bliddy
stage'll be *floatin*' before the end.' Tony moved off to relay this
information and his mother called after him, 'But if the aulder
wans hivnae been, make sure they go.'

'I think I'll move in now,' I repeated.

'I'll come in wi' ye,' Delia said. 'Somebody has tae be there tae
catch the buggers comin' doon the stair.'

I was desperately aware of people looking at us as – on her
insistence – we marched arm-in-arm back to the auditorium.

'Whi' *is* your name, son?'

'Bill Thompson.'

She squeezed my arm. 'A'm awful glad Tony's found a pal.
He's been such a solitary boy.'

'Perhaps he prefers his own company.'

'Aye, but ye know where that leads,' she said cryptically.

As it turned out, that journey back in the bus was not a *minor*
sacrifice. Given the choice again, I'd prefer crucifixion. As we set
off the noise was incredible. Each member of the coach-party was
either singing or shouting at somebody who was singing. Every
now and then they changed about and apparently there was no
one song that any *two* people wanted to sing, or hear. Meanwhile,
those who could still lurch were lurching up and down between
the seats and across the seats. Either way, they had to squeeze
round Big Delia – who was everywhere. Adding impetus to this
mêlée was the coach driver who decided to dispense entirely with
first gear and attempted racing starts whenever he'd been stopped
by lights or heavy traffic.

But such a prodigious output of energy could not be sustained
and by the time our kangaroo progress reached Erskine it was
possible to hear yourself speak. The person who spoke to me,
when Tony thrust her down beside me, was a beautiful dark-
haired girl. She had a slow, demure smile and abruptly pushed
her thigh against mine.

'This is nice, isn't it?' she said, ostensibly referring to the coach
run.

'Yes.'

She reached across to unfold my arms and take my hand.

'I don't always come in the bus,' she remarked, or warned – it
was difficult to tell which meaning she intended, for her body
seemed to have a mind of its own.

'I never do,' I told her. 'Oh! I'm sorry, I'm sitting on your
hand.'

'That's all right. If ye just open your legs a bit.'

'Ah! . . . Yes.' I laughed. 'These seats are a tight fit.'

'I'll bet everything's a tight fit for you.'

'Pardon?'

'A mean, ye're a big fella. An' gettin' bigger . . .'

'What?'

'. . . I expect.'

I coughed as though I was just clearing my throat. 'The Fol De Rols are a favourite of mine.'

'Me tae!'

'I often saw them in Brighton.'

'Brighton!' She snuggled closer and with her free hand placed one of my hands on her breast. 'Did ye go by yersel'?'

'Usually, yes.'

'How was that?'

'I preferred it.'

'That's a shame. Can ye no' manage they buttons?'

'What?'

'On ma blouse. There! It's quite easy.'

Again I cleared my throat.

'I never bother wi' a bra,' she told me.

Big Delia loomed above us, her bosom rolling over the top of the seat in front. 'Everybody pull up yer drawers, we're nearly there!' she shouted to the bus in general. 'And that means you tae, Ishbell!' Her plump hand, weighted with bracelets, pointed at the girl beside me as though cancelling a normal exemption. Then she raised anchors and went surging back down the bus, repeating the same message.

'Do you know that woman?' I asked, cautiously.

'A certainly do!'

'Your mother,' I guessed with fatal certainty.

'That's her,' said Ishbell.

Despite her mother's warning, the girl went right on doing what she was doing in the bus. And before we got *off* the bus – in exchange really for allowing me off – we arranged a date for the pictures the following Wednesday.

She insisted that I was to have my tea at her house and gave me the name and address. Looking back on it, I can see – anyone can see – the inexorable pattern in all of this, but at the time I did not catch even a glint of the trap until the jaws started closing upon me at that address. It was a ground-floor flat and the door was open. In fact, there was no way of closing the door. And no point, since children were running in and out all the time. Big Delia

Liddle was devoted to children. She gave *me* a big welcome, too, when eventually I found her stirring an enormous pot in the kitchen.

'Hello, son! Are ye comin' tae gie me a haun?'

'I did knock . . . at the front door.'

She laughed, 'Buggerall use that'll dae ye! The only man that chaps *ma* door is the rent man, so naebody'll answer it.' She left the pot and busied herself for a moment chopping vegetables with amazing speed and precision.

'Is Ishbell in?' I asked.

'Oh, it's Ishbell ye've tae see? A thought ye were Tony's pal.'

'Didn't she tell you I was coming?'

'Naw. But it disnae make any difference. A always make extra.'

'It smells delicious.'

She chuckled. ' "Delicious" – God, where did she get you?'

'On the bus.'

'She's an awful lassie, Ishbell!'

'You're very busy, Mrs Liddle. I'm sorry to disturb you.'

'Ye're no' botherin' me, son. Could dae this wi' ma eyes shut by touch and smell. Aye! An' wi' two dozen mad Italian waiters jumpin' across me shitin' theirsels.'

'You're a professional cook?'

'A was. Wan o' the best in ma day.'

'Why did you stop?'

'Tae look efter ma weans, before the eldest were auld enough.'

'That's a pity.'

'Whit's a pity?'

'That you had to give up your career.'

'Career, b'God,' she snorted. 'You in trainin' tae be a manager?'

'No, an engineer.'

'A'd a thought ye could dae better for yersel'.'

'That's what I want to be. A marine engineer; so my father thought I should start on the Clyde.'

'Fancy!'

'This is where he served his time.'

'They've got nae shipyerds in England, A suppose!'

'Yes. But a Clyde apprenticeship counts for more.'

'Then it's a wonder they hivnae diverted the bliddy river through London.'

I laughed. 'It wouldn't be the same.'

'Naw! It wid be cleaner. They'd see tae that.'

'And London already has a river.'

'Only the wan?' She raised her head briefly from the utensils and steam to remark, 'That's Tony, noo. A know their feet, every wan o' them.'

'I think I'll go and have a chat with him,' I said.

'Sure thing! You go an' hiv a chat.'

The younger children didn't seem at all curious about me as I wandered through the flat. They dodged past me or, height permitting, between my legs. In contrast to the spotless and orderly kitchen, the other rooms were a mess. As I picked my way between the debris of discarded toys and stacks of cardboard cartons a man's voice called, 'Is that you, Delia?' I called back, 'No!' and continued my search for Tony. He was wriggling out of very oily dungarees when I came upon him at the end of the lobby. He disposed of the overalls by kicking them under one of the two beds in the tiny room.

'Ye're here early.'

'I wasn't sure how long it would take me to find the place.'

He pushed past me. 'A've got tae get washed,' he said and went off towards the bathroom. 'C'mon!'

'That you, Delia?' called the voice again, but Tony ignored it. The voice was old, weary, and curiously tentative – as though the caller did not know if it was even possible to receive an answer.

'Is your father ill?' I asked Tony as he turned on the tap.

'How the hell dae A know? Whi' put that in yer mind?'

'The man, there, who was calling. Isn't he . . .?'

'A've nae idea *who* he is.'

'Oh! Well, he seems to want something.'

'Aye. An' he'll get it, I expect.' He turned his dripping head towards me as he reached for a towel. 'Ma faither's at sea.'

'Is he an engineer?'

'That, A couldnae say.'

Elsewhere in the house children shouted and banged things, someone laughed and a radio played Fats Domino singing 'Blueberry Hill'. No two of the many people in that flat seemed to be together. They didn't know who was in and who was out or who was expected. I stared at Tony's narrow, thin shoulders as he faced the mirror, combing his hair – trying to coax it into a DA without much success because his pale hair was too wet. Never had I been so alien. And suddenly I felt sad for him, so vulnerably preoccupied with his hair, that he should be tied to this casual and – it seemed – dangerously unstable household. I was beginning to understand his habitual expression of worry.

'Whi's up wi' *your* face?' He was staring at my reflection in the mirror.

'I was . . . listening to the music.'

'Liar!' He prepared to brush his teeth.

'Why don't you brush your teeth *after* you've eaten?'

'A dae it then as well.'

'Oh.'

'Whi' *were* ye thinkin'?'

'I was wondering how many people there are in the house.'

'Includin' the weans?'

'Especially.'

'Well . . . when we're a' thegither – an' that's no' often – there must be . . . nine. Ten, maybe.'

'Are you the eldest?'

'Naw! A've got a big brother.' He chuckled. 'A *really* big brother. Neil. He's aboot twenty-five. Then there's me, an' then Ishbell.'

'What does Neil work at?'

'That's his business. If ye've got tae know, ask 'im.'

'I'm sorry. I didn't think it was . . .'

'The sooner ye get oot o' thinkin' that we're like you, the better.'

'Yes, I see that.'

'A don't mean tae chib ye, Billy. The thing is, you think ye kin talk aboot anything you know or want tae know. But there's a lot o' things aboot us, even *we* don't want tae know. Okay?' I nodded, but I didn't understand. Yet, I could believe it. Certainly there was something gravely secret about Tony.

'I don't mean to pry,' I said.

'Ye dae mean it,' he asserted. 'How other people live means a lot tae you, an' I'll tell ye how.'

'How? I mean, why?'

'Because you don't.'

'Don't what?'

'Live.' He grinned. 'How'd ye get on wi' Ishbell?'

'Fine. We're going to the cin . . . pictures.'

He held the toothbrush in mid-air and turned directly to me. 'When?'

'Tonight.'

'Don't think so,' he said. Again his voice was tight and bleak. 'She must've forgot.'

'What?'

'This is the night we start collectin' fur the Store Quarter.'

'Does she collect for that?'

'We a' collect fur that,' Tony said grimly and applied himself to his teeth with angry vigour. 'Bloody Store Quarter!' he spat.

Until then my knowledge of Quarter Days was limited to pleasing names such as Lady Day, Midsummer, Michaelmas and Christmas – which were of interest only to people living by the Inner Temple. For people living in Scotland, however, and on tick, they were days of judgment and despair. These awful days were visited upon Co-op customers the first week in March, June, September and December.

Now I learned that there is no institution less co-operative than the Co-op when bills have to be paid. It was fear of Co-op retribution that led many people to deal instead with a middle-man – or middle-woman, such as Big Delia. That evening, as we ate her marvellous dinner, she marshalled her forces to *collect*. Beside her plate she had a huge pile of invoices and a tattered notebook.

'Neil! This time A want ye tae put the fear o' God in that wee sickener, Bilsland. Ye let him aff too light at Christmas.'

'His wife'd jist had a wean,' said Neil.

'Well, A'm no' gonnae wait tae the bliddy wean's auld enough tae work for ma money. You see 'im the night and tell 'im, Friday definite.' She handed over a pile of papers. 'There's a' his orders.'

Neil folded them and slid them under his place-mat at top position. He was, as Tony had told me, a *very* big brother with a slow, deep voice and the height and build to put the fear of God in anyone. 'Are they added up right?' he wanted to know. 'Sometimes they chisel me aboot the sums no' bein' added up right.'

Delia nodded. 'Tell him, if ye add it up again it might come tae mair.'

'An' tell him ye're comin' on *Saturday*, so that he'll be in on Friday,' said Tony.

'Right enough!' Ishbell agreed.

'Ishbell!' her mother said, 'if you dae Chisholm, Turner an' Gillies, ye'd still be in time fur the pictures.'

'She always gets the easy wans,' Tony complained.

'Turner's no' easy,' said Neil. 'She came at me wi' a knife, wance.'

'Tae stab ye in the *knee*?' Ishbell asked. Everyone laughed, including the old, white-haired, haggard man to whom I was not introduced but was probably the unseen caller from the bedroom. Four of the younger children were also at the table; blessedly silent and well-behaved.

But Big Delia knew what she was doing. 'It's better tae send Ishbell tae the single women.'

'Aye, we don't want any payin' in kind,' said Tony under his breath, winking at me.

'Whi' was that?'

'A'm sayin' there'd be nae dividend in how they might pay Neil.'

'Watch yer mooth,' his mother warned.

'Whit's he talkin' aboot?' Neil asked. Evidently he was not the brightest of the family.

'Never mind. Tony's too smert fur his ain good.'

'An' naebody wid want tae pay him *except* wi' money,' said Ishbell, and for the briefest moment an expression of real pain creased her brother's face. If the girl noticed it she did not care.

'Do they always have the money?' I asked.

'No' always, but usually,' Tony said. 'If ye keep at them they remember where they put it, or where they can get it – if it comes tae the worst.'

'But what if they just haven't got it?'

'Then ma Maw has tae put it up hersel',' Ishbell told me.

Delia consulted her notebook. 'A'll dae Timmins, the two Kerrs, Devine an' Grant.'

Tony groaned. 'Aw, Ma! That leaves me wi' the same lot as last time.'

'Eat yer food!' Delia told him.

'But that's twice as many as Neil an' Ishbell!'

'Tony, son, A *know*! An' why? Because you're good at it.' She turned to me, with evident pride. 'If A ever started a protection racket that boy wid be worth a fortune.'

Ishbell said, 'They pay him because he's wee and skinny.'

'Naw!' his mother noted perceptively. 'They pay him because he's dangerous.'

'That's true,' Neil sighed regretfully.

'May I have some more vegetable, Mrs Liddle?'

'Certainly, son! Here ye are. Does your mother hiv any o' this bother wi' the Store Quarter?'

I choked at the thought of it. 'Hmmm . . . No.'

'Surely they've got the Co-op in England b'noo?'

'Oh, yes. They have it. But my mother doesn't shop there.'

'Silly wumman. It's a lot cheaper fur the groceries, at least.'

'As far as I know, she doesn't . . . shop for groceries. At all.'

The cutlery fell silent and each of those holding it stared at me for a long moment before Delia loudly filled the silence. 'An' how the hell dae yis eat?'

'We have a cook,' I said; aware – too late – that I was ruining the rest of the meal for all of us. I lowered my head to avoid their eyes, but not before I saw Tony and Ishbell exchange an identical slight nod and even slighter smile.

The great attraction of Ishbell, for me, was that she made all the effort. With her, the promise of sex was more of an affidavit. For someone as shy as I was then, such rare bounty could not be ignored. I went with her to see Chisholm, Turner and Gillies. As we walked along we took occasional advantage of the wretched street lighting in that part of the town. I also tried to find out more about such a remarkable family.

'It must be difficult for your mother coping with all this on her own,' I said.

'She's never on her own.'

'I mean, with your father at sea.'

'Ma father's in jail,' said Ishbell.

'But Tony told me he was at sea.'

'That's right. His father *is* at sea.'

'Then your mother was divorced?'

'Divorced?' Ishbell's soft, rather timid, voice betrayed a slight impatience. 'She never even got *married* for most o' us. Just Neil's father. She was married tae him; she says. But he died.'

We walked in silence for a while then I asked, 'What is your father in jail for?'

'Gettin' caught,' Ishbell said, weary of an old joke she had often told.

'Your mother must make things very awkward for all of you.'

'Awkward?'

'The way she lives.'

'My mother lives the way God made her,' Ishbell stated with no trace of timidity. 'And she's the kindest woman you're ever likely tae meet.'

'Yes, I'm sure she . . .'

'That's how all this started, y'know, wi' the Co-op. People came tae her and she got them what they needed. Kindness! And she was the one had tae pay up when they couldnae pay her. An' some o' them denied they got anything at a'! That's what ye get for kindness.'

'She's certainly a marvellous cook.'

'You'll know aboot that.'

'I'm sorry, I didn't mean to criticise her in the least.'

'It wisnae till Tony and me got older she could be sure o' gettin' her money. Somehow!'

'I just thought people must be critical of you, because of her.'

'If they are, they don't tell me.'

'Stop here a minute.'

'Let go! We havnae got time.'

'We've had time until now!'

'Ye've put me aff it.'

'What did I do?'

'Ye asked questions. Ye'd dae better if ye kept your mouth shut and your flies open.'

Tony didn't go up to Glasgow Tech. that Friday. It was final collection night. I didn't envy him the job of trudging around from door to door through the sleet and against a wild blustery wind. Even the short walk from Central to George Square left me miserable and exhausted. And, for once, I welcomed the stupefying heat in the basement of the Tech. We stood at the physics benches oozing pools of water on the polished wooden floor round our feet while steaming gently from the tops of our heads. The experiments had to be done by students in pairs, since it was the naïve belief of our tutors that each would check and verify the written results obtained by the other. In practice we did the experiments then, quite separately, wrote the results which had been obtained five or ten years earlier by long-gone apprentices who'd prudently sold their notes. We did alter the odd fourth decimal point to avoid suspicion. My partner was Deanie.

'Got yer car yet?'

'No. I'm getting it next week.'

'We could'a done wi' it the night.'

'Yes. I could. Shall I do the experiment first?'

'Tell me this, how can they call it an experiment when people hiv been daein' it fur years?'

As I set up the apparatus the logic of the question bothered me. Deanie, however obscurely, had a point. 'I suppose it *is* an experiment for each person who does it for the first time.'

'Aye, except that – even the first time – we're expected to get that bloody stuff tae dae what somebody else *knows* it does.'

'Yes.'

'An' if we get it tae dae somethin' diff'rent – like a real experiment – we lose marks. Right?'

'Right.'

Pleased with my support he grew enthusiastic. 'Christ! Jist

wance, I'd like tae make the bloody li'mus-paper turn *black*! They'd aw hiv kittens!' He laughed and stamped about in his puddle, delighted at the idea. 'Eh, Billy? We could put the entire li'mus-paper *industry* oot the gemm.'

'And the chemical industry,' I suggested, beginning to like Deanie.

'Sure!'

'What else?'

'A know how tae find gold.' He paused to see if I was interested.

'Tell me.'

'The elements hiv a' got their ain frequency y'see, so ye jist get a wee radio transmitter tuned tae exactly that frequency and point it at the hills. It beats paddlin' in burns wi' them big bowls.'

'Sounds a good idea.'

'There's jist wan thing – ye don't happen tae know the frequency o' gold, dae ye?'

'Seldom,' I told him. 'Anything else?'

'Listen! Last week A wis tellin' wee Liddle a great idea. See a' them things that make the wavy lines . . .'

'Oscilloscopes.'

He nodded eagerly. 'Whit's tae stop us convertin' them intae dinky wee television-sets?'

'We haven't got the time,' I told him. 'What did Tony Liddle say?'

'He said we'd make mair money jist floggin' the . . .'

'Oscilloscopes.'

'Aye. An' he should know – he's probably done it. A usually work wi' him, y'see. He's always thinkin' aboot makin' money, or stealin' it. Widnae surprise me if another sub post-office gets busted in Grcenock th'night.'

I was incredulous. 'Rob a post-office?'

'He's done it before. Wisnae caught, but he done it all right.'

'At the beginning of March?'

'Don't think he's fussy. Naw, the Christmas before last, it wis. Tae get presents, maybe.'

'Do you know his family?'

'Know Big Delia. She's a case! She'll pick any auld ratbags aff the street and gie them a square meal if they look like they need it.'

'She seems a very . . . cheerful woman.'

'Oh, aye! When she's sober.'

Shortly, I was to discover what she was like when drunk. The train pulled into Greenock station and almost immediately,

through the billowing steam at the barrier, I saw Tony waiting for
me. He stood, hunched and intent, wearing a tightly belted
raincoat. He watched me approach and even at that distance I
could sense disaster.

'What's wrong?'

'I need your help, Billy.'

'What's happened?'

'A've no' been hame yet. Wid you come wi' me?'

'Now?'

'Aye.'

'It's nearly eleven o'clock. You could come to my digs; it's
nearer.'

'That's no' the point.'

'We could talk there.'

'A don't jist want tae talk. Honest! Ye've got tae come wi' me.'

'Could I go to my digs first?'

'Naw. Right away. I've been waitin' on ye fur an hour an' a
half!'

We moved out of the station and braced ourselves for a long
walk against the wind and sleet. Tony said, 'If A go hame masel'
she'll kill me.'

'Your mother?'

'A couldnae get it a'. The money. No even maist o' it!' His
voice, pitched against the wind and traffic noise, had the edge of
panic. 'She'll go bloody daft!'

'What can I do?'

'It'll help me. Wi' a stranger there she'll no . . . She'll no' dae
anythin' . . . *desperate*.' Then he used a word I was perfectly sure
he'd never used before in his life. 'Please!'

I went with him.

Delia could be heard as far away as the end of the street. The front
door was wide open, letting the sound of her shrieks ricochet and
amplify in the tunnel of the close before spreading wide in the
open air. When Tony and I went in she was leaning over Ishbell
who sat tight-lipped at the table, still wearing her raincoat and
hood. Delia herself seemed to have risen from bed. She wore a
thin, low-cut, petticoat which exposed the threatening mass of her
breasts and, over it, a long untied dressing-gown. Her feet were
bare and when she looked up to confront us we could see the tears
of sheer anger running down her cheeks. She stumbled a little
towards Tony. 'Oh, ye've come back ya sleekit' wee bastard!
Well?'

'Ma! Couldnae get it a' . . .'

'*You* couldnae!'

'They hivnae got it, honest.'

'How much!' She rushed at him and gripped his hair. 'Holy God, ya runt, how much?'

Tony stumbled against me and I, moving further into the room, caught sight of the drained faces of two younger children hiding behind the armchair at the fire. Tony cried, 'Oh, ma hair! Don't! Maw, don't!'

'How much?'

'A only got . . .'

'*Only!*'

'. . . Simpson an' . . . Ooooh! White.'

Delia roared, 'White! Shite! Ye got nothin'. An' that wee hooer didnae get wan o' *hers*! Did ye?' She whirled around and slapped Ishbell squarely across the face.

'Mammy!' the girl cried. Her chair toppled over.

'Stop!' I shouted but my voice was constricted with fear.

Delia ignored me and almost trotted up and down the room in frustrated fury.

'Whi' am A tae dae! Tell me! Whi' am A tae dae? An' whi'll happen tae the weans? C'm'ere, hen. C'm'ere tae yer mother.' She halted unsteadily and spread her arms wide for one of the small children. The child didn't budge.

'She's frightened, Maw,' Tony protested.

Delia bawled with all her might, 'COME HERE!'

Before worse could happen Ishbell scrambled up and delivered the hostage to her mother's arms. 'There. There ye are, Mammy. She was jist frightened.'

Delia clasped the child to her and stood swaying in the middle of the room. 'Efter a' A've done for them, this is whi' A get! Ma weans'll be taken on the Parish. Poor wean, d'ye understand? Yer Mammy's finished.' Her voice swooped to the maudlin as she stroked the child, but almost immediately leapt again to rasp, 'An whose fault is it? Whose bastard'n fault?' She lunged again at Tony but tripped slightly on the trailing cords of her dressing gown. I grabbed the child and set her down out of reach. Delia kicked her foot free of the cord then kicked at Tony. 'Yours! Comin' back here wi' nothin'! Nothin'! Nothin'. Oh, you'll rue this day. A'll make ye rue the day ye welched on yer mother!'

'A cannae help it, Maw.' Tony tried to sound soothing but the unaccustomed attempt was not convincing.

'Ye'll hiv tae help it! There's nothin' fur ye but that. An' before Monday. D'ye hear me? Before Monday or your life'll no be worth livin'.' She gripped his hair with both hands, forcing his head back, and screamed in his face, 'D'ye hear me?'

Tony did not struggle and he let his arms hang, swinging, at his sides.

'Mrs Liddle, maybe if . . .'

'Shut your face! Whi' are ye daein' here anyway? Lookin' fur *anither* cook, eh? Ya stuck-up English pig! Got a place fur me in yer scullery? Christ, that's a' A'll be fit fur efter this, if A'm no' emptyin' piss-pots in jail.'

Ishbell tried to placate her. 'Neil got a' his.'

'He did! He did that!' Her tone altered and for a moment it seemed she would be diverted. 'He's a good boy. An' good tae me!' But then she resumed with evil intensity, 'An' he's a *decent* boy, because he wis put intae me in *ma man's bed* – no' up against a wa' like you. An' you! Ya clap-scarred, poxy bastards!' She staggered past us, pushing Tony aside, and shouted down the lobby, 'Neil! Neil!' She stood swaying and hanging onto the edge of the door until he appeared. He must have been lying in bed listening to all of this for he wore only a pair of underpants. Delia threw herself in his arms, weeping.

'It'll be a'right, Ma,' Neil said. 'We'll get the money somehow.' Awkwardly, he stroked her head and she erupted in a sustained sobbing wail.

Neil repeated, 'A'right.' He tried to lead her to a chair while she flexed her hands gripping his shoulders and rubbed her face against his chest. Very softly, almost crooning, he reassured her, 'We'll get it. We'll get it.'

Tony whispered urgently, 'Ishbell! You'd better get tae yer bed.'

'Whi' aboot him?'

'Billy's a'right wi' me. Go on! When she's quiet. An' take they weans.'

Hidden by Neil, and with his complicity, Ishbell took the two young children out of the room. Unfortunately, she tried to close the door behind her and the sound alerted Delia.

'Whi's that?'

'Nothing, Ma,' Neil tried to block her view. 'Sit there.'

But she surged out of the chair. 'Where . . . Where is she? Skinned oot?' Tony stood with his back pressed against the door. She would have thrown him aside but Neil caught her arms and held her back. Thwarted, she wrenched her head from side to side, roaring, 'I'll get ye! A'll *swing* fur ye, ya rotten wee spunk-bag!' Now all her venom was directed at Tony.

'But A've got you, toerag . . .'

'Maw! Don't!' he pleaded.

'Don't whi'?' She threw off Neil's grip. 'Let go! Neil, son, get me a knife.'

'That's enough,' Neil protested, moving in front of her.

'Get me a knife! A'm gonnae mark that skinny weasel for good!'

'Naw, he'll get the money. He will.' Again the big man tried to soothe her.

'Where?' she cried. 'Where?'

'He'll get it.'

'If he disnae A'll end 'im, sure as Christ!'

Neil continued to stroke her. 'Take it easy. We'll manage. There!'

I looked at Tony who had moved to the far side of the room. He nodded at the door and I opened it and, as his elder brother slowly moved Delia back to the chair, he slipped out. She knew he had escaped but now, it seemed, she was even more aware of the warmth and strength of the arms that held her. She began to enjoy being comforted as though not by her son but by this desirable man who embraced her. She pressed herself against him and he seemed prepared to take on the new role.

'Aw,' she sighed. 'You're a fine big fella!'

'Aye. Come on, sit doon.'

'Ower here. Oooh, A love ye!'

'A know.'

It started like a predetermined ritual. All this had happened before and would happen again. Neil knew how to calm his mother. Horrified, I moved carefully out of the room.

Tony was sitting on the edge of the bath and he beckoned me in. 'Lock the door.' I turned and pushed the substantial bolt. 'That's the only door that locks in this hoose,' he said. Then, feeling more secure, he slumped forward resting his elbows on his knees. 'Oh, God! Whi' am A gonnae dae?'

'She seems quieter now.'

'For how long? There's the rest o' th' night and the morra.'

'How much money should have been collected?'

'A'thegither?'

'Yes?'

'Too much! Faur too much. A've got a list.'

As he stretched to delve into his coat pocket I noticed that the toe-cap of one of his shoes was practically ripped off and his feet were soaked through.

'Roughly, how much?'

'Hivnae added them up yet. But there ye are. There's the exact amount, against each name. Tried everythin'! They hivnae got it tae gie me!'

I looked at the names. 'There must be over a dozen people. That's . . . thirty two pounds, seventeen, forty, twenty one . . .'

'Don't tell me!' he protested. 'Add it up.'

'It comes to nearly four hundred pounds!'

'Ohhhh!' He slumped forward again. 'She'll kill me. She'll kill me. A darenae face her again.'

'I'd no idea it could be as much as that.'

'Aye. It's the March quarter, y'see. Noo's when they should pay for a' the stuff they got at Christmas. The March quarter's always the worst.'

'Four hundred pounds.'

'If A could even get a *loan*. But nae bugger's gonnae lend tae me, or the *likes* o' me!' He reached out and gripped my hand. 'Oh, Billy! Whi' am A gonnae dae?'

'I'll give you the money,' I said.

He didn't seem to take it in. '*Lend* it tae me?'

'No. I'll give it to you. Then you won't have to do anything . . . stupid, to try and pay it back.'

He stood up, staring at me with a dazed, almost wild, expression. 'You'll *gie* it tae me! The whole four hundred? But where'll *you* get it?'

'I've been saving up to buy a car,' I told him. 'I was going to buy it outright for six hundred pounds.'

His response came most acutely. 'Then ye'll still hiv enough tae lay doon a deposit.'

'I could, but I won't.'

'An' ye're gonnae gie me maist o' the money ye saved! Billy, ye've nae idea whi' that means tae me.'

'Do you want to go and tell your mother now?'

'Naw! She'd never believe us. She'll no' believe us till A've got the cash in ma haun.'

'I'll get it for you when the banks open on Monday morning.'

'That's great! So, A'll be doon at the yerd gate at dinner-time.'

'All right.' I unbolted the door.

'Billy!'

'Yes?'

'A want ye tae understand . . . wi' ma mother . . . she's that *proud* y'see. And the drink. She's no' hersel' when she's'd too

much tae drink. Thing is, she'll no' be right sober tae the quarter's
by. Her nerves are no' up tae it, noo.'

'What about your nerves?'

'Aye, but A hivnae had her life.'

'I can't understand why you stay here.'

'Whu's that?' For the first time that evening the bleak, hostile,
tone was back in his voice.

'I don't know how you can bear it, here!'

'Where else wid A be?'

'You could get digs. I'm in digs.'

'So ye are. But *your* mother's no' at her wits' end thinkin' o'
weys tae keep a' they weans, an' us, under wan roof.'

'No.'

'No! *Your* mother disnae rely on the Store dividend tae feed
them. An' she doesnae depend on *you* for any damn thing at a'.'

'Not at the moment. But she expects a great deal from me in
the future.'

He expelled his breath disdainfully. 'How dae ye get tae the
future? Tell me that, Billy. How dae I *get* tae the future when A
don't even know there's gonnae *be* a future?'

'I mean, when you're qualified.'

'Oh, A'm gettin' qualified all right.'

'Not like this.'

'If ye're me, ye cannae pick an' choose.'

'Other families get along.'

'Sure. But A wis born intae *this* family. An' there's naebody
thought o' changin' it – jist tae suit me.'

'You are all separate people, though.'

'No. This family depends on each other for everythin'. Nae
other wou'l!'

'Yes. I understand.'

'A'm *responsible* here!' Suddenly the strain caught up with him
and he was weeping. 'A'll . . . always be . . . re . . . responsible.'
He turned away and stared at his own swimming eyes in the
mirror.

That Friday night taught me a number of things, but I did not
learn them. Since I'd been educated at a public school, the idea of
being a separate person from my family was forced upon me at an
early age. My father was often abroad and my mother devoted
most of her time to music. Clearly, they were quite separate
people, too. The idea of a family as a self-destroying, self-renew-
ing organic unit was quite alien to me when I saw it in action that

Friday. On the Saturday morning I went to the car showroom and told the salesman I'd changed my mind. He didn't take it at all well. In fact, he seemed more disappointed than I was. He stared through the plate-glass after me, like a man betrayed. By staying away from my digs for the rest of the day I hoped to avoid whatever news of disaster there might be from the Liddles.

Sunday I spent studying but couldn't concentrate for straining to hear that knock on the door heralding Tony or Ishbell or even worse – I saw it clearly – the white face of one of those terrified children. I asked my landlady, Mrs Mulvenny, if she was a 'Store' customer. She said she was, but if I wanted her to get me something I'd have to wait until Tuesday because Monday was the Store Quarter. I told her I knew that. On Monday morning I applied to the foreman for a 'Pass Out' on 'vital family business' and withdrew my savings. I felt like a thief, carrying all my own money back through the streets. At lunch-time, Tony was waiting for me at the yard gate and I handed over my only chance of insulating myself from my apprenticeship.

It was on the following Sunday that I had a visitor. 'Mrs Liddle!'

'Hello, son. How are ye gettin' on?'

'I'm fine. How are you? Please, sit down.' She really looked quite striking in a dark blue wool suit, a hat with a veil and – to my astonishment – gloves. 'You're looking very well.'

'Thanks. Where will A put this?'

'What is it?'

'It's a special cake I've made for ye.'

'Thank you very much. I'll . . . put it here.'

'A've came because A thought A should apologise fur bein' in a bit o' a temper when ye came tae see Tony last week.'

'Oh!'

'A wis that worried, y'know, aboot collectin' fae the customers.'

'Yes.'

'An' then wi' Tony kiddin' me on aboot no' gettin' the money – that wis a silly thing tae dae.'

'That I did?'

'Naw, naw. You didnae dae anything. A'm sayin', *Tony*. You were there when he said it. That he couldnae get the money.'

'Yes, I heard him say that.'

'Well – he had it a' the time! Collected fae every wan. He wis at the Store first thing on Monday, waitin' fur me, an' we cleared the whole account.'

'That must have been a great relief to you.'

'A'm tellin' you it wis! Anyway – A'm very sorry if A upset ye when ye were in at the hoose. An' A hope ye enjoy that wee present.'

'I'm sure I shall.'

'An' mind! The next time ye're passin' you come in an' see us. The weans were a' tickl't wi' the funny wey you talk.'

'Really! Er . . . I didn't see Tony at the college this week.'

'Naw, he didnae go. Hisnae been at work either. Seems tae hiv caught an awful bad chill, so A'm keepin' him in his bed. Better get back an' see if he needs anythin'.' She rose with ease onto her perilously high heels.

'Oh, please don't go yet. I think Mrs Mulvenny is making some tea for you.'

'I'll tell her no' tae bother.' She laughed – for a moment very much the grand lady visiting the needy. 'Tae be honest A hivnae got the time.' She moved to the door. 'But whenever you want a good meal, remember, ye're always welcome.'

I stood in the centre of the room, dazed. How could this possibly be the same woman? And, if it was, how could she possibly describe the raging behaviour I'd seen as 'a bit of a temper'? Yet it was she. And there was the cake to prove it. And the venomous foul-mouthed virago *was* the rather superior woman now chatting, somewhat condescendingly, to my landlady. Obviously Tony hadn't told her he'd got the money from me. Considering his status in the family and his sense of responsibility I could understand his need to claim a full score as chief collector. What was absolutely inconceivable was her belief that Tony was just kidding her when he reported that he'd failed. Who, I wondered, in his right mind, would kid Delia, about *money*, when she was drunk! I went into the lobby and called her back.

'Excuse me, Mrs Liddle!'

'Aye? What is it . . . er, Billy?' She re-entered the room.

'That *was* a silly trick for Tony to play on you – pretending most of his customers hadn't paid.'

'As long as it was a trick. A suppose he jist wanted tae know whi' A'd say.'

'Yes. And he certainly found out.'

Her tone hardened. 'Whi' was it ye wanted tae ask me, Billy?'

'Well, you see . . . I was sure he meant it. That he wasn't pretending.'

'That's because you don't know him as well as me.'

'I hardly know him at all.'

'Is that right? Oh, A thought you an' him were great pals.'

'I wondered if, perhaps, you'd seen any of his customers since then.'

'Make a point o' it, son! His customers are ma customers. Efter the Quarter A go roon and see them a'. Tae thank them, an' that. An' tae let them know, if there's anything mair they want me to get fur them they've only tae ask.'

'And those that Tony collects from had all paid?'

Delia grew impatient. 'Son, A don't think you're followin' this very well. That's three times A've telt ye. *Aye!* Tony got the money fae every wan o' them. D'ye understand noo?'

'Yes. Now I understand.'

She turned, once more, to go. 'Well, A'm glad A've cleared that up fur ye,' she said; then added not entirely under her breath, 'Bring a cake an' get the bliddy Means Test!'

'Good bye, Mrs Liddle, and thank you.'

'Right ye are.'

Tony got over his chill by the following Friday and he was back at the Tech. – again partnering Deanie. He gave me a wave across the bristling laboratory benches. I nodded, but waited until the others had left the compartment in the train back before letting him know what I knew. He was far from overcome with shame. He adjusted his position in the corner seat so that he faced me diagonally across the compartment.

'A wid've been a mug *no*' tae take that money aff you,' he said.

'But you didn't need it!'

'Wrong. A need it. Ma *mother* didnae need it – this time.'

'What do you need it for?'

'Debts. Gam'lin'. Fines. You've got nane a them tae take care o', hiv ye?'

'But all that's your own fault.'

'Sure. But A cannae pay them by sayin' sorry.'

'You could say sorry to me.'

'Wid that be enough?'

'No. But it's the least you could do.'

'Sorry, Billy, that A took yer money. Ishbell's sorry tae.'

'Ishbell?'

He gave a little bark of a laugh. 'She's sorry because it wisnae her that got it.'

'Did she know what you were doing?'

'Christ, fella, we were *baith* ontae ye. Set ye up for it. You were gonnae lose that money wan way or the other. An' A must say if ye'd tried the other, ye'd a got mair satisfaction fur yer money than a cake.'

'I see.'

For a few moments there was only the sound of the train's progress as I stared out of the window and he watched me staring out of the window.

The silence seemed to annoy him. 'Ye were askin' fur it!' he protested. 'Talkin' aboot buyin' cars, saved up, cash down. Whi' the hell dae ye expect?'

'I gave you the money because I was sorry for you.'

'A *know*.'

'I would have done anything to prevent a night like that one happening again.'

He snorted. 'Again? When Big Delia's drunk, a night like that is rou*tine*. It's no' jist the Store Quarter that annoys her, y'know. The night, maybe, when A go in – it'll be the same thing. Different reason, but the same wumman you saw that night.'

'You're going back to that?'

'Likely.'

'How can you bear it?'

'Practice. Never known anythin' else.'

'Then you deserve the money.'

He nodded and seemed affected by that thought. 'Aye,' he sighed. 'Better still – A deserve tae hiv been born *you*!'

Now that I knew the Liddle family, I seemed to see or hear of them all the time. The local paper frequently reported the various social enterprises of Mrs Liddle and often Big Delia's bright-eyed face leapt at me from press photographs of one line-up or another. Now and then I saw Ishbell in the street and one hot summer day when I was on my way to Glasgow she occupied the seat in front of me on the bus.

'How's the family?' I asked.

'No' quite ready yet,' she said, and invited me to lean over the back of the seat. She was pregnant.

'Oh! Congratulations!'

'Tae the faither?'

'No, to you.'

'Huh!' She shook her head and turned to face the front. 'It wisnae my idea. I'm just too good-natured.'

I was rather shocked by the observation but Elsie, the girl who was with me, gaffawed with delight.

As Tony had predicted, I did pass all the necessary exams and so, with day-release, my weekly visits to the Tech. were over. Tony himself was once or twice reported in the paper. In the exam results, I noted that he'd passed his LNC. In police court proceedings, I noted that he was less successful at burglary. We didn't meet again for a long time. But, though many Quarter Days went by, not one passed without acute unease on my part. So I had the Liddles in mind when Archie Hemple stopped at my board in the Drawing Office.

'Have ye heard aboot Big Delia?' he asked.

'She's started a protection racket,' I suggested.

'No. She's dead.'

'What!'

'Some weans ran intae the polis office this mornin'. They went tae the hoose an' found her stabbed. They've lifted Neil for questionin'.'

'It wasn't Neil,' I said.

'How dae you know?'

'He didn't *care* enough.'

'Whi' are ye talkin about? They think he might have *stabbed* her.'

'That's what I mean. He wouldn't.'

The police went through the usual elaborate shadow-boxing exercise in their information to the newspapers. And the newspapers, as usual, managed to make all those involved seem quite unreal. I knew Tony would give himself up and, before the end of the week, he did.

'It wis Tony, efter a',' Archie marvelled. 'Can ye credit it?'

'Easily.'

'Whi' wid make him dae a thing like that?'

'Self-defence?'

'It's no' somethin' tae joke aboot. She wis an awful kind wumman, Big Delia.'

'Yes, and she expected as much as she gave.'

'Ah, well,' said Archie. 'Ye can never tell whit a homo's gonnae dae.'

'Pardon?'

'Tony Liddle.'

'Yes. What did you say about him?'

Archie was obviously astonished at my ignorance. 'Ye mean you didnae know?'

'What?'

'That he's a homo?'

'You don't mean homicidal?'

'Naw! A mean homosexual.'

'How do you know that?'

'Because a pal o' mine used tae get intae him, regular.'

Perhaps unjustly, I immediately thought of Deanie. 'I don't believe it,' I said.

'Ho!' Archie scoffed. 'There's many a wan – that should know – will tell ye the same thing. And some o' them got money out of him tae keep it quiet.' He nodded firmly. 'I'm tellin' ye – real Mamma's boy, wee Tony.'

Rather weakly I commented, 'I didn't know that you knew so many homosexuals.'

'Naw, *they're* no'. He is.'

'I see.'

Unwilling to contemplate the possibility that some of my money had gone to pay blackmail, I disregarded this information. But later in the year, when all the circumstances were set out at the trial, that fact could not be avoided. Nor could the facts of the murder. Tony's lawyers claimed mitigating circumstances. Neil, Ishbell and several neighbours testified to that and he got fifteen years.

Some months later I had an appointment in Glasgow to be fitted for my Merchant Navy uniform. I applied for a visitor's pass to Barlinnie the same day. Tony, in his uniform, looked even younger than before.

'Well, Billy! You're the first, apart fae the family.'

'How is the family?'

'All right, A suppose. Ishbell's runnin' the hoose and Neil's got a steady job.'

'Good.'

'So they don't really need me.'

'It's a big family to provide for.'

'Aye, but Ishbell's no' proud. She takes charity. That's somethin' ma Maw wid never dae.'

I was shocked that he should mention her, but foolishly determined to show that I was not shocked. 'No. Your mother was a very . . . enterprising woman.'

'There wis nae stoppin' her,' he said admiringly. I couldn't think how to respond to that and we faced each other in silence for a few moments. Then he asked, 'Did ye ever get a car?'

'No. And now I don't need one. I'm going to sea.'

'Ye didnae need wan then, either. Ye jist *wantit* wan.'

'That's true.'

'So?'

'What?'

'Whi' did ye dae wi' the money ye had left? A often wondered aboot that.' His cold eyes were friendly enough. He just wanted to know if I'd wasted money he could have had.

'I invested it.'

'Invested! Holy God, there's nae beatin' you either.'

'How are they treating you here?'

'No' bad.' He repeated it loudly for the officers. 'No' bad at a'.'

'And the family visits you.'

'*Only* the family. Why did you come tae see me?' .

'Because I . . . well . . . curiosity, I suppose.

'Aye. Ye were always a nosey bugger. So – whi' dae ye want tae know that ye don't know already?'

'Whatever you'd like to tell me.'

'Right. A'll tell ye this. She wis the only human bein' that gave a damn aboot me. An' the only wan ever *likely* tae. Wi' her gone A'm no' missin' much bein' in here.'

I believed him. At least, I believed that he thought so. There was nobody now to test his ability; and no one to whom he must prove it.

Perfect Pitch

MOST PEOPLE WHO'VE heard of *The Tales of Hoffmann* limit their familiarity to the Barcarolle. The record I never tire of playing is from another tale – that of Olympia, Hoffmann's first love. She is a fabulous doll who comes to life; and sings a most testing aria to prove it. My record of Olympia's aria is very worn because I often want to be reminded of Greenock. And she does it; bringing back the smell of tarred rope and the sound of a factory whistle – each of them potent Greenock locators on my map of the interior.

Other people are content enough to find Greenock where it is – strung out along a narrow shore on the rainier side of the Clyde estuary. There's a saying: 'If you can see Greenock, it's going to rain. If you can't, it is raining.' It was there I served my apprenticeship, twenty-five years ago. It was there I met Elsie.

Quite near the shipyard where I worked there was a rope factory which employed a large number of girls. They were a rough and ready lot, occasionally foul-mouthed but always merry – or 'cheery', as they say there. During the lunch-break they lined up on the wall outside the factory, reeking of tar, to survey whatever male 'talent' might be passing. They were not easily pleased. And not reticent in alluding to – or shouting to each other – the precise nature of their misgivings. When I was nineteen I was barely brave enough – even supported by Frank – to run that gauntlet. And it was only for his sake that we did it. He fancied one of those girls.

'Which one?' I asked him.

'Her in the middle, beside the gate.'

'With the red hair?'

'Naw! The quiet wan, beside her. Come on.'

Before dodging through the traffic in Frank's impetuous wake, I paused in the bustling midday street to fix the target. She had dark hair and was, I suppose, the most demure of the bunch; which is to say, the least raucous – which is not to say a great deal. I joined Frank on the other pavement and we sauntered past them with hands deeply delved in dungaree pockets. Our casual passing was logged, interpreted and loudly noted by the red-haired girl.

'Hey, Ada!' she shouted to Frank's fancy, who sat immediately beside her.

'Whit?'

''Er's them two again! D'ye think they're auld enough tae be ower it?'

'Ower whit?'

'The knot, ya stupit bitch!' She gave a yelping laugh then shouted directly at us, 'Hey, son, are ye?'

I guessed that she was enquiring about a facility we acquired at puberty.

'Whit dae ye want?' Frank shouted back.

The one who was not Ada gave an ecstatic shriek. 'Ooooh! Whit dae A want? As if you could gie me anything A'd want!'

Ada said, 'Leave him alane, Elsie!'

Elsie tossed her red hair – which was too short and frizzy to convey much hauteur. 'A've every intention o' leavin' him alane. Christ! That wee fella must be still wankin' dry.'

'You watch ye gub!' warned Frank.

'You watch it, you've got a better view.'

Frank put his shoulder behind mine and, with a brisk shove, urged me out of range. 'Come on.'

But Elsie hadn't dealt with me yet. She called after us. 'Does yer big mate no' talk? Whit's he haud'n on tae?'

'Nothing,' I called back.

Elsie seized on that. 'Another wan wi' nothin' in his pocket! Honest tae God, Ada, we never hiv any luck. They must breed bloody eenochs in that yerd!'

Correcting the pronunciation I replied, 'Eunuchs!' but she chose to treat it as confirmation.

'There ye are.' She jabbed Ada with her elbow. 'Whit did A tell ye? He gives in!' Her loud laughter was interrupted by the high piercing note of the factory whistle. 'Holy God! Time's up a'ready.' She jumped off the wall and, as she paced slowly backward through the factory gate, continued to call to me, 'See ye the morra, son. Maybe somethin'll sprout durin' the night . . . if ye watter it!'

That was our first encounter and, to be honest, I wasn't very hopeful about Frank's chances for a lasting relationship. But in that, as in so many other things, I had misjudged the spirit of the occasion. In my simple English way, I had mistaken the sound of insult for an intention of insult. Frank knew better.

'Well, whi' d'ye expect her tae say? "Pleased to meet you"?'

'Maybe not. But your dark-haired one didn't say anything.'

'Aye, she did.'

'What?'

'She tell't the red-heidit lassie tae leave me alane.'

Frank knew what that meant. He knew what everything meant. When I'd come up from England to start my apprenticeship it was Frank who took pity on my ignorance of the language. He thought my accent was mildly hilarious and wondered how long I could keep it up. And he was very sympathetic when he found out I couldn't help it. Anyway – he knew that if the dark-haired girl told the red-haired girl to leave him alone, it meant that – however distantly – *she* fancied *him*. Next morning, while working together at the marking-off table, we discussed strategy.

'It wid be easier if they werenae always thegither.'

'Yes. And maybe it would be better if you walked by on your own.'

'Naw, naw.' Frank saw the danger in that. 'Then she wid think that I fancy *her*.'

'I thought you did!'

Frank was immediately belligerent. 'Whit if A dae?'

'Well . . .' The intricacies of this were beginning to tire me. 'Wouldn't that help?'

He promptly took refuge in our common task. 'Are you supposed tae be workin' on this or no'? Whit aboot that corner ye havenae pasted?'

For a few silent minutes I set about my job of applying the whitewash to the surface of the brass plate; on which Frank, when it had dried, could mark off the drilling pattern with a metal 'scribe', hammer and dab. It was a very soothing occupation and soon I felt the conversation could be continued.

'Do you want me to go with you, then?'

It was too soon. Frank was still on the defensive. 'Look Bill, if you've got somethin' else t'dae, don't bother yer arse.'

'No. Nothing.'

'A widnae want ye tae be affrontit,' he said, using the hammer and dab as punctuation, 'wi' aw they bad lassies usin' sweery words.'

'I don't mind that. I think it's quite funny.'

'They're no' daein it tae be funny.'

'So – we'll go by again today at lunchtime?'

'Dinner-time!' Frank corrected wearily.

'Yes.'

'An' you can chaff the ither yin.'

'What?'

'The red-heidit wan – she's yours!' he expansively granted.

This was rather more than I was willing to do on his behalf. 'What shall I say to her?'

'Tell her whit ye've got in yer pocket.'

'I think she knows.'

Frank gave a shout of laughter. 'By God, she knows! I'll bet she's seen mair o' them than a lavatry wall.'

'She seems very defensive.'

'What?'

'As if she were afraid of something.'

'Get away!'

'Afraid of being taken seriously.'

He did not spare that idea a moment's thought. He said, 'She'd be a nice enough lassie, if her mouth was shut. Tell her that. Maybe she'll try it.' Spread flat on his stomach across the condenser plate he applied a series of delicate taps to the point-illist drilling design. 'Anyway, you've tae keep her muzzled while I talk tae the ither yin.'

'Ada.'

'How d'ye know that?'

'That's what Elsie called her.'

'Who the hell's Elsie?'

'Mine. Weren't you listening?'

He reared up by arching his back. 'Ada? Funny name, that!'

'Maybe you'll get used to it, when you know her better.'

He gave me a very lewd grin. 'There's only wan thing A want tae get used tae, when A know her better,' he growled, and executed a few humping movements on the whitewashed surface.

I sighed at this display. 'Frank! It's me.'

'An' whitsa different about you?'

'You don't have to *bluff* me.'

He threw down the hammer with an angry clang. 'And you don't hiv tae *tell* me. Right?'

'Sorry.'

Frank had integrity, there's no denying that. If you called his bluff he'd admit it. As long as you didn't try it very often.

He was short, energetic and wiry; with wiry hair and a big nose which he'd aim at you in a menacing way – as though he'd already released the safety catch. Come to think of it, there was a hair-trigger immediacy about everything he did. For him, Do It Now was the only way to live. So, phase two of Operation Ada could not be delayed. I paused on the waste ground outside the canteen to arm myself. Frank was already well ahead, walking towards the rope factory. As I caught up with him he instructed me. 'Try and get them tae separate – okay?'

'You mean, pull mine off the wall?'

'As long as ye get her aff ma back.'

Elsie saw us coming from a long way off, but waited until we were comfortably within earshot before loudly asking her companion, 'Hey, Ada! Hiv you got yer horns oot, hen?'

'Naw, how?'

''Cause here's a coupla peasants starin' at us.'

Frank's urgent shoulder indicated that I get on with the chaff. 'Hello', I smiled. 'Your name's Elsie, isn't it?'

'Holy God!' the girl exclaimed. 'It's no' a peasant at a'. It's an English nancy-boy.'

'No – I'm not.'

'Well, ye *sound* English.'

'I've got something for you,' I declared.

'In there? A doubt it.'

From my dungaree pocket I drew the long stem of the foxgloves which abounded behind the canteen, 'There you are!'

'Jesus!' She stared at the flower and then at me as though I were mad. Clearly, I had gained some sort of advantage. 'Whit am A supposed tae dae wi' this?' she asked.

'Clench it between your teeth.'

She laughed with genuine amusement and, I thought, appreciation at the suggestion. And she continued to hold the flower in her hand while she answered my few pointless questions about her work. Meanwhile, Frank did his best with Ada at close range. Before long, my conversation with Elsie began to pall on both of us. I glanced at my watch once or twice and she threw back her head to catch some rare sunlight under her chin. Then, not a moment too soon, it seemed we heard the Works whistle. All the girls, except Elsie, scattered and ran for the Works gate, to be in while the whistle was still blowing and avoid being 'quartered'. That is, losing quarter of an hour's wages. The whistle faded and Elsie brought her head forward to face me; her eyes sparkling, a mischievous grin on her face. 'Ye're damn all good at the patter, Billy, I'll tell you that,' she told me. 'Get yer mate tae gie ye a few tips.' She jumped down from the wall and sauntered alone through the gate. She was safely inside, unquartered, when the real whistle sounded.

'What the hell are they playin' at?' Frank wanted to know.

'It's exactly on time.'

'But that's the second time they've blew it.'

I shook my head delightedly. 'No. The first time it was Elsie. She hit exactly the right note, on the button, and held it!'

I wish I could say that *gradually* it occurred to me where this remarkable ability of Elsie's might lead. The slow realisation of her potential value would be much more interesting. But it didn't occur to me gradually at all. It struck me instantly. Falseness is very hard to spot, but who doesn't know the truth when they hear it?

The truth was that Elsie had an amazingly accurate, pure and powerful singing voice. More could be done with it than imitating factory whistles. Probably I would not have reached such an adamant conclusion, even at nineteen, if I had not been brought up in a 'musical' atmosphere. My mother devoted a lot of her time to music – mainly operatic – and it was she who had told me of that rarest of creatures; that fabulous unicorn among singers – the voice which has perfect pitch. That, as I say, was what I knew instantly. Proving it took much longer. To start with, it meant making a date with Elsie.

She agreed readily enough – at our third tryst by the Rope Works wall – but she wanted to see *The Inn of the Sixth Happiness* which had recently opened its doors in Greenock, and I wanted to spend the evening in a particular café.

'Whi' fur?'

'So that we can talk.'

'Talk!' Not her idea of a date, apparently. 'Whi' d'ye want tae talk aboot?'

'Different things.'

'How, different? That café hasnae even got a juke-box.'

'I know.'

'Be a real cheap night fur ye, that.' She again essayed the disdainful tossing of her head and again her short hair refused to swish. It only bounced a little round the ears. It occurred to me that she couldn't know how short her hair was.

'We could go on to the second house at the cinema.'

'And miss the *wee* picture?' she exclaimed – incredulous.

'Well – it's Ingrid Bergman you want to see, isn't it?'

'Dae A hell! It's Curt Jürgens A want tae see.'

So, we settled for that; missing the supporting feature but seeing all of Curt Jürgens. The choice of that particular café was part of my underhand plot to seduce Elsie into believing in herself as a singer. It was a modest little shop owned by a man who played

subdued and *tuneful* music on a gramophone under the counter. I
took a record with me. As we walked in, Elsie made it plain that
she was not impressed with the dim interior or the softness of the
music. She halted just over the threshold. 'Christ Almighty! Has
there been a death in the family?'

'I think it's quite pleasant.' I urged her forward to a table.

'Oh, aye. Pleasant enough – as long as we get oot before "Abide
wi' Me".'

'Do you sing?'

'How? Are ye gonnae take a collection?'

'No. I mean . . . *can* you sing?'

'Don't be daft,' she said, spacing her forearms on the table as
though at a card school. 'Everybody can sing.'

To her that was a fact and the subject needed no further
comment. She looked around at the few other, older people in
the café, then – making the best of a bad job – brightly back at me.
'Now! Wha' d'ye want tae talk about?'

'Well . . . you!'

'Wha' d'ye want tae know aboot me?' She twisted round in her
chair with the intention of obtaining service. 'Where the hell's the
man?'

'I think he's in the storeroom.'

'He's quite right. It'll be livelier in there, A should think. Wha'
aboot me?'

'What age are you?'

She laughed. 'Don't worry aboot it. I'll tell them A led ye on.'

'No, but really?'

'Sixteen, how?'

'You seem older.'

'I should bloody well hope so! Or A've wastit money on this
make-up. Who dae A remind you o'?'

'Amelita Galli-Curci.'

'Where's she come fae?'

'Italy.'

Plainly, Elsie was disappointed. 'I don't like Italian film stars.
They're a' too big in the boobs.'

'Yes.'

'I mean, whi' *American* film star dae A remind you o'?'

'I can't think of anyone.'

'Oh, thanks very much! Hiv you any idea how much this
mascara cost me?'

'Not enough, or you would have used less.'

Again I saw that surprised and appreciative glint in her eyes before she laughed. 'That's quite good, that. Cheeky bugger! Of course, it's all right for you. You're well-aff. So yer mate tell't Ada. But A knew that right away.'

'I'm a fourth-year apprentice – if you call that "well-off"!'

'Aye. But yer family's got money. That's how I'm hingin' in wi' ye.'

'Oh.'

She clicked her tongue in annoyance, thinking she'd offended me. 'That's a joke. At least, ye're meant tae *take* it as a joke.'

'I see.'

The proprietor emerged from the storeroom and I asked him for tea and Elsie's firm preference of orange Club biscuits.

'Ye're no' very sharp, are ye, Billy? Still, A suppose you've never hid tae be. Ye'd starve fur want o' a shout in oor hoose.'

'What about your family?'

'They can look after theirsels.'

'Are there many of you?'

'Six weans an' me. I'm the eldest.'

'Seven!'

'At the last count,' she grinned. 'But hell, wi' ma Maw ye never know the minute.'

'And your father . . . is he . . .?'

She gave a yelp. 'Oh! It's him that dis it, all right!'

'What does he work at, though?'

'Whi' *is* this, an examination?'

'I'm sorry. I'll go and get the tea.'

'Sit on yer erse! Jist gie him a shout an' he'll bring it ower.'

'No. I want to . . . ask him something.'

'Suit yersel'. Whit's the record?'

I'd hoped she wouldn't notice that. But, anyway, I managed to smuggle it to the counter without further question. I'd already arranged with the proprietor to have it played and he accepted it without surprise. There weren't many people in the café and none of them looked downright anti-operatic. I returned to the table with the tea and biscuits.

Elsie was worried about her appointment with Curt Jürgens. 'Whi' time is it?'

'We've got plenty of time.'

'Fur whit?'

'To get to know each other.'

Elsie loudly snapped her Club biscuit in half before she removed the foil, 'Aw, is that whi' we're daein'? Gettin' tae know each other wi' a table between us?'

The background music now moved perceptibly into the foreground and we heard a soaring soprano voice in a bravura piece full of dramatic leaps and staccato repetitions. I brought the sound to Elsie's attention. 'Listen!'

'What?'

'Listen to her voice. Could you do that?'

'That's no' singin' – that screechin',' was Elsie's opinion, but she listened and upon one of the more intricate and testing repetitions she joined in – making a credible duet of the solo record. It was astonishing to hear that achingly pure sound come from that snub-nose, tiny girl with frizzy red hair leaning casually back from the café table. On one hearing she followed the piece, note for intricately pitched note as they tumbled after each other at dazzling speed. When the duet was over all the people in the café joined me in applauding Elsie.

'Marvellous!' I cried.

Elsie nodded – pleased with herself, now that I was pleased – and asked, 'Who was that singin'?'

'*That* was Galli-Curci! And *you* are amazing!'

'I was only imitatin' her.'

'Yes, I know. But, don't you see – you *could*! You heard it once and you followed her perfectly. That is amazing.'

'Aye, but what good is it? Ye cannae rock an' roll tae that kinda stuff. Ye couldnae even get intae a skiffle group.'

Then, and on other occasions, I did point out to her that successful opera singers make a lot of money. She conceded that maybe they did – but nobody ever heard of them; an assertion which would have caused Madame Callas a twinge, since she was then at the height of her powers. But I could see the point. Nobody that Elsie knew had ever heard of Maria Callas.

Frank hadn't heard of her either, but he was fascinated by my interest in Elsie. Early that summer – which was to prove one of the sunniest on record – we took our bikes on the ferry across to Kilcreggan from where we started the ritual circuit of The Three Lochs. I was glad to get away from my digs and Frank was glad to have a cycling companion not nearly as fit as himself.

We arrived back at the pier as the gloaming started to slip into darkness and the scanning beam of the Cloch Lighthouse was bright enough to make the sweat on our faces shine as it swept the shore at unvarying intervals. Frank returned to the subject of promoting Elsie's ability.

'Suppose ye do get somebody tae listen tae her . . .' He threw a pebble far out into the water and paused to hear the effect before continuing; '. . . y'know, somebody that would allow her tae get on . . . She'd hiv tae go away, wouldn't she?'

'Mmm,' I agreed.

He bent down to find another suitable pebble. 'Tae London, or abroad, maybe?'

'Probably.'

'Well . . . if . . .' He threw again with even greater effort. 'If she was away – whit good wid that be tae you?'

'I'd be very pleased.'

'Aye – but she widnae bother aboot ye then.'

'She doesn't bother about me now! I wish she would.'

'Dae ye?' There was a new, more alert note of interest in his voice.

'Of course. I wish she'd take my advice and make some effort to . . .'

'Aw . . . that! I thought maybe ye were serious aboot her.'

'I *am* serious. She has a marvellous voice.'

'Aye. But her voice is no' *her*, is it?' The alertness was gone and now there was some impatience. 'How are ye gettin' on wi' *her*?'

'What do you mean?'

Frank's words picked very decorously at what he saw as the situation. 'She thinks you're too . . . shy. So Ada says.'

'How are you and Ada getting on?'

'All right.' He altered his pitching position for a 'skimmer'. 'Sort a . . . steady . . . y'know. She's quite a nice lassie, but . . .'

'But, what?'

'She hasnae got much life in her.'

'That's what I thought. But Elsie has plenty of spirit.'

'She has that! Dae you no' *care*?'

'Care?'

'Aboot anybody? I mean . . . personally!'

'Yes.'

'You hivnae any idea whi' A'm talkin' aboot.'

'I don't think you realise how rare Elsie is.'

'A know. A know, A know! She's got "perfect pitch" – whatever that is. Or so you say.'

There was silence for a few minutes during which the Cloch scanned us with its brightening beam. I tried to think of some way to explain the remarkable nature of Elsie's ability. I tugged at Frank's singlet and pointed. 'Do you see that can, floating right out there?'

'Where?'

'Wait until the light comes round again. There!'

'I think so.'

'Wait . . . There!'

'I saw it that time. That's quite a distance.'

'Sure. But if you had just the right pebble and you used all your strength – you could throw it that far.'

'Maybe.'

'And if you were very, very accurate, you could hit that can – once.'

'If I could see it.'

'And if you were lucky.'

'So? Whit's a' this aboot?'

'Think!' I got to my feet in the excitement of what seemed a perfect analogy. 'If you had just the right pebble, if you could get all your strength into one throw, if you were amazingly accurate and very lucky – you could hit that can out there. With all that, and if you could see it, you could hit it – once. Compare that to Elsie's voice. She's able to hit that can any time she wants to – dead on, every time. And in the dark.'

For a long moment Frank stood perfectly still, staring out over the water, then in a voice soft with wonder he murmured, 'Christ!' However, the competitive urge quickly reasserted itself. 'I'll bet you couldnae hit that can.'

'No, I couldn't. But I do know it's there.'

'Oh, grandeur, b'Jesus!'

'I do, and I'm prepared to say so.'

He shook his head dismissively. 'You're a funny bloke.'

'So you say.'

'So everybody says – an' a lot mair!'

'Oh?'

'D'ye know what I used tae tell them, when we startit here?'

'That I was daft.'

'Aye, but apart fae that – I tell't them you've got a bad heart.'

'I haven't.'

'A know! A know, ye havenae. It was jist in case ye got intae a fight – tae make them go easy on ye. In case ye died on them.'

'Thanks a lot.'

'But noo I think there *is* somethin' wrang wi' yer heart.'

'Oh?'

'Whit dae ye call they things musicians use – that wag fae side tae side?'

'A metronome.'

'That's it! That's whit you've got, tickin' away in yer chist.'

'I'm sorry you think so.'
'So am A, pal. So am A.'

Now that Frank was converted on the value of 'perfect pitch', he convinced Elsie. Since he was not a fanciful outsider who just happened to be passing through, she believed him. We called a joint meeting of four in the café to hammer out what should be done.

'There must be somewhere she could go,' Frank said. 'Tae start wi', at least. Is there no' any night-school for singers, or anything like that?'

'A don't want tae go tae night-school,' Elsie stated.

Ada was morosely philosophical. 'Ye've got tae start some-where, Elsie.'

I shook my head. 'There's only musical appreciation classes. What Elsie should have is training.'

'Where?'

'There's the Academy of Music in Glasgow,' I suggested. 'We could write to them and see what they say.'

That was too indecisive for Frank. 'Don't bother writin'. You an' Elsie go up and see them.'

'If we did that they'd probably want to hear an audition piece.'

'A whit?' asked Elsie.

'They'd want to hear you sing pieces from opera.'

'But a' they songs is in a foreign language!'

Ada was appalled. 'Oh, God! Ye hiv tae learn a foreign language next.' I was beginning to doubt the usefulness of Ada at this meeting.

'No,' I said firmly. 'She doesn't.'

Frank was glad to take up my denial. 'Naw, she doesnae, ya stupit bitch.' But he gave me a worried, enquiring, look to discover why this should be so.

'You can learn the words without learning the language. As long as you know what they mean.'

'Right!' said Frank. 'There must be a teacher in Greenock that could learn ye a coupla songs. So – that's the first thing. Eh, Bill?'

'Yes.'

'Ada! Run oot an' get us the night's paper.'

'Och!'

'Go on! We hiv tae look up the adver*tise*ments.'

We watched Ada as though the world was waiting for her to leave in search of the local newspaper. And she took her time about it, fiddling with this and that before she even scraped back her chair. She knew it was the most attention *she* was going to get all night. When she'd gone, I tried to establish other possibilities of advancement.

'What do your parents suggest?' I asked Elsie.

'Nothin'. I havenae tell't them.'

'Why not?'

'Whit could they dae?'

'She's right,' said Frank. 'An' they might try an' stop her.'

'Surely not! They must be interested in . . .'

'Naw!'

'Never!'

They adopted identical expressions, shaking their heads slowly and smiling tolerantly at my naïve assumption.

'They've got enough tae think aboot,' was Elsie's summary. 'They don't need me tae cause any mair bother. As long as A'm workin' they'll be quite happy.

Frank nodded. 'Sure thing. She's got tae keep her job while she's daein' this trainin', ye know!'

'I don't think that would be possible.'

'Then ye kin forget it!' said Elsie flatly.

We all looked down at our empty cups and at the little mound of coloured foil from a good half-dozen orange Club biscuits. At that moment I felt like forgetting it. Around me, I became aware of the murmured conversations of other people in the café for whom a dream was not, so suddenly, evaporating. And behind that murmur, supporting them, was the discreet music of a Gilbert & Sullivan favourite in an orchestral version. To me it was incomprehensible that Elsie's parents and friends, not to mention Elsie herself, could so misjudge what should have been the order of priorities. I glanced across to Frank for help in this embarrassing situation. And he came through. 'Here! Wait a minute. Is there no' Grants or Scholarships?'

I jumped at the idea. 'Yes! Of course there are. I'm practically sure there are.'

'Ye see, Elsie, they wid pay ye money while ye were trainin'.'

'Fur singin'?'

'Aye!'

'Then they should hiv their heids looked,' was Elsie's opinion.

'That's something we could ask about at the Academy.'

Ada, apparently exhausted, walked towards us carrying the *Telegraph*. She explained, 'A had tae wait for the fella comin' oot o' a pub. But there ye are!' She threw it down on the table where it was immediately seized by Frank.

He asked, 'How much dae ye think a singin' teacher wid take fur a coupla songs?'

'That would depend on how long it took Elsie to learn them.'

Elsie brightened a little. 'A widnae take long. Y'know, maybe if A wis singin' in a foreign language, A widnae sound like a wee scrubber.'

'Right!' Ada said. 'Maybe that's how a' they other singers dae it.'

Elsie laughed. 'Is that right, Bill? Whi' aboot that wan A wis imitatin'? Wis she a wee scrubber?'

I gasped at the accuracy of this. 'Yes! As a matter of fact, she was – about sixty years ago, in Milan.'

'Well, there's hope fur me yet.'

It was at that moment the splendid idea occurred to me which was to have so much importance in our plan. 'Yes! Yes! And she's still alive!'

'Whit's up?' Frank was startled at my vehemence.

'Madame Galli-Curci is still alive! In her late seventies, she must be – but she's still alive.'

'So what?'

'We could record Elsie's voice on a tape and send it to her. She lives in America. California, I think. We could send her the tape and ask for her help. If *she* liked it everybody would listen to her opinion. She could lift Elsie right out of this place; in the same way that she was lifted out of the slums in Milan.'

Ada saw the justice in that. 'Noo she's really famous, this woman, is she?'

'Yes! Oh yes, she is. And she must still remember how difficult it was when she was starting.'

Frank wasn't so sure. 'She must get hundreds of people askin' her tae speak for them.'

'I expect so. But how many have the quality Elsie has? This isn't just another person asking for help; it's somebody who deserves it.'

Elsie punched my shoulder. 'I wish A wis as sure as you are.'

Frank quickly returned his attention to the small ads, but I knew he was about to latch on to the next positive step. 'There's a place in Glasgow where ye can make records,' he said, without looking up. 'But that'll cost money as well. An' if ye're gonnae make a job o' it, you'll need tae learn the songs. There's a wumman here that might dae.' He slid the paper towards me.

'How much does she charge?' Elsie wanted to know.

'Not very much.'

'Good. 'Cause A hivnae got very much.'

'Who has?' observed Ada.

'Aye,' Frank said, 'the money's another thing we've got tae think aboot. Maybe we could hiv a whip-roon some o' your mates, Elsie. Hauf o' them must be on the gemm.'

'Are they hell! They a' dae it fur nothin'.'

'A don't dae it at a'!' Ada protested. 'Don't you call me a hooer.'

'Wish A could,' growled Frank.

'Aw – poor fella!'

It bothered me a little that they could joke about raising money but I tried to sound reassuring. 'I'm sure we could raise enough for a few lessons and for the recording.'

Even the assurance that the money could be raised was enough for Frank. 'Right! First, the lessons. We'll go and see this wumman.'

'Now?'

'Aye, "Now"! But no' you. If this teacher heard you talkin' she might double her price for a kick-aff.'

'True enough,' said Elsie. 'Me an' Frank'll go. You jist write doon the songs ye want me tae learn. Here, write it on the bottom o' the paper.'

Frank grunted. 'Oh, naw! Bill's got a notebook. Haven't ye, son? Bugger never moves without his notebook.'

'Whit does he cairry a notebook fur?' whispered Ada.

Frank whispered back, 'Tae prove he's livin'.'

I tore out the page on which I'd listed three arias. 'There you are. Tell her these are just suggestions.'

Elsie and Frank set off immediately and I was left with the dolorous Ada to our mutual unease and silence. 'Well', I said at last, 'I'd better get back to my digs.'

'Who is it ye're ludgin' wi'?'

'A family called Mulvenny.'

'Is it nice?'

'Not very. The husband's an invalid, so I have to do all the odd jobs around the house.' Silence fell again. 'Well – I'd better go.'

'So ye said.'

'Yes.'

'That wumman in America . . .?'

'Galli-Curci!'

'Did she get mairrit?'

'I don't know. Does it matter?'

'It wid ma'er tae Elsie. Aw she talks aboot is gettin' mairrit an' havin' a squaad o' weans.'

The next few weeks leading up to the Fair holidays were devoted to activities aimed at promoting Elsie. There were rehearsals of her audition pieces; bus journeys to Glasgow in search of records by other singers and, on the way home, a crash-course in operatic plots. Elsie seemed to enjoy those top-deck viva voce examinations as assorted drunks on *their* way home kept up an interminable serenade.

'Tell me about Gilda,' I prompted.

'Gilda. Gilda is the hunchback's daughter. The hunchback wants the other man tae kill the Duke. But the daughter fancies the Duke . . . so . . . she gets dressed up as a man and walks right in tae get knifed. Then they put her in a bag – bleedin' like a pig, but still alive. Then they gie the bag tae the hunchback and, er . . .' The laughter she'd been fighting to suppress burst through. She struggled to resume. 'They gie this bag wi' Gilda in it tae the hunchback . . . *and* . . . he's no' very pleased. They let her oot the bag tae sing, but then she dies.'

Much as she liked the plot of *Rigoletto*, she found *Tosca* even more hilarious. Indeed, she was quick to discover a basic lack of savvy – or even common sense – in the behaviour of people in opera. 'They seem determined tae get kill't,' she said. 'Especially the weemin!' I explained to her that these were tragedies. She wouldn't accept it. Anything as unnecessary and basically funny as *Tosca*, she thought, couldn't become a tragedy just by calling it that. 'Who,' she wanted to know, 'dae they think they're kiddin'?' She saw much more sense in 'real fantasy' because everybody knows it *is* fantasy, and she became quite attached to the story of Olympia in *The Tales of Hoffmann*. That was what she concentrated on in the few more singing lessons that could be afforded. As the weeks went by, Frank became more and more impatient. One morning, as he scorched away at the grinder in the Fitting Shop, he told me, 'She'll no' dae it any better than she's daein' it. Make her an appointment.' So – I wrote to the Academy of Music in Glasgow.

Elsie and I took the afternoon off. It was a Thursday. The weather was hot and sticky. The bus was crammed and we were crushed against the window on the long upper-deck seat; Elsie trying to keep her sheets of music flat and I trying to avoid leg-cramp by using the jolts to alter position.

Very gradually, the Clyde narrowed, darkened, then disappeared among the docks and grimy warehouses of the city. The current of nervousness grew between us and that charged all the latent doubts we'd had about this odd enterprise. Swaying through the grim streets under the glare of that sunlight, our assurance oozed away. It just did not seem possible that a world-famed career in opera could begin this way. And yet, if it did, how satisfying success would be. From the Rope Works to Covent Garden. If Galli-Curci could do it in Milan why couldn't Elsie do it in Glasgow, fifty years of progress later?

I glanced at Elsie; her make-up already in need of repair, wearing an over-elaborate dress she'd bought to be a bridesmaid some time ago. But her voice, I kept telling myself; they must recognise what a marvellous voice she has.

Eventually, after two mistaken changes of bus and a long exhausting trek up Buchanan Street, we presented ourselves at the desk of the Academy of Music. And for the entire interview we stood, right there at the desk. No, they did not want to hear her sing. No, they did not think there would be any point in seeing anyone else. No, scholarships were not awarded to outsiders. No, she could not become a student without passing an examination which would show she had reached the academic standard required. 'Good afternoon', and we were out on the dusty pavement again.

Elsie grinned. 'They certainly know what they *don't* want, eh?'

'I'm sorry.'

'Don't you worry aboot it, Billy. You did your best fur me, and that's that.'

'No!'

'You heard whi' the man tell't ye! They only want well-educated singers that don't hiv tae earn a livin'.'

'To hell with them!'

'Good fur you! That's whi' A think. If A wis well-educated an' didnae hiv tae earn a livin' A'm damned sure A widnae go near that place. They've nae bloody chairs, for a start!'

We both laughed. 'So it seems. But you're still going to make that recording. Today. If only we can find someone to accompany you.'

'Whi' fur? A can sing they songs withoot a piana.'

I grasped that defiant little figure in pink chiffon by the arms and whirled her round, cutting a clear circle in the flow of the sweating pedestrians. 'Of course! Of course you can. All right! We'll record it and send it off today. Since that stuffy lot wouldn't have you, we'll send a gift to Galli-Curci!'

★

'And has she replied?' asked my mother.

'Not yet. But that was only a few days before I came down here.' I was spending a week of my holidays with my parents in Sussex and told my mother the story as I followed her round the garden.

'I'd no idea Galli-Curci was still alive. We saw her in New York when I was a girl.'

'What was she in?'

'Probably *Traviata*. She did that a good deal. She never sang in England, though. I can't think why.'

'Perhaps she wasn't well enough educated.'

'What, darling?'

'Nothing.'

My mother did not pursue it and, for a few moments, gave most of her attention to flower selection. On the garden path in the warm sunlight we seemed to be wading in a sluggish stream of perfume which was stirred and lifted by our movement. My mother added, 'Her most famous role was Gilda in *Rigoletto*.'

'Elsie would be a perfect Gilda, though she might refuse to die in a sack.'

'I wish you'd brought the recording down with you, instead of sending it off to California.'

'It was important to send it that day.'

'Why?'

'To make up for a disappointment.'

'Ah, yes.' She did not pursue that either. My mother had a great knack of gracefully minding her own business.

'Isn't there anyone you could interest in hearing her?'

'I don't know.'

'Would you try to think of someone?'

'This afternoon?'

'All we need is a well-known musician whose opinion is respected.'

'Aren't there any respected opinions in Scotland?'

'Only on education. We need somebody in opera. What about all those parties you go to – and the fund-raising? You must know hundreds of suitable people.'

'Less than a hundred and I'd know far fewer if I kept thrusting aspiring Gildas at them.'

'I'm not asking you to keep on doing it. I'm asking you to do it once, for one girl.' It seemed to me the pace of this conversation was far too slow and detached. Now it stopped entirely in another foray of snipping.

'She must be a remarkable girl,' said the lady, a little too evenly to be entirely casual.

'She is!'

'Then why hasn't she made some effort on her own behalf?'

'Because she's only sixteen and she's too busy helping to feed her many brothers and sisters.'

'I'm sorry. That was a foolish question.'

'It was, rather. You've no idea how they live. And nobody cares.'

'Except you,' said my mother, smiling to herself. Then she conjured up a name. 'Eric Delber!'

'What?'

'The conductor – Eric Delber. He's doing a tour, including Scotland.'

'When?'

'Ah . . . When did he tell me it was? Or maybe it's over.'

'How can we find out?'

'We'll call his wife.'

'Now!'

'No – when I have filled this basket. You realise, of course, that I would have to hear her before I could recommend her to Eric.'

'Oh! I don't think she could manage to come down here.'

'Of course not. I've been promising to visit Mrs Mulvenny again. Perhaps she'd let me use her piano to hear Elsie sing.'

'That wouldn't be a good idea – I mean, coming to the Mulvennys. Mr Mulvenny is at home now.'

'Ah!' She did not want to know why that was a deterrent. 'Well, no doubt we'll be able to manage somewhere else.'

We'd been back at work a couple of weeks when I burst upon Frank in the millwright's 'howf' where he was doing a rush 'home-job'; hammering away at an immovable gas valve as though his life depended on it. I had to shout for him to notice me at all. 'Frank! Frank, stop that for a minute!'

He continued hammering and shouted over the noise, 'Whit's up?'

'Look!' I brandished the letter under his nose.

'Whit's that?'

'A letter from California. I got it this morning.'

'Whi' does she say?'

'It's from her secretary. It says, "Dear Mr Thompson, Madame Galli-Curci thanks you for your gift." '

'And . . .? Whi' else?'

'That's it. "Madame Galli-Curci thanks you for your gift," and nothing else at all.'

'Christ! She's got a hard neck.'

'Maybe she didn't understand what I wanted her to do. But I did explain.'

'Aye. She understood all right.' He started slapping the head of the hammer against his palm and I could feel his anger building up.

'Or maybe she's forgotten what it felt like to be in Elsie's position.'

'Naw!' He dealt a blow against the jammed valve which rocked the vice. 'Mair likely she disnae want tae remember. There's nane wi' a hazier idea o' poverty than them that's got by it.'

'I don't believe that.'

'You! Whi' the hell dae you know aboot poverty?' He was perfectly willing to seize on anything as a source of irritation.

'And I don't believe she even saw the letter. It must have gone straight to her secretary and she sent a stock reply.'

'Either way, it wulnae dae Elsie any good.' He started on an accelerating barrage of hammer blows which turned the rest of our exchange into more of a shouting-match than a conversation. 'An' whit's worse . . . ye've spent money . . . on a present . . . tae a wumman that disnae need it . . . an' disnae want it!'

'We agreed! It was worth a try.'

'It wis your idea.'

'Maybe . . . Frank! Maybe Eric Delber will do something for her.'

'Oh! Maybe he will. Maybe the Academy will take her on. Maybe an auld wumman in America'll wave a magic wand. Maybe she could win a scholarship.' He paused from sheer physical exhaustion of hammering to shout into my face. 'Ye're full o' fuckin' maybees, an' ye've got that wee lassie's heid wastit.' I stared at him with my mouth open. I'd seen him angry before but never as now, vulnerable to the anger. Something in my expression must have taken the heat out of the moment for he went on in a curiously sad and flat voice, 'Maybe it's jist no' worth a' the bother.'

Eric Delber's tour included a week in Glasgow. My mother came up a few days earlier and booked a room in the hotel where the conductor was staying. That Saturday was Elsie's birthday and I took her to Glasgow for tea. It was agreed we would meet my mother in the lounge at three-thirty to have a chat first. When we eventually arrived mother signalled the waiter at once, then extended her hand to us. 'Darling! I was beginning to give up hope.'

'The bus was waylaid by a crowd going to a football match.'

'And you are Elsie! I'm delighted to meet you.'

'How do you do, Mrs Thompson.'

'Sit beside me, my dear.'

As Elsie settled herself on the sofa, as though preparing for a siege, I further explained our delay. 'They all wanted to get on our bus, but the conductress wouldn't budge with more than five standing inside. There was quite an argument.'

'Surely they could count to five!'

'Yes. It was a question of *which* five.'

'A right bunch o' neds!' Elsie reported.

Mother smiled in agreement and touched Elsie delicately at the wrist. 'I do like your coat,' she said; and probably she did. Anyway, Elsie was visibly cheered and the waiter laid the tea things before us. 'How is the family?'

'They're a'right.'

'Good.' She thanked the waiter and seemed preoccupied arranging the cups while really waiting to see if the girl was going to say anything. Failing that, she went on, 'There's a music room here they will let us have the use of. I hope I can do you justice, Elsie.'

'Pardon me?'

'In the accompaniment,' mother explained.

'Dae you play the piana?'

'Yes; though not as well as I used to. Oh, Bill!'

'Mm?'

'I've forgotten to bring down the music – would you get it?' She handed me the key to her room.

'Where did you leave it?'

'I can't remember that either. Just look around and you'll find it.'

'Excuse me,' I said, and left them side by side. It was not until a long time later that my mother felt willing to give a report on that conversation.

Elsie had immediately decided she would have to make *some* contribution. 'It's very nice o' ye tae come a' this way tae hear me.'

'Well – it wasn't only to hear you. I've been promising for a long time to visit Bill's landlady and I did also want to hear the programme Mr Delber is presenting in Glasgow.'

'That's good.'

'Do you know it?'

'Naw. A mean, at least ye'll get somethin' oot o' the journey.'

'You're being far too modest. Bill has a very good ear and he says you're wonderful.'

'Maybe that's jist whi' he wants tae believe.'

'I'm sorry?' Mother was having difficulty coping with Elsie's unfenced vowels, as well as her imperviousness to flattery.

'Bill's a nice fella, but he's awfa easy takin in.'

'Is he?'

'Dae *you* no' think so?'

'Probably I do think so, but I'm not sure that I understand you.'

'He's a bit up in the air, y'know?'

'Yes, he is!' She was relieved at getting that bit. 'And you are not.'

'Me? Naw! That's no' ma style at a'.'

'I'm glad to hear it.'

'For ma sake, or his?'

The pertinence of this question threw mother for a moment, but she was getting into the swing of the very direct approach. 'Well . . . for both your sakes.'

'Ye don't hiv tae worry aboot that.'

'About what?'

'Aboot whi' was worryin' ye.'

Again she had scored a bull's-eye and they busied themselves with the tea in silence while mother came to terms with this very practical woman who'd just turned seventeen. She began, 'You're a very astu . . . You're a very clever girl, Elsie.'

'Well – A didnae come up the Clyde in a barra'. An' *you* didnae forget tae bring doon yer music.'

Mother laughed. 'That's true!' She realised that she was actually enjoying this conversation.

'No' that A don't fancy him, mind ye. But when he looks at me a' he sees is a coupla tonsils jiggin' aboot.'

'Oh, come now! I don't think that's quite fair.'

'It's *no*' fair. But it's true. He disnae see me at a'.'

'Then he's missing quite a lot.'

'Naw! He'll never miss whi' he never wantit.'

'But he does want you to be recognised and valued for your ability.'

'Sure! A know. So, A'd better be good, eh?'

★

And she was. My mother was certainly impressed enough to recommend her to Eric Delber who saw Elsie, alone, the following day. It was a relief that, now, other people were doing things and I was very glad to let them get on with it. If Elsie was going to make any headway, I couldn't always be there. So, it was mother who went backstage after the concert to hear Mr Delber's opinion.

'Eric!'

'Marianne! My dear, how sweet of you to come round.'

'Congratulations! It was a wonderful performance.'

'Thank you. And the audience was much better, too. Of course, they have a good Ear, Nose and Throat hospital in Glasgow.'

'What do you mean?'

'A Glasgow audience will always hear, rarely sneeze and cough only when it is absolutely necessary.' They laughed together. Delber set up another wine-glass and offered to pour. 'Will you have some of this?'

'Yes, thank you. Then I can drink to your success.'

'Oh, no! We will drink to *your* success.'

'Mine?'

'Yes. To your discovery. I heard her sing today. I couldn't understand a word she said, but when she sang . . .!'

'I am glad you liked her.'

'I'm going to call Chicago when I get back to the hotel.'

'Chicago!'

'The opera-school there. I have a roving commission from them to find a coloratura. Well – I've found her. Or, rather, you found her for me. And she's young enough to take the full training. They'll be delighted about that. Should be ready for the 1962–3 season.'

'I'm so glad that something can be done.'

'And she seems a very level-headed girl. Quite . . . resilient . . . really.' The word he'd thought of was 'tough', as they both knew.

My mother came instantly to her defence. 'I suppose she's had to be. But with three years' training, I wonder how her family will manage.'

'You needn't worry about that. She and her family will be very well taken care of and provided for. Let me give you a lift back to the hotel. My car's waiting.'

'Thank you. I really am most grateful to you, Eric.'

'It's Chicago and I who are grateful to you. I think we and you

and all of opera can look forward to Elsie's career with great
satisfaction.'

From then on everything was taken entirely out of my hands.
Delber had made a recording of his own to send to Chicago. They
responded as enthusiastically as a cable would allow. Or so
Delber's wife told my mother, who sent me a note. Elsie herself
seemed to be avoiding me so I had no idea how closely they kept
her informed of progress, but around the middle of September it
was settled that Elsie would make a preliminary visit to Chicago
for final approval and signing the contract. About that time, too,
Frank suggested that we make a last-of-the-year circuit of the
Three Lochs. It wasn't a successful outing. Most of the time he
just grunted at my questions. He seemed anxious to keep going,
so we reached the final stretch much earlier than usual. But that
long steep hill over the back of the Roseneath peninsula was too
much for me.

'Frank!'

'Save yer breath!' he shouted from several yards ahead, pedalling strong.

'I've got to stop!' I gasped and just tumbled off at the roadside.

He kept going. 'We're nearly there!'

'I've got to take a rest.'

He glanced back then practically stood his bike on end as he
whipped an about-turn. As he free-wheeled down to me he
shouted with that edge of impatience he'd been displaying all
day. 'Whi's the matter wi' ye? We're nearly at the crest.'

'What's the matter with *you*?'

'A could've made it if A wis masel'.'

'You might as well have been,' I told him, controlling my
breath with painful difficulty.

'Whi' that?'

'You've been acting as though I weren't with you. Sit down for
a minute.'

A car passed us, grinding slowly up the hill in second gear and
for a moment polluting the clear scent of early Autumn with
fumes of unburned petrol. Aided by overcoming the sound of the
engine, Frank was able to shout – accomplishing an even quicker
than usual transition from impatience to anger, 'Christ Almighty!
It's no' a picnic.'

'Frank!'

'"Frank!"' he mimicked. 'Jesus! Aw, away an' pick some
heather.' He slumped down beside me on the grass verge. I

waited and he went on, more quietly, 'What? What d'ye want me tae say?'

'Whatever it is that you've been trying not to say.'

He gave me a hard, cold look and did exactly that. 'Right! Elsie and me is goin' tae get mairrit.'

'Oh!' That was nowhere near what I expected him to say. 'When she comes back, you mean?'

'Naw! Next month, A mean.' He paused. 'She asked me tae tell ye.'

'But what good will that do? She'll be in America for three years.'

'She's no' goin' tae America. At all! She'll no' sign the contract. She'll stay right where she is.'

'Oh!' An area of coldness was beginning to expand in my stomach and I became acutely aware of the coarse texture of the grass stubble under my fingers. 'Why?' I asked him.

'Because she wants tae get mairrit! Tae me!'

I recalled Ada's words. ' "An' hiv a squaad o' weans"?'

'Likely! She'll hiv wan anyway – in the spring.'

'Oh.'

'For God's sake! Will ye stop saying, "Oh"!'

'But everything has been arranged for her. Does she really want to get married?'

'Aye. That's whi' she wants. That's whi' she's always wantit. She's no' a bloody puppet, y'know, that can be wound up tae dae whi' you an' yer fancy freens want.'

'But she'll do what you want?'

'I want tae marry her. That's different. And there's another thing A've tae tell ye . . . *ask* ye.'

'What?'

'A'd like you tae be ma best man.'

'Why?'

'Whit dae ye mean, "Why"? Because you're ma mate – an' ye know how tae dae things right. Will ye?'

'Yes,' I said, wondering a little how I could be both a source of irritation and a pillar of support. 'I'd like to.'

'Great!' He sprang to his feet, smiling for the first time that day. 'You've been a good pal tae me, Billy. An' ye certainly picked me a winner. Noo, come on!' He raised his bike and set it on the road with one hand. 'I'll race ye doon tae the boat.' Relieved of the burden, he pulled strongly away – up the last yards of the hill. He disappeared over the crest with a triumphant wave of his arm.

★

All that was twenty-five years ago. A year after Elsie's first baby was born – and while she was carrying her second – I finished my time and went to sea. Frank, having done his home service, went off to do his National Service. I never heard from them again and never forgave them for that loss and that waste of talent. But I do hope they've been happy. To deprive us of another Galli-Curci, the least they owe us is to be happy. Oddly enough, Madame Galli-Curci died in 1963 – the very year that Elsie would have made her début. Shortly after that, the tape we had sent to California was returned to me. I have it still. Elsie singing Olympia's 'List' to the Song of My Heart' – the plea of the fabulous doll in *The Tales of Hoffmann*. I have her voice, but Elsie, herself, was never the sort of girl to be turned into a puppet; no matter how beautifully it may sing.

Lord Sweatrag

MY FINAL YEAR was spent in the Drawing Office among the soft-talking, paper-rustling, élite of the shipyard where I learned to fashion the ultimate and perfect 4H chisel-edge pencil, capable – if used – of making the very whisper of a line which had direction but no thickness. A line capable of transporting any female tracer to a distraction of delight and possibly an eye-specialist. There, too, I found the solution to a mystery which had previously baffled me and my colleagues on the shop-floor for many months. It was the secret cause of the bitter feud between a senior apprentice, Jock Turnbull and the labourer, Lord Sweatrag. The whole affair was inexplicable. Lord Sweatrag's action, which had been such a bizarre starting point in the middle of the Heavy Turning bay, the mysterious and secret management discussions that had followed it and then the weird change in Jock's behaviour were all connected – but how? It seemed entirely apt that, like so much information desperately required by 'the shops', the Drawing Office kept the facts to itself. On my first day there I learned more about the strange labourer than I'd managed to gather in the four years when I'd seen him practically every day.

He was called Lord Sweatrag in recognition of his taciturn, aristocratic, manner and his domination of the sweat-rag trade. A sweat-rag was a nine-inch square of loose-woven stringy cloth used for wiping muck off the hands and never, to my knowledge, sweat off the brow. I have no idea, now, why they were so fiercely coveted, but I did not question it at the time. Initially we were issued with two clean rags every Wednesday *if* we could hand in two dirty ones. Given lucky finds, seniority or theft, that number could be increased. Theft was simple because custom dictated that the sweat-rag was worn, not in, but hanging out of the right-hand trouser pocket. However you came by them, you got back exactly the number you offered. Lord Sweatrag was adamant about that. He had a little single-entry cash book in which were listed all our names and with the £ s. d. columns converted to note: 'Lifted', 'Supplied' and 'Date'. After my first couple of

weeks I tried to make friends with this odd man that all my
workmates sneered at.

'How many?' he asked, standing at the other side of my
machine, account book at the ready.

'Two,' I said.

'Still only two?' He made the appropriate note in his book.

I didn't know if he was deriding my lack of enterprise or
commending my honesty. And I didn't know what to call him.
All I'd been told was, this is Lord Sweatrag and he's a loony. He
deposited the soiled rags at the front end of his barrow and lifted
two clean ones from the back. Before handing them over, one by
one, he snapped them in the way shopkeepers used to snap the old
five-pound notes.

'There you are. One . . . and . . . one.'

'Thank you, Mr . . . er . . .'

'What?'

'I've forgotten your name.'

'It's Chinese,' he said, without a smile. 'Hey-You!'

I laughed. 'Yes. But what's your English name?'

'My Scottish name is Dalziel.'

'Sorry.'

'There's no need to apologise to me,' he said, and moved his
barrow on to the next machine.

He was, then, a man in his mid-fifties, thin, with a military
bearing and a razor-edge parting in his sleeked-down grey hair.
He'd been in the Army – a Quartermaster Sergeant, I'd been told.
The charge of being a loony seemed to arise from nothing more
than his attitude to his work. He treated the filthy, menial job of
labourer with the fastidious care of an exacting professional.
There was also the fact he didn't like people, but I could see
nothing loony about that. More suspect, in my view, was his
obsessive interest in the Drawing Office. He desperately wanted
to work there among 'the gentlemen at boards' as he always called
the draughtsmen. The fact that, as a matter of course, I would
finish my time there was enough for him to treat me with special
interest.

I never did manage to acquire more than the regulation two
sweat-rags and that seemed to please him. He placed great trust in
regulations, but none at all in his fellow man. And he saw
everything that was going on. Often when there was some upset
or accident – or even argument – the one person not moving or
shouting or perturbed would be Lord Sweatrag. He would stand
an even distance away, almost at attention, his shrewd, unblink-

ing eyes taking in every detail. When I was in imminent danger of
being greased it was he who suddenly materialised and thwarted
the attempt. By then we were on speaking terms. That had come
about because of a book I was reading at lunch-time. A shadow
fell on the page and I looked up to find him poised over me.

'What are you reading?' he asked. It was meant to be con-
versational but, with his lack of practice, it came out a shade
peremptory.

I lifted the book to show him. '*The Republic*. Plato.'

'Why?'

'Pardon?'

'Are you reading it because it's a fine book to be caught
reading, or because you want to find out if he agrees with
you?' This question was delivered literally over my head, but
then he gave a quick downward glance which warned me that it
might be a trick question. I gave the matter a little thought. The
pause did not please him. 'If you're as unsure as that you could
have saved the Greenock Public Library the bother of getting it
for you.'

I said, 'I'm reading it because other writers, that I've enjoyed
reading, speak highly of it.'

He raised his eye-brows wearily. 'And don't you think they
might speak highly of it for one of the two reasons I put to *you*?'

'I hadn't thought of that.'

'Even writers you enjoy reading have their vanities.'

'Have you read it?' I asked.

'Good,' he said and raised his hand to give my question a one-
finger salute. 'Good. A knight's move question.'

'How is that?' It occurred to me that he may have rehearsed all
this before he approached me. On the other hand, it could be that
I was just slow on the uptake.

'You've dodged one square to the side of the two squares I put
in line – which places you in a good position to attack, whatever I
say.'

'And what do you say?'

'I say, yes, I have read *The Republic*. And I made notes on it. I
always made notes on any serious books I was reading. Do you
keep notebooks?'

'No.'

'You should. You'll never be young again. This is the most
important time to remember. Your training. Accuracy. Have
something certain in your life – even if it's past.'

'I have my class notebooks.'

'I'm not talking about that. No, no. It's not the academic stuff that's important. What I mean is organisation, records, planning. That's the sort of thing they'll want in the Drawing Office.'

'Do you keep records like that?'

'Certainly. I can tell you to a penny how much I spent in any week five years ago – *and* all the comings and goings of the people I was working with.'

'But what use is it?'

'I'll tell you. It demonstrates a well-ordered mind.'

'To whom?'

'To whom it may concern,' said Lord Sweatrag severely. 'I showed some of my notebooks to the Chief Draughtsman when I was interviewed for the post of Clerk to the Drawing Office. I could tell he was impressed.'

'It's a shame you didn't get the job.'

'Yes. I'd be better alongside the gentlemen at boards than among this rabble. It would be much more fitting.' He said it as though, fairly soon, he expected God to admit a gross oversight.

'Who did get the job?'

'A foolish old-wifie of a man that happens to be a cousin of the Chief Draughtsman's wife. He will not last long.'

'Surely he'll always be a cousin of the Chief's wife?'

'A cousin aged about sixty is one thing,' said Sweatrag. 'A cousin in his dotage is quite another.'

For the next few years I moved from one department to another 'gaining experience'. But in whatever part of the sprawling Engine Works I stowed my tools I could be sure to see the aloof, alert, figure of Dalziel. I half suspected that he was watching over me, but I suppose he was just watching over everybody. Jock Turnbull, the senior apprentice, had a theory that the enigmatic labourer was really a management spy.

'You watch him,' he said. 'He's got a microphone hidden in the bristles o' his brush.'

'Surely not!'

Jock crossed his heart with wide strokes.

'Why?'

'Well, it's easier than keepin' his *ear* tae the ground.' He laughed, as he often did, at his own joke and it was such a childish, infectious laugh that it would have been churlish not to join in.

'What does he do with the information?' I asked.

'Transmits it tae they other loony bastards in Personnel.'

One of the messiest jobs that labourers performed was cleaning out the machine sumps. Almost all the machines used soluble oil to cool and lubricate the cutting edge against the metal. Driven by a pump, the mixture of oil and water gushed like a jet of milk from the nozzle above the tool and ran down to accumulate in the sump under the machine. Much else accumulated there, too, and over a period of months the stagnant oil, various droppings and debris thickened into a black, evil-smelling, treacle. This had to be swabbed out by hand and emptied into buckets. Whereas any labourer could be told to do the job, in the Heavy Turning bay it was usually Lord Sweatrag whom the Turners preferred. He made such a good job of it. Practically every working day I'd see him, sleeves rolled neatly well above the elbow, kneeling in a semi-circle of buckets behind a lathe, enveloped in a sickening stench.

I remarked to Jock, 'He seems to take a masochistic pleasure in it.'

'Aye.'

'Like T. E. Lawrence cleaning the latrines.'

'Who?' Jock asked.

'Lawrence of Arabia.'

'In Arabia?'

'No. The latrines were in England.'

'Eh!' Jock gave a bellow of laughter. 'That's a helluva journey for a shite.'

I laughed. There were few pieces of information that Jock could not turn into a joke. He was a big, jovial, young man with large brown eyes which shone with a constant gleam of pleased anticipation. It was his task to enlighten me on the art of 'bedding the bearings' on the big diesel shafts. This he did by letting me watch him do it. There was no question of letting me try it for myself. Nor did he tell me what he was doing, nor why. Instead, he reported at length on the appearance, conversation and behaviour of Helen. He was consumingly in love with a girl called Helen. They'd been engaged for almost a year and he wore a heavy-looking gold ring to prove it. When he thought he wasn't being watched he would polish it and, often, when he rested his strong brown hand on the polished surface of the bearing he seemed to be hypnotised by the astonishing fact of that ring; and the fact that Helen was going to marry him. He thought himself a very lucky young man and worried about his luck holding. But she had promised that as soon as he'd finished his time they would marry. Her one condition was that Jock should not go to sea.

'That must have been a hard decision,' I said. Jock, like nearly

all the apprentices, lived in the constant anticipation of the
freedom and adventure offered by the merchant fleet. The five
years in a shipyard was the ransom we were paying for that.

'Aye, it was hard,' he agreed. 'But I had tae give in. She'd made
up her mind.'

'Helen must be a very determined girl.'

'She is that.' His voice had a husky catch of admiration. 'An'
she'll be the makin' o' me. Christ, A'd kill masel' if she found
somebody else before A'm out o' ma time.'

For the first few weeks I worked with him he kept me informed
on how fast that time was passing. Then, quite suddenly his
manner changed. There were fewer reports on Helen and far
fewer jokes. He became moody and preoccupied. He started
having fainting fits; 'blackouts' he called them. It was incongruous that such a big, healthy young man should faint. Fortunately,
the job required him to sit on a low stool leaning over the shaft
bearings – which meant that usually he did not so much fall as
slump unconscious. He was always given prompt First Aid but
nothing could revive him for at least five or six minutes. He
reported that he'd seen his doctor and was given pills but I never
saw him take any. In fact he seemed curiously resigned to the
whole business. He laughed about it, although there must have
been great danger to him if it happened in the street. At work,
because it was Jock, everyone tried to save him any embarrassment. And the foreman didn't insist on sending him home
because when eventually he regained consciousness he was
perfectly all right and it was known he needed the bonus for
the new house. I wondered if he did. It seemed to me likely that
the cause of these 'blackouts' was trouble with Helen, maybe the
engagement broken off; though he still wore the broad gold ring.

Once he did fall full-length between two rows of machines. He
fell back and lay sprawled across the clear alley. I was some way
from him and walking towards him when it happened and,
though I started running, the first person to reach him was Lord
Sweatrag. He came swiftly from behind a machine, bucket in
hand and without hesitation emptied a stream of oozing black
sump muck over Jock's face and neck and chest. Everyone who
had been moving froze in sheer astonishment. Jock instantly
revived, spluttering and raising himself into a sitting position.
He knew what had happened and who had done it but it took him
a few moments of violent coughing before he regained his breath,
then, with the thick oil still running down his face he shouted, 'Ya
evil loony cunt! I'll flatten you. Whit did ye dae that for?'

'To save you the bother I've had,' said Lord Sweatrag calmly. Whatever that meant, Jock seemed to know. His angry stare flickered. The labourer added, 'Try not to spread that stuff in the alley.'

The patient was incredulous. 'Ye mean I've tae let it soak intae ma boiler suit?'

'If you can,' said Lord Sweatrag. He turned smartly about and marched away swinging the empty bucket.

Several people made tentative gestures indicating their intention of helping Jock to his feet. As he was now completely covered in wet filth they delayed just long enough to let him prove he didn't need any help. He was standing upright, like a huge black candle which was rapidly melting, when the foreman arrived. Jock shouted, 'I want that mad bastard sacked. Today!'

There was a general murmur of agreement and I saw the foreman note it. They all liked Jock and they did not like the autocratic labourer. He had a way of making many of them feel uncomfortable, even without pouring sump oil over them. The foreman himself had often been at a severe disadvantage in dealing with Lord Sweatrag, who had detailed knowledge of the whole administration of the Engine Works and of the very few inalienable rights of a labourer. He nodded reassuringly to Jock. 'Get cleaned up then come and see me in the box.'

When Jock had gone, a bemused group remained around the spot where the black footprints started. The certainty was growing that Sweatrag would have to go or it would be a Union matter. I said, 'Maybe he was trying to help.'

'Help?'

'To bring Jock round when he fainted.'

'Wi' sump oil?'

'But it did revive him.'

'Don't be daft. Suffocation! If he was unconscious it could've killed him.'

'That's true,' I said. They took it as an admission of my stupidity but I was thinking of that odd moment of complicity between Jock and the labourer.

The foreman's box became the focus of attention for the rest of the morning and the foreman's powers were acutely weighed in various discussion groups, the members of which were ostensibly consulting each other about work. Each carried a token piece of machinery or a machine-drawing to be flourished occasionally. And the news spread. Eager emissaries from other shops arrived, work token in hand, to be briefed on what might be the first flash

in a full-scale labourer revolt. Others went in search of Sweatrag
and came back to report that he was still sweeping and saying
nothing. Attention turned to what would happen now. Best
opinion was that whereas a foreman could certainly sack one
of his own men on the spot, sacking a labourer – who was
technically part of a general utility, like running water – was
more than a 'soft-hat' could do. That would require a 'bowler'.
And sure enough, before Jock had finished cleaning up, a manager wearing his bowler hat arrived at the box. The charge-hand
opened the door for him; and did not fully close it. A few minutes
later, he was called in. He came out again immediately and
walked straight towards me.

'Billy, you saw what happened, didn't ye?'

'Yes.'

'Ye've tae tell the boss what ye saw. Come on.'

The charge-hand and I walked like priest and acolyte through a
discreetly avid congregation. It made me blush to feel all those
eyes following every step I took. The manager had pushed his
bowler well back on his head as he lay sprawled in the foreman's
little swivel chair. The foreman stood and so did I. There were no
introductions.

'Well? What happened?' asked the Bowler.

'Jock was walking towards me when he fainted. Mr Dalziel . . .'

'Who's that?'

'Sweatrag,' said the Soft-Hat.

'Is he a Dalziel?'

'Seems so.'

'Bloody clown,' said the Bowler impartially and nodded to me
to continue.

'Mr Dalziel tried to revive him.'

The Bowler smacked his lips disapprovingly and grimaced.
'You mean he tried to drown him in sump shit.'

'Perhaps he thought it was water. Mr Dalziel always has a
bucket of clean water when he's doing sumps – to prime the pump
when he's finished the job.'

The Bowler glanced questioningly at the Soft-Hat. He
shrugged to indicate that this was a possibility then turned to
me as to a hostile witness. 'That's what Sweatrag told you, I
suppose?'

'No. I haven't spoken to Mr Dalziel at all about this.'

'Was there any argument between Jock and this labourer?' the
Bowler wanted to know. 'Just before it happened. Any struggle?
You say Jock fainted.'

'Oh, yes! He often faints.'

'Often! Then what the hell's he doin' at work?' demanded the exasperated manager of his subordinate.

The foreman glared at me. 'That's all, Billy, thank you.'

As I left the box, Jock was waiting to go in. 'Did ye tell them whit happened?'

'I told them what might have happened.'

Jock patted my shoulder, misinterpreting my contribution. 'Aye, right enough, he might have suffocated me.'

For the watching eyes I took out my Works ticket and headed in the direction of the lavatories. They would readily believe that the honour and excitement of being questioned by a manager would bring on the craps. But instead I went in search of Lord Sweatrag. I did not have to search far. He was exactly where he should have been and fastidiously continuing with his work.

'Mr Dalziel!'

He gave a tight little smile at this rare use of his name but did not immediately look up. 'Yes?'

'I've been talking to the manager about you and Jock . . .' He went on sweeping with measured strokes. 'They asked me because I saw what happened.'

'Yes?'

'And I told them you probably picked up the wrong bucket. I mean, that you intended to pick up the bucket of clean water.'

He straightened his back and leaned on the brush. No. He rested his open palm on the top of the brush handle as though it were a magisterial staff. 'There was no mistake,' he said. 'I know which bucket is which and exactly where they are placed about me.'

'But you don't have to tell them that.'

'I don't have to tell them anything,' replied Lord Sweatrag, looking at me with weary condescension. 'Was there something you wanted me to do for you?'

'No. I came to tell you that. To give you an excuse.'

'Excuse! What makes you think that *I* would want an excuse?'

'Well – they may sack you.'

'They can do that whenever they want – with or without an excuse.'

'But if you had a good reason . . .'

'I have a good reason.'

I waited but, apparently, the audience was over and he resumed sweeping. I should have learned then that there was no point in trying to help Lord Sweatrag. He took complete responsibility for himself, however perverse his actions. Back in the shops there was a lull filled with conjecture while we waited for the accused to be brought up. It was just before lunch when he was summoned to the box to be sacked. We all knew he would be because after *his* interview Jock had told us that the manager had more or less promised to rid him of this turbulent labourer. Jock had also been told of my hypothesis, which he took as a kind of betrayal.

Sweatrag strolled to the box with maddening composure. He bore himself so upright that he seemed to be leaning backwards. Just before he stepped inside he paused and surveyed it, as though doubting the safety of such a flimsy structure; but he went in, anyway. Then we gasped as the foreman came out, presumably at Sweatrag's request. Our boss was far from pleased at this temporary eviction from his power-base and immediately engaged the hovering charge-hand in conversation about a job – as though *that* was what he'd come out for. The manager and Sweatrag were alone together for quite a while before, to everyone's surprise, Jock was recalled. 'I'm no' gonnae accept any bloody apology, I'll tell ye that,' he told us as he went. There were murmurs of approval. Nobody wanted the climax to be spoiled with an apology from the ridiculous loony. The foreman, under guise of ushering Jock in, went in again himself. We waited. However, the climax was spoiled by the horn blowing for lunch. The fascination of box-watching had distracted most of the men from their usual preparations and they cursed at having to wash their hands in their own time. And they kept glancing back as they headed for the canteen.

I decided to wait and see what happened, mainly because I was sure that Lord Sweatrag would never offer an apology. My pal, Frank, was unsettled by my failure to obey the call of the canteen.

'Come on! Don't be daft. Ye'll miss yer dinner!'

'I'll have it tomorrow.'

'Mair than likely. But ye've paid for it th'day as well.'

'I want to see their faces when they come out.'

'They'll still hiv the same faces *efter* ye've had yer dinner. Come on, Billy.'

'You go on.'

'Ye're a stubborn bugger,' he muttered as he sprinted away, overtaking the charge-hand who'd thought he was the last to leave.

Now that all the machines were off, there was a startling silence in the shop. I was reluctant to move in case the sound would be amplified and carry to the four men in the box. Gradually, I became aware of their murmuring voices, though over the distance of a hundred yards I couldn't tell which of them was speaking. That murmuring continued for twenty minutes. Then it was Jock who was first to emerge. He walked quickly to the far end of the shop where there was a water tap and a can of soluble oil. I followed him.

'What happened?'

He glanced at me with an air of suspicion or, I thought, fear. As though I knew what had happened and was trying to trap him. 'Nothing.'

'Has Mr Dalziel been sacked?'

' "*Mister* Dalziel"!' He lathered his hands with the soluble oil, in lieu of soap, and began rinsing them, turning the oil magically from golden-brown to milk-white. Obviously, he did not want to discuss the matter. In silence I watched him complete the washing and the drying of his hands with a clean sweat-rag. 'Did he apologise?' I asked.

'He did not.'

'And he hasn't been sacked.'

'You seem tae know.'

'I'm just guessing.'

'Like ye were guessin' he picked up the wrang bucket.'

'What did Dalziel say?'

'Ye'd better ask him,' said Jock, and strode away in a manner which forbade any further exchange. He put on his jacket and went home.

I knew it would do no good asking Lord Sweatrag about his private conversation with the manager. And, since the foreman had been excluded from it, the normal process of information filtering from him through the charge-hand had to be excluded as well. For the rest of that week the Machine Shops were in a ferment of baffled curiosity. There was Lord Sweatrag with an air of amused superiority, and there was Jock Turnbull, muted and depressed. And Jock did not suffer any more 'blackouts' that week or in the weeks that followed. In fact he never fainted again. One might have thought he'd be grateful to Dalziel for curing him with a bucket of sump oil. Instead, he developed an obsessive hatred of the labourer, even if he had to remind himself of it from time to time – since he'd no previous experience of hating anyone. It meant remembering not to look up when Dalziel came to collect the sweat-rags and to throw them on the ground instead of handing them over. He had to remember to find Dalziel when there was any heavy material or tools to be collected from the

store and to push the requisition slip into the labourer's top
pocket without a word. These and many other petty actions,
ritually repeated, reduced the bright-eyed, ebullient senior apprentice to an edgy bitterness. And the fact that he avoided any of
his previous friendly banter with his workmates, in case they
raised the subject of Lord Sweatrag, gradually isolated him. As for
Lord Sweatrag, he had always been isolated – and the object of
derision. He bore the efforts of an amateur hater with ease. But no
secret is a secret forever, or we would not know that a secret
existed. The clue came from the Drawing Office and from the
'old-wifie' of a man that Sweatrag had told me about.

Before I discovered it, though, I had to take leave of 'the tools'.
Naturally my colleagues had a ceremony for that. And, inevitably,
it involved genital exposure. Whereas an apprentice starting work
at the tools was greased, anyone elevated to the 'staff' was washed
– with a hose-pipe. You could have it stuck down the front of your
trousers or you could take off all your clothes. Nor was there any
consolation in the fact that they also undertook to dry the crucial
area, for that was done with compressed-air nozzles. Is there any
wonder, I thought, that men in the Drawing Office were said to be
impotent? In my case it was remembered that, four years earlier,
I'd escaped greasing. So they did the greasing first, then applied
the hose-pipe, followed by the freezing jets of air. In fact the only
indecent exposure I missed was the pre-nuptial rite; which is the
messiest of them all. I'd seen Frank go through it and there was
gleeful anticipation of Jock Turnbull.

Apart from being desperately uncomfortable, I thought the
'leaving the tools' ceremony was quite unnecessary. Going into
the Drawing Office was just another aspect of the same job.

'Not at all,' said Frank. 'We're the workers, they're the staff.
And *they* never let ye forget that.'

'It's still part of my apprenticeship.'

'But if ye stayed there ye'd be a Draughtsman – and that's
middle-class right away.'

'Frank, I *am* middle-class.'

'Aye, *you* are. But the other fellas that go up there arenae. It's
goin' through that shiny door changes them. Anyway, I'll miss
ye.' To my embarrassment he took my hand and shook it. 'An'
don't say A didnae look after ye while ye were here.'

'I'm very grateful to you,' I said, trying to match my tone to that
of someone embarking on a long hazardous voyage. 'Give my
regards to Elsie. How is she, by the way?'

'Fine, fine. The baby's due early in May.'

'I hope everything goes well.' Then the sham solemnity over-
came me and I laughed. 'Oh, this is ridiculous. I'm going to work
only three hundred yards away. I'll be down to see you regularly.'

'Sure,' said Frank.

'I shall,' I promised.

'Aye, at first. But even then ye'll no' be the same.'

'Why not?'

'Because you're "staff" now, Billy, an' I'll never be "staff".'

'What's to stop you?'

'Lack o' brains,' Frank said.

I shrugged and turned away, walking up the long humming
alley of machines for the last time in dirty dungarees. I passed
Lord Sweatrag, busy as usual, bending over a sump. I thought he
didn't see me but when I glanced back he was on his feet – almost
at attention – staring wistfully after me as though at someone
departing for the promised land. I reported at the Gatehouse and,
with some little ceremony, gave up my 'ticket'. No longer was I
No. 875; I was one of the gentlemen at boards and a man of
honour who would be trusted to arrive for work in time and to
leave it only with the greatest reluctance.

The following Monday I went in by a different gate and was
immediately taken into custody by the man who'd got the job
Lord Sweatrag wanted. As Drawing Office clerk it was his duty to
note all my particulars and he seemed perfectly happy to devote a
whole morning to the task. His name was Weatherby and,
fortunately, he was a terrible gossip. I steered him round to
the onerous nature of the position he held and wondered idly
how he came to be there.

'Well, they couldnae dae wi' any roughnecks in here,' he said.

'No, of course not.' I looked down the length of the huge,
hushed room and at all the heads bent over boards in waxwork
concentration.

'And they want somebody they know they can trust. I mean tae
say, I have access tae all the confidential records that come
through this office.'

'Were there any other applicants for the job?'

He laughed – though very softly. 'Oh, aye, there were. But, of
coorse, preference is given tae them that's already inside the firm.'

Not to mention inside the family, I thought – but asked, 'Did
no one else in the firm apply?'

'Just Ian Dalziel,' said Weatherby. 'An' tae be honest, I thought
he would have got it. I think it was his health trouble that put

against him.' He agitated his jowls at the sadness of this. 'He spent
eight years in an asylum, y'know – efter he came oot the Army.
Then they found oot he wisnae mad at a'.'

'Really?'

'But it was his ain fault, the silly man. He worked his ticket,
y'see tae get oot o' the Army and then . . .'

'Sorry?'

'Dalziel kidded on he wis mad, so that they'd gie him his
discharge papers. They believed him and they discharged him.
But when he got out, everybody else believed him as well and they
put him away.'

'I see.' And what I was seeing was Lord Sweatrag standing,
sump bucket in hand, asserting that he wanted to save Jock the
trouble *he'd* had. Weatherby babbled on, then, near the end of our
marathon interview, he mentioned the point which nudged the
other part of the mystery into place.

The clerk referred to my written application. 'Now, ye say here
that you'll be joining the Merchant Navy as soon as ye finish yer
time.'

'Yes. I have an agreement that Holts will take me.'

'Ye'd better let me have a copy o' that tae send on tae the
MOD or ye'll get called up straight away for yer National
Service.'

'National Service.' I sighed at the sheer simplicity of the
solution. It hadn't occurred to me before because I knew I
wouldn't be doing National Service. But Jock Turnbull was
not going to sea. He was going to get married as soon as his
time was out. And, as soon as his time was out, he'd be called up
to do two years in the armed forces . . . unless. Unless he failed
his medical. That's what all the 'blackouts', the fainting fits had
been for. He was preparing to fail his medical. He was 'working
his ticket' in advance. As I sat at the empty vastness of my drawing
board, perched high on my brand new stool, I wondered if it had
been Jock who'd thought of the deception. No; he was too
ingenuous for that – or he had been. More likely it was the idea
of the redoubtable Helen. Apparently she was a young lady who
always got her own way; she'd have had no intention of spending
the first two years of her married life alone, on National Service
pay. But if Lord Sweatrag had effectively thwarted the fainting
ploy would she not think of other means? I'd been told of
apprentices who pierced an ear-drum, or took small but not fatal
doses of poison, or lapsed into provable sodomy in order to
escape the soul-destroying boredom and bull of two years' futility.

And to judge by our former colleagues who came to see us on leave, such desperate remedies were worth taking. National Service could ruin a man for life.

As I settled into my new job and concentrated on assimilating a flood of complicated information, Jock's dangers were pushed out of my mind. It was a few weeks before I came upon another nugget known to everyone in the office. Weatherby was about to retire. This was something Lord Sweatrag would have to be told at once. And in return there was something I wanted to question him upon. Perhaps there was a way in which he could help Jock and save the situation he had aborted. I couldn't very well discuss it with him in the shops where I'd now have to wear a glaring white boiler-suit as a visiting member of staff and to avoid contamination. I would go to see him at home. Old-wifie Weatherby was sure to have the address in the records. And on his own ground Lord Sweatrag would not be able to use the defence of inverted snobbery. I was determined to be firm.

'Good evening, Mr Dalziel.' He seemed much shorter wearing cardigan, corduroys and slippers. 'May I come in?'

'Mr Thompson.'

He opened the door wider to reveal the tidy lobby of the single-end which was on the top floor of a fairly respectable tenement in the West of the town. I felt his sharp blue eyes on me, assessing the situation, as he closed the door and gestured with the evening paper for me to precede him.

'I hope you won't think me presumptuous,' I began.

'That's no way to begin,' he said. 'Sit down. And tell me, how are you liking life in the Drawing Office?'

'It's very quiet.'

'And civilised, and clean, eh?'

'Clean, certainly.'

'And nothing heavier than paper,' he sighed and eased himself into a small chair which had never been sat in before.

'There are two things I want to talk about. First . . .'

'That's better. Always begin with the first,' he said. It was as though, in a very supercilious way, he was patting my head.

'I wanted you to know that Mr Weatherby is retiring soon.'

'Not a moment *too* soon,' Dalziel crisply observed.

'The advertisement for his replacement hasn't been published yet, so you've got time to prepare your application.'

'What application?'

It was maddening. 'Your application for his job. You're sure to get it this time.'

'But I'm not so sure that I want it, now.'

'Of course you do,' I exclaimed, and realised at once that it was the wrong attitude to take with anyone as prickly as Sweatrag. In his book – no doubt in *all* his books – wanting something was a weakness. He shifted irritably in his little unrequired chair.

'I'm not your labourer *here*, Mr Thompson,' he said.

'No, no. I meant, you *should* apply. That office needs someone with your ability. I'm afraid Weatherby has let things get into a mess. Disorder and lack of discipline. I can't think of anyone better than you to set it in order.'

He continued to glare at me then said, 'And I'm not easily taken in by flattery.'

'You must please yourself, of course.' But I knew he would apply and I knew that, although he dare not show it, he was grateful. Gratitude was another weakness. We maintained a silence for a few moments and I noted that his 'set-in' bed was made; and made in the impenetrable fashion of beds in hospitals. It occurred to me that there must have been many aspects of the strict regimentation of a mental hospital that he relished. This stark private room could well have been the room of a private patient; with the single, uncomfortable, chair for visitors who never came.

'What was the other thing?' he asked.

I gulped. If telling him good news was so difficult, how would I manage to ask him a favour? 'I'd like to talk to you about Jock Turnbull.'

'Ah!'

'I believe you spoiled his chance of avoiding National Service.'

'Do you?' His eyes widened and he smiled. It was the first time I'd seen him smile. 'Is that what you believe, Mr Thompson? And why would I do that?'

'So that he wouldn't lose his job through being unfit for work.'

'He's perfectly fit,' said Dalziel with his usual asperity.

'Yes, you knew that. And now I know that. But the manager wanted to have him signed off. Immediately.'

'There you are, then. What good would it do him evading the Army if it meant losing his job?'

'That's what I said.'

'Yes, yes.' He gave several sharp nods. 'So you did.' He smiled again – this time directly at me – evidently it was not going to be so difficult after all. 'Well, what do you want *me* to do? You've obviously got something in mind, Mr Thompson. What is it?'

'I'd like you to suggest some way in which he could still fail his medical.'

He was about to deny any knowledge of such things, but circumstances indicated that I knew better. Rather bravely he asked, 'Short of madness, you mean?'

'Preferably.'

' "Preferably",' Lord Sweatrag chuckled. It seemed he was proud of having beaten the system, and pride was *not* a weakness. 'No, no. We can't have another loony. And he'd be no good at it anyway. He hasn't got the intelligence to be mad. He can't even faint right.'

'There must be something he *can* do.'

'I wouldn't be so sure. He's a very simple-minded young man.'

'And very likeable.'

'Is that why you are so anxious?'

'I'm afraid he'll do something stupid to please his fiancée.'

Dalziel stood up abruptly. His voice was again edged with irritation. 'In that case, you've come to the wrong person, Mr Thompson. You should go and see his fiancée.'

'I would if I thought she'd had any experience of Army medicals.'

He held his impatient pose for a few seconds, then just as abruptly sat down again. He cleared his throat. 'What I meant was, why are you taking such an interest? Surely it's none of your business.'

'It was none of yours either, but you drenched him with sump oil.'

After a long pause: 'Sump oil,' said Dalziel quietly. 'The very thing.'

'What?'

'Suppose he swallowed some of that filth? It could bring out the impetigo. There's nothing these new men detest more than an infectious skin disease. They'd mark him unfit from the other side of a glass door.'

'But he hasn't got an infectious skin disease.'

'I can't think why he hasn't. In fact it's difficult to see how a lot of them avoid it – saturating their hands in that soluble oil. That's just asking for trouble.'

'The oil doesn't affect him.'

'It would if he swallowed it,' said Dalziel. 'And now he's done that, he has a likely cause of infection. Bacteria breeding in the nose and throat transferred by the hands to the body.'

'How long would we have to wait for the symptoms?'

Dalziel looked at me pityingly. 'I'm not suggesting he should really have it,' he explained. 'He has a likely cause of it, that's the main thing. The symptoms are easy to apply.'

'How?'

'A few cheap chemicals mixed into a powder he can rub on his skin. That'll give him a rash of blisters wherever he wants them. His fiancée could catch it as well, if she's keen.' He reached over and lifted a notebook from his bedside table. 'This is the mixture. Tell him to get each of these things from different chemists and then mix them in equal parts.'

'The rash wouldn't be permanent, would it?'

He shook his head. 'No. But it's got to be the right kind of blister in the right places. Any medical book will tell him where, what they should look like and what they should feel like. Impetigo – or ecthyma which sounds better. I'll make a note of that for you.'

'Why didn't you catch that, instead . . .?'

'Instead of what?'

I hesitated to say it and compromised. 'Instead of doing it the hard way.'

'Huh! It was during the war and as long as you could march and point your rifle in the right direction, they didn't care if you had leprosy.'

'Surely you could march?'

'Aye. But quite often I pointed my rifle in the wrong direction – *and* pulled the trigger.'

'Did you hit anyone?'

'Only once. A fat sergeant didn't jump high enough and the bullet went right through the calf of his leg.'

'What did you dislike so much about the Army?'

'The noise. That, and being at everybody's beck and call.'

I did not say so but it seemed to me that, as a labourer in the deafening Machine Shops, Lord Sweatrag hadn't managed to escape anything.

Next day, clutching my counterfeit impetigo formula, I put on the starched white boiler-suit which hung by my peg in the Drawing Office cloakroom and went trotting down to the shops in search of Jock. I'd made up my mind that I would not tell him who had devised the plan. But even then I foresaw difficulties in raising the subject. He'd have to be willing to admit the first sham to me before I could offer the better sham. As usual for him now, he was working alone, grimly rasping away with a de-ragging file. I approached him, smiling, and was about to start on my rehearsed spiel when it struck me forcibly that I might be wasting my time. The broad gold ring was missing from his finger. I waited a few moments to see if he was going to stop working, but he didn't.

'Hello, Jock.'

'Billy.' He went on filing.

'How have you been since I saw you last?'

'Fine. Just fine. A1, in fact.'

'Oh.' It was clear what that meant. I'd come too late.

'As far as the Army's concerned, anyway.'

'You've had your medical.'

'I've had it. And I've passed it.'

'That's rotten luck. When do you expect to go?'

'At the end o' next month.'

'What does Helen say?'

'Helen? Helen says it's off.'

'Your engagement!'

He nodded heavily, as though my questions were blows on his head. 'She says it's no' worth it – for her. The waitin', y'know.'

'You did all you could.'

'Aye. Gave up the chance tae go tae sea.'

'I think she's being unfair.'

'No' her fault,' Jock said. 'But I sure as Hell know who's fault it wis.'

I crackled sadly back to the office vowing that never again would I try to help anyone. I could not afford these vicarious disappointments. Another vow, which even at the time I doubted if I'd keep, was to avoid getting involved in matters that were not my business. Tony Liddle had told me something about that. I couldn't remember what it was but probably he was right.

The day after the internal notice appeared inviting applications for the post of Drawing Office Clerk, Dalziel's application was received in the office. Old Weatherby, remembering that he'd told me about the man, showed me the letter of application and I almost wept at the many pages of achingly clear copperplate writing in Indian ink, and at the care with which it had been composed. He must have started the first draft of it immediately I left him that evening. Clipped to the document was a signed chit from the department manager acknowledging that he knew of the application. The manager had to know and he would tell the foreman. If the foreman knew, the charge-hand knew. And if the charge-hand knew then everybody in the shops would know that

Lord Sweatrag was attempting the impossible. I could well imagine the additional barrage of derision he would have to face that morning.

Meanwhile I did my bit in the office, telling the draughtsmen how intelligent and conscientious Dalziel was and how he really shouldn't have been a labourer at all. It surprised me how willing they were to take my opinion. I mentioned this to Archie Hemple, who was the only person I knew in the place.

'I must be very convincing.'

'It's no' you,' Archie told me, 'it's your accent. Anything said in an English accent *must* be right, as far as this lot's concerned.' I laughed but he insisted. 'Naw, true enough. I'm tellin' ye, that voice is worth five years' seniority and an honours degree among these fuddy-duddies.'

To me it seemed more likely that Lord Sweatrag was called to an interview on the strength of his written application alone. He must have taken the Wednesday morning off to get dressed and ready for it because I hardly recognised the distinguished-looking gentleman who went in to see the Chief. He wore a tweed hacking jacket, cavalry twill trousers and brogues. And he carried a slim but very expensive document case, probably for a sample of his notebooks. He looked like a county squire. The interview seemed to go well because the Chief came to the door with him and they were joking together. The Chief called old Weatherby over and the three of them stood chatting amiably together for some time. Oh yes, I thought, this is where Lord Sweatrag belongs.

In the afternoon I went down the shops to congratulate him on the splendid impression he'd made, and came upon disaster.

'Sweatrag's for it this time,' Frank told me. 'They caught him wi' stuff he stole fae Jock.'

'I don't believe it!'

Slowly and solemnly Frank nodded his head. 'They found the stuff in his locker, I'm tellin' ye.'

'What stuff? What stuff could he want, much less *steal* from Jock?'

'Personal belongings. Tools and gauges, they say. He could always sell them, y'know.'

'When did they find it? Who found it?'

'This mornin'.'

'While Dalziel was up in the office for his interview?'

'Seemin'ly.'

'Somebody forced open his locker and found the stuff?'

'Charge-hand says the locker wisnae locked.'

'Frank!'

'A know it sounds funny but . . .'

'It sounds ridiculous. It *is* ridiculous. And who found the stuff in the locker that wasn't locked?'

'Wan o' the other labourers. He wanted tae get the book tae check on the sweat-rags.'

For, of course, it was Wednesday and another labourer would have to take over Dalziel's usual chores. And certainly there was likely to be at least one argument about the sweat-rags to be issued. The same arguments broke out every week with labourers all over the Engine Works and were settled by whoever could shout loudest. However, the stand-in labourer in this department knew of a trouble-free way to check. There was the unassailable log book in Dalziel's locker. I marvelled at Jock Turnbull's patience and care. He had waited for his chance and had taken advantage of the ideal circumstances to get rid of the labourer he hated. And if Dalziel was sacked from the shops for theft there was no hope of his being employed in the Drawing Office. To make certain there would be no wriggling out this time Jock also insisted on having the police called.

In some desperation I cast around for a way of defeating Jock's astonishing vindictiveness. What, I wondered, if I told him that Sweatrag had given me the means for him to avoid the Army and that it was my fault it wasn't passed on in time? Would he then retract his accusation? Probably not, because then he'd still have to admit the sham 'blackouts'. And Sweatrag would have to admit his secrets, too. I was hemmed in by confidences which were the only way of explaining the sequence of events and this blatant revenge. Jock, having failed to get Sweatrag sacked for something he *did* do, was plainly elated at the prospect of getting him sacked for something he *didn't* do. He stood at his bench, happy again in a group of his former friends, as we all waited for the police to arrive. Next, I thought of going back immediately to the office and giving all my information to the Chief Draughtsman personally. But what could I prove? And even if I could prove it, the Chief – who normally would, and often did, sail against all opinion from the shops – must be chary of taking on a man who'd been questioned by the police.

First the gossip-runners brought news that Sweatrag had bolted and couldn't be found. Almost immediately the charge-hand corrected that. Sweatrag had asked for the whole day off. A policeman had gone to his home to fetch him and, no doubt, make a casual search of the premises for other stolen goods while

he was there. Every quarter hour's delay increased the speculative
haul which was being loaded into the police van. Then came an
eye-witness report that a policeman was examining Sweatrag's
locker very carefully. I paid close attention to Jock's face when
that fact was relayed to his group. Surely he must have broken
into the locker in order to plant the stuff. He betrayed no sign of
alarm. To me that meant that he had not forced the lock but had
unscrewed the back – as, on more than one occasion, I had done
with my own locker when I'd lost the key. Someone was posted to
keep a look-out for the police van arriving. I looked around from
group to group of faces. There was a common expression and it
was one of patient, expectant exultation. To my mind that small
police van now moving through the streets of Greenock became a
tumbril bearing a very elusive aristocrat. I said to Frank, 'All *we*
need is some knitting.'

'Knittin'?'

'Round the guillotine.'

'That'll be right,' he said, not understanding and too engrossed
to require an explanation.

Suddenly, *there* was Lord Sweatrag. Accompanied by a police
constable he strolled down the alley that he himself kept meticu-
lously clean. He was dressed as I had seen him in the morning and
many of those watching thought at first that this was a very smart
plainclothes detective with the constable in attendance. If anything, his look and bearing were more autocratic than ever and it
occurred to me that he was acting the part, just a little. They went
into the box where the manager already stood, guarding the
recovered valuables. Jock could not wait to be summoned. Straining to keep a triumphant smile off his face he walked up to the box
and went in. We prepared ourselves for another long wait while the
charge was made and denied, the articles identified and examined
and the labourer who 'found' them was called to give his evidence.

We were mistaken. No more than a minute elapsed before the
whole sequence that we'd watched almost a year before was
repeated. Again, it was Jock who came out first looking bewildered and angry. There was an audible sigh of disbelief from most
of those watching. Surely the labourer hadn't got off again. Our
eyes moved from the slow, weary figure of Jock to the door of the
box where Lord Sweatrag emerged, head high and undeniably
pleased with himself. Our attention switched back to Jock who
had now reached the group at his bench. They stared at him,
demanding the news which he managed to give only with great
difficulty. 'He admitted it,' said Jock softly, then loud enough for

all the shop to hear – 'the loony bastard admitted it!'

I felt as though a lump of joy had exploded in my chest. Spluttering at the sheer effrontery and neatness of it, I realised at once that Sweatrag had stolen – not what he was accused of – but a victory. He'd found the only way to beat Jock and he had won. Jock knew it. His face and the tone of his voice proclaimed that he knew it. And suddenly I realised that practically everybody watching him had been aware that he'd planted the stuff in Sweatrag's locker. They shared Jock's dismay and, somehow, they too were defeated.

Lord Sweatrag, now dismissed, walked away as Mr Dalziel to collect his cards. The constable, who would then take him to the police station, was now clearly an officer in attendance; and I was, too. I couldn't resist following in the wake of that stately exit. It was like Charles I strolling down Whitehall on his way to the block. Better, it was like *Alec Guinness* strolling down Whitehall on his way to the block, for Sweatrag was acting too. All through the shops, men came to the edge of the alleys to see him pass. He smiled occasionally and nodded. Oh yes. He was acting. He was certainly acting, but with what *style*.

Old-wifie Weatherby retired at the Fair holidays and was replaced by a man who looked even older. There was no news at all of Lord Sweatrag once he'd served his short sentence in prison. Jock Turnbull, though, made the obligatory visit to his friends down the shops and added to the horror stories of life on National Service. Frank said he was a lot thinner but looked very well in his uniform.

'Did he say anything about the theft?'

'Naw, naw. All that's over an' done wi',' said Frank. 'Jock's no' the sort o' bloke tae bear a grudge.'

'Really?'

'Anyway, he's too taken up wi' the weddin' tae think aboot anythin' else.'

'His wedding?'

'Aye. Him an' Helen. She came back tae him, seemin'ly.'

'Oh! I wonder why.'

Frank gave me a sidelong, old-fashioned look. 'Because she couldnae find such another soft-mark tae take her, I expect.'

I nodded, for that seemed likely. It also seemed inevitable that all of the effort had been wasted. Jock's effort, Dalziel's effort and – less significantly – my own, had all been made pointless through time. And the gentlemen at boards who would not notice my

return – indeed, who would not notice if I never returned – did
not care, either, who sat at the Clerk's desk. For I now knew that
to them he was just a labourer. Maybe it was fortunate that Mr
Dalziel was prevented from making that discovery.

'What are you smilin' at?' Frank asked me.

'I was just wondering if there will ever be anything I do which
turns out the way I want it.'

He shook his head. 'Shouldnae think so.'

'Why not?'

'Because naebody's *got* what you want.' My long-time guide
and interpreter looked closely at me to see if I understood that.
And, presumably judging that I could bear it, he went on, 'What's
worse, everything *you've* got is only valuable tae *you*. D'ye see whi'
A mean?'

'I'm beginning to.'

He grinned. 'It's took ye a while.'

'Nearly five years.'

'Never mind, when ye qualify ye'll make a great Owner's man.'

That was less a compliment than it sounded. Everyone in the
shipyard from directors to apprentices tried to steer clear of the
shipowner's representative. They were civil to him, of course, and
they tried to please him with bluff or excellence, but he was the
enemy. He was an alien with rights and powers unfairly granted; a
sort of turncoat who'd trained with the men who built ships then
went over to the side of men who merely bought them.

'I'll never be an Owner's man,' I protested. But, of course, that
is what I became. In a way, that's what I'd always been. No matter
how devotedly I sought to become just another apprentice, and
no matter how genuinely they tried to accept me, there was always
the feeling that, after all, I was really a dilettante worker. And,
perhaps, a dilettante human being.